Resounding praise for
New York Times bestselling author
KYLE MILLS

"The new master of gripping and intelligent
page-turners. If you haven't read Kyle Mills yet,
you should. I do."
Tom Clancy

"A skillful and riveting writer."
Denver Post

"Kyle Mills is that special kind of thriller writer who
knows how to keep an ominous chill lurking
on almost every page."
Allan Folsom, author of *The Day After Tomorrow*

"Mills writes with pace and style."
San Antonio Express-News

"A writer with a brilliant future."
Stephen Coonts

"Mills is definitely someone to watch."
Publishers Weekly

"One of the world's master storytellers . . .
Mills keeps readers breathless, transfixed,
and turning pages."
Tulsa World

Books by
Kyle Mills

BURN FACTOR
FREE FALL
STORMING HEAVEN
RISING PHOENIX

Rising Phoenix

KYLE MILLS

Storming Heaven

AVON BOOKS
An Imprint of HarperCollinsPublishers

Rising Phoenix was originally published in hardcover by HarperCollins in August 1997 and in paperback by HarperPaperbacks in July 1998.

Storming Heaven was originally published in hardcover by HarperCollins in July 1998 and in paperback by HarperPaperbacks in January 2000.

HarperCollins books may be purchased for educational, business, or sales promotional use. For information please write: Special Markets Department, HarperCollins Publishers Inc., 10 East 53rd Street, New York, NY 10022.

FIRST EDITION

ISBN-13: 978-0-06-089469-6
ISBN-10: 0-06-089469-5

06 07 08 09 JTC/RRD 10 9 8 7 6 5 4 3 2 1

Rising Phoenix

To my dad
The get-things-done guy

ACKNOWLEDGMENTS

I have been told, on a number of occasions, that the care and feeding of a first-time novelist is no small task. I would like to thank the following people for all their help and/or tolerance:

Darrell Mills for unwittingly immersing me in the FBI culture for most of my life—see, I do pay attention. Also, for putting his inexplicable marketing genius to work for me. I never doubted for a second.

Elaine Mills for her unwavering confidence that I could translate my grade school short story career into an adult novel, as well as for her occasionally scathing editorial comments.

My "test market" critics: Steven Summers, Chris Bruno, and Lori Adams.

Kelly Meier, my Baltimore connection, and Deb Michael for a brief lesson on the criminal justice system at the Wharf Rat.

Robin Montgomery at the FBI's Critical Incident Response Group for his help with the FBI's SWAT capabilities.

Tim Sandlin for spending God knows how many hours combing though my manuscript and scrawling comments. I promise not to stick you with the next one.

Allen Thomas for his many inspired title ideas.

Tom Clancy, for helping to put me in touch with the right people and for all his support.

John Silbersack and Caitlin Blasdell at Harper-Collins for their insightful editorial comments and for teaching me a little about the business.

Robert Gottlieb and Matt Bialer, my miracle worker agents at William Morris, for taking a chance on a first time novelist and borderline climbing bum from Wyoming. And, of course, Maya Perez for always being there to answer a dumb question.

And finally, my wife, Kim, for reading the manuscript more times than I had a right to ask and for always prefacing criticism with, "It's really good, but . . ." For doing my chores while I hammered away at my keyboard, and, of course, for everything else.

There is nothing more difficult to take in hand, more perilous to conduct, or more uncertain in its success, than to take the lead in the introduction of a new order of things.

—Niccolò Machiavelli
The Prince

PROLOGUE

Baltimore, Maryland,
August 23, 1985

Mark Beamon jabbed at the air-conditioning button one last time as he eased the car to a stop next to a faded yellow curb. It was pointless, he knew—the mechanic who cared for the FBI's pool cars hated him. One little practical joke and he was condemned for the rest of his time in Baltimore to driving these subtly sabotaged vehicles. In the summer it was always the air-conditioner. In the winter, of course, it was the heater. Spring and fall usually found the windshield wipers disconnected.

Some people just had no goddam sense of humor.

He stepped from the car and stood motionless on the sidewalk for a moment, enjoying the gentle, salt-scented breeze coming off the water. He wasn't familiar with the neighborhood, but it didn't really look any different from most others in this part of town. The endless brick row homes that set Baltimore apart from other major U.S. cities also contributed to a mind-numbing architectural monotony.

Beamon jogged quickly across the street, his sweat-soaked shirt slapping audibly against his skin. He slowed to a walk when he reached the sidewalk, already slightly out of breath. The house he was looking for was halfway up the block.

He rapped hard on the door. No answer. He tried the knob and, finding it open, entered. It took a moment for his eyes to adjust to the gloom inside the narrow living room.

John Hobart, the DEA agent he had been temporarily partnered with, was sitting on the sofa at the far right. A younger, painfully thin man was lying on the dirty carpet at Hobart's feet. Beamon assumed the man on the floor was the informant that Hobart had suggested he meet.

"Nice of you to show up, Mark."

Beamon pushed at the door behind him. It was warped with age, and took nearly his full weight before it clicked shut. "Yeah, yeah. Too goddam hot to rush." He nodded toward the figure on the floor. "Is this Peter Manion?"

"That's Peter."

Beamon walked over to the young man and peered down at him. "What's wrong? Didn't get his fix today?"

Hobart remained silent as Beamon crouched down to get a better look at Manion's face. He pulled on the young man's arm, trying to roll him over, but let go when Manion cried out.

"Jesus, John, what happened?" Beamon asked, poking at Manion's arm again and getting a similar response.

"Peter here was bullshitting me." Hobart leaned forward on the couch. "Weren't you, Petey?"

Manion whimpered a noncommittal response as Beamon examined his arm. A delicate-looking bone was protruding from the top of his wrist. The blood drying onto Manion's hand had a distinct waffle pattern.

"What the fuck's going on here, John?" Beamon said, tying his handkerchief around Manion's wrist.

Hobart's face remained serene. He didn't reply.

Beamon stood and looked down at his partner. At first glance, he didn't look like he was capable of this kind of violence. He stood less than five foot eight in stockinged feet and couldn't have weighed more than one hundred and forty pounds. His size, combined with his sharp features and fine skin, made him look almost feminine. This impression was quickly dispelled, though, by his seething intensity. The little quirks that combined to form a person's humanity seemed to be lacking in him.

The vague misgivings that Beamon had had about his new partner's soul, though, had been lost in his admiration for Hobart's uncanny eye for detail and unwavering dedication to his work.

Until now.

"Take it easy, Mark," Hobart said finally. "The arm was an accident. He fell into the edge of the table."

"Then why are your fucking shoe prints all over his hand?"

Hobart shrugged. "His wrist was already broken, Mark. Might as well take advantage of it."

Beamon opened his mouth to say something but Hobart cut him off. "Come on, Mark. I was there when you slapped Terazzi around, remember? Don't even think of lecturing me about this."

"Bullshit! There's a difference between slapping a mob enforcer a couple of times and this." He pointed to Manion. "Terazzi was intimidation. This is torture."

Hobart crossed his legs and stretched his arms across the back of the sofa. "You say tomato . . ."

Beamon stared at his partner, slack-jawed. He'd seen it before, but usually in cops who had been on the beat for twenty years. Hobart had completely distanced himself from Manion and others like him. He no longer saw them as human, only as problems to be solved.

Beamon stooped down and grabbed Manion by the back of his shirt. The young man cried out in pain as Beamon dragged him to his feet, but managed to stand with minimal support. Beamon wrapped an arm around Manion's torso and began hobbling for the door.

"Where the hell do you think you're going, Mark?"

Beamon turned to face his partner. "To the hospital."

Hobart shook his head slowly. "Manion's the key to this investigation. You know that. I'm not going to let you blow this bust just because you have a weak stomach."

Beamon's eyes narrowed. "Blow this bust? I'm gonna blow your entire career, you sadistic son of a bitch."

Beamon began to turn back toward the door but stopped when Hobart reached for the gun resting on the coffee table in front of him.

"What are you gonna do? Shoot me?" Beamon had to struggle to keep the nervousness out of his voice.

Hobart put his feet up on the coffee table and rested

his gun hand on his knee. The barrel, and Hobart's eyes, were pointing directly at Beamon's chest.

Beamon turned and began moving slowly for the door, pulling Manion's near deadweight along with him. He held his breath as he reached for the knob.

1

Washington, D.C., October 15, Present Day

Things were looking good for Wile E. Coyote. His rocket-propelled roller skates gushed fire as he streaked across the dramatic desert landscape. It didn't matter, though. In the end he'd lose, left in the dust by that smart-ass Road Runner.

Leroy Marcus understood the coyote. He understood wanting and not having. And, though he had only just turned fifteen, he understood disappointment.

He punched the volume button on the remote, effectively drowning out the loud coughing coming from his mother. It looked like the coyote was about to take another spectacular fall to the earth, and he loved the low whistle that always seemed to accompany The Plunge.

"Leroy, get your mama some sugar."

He ignored her and stabbed at the volume button a couple more times.

"Leroy. Did you hear me? I need me some sugar!"

The quiet desperation in her voice cut through the screech of ACME rocket skates.

He thought back to the days when his mother used to come home from work and ask for sugar. He and his older brother would run to her and bury their faces in her skirt and she would laugh and pat their heads affectionately.

But his brother had been dead for almost a year, and his mother no longer rushed out the door every morning, fussing that she was late. Now when she asked for some sugar she wanted more than a kiss. She wanted her fix.

"Leroy!"

He turned his head slowly and peered around the overstuffed chair that engulfed him. His mother sat in the kitchen, legs splayed out unnaturally under the table. She stared back at him with watery eyes.

The volume of the television increased again, this time on its own. The cartoons were over, replaced by a small leprechaun extolling the virtues of Lucky Charms. He turned away from his mother and pulled his knees to his chest.

"What you waitin' on, boy?"

Reluctantly he lowered his feet to the floor and maneuvered through the worn and broken toys that his five-year-old sister had scattered across the room. He paused for a moment to look down at his mother. She turned away and reached for a pack of cigarettes.

His sister appeared in the doorway of their mother's bedroom and ran to him. He knelt down and ran a hand through her hair.

"What you been up to, Diedre? Your braid's already

falling out. Took me a half an hour this morning to make you all pretty."

She giggled and chewed on her knuckle.

"I gotta go out for a little while, okay? You gonna be good for Mama?"

She nodded. Her smile had a way of making him forget who he was. He took care of her—and that made him as important as any rich white man. Maybe even more important.

"Okay. I'll be back in an hour. If you're good, I fix that braid. If not, you have to walk around all lopsided for the rest of the day."

She turned and ran back to their mother's bedroom. He watched her until she disappeared, and then he punched the redial button on his cellular phone.

The wind that had been flowing through the streets like a river for the past two days had finally blown itself out, leaving Washington blanketed in a cold mist. Leroy surveyed the dark sky from the doorway of the housing project that had been his home since he was born. His 'hood was particularly depressing in the rain. It was true that the sun accentuated peeling paint and cracked sidewalks, but it also spurred activity. Children ran across asphalt-covered playgrounds. Teenagers smoked and drank on street corners. Even the foul smell that the sun wrung from the neighborhood was something. Rain made it all look like a faded black-and-white photograph.

He shoved his hands into baggy jeans and began splashing slowly down the stairs. At the bottom he turned right and started up the street, covering his head with the hood of his sweatshirt. Through the mist, he could just make out another lone figure framed by a severely leaning doorway. As he approached, the figure came to life and started toward him. "Tek! Whassup?"

Leroy had earned the moniker a little over a year ago from his prolific, though less than skillful, use of a Tec-9 machine pistol. It was his weapon of choice, and an item that he was never without.

"Ain't nothin' goin', 'Twan. You ready?" The wet air seemed to suck up sound.

"Shit, yeah. Nothin' much doin' on a day like this."

They continued up the street, not talking. It took less than ten minutes to arrive at the small white house that was their destination. They paused on the side-walk, scanning for danger signals.

The house's roof looked ready to cave in. The thick boards covering the windows seemed to be the only structurally sound materials that had been used on it. There was no yard to speak of, just wet garbage cling-ing to overgrown weeds. To the uninitiated, the house would have appeared abandoned. They knew better.

'Twan held back by the street as Tek walked casu-ally to the front door, resisting the urge to look around him. He rapped three times with his knuckles, paused, then hit the door twice with the soft flesh on the side of his fist.

"Yeah, who is it?" came a muffled voice on the other side of the door.

"Yo, man, it's Tek. Open up, it's fucking pouring out here!"

The door opened about two inches, stopped, then opened the rest of the way.

"Who's that?"

Tek examined the man pointing at his friend on the sidewalk. He looked like a mountain.

"He's with me," Tek explained simply, trying unsuccessfully to step around the man and out of the rain.

"You come in. He stays out."

Tek gave his friend a quick wave. 'Twan remained motionless, staring at him through the dark wraparound sunglasses that seemed to have become part of his face over the years.

The light in the room was dim, supplied by a single shadeless lamp in the corner and what little daylight could filter in through the boarded-up windows. The interior of the house was divided in two by a single wall, making it impossible for Tek to see into the back room from his position by the door. There was no furniture, though he imagined that behind the wall was a table full of the stuff he was there for.

A tall man with mottled skin appeared from the back. Tek had met him twice before and knew him only by his street name—DC.

"Tek, my man! How you doin?" His warm smile made Tek vaguely uneasy.

DC turned away for a moment and spoke to the large man who had positioned himself in the far corner of the room. "Hey, Split—this is my man Tek. He's the exclusive supplier to the Waring apartments." Split nodded in Tek's direction. If he was impressed that someone Tek's age could control such a prestigious territory, he didn't show it.

"What can we do for you?" DC asked. His tone was light.

"I could use some rock, man. Havin' problems with my supplier and I thought we could do business."

"Love to, man, love to. What you need?"

"Got a thousand, man. What'll that get me?"

"A thousand! Shit, maybe I can get you our preferred-customer volume discount. Allow me to confer with my associates." He disappeared into the back again, and Tek was left under Split's watchful eye.

A few minutes passed before DC poked his head back around the wall. Tek was feeling more and more exposed standing in the empty room.

"You lookin' to buy right now?"

Tek nodded impatiently. Why else would he be here?

DC walked back into the room with an exaggerated look of disappointment on his face. "We don't have that much stuff ready, man, but it's no problem. Tell you what—why don't you just leave the money here, and I'll have Split come by in a couple of hours and bring you what you need."

Tek's heart began to pound forcefully in his chest, though his face remained expressionless. DC knew damn well that he wasn't going to leave a thousand dollars in cash with a man he had never done business with.

Out of the corner of his eye Tek saw Split's arms drop to his sides. He quickly sized up the situation, once again becoming aware of the comforting weight of the machine pistol tucked under his rain-soaked sweatshirt.

There was no way he was getting out without shooting his way out. Twan could be trusted to back him up, but the door had been locked behind him when he'd entered. The trick was going to be surviving the twenty seconds it would take for his friend to run to the house and take out the lock.

"Thanks anyway, man," he heard himself mumble. "I'll just come back later and pick it up myself." He looked directly at DC when he spoke, but his mind was focused on his peripheral vision and Split.

"Shit, man, it's no problem. Split would be happy to do it. Wouldn't you, Split?"

The mountain nodded but didn't look enthusiastic.

DC's words confirmed Tek's first impression. Talking was a waste of time. Better to go for his gun first and get the edge.

Tek stepped slowly out from in front of the door that he hoped Twan would be shooting at in a few seconds. With one quick motion, he reached under his sweatshirt and leveled the machine pistol at Split's chest. He'd gotten more of a drop on them than he'd expected. Taking full advantage of his good fortune, he pushed the gun out in front of him and squeezed the trigger.

Through the flash of the muzzle, Tek watched his target clawing for the gun stuffed in his pants. He ignored DC, who was diving for the back room, reaching under his jacket as his body twisted through the air.

Split's gun had cleared his pants and was nearly level with Tek's chest when it was torn from his hand. A second bullet impacted his chest, spinning him around to the right. He hit the wall face first and was suspended there for a moment, framed by fresh bullet holes.

Tek turned his attention to more pressing matters as

Split's lifeless body slid slowly down the wall, ending up crumpled in the corner. DC hadn't reappeared and Tek stood motionless for a few seconds, ears ringing in the sudden silence. He thought for a moment that he'd lucked out, that DC had taken off through the back door and was at that moment sprinting through the wet streets.

The moment didn't last. As he turned to make a grab for the front door, someone started shooting at random through the wall that separated them. The rate of fire suggested some kind of fully automatic machine gun. Tek dove onto the floor and shot back through the wall. Behind him, pieces of the front door began tumbling through the air as 'Twan fired relentlessly at the lock.

In front of him, the wall was becoming so riddled with bullet holes that he was beginning to be able to make out movement on the other side. The realization that he wasn't going to survive another fifteen seconds struck him without warning. The feeling of immortality that seemed to go hand in hand with youth drained from him. For the first time, he could picture his own death.

It was getting hard to breathe and progressively harder to see. The lamp that had stood in the corner hadn't survived DC's first volley. Gun smoke and particles of shattered drywall floated lazily in the air, choking him and burning his eyes. Tek dropped the empty pistol and rolled onto his stomach. The smell of mold in the carpet mingled with the overpowering smell of gunpowder.

It was time to get out. The boarded-up window in

front of him emanated a few small beams of natural light that were quickly swallowed up by the thick air. Holding his breath, he jumped to his feet and ran crouching through bullets and flying debris, throwing himself headfirst at the window. He fully expected either to be shot in midair or to hit the boards covering the window and bounce back into the gauntlet. To his surprise, the combination of dry rot and gunfire had weakened the boards to the point that they offered no more resistance than glass.

He landed hard in the garbage-strewn side yard of the house, but managed to struggle to his feet and begin limping around to the front. As he came around the corner he saw 'Twan standing in the now open doorway, holding his Uzi sideways in front of him, spraying bullets wildly into the room and shouting obscene insults at no one in particular.

"Let's get out of here!" Tek shouted over the crackling gunfire.

Miraculously, his friend heard him, and they began running, side by side, back the way they'd come. Tek grabbed his friend's gun and began firing blindly behind them as they ran, hoping to discourage pursuit.

In a house two doors down from the one the two young men were fleeing, Katerina Joy Washington was sleeping on a couch in her cluttered living room. Gunfire was no more unusual to her than the sound of laughter or car engines, and she barely stirred. Yesterday had been her third birthday, and she was still clutching the doll her mother had given her. It hadn't been out of her hands all day.

If someone had been standing next to the sofa,

looking into her serene face, they probably wouldn't have noticed anything unusual. Her head jerked slightly as though she had sneezed. Or maybe it was a bad dream. Then she lay perfectly still, a crimson stain spreading out behind her head like a halo.

2

Greenbelt, Maryland,
October 15

The Reverend Simon Blake felt the sweat trickling down his back as he paced back and forth under the glaring stage lights. He stopped short, wiping his brow with an exaggerated flick of his hand.

"I have something important I want to talk to you about. It's something that threatens our families, our country—threatens Christ himself," he confided to the five thousand eager faces looking up at him. Continuing his pacing, he pulled the microphone close to his mouth.

"It's Satan's greatest weapon. His greatest curse—drugs."

Blake was near the end of his weekly service. In addition to his sermons, the two hours were filled with inspirational music, interviews with public figures, and Christian news stories. The show was translated into three languages and broadcast to seven different countries. An eighth would be added next week, if his attorneys were earning their exorbitant salaries.

The walls of his church soared above him but somehow didn't have the effect of making the preacher look small. On the contrary, he seemed to be one with the vast complex, woven into the fabric of the concrete and glass. Part of his congregation's growing excitement.

As his voice echoed through the church, amplified by its state-of-the-art PA system, the pitch of the crowd changed perceptibly. Sex and drugs were always sure-fire attention grabbers.

Fifteen years ago, his sermons had been full of God's love and salvation. He had thought that he could change the world from his little chapel in western Maryland with a simple message of hope. How naive.

The years had changed his message. Selections from the Bible had been replaced by quotes from prominent politicians. The concept of universal love and peace had succumbed to an ultra-conservative political agenda.

The cathedral had been completed nearly ten years ago and had cost almost ten million dollars. As his message evolved, he had outgrown the small chapel and loyal congregation that had been so important to him in his youth. He'd gladly given up recognizing the faces looking up at him for the opportunity to command the souls of an entire world.

"The Lord has told me over and over again to save the children—that they're the future." His congregation shouted its agreement.

"He's told me that Satan wants us all, but mostly he wants the little ones. Evil is always plotting, always looking ahead."

He paused, holding himself completely still, scanning the crowd. He stood there for almost a minute, mouth moving in silent prayer. It was one of his favorite dramatic devices, giving the impression that God himself was sending a confidential message—right then and there. The audience responded, as they always did, and their shouts flowed through the cavernous interior of the church, building power, until they hit him like a tidal wave. Blake stood, arms outstretched, feeling the hearts and minds of his congregation open to him, waiting to be filled with his wisdom. The wisdom of God.

"Do you know what his weapon is?" Blake said quietly into the microphone. The congregation went silent so quickly that it seemed as if a transparent wall had been suddenly dropped in front of the stage. He repeated himself for the benefit of those who hadn't been able to hear him over the din.

"Do you know what Satan's weapon is?" He answered his own question. "Drugs."

Once again, the crowd shouted its agreement.

Years ago, the growing use of narcotics—especially by the young—had alarmed him. Now it consumed him. Users were everywhere—even in his church. He could feel them. Weekend Warriors, he called them. The men and women who joined his congregation to be entertained and to relieve their guilt. When they left, though, they went home and forgot about God until Sunday once again rolled around. At home, they fornicated, drank, and smoked marijuana. Or worse. These hypocrites would pay for their weakness and burn in the fires of hell for all eternity, he knew, but not before they corrupted others. And the Lord had charged him with putting a stop to it.

Blake marched to his podium, picking up a well-worn Bible that had been given to him years before by his father. He held it over his head.

"The Bible warns us about the evils of strong drink," he continued angrily. "But Satan didn't stop at alcohol. No, he invented more seductive things to enslave mankind. Now we have heroin. We have cocaine. We have marijuana. And don't kid yourselves that it's not in your neighborhood, not in your children's schools. It's everywhere!"

He was shouting into the microphone now. Sweat and spit flew as he ran up and down the stage.

"And don't bother looking to the government to protect you from this plague. The liberals like to say that they are on the side of the working man, but I know the truth." He motioned to the crowd. "We know the truth!"

Blake put the Bible back and waved his free hand in the air frantically.

"They just want to make sure that they don't offend any of the drug pushers." He effected an outrageously deep voice and spoke to an imaginary woman next to him. "Sorry if you got mugged yesterday, Mrs. Smith, but we wouldn't want to punish anyone—that might violate their civil rights."

Blake chuckled into the microphone, shaking his head. The crowd laughed with him. He had always thought of his sermons as a roller coaster ride. Intensity had to be matched occasionally with humor and informality to have maximum effect. Otherwise you just exhausted the poor creatures.

He returned to his confidential tone. "I have something I need to tell you all." He shook his head sadly. "I just need a moment to pull myself together first."

He sat down and once again looked out over the crowd. Through the glare of the lights, he could make out the concerned faces worn by the people in the first few rows. He motioned to the director of the choir, who turned and began "The Old Rugged Cross." As the rest of the choir joined in, Blake allowed a sad smile to cross his lips. It was a song he found particularly inspirational.

When he sat in his chair listening to the choir and surveying his church, he always felt a pang of regret. There was no disputing that the space was functional. It seated thousands, was acoustically perfect, had sufficient parking, and hid television and sound equipment with ruthless efficiency. It was the feel of the structure that bothered him. He had hoped for a more gothic look, a church full of interesting stone work and stained glass. What he had ended up with was a stark tribute to mankind's intellect and not the monument to the human spirit that he'd expected. The harsh angles and blank walls spoke of mathematics, not of soul.

The architects, whom he was still suing, argued that they had shown him the drawings every step of the way and that he had approved them all. But what did he know of blueprints and construction? He was a man of God.

The completion of his cathedral had marked the beginning of Blake's dominance in the highly competitive TV evangelism game. His ministry had expanded quickly, as he knew it would, and his fame had been bolstered by an endless procession of ghostwritten books, a small university in Tennessee, and an ever-growing group of powerful political allies. Blake had discovered early in his career that if the Lord wouldn't provide, there were probably any number of congress-men who would. To ensure his good standing with the men in power, he continually donated substantial funds to various campaigns and gave his allies ringing endorsements through his complex and constantly expanding network.

Of course, these allies were as godless as any man on death row. Hedonistic men who cared only about maximizing their own power and influence. Whores. But the Lord had taught him that it was just those flaws that made these men so painfully simple to manipulate. He ignored the darkness and lust that they nurtured in their black hearts. Their intentions were irrelevant—they were tools. And through him they had unwittingly become God's tools.

As the final stanzas of "The Old Rugged Cross" filled the church, Blake walked back to his podium, head bent forward in defeat. He took a long deep breath that echoed through the church.

"I don't know how to say this, it grieves me so," he began. "One of our congregation's children was mur-dered last week."

Cries of "No!" and "Lord save us!" floated up and seemed to hang in the still air. Blake held up his hand, calling for silence.

"Bobby McEntyre was sixteen. He was on his high school's varsity football team. He was a good student, and was active in his church." Blake's eyes began to mist, and a tear dripped down his cheek. He ran the sleeve of his dark suit across his face, wiping it away. His congregation shouted its support.

"Bobby and a couple of his friends were driving to a Safeway in East Baltimore." Blake shrugged dramatically. "It was just another Wednesday night—not late—about eight o'clock. It took a few moments for Bobby's friends to grasp what had happened after the windshield shattered." He paused. "The police say that a couple of drug pushers got into an argument, and these good Christian boys were just in the wrong place at the wrong time." Blake turned and looked up at the large sculpture of Jesus crucified in front of the organ pipes at the back of the stage. "The wrong place at the wrong time," he repeated to the Savior. His voice cracked.

His wavering tone was the cue for the technicians in the booth to cut to a video of a laughing Bobby McEntyre tossing a football with his younger brother. When this appeared on the monitors in the church, as well as on the TVs of millions of viewers, a woman in the audience began to cry. He walked to the end of the stage, squinting against the lights.

"Mr. and Mrs. McEntyre, please come up here." He held his hand out to help a heavyset woman in her early forties onto the stage. Her husband followed close behind. Both had tears in their eyes. Blake hugged them and turned them to face the crowd and cameras.

"I wanted to bring the McEntyres up here so that we could all express our sympathy and to tell them that they will be in our prayers." The congregation mumbled its agreement. "I also wanted to tell them that I'm beginning a scholarship to Lord's Baptist University in Bobby's name."

The McEntyres hugged Blake again, tearfully expressing their gratitude and telling him how happy the scholarship would have made their son. A few people in the crowd clapped at the gesture. Blake watched the McEntyres as they were ushered back to their front row seats.

"I know that Bobby is in Paradise now, but he must feel great sadness in his heart at leaving such a wonderful family."

A man at the edge of the stage signaled that there were only five minutes left in the broadcast. Catching him out of the corner of his eye, Blake nodded imperceptibly and walked back to his pulpit. It was important not to let the realities of television interfere with the electricity of the Lord's presence.

"I want everyone in this church and everyone watching from home to join the Lord's mortal battle with drugs. Write your congressman! Write your senator! Write the President! Tell them that we have had enough!" Blake pounded his fist on the podium, creating an exploding sound over the PA system.

"Don't wait until tomorrow—write today," Blake insisted. "We can take back America from the pushers, but it's got to start with us! I don't want any other parents in my congregation to suffer like the McEntyres have."

He pushed himself away from the podium and walked to center stage. He stood there with his arms straight up in the air.

"God bless all of you," he shouted without the aid of

his microphone. Thanks to the near-perfect acoustics of the building, his voice made it to all corners of the structure. It was his signature end to the service.

The choir began their final song as Blake disappeared through an inconspicuous door at the back of the stage.

As he walked toward the rear of the church, his chauffeur fell into step next to him. "Straight back to the office, Reverend?"

"Yes. Can we make it there by one-thirty?"

Carl looked at his watch and frowned. "I'll do my best, but it depends on traffic."

Despite its considerable bulk, the black limousine slipped effortlessly through the light afternoon traffic, a tribute to the man behind the wheel. Blake sat in the back sipping a Coke and flipping through the *Washington Post*. *The New York Times* and *LA Times* sat untouched next to him on the soft leather seat.

The front page of the *Post* was dominated by a picture of a young black boy. It was unmistakably a reproduction of a school photo. The boy mugged uncomfortably, hair and collar neater than they had a right to be on a child that age. The accompanying article caught Blake's eye. He grimaced as he scanned through the first few paragraphs.

They told a story of a young boy living in downtown Washington who had repeatedly refused to get involved with drugs, despite escalating peer pressure. His abstention had irritated the local pushers sufficiently to inspire them to douse him with gasoline and set him alight. Blake flipped the page, finding another picture of the boy. This time he was lying in a hospital wrapped in bandages. The only skin visible was a small patch on his right shoulder. His eyes were covered with large round pads that looked like something used to wax a car. Clear plastic tubes ran from his nose to a complex machine by the bed.

Disgusted, Blake tore out the article and stuffed it into his briefcase. Too bad the boy wasn't white—a story like that could break collection records.

Blake scooted into the corner of the back seat so that he could see his driver's face. "Did you read about the boy in Washington who was set on fire?"

"I sure did, Reverend. Breaks your heart, don't it?"

"Why is this happening? What can we do to keep these kids away from drugs?"

Carl was one of the few black people that Blake knew well. He was under the impression that the black community was completely homogeneous and that his chauffeur was its spokesman.

"Don't know, Reverend. Most of the kids I see don't have much of a home life. And even if they did, it wouldn't do any good. The pressure to be cool, do drugs, you know—all that stuff—it's pretty strong. Comes a time when kids don't want to listen to their folks anymore. It's the same old problem, really. Kids want to feel grown up. They want to feel important."

Blake smirked. Carl had a God-given talent for understatement. "I remember being a kid—how important it was to fit in," Blake agreed. "But I don't remember the unpopular kids being set on fire." He scooted back to the middle of the seat and flipped on a small television, signaling that the conversation was over.

The traffic thickened as the highway melded into a two-lane Baltimore city street. Carl continued north, past the new Camden Yards baseball stadium, and took an indirect route to the parking garage under the building that housed the church's main offices. Blake jumped from the car, almost forgetting his briefcase, and walked quickly through the gloom to the elevator. His watch read 1:35, and he knew that John Hobart would have been waiting for precisely five minutes. Tardiness was not one of Hobart's failings.

Blake's organization took up the entire fourteenth floor of a hundred-thousand-square-foot office building that passed for a skyscraper in Baltimore's Inner Harbor. Anyone accidentally getting off on the floor occupied by the church would probably mistake it for a large law firm. The space was tastefully decorated with plush beige carpet and thick wood paneling. Crystal vases filled with dried flowers sat on antique mahogany tables. Walls were sparsely covered with original artwork, and employees were dressed in dark suits or well-pressed skirts and blouses. Only the light religious music playing over invisible speakers hinted at the true nature of the tenant.

Blake strode purposefully past the reception area near the elevator doors, not returning the greeting of the young woman sitting behind the desk. As he walked into his office suite, his secretary motioned toward his office, indicating that his appointment was waiting. Blake threw his coat on the sofa and walked though the open door of his office.

"Afternoon, John, sorry I'm late."

"No problem, Reverend, I just got here myself," John Hobart replied, looking up from the yellow legal pad resting in his lap.

Blake sat down across from him and pulled a pen from his pocket. He could feel Hobart watching him as he dated the first page of the pad. He didn't immediately meet his gaze. Hobart had a lifeless stare. His eyes had a way of eliciting a nervous laugh from all but the most powerful of men. They seemed to be able to see things that people didn't want seen.

Blake had hired him five years ago as head of church security, a move prompted by his growth into a full-fledged public figure. He hadn't liked Hobart when they'd first met, but the man's qualifications had been undeniable. Hobart had spent two tours of duty in Vietnam attached to a special forces unit, and had been highly decorated. Upon his return, he had gone to work for an accounting firm, getting his CPA less than a year later. Despite his success there, he had joined the Drug Enforcement Administration in the late seventies. He had explained to Blake that the boredom and irrelevance of the accounting business had finally worn him down.

Blake's initial dislike for Hobart—his son would probably say that John gave him the creeps—had prompted him to continue his search for a security manager. He had spent weeks weeding through steroid-enhanced bodyguards, sleazy private investigators, and classless ex-cops. After all of the interviews were finished, he found himself rereading Hobart's résumé. Despite the fact that a polite rejection letter had already been sent, he called Hobart back for a second interview. It hadn't changed his opinion of the man, and in fact, his feelings about Hobart still hadn't changed. In the end though, Hobart had seemed to be the smart choice.

There had been no cause to regret his decision. Hobart had created a security force that the Mossad would respect. His less than sunny personality and ambiguous religious leanings were no great hardship when Blake weighed them against his own personal safety and the safety of his family.

In addition to his security expertise, Hobart's accounting knowledge had become indispensable in handling the church's less-than-above-board transactions. While the Reverend liked to see himself as an honest man, he had grown accustomed to the finer things in life. He had also become increasingly addicted to political power, which had a price. His donations to various government officials didn't always meet the current definition of legality, and could be extremely embarrassing to a great number of people if they were to become public. Hobart seemed to have a special genius for setting up shell corporations and foreign accounts that looked completely legitimate, even under heavy scrutiny.

Blake's secretary poked her head into the office. "Sorry to bother you, Reverend, but Senator Haskins is on line one."

Blake stood and marched over to his desk. "Thanks, Terry."

Hobart went silently back to the legal pad sitting in his lap. He spun his chair so that his back was to his boss, and suppressed a smile.

The family-values senator and the family-values preacher.

Blake had spent the last five years throwing money at "return to family values" campaigns. A shameful waste of resources, as far as Hobart was concerned. The Reverend came from a nice, white, middle-class family in western Maryland. Dad was a preacher, and Mom stayed home making pies and taking care of her 2.5 children. Blake seemed to think that people who wavered from that cosmic norm did so by choice. He thought that he could simply convince them of the superiority of a wholesome and fulfilling home life, and when convinced, they would come around instantly.

Hobart knew better. He'd grown up in a poor, blue-collar family in New York that couldn't have been farther removed from Blake's idyllic childhood.

Young John had been a disappointment to his father, and after a few drinks the mere sight of John would set his father into a violent rage. Like most men, he had hoped that his son would be a younger version of himself. He had wanted an athlete. He'd wanted a boy who would turn into a tough-talking, hard-drinking man. What he'd ended up with was a son who was much smaller than his peers, pale and reed-thin. He seemed to blame John for his small stature, as if the boy had kept himself from growing just to irritate him. Athletics held no interest for John. His first love was chess, a game his father's limited intelligence couldn't grasp.

A few days after Hobart's fifteenth birthday, his

mother had been walking up the street with an arm-
load of groceries, as she always did on Tuesdays.
When she'd come around the corner, the flashing
lights of two police cars parked in front of her home
had momentarily blinded her. She hadn't waited to
reorient herself, but had dropped the bags and run to
the house. The injuries that she and her son had suffered as a result of her husband's binges had been getting worse. She was convinced that her son was dead.

She burst through the door only to find John sitting
on a kitchen chair, swinging his legs back and forth,
sucking on a popsicle. A large policeman was
crouched next to him, talking softly into his ear. He
turned when he heard the door slam. There had been
an accident, he told her. Her husband had fallen down
the stairs. His neck was broken.

She'd gone numb. Not at the sight of her husband's
limp body at the bottom of the stairs, but at the look
on her son's face. The policeman followed her gaze to
John's emotionless expression and explained that they
thought he might be in shock. She'd walked over and
knelt down in front of him, looking in his eyes. It was
there that she found the truth about what had happened that day.

That incident had formed John Hobart's entire philosophy on life. Most of humanity's problems were
rooted in centuries of misguided and often contradictory moral teachings. For a man with the intelligence
and resolve to rise above this tangle of right and
wrong, there was no problem that couldn't be solved
simply, quickly, and finally. Despite its simplicity,
Hobart had never met anyone besides himself who

truly grasped this philosophy and had the inner strength to live by it. There had been a few men in Vietnam who were beginning to understand, but they had all become addicted to the killing—dependent on the brief sensation of ultimate domination to mask their feelings of guilt and horror. Hobart saw killing as nothing more or less than an effective tool, and he used it with the thoughtless precision of a master craftsman.

"Sorry about that," Blake apologized again, replacing the receiver. "What's on our agenda today?"

Hobart stood and quietly closed the office door. "Nothing too interesting, Reverend. I wanted to confirm that we'd funded Senator Haskins the money he requested—but it seems that we did." He pointed to the phone. "Also, I wanted to let you know that I negotiated our own elevator when we renewed our lease. Starting next week, you'll have a key to the far-right elevator downstairs. None of the others will service this floor, except in emergencies. I've been a little concerned about the easy access to your office. As it stands now, some crazy drug addict could waltz right up here and mug your secretary."

Blake nodded. He wasn't thrilled about being imprisoned in his own office, but he deferred to his security chief's expertise. Operational details, necessary as they were, bored him to tears.

"Did you read that article in the *Post* today about that young boy getting set on fire because he wouldn't do drugs? I was looking at it on the way here."

John gave a short laugh, trivializing the incident. "It's a crazy world, Reverend." He flipped a page on his pad. Blake could see the heading at the top of the page. Offshore Investment Accounts. He wasn't yet ready to be immersed in numbers.

"How much does the U.S. spend on trying to stop illegal narcotics?"

Hobart frowned and looked at his watch. Blake had seen that particular phrase of body language a thousand times, and it still irritated him.

"Well?" he prompted, letting his anger seep into his voice.

Hobart dropped his pad onto the table, looking frustrated. "Annually? Somewhere in the fifteen billion dollar neighborhood, I guess."

"And how much of the church's money did I spend supporting law and order politicians last year?"

Hobart thought for a moment. "That's a tough figure to put your finger on, Reverend. We don't break it out anywhere."

"Guess."

"It must be in the two million range. Give me a few days and I'd be happy to pull it off the computer."

Blake waved his hand dismissively. "No thanks."

Hobart reached for his pad again, obviously anxious to finish their meeting and go home. Blake knew he hated working on Sundays.

"So am I wasting my money?"

Hobart released the pad with a sigh, but didn't answer.

Blake repeated the question.

"I don't know, Reverend. Is it a waste of money to try to do something good?"

Blake laughed out loud at his security chief's

attempt at Christian philosophy. "I'd appreciate a straight answer, John."

Hobart gave a defeated look. "Okay, Reverend. If you're asking me whether your giving these congressmen a few million every year will stop the spread of narcotics in America, the answer is no. Teen drug use has more than doubled in the last few years—you've seen the surveys. Coke use is up almost two hundred percent. Pot's up a hundred and fifty percent. Heroin's doubled."

Blake leaned back into his chair, taking a passive role in the conversation. An unusual position for the preacher.

"Then what would you suggest? We have considerable resources and will. How should we allocate them to win the war?"

Hobart started slowly. "Look, Reverend, illegal narcotics are a serious problem—and serious problems demand serious answers. That's where things break down. The best way for a politician to get reelected is for him to look like he's doing great things for the country, but not actually do anything at all. That way everybody's happy and nobody's mad enough to mount an effective negative campaign."

"That's a pretty cynical view of the government of the greatest country in the world."

Hobart chuckled. "The greatest country in the world. Why? The Japs have a stronger economy. Man for man, the Israelis are better fighters. The European children test better than ours. And hell, I'd feel safer walking a dark street in Trinidad than I would West Baltimore. Yeah, we were the greatest country in the world once, but now we're on our way out. In the next twenty years the rest of the world's gonna run over us like a steamroller."

A flush had risen from Blake's collar. Insulting the United States of America wasn't much better than insulting the Lord himself. But there was truth in what Hobart was saying. He couldn't deny it.

"So what do we do to stop this slide?"

"Hell if I know, but I think you're right in starting with the drug problem. There are, oh, say, thirteen million regular users in the U.S. About a third of those are heavy users. Quite a bit of the crime and violence that's eating this country up can be directly or indirectly traced back to those addicts."

"So what, then?" Blake said in a frustrated tone. "Should the government just execute anyone caught dealing drugs?"

"Waste of time, Reverend. You'd break the bank, keeping that many people on death row. Not to mention the cost of the appeals. Besides, you're talking about changing the way the judicial branch works to make it an effective policy. Not likely."

"I'm sick of people telling me there's no solution. The Lord has told me that there is a way. And he's charged me with finding it."

"There are a lot of ideas out there, Reverend. One is legalization and regulation." Blake frowned and opened his mouth to give a well-practiced argument to this proposal. Hobart cut him off. "I know you're dead against that option, Reverend, but it's not as bad as you think. It increases tax revenue and takes the criminal element out of the drug game. The effect would probably be something like the repeal of Prohibition back in the twenties. Of course, it wouldn't do anything to decrease drug use. It'd probably increase it a little, actually."

Blake folded his arms across his chest, indicating that he was looking for a better idea.

"Another idea is to have the U.S. buy all of the world's drug output and destroy it. Of course, that doesn't do anything for manufactured drugs like speed, X, or LSD. Also, you'd probably have every country in the world with ten feet of soil growing poppies—and you'd still have black market dealing. Other than that, we just keep on doing what we're doing."

"Which isn't the least bit effective."

Hobart shrugged. "Complete waste of time and money."

"That's it, then. I should just save my money and let my children grow up in a country where they could be shot down in the streets at any moment." Blake was pounding on the conference table. Always the preacher.

"There is a way, actually. It's something we used to bat around late at night back at DEA. It'd put an end to drug use and trafficking almost overnight."

Blake leaned forward in his seat. "How?"

"When you think about it, all you'd have to do is change the mission of the DEA from confiscating drugs and jailing dealers to confiscating drugs, poisoning them, and then putting them back out on the streets."

Blake turned his eyes to the large window overlooking the Inner Harbor and began chewing on his eraser. After almost a minute, he stood and walked to the window. The fall sun reflected off the water. Small sail-boats appeared and disappeared in the glare.

In the distance, he could see a stark white Coast Guard cutter heading out to sea. Next week they would probably be chasing a Colombian boat with a cargo hold full of sin and death.

"Think about it, Reverend, it's a win-win proposition. Hard core drug users, who are leeches on society anyway, would either have to clean up their act or die. That would include dealers, who are mostly heavy users. Anyone with half a brain would decide that the risk was too great and would stop using. Remember a few years back when the FDA found a couple of grapes with a little cyanide in them? You couldn't pay people to eat those things. And as I recall, it wasn't even enough to make you sick."

Blake grunted. He himself had sworn off grapes.

"The other plus in this kind of an operation is the cost. After you started it up, it would probably be self-sustaining. The DEA confiscates the drugs—in essence, gets them free—then puts five dollars' worth of poison in them and sells them for one hell of a profit. Besides, after a while you wouldn't have to do much poisoning. Fear would do your work for you."

Carl pressed a button on the remote clipped to his key chain and slowed the limousine to a crawl. The imposing gate guarding the entrance to Blake's estate swung open obediently. As they drove through, Blake caught a glimpse of a man in a dark suit standing partially obscured by a hedge, and recognized him as one of the guards who had been assigned to the house. He had initially resisted having men at the house, but finally acquiesced when Hobart promised to keep them out of sight. As always, Hobart had kept his word. Blake had actually been forced to introduce a couple of them to his young daughter, who became convinced that they were well-dressed ghosts. While he didn't normally tolerate talk of the occult from his children, he really couldn't blame her. Sometimes he thought they were well-dressed ghosts, too.

The drive was nearly three quarters of a mile long, and climbed a gentle hill to the main house. The rise of the hill and the carefully calculated placement of trees kept the house completely hidden from the road. Carl stopped the car under the portico growing from the front of the large white Tudor and walked quickly around to open his boss's door.

"Will you be needing the car anymore this evening, Reverend?"

"I don't think so. Be here at seven-thirty."

Carl touched the brim of his hat, climbed back into the car, and pulled slowly away.

"Hello!" Blake called, dropping his shoes on a priceless Oriental carpet centered in the large entry hall. Directly across from him, a black antique screen partially obscured by a potted tree depicted Japanese women washing in a stream.

"Erica! I thought I told you to get rid of this thing!" he shouted.

Blake wasn't crazy about the Oriental theme that his wife had chosen for their home. He considered the inhabitants of the Far East to be a godless people, and had developed a disdain for their culture based on the few business dealings he'd had with them. His wife's last purchase had finally pushed his good nature too far. He'd be damned if the first thing his guests saw when they entered his home was a bunch of half-naked heathens immortalized in lacquer.

No one answered his call, so Blake followed the sound of Beethoven's Ninth Symphony. He padded through the immaculate home in his stockinged feet, his nose latching onto the unmistakable smell of garlic and oregano.

"Did you have a good day?" Erica Blake asked as she stirred a seafood steamer full of spaghetti with a ridiculously long wooden spoon.

"Why is that screen still in the entry?"

Erica turned away from the stove. "I put a tree in front of it, honey. I thought . . ."

Blake cut her off. "I want it gone when I come home tomorrow. I don't mind you collecting these things, but I won't have obscenities at my front door. You can put it in your bedroom if you like."

Erica nodded and silently turned back to her pasta.

Blake sighed and headed for his bedroom to change.

Erica had been the perfect wife when he had still been at his little chapel in western Maryland—reserved, God-fearing, and supportive. The further his star had risen, though, the further she had retreated into her furniture collecting, painting, and childrearing. While her increasingly introverted nature was not really a hindrance to him, he had hoped that she would develop into a formidable ally.

He still saw himself as a preacher, but he needed a politician's wife.

Ten minutes later Blake reappeared in loose-fitting khakis and a Polo shirt. His children, Joshua and Mary, were already seated, and Erica was spooning sauce onto plates heaped with pasta.

"Hi, Daddy," Mary said, waving her little hand. Josh remained unusually quiet and did not meet his father's gaze.

"Hello, Princess. Did you have a fun day today?" She smiled and nodded her head.

Blake turned to his son, who had begun junior high the month before. "How was school today, son?"

A strange look flashed over Joshua's face. Fear? Then it was gone.

"Fine, Dad." He studied his food.

"Something wrong?"

"Huh-uh."

They finished the meal in silence. Blake resisted the urge to have a second helping. His pants were starting to feel a little tight.

"You all finished, honey?" Erica asked her daughter. She smiled and nodded again.

"Why don't you wipe all that sauce off and go watch some TV?"

"Can I?" she dragged a napkin across her face and took off before her mother could change her mind.

Dinner had left Blake a bit confused. Their usual lively conversation had been replaced by the quiet clinking of forks against porcelain. And now Erica had suggested that Mary go watch TV, a device that she could effectively argue was the root of all evil—

though she would never dare to do so in front of him.

"Josh has something he wants to talk to you about," Erica said as the sound of their daughter's footsteps faded into the distance. She was talking to her husband but looking directly at Josh, who squirmed uncomfortably.

She prodded again. "Josh?"

"It's about Jimmy," he said, still working to find a comfortable position in his seat.

James Miller was Josh's best friend. They had met in the fourth grade and had been virtually inseparable ever since. Two peas in a pod.

"What about Jimmy?"

Josh looked to his mother for support. She wasn't offering any.

"He, uh, got expelled today."

At first Blake thought that he hadn't heard correctly. "Expelled?"

Josh nodded.

"What? Why? Was he cheating?" Blake couldn't imagine Jimmy doing anything warranting expulsion. There must be some mistake.

"Uh, no."

Josh didn't seem able to continue. He stared at his plate. Blake looked at his wife. "What?"

She was silent for a moment, but finally decided to jump in and help her son. "They found some marijuana in his locker, Simon."

He fell silent, staring dumbly at his wife. Finally he turned back to his son. "Did you know that Jimmy was using drugs?"

"Not really, I . . ."

Blake exploded, slamming his hand down hard on the table. The drinking glasses swayed dangerously as Josh scooted back in his chair, putting some distance between him and his father.

"Don't give me that 'not really' crap! Either you knew or you didn't!" The flames of hell began to glow alarmingly bright around his son's head.

Tears welled up in the boy's eyes. His mouth moved, but at first no sound came out. "He just told me a few days ago."

"Bullshit!" Blake yelled, reaching across the corner of the table and grabbing Josh's arm. "Have you been using drugs? Answer me! Have you been using drugs?"

Josh looked to his mother again, and in that brief moment Blake saw the truth in his son's eyes. He let go of the boy's arm and slumped back into his chair. A wave of nausea hit him violently and then subsided.

"It was nothing Dad. Really, I . . ."

"Get out of my sight," Blake said quietly.

Josh stood and walked slowly from the room wiping at his eyes with his sleeve.

Erica reached across the table to take her husband's hand, but he pulled away.

"We'll talk about this later," Blake said in a slightly threatening tone. He pushed his chair back and began walking slowly to his den.

There wasn't anything Oriental in his den. The cluttered room was dominated by a large desk in the far corner. Books on various aspects of Christianity littered poorly organized book shelves. But it was the overstuffed chair by the fireplace that he was interested in at the moment. He did his best thinking in its embrace.

Blake grabbed some kindling out of a bronze bucket and carefully organized it in the fireplace. When the fire was roaring to his satisfaction, he sat, regretting for one of the few times in his life that he didn't drink.

It was too quiet. He grabbed the TV remote and flipped quickly through the channels, finally deciding on a local newscast. He didn't have much interest in what the well-groomed anchorman was saying, but the background noise was somehow comforting.

". . . young Katerina Washington was found dead in her home in Washington, D.C., this evening." Blake turned his attention from the dancing flames to the television as the scene cut to a shot of a dark D.C. neighborhood. Four police cars were parked haphazardly in front of a small gray house, their blue lights giving a sick swirling effect to the scene. A small lump under a white sheet was being rolled down the sidewalk as a growing crowd looked on. The cameras turned and focused on a young woman sitting in the back of one of the squad cars. The powerful lights glared off of the glass, partially obscuring her tear-streaked face. A man with a microphone stepped into the picture, successfully stopping a policeman who seemed to be walking toward the house.

"Lieutenant, can you tell us what happened here?"

The cop looked bored. His eyes met the camera as the reporter pushed the microphone into his face. "The victim was found by her mother about an hour ago. It looks like a bullet came through an open window and struck her in the head. She was killed instantly."

"Do you have any suspects?"

The cop shook his head. "Nobody seems to have seen anything. There's a lot of drug trafficking in this neighborhood. Seems pretty likely that it was a stray bullet from a gunfight that took place earlier today."

"Shit!" Blake yelled, throwing the remote at the TV. When it hit, the channel changed to an old episode of *Father Knows Best*. He turned his attention back to the fire. The television played on, recalling another time. A time when America was on the right track. A time before drugs, before hippies, before Vietnam.

After about ten minutes he rose from his chair, turned off the television, and walked to his desk. Glancing back to make sure that the door to the den was firmly shut, he picked up the phone.

John Hobart was sitting in the small office that he kept above his garage. The room was lit only by the screen of his personal computer and a small halogen desk lamp. For the past two hours he had been reviewing the status of Blake's offshore accounts, a job that was becoming easier and easier with recent advances in technology. And that concerned him. The thought of an overzealous reporter finding an MIT whiz kid to dig up embarrassing information about the church had been bouncing around in his mind for some time. But he had done, and was doing, everything possible to prevent that kind of thing from happening. There was no point in spending time worrying about things that were beyond all control.

His concentration was disrupted by the phone sitting on the credenza behind him. He picked it up on the first ring. Not surprisingly, it was Blake. He gave very few people his home number.

"What can I do for you, Reverend?"

Blake's voice was low and quiet. There was something in his tone that could only be described as despair.

"Remember what we were talking about today? Your simple solution to America's problems?"

"Yes." Hobart was cradling the phone in the crook of his shoulder, half listening, as he punched instructions into his computer.

"I recall you saying that one of the best things about this, uh, operation, was that maintaining it wouldn't take much manpower."

"I don't know if I used those exact words. What are you driving at, Reverend?"

There was a moment of silence on the line. "Could a small organization with substantial financial resources carry out a course of action like we discussed without the involvement of the government?"

Hobart stopped tapping at the keyboard and focused for the first time on the conversation. "That's an interesting question, Reverend." He thought about it for a few moments. "Sure, I don't see why not."

"Would you be interested in being involved in an organization like that?"

Hobart couldn't believe what he was hearing, and for a moment thought he had misunderstood Blake's meaning. Replaying the conversation in his head, he decided that he wasn't mistaken.

"I'm probably the only man for the job," Hobart replied honestly. Other men would crack in the face of mounting casualties, he knew, or would make mistakes that would lead the FBI to their door. Hobart's amoral nature and intimate knowledge of investigative procedure combined to make him perhaps uniquely qualified.

"Let's discuss it tomorrow. Eleven A.M." The phone went dead.

Hobart sat quietly in the semidarkness of his office, still stunned by the conversation. He had seen the Reverend act rashly before, but he usually came to his senses within a few days. Hobart suspected that his boss would regret this conversation in the morning, and by eleven o'clock would have forgotten all about it. He'd seen it before.

He flicked off the computer and the lamp and sat in the dark silence of the office. His mind raced, running endless scenarios for the operation and for his meeting with Blake the next morning. He would have to downplay casualties and cost, but most important, he would have to devise a plan that would insulate Blake from any personal risk.

Hobart pulled his knees to his chest, balancing his heels on the edge of the chair. Until now, he hadn't realized how much of the frustration and resentment he'd suffered at the DEA was still with him. He had spent years trying to compete against the world narcotics machine using conventional legal tactics, and had suffered defeat after defeat at the hands of men of vastly inferior intellect and capability. Now he had a chance to level the playing field, to use methods that would make the most ruthless cartel enforcer cringe. A chance to beat them at their own game.

3

Baltimore, Maryland, October 16

The Reverend Simon Blake stared silently at the blank piece of paper lying on his desk. He reached for the mug of coffee next to him, but feeling that the cup had gone cold, withdrew his hand and leaned back in his chair.

It was a little after ten o'clock on Monday morning. Sermon-writing morning.

Usually Monday was his favorite day of the week— the day that he created the message that would keep millions of viewers glued to their televisions and on the virtuous path. But today the words wouldn't come.

As soon as he had settled in behind his desk, his thoughts had turned to his son. Pictures of Josh's "innocent" experimentation with marijuana flashed through his mind, gaining mass and speed. Soon the image of his son taking his first hesitant puff on a joint was replaced by that of an older Josh sitting alone in front of a mirror piled high with cocaine. Finally he saw his son, old and emaciated, lying in a garbage-strewn alley with a needle in his arm.

Blake knew that he couldn't let that happen.

A knock at his office door jolted Blake back to reality. He straightened up in his chair and ran a hand through his short hair.

"Come in."

John Hobart strode through the door, closing it firmly behind him. "Good morning, Reverend. You ready to talk?"

Blake stood and walked silently to the conference table near the door. Hobart sat down next to him.

"Have you made a decision, Reverend?"

Blake shook his head slowly. "I'd like to hear some specifics."

Hobart's tone was casual. "What do you want to know?"

"You talk, and I'll tell you if I'm getting bored."

Hobart cleared his throat. He'd hoped to avoid getting into details. They'd just give the Reverend ammunition. He was too close to blow it now.

"Well, at first, we would concentrate on coke and heroin—those drugs, and drugs based on them, seem to be the major problems right now. I would expect that after the first few . . . casualties, the media would saturate the country with the story. Every addict would be on the alert. I think we could expect a substantial drop in use almost immediately."

Blake broke in. "What about the truly addicted? Do you think that they would be capable of just stopping?"

"I think so. There are programs out there to help

people like that, they just haven't had much of an incentive to go."

Blake looked satisfied with that answer and signaled for Hobart to continue.

"The fact of the matter is that casual users—not addicts—account for the vast majority of drug consumption in the U.S. I think we can count on them to stop purchasing right away. And that's going to throw a real monkey wrench into the drug dealing and manufacturing machinery. They work just like any other business—credit, cash flow, profitability, inventory—all words you'd hear at a cartel meeting, I guarantee you. Suddenly they can't sell the product they paid so much to produce and ship. The same thing that'd happen to Ford if it suddenly couldn't sell cars, is going to happen to them. In essence, they'll go bankrupt. And without their phenomenal cash flow, they won't be able to pay for the political influence, police protection, and muscle that has kept them in business for so long. I think their infrastructure would collapse faster than anyone expects."

"You mentioned casualties. How many?"

It was a subject Hobart had hoped to stay away from. He lied. "Not many. Drugs are a recreational item, nothing more. I think people would be quick to give them up with that kind of a threat hanging over their heads, don't you?"

He knew Blake's answer to that question. The preacher couldn't understand why people used drugs in the first place. .

"Cost?"

"About a million five, total. It should be a self-sustaining operation after the initial start-up." Blake didn't even flinch at the number.

"And my involvement?"

Hobart smiled. "None whatsoever. You give me the okay to drain the money from your accounts, then you fire me. There would be absolutely no way to trace anything back to you. In the unlikely event that anyone ever comes sniffing around, I'll make it look like I embezzled the money."

Blake stood and walked once again to the wall of glass behind his desk. He stood there motionless with his hands clasped behind his back.

"This is it, Reverend. Your chance to smash the cartels and bring America back on course." Hobart felt an excitement he hadn't felt for years. The government, with all its whining bureaucrats and human rights fanatics, had lost its battle with drugs. He wouldn't.

Of course, there were drawbacks that Hobart hadn't elaborated on. Casualties would undoubtedly be significant—but that was all to the better. America needed to have its population thinned. It was like laser surgery. Cut out the cancer and leave the healthy tissue.

And then there was the FBI. They could be counted on to do everything in their considerable power to spoil the party. It would be one hell of a tough investigation, though. No traceable motive, victims who would be reluctant to talk, and an opponent who knew their investigative techniques backwards and forwards.

They might eventually get close enough to make him run, but by then it would be too late. The users would be gone—one way or another. The memory of the initial casualties would be fading in the minds of the population, but new drug-free neighborhoods would be right out their front door. The pressure would be on for the government to maintain the new status quo.

Hobart suppressed a smile. Someday he might be recognized as one of the most important figures in American history.

"It looks like I've got some thinking to do, John," Blake said from his position by the window. "Let's talk tomorrow."

Simon Blake didn't move from the window as he listened to his security chief walk quietly out of the office.

The moment was at hand. His moment. God had chosen him for a great mission. He was destined to drive Satan from the hearts and minds of America. Until today he had thought that he was to accomplish this through his expanding television ministry and political influence. Now he knew the truth. God didn't want a messenger—it was too late for that. He wanted a soldier.

John Hobart was already waiting when Blake walked into his office the next morning. He was sitting cross-legged with his back to the door, bouncing a pencil impatiently on his knee.

"Early start today, John?"

"You know me, Reverend." He put the pencil down next to his leather-bound legal pad.

"I guess you want my answer on your proposal." His tone was aloof.

Hobart smiled. The Reverend's tone and choice of words spoke volumes. He was already distancing himself from the project. There was no need to distance yourself from something that wasn't going to happen.

Blake sat down behind his desk. "My answer is a conditional yes. But I think that we have some moral obligations here."

Hobart's smile faded. Moral obligations had a way of turning a workable concept into a disastrous operation.

"I feel that you have to warn the public of your intentions. Also, I don't want marijuana tampered with. There are just too many basically good kids involved."

"I never had any intention of going after pot," Hobart stated. "But could you be more specific about the warning?"

"Large ads in three or four major newspapers ought to do it. Say, three days' notice."

Three days. Hobart wondered if the time frame had a biblical origin.

"No, I don't think that's a good idea. It's going to complicate an already complicated operation and increase my exposure. I strongly advise against it." Hobart leaned forward, punctuating his words by locking eyes with Blake across the office. The Reverend looked unimpressed.

"Nevertheless, that's the way it's going to be, John. If you don't think you can handle the added risk then maybe you're not the right man for the job."

Hobart didn't let his anger show in his expression.

Someday he'd take a knife and carve that smug look right off Blake's face.

"I'm going to have to research how much ads like that cost and increase my estimate."

"Just take two million—that ought to cover it. I assume that I can afford it?"

Hobart nodded, knowing that the church could probably afford ten times that amount.

"Is there anything else?" Blake was obviously anxious to end and forget this conversation.

Hobart nodded. "Only one thing—my termination."

4

Washington, D.C.,
November 1

Mark Beamon waved wildly at Tom Sherman, associate director of the FBI. Sherman stood nearly motionless at the entrance of the bar, carefully scanning the crowd. Understandably, he was unable to see Beamon, who had effectively hidden himself behind two half yards of beer balanced precariously on the table. Beamon stood, crossing and uncrossing his arms over his head. Sherman spotted him and began weaving through the tables.

"Nice place, Mark." They shook hands warmly.

"Oh, don't be coy. The bartender tells me they have to roll you out of here most weeknights," Beamon joked, taking his seat and sliding one of the half yards to his friend. "So how was it?"

Sherman had just returned from New Mexico, where he had attended his daughter's college graduation.

"Not so good. She's staying. Sprang it on me just like that. An accounting firm in Santa Fe made her a pretty good offer."

"So what's not so good? Getting a job's tough these days, Tommy. It's not like when you and I were kids. The competition out there's pretty bitter."

Beamon watched his friend take a long pull from the beer. He knew what was bothering him. Sherman doted on his daughter—always had. Having her a thousand miles away for four years was one thing, but having her that far away permanently was another.

"It's a lot of miles, you know."

"Yeah."

Sherman looked like he wanted to say something, but he didn't. He began scanning the bar again, looking at the young faces that surrounded them. "Did you get us any food or are we on the Mark Beamon beer diet?"

"I got some of those mozzarella sticks and a plate of nachos—oh, and buffalo wings." Beamon ignored the pained look on his friend's face. Sherman had been an insufferable health nut ever since he'd quit smoking. "I might've gone a little overboard, but I figured you'd be bringing Leslie. She must be pretty worn out from the trip, though, huh?"

Sherman shook his head. "No. I thought just you and I could have a talk."

Beamon wrestled his glass out of its wooden stand.

"You really did it this time, Mark."

The waitress intruded on their conversation, sliding the platters of junk food onto the table. Beamon assured her that they weren't quite ready for another round of beers as he eyed the food guiltily. The roll of fat around his midsection—popularly known as the Bureau Bulge—was expanding at an alarming rate.

Worse yet, the extra weight was spreading to his face, making his eyes look like they were sinking into his thickening brow. But what the hell, too late for a career in modeling anyway. He reached for a wing.

"C'mon, Tommy, the press made half of that stuff up."

"Mark, you called the war on drugs a waste of time right in front of Calahan and two guys from the *Post*. And you did it so loud, half the room heard you."

Beamon grimaced at the name of the current Director of the FBI. He had met William Calahan for the first time at a retirement party for the outgoing Director, and Beamon had taken an instant dislike to him. It had been only three days since the announcement of Calahan's appointment, and the new Director seemed to have already sized up the entire organization and found it wanting. He had talked at Beamon nonstop for fifteen minutes about what he saw as the Bureau's numerous failings, keeping the distance between their noses at less than two inches. Following this discourse, which left Beamon thinking that the new Director was dangerously ignorant and conceited, he had immediately changed the subject to his rebirth as a Christian in the mid-seventies, and the fact that he felt that most of the Bureau's senior staff were alcoholics.

When Calahan had finished his little speech, Beamon had taken one step backward and drained the full bourbon and water he'd been holding. After a quick "nice meeting you," he had turned away and rushed off to find Tom Sherman and a few more drinks.

The Director had never forgotten this inauspicious

first meeting, and his initial disdain for Beamon had turned to dislike, then to hatred. It had been hovering in the loathing stage for the past year.

"I can handle Calahan," Beamon said. "Jesus, Tommy, I'm the best investigator the Bureau's got. What's he gonna do? Get rid of me?"

"Goddam right. You pushed him too far this time, Mark. Calahan spent half the morning in my office literally screaming at me."

Beamon reached for another buffalo wing and submerged it in ranch dressing.

"What's the worst job you can imagine, Mark? How would you like to spend the next five years in charge of a task force reviewing the Bureau's filing systems? I'm not making that up—he actually suggested it."

The table next to them broke out into a drunken rendition of Happy Birthday, serenading an embarrassed girl who must have just turned twenty-one. Beamon watched them for a long time as they swayed happily to the tune. Finally he turned back to his friend. "What's the bottom line here?"

"Houston."

"Huh?"

"Houston, Texas."

Beamon stared blankly at him.

"You know. That big state near Mexico."

Beamon broke from his trance. "What's in Houston?"

"Assistant special agent in charge. A slot just opened up. You'd be Steve Garrett's number-two man."

Beamon leaned back in his chair and lit a cigarette. His entire career was flashing before his eyes. He'd been known as a miracle worker. Impossible case? Call Beamon. He'd devoted more of his life than he liked to admit to the Bureau, taking on the cases that most people ran from—investigations that would take years of legwork to solve. And instead of fading into anonymity toiling on an unsolvable case, he had, with a few notable exceptions, successfully concluded them within six months.

And now his reward. A demotion and banishment to Texas. He'd always known it was coming, but the reality of it, sitting there in the Tibre Creek Inn, was more than he'd bargained for.

"Fuckin' hell, Tommy. An ASAC? You know I don't work and play well with others. Give me a shitty office, but for God's sake put me in charge."

Sherman shook his head sadly. "You know I can't do that Mark. Special agent in charge would make you too high-profile. You've gotta disappear or you just won't survive. You knew this was coming, Mark. You had to. You never gave an inch your whole career. You refused to play the game and now it's time to pay up."

Beamon drained the enormous glass in front of him in under two seconds, eliciting a sincere round of applause from a group of college students sitting at the adjacent table. Beamon smiled and nodded in their direction. He waved at the waitress and held up two fingers. "Right back where I started," he said, turning back to Sherman. "I grew up near there."

"I know."

Beamon took a thoughtful drag on his cigarette. "Houston, huh."

"Houston," Sherman agreed.

"What did Garrett say?"

"He was excited to get you."

Beamon frowned. He didn't know Steve Garrett well, but he knew him better than that. "What did he really say, Tommy?"

Sherman waited for a moment before answering. "He asked if you were as big a prick as your reputation."

"And you said?"

"Bigger."

Beamon laughed. "Oh, thanks, bud. Go ahead and put in a good word for me."

"But then he asked if you were as good as your reputation."

"And you said?"

"Better."

John Hobart brought his new Jeep Cherokee to a stop, and watched a thick knot of people disperse across the road. The sun was shining for the fourth day in a row and the temperature had risen to a near record sixty-two degrees. It was lunch hour, and the Inner Harbor was crawling with local business people, sightseers, and well-dressed conventioneers.

Hobart knew from his former place of employment that a national Baptist conference was in town for the entire week. Thirty thousand holy rollers had descended upon Baltimore, along with their three hundred buses, which were having a disastrous effect on downtown traffic.

The light changed and Hobart stepped lightly on

the gas, eliciting dirty looks from the last-minute stragglers hurrying across the street.

He would never get used to the new Inner Harbor. Baltimore had turned its downtown into a gleaming example of urban renewal. The streets were well lit, and the buildings were tall, clean, and modern. Street performers juggled, sang, and joked in front of glass shopping malls and food courts. Across the water, he could see the strangely angled roof of the National Aquarium. A tourist attraction extraordinaire, it was constantly engulfed in a sea of humanity impatiently waiting to get inside.

Fifteen years ago, the Inner Harbor had been infested with rats and old rusting cargo ships. Back then, anyone unfortunate enough to work downtown ate their lunch in their office and left as soon as the bell rang.

The only noticeable holdover from that era was the garbage floating in the murky harbor water, and the hordes of homeless men begging for money from families that hailed from places like Kansas and Iowa.

Hobart couldn't help glancing in the rearview mirror as the building that housed the church's offices disappeared from view. He had spent so much time there over the years that his spacious office had started to feel like home.

It was funny how things worked out. He had taken the job with Blake as a short-term arrangement; the money was good and the security work wasn't particularly demanding. As Blake's focus moved away from pure religion and toward politics, though, the job had become more and more interesting. Using the church's finances to pull the strings of some of the most powerful men in America was a hell of a lot more stimulating than protecting Blake from a bunch of overzealous Bible bashers.

Hobart had spent the first three days after his meeting with Reverend Blake tied to his computer, shifting and manipulating the church's accounts. Money had been deposited across the U.S. and in a number of foreign countries under various individual and corporate names. In all, Hobart had siphoned exactly two million dollars from the church, mostly in the form of payments for phantom services. Unless an accountant was willing to travel across the third world verifying various purchases, construction projects, and donations, the money would never be missed. Hell, even if a Big Six firm was hired specifically to look for wrongdoing, it would take them at least six months and a million miles to sort things out. And when they did, the police would show up at someone else's door, not his.

When he had been completely satisfied with the financial stability of his new organization, tentatively called the Committee for a Drug-Free Society, or CDFS, he had made his way back to the office for the last time.

Blake had been perfect. And why not? He did this type of thing for a living. Hobart had slammed through his office door, "accidentally" not getting it entirely closed. They had argued loudly, Blake making vague accusations, and deriding his attitude. Hobart had constructed an equally vague defense. Finally the Reverend had told him to get out. Hobart had slammed the office door behind him, getting it closed this time, and walked quickly past the four people waiting in Blake's outer office. He had felt their eyes on him as he strode purposefully down the hall.

When the elevator doors opened into the lobby, the front desk guard was standing directly in front of him, blocking his exit.

"Reverend Blake called down and asked me to take your elevator key," he had said nervously. His right hand shook slightly as he held it out in front of him.

Hobart silently complimented his former boss on his thoroughness as he slid the key off its ring and placed it in the guard's outstretched hand. He forced his way around the man and walked through the sunlit lobby. As he opened the first set of glass doors, the guard called after him. "The Reverend told me to tell you that he'd have your personal belongings sent to your house."

Hobart left the building shaking his head. He'd make a covert operative out of Simon Blake yet.

But now that part of his life was over and a new chapter had begun. He gunned the Jeep through a yellow light. He had an appointment in less than two hours, and he had at least an hour's worth of work to do at home first.

Hobart jerked the wheel right, almost missing the narrow side street. He was nearing Canton, about two miles east of the Inner Harbor. Recent years had seen the transformation of this waterfront area from a poorly maintained warehouse district to a yuppie haven. He was a few blocks north of the water, though, and the neighborhood was typical Baltimore. Narrow brick row homes and crowded, potholed, car-lined streets. Elaborate Catholic churches adorned street corners, recalling another time.

Hobart scanned the streets as he drove. It seemed that every other doorstep held a dull-looking chain smoker taking advantage of the unseasonably warm weather. Shouted profanity floated through his open window as women yelled at their children or at the dogs running loose in the street.

He continued on, glancing back and forth from the street to a small Post-it note stuck to his dashboard. Cresting a hill, he could see the blackened metal roofs of the city as they melded together into a black and silver tapestry.

Only a few blocks from the waterfront, he found what he was looking for—a small brick warehouse with a professionally dressed woman in a wheelchair gliding back and forth in front of it. He swung his car into the nearest available space and jogged across the street. Hearing him coming, the woman turned and gave him a practiced smile.

"Mr. Severen, I presume. I'm Karen Styles." She held out her hand, keeping the other one firmly around the chair's left wheel.

He took it. "Please call me John."

In between bouts with the church's various bank accounts, Hobart had managed to contact an old acquaintance who had a talent for forgery. He'd provided four different identities, complete with passports, driver's licenses, birth certificates, and even library cards. The license in the name of John Severen pictured him as having sandy brown hair and a thick mustache. Hobart had made the appropriate changes to his appearance with the help of a well-stocked theatrical makeup shop. He still wasn't used to the change. It was disorienting to look in the mirror and not see his closely cropped black hair and smoothly shaven face. Worse yet, the mustache itched mercilessly.

"Let's take a look," the Realtor suggested, using the key in her hand on the heavy metal door to the warehouse. Hobart reached over to help her. She found the lights and he followed her in.

They entered a small outer office. The walls had been painted yellow sometime in the distant past but had faded to an uneven tan. Hobart walked across the stained carpet and through a door at the back. It led to a nearly identical room. Two large windows had been cut into the wall to the left of him. Judging by their crooked appearance, the work had been done long after the sturdy brick building had been erected.

"If you walk back around here, you can see the bathroom and the entrance to the warehouse section." He followed her, examining her thin neck as she maneuvered the wheelchair through the narrow hall. It would take less than a second to snap it. She'd never know what happened. He frowned. Too dangerous. She was a loose end that he would have to tolerate.

The bathroom was small and basic. A sink, toilet, and mirror. It had the same faded yellow walls but they were stained by mildew, causing wide black streaks that at first glance looked like wallpaper. Karen stopped at another formidable-looking door and tugged at it with all her might. It didn't budge. She looked at Hobart who, finished with his examination of the bathroom, pulled it open. She wheeled through with a grateful smile.

It was just about the right size, close to fifty by fifty feet, with a twenty-five-foot ceiling height. The walls consisted of old brick, occasionally obscured by dirty wooden shelves. At the far end was a tall garage door. It looked large enough to back in a semi. Hobart wandered around aimlessly, stirring up the brightly colored sales flyers littering the floor and ignoring the Realtor's sales pitch.

"Until two weeks ago the warehouse was occupied by a T-shirt company." She reached down and picked up one of the flyers. "That's where all these flyers came from. Obviously, it will be broom clean if you decide to take it."

"And there are apartments above?"

"Two. I confirmed that they're both available, but I hear that they're not that nice."

"You said eight hundred dollars for the warehouse?"

She nodded.

"How much for the entire building?"

She chewed her bottom lip. "Probably double that, sixteen hundred. Keep in mind that there's no access to the upstairs from here."

He took another quick turn through the space. "I'll take it for a year with a one-year option. It'll need some work, though. I assume that the owners wouldn't mind if I made a few improvements—at my own expense, of course."

"What kind of improvements were you considering?"

"Nothing special. A little paint, a new carpet, maybe an alarm system."

She shrugged. "I can't imagine that would be a problem. What kind of business are you in, John?"

"Wholesale antiques."

"Really? That's interesting," she said in a slightly bored tone. "Let me pop out to my car and call the owners. I want to make sure that I quoted you right on the apartments, and ask them about the improvements. If everything's all right, we can go back to my office, fill out a little paperwork, and it's yours."

"Fine."

It was almost five o'clock when Hobart left the realty office in Fells Point, an area known for good seafood and dive bars. The smell of steaming crabs hung in the air, inviting him into the restaurant directly across the street. He glanced at his watch. Dinner would have to wait.

Hobart pulled his car into a narrow space about a block from his final destination. He fished a small scrap of paper out of his pocket and dialed the number written there on his cellular phone. It rang four times before being picked up by a machine.

"Leave a message," was the only greeting, followed by a loud beep. He didn't. Instead he pulled a small black knapsack off the floor of the Jeep and walked across the street, straining to make out the numbers on the houses in the waning light. When he got to 619 he turned and walked into the narrow passageway between it and the house next door. The cracked cement under his feet was under two inches of sudsy water. It smelled like laundry detergent.

The passageway eventually opened into a small backyard separated into two parcels by a short chain-link fence. Hobart entered the gate on the left. He looked around to confirm that no one was watching from the windows of the surrounding houses, and pulled out a large screwdriver. It turned out to be unnecessary. The door swung open when he grabbed the knob. Smiling, he entered the kitchen.

Dishes were stacked everywhere, and judging from the smell, they'd been there for some time. Hobart's gaze fell on a small pile of bones lying on the floor and he froze. He stood perfectly still for almost a minute listening for any sign of a dog. Hearing nothing, he padded quietly into the living room. No self-respecting canine could have missed his less-than-silent entrance.

He made a quick walk through of the house, confirming that no one was home. The other rooms were in a condition similar to the kitchen. Plaster was falling from the ceiling in places and half the lights seemed to be burned out. The furniture—what little there was of it—looked like it had been retrieved from city dumpsters. The single bedroom didn't actually have a bed, only a foul-smelling mattress lying on the floor.

He moved quickly, placing listening devices in the phone, the living room, and bedroom. He was thankful for the surgical gloves covering his hands—he wasn't anxious to touch anything with his bare skin. No telling what you could catch.

When he was finished, he situated himself in a worn

out La-Z-Boy next to the front door. It wasn't particularly comfortable. It didn't recline and it looked like most of the foam had rotted and fallen out onto the carpet. Other than that, the chair was ideal. He couldn't be immediately seen from the door, and it was more sanitary than sitting on the floor—though only marginally.

Next to him was a large shelf overflowing with books. He leaned over and scanned the titles. No novels or fiction, just textbooks on subjects like physics and chemistry. Archaeology also had a place, but the thick dust on the covers suggested that the subject had fallen from grace. He was glad to see that his old friend was keeping his mind sharp.

The friend he was waiting for was one Peter Manion. Hobart had flipped through a bootleg file on his ex-informant the day Blake had given him the go-ahead. He hadn't seen Manion for years—not since his DEA days.

Manion had been born on the east side of Baltimore to a working-class family in 1957. He'd shown an early aptitude for math and science and was encouraged by his mother, a particularly strong woman whose interest in education belied her lack of one. His father hadn't shared her convictions and had constantly belittled his son for his shy, quiet demeanor. In the end his mother prevailed, and Manion won a full scholarship to Johns Hopkins. It was there that he became interested in the darker side of chemistry.

One evening in the last half of his sophomore year, Manion had been befriended by a pretty psychology student. After a few weeks, his new friend brought up the possibility of Manion cooking up a batch of LSD. He'd resisted at first, but the promise of quick and easy money finally seduced him. When he finished that first batch, curiosity had overwhelmed him and he tested his handiwork.

That had been the beginning of a drug problem that engulfed his life and ended in his addiction to heroin. He left JHU in 1978, the middle of his junior year, and had been in a drug-induced fog ever since.

They had first met during Hobart's tour as a Baltimore DEA agent in the early eighties. Manion's intelligence, connections, and paranoia had made him an ideal resource for the young John Hobart. While he never actually informed on individuals, Manion had been a fount of information on the manufacture of designer drugs and the refinement of biological intoxicants.

Hobart hadn't seen him in almost ten years, but hadn't had any difficulty in finding the addict. He lived only three blocks from the house that he'd occupied the last time they'd met, and his phone number had been in the book. Drug dealers could only afford so much anonymity.

At six-thirty Hobart heard the unmistakable sound of a key turning in the lock on the front door. He pulled his .45 automatic from its place under his left arm and quietly stood. By the time the door finally swung open, he had flattened himself against the wall about a foot away from the doorjamb.

The man who entered was taller than Hobart, but his body seemed to sag from some unseen weight, bringing his head to eye level. Hobart recognized him immediately, though the years of inactivity and drug use had taken their toll. He maneuvered himself behind the man and pressed the barrel of his gun snugly into the back of his neck.

Peter Manion froze. "Darren, is that you? I told you I'd get you your money next week, man. I got some stuff cooking. I swear you'll get every dime." His voice was thin and Hobart had to strain to hear despite the fact that he was right behind him.

"Have you not been paying your bills, Petey?"

Manion's body snapped straight, forcing Hobart to adjust the barrel of his pistol. Manion obviously recognized his voice.

Hobart slowly circled around to face him, drawing the gun along the slack skin of his neck.

Manion looked straight into Hobart's eyes, ignoring his elaborate disguise. He began unconsciously rubbing the wrist that Hobart had broken so many years before.

"How you doing, Peter? Long time no see." Hobart grabbed the front of Manion's filthy sweater and pushed him onto the La-Z-Boy that had been his home for the last hour.

He sat down on an old army footlocker that passed for a coffee table. "You look like you've lost weight—been working out?" The haggard face across from him continued to stare blankly. Finally it spoke. "I heard they drummed you out of the DEA."

Hobart shook his head at the feeble attempt at bravado. "That's what everybody thinks. Fact is, I just switched organizations."

"Who you working for now? FBI?"

Hobart shook his head.

Manion's eyes widened. "CIA?"

Hobart smiled and nodded almost imperceptibly.

Peter Manion had always been a borderline paranoid schizophrenic. Hobart still remembered his fantasies involving the CIA and how they were behind everything from Kennedy's assassination to the closing of the local Seven-Eleven. Manion saw the CIA as a faceless, all-powerful organization with operatives behind every corner. Hobart intended to put that paranoia to good use.

Manion pulled his knees up against his chest and cradled them in his bony arms.

"What do you want, man?"

"Just a little information. Should be right up your alley."

Manion remained silent. He looked like he needed a fix.

"We're getting a little operation together and I need your expertise in chemistry." Manion perked up a bit at the word "chemistry."

"The Company's getting fed up with all this narcotics money that's running around. It's keeping some governments afloat that we'd prefer to see sink. You understand what I mean?"

Manion was looking desperately around the room as Hobart spoke. He seemed to not be paying attention.

"We need to cut off their money—so we're going to poison the U.S. narcotics supply."

Manion's hands popped open and his feet fell to the carpet with a thud. "You're crazy!" His eyes continued to dart around the room. Hobart wasn't sure if he was looking for somewhere to run or for CIA agents hiding behind the furniture.

"I have my orders. We'll make it worth your while. Ten thousand dollars and a lifetime supply of top-quality heroin. Poison-free, of course." He punctuated his words by pulling a wad of bills from the bag at his feet and slapping them down on the sofa next to him.

"No way, man. There's no way you can make me help you. I got rights." The last part sounded more like a question than a statement.

"Of course you do," Hobart said soothingly. "This is a great deal, though, if you think about it. We're going to do this with your help or not. So why not make it easy on yourself?"

"No fucking way, man!" The spit that sprayed from his mouth mingled with the dust in the air.

Hobart looked down at his feet, where a can of lighter fluid sat. His old informant didn't seem like the barbecuing type. No doubt the stuff was used to manufacture some kind of high.

He reached down and picked up the greasy can, studying it. Manion was hugging his knees again, rocking back and forth, mumbling as though in prayer.

"You know, Peter, I was watching an interesting show on PBS last night. It was on those monks in Vietnam who set themselves on fire to protest the war. Remember them? I saw one of 'em do it when I was over there. Nasty." He turned the can and began reading the back. "They said that burning is the most excruciating way to die. They also said that a person's sense of smell is the last thing to go. Do you believe that?"

Manion shook his head miserably, sweat dripping down his forehead. Hobart was starting to enjoy himself.

"Awful smell, burning flesh—must be even worse when it's your own." Hobart picked up a steak knife from a half-empty plate on the floor and put it to Manion's throat. With the other hand he squirted the lighter fluid on his head. Manion buried his face in his knees, protecting his eyes. The knife pressed to his neck kept him from rising.

"Last chance," Hobart advised, tossing the nearly empty can behind him and pulling a lighter out of his pocket. Manion's face came out from behind his knees at the familiar sound of the sparking lighter. He looked like he was about to scream, and Hobart pushed harder with the knife, diminishing the cry into a pathetic whimper. He held the lighter a safe distance from Manion, whose eyes were locked on the quivering flame.

Hobart fully intended to kill him if he didn't agree. He'd be forced to pick a less dramatic method though. A screaming ball of flame running around the house was bound to attract attention.

Manion closed his eyes and began sobbing quietly.

Hobart was getting impatient. "C'mon, Petey, what's it going to be?"

5

Near Cumberland, Maryland, November 1

John Hobart set the cruise control at sixty-six and leaned his seat back into a more comfortable position. It was a beautiful night. Cool, but not cold, and crystal clear. The new Jeep rode as smoothly as a Rolls-Royce down the empty highway, allowing him to gaze through the glass sunroof at the stars. He occasionally glanced back at the road to confirm that he wasn't straying over any important lines.

He'd left Peter Manion's house just before seven o'clock, maneuvering through the thickening city traffic and onto the highway out of Baltimore. City had turned to suburbs, and finally the suburbs had given way to the grassy hills of rural Maryland. The radio was beginning to fade, erupting in loud static every few minutes. He fed a classical CD into the dash.

It was almost another hour before he saw his exit rushing to meet him. He tapped out the complex rhythm of the last concerto on the CD as he swung his car off the highway. It wasn't an exit ramp in the true sense of the word, more of an ill-kept asphalt road breaking off from the main thoroughfare. The night closed in on the car as he sped away from the interstate. The faded gray asphalt climbed a steep grade into the darkness.

Eventually the road turned to gravel and then to dirt. He switched on the four-wheel drive and struggled through deep ruts, slowing to under ten miles per hour. The road narrowed to the point that tree branches swished against both sides of the car. The air, moistened by the dense trees, had turned into a swirling fog. Hobart leaned closer to the windshield, resting his chin on the steering wheel.

Finally the headlights illuminated a small break in the trees to the right. He turned carefully into it, hearing the bottom of the Jeep scrape as he maneuvered down a steep incline. When he leveled out, a small cedar cabin nestled in the trees became visible about twenty yards away. He cut the engine and coasted to a quiet stop next to its large redwood deck.

His breath came out like steam, illuminated by the light still on in the interior of the car. His boots made a satisfying crunching sound as he walked around to the back of the car and pulled a large black suitcase out of the cargo space.

The cracked and faded exterior of the cabin, illuminated briefly by the Jeep's headlights, didn't fit with the interior. While the furniture had a hand-me-down look common to weekend retreats, the cabin was immaculately maintained inside. Floors were swept and oiled, and the kitchen was well stocked. Flashlight in hand, Hobart weaved his way through the dark living room and lit a propane lamp on the wall. The flame came to life, bathing the inside of the cabin in a soft blue-white glow.

After unpacking his suitcase in one of the cabin's two bedrooms, he went back out to the car and pulled a large cooler out of the back. It was full of perishables that couldn't be kept at the cabin during his long absences. He switched on the refrigerator and loaded in the food, keeping a cold beer on the counter for himself. He started a fire in the wood stove and settled onto the sofa. The sound of the wind blowing through the tall pines that surrounded the cabin lulled him to sleep.

Hobart jerked as the hot grease spattered on his arm. He quickly threw a lid on the pan, hiding the cooking bacon within. Last night's fog was only a memory, and the sun was beginning to filter through the skylights high above him. In the light, the house took on a colder feel. The cabin had the same unlived-in look as his home in Baltimore. The motion in the kitchen and the smell of bacon and eggs seemed out of place in the sterile atmosphere.

He was halfway through eating his breakfast when he heard the unmistakable sound of tires rolling down the steep hill to the cabin. He looked at his watch as he pushed the chair back and wiped his mouth on a napkin. Fifteen minutes early.

Hobart waved as he walked out the front door and onto the deck. Robert Swenson returned his greeting by sticking an arm out of the window of his beat-up

Cadillac. Pulling to a stop next to the Jeep, he jumped out and slammed the door behind him.

"What the hell's going on, John? A week ago the Reverend comes into my office and tells me he fired you. You don't return any of my calls, then I get that cloak and dagger message from you on my voice mail."

Hobart ignored his question. "You didn't tell anyone you were coming here did you?"

"Hell, no, your message was pretty clear on that subject. So what's going on?"

"Come on in," Hobart said, turning and starting back into the house. "I'll tell you all about it."

Once inside, Hobart repositioned himself in front of his breakfast and started in on it again. "Can I get you something?" he asked, watching Swenson drag a chair in from the living room.

"Nah, I grabbed an Egg McMuffin on the way. So what happened?"

"Nothing all that interesting, Bob. Just got sick of that prima donna, you know? We had it out and he fired me."

Swenson shook his head knowingly.

Hobart had first met Robert Swenson in Vietnam when their Special Forces units had been temporarily combined. After the war was over, their lives had continued on similar paths. Hobart had joined the DEA, and Swenson, the L.A. Police Department's narcotics division. Later, when Hobart had taken the security chief post at the church, he'd brought his old friend in as his right-hand man.

"Shit, John, he'll probably change his mind next week."

"Not that big an issue, really. There's some stuff I've been wanting to do and this'll give me a chance to do it."

Swenson snatched an untouched piece of bacon from Hobart's plate. "What do you have going? Starting a private contracting business?"

"In a way. Actually, I asked you to come here 'cause I want you to come and work for me. I think I've got something for you that you'll find more fulfilling than chasing Simon Blake around."

Swenson looked interested, as Hobart knew he would be.

Swenson had been married for almost six years when his wife had been killed in a car accident. They seemed to have had a perfect marriage—she was one of the few women able to adjust to the life of a cop's wife. Between that and Swenson's rare talent for separating his personal life from the job, it looked like a relationship that was going to last. Hobart couldn't remember exactly when she had died, but it was sometime in the mid-eighties—maybe '84.

As he recalled the story, it had been a clear night in Chicago and Helen had been returning from a college where she was taking classes. The stretch of road where she died was perfectly straight. Inexplicably, a car coming in the other direction ran off the road, through a grass median, and head-on into her Volkswagen Rabbit. The other driver survived, protected by his one-ton pickup. Helen had been decapitated. Later it was discovered that the driver had been hopped up on some drug or another.

"So?" Swenson prompted.

Hobart had spent most of the drive to the cabin trying to figure out a way to hedge on his offer to Swenson. Not to give too much away. He hadn't been able to come up with anything practical. There seemed to be no alternative to jumping in with both feet.

"I intend to stop the illegal narcotics trade in the U.S."

Swenson laughed and gnawed on the piece of bacon. "Don't tell me the DEA's taking you back."

"I'm serious, Bob. America's being torn apart by drugs—you ought to know that better than anyone. I've decided to put a stop to it."

"Never knew you were such a patriot, John."

"I think of it more as an interesting challenge." He wasn't joking, and from Swenson's expression, it looked like that was beginning to sink in.

"Hey, I'm with you in theory, John, but let's face it, the war on drugs is a joke. You and I devoted some of the best years of our lives to chasing our tails."

Hobart put his fork down and took a deep breath. "That's true, we did. But now I think I've found a way to make up for that lost time."

"Planning on running for President? I don't see you as the baby-kissing type."

"I'm going to poison the drug supply."

Swenson dropped what was left of the strip of bacon onto the table and stood. He walked back into the kitchen and poured himself a cup of coffee. Hobart went back to his breakfast.

"You're serious," Swenson said from the kitchen. It was a statement and not a question. He came back around and took his seat, sipping at the steaming mug.

A deep crease appeared in his forehead as he mulled over what he'd just heard.

"Why not? I assume you agree that it would take care of the problem."

Swenson nodded. "Yeah. It'd work. Given the right scale."

Hobart had expected a more enthusiastic response than the blank stare he was getting. Had it not been for Swenson's wife being killed by a narcotics user and his subsequent bitterness, Hobart wouldn't have dreamed of trying to recruit him for this operation. If Helen were still alive, Swenson undoubtedly would have marched into the nearest FBI office and turned him in. She wasn't alive though, she was lying in a coffin in two pieces somewhere in Chicago. And that made all the difference.

Hobart reached discreetly under the table and closed his hand around a hard piece of wood. That morning he had sawed off a baseball bat to a two-foot length and taped it under the table. Robert Swenson was the closest thing to a friend that he had, but his friend either had to get on board or disappear.

It wouldn't be difficult. He would put Swenson's body back into the Cadillac and run it off the edge of one of the winding mountain roads that crisscrossed the area. It was risky, but the local cops weren't rocket scientists. And it was less of a hazard than having someone not involved in the operation running around knowing who was behind it.

Swenson was silent for almost five minutes and Hobart's hand began to sweat, making the handle of the bat damp and slippery.

"I'm in," he said finally. Hobart's hand loosened on the handle.

"But we're gonna have to put together a decent amount of money to get something like this off the ground."

Hobart's hand dropped completely from the handle at the word "we." He wiped his wet palm on his slacks. "Already taken care of."

"Blake's in on it, then?"

"No." Hobart's tone and expression made it clear that Blake's name should never be mentioned again. Swenson took the hint and changed the subject.

"How many people do you figure we need?"

"About eight more. I've already scheduled meetings with them here. The first one arrives at three."

"People you've known for a long time?"

"For the most part," he replied vaguely, beginning to clear the dishes off the table.

"What if you ask them and they aren't interested?"

"That's my problem. I'll take care of the recruiting. You go tie up any loose ends you have in Baltimore."

"Just tell me one thing before I leave."

"Sure. What?"

"How the hell are we gonna pull this off?"

Three o'clock rolled around quickly. Swenson had gone less than an hour ago. They'd spent a productive day going over operational details. It was surprising how much it helped to have someone to bounce ideas off of. Things that seemed brilliant alone in front of the fire could sound stupid out loud.

"Johnny! How you fuckin' doing!"

Hobart's second recruit had arrived and was making his way to the house.

Bill Karns had been a narcotics cop in Chicago when they'd first met. Since then he had quit the force and become a private investigator. His wife died a few years back, leaving him without any surviving family. Given the pick of the litter, Hobart probably wouldn't have chosen him. In his opinion, the man was brainless and undisciplined. On the other hand, he knew that Karns would go for this plan in a big way. His bigotry ran deep. Almost as deep as Hobart's own.

"Looks like you put on a little weight since I was last in L.A.," Hobart observed sternly, slapping the roll of fat adorning Karns' waist.

"You know how it is, Johnny." Karns was the only person in the world who called him Johnny. He'd forgotten how irritating it was.

"Come on in."

Karns was sweating profusely despite the damp cold of the woods. Hobart maneuvered him to the chair that Swenson had occupied earlier that day and got them both beers. Karns grunted his thanks and twisted the top off.

"Good to see you, Johnny. It's been too goddam long."

"You didn't tell anybody you were coming up here, did you?"

"Shit, no. In my business you understand the word 'confidential.' He took a pull from the bottle, almost emptying it. "You needin' a good private investigator?"

"No. But I do have a job for you. Good pay, but you'd probably do it for free."

Karns looked interested, but not so interested that he didn't finish the beer in one large gulp and begin looking woefully at the one across from him. Hobart got the hint and pushed it toward the still-perspiring man. Then he smoothly slipped his hand under the table and around the bat.

"I'm putting together an organization that's going to stop the use of illegal drugs in the U.S.," he said simply.

Karns laughed. "My ass. How the fuck you gonna do that?" He lifted the beer bottle.

"I'm going to poison the narcotics supply."

The beer stopped about four inches from Karns's mouth. "The fuck you are."

"The fuck I am." He could see the wheels in Karns's head slowly turning. It was their only speed.

Karns scooted his chair back and slapped his knee, laughing. "Shit! That oughtta just about piss off all the niggers and the spics!"

Hobart smiled. "I expect it will. So you're in?"

Karns banged his beer bottle down on the table. "You're really serious?"

Hobart pulled a briefcase from the floor next to him and laid it on the table. He opened it, exposing neatly bundled stacks of hundred-dollar bills. "That's fifty thousand dollars. Your advance."

Karns's eyes were glued to the briefcase. He reached blindly for the bottle of beer, almost knocking it over.

"So are you in?"

"Fuck, yeah!" He reached out and caressed the bundles, pulling one out and flipping the edge like a deck of cards. He looked up at Hobart. "You're right, you know."

"About what?"

"I would have done it for free."

He'd been luckier than he deserved. The bat was still taped to the bottom of the kitchen table at his cabin, unused. The remaining six recruits had come and gone over the last week. They had taken quite a bit more work than Karns, whose life could be summed up on a postcard. Hobart had served meals, hiked, boated, and hunted with the rest. He'd probed deeply into their lives, looking for serious girlfriends, jobs, homes that they were attached to, sick relatives, set-in-stone future plans. Only when he was completely satisfied with their answers did he wrap his hand around the bat and pop the question.

There had been a few tense moments of indecision and varying degrees of enthusiasm, but in the end they had all agreed. Hobart had counted on at least one of them having to disappear. Two was probably more likely. He had been dreading the added exposure.

The remaining recruits were all of better quality than Karns, though they lacked his blind loyalty and single-mindedness. Karns would stay with him to the end, no matter what the circumstances. The rest would be wary of the FBI and dealers, and would get out when it got too hot. While they lacked Karns's simple predictability, they made up for it with intelligence and experience. Every one of them was capable of running a top-notch undercover operation.

Hobart slowed his car to match the speed limit as he closed in on Baltimore. He hoped to avoid the police completely over the next year.

"Peter! Good to see you!" Hobart was sitting in his favorite chair by the door as Peter Manion walked into the dimly lit room. His .45 rested next to him on what passed for a table. Intimidation value.

"Hi, John," Manion mumbled. He squinted his glassy eyes to see his guest more clearly. His speech was a bit slurred.

The fact that Manion hadn't been startled by his presence confirmed in Hobart's mind that he probably had fortified himself with a healthy dose of heroin in honor of their meeting. The ten thousand dollars that he had left behind on his first visit had been put to good use.

"What have you got for me?"

Manion walked over to a large pile of books that hadn't been there the last time they had spoken. The jackets were free of the dust and drink rings that covered everything else in the house.

"Orellanin," Manion said, holding a book up as though Hobart could read it through the cover.

"Come again?"

"Orellanin. That's what you've got to use, man." Manion was starting to warm up to his subject. The combination of drugs and his fanatical interest in science appeared to have made him forget the real reason that they were speaking. To him, it had become nothing more than a conceptual exercise in biochemistry.

"Never heard of it."

"I'm not surprised, man. It's distilled from a mushroom that grows mostly in Poland. The *Cortinarius orellanus*."

Hobart was shocked. Manion was yanking his chain. For a moment he wondered if the police were standing right outside the door, but quickly dismissed the idea. He'd reviewed the tapes from the bugs he'd planted and gone over the house with a fine-tooth comb before its owner had arrived. He picked up the .45 and aimed it at a surprised Peter Manion.

"I'm not in a joking mood today, Petey my boy. Not at all."

Manion dropped the book and backed slowly into a corner, his hands out in front of him. "Don't shoot, man. I *am* serious. This stuff's perfect."

Hobart lowered the gun slightly. "I'm listening. But you damn well better dazzle me with your genius."

Manion moved slowly around to the ragged sofa, keeping his back against the wall the entire way. When he sat down, a cloud of dust rose around him. "Listen. The problem with poisoning coke and heroin when it's being processed isn't getting it into the drugs—that's easy. The problems are in distribution."

Hobart leaned back and pulled a small pad from his jacket. He fished around for a pen. "Go on."

Manion, looking more comfortable, continued. "Let's say you just dump a bunch of, say, arsenic into a vat of coke while it's being refined. No problem, you're done, right?"

Hobart nodded.

"But it wouldn't get you anywhere. Distribution would totally fuck you up. Most times, when the stuff is sold, some dealer or another tries it, right? If not, they could just be getting twenty keys of baby powder. So, they try it and drop dead. Who's gonna buy it then?"

Hobart shrugged. It was a good point. "So what's the answer?"

"I already told you, man. Orellanin." Manion picked up the book that he had dropped while looking down the barrel of Hobart's .45, and held it to his chest. Hobart could just make out the picture of a mushroom on the front.

"The beauty of this stuff is that it has like a two-week delayed reaction. Say you shoot it," he pantomimed using a syringe on his arm. "You feel great, while the poison's making its way to your liver and kidneys. By the time you start feeling shitty, you're fucked. Your major organs are toast. The only way they're gonna save you is a transplant—and there isn't gonna be time for that."

"What if a doctor found out early? Could he give the patient an antidote then?"

"Is none, man. I think a few people who've eaten the mushrooms have been saved by getting their stomachs pumped, like, right away. That wouldn't really apply here, since you don't eat coke and horse. Of course, a full blood transfusion might do it—totally change out the guy's blood right after he's been poisoned. I'm only guessing on that, though."

"So I need to crush up a bunch of mushrooms?"

"Not exactly. The poison has to be extracted. It's pretty much a no-brainer, though."

Hobart smiled. "I'm sure you won't have any trouble at all."

"Hey man, I didn't mean . . ."

"I've got a nice warehouse," Hobart cut in. "We'll set you up with whatever you need. Hell, we'll put together a lab that'll put Hopkins to shame."

Manion perked up at that. The thought of being surrounded by steaming beakers, Bunsen burners, and microscopes seemed to agree with him. It had been a long time.

"Okay, Peter, how many of these mushrooms do we need?"

"Depends on how much stuff you want to hit."

"Say fifty keys."

Manion tapped his chin and did some quick calculations. "That's gonna take a lot of 'shrooms, man. You're in the neighborhood of a ton there."

Hobart took a deep breath and let it out loudly. "About a ton. Shit. Is there anything else I can use?" This was becoming more complicated than he'd bargained for. As was often the case, the concept had looked better without the details.

"As far as hitting the stuff at the manufacturer, probably not. You need that delay, man. That's what makes it all work. You could get a shorter delay out of paraquat."

That one rang a bell with Hobart. The DEA had used it back in the seventies. "The defoliant?"

"Yeah, it's a herbicide. Two-day delay—easy to get. I think they call it StarFire or something, now. Two days isn't gonna get you far, though."

Hobart's mind was racing. Manion was right, it

wasn't enough. It had to be the orellanin. "What about downstream stuff, Peter? The stuff we hit right before it makes it to the street?"

"No need to get fancy on that. Go to Safeway and buy rat poison with cyanide in it."

Hobart nodded. "So how do I hit the stuff at the refinery?"

Manion picked up a potato chip from a plate full of molding food and began munching on it. "Oh, shit, getting it into the stuff—that's the easy part."

6

Warsaw, Poland,
November 21

The Krolikarnia was considered a moderately nice hotel, though through the dirty glass of the car window it looked more like a Harlem boxing gym. Hobart eased himself out of the cramped interior of the cab and straightened his body out for the first time in what seemed like ages. He took a deep breath, cleansing his memory of the knuckle-whitening landing at the Okecie Airport, and even more nervewracking ride from airport to hotel.

Hobart doled out twenty American dollars to the cabby and walked around to pull his bags from the trunk. The ex-communist cabbies hadn't yet warmed to performing this service. He had barely begun to pull at his suitcase when, with an unintelligible shout, the driver merged the cab back into the heavy afternoon traffic. His sudden acceleration almost slammed the trunk shut on Hobart's hand.

An atmosphere of lawlessness pervaded Warsaw, and nowhere was it more evident than in the traffic patterns. It seemed the Poles felt that their newfound freedom extended to a considerable amount of artistic license on the road.

The fumes expelled by the cars racing by were beginning to choke him, so Hobart hefted his bags and entered the hotel. A bored-looking woman sitting at the front desk watched him approach. Except for her, the small lobby was empty. She smiled wearily as he approached, but remained silent.

"Hi, I'm Dr. John Stapleton," Hobart said with a thick Southern drawl that was obviously lost on the desk clerk. "I think y'all have a reservation for me."

Still not uttering a sound, she flipped through a well-worn leather book lying on the equally worn desktop. Computers hadn't found their way to the Krolikarnia yet.

"I have it," she said in a thickly accented voice. "Please, you sign your name here."

He obliged and she handed him a key attached to a six-inch-long piece of wood. The number 414 was burned into it.

"Thank you," she said, sitting back down and turning her eyes to the front door. Hobart got the feeling that he'd heard her entire repertoire of English.

No eager bellhop materialized, so he hefted his luggage and walked into an old iron-gated elevator directly opposite the desk.

The sun streamed through an open window in his room, illuminating the sheer white curtains blowing in the breeze. The space was so small that it was difficult to walk around the single twin bed in the middle of the room.

Hobart pushed a Kleenex into the ancient keyhole

from the inside and lay down on the lumpy bed. International travel always sapped his energy, and the effect was getting worse as the years passed.

The room looked like something out of a 1950s gangster movie. It was a simple small cube. A sink stood in the corner with a large painted pitcher teetering on its edge. There was no television; the furniture consisted only of the bed, a lamp resting on a nightstand, and a broken wooden chair sitting next to the window.

Glancing at his watch, Hobart saw that he had a few hours before his meeting. He hated to take a nap—it always seemed to prolong jet lag—but he decided that he should stay sharp. It would probably be impossible to sleep anyway. The disguise he was wearing had been driving him crazy since he put it on. Effective, though. It was getting so he didn't even recognize himself anymore.

A gray wig of nearly shoulder-length hair adorned his head and was tied back in a neat ponytail. The full beard was a bit darker. The proprietor of the costume store had insisted that no one ever had a perfectly matched beard.

He wore wire-rimmed glasses with clear glass, and beneath them his eyes were tinted green by contacts. Having perfect vision, he'd never had to deal with contacts before. So far they had been more trouble than they were probably worth.

The disguise was completed by a tan corduroy jacket covering a reddish wool sweater and well-worn jeans. It was a bit stereotypical, but he doubted that his new associate would notice. It seemed that the Europeans

looked at Americans as one stereotype or another anyway. They seemed disappointed when they saw one
that didn't fit their categories.

Hobart awoke to the sound of knocking on his door
accompanied by a comically accented voice. "Yoo
hoo. Professor Stapleton—are you asleeping?"

He had never actually spoken with Lech Orloski on
the phone, but the voice was exactly what he had
expected.

Hobart had located the man on the Internet
through a loosely knit group devoted to exotic mushrooms. The strange and elaborate subcultures that
inhabited the world never ceased to amaze him. There
seemed to be a club, organization, or magazine built
around every subject imaginable.

When Manion had first suggested using orellanin,
Hobart had been concerned about the complexity of
gathering the mushrooms. In the end it had been simple. His Internet search had no potential to expose his
true identity, and all communications, until now, had
been carried out by computer.

Hobart had simply e-mailed Orloski as to the type
of mushroom that he was interested in and the fact
that he needed about a ton. This had produced more
than a few questions, but he had managed to answer
them to the Pole's satisfaction.

Orloski had, of course, been familiar with this particular type of fungus and had e-mailed Hobart that it
would be a simple matter to collect them. He had
even arranged for a shipping method that would

bypass U.S. customs. That last little service had cost plenty.

Hobart swung his stockinged feet off the bed and walked quickly to the door, effecting a scholarly stoop in his shoulders. He opened it to find Orloski just as he had pictured him—tall, round, and with an enormous beard spilling across his chest.

"Professor!" the Pole cried as the door opened. "It is so good to finally see your face!" He grabbed Hobart's shoulders and kissed him hard on both cheeks.

Hobart took a step backward when the Pole released him, still trying to shake the gauze out of his brain. "It's good to finally meet you, too, Mr. Orloski."

"Please, call me Lech. My car awaits. Are you ready?"

Hobart grabbed his shoes and coat off the floor and motioned toward the door.

The wind was blowing with surprising force, making it necessary for Orloski to put his full weight behind opening the front door of the hotel. He held it long enough for Hobart to slip through, and then made for a tiny European car illegally parked in front of the hotel. Hobart watched the man pour himself into the car and expand into the limited space inside. When Orloski was down to one leg outside the vehicle, Hobart jogged around to the passenger side. His diminutive stature benefited him occasionally, and this was definitely one of those times. Orloski's bulk spilled over the console between the seats, and Hobart found himself sandwiched between the Pole's fleshy shoulder and the car door, the handle of which had settled uncomfortably into his ribs.

"Are you comfortable?" Orloski's tone suggested that the car was a Rolls. The pained look on his passenger's face seemed to escape him.

"Oh, sure, Lech. Just fine."

"Wonderful!"

Armed with the knowledge that his client was happy, Orloski jumped on the gas and sent the small car hurtling into traffic. He took the long route through the city, detouring around endless traffic circles and pointing out historically significant sights by the dozens. He would get halfway through a dissertation on one landmark when another would appear. The prior story was instantly forgotten as he began a half lecture on the next. This went on for about an hour before they broke out of the city and into the rolling countryside.

The wind that had been blowing in Warsaw grew stronger, unhampered by the narrow streets and sturdy stone buildings. The gentle rocking of the car and Orloski's habit of racing up behind other vehicles and slamming on his brakes was making Hobart queasy. He concentrated on the mist-covered landscape and ignored his host's dissertation on Polish family life and the sad history of his ancestors.

After about forty-five minutes, they passed a large group of peasants collected on the top of a windy knoll to their right. They walked bent at the waist, reaping phantom crops from the scrub that blanketed this part of Poland. Orloski changed subjects without taking a breath.

"There are your mushrooms." A fat finger pointed to the slowly circling peasants, almost touching the glass of the passenger-side window. He swung the car carefully onto a muddy side road and stopped. Throwing the door open, he began the laborious project of getting out. He had to hurry to catch Hobart, who had started immediately up the road toward the center of activity. Orloski was breathing heavily as he pulled alongside.

"I found this place a few days after we spoke," he said between gasps. "The man who owns the land allowed us to pick the mushrooms for a small fee. In fact, I believe that I hired some of his family to help." Orloski scanned the distant men and women intently, trying to pick out one of the owner's family members. Not interested in meeting anyone else in Poland, Hobart changed the subject.

"How many people do you have working here?"

"Oh, quite a few. I would guess around fifty. You needed the mushrooms so quickly, you know. I think I am employing nearly every person over ten and under seventy from Takestek.

"Takestek?"

"A nearby village. The citizens are very happy to work for the fair wage I pay them."

Hobart wondered what he considered a fair wage. A dollar a day? Less?

As they crested the hill, Hobart could clearly see the workers' path. In front of the brightly dressed peasants, the mushrooms grew surprisingly thick. Behind them lay a smooth brown-green carpet of grass. About fifty yards ahead, an old flatbed truck was parked in the middle of the muddy road. A young man in jeans and knee-high rubber boots was picking through a pile of mushrooms at his feet.

He looked up from his task briefly, catching a glimpse of Orloski. He waved and stepped carefully around the pile. They met halfway and the boy, who looked much younger close-up, kissed the Pole on both cheeks and then offered his hand to Hobart.

"This is my eldest son, Paul. Paul, I'd like you to meet Dr. Stapleton."

"A pleasure to meet you, Doctor." His English was only lightly accented.

They walked side by side back to the truck, listening intently to Paul's status report.

"I believe that we have about the amount you asked for in the truck, but we have paid the workers until three o'clock, so I thought we'd keep going until then. I assume that you won't mind a few extra kilos?" He looked at Hobart, obviously expecting a show of gratitude for his extra work. Going above and beyond for a customer wasn't a concept that had taken Poland by storm.

"That would be fantastic," Hobart gushed. "The more of these I can get, the more people I can help."

Hobart had told Orloski that the mushrooms were part of a research project at the University of North Carolina Medical School. The mushrooms, he had said, contained a chemical that could be helpful in treating cancer.

"How much longer?" Orloski asked.

"It's two-fifteen now—forty-five minutes."

"Would you like to inspect them now or wait until Paul is done?"

"Oh, I don't think that I want to inspect them at all," Hobart said. "I'm a chemist, not a botanist. That's why I hired the foremost expert in Eastern Europe."

Orloski swelled with pride. "Let's return to my car, then. I have a bottle there that will help keep this damp chill away."

Hobart's second drink, and Orloski's fifth, was interrupted by a shout from Paul. The large pile of mushrooms in front of him had dwindled to nothing, and the workers had straightened up and were walking slowly across the field. Back to their village, Hobart assumed. The two men walked quickly up to Paul and the truck.

"All ready," he announced. The mushrooms had been sealed into six large wooden crates that were tied securely to the back of the truck.

"Wonderful! Dr. Stapleton and I will be taking the truck to the docks so that they can be shipped out immediately. Very perishable, must hurry."

Paul nodded knowingly, and took the keys offered by his father. After a short good-bye, he ran down the hill and sped off in the little car that had brought them there.

Lech pointed to the open door of the driver's side. "After you." Hobart looked at him with a confused expression. "The passenger's side door doesn't open, I'm afraid," Orloski explained.

Hobart surveyed the truck skeptically. It looked as if it had been welded together from spare parts. Rust had eaten away the bottom of the body, which now seemed to float magically above the chassis. All in all, though, it looked a hell of a lot safer than the go-cart they had arrived in, so he climbed aboard. Orloski followed, having some trouble getting himself into the elevated cab. The whiskey hadn't improved his limited mobility.

With a loud grinding noise, they were off. The truck swayed down the mud and gravel road and onto the highway. Orloski pressed the accelerator to the floor, increasing their speed to the truck's maximum of forty. It seemed too fast.

"There haven't been any problems with the shipping arrangements, I hope," Hobart said.

"Of course not. Everything has been taken care of."

Hobart nodded gravely. "Normally, I would never ask your help on something like this. It's just that U.S. Customs can be so unreasonable sometimes. I'm afraid that your mushrooms might sit in quarantine forever before they release them. If they begin to rot and lose their potency, my experiment will be ruined."

The first indication that they were approaching their destination was the smell. The fragrant dampness of the Polish countryside began to fade, replaced by the stench of industry. A cloud of smog on the horizon closely followed the noxious odor, and Orloski started into an animated history about the small river port that was their destination.

The city lacked the hustle of Warsaw. It also lacked the architecture and recent renovation. It was a town of abandoned houses, cracked concrete, and most of all a pervading stink that seeped into every crevice of the old truck. Occasionally a small child could be seen playing in a large pile of bricks or rolling an old tire. Mostly, though, the streets were empty. Orloski pointed the truck down a desolate road leading to the docks. His speech on the history of the area had ended somewhere in the 1600s. He seemed to have no interest in the city as it existed in the present. Hobart was thankful for the silence.

"Here we are," Orloski announced, parking the truck next to a group of wooden crates with large red lettering on all sides. Docked at the end of the pier was a smallish gray-and-white freighter. Rust began at the decks and sprayed out over the sides as though someone had dumped brown paint from the edge.

"Please wait here, I'll be back in a moment," Orloski said, sliding out of the cab and hurrying across the dock to a small knot of men huddled near the ship. He disappeared into the middle of the group. About five minutes later, he reemerged with one of the men in tow and hurried back to the car.

His companion was enormous—well over six feet tall, with heavily tattooed forearms that looked as thick as telephone poles.

Hobart jumped out of the cab, relieved to nearly be done with this phase of the operation.

"John, I'd like you to meet Mikhail. He is the man I told you about."

Hobart offered his hand, but Mikhail just stared down at him. It appeared that he was waiting for Hobart to speak.

"It's nice to meet you, Mikhail. I understand that you can help expedite my shipment's arrival in the U.S." Orloski translated as he spoke. Mikhail listened intently and replied in Polish.

"Mikhail would like to know where you would like your shipment delivered."

"Norfolk, Virginia."

This needed no translation. The man nodded slowly and spoke directly to Orloski.

"He says that there is quite a bit of Naval activity in that area, making his job more difficult. It will cost you another five thousand dollars." Orloski looked apologetic.

Hobart knew that he was being played. Aircraft carriers were not in the business of stopping freighters to look for illegal produce shipments. If there was any additional expense, it was the result of his translator taking a healthy cut of the proceeds.

He was not inclined to generate any ill will by haggling over insignificant amounts of money. It was critical that the product reach the U.S. More important, Hobart wanted Orloski happy. The FBI would undoubtedly be speaking with him in the coming months, and the happier he was now, the more forgetful he might be then.

"That seems fair, Lech, but there is something I need to know," Hobart said in a serious tone.

"What's that?"

"Your friend here is reliable, right? You know how important my research is."

Orloski looked insulted. "Of course he is! I personally guarantee their safe arrival."

Hobart considered himself a good judge of character—a near prodigy, in fact. Orloski would skim as much as he could, but he would deliver. In fact, if he had it to do over again, he would have never made a physical appearance in Poland.

The shipping arrangements had been a difficult decision. Hobart had originally considered taking the mushrooms into the U.S. legally. In the end, though, he had decided that the added scrutiny was a risk he'd rather not take. His passport was good, but he wasn't anxious to subject himself to any undue attention from customs or any other government agency. While smuggling carried its own risks, they weren't resting on his shoulders.

"When can I expect my crates to arrive in Norfolk?"

As Lech translated, Mikhail produced a full-sized clipboard from behind his back. His brow creased with concentration as he silently ran a finger down the grease-streaked papers.

"December fifth," Orloski translated.

"Fine. I have traveler's checks amounting to three thousand dollars with me. I'll give him the other two upon delivery." Lech looked doubtful, but translated as Hobart spoke.

Mikhail shook his head furiously. He and Orloski argued for almost five minutes in Polish. Mikhail seemed to be winning.

"Lech," Hobart broke in. "Tell him that he gets an additional three thousand if they're on time."

Orloski smiled and started in on their heated conversation again, every once in a while shooting a glance in Hobart's direction. Finally the debate ended and Mikhail yelled something to the group of men behind him. For a moment Hobart thought that they were going to be physically thrown off the dock.

"He has agreed to your terms," Orloski said happily. "It wasn't easy, but I finally convinced him that you are an upstanding member of the American academic community. You would be surprised at Mikhail's respect for higher learning."

The group of men hurried past them and began pulling the crates off the truck.

"Mikhail would like to know where he can reach you."

"He can't. I'm going to be on the road for the next month," Hobart lied, leaning against the truck. "I was hoping that I could stay in touch with you, and you could let me know when my assistant should meet the ship."

"I'm sure that can be arranged," Orloski replied. "We'll discuss it on the ride home. And you can describe to me what it is like to live in North Carolina—I hear it is a wonderful place."

Hobart walked toward the truck, glancing back one last time at the crates being moved across the dock. Leaving them there with no receipts, not even a handshake, was tying his stomach in knots.

Hobart snatched his last suitcase off the conveyor and headed toward the glass facade of the Baltimore-Washington International Airport. He started to jog as he passed through the automatic doors, his heavy luggage throwing him slightly off balance. The plane had been almost an hour late arriving, having sat on the runway in New York for what seemed like a lifetime. Bob Swenson was expecting to meet him in ten minutes.

He gunned his Jeep up 295, and in fifteen minutes was only a few miles from the warehouse. It had been nearly two weeks and five thousand miles since he'd left his hunting cabin. It felt like two years.

As he pulled up to the rented warehouse in Canton, little had changed. The only noticeable difference in the building was the new front and loading dock doors, and the tasteful but sturdy-looking bars on the first-floor windows. Venetian blinds had been installed inside, and were closed.

He jumped out of the car and walked up to the new front door. A small metal box, painted the color of brick, was discreetly bolted to the door frame. He rapped on the door. Swenson let him in almost immediately.

The outer office had been completely renovated. A fresh coat of white paint covered the walls. Two antique sofas sat on plush beige carpeting. A small tree grew in the corner, enjoying the light filtering through the blinds.

"How was your trip?"

"Productive."

"Good. You ready for a tour?"

Hobart checked the bottom of his suitcase for dirt, then laid it on one of the sofas. "Sure."

Swenson led him into the back office. It was furnished in the same style as the reception area, though a large desk stood in the place of the sofas. A new-looking computer took up most of the top. A map of the United States was framed over a small love seat opposite the desk. Colored pins were stuck in New York, Chicago, Washington, D.C., Los Angeles, and Baltimore. A plaque on the desk was engraved with the words JOHN SEVEREN, PRESIDENT, CLIPPER CITY ANTIQUES AND ODDITIES. A crystal tray held business cards with the same inscription.

"Looks pretty good."

"Yeah, they just finished. I'd rather deal with ten

pissed-off coke dealers than one Baltimore contractor." He sat down behind the desk. "I've barred all the windows and replaced the doors with steel. We've got motion detectors in the reception area, the office, and the warehouse. All the windows and doors are wired." He threw Hobart a key chain. "The small key opens the panel on the keypad out front—you probably noticed it as you came in the door."

Hobart nodded.

"The large gold one opens the front door. You can't open the loading dock from the outside. The two silver keys are to the apartments upstairs. You've got the one on the second floor. The boxes you wanted me to pick up at your house are in the bedroom."

Hobart fished his keys out of his pocket and added the new ones to the ring.

"So when do we get the mushrooms?"

"They tell me December fifth." Hobart took a piece of paper out of his wallet and tossed it on the desk. "Give this guy a call and tell him you're working for Professor Stapleton. He'll let you know if the shipment's going to be on time. It'll be coming into Norfolk."

"Where're you gonna be?"

"Bogotá. I'm flying out in a couple of days."

Swenson's eyes moved across the piece of paper. "No problem, I'll take care of it."

"How're our guys doing?"

"Better than we expected, actually. I got them all their IDs within a couple of days and they're all on location. The guy in New York has a lead on a warehouse owned by Anthony DiPrizzio. Word on the street is that he ships a lot of stuff through there. He's trying to get hooked up with a job. Miami's actually set up a bogus trucking company and is putting the word out that they don't much care what they ship. They seem pretty sharp."

"They are," Hobart replied. "I figured we'd send our best two guys to Miami. Should be some opportunities to hit big shipments."

Swenson nodded his agreement and continued. "Let's see . . . The guy in D.C. has set himself up as a supplier to street dealers. Not a real sexy operation but he says he's done some deals already. Chicago set up a lab and is making designer stuff—speed and acid mostly. They say they'll probably start doing deals in about a week. The guys in L.A. are setting themselves up as midlevel operators. They say things are moving along but that it could be a couple of months before they get things really rolling."

"How are the finances holding up?"

"Pretty good so far. The warehouse cost us a few bucks, and your last-minute plane tickets are a hell of a lot more expensive than I thought, but we should be okay. Look, I've got a full report for you on the computer. Let me reel it off the printer and you can go through it tonight. The shredder's out in the warehouse."

Hobart sat quietly as his associate punched at the keyboard. Swenson gave a sharp push on the front of the desk, sending him and his chair rolling to the printer which had just come alive. "Oh, I almost forgot, the security code on the door is HEAT. The one on the computer is TIME. I think words are easier to remember than numbers. He pulled the pages off the printer and handed them across the desk. "Why don't you go check out your apartment and get some sleep."

The apartments hadn't been renovated to the degree that the office had. The carpet was clearly new, and there was a new coat of paint on the walls, but the appliances, cabinets, and bathrooms were vintage 1970s Baltimore. On the positive side, the rooms were spacious and well lit, and the furniture was comfortable, if not luxurious. Even better, his partner had stocked the refrigerator with food and beer. Hobart screwed the top off of a Budweiser and settled onto the sofa. The TV remote was on the coffee table and he used it to flip to CNN. Settling back, he scanned the report in his hand. It was headed CCAO, Clipper City Antiques and Oddities.

Swenson had used clever euphemisms for their operation, and the report ended in a cash flow statement and balance sheet. Hobart had no difficulty understanding the real contents of the pages, but anyone picking it up would read a rather confusing antique company financial report. Clever. He was lucky to have Swenson on board.

He took a last gulp of beer and headed for the shower. It was early, but he knew that he should get sleep when he could. Things were going to start moving pretty fast.

"Howdy, ma'am," Mark Beamon said with a deep Southern drawl.

The young woman sitting at the desk in front of

him leaned forward to get a better look at the ornate silver plates adorning the toes of his boots. Then she leaned back, taking in the enormous ten gallon hat perched on his head.

"Can I help you, sir?"

"I'm the new deputy marshal in town. Marshal Beamon."

"You're Mark Beamon?" She jerked to her feet.

Beamon pulled a long piece of hay from his pocket and began chewing it. "I shorly am. And you're Christie—my new secretary, right?"

She stuck out her hand. "Welcome to Houston, Mr. Beamon."

"Mark, please." He pointed behind her.

"So is this my office?"

"Yes, sir. Let me give you the tour." He followed her into the small office. She stood in the center of it and spread her arms wide. "Here it is."

Beamon tossed his hat at a picture of the President, attempting to hook it on the edge of the frame. Both the picture and the hat fell to the carpet.

"Great tour, Chris. Have a seat." He tested his chair like a bather trying to sit in water that is too hot. Finally he settled into it, satisfied. He looked across the tidy desk at his new secretary. He had checked her out before he came. Top scores from all polled.

"So do I have anything to do today, Chris?"

"Yes, sir. Steve said he wanted to see you as soon as you got in. He should be in his office. Straight down the hall. Last door on the left."

"How's his mood?" Beamon asked out of habit.

Director Calahan's emotional state was always in question. Realizing he wasn't in Washington anymore, he held up his hand. "Never mind. Do I have lunch plans?"

"Not that I know of."

"Do you?"

"No, sir."

"Inexplicably, I was passed over by the Queen for a knighthood. Just Mark, please."

She smiled. "Okay, Mark."

"Better." He rose from his chair and headed for the door. "What say you and I do lunch around noon?"

Beamon peeked his head around the doorjamb of his new boss's office. "Steve! How you doin'?"

Steve Garrett stood up from behind his desk and walked across the room. They shook hands warmly.

"It's been a long time, Mark."

"Five years?"

"It's gotta be."

Beamon headed for a sofa in the corner. Garrett closed the office door and sat down on the love seat across from his new ASAC.

"So how's your first day so far, Mark?"

"Good. I just met Chris—she seems great."

"Yeah, you lucked out. She's one of the best."

There was an awkward lull in the conversation. Beamon wanted a cigarette but resisted. Garrett's move.

"So where do we stand, Mark?"

Garrett wasn't going to get off that easy. "Whatever do you mean, Steve?"

Garrett looked down at this thumb and began cleaning imaginary dirt from under the nail. "A high flyer like you can't be too happy about being banished to Houston to work for a . . . conservative guy like me."

Beamon shrugged. "I'm not gonna bullshit you, Steve. Was this my first choice? Nope. I thought I was due an SAC slot. But Tom Sherman disagreed. Probably for good reason—he's a lot smarter about stuff like that than me. So here I am."

Garrett nodded thoughtfully. "And how are you gonna play it?"

Beamon smiled. "Any way you want me to, boss."

"I'm serious, Mark. Tom tells me you live up to your reputation as the best investigator in the Bureau. But I also hear you can be . . ."

"Go ahead and say it, Steve."

"I don't need a lot of problems, Mark. I'm getting old."

Beamon's tone turned serious. "You're not gonna have any, Steve. Look, I need some latitude to do my best work, I'm not gonna deny that. The whole solemn dignity thing never worked for me. But give me a little rope and I can be a hell of an asset to you. I'm looking forward to working here. I really am. Calahan's a thousand miles away, and I get to help a bunch of young energetic FBI agents turn into top-notch investigators."

Garrett frowned. "Try to impart the skills and not the attitude. I can live with one Mark Beamon, but fifty'd be a bit much."

Beamon laughed and pantomimed spitting in his right palm. He stuck out his hand. "That'd be too many even for me. Friends?"

Garrett stared at his hand with mock suspicion for a few seconds, then reached out and grabbed it.

7

Above Bogotá, Colombia,
November 26

At the request of a pretty Hispanic stewardess, John
Hobart put his seat in the upright position for the final
approach into Bogotá's Eldorado Airport. He watched
with mild interest as her ample bottom swayed gracefully through the narrow aisle, jiggling seductively as
the plane shuddered through the Andean turbulence.

He hated flying. It wasn't that he was afraid of
crashing—irrational fear was not one of his failings. It
was the inactivity that put knots in his stomach. Most
people could put their flying time to good use, but
there was something in the white noise that wouldn't
let him think. He could only wait until the wheels
touched the ground and the dull hum of the engines
faded into the rustling of the passengers reaching for
their belongings.

He looked out the window for the thousandth time.
There wasn't a cloud in the sky. The captain promised
a temperature of sixty degrees and a light westerly
breeze.

Hobart hadn't been to Colombia in almost fifteen

years, but little had changed. A cabby dropped him in front of his hotel, still trying to convince him that he knew of places more suitable. It could have been the same man who had chauffeured him around the city in the early eighties.

Hobart stood for a moment on the sidewalk and ran his hand through his newly colored jet-black hair. A combination of sunlamps and dyes had darkened his skin considerably. Contacts turned his eyes brown.

The effect was marginal. Between his European features and accented Spanish, he would pass as a half-breed at best.

His two large black bags had sailed through a disinterested Colombian customs checkpoint without so much as a glance from the officers on duty. He hated leaving things to chance, but sometimes it was unavoidable. Had he been unfortunate enough to have been stopped, the officials would have undoubtedly been very interested in their contents. Fortunately, people were not generally in the practice of smuggling things into Colombia.

The hotel was far worse than the one in Warsaw. Buildings on the Continent aged more gracefully than their counterparts in other parts of the world. Cracked plaster and broken tiles just seemed to add character— a reminder of Europe's colorful past. In South America, run-down was just that, run-down. The hotel looked like it had been built ready to fall down.

The room was about what he'd expected. A filthy cubicle with no furniture other than a twin bed with a single blanket and a folding chair. A mirror hung across from the bed. Judging from the discoloration on the wall, it had at one time adorned the top of a bureau.

Hobart shoved his suitcases under the bed and pulled a crumpled street map out of his back pocket. As near as he could tell, the bar that his friend had suggested for their meeting was about twenty blocks from the hotel. He had two hours before they were to meet, so he decided to walk. It would give him a chance to acclimate to his surroundings. The air and exercise would do him good. Bogotá's eighty-seven-hundred-foot altitude was giving him a splitting headache.

It was almost four o'clock by the time he left the hotel, but the winter sun was still powerful. It heated his black T-shirt, making the jacket he was carrying unnecessary. Pulling a pair of sunglasses out of his pocket, he began his hike across town.

Bogotá seemed to be trapped in time. The feeling that he had stepped back to the early eighties grew in him as he walked. The streets were bursting with people in clothes that hadn't been in style for years. The small houses that lined his route were painted with little thought to the color of the houses next door. Garbage was piled high in the yards of many of the homes that would have looked abandoned had it not been for the people sitting on the porches.

Every few blocks or so a group of dirty children surrounded him, begging for pesos. He noticed that he was one of the few people being mobbed, making him feel self-conscious about his disguise.

Slowly the houses became more and more scarce, appearing only occasionally, sandwiched between colorful shops and bars. Music blared from the small cantinas, replacing the squeals of children playing in the streets and the cautioning shouts of their mothers. Despite the early hour, drunk patrons stood elbow to elbow in the cramped cantinas, swaying maniacally to the volume-distorted Spanish rhythms. An old man stumbled out of an open door, nearly knocking Hobart over, and finally landing on his back in a pile of bulging garbage bags. He sank deeply into their soft contents, and that, combined with his altered equilibrium, was making it impossible for him to get up. He apparently found his predicament hysterically funny and began a drunken, coughing laugh that could be heard clearly over the noise of the bar ten feet away. Eventually a woman stumbled out of the same door and pulled him to his feet. They walked off, clutching each other for support.

Hobart jogged across to the quieter side of the street, continuing his search for the place where his friend had promised to meet him.

The man that he was in Bogotá to see was Reed Corey. They had been attached to the same Special Forces team in Vietnam, and as far as Hobart was concerned, Corey was one of the finest jungle fighters in the history of the U.S. Army. Since his discharge after the war, Corey had wandered aimlessly through Asia and South America. He seemed unable to assimilate back into polite society. Hobart understood his predicament. After three tours in Vietnam where his team had made its own law, returning to the U.S. had been strangely confining. While Hobart had forced his own personal transition, Cory had resigned himself to living in the less genteel countries of the world.

Corey was prone to excesses. He always had been. Drinking, fighting, sex. One thing Corey could not abide, though, was drugs. Hobart remembered sitting idly one time in a small village not thirty miles from Saigon, watching Corey beat one of his men nearly to death—something that he couldn't do as an officer. Corey had discovered a stash of heroin in the man's duffel. He'd never understood other men's need to occasionally escape the grim reality of the war. The things that drove other men to the edge—the heat, bugs, rain, brutality—all seemed to go unnoticed by him.

Why rot your brain when you could be blowing some gooks out? he used to ask. All in all, a perfect recruit for this operation.

On his second pass down the street, Hobart found what he was looking for. He turned off the sidewalk and hurried through the thickening traffic. The entrance to the Piñata Verde was doorless, basically a hole cut in a galvanized metal wall. He stepped through and scanned the room. It was nearly empty. A few tired-looking patrons sat alone at tables with lines of empty shot glasses extending in front of them. The bartender sat on a stool behind a plywood bar, concentrating on an American game show dubbed in Spanish—Hobart couldn't place which one. No one acknowledged his arrival. The only sound in the room came from the television and the bartender trying to beat the game show contestants to their answers.

Hobart padded quietly to the back of the bar, keeping his eyes on the booths to his left as he passed them. He slid into the last booth, and began reading the graffiti carved into the cheap wood table. It looked like Corey would be a little late.

A lone figure at the bar came to life. Ordering two drinks, he jumped unsteadily off his bar stool and started to make his way to the corner booth where Hobart sat. The man was clearly not native. His matted light brown hair came down straight onto his shoulders, framing a tangled full beard. The tie-dyed shirt, baggy shorts, and Birkenstocks completed the effect of a hippie-era throwback. Hobart studied him as he approached.

The man slid into the booth and pushed a full shot glass across the table to Hobart. His ample belly brushed the table.

"Almost didn't recognize you, John. You look like a fucking spic." Reed Corey lit a cigarette, cupping his hand needlessly in the stagnant air. As the flame briefly illuminated his face, Hobart recognized his eyes. They were watery and red-rimmed, where they had once been clear and sharp, but there was no mistaking them. He stared quietly at what was left of his old army buddy, and Corey stared back. "It's good to see you, John. Been a long time." He wiped at his nose with the back of his hand and sniffed loudly.

"It's good to see you too, Reed. . . . You've changed."

Corey laughed at the comment, patting his round stomach. "Yeah, a little too much of the good life." He went through his nose-wiping ritual again.

It was clearly time to switch to plan B. Hobart had come to Colombia expecting to convince Corey to hit the drugs. His training, talent, and knowledge of the area made him the perfect candidate for the operation.

Or so he had thought. The man in front of him looked like he'd have a hard time getting up two flights of stairs. Hobart hoped Corey had enough of his faculties left to at least provide some information.

"So what are you doing in Bogotá? And why the getup?" Corey asked, turning sideways and putting his feet up on the bench. He sniffed deeply.

"Working on a little operation," Hobart replied hesitantly. His old friend could no longer be trusted. Corey's condition screamed drug habit, and while that could work in his favor for getting information, it would work against him in trying to coerce Corey to keep his mouth shut. Addicts tended to quickly forget past promises and fears in their eagerness for their next fix.

On the other hand, he was the only game in town.

"I could use a little information and you came to mind."

"What kind of information?"

Hobart scooted closer and lowered his voice. "Information on cocaine manufacturing."

Corey looked surprised. He took a long drag on his cigarette. "I heard you got booted out of the DEA. They decide to take you back?"

"Nope. Working for myself."

Corey scooted even closer and craned his neck unnaturally. His position obscured his mouth from the other people in the bar. Hobart wondered if lip-reading eavesdroppers were common in Bogotá's seedier bars.

"So what do you want to know exactly?"

"I'm looking for a large coke manufacturing plant

that supplies the U.S. I need to know its exact location, who runs it, and where they get the chemicals they use for processing."

"Which one?"

Hobart shrugged. "Doesn't really matter."

Corey laughed quietly and scooted back to his side of the booth. "What're you up to?" He lit a new cigarette with the waning embers of the old one.

"What's the difference?"

"None, I guess."

"I could use a .22 pistol, too."

"Jesus, John. Anything else? Maybe a fucking invitation to Luis Colombar's birthday party?"

Hobart recognized the name. Colombar was the most powerful of Colombia's cartel leaders. "I don't think that will be necessary."

"Pretty tall order—and it's gonna cost me to fill it. I don't have to tell you that asking those kinds of questions can get you killed. You know what I mean?" His expression was vaguely hopeful.

Hobart looked on with a bored expression. He was being buttered up for the price tag. He knew damn well that the information he needed was already locked in Corey's coke-addled brain. He decided to move things along.

"How much?"

Corey made a show of calculating the amount. "I can probably get you the information for, say, five thousand dollars. The gun will cost you another thousand. That's cost, John. I'm not making anything on the deal."

"I can trust your information, right?"

He looked insulted. "Have I ever steered you wrong?"

He hadn't. Hobart hoped that the drugs and years had left just a fraction of the unfailing reliability that he'd counted on in Vietnam.

"Six thousand it is. When?"

Corey thought for a moment. "Wednesday. I'll meet you at the bar directly across the street at eleven-thirty."

Hobart scowled. He wasn't looking forward to spending nearly a week idle in Bogotá.

Changing the subject, Corey held up his shot glass. "To old times."

Hobart picked up the glass in front of him and gulped back the cheap tequila.

Corey stumbled out of the Piñata Verde at two-thirty a.m. Hobart watched him from the garbage-strewn alley where he'd been standing motionless for the last six and a half hours. He let the drunken man get a fifty-yard lead, and walked quietly out onto the street after him. Corey took him straight north for almost a half an hour, though his weaving gait didn't get them very far in that time. Finally he turned east through a narrow alley, exiting onto an empty four-lane road. About half a block from the alley, he turned again and made his way up a set of stairs to a white house with a sagging roof. It took him almost a minute to find the lock with the key.

Hobart watched until he disappeared into the house. Shivering slightly, he turned and walked back the way he came. Five minutes of vigorous waving found him a cab that took him back to his hotel.

He lay awake on the hard mattress until the sun appeared in his window and the light began inching across the stained vinyl floor. Unexpected changes in plans always made him nervous. There were so many angles to consider. But he had five days until their next meeting and nothing to do but think.

Hobart paced slowly across the small room that had been his home for almost a week. It was ten o'clock Wednesday night. Almost time.

The week hadn't been wasted. He had had time to explore Bogotá and many of the surrounding mountain roads. Talking with everyone who would listen, he had also managed to put a little polish on his rusty Spanish. On the whole, though, he had felt like a horse stuck in the starting gate of a race. But the gun was finally about to go off.

With his newly acquired knowledge of the city, Hobart maneuvered his rented car through the back streets and alleys of Bogotá, ending up in a parking space three blocks from his final destination. It was 11:28. He hurried up the well-lit street and entered the bar across from the one he and Corey had met in almost a week ago. There was no name on it, only a hand-painted sign welcoming its patrons. The bar was wall to wall with sweat-drenched revelers, grinding and shaking to an ear-splitting disco song. Hobart couldn't remember the artist, but he remembered the year: 1977.

He paused in the doorway. There was no way to easily circle the crowd. All of the tables had been moved to the sides of the large room, and patrons had spilled from the dance floor and were gyrating in every open space they could find. Light was supplied almost exclusively by a spotlighted disco ball.

Hobart took his last gulp of fresh air and began pushing his way methodically through the crowd. He started at the left. When he hit the back wall, he moved a few feet to his right and plunged in again. Wet bodies ground against him, and disgruntled dancers mouthed silent insults as he pushed by. An elbow, inadvertently thrown by a large man with a gold tooth, dazed him. Hobart wondered angrily why Corey would choose this place to meet. It seemed that anonymity could be found in more convenient locales.

Finally, a lone brown head bobbed up in the sea of black. It was less than ten feet away, and Hobart adjusted his trajectory accordingly. It took a full five minutes, but he finally found himself standing alongside his old friend. He felt conspicuous when he stopped and began swaying to the rhythms in an effort not to stand out. Corey glanced at him and twirled around. For a moment he thought that his old friend hadn't recognized him, and pulled a hand back to give him a sharp jab in the ribs. Before he could, though, he felt a large padded envelope being pressed into his stomach. He grabbed the heavy package, and pulled an envelope with six thousand dollars in cash from his waistband. Corey took it and disappeared, deftly swinging a rather overweight woman between them. By the time Hobart was able to work his way around her, Corey was gone.

Back in his rental car, Hobart ripped open the package with his teeth and pulled out of his space and into traffic. He didn't have much time if Corey had left right after their meeting.

He had driven the route between the bar district and Corey's home a number of times during his exploration of Bogotá.

The late-night traffic was making it unnecessary to concentrate very hard on driving. He dumped the envelope out on the seat next to him and began sorting through the contents with his free hand, occasionally glancing up at the road.

They consisted of a .22 caliber semiautomatic pistol, twenty or so shells—which were now bouncing all over the passenger seat—a folded topographical map, and an empty envelope with handwriting on it. The envelope had the names of various chemicals used in the processing of cocaine, with company names and addresses next to them. The map had a small circle near the center with something scrawled next to it. The light in the car was too dim to read the blue pen against the blue-green of the map.

Hobart stuffed everything back in the envelope as he approached Corey's neighborhood. Pulling over into an empty spot about three blocks away, he collected the remaining shells off the floor and threw the repacked envelope into the trunk of the car.

After double-checking that the trunk was locked, he walked briskly across the street and into the alley that Corey had led him through a week before.

Hobart found a comfortable spot between a Dumpster and some garbage cans, and settled in. From that position he could just see Corey's front door around the corner of the alley, but would be invisible to anyone walking by. He pulled a long thin knife out of the sheath taped to his calf, and laid it on his lap. The black blade didn't reflect the light from the street.

Hobart checked his watch for the twentieth time—he could just make out the hands. They read four-thirty A.M. He had been sitting motionless, surrounded by garbage, for almost four and a half hours. In that time only three people had walked through the alley. None had seen him, or at least none had acknowledged his presence. People sleeping in alleys were hardly a novelty in that part of Bogotá. The only attention he got was from the rats, upon whose turf he seemed to be intruding. Every fifteen minutes or so another cat-sized rodent would stroll within five feet of him, stop, and stare. He stared back, occasionally he considered throwing something, but knew that the minute he did, Corey would come around the corner. Murphy's Law.

His legs were starting to cramp from his partially crouched position, and that worried him. Corey might be a fat drug addict now, but his days as a killing machine were still fresh in Hobart's mind. It had to be over in a few seconds. He didn't want to give Corey's body the chance to produce enough adrenaline to bring him out of his stupor. A fight with Corey, even at half of his former capacity, could prove lethal.

To the degree that Hobart felt emotional pain, this had been the most painful decision he had ever made. Seeing his old friend brought back memories that he thought were dead and buried. Memories of Corey on point, gliding silently through the jungles of Asia. He had always taken the point and Hobart had always been a few feet behind him, following his footsteps through thick mud or tangled living carpet. Corey's instincts and sharp eyes had kept him and his team from getting their asses shot off more times than he could remember.

Corporal Reed Corey was gone though, and in his place stood a drug-soaked impostor. An insult. To Hobart, Corey was already dead—he was just going to make it official. The regret wasn't for the act of sliding the knife into the back of his head—it was for the memories of Corey that would be forever overshadowed by this last meeting.

There was no alternative, Hobart had decided, though he'd made little effort to find one. Corey was now completely unreliable. Should he put two and two together and figure out that it was Hobart behind the drug poisonings, he would undoubtedly sell that information to the highest bidder. The thought of dodging cartel enforcers as well as the FBI didn't sit well with him. This was the most effective solution to the problem.

At about seven, Hobart noticed shadows beginning to appear. The light of the coming dawn was turning him from an invisible stalker to a derelict bum sleeping in an alley. It was time to move on. Corey was a no-show and he was bone tired.

It was difficult getting up initially, but the blood started flowing back into his legs as he walked up to the house that he had seen Corey go into a week before. As he passed by, he noticed an envelope taped to the door. It was almost invisible against the peeling white paint. Hobart jogged casually up the steps and grabbed the envelope, hoping that it might give some indication as to Corey's whereabouts. To his surprise, it was addressed to him. The letter inside was in the same precise lettering as the list of chemical wholesalers in his trunk.

John,
    I don't know what's going on, but knowing you, it's something heavy. If I were you, I wouldn't want some small-time coke dealer running around with too much information. I know you hate loose ends even more than me—remember Pyon Te? So I thought I'd take your money and go on a little vacation.
    I want you to know that the info I gave you is totally accurate and that I'll take our conversation to my grave.
    Good luck with whatever the hell it is you're doing.

It was unsigned.
Outsmarted by a coke addict. He tore the note up into small pieces as he walked back to his car, throwing the pieces on the ground with frustrated snaps of the wrist.
Pyon Te.
He vaguely remembered the name. Just another nothing village somewhere in southeast Vietnam. His

team had been sent there toward the end of the rainy season in what—1969? It had been a routine operation. Round up the occupants of the village and question them regarding reports of VC activity in the area. What had happened there that rated a mention twenty-odd years later?

It came to him as his key hit the lock of the rental car.

The rain had been coming down in sheets all day. It had slowed them down sufficiently to put Hobart and his team more than two hours late in arriving at the village. The light had been waning as they surrounded the small group of huts and began creeping through the mud toward them. Corey had taken the lead, as he always did, and by the time Hobart arrived in the center of the village, almost all of the twenty or so inhabitants were kneeling in a deep puddle at the edge of the swollen river that wound its way through the region.

Hobart had been questioning a particularly stubborn villager when he'd caught a hint of movement through the rain about fifteen meters south. The downpour had quieted enough for him to recognize the figure as a child of ten or eleven. He had calmly raised his pistol and squeezed off a single shot. The bullet hit the child squarely in the ear.

Inexplicably, Corey had been shaken by the incident. He had stood over the small body for some time. For a moment Hobart had thought he was going to cry. In Hobart's mind there had been no choice. The girl could have made it to any number of adjoining villages in less than an hour, and if the village was indeed

VC-controlled, his team could have ended up with more than they could handle. Corey hadn't seen it that way.

No loose ends.

Back at the hotel, Hobart spread the contents of the envelope onto the bed. He picked up the .22, loaded the magazine, and stuck the rest of the shells in his pocket. The gun looked like it had been well maintained, but he regretted forgetting to ask for a holster. Next he smoothed the map out on the bedspread. A small blue circle was drawn on a mountainous area about fifty miles from Bogotá. Next to it was printed an exact latitude and longitude that ought to get him within a hundred feet of the refinery. He smiled. Where Corey had found precise coordinates escaped him. Still a miracle worker.

He put the gun and map under his mattress and focused his attention on a small white envelope. Running a finger down the list written on the back of it, he saw what he was looking for.

KEROSENE: GARCIA QUÍMICO: 12 ROHO

8

Bogotá, Colombia,
December 2

Hobart spent almost the entire next day looking for a Global Positioning System. These units were relatively new on the American market, having become more reliable following the recent launch of additional navigational satellites. The concept was simple: The small handheld unit tracked as many synchronous satellites as possible and triangulated its position to within a few feet. Hobart had assumed that Corey would give him a general area on a map and that he would have to search that general area for the plant—necessitating the use of his rusty orienteering skills. He had to admit that Corey had come through. That is, if the refinery was at the coordinates scribbled onto the map.

He finally located a GPS at a high-end electronics store in one of Bogotá's ritzier sections. He paid probably double what it was worth and started the long drive into the mountains.

It was almost ten P.M. when he reached the outskirts of Bogotá. Another thirty miles of highway driving brought him to a gravel road that wound its way into the mountains. The night was clear, though the moon was only a sliver. The waning moon, in combination with the thickening jungle canopy and narrowing road, gave the illusion that the world ended at the edge of his headlights.

Almost an hour into the mountains, he was forced to reduce his speed to a slow crawl. He cursed himself for opting for an economy car instead of a more sturdy four-wheel drive. Pressing a button on the front of his GPS, he watched it light up and read out his coordinates. He punched another series of buttons and the unit calculated the direction and distance to his pre-programmed objective. It read just over six miles and the directional arrow pointed northeast. He had been heading roughly north for the last hour, and hoped he could cover the rest of distance in another hour.

In the end, it took him almost ninety minutes to cover four miles. The road never seemed to go straight for more than ten feet and in many places deep ruts had been carved by the heavy Andean rains. When the GPS read out two miles to his objective and the arrow had moved to point more or less west, Hobart eased into a small clearing in the jungle. He could get the car only about five feet from the edge of the road—any farther and he would risk getting stuck.

The smell was somehow different from Asia, he noted as he jumped out of the car and retrieved his bag from the trunk, but the sights and sounds were enough to cause an uncomfortable sense of déjà vu. Pushing it away, he laid his bag on the ground and pulled out a pair of night vision goggles, which he strapped to his face and turned on. The jungle around him was bathed in an eerie green light. Despite the goggles' ability to amplify existing light ten thousand times, his vision was still murky. The weak mix of moon- and starlight was being diffused by the thick canopy of the jungle.

He quickly changed into fatigues and military boots and stuffed the bag under a dense bush. He rose, walking quickly to the car, and let the air out of the driver's side front tire. Anyone noticing it would assume that the driver was out looking for help. A necessary trade-off. The flat would slow his getaway if things got hairy.

Hobart stuffed the .22 into the thigh pocket of his pants, took one last reading on the GPS, and started out at a slow pace. The foliage was dense, impassable in places, and he made poor time. He used the GPS sparingly, stopping every fifteen minutes or so to correct his direction. The unit was having some difficulty tracking satellite through the trees and mountainous terrain, but in the end he was able to get the fixes he needed.

Hobart had been in the jungle for a little over two hours when he checked his position for the last time. He was sweating profusely despite the cool temperatures—every step had been an adventure of bogs, tangled vines, and jagged rocks.

He was pushing the GPS back into his pocket when he heard the unmistakable sound of a human voice—startlingly out of place amidst the white noise of rustling trees and a billion insects. The jungle seemed to change instantly with the presence of another human being. Hobart slowed his pace to a crawl, working his way toward the voice. In less than a minute, the sensitive photo cells of his goggles began to pick up a green glow through the trees. In another minute, the world began to look like an overexposed photograph, and he pulled the goggles off. Dropping to his belly, he crawled toward the light and activity. His progress was slow, every motion setting off a chain reaction of rustling foliage. He was forced to match his speed to that of the weak breeze. Another one hundred yards and he could see his objective. Corey hadn't let him down.

It was less impressive than he had expected—just an old shack. Constructed out of native trees and woven with large leaves, it could easily be mistaken for the residence of a poor farmer. The tip-off was the four dirty-looking men with rifles, sitting with their backs pressed against the hut, warming their hands around a small fire.

Next to the structure was a grouping of metal barrels, each about three feet high and two feet across— he counted six. While he could see them clearly from his position in the dirt, they would be completely invisible from the air. The tops had been covered with a thin layer of leaves and vines. The barrels were what he was looking for. The only chemical needed in quantity to process coke was kerosene.

He watched the four men pass a bottle between them, laughing loudly. He was close enough to see the rotting teeth of the one on the right before the man hid them with the bottle.

Hobart lay there quietly watching for nearly two hours. Two things struck him. The first was the incompetence of the guards leaning against the hut. He guessed that not one of them could hit the broad side of a barn with their rifles dead sober—which they certainly were not. He also doubted that they had a combined IQ over ninety. Their conversation seemed limited to the sizes of women's breasts and the sizes of their respective penises. Their laughter came on cue just before the punch line, suggesting that the dialogue was the same every night.

Hobart calculated fair odds that he could walk up, kill all four with a knife while singing the "Ave Maria" at the top of his lungs. Not that he faulted Luis Colombar's choice in manpower. The Colombian police weren't any kind of real threat to the most powerful organizations—cops were too easily dissuaded. And at the moment, the different local factions seemed to be enjoying an uneasy peace. The guards were more for show than anything else.

The only thing that made the "Ave Maria" plan unworkable was the second thing that struck him. Since he had arrived, at least twenty people had come out of the hut for a smoke or a quick stroll around the clearing. He seriously doubted that the ten-by-ten structure could hold such a crowd, so the actual refining must be going on underground. It was impossible to estimate how many people were beneath him. Fifty? A hundred?

Hobart didn't hear the rumble of the Toyota Land Cruiser's engine until after its headlights had washed over the dense foliage that he had hidden himself in. He buried his face in the soft earth, presenting his newly dyed black hair to the light. He lay perfectly still, straining to hear what he could no longer see. The vehicle skidded to a stop with a deep gravelly sound. He heard the engine die and two doors open. When the lights blinked off, he slowly raised his head.

He was safe. The guards crowded respectfully around a heavyset Hispanic man as an impeccably dressed Japanese man in his mid-fifties walked around the back of the truck.

"Quit hovering around me," Luis Colombar shouted, giving the man closest to him a hard shove. He was in a particularly dark mood. Since he had broken the back of the Cali Cartel and become the most powerful narcotics manufacturer in Bogotá, he had gotten used to doing whatever he wanted to do, whenever he wanted to do it. And what he didn't want was to be touring one of his refineries in the middle of the night when he should be at home in bed with his beautiful young wife.

It was his assistant's doing. Perez had been insisting for years that Japan's youth were getting restless. The thought of working eighteen-hour days and living in a one-bedroom apartment in a smog-filled city wasn't as satisfying as it had been to their parents. And where there was discontent, there was business opportunity.

Colombar turned, acknowledging his guest's presence for the first time in an hour. He hated the Japanese. All business and no fun. He'd personally picked up the little yellow bastard from the airport not two hours ago. He had a big evening planned. Some of the finest women, food, and liquor in Colombia were waiting for his guest at Colombar's estate.

Despite his protests, his guest—reportedly the most powerful organized crime boss in Japan—had insisted on coming straight to one of Colombar's refineries. He wanted to see how it was all done. Fucking nips.

"This way, Yakashiro," Colombar said in English. The Japanese man walked past him, eyes focused on the door of the small hut in the center of the clearing. Colombar followed him through the door and opened a trapdoor under the mats on the floor. They descended a ladder to a dirt floor twenty feet below.

The room at the base of the ladder was the exact same size as the hut and gave the impression of an Old West mine. The crumbling dirt walls were held at bay with rotting timbers, and light was provided by a single rusty oil lamp. At one end of the room was a metal door. It too was covered in dust and mud, making it look less out of place than would be expected. It opened, as if by magic, when Colombar approached.

The underground structure took on a much different look as they passed through the door. Timbers were replaced by cinderblocks painted a uniform white. Light was provided by overhead fluorescent fixtures. This room was only slightly larger than the first and was lined with wooden benches. Four serious-looking men sat on them, eyeing the Japanese visitor suspiciously.

Colombar pulled two respirators off a hook at the door and handed one to Yakashiro. They silently affixed them to their faces. One of the guards pulled another heavy door open and the two men entered, still adjusting the straps on the sides of their masks. Colombar paused halfway through the door. "You don't have a lighter or anything that could produce sparks on you—do you?" The Japanese shook his head gravely. Colombar wondered if his guest really understood anything he was saying.

The room was long and narrow. Large open vats were lined up along the walls, three to a side. Two men paced up and down the length of the room trailing thick black air hoses attached to elaborate masks similar to those worn by firemen. Colombar began to explain the scene as his potential associate pulled up alongside of him.

"The first stage of the refining process takes place in this area." He spoke slowly. Yakashiro's English was poor, and he was obviously having trouble understanding Colombar's accent. The masks didn't help, either.

"The vats are full of coca leaves. First we cover the leaves with potash and let them sit for a while." Colombar walked to the first vat and motioned Yakashiro over. The Japanese man looked into the vat with a look of mild interest.

"The ash begins to separate the alkaloids from the leaf. At that time the mix is doused with kerosene—explaining why we have to wear these masks."

He pointed to the men at the far end of the room and the hoses trailing behind them. "Actually, we found that these masks are only safe for temporary exposure to this room. We had to install those hoses that vent to the outside for the people that work here regularly." The truth was that he had resisted the expense of installing that particular amenity as long as he had been able to. After the death of the sixth worker, though, it had become difficult to find replacements.

They walked to the next vat, which was filled with kerosene almost to the rim. Colombar grabbed a large stick leaning against the wall and gave the leaves a quick stir. "As the leaves soak, the alkaloids begin to float in the kerosene. We squeeze the kerosene from the leaves and put it into drums—they're stored in the next room."

They passed quickly through the door at the other end of the room. Colombar hung his respirator on a naïl and motioned for his guest to do the same.

He pointed to a group of metal drums neatly lined up against the wall. "Sulfuric acid and water are then mixed with the kerosene-alkaloid solution. The acid helps to transfer the alkaloids to the water, which sinks to the bottom. The kerosene is then removed, leaving a mixture of water and cocaine, which is then dried into a paste."

They walked past the drums to a bank of tables guarded by no less than five dim-looking men. They stood as Colombar approached. He ignored them and broke off a baseball-sized chunk of what looked like off-white Play-Doh. He handed it to Yakashiro. "We call this *pasta*. It is cocaine in its most raw form."

Yakashiro squeezed and rolled the cocaine paste through his fingers, remaining silent.

"The process to transform the pasta into cocaine's final form is even more complicated. Let me show you. Right through here."

* * *

Hobart slid his body straight back, putting fifteen feet or so between him and the clearing. Rotating to the right, he began a slow crawl around the perimeter. Occasionally he caught a glimpse of the hut from a different angle through the trees. It took him almost two hours to make a three-quarter turn, but he finally found what he was looking for. A rusting flatbed truck sat idle in a narrow slot cut into the trees. The canopy of the forest hung low over it, shielding it from flying eyes. Poor farmers didn't keep trucks any more than they did barrels of kerosene.

He crawled closer, the faint smell of kerosene reaching his nose when he was less than four feet from the rear of the truck. The license plate was barely readable at this distance, and he committed it to memory.

Peter Manion had devised a simple, yet elegant, plan for the actual poisoning. Hobart had envisioned a risky commando-style operation in which Corey— now he—would have to actually infiltrate the factory and dump poison into the product before it was packaged. The final plan was a hell of a lot simpler.

As it turned out, orellanin had properties not entirely unlike cocaine. In essence they were both biological toxins, only with very different effects. All he had to do was poison the kerosene. As the alkaloids melted from the coca leaves and were transferred to the kerosene and water, the orellanin would combine with the cocaine molecules and transfer smoothly and evenly into the final product.

It looked like the act of actually poisoning the

kerosene was going to be even more simple than he had imagined, as well. The open flatbed would allow him to hit the shipment as it went from the supplier to the refinery. He had originally planned to infiltrate the warehouse in Colombia—adding the local police and security guards as a complicating factor. Not to mention the problem of deciding which barrels to hit.

Having found all he had come for, Hobart crawled directly away from the clearing until the light from the guard's kerosene lamp faded to a faint glow. Switching on his night vision goggles, he stood and walked briskly back to the car, the coordinates of which he had programmed into the GPS before leaving the road. He stuffed his fatigues and gear into the bag and changed back into the dirty jeans and T-shirt that he'd been wearing for a week. Pulling a can of Fix a Flat out of the bag, he filled up the tire and began the slow journey back into town.

Hobart couldn't remember feeling this good in years. He adjusted the air vent above him and took a sip of ice cold Jim Beam from the plastic cup in his hand. His hatred of flying was overcome by the joy of being freshly showered and in clean clothes. He'd spent just under four weeks in Bogotá. With no intervening baths, his disguise had improved dramatically. Something he'd have to remember.

It had been an exhausting trip. He'd spent nearly every night on his belly near the clearing that housed Colombar's refinery and every day tossing and turning on the uncomfortable mattress in his filthy hotel room.

The refinery seemed to be a very professional operation, and that worked to his advantage. They had a production schedule, and they stuck to it. He imagined that the penalties for falling behind were more severe than a light Christmas bonus.

They used two barrels of kerosene a night, without fail. Two of the guards took the old truck up to the chemical plant specified in Corey's note and purchased fourteen barrels every Wednesday. Production went on around the clock, seven days a week.

Hobart took the pillow offered by the stewardess and propped it against the window. He fell asleep with his drink still in his hand.

9

Baltimore, Maryland,
December 26

"John! How'd it go?"

Hobart fell onto the sofa in the reception area of the office. It wasn't as comfortable as it was stylish. "Good and bad, I guess. Reed's . . . unreliable."

Swenson frowned and sat down on the sofa across from him. "So what did you do?"

"I paid him for the information I needed and reconned the refinery myself."

"How'd that go?"

"That's the good part. They run on a tighter schedule than Du Pont. Unless something weird happens in the next couple of weeks, getting to the kerosene shouldn't be a problem."

The frown on Swenson's face melted into a relaxed smile. He stood and disappeared into the next room, reappearing a moment later with two beers in his hand. He gave one to Hobart. "Things have been shaping up around here, too."

"I saw the new addition." Hobart pointed through the door behind him to a large TV suspended near the ceiling.

"Yeah, I figured that when things start popping, CNN'll probably have some interesting programming."

Hobart nodded his agreement and rubbed his eyes. He'd put off the subject long enough. "Did the mushrooms arrive?"

"Yup. Two days early in fact. I picked 'em up in Norfolk last week. You wanna see 'em?"

Hobart sighed with relief. The shipping arrangements that he'd been forced into had been gnawing at him since Poland. He stood and waited for his partner to lead the way.

They walked back through a narrow hall leading to a heavy metal door. Next to the door, two respirators and two pairs of goggles hung on a long nail. Swenson took one of each for himself and handed Hobart the others. "Potent stuff," he explained.

Hobart took him at his word. When they had secured the goggles and masks to their faces, Swenson pushed the heavy door open and walked through.

The warehouse had changed dramatically since Hobart had last seen it. Cheap antiques and dirty wooden crates were stacked everywhere. Old metal signs advertising long-defunct household products hung thick on the walls. Rolled-up rugs were stacked between the legs of overturned chairs.

"Follow me."

They began what seemed like a random route through the stacks of furniture that had looked completely impassable a moment before. The haphazard mess had obviously been created by careful design. Someone coming into the warehouse through the office wouldn't even consider trying to cross to the opposite side. But following Swenson, a well-hidden path appeared as if by magic.

About fifteen feet from the back of the warehouse, a wall of furniture that rose almost halfway to the ceiling stood in front of them.

"How much did all this shit cost?" Hobart asked, jabbing a tattered armchair with his finger. His voice sounded artificial through the respirator.

"About ten thousand. It's all junk—I just needed volume. I'd say we look like antique dealers now, though."

"I'd say," Hobart agreed.

Swenson pushed aside an Oriental rug and ducked under a large dining room table. Hobart followed him, noting that some of the pieces in the furniture wall had actually been nailed together.

As they emerged from under the table, a fifteen-by-forty-foot space opened up in front of them. It was dominated by five large wooden crates stacked against the wall and a long folding table that would have looked at home in a grade school cafeteria. Three empty crates sat in the far corner next to their splintered tops.

A thin figure in a white coat, thick rubber gloves, and an apron was stooped over an iron bathtub throwing in handfuls of mushrooms. The smell of alcohol was strong, even through the respirators.

"Peter! Look who's here," Swenson called.

Peter Manion glanced back and, seeing Hobart, snapped upright. He was wearing the same goggles and respirator.

"Quite a setup you've put together here, Peter," Hobart said, walking the length of the table. It was piled with glass beakers and a mystifying array of other equipment. Hobart wondered how much of it was really necessary and how much was for Manion's personal enjoyment. No point in dwelling on it, he barely knew a test tube from a Bunsen burner.

"So, what are you up to?"

"Uh, I'm converting the active agent in the mushrooms to a concentrated powder form. You see . . ."

Hobart cut him off. Despite his nap on the plane, his eyes were burning from lack of sleep. The last thing he needed was a two-hour blow-by-blow on the chemical processes involved in distilling poison. "How much have you gotten done?"

"Oh, I'd say about a fifth of it. I've got another week or so to finish."

Hobart walked over to a large metal drum much like the ones that he'd seen full of kerosene in Colombia. Out of the top grew a transparent rubber tube capped by a cork stopper. "So you're putting it in here?"

"Yeah. As soon as it's dried into a powder I pour it in there. It's a slow process—you don't want to get any powder in the air. It's real concentrated."

"So how much of this stuff am I gonna need?" Hobart sat down on a rickety chair next to Swenson.

"Depends. Are the drums the same size as this one?" He pointed a shaky finger at the barrel with the tube in the top.

"Yeah."

"I'll have to do some calculations, but probably a half a pound per drum—something like that."

As Manion turned, the reflection fell away from his goggles and Hobart got a good look at his eyes. He was flying. No doubt this was the reason for his enthusiastic cooperation. Hobart wondered if he even remembered why he was working with the mushrooms, or if he'd just pushed it to an unused part of his brain. In any event, he seemed happy, and Hobart wanted to make sure he stayed that way until the job was done.

"How you fixed for money, Pete?"

Manion looked at the ground. "Well, you know, okay, I guess."

"Bob, see that Peter gets a thousand bucks before he goes home tonight." He stood and turned toward the exit, letting Swenson go ahead of him. He wasn't sure if he could make it back through the maze.

"Keep up the good work, Peter."

Back in the office Swenson popped the top off another beer. "So when are we leaving?"

"We'll let Peter finish what he's doing—get that all tied up. Then we'll go. How're our guys in the field doing?"

"Things are getting set up pretty quickly. They all seem to have their covers set. Most of them have made at least one clean transaction."

Gaining a reputation for dealing good drugs at a fair price would deflect blame to other parts of the distribution chain when they began introducing the orellanin into the mix. At least that was the theory.

Out of the top drawer of his desk Swenson took a few sheets of paper held together by a paper clip, and handed them to Hobart. "Here's a full report. It's pretty current, I did it a couple of days ago. You were a little later getting back than I thought."

"Yeah, me too." Hobart rose slowly from his chair. "Hopefully Peter won't go too fast. I need the week off."

A well-rested John Hobart sat behind his desk punching numbers into a LOTUS spreadsheet. CNN was providing background noise.

The figures represented a one-year financial projection for Clipper City Antiques and Oddities. Things looked like they'd get a little tight in about twelve months, but it wasn't worth worrying about. Who knew what the next year would bring?

He had been in Baltimore for a little over a week— plenty of time to slow down and focus on the details. He was completely up to speed on his four undercover teams and had spent some time thinking about the future of the project. So far he was happy with the plan that he'd originally devised. A few holes had appeared, but they were easily filled.

Swenson peeked his head around the corner of the office door. "He's done."

Hobart saved the file he was working on and walked slowly back to the warehouse. Swenson was standing next to the entrance, waiting for him, when he walked up and pulled a respirator off the wall.

"You won't be needing that, actually. The lab's clean. I'm getting rid of all the waste this afternoon."

Hobart hung the respirator back on the nail and followed his partner into the warehouse, weaving his way through the furniture with practiced ease. They found Manion tying up a large Hefty bag. All of the lab equipment was gone, and the floor and walls looked as though they'd been freshly scrubbed. There was still a puddle of water near a drain in the floor that Hobart had never noticed before. Near the loading dock door, a pile of garbage bags sat next to the remnants of the wooden crates that had protected the deadly mushrooms on their voyage from Eastern Europe. In the corner opposite the refuse, a stack of Tupperware containers sat, each sealed in its own Ziploc bag.

Swenson pointed to the containers. "I had Peter break the orellanin into smaller containers. The ones marked with red tape are for you. He figured out the exact amount you need."

"That's it," Manion said, tossing the last bag onto the stack. "It's ready to haul away." He was breathing hard, unaccustomed to the physical demands of cleaning.

Swenson put his arm around Manion's narrow shoulders. "We really appreciate your help, Peter."

He really knew how to play the addict. Hobart noticed that Manion actually seemed to have taken a liking to his partner, who was pulling a wad of bills from his pocket. Swenson pressed them into Manion's trembling hand and began walking back out to the office with him, leaving Hobart alone. He walked over and ran his hand across the innocent-looking Tupperware, remembering that his mother had used similar containers to store leftovers.

It was almost time to find his place in the history books.

* * *

Hobart settled into the ragged easy chair for the last time and surveyed the dark room around him. Very little had changed. The same dishes sat on the coffee table, the food on them perhaps slightly more petrified than it had been a month before. The same books were stacked on the floor, though they seemed to have collected quite a bit of dust in his absence. The same closed-up smell assaulted his nostrils. He found all these things comforting in a way. He hated surprises.

Most of the money that he had given Manion he found stuffed in an envelope between his mattress and the filthy carpet. For all his brains, Manion just wasn't very sneaky—something Hobart appreciated in a flunky. His usefulness was waning, though. Swenson had stayed close to him throughout the distillation process, asking questions constantly. Manion, who loved to talk endlessly about physics and chemical reactions, would have made a great college professor in another life. The reward for teaching Swenson everything there was to know about the distilling process wasn't tenure, though.

Hobart had almost dozed off when he heard a key hit the lock. Looking at his watch, he registered that he'd been there for almost three hours. He watched Manion's unmistakable figure come through the door, leaving it open behind him. A moment later a young girl walked through and pulled the door shut behind her.

She was just a waif, really. All skin and bones

beneath a billowing, full-length chiffon dress. She shared Manion's pale complexion and red-rimmed eyes, though she was much younger. Eighteen at the most.

"Who's your friend, Peter?"

They both spun around, startled. The waif almost fell over.

"John! What are you doing here? I'm finished!" He backed himself against the wall. The waif was over her initial fright but wasn't sure what to do. She stood in the middle of the room nervously shifting her weight from one foot to another.

"Just one more thing, actually." Hobart rose from his chair, stuffing his hands in his pockets. They were covered with surgical gloves and he didn't want Manion to panic. He walked up to the young girl and looked her over carefully. His first impression had been correct, she was definitely no older than eighteen. A closer inspection revealed that she was really quite pretty, in a sort of fragile way. Also, she didn't seem to share Manion's shoddy personal hygiene habits.

"You didn't answer my question," Hobart said, not taking his eyes off the girl.

"Tracy. Her name is Tracy."

"She looks a little young for you."

Tracy was squirming beneath his gaze but hadn't mustered the will to move yet.

Hobart bent and picked up a black satchel lying on the floor. He continued to focus on the girl's face. There were no lights on, and it seemed to glow in the semidarkness of the room.

"Come here a sec, Peter."

Manion did as he was told and took a place next to Tracy.

"Who is he, Peter?" She seemed even younger when she spoke. Her voice came out a high-pitched whisper.

"It's okay, Tracy. He'll leave soon, I promise."

"He's right Tracy, with any luck at all, I'll be out of here in five minutes, tops."

With that, he drew his .45 and pointed it in their general direction. Tracy let out a squeal and Manion put his arms straight up in the air, like a train robbery victim in a bad western. Hobart put his index finger to his lips, silencing them both. Reaching into his bag, he pulled out a couple of handkerchiefs and handed one to each of them.

"If you would be so kind as to stuff these in your mouths?"

They stared blankly at him.

"C'mon, start stuffing," he prompted, leveling the gun at Tracy's nose. That seemed to be enough incentive for her, and she began pushing the cloth into her mouth. Manion followed suit.

"Get all of it . . . good. Now please turn around. Hobart pulled two bandannas out of the satchel and blindfolded both of them.

"Now, why don't you both lie down on the floor and relax." They both sank awkwardly to the floor.

Digging around in the satchel, he pulled a full syringe and a two-foot length of rubber tubing. He reached in again, fishing around the bottom of the bag until he found another syringe, brought along for just such a situation.

He wrapped the tube tightly around Manion's upper right arm and unbuttoned his sleeve. The vein was adorned with an endless trail of holes and bruises—the result of fifteen years of daily injections.

Manion began grunting and wiggling until Hobart pressed the .45 up under his chin. The cold metal froze him. When he'd calmed down, Hobart plunged the syringe into a vein and depressed the plunger. Manion jerked with the initial prick and then relaxed deeply as the heroin flooded him.

Hobart turned his attention to Tracy, who seemed to be straining to hear what was going on. He unbuttoned her sleeve, but found no tracks. The other arm was also clean. He sat confused for a moment. She had the look of an addict and was hanging around with Manion . . .

He grabbed the hem of her skirt and began pulling it up. Her hands came to life, grabbing her thighs to stop the progression. The barrel of the gun under her chin was just as effective on her as it had been on Manion. She went limp and began sobbing quietly through the handkerchief in her mouth.

He pulled her dress the rest of the way up, exposing her pale thighs and a pair of faded pink panties. Pulling her legs apart, he found what he was looking for—track marks scrawled across her inner right thigh.

He drew his glove-covered finger up the soft, cotton covered cleft between her legs and then back down the edge of her panties, where wispy blond pubic hairs peeked out from behind the fabric. Her sobbing grew louder, and she began choking on the handkerchief in her mouth.

He moved quickly, repeating the procedure performed on Manion. He felt his fingers dig deeply into her thigh as the heroin relaxed her muscles, and he let go abruptly. A hand-shaped bruise on the girl's thigh would probably go unnoticed by the overworked Baltimore coroner, but it didn't pay to be careless.

Hobart pulled the handkerchiefs out of their mouths, removed their blindfolds, and stood up, stretching his back. As he was throwing his things into the satchel he looked carefully around the room, making sure that he hadn't left anything but the syringes with the appropriate fingerprints pressed onto them. Manion's breathing was becoming increasingly labored as Hobart padded silently out of the living room and through the back door. Each of the syringes had contained enough heroin to kill two, maybe three people.

The dampness of the soil had finally managed to soak through Tek Markus's jeans, making it impossible to sit still any longer. He lifted himself up a few inches and scooted farther back into the bushes, showering himself with droplets of icy water in the process.

It was too cold to wait any longer. Rico Washington's mother had left for her night job more than ten minutes ago and Tek was starting to lose the feeling in his hands. He cupped them to his mouth and blew. The gray smoke of his breath slithered through his fingers and disappeared with no effect.

Tek kicked his friend's leg gently, being careful not to bring down another waterfall. "Put that forty down and let's get busy, man."

'Twan finished peeling the label off a half-empty beer bottle and then smoothed it back on with his palm.

"Wake up, man. What's wrong with you?" Tek said.

'Twan finally looked up. "This is bullshit, man. Rico ain't gonna do nothin'. He's okay, you know?"

"That's easy for you, man. He ain't been dissin' you all over the 'hood."

'Twan renewed his attack on the label in silence, but Tek could read his friend's expression in the twilight. He was in. He might not be happy about it, but he was in.

Rico had started shooting his mouth off about getting revenge a few days after his sister's funeral. At first, Tek had just ignored it. After all, he hadn't shot her on purpose; it had been an accident. Besides, Rico was a nobody—by all reports, he didn't even own a gun.

But now almost two months had gone by and the verbal attacks just kept on coming. If anything, they had become more frequent and bitter. People were starting to ask Tek what he was waiting for. Starting to speculate that he was scared.

Tek grabbed a small tree with his left hand and 'Twan's arm with his right, and hoisted both of them to their feet.

'Twan mumbled something unintelligible, but followed solemnly as Tek made his way to the front door of the small gray house. Tek stopped at the door and looked over at his friend, who was shifting his weight nervously from one foot to the other and chewing desperately at his lower lip. Frowning deeply, he knocked on the door and stepped back two paces.

When the door began to open, Tek used the added

distance to build up momentum. He drove his left shoulder hard into the door and managed to wedge a foot inside the house. Grabbing the thin bronze chain stretched tight in the narrow gap between the door and the jamb, he used his foot as a lever until the chain broke free and he was able to slip gracefully into the house. He pulled a machine pistol from his waistband as 'Twan closed the door behind them and circled to the back of the room.

Rico Washington stood three feet in front of him, wide-eyed and wearing only a pair of red boxer shorts and a Georgetown Basketball sweatshirt. At seventeen, he was two years Tek's senior and a full foot taller. He had started shaving recently and it had raised an uncomfortable-looking rash on his cheeks.

"Whassup, Rico?" Tek said, leveling his machine pistol at the boy's chest.

Rico backed up a step and looked past Tek. "'Twan—what's going on, man?"

Tek held the gun steady, but looked back at his friend. 'Twan had both hands thrust into his pockets and had squeezed his body between an empty book-case and the wall. He was looking at his shoes as though it was the first time he'd ever seen them.

Tek knew now that bringing him along had been a mistake. 'Twan and Rico had grown up two doors from each other. They had been fast friends until about the fifth grade, when 'Twan's interests had turned to the streets that Rico wanted so much to escape. They hadn't spoken a full sentence to one another in years, but the memory of their friendship hadn't completely faded, either.

Tek turned his attention back to Rico, satisfied that Twan was not going to interfere one way or the other. "What you thinkin', dissing me around the 'hood? You lookin' to die?"

Rico straightened his shoulders and thrust out his chest, trying to use his considerably superior size to psychological advantage. Tek wasn't impressed. He was used to killing men older and larger than himself. Nobody was bullet-proof.

"I asked you a question, Rico."

"You killed my sister, man. You fucking shot her in the head."

"You're nothin', man. Look at you—I kill your sister and you don't do shit," Tek yelled back, his voice dripping with hatred and contempt that he didn't really feel.

Rico stared back at Tek, eyes burning with rage and frustration.

"What's your sister think of you now, huh? Now that she knows her brother's too much of a pussy to take out the guy who killed her and just runs on at the mouth instead?"

Rico's eyes softened perceptibly and he looked away.

It was useless. The spark of anger that Tek had been carefully fanning since breaking through the door just wouldn't burn. Shooting a boy he hardly knew just for being pissed about the death of his sister was harder than Tek had planned. But it had to be done. Without his reputation, he was nothing.

Tek looked at his right hand. It was still numb from the cold. He couldn't feel the rough grip of the gun on his palm, or the cold steel of the trigger under his index finger. The only sensation was a vague burning as the heat of the room seeped into his skin.

He moved his eyes back to Rico and pretended that the finger on the trigger belonged to someone else. The gun jerked twice as the ghost hand tightened and Rico sank to his knees, then pitched forward. Tek jumped to the side, barely avoiding being knocked over by the falling body.

"Oh, fuck man, you killed him," a very young-sounding voice behind him said.

Tek twirled around on his heels, gun stretched out before him, but it was only Twan.

"No shit. Let's get out of here."

10

Western Maryland,
January 5

Hobart was starting to feel as if all he did was travel. He was looking forward to the day the preliminaries would be over.

The sun was rising directly behind him and though it was still low in the sky, he reached for his sunglasses. He had been driving for almost an hour, heading west to Saint Louis. His back was already starting to ache—probably due to the anticipation of being in the same position for the next thirteen hours. Leaning the seat back helped, though it put his arms in an uncomfortable position. Switching back and forth was probably the answer.

This was the part of the operation that put him on edge. Full-page ads explaining the CDFS's actions would only save those who would be better off dead, and give the FBI another thread to pull on. The Reverend had made his decision, however, and Hobart had given his word.

He had originally thought to just shove cash into three FedEx envelopes and mail them off with the ad. After some research into the costs of the ads, though, he had reconsidered. It wouldn't be wise to send the better part of two hundred thousand dollars accompanied only by an anonymous letter. Three ad clerks would most likely be driving Corvettes the next day.

After some thought he had decided that the best bet would be to have cashier's checks issued and to enclose them with the ad. The problem was that he would have to walk into a bank to get the checks, and that it would take the FBI less than a day to swarm all over the issuing branch. Not a thrilling prospect, but there seemed to be no alternative.

It was almost four o'clock by the time the Gateway Arch began to emerge from the haze. Hobart maneuvered his car through the light traffic for about ten minutes before exiting the freeway. He slowed and swung the Jeep right for no particular reason and continued on until he spotted a small branch bank on his right. He drove for almost another fifteen minutes, finally turning into a strip mall and parking in the sparsely populated lot.

He looked in the rearview mirror and examined his disguise for flaws. He wore a gray wig of slightly long but well-groomed hair, and a closely cropped gray beard. His eyes were tinted blue by contacts and partially hidden by wire-rimmed glasses.

He had darkened his skin somewhat with a foundation and accentuated the wrinkles around his mouth and eyes. This, combined with a slightly stooped walk perfected in Warsaw, made him look much older than he actually was. Looking in the mirror with a dispassionate eye, he guessed mid-fifties. He hoped everyone else would, too.

After putting on a pair of blue leather gloves and a matching topcoat, he grabbed the black satchel lying next to him on the passenger seat and walked quickly back to the main street. It took another fifteen minutes to hail a cab, but mercifully one pulled over just as it began to rain.

"Where to?"

"First Missouri. The one on the corner of Pine."

The cabby nodded and eased the car back out into traffic.

"What can I do for you, sir?"

The thin young man behind the teller window didn't look like a bank employee. His long blond hair was tied back in a ponytail that seemed to go quite a way down his back. Despite his youth, his skin had a ruddy complexion, suggesting that he spent most of his spare time outdoors. The nameplate next to him introduced him as Lance.

"Hi, Lance," Hobart said, hoisting the satchel into the teller window. "I'd like to get a couple of cashier's checks made."

"Oh, I'm sorry sir, you don't do that here. Our customer service representatives are the ones that take care of cashier's checks. That lady right there can help you." He pointed to a graying woman sitting at a neat desk near the front of the building.

"Thanks." Hobart dragged the satchel off the counter and maneuvered back through the line of people waiting behind him.

"Hi, may I help you?"

"I hope so. Lance over there told me that you were the person to see about having cashier's checks made."

"That's me. My name's Jennifer. Have a seat."

"Actually, I have a lot of cash in this bag. Is there an office we might use?"

Jennifer frowned with concentration for a moment. "Maybe. I think that my boss might have taken an early lunch. Why don't you wait here and let me check." She dashed around her desk and disappeared around the corner. She reappeared in less than a minute.

"We're all set. Could you just follow me?" Hobart trailed her around a corner and into a small office alongside the teller line. Jennifer sat behind the desk and motioned to one of the two chairs in front of her.

"If you could tell me the amount of the checks you'd like made, and who they're to, I can get them going. Did you say that you were going to pay cash for the checks?"

"Yes, if that's not a problem."

"Oh no, no problem at all. Now, what do you need?"

"Let's see. I need one made out to *USA Today*." Jennifer scribbled on a legal pad. "That one should be in the amount of $57,500."

She looked up. "You said that you were going to pay for these checks with cash?"

"If it's not a problem," Hobart repeated.

She shrugged. "No, I guess not."

"The second one is to the *Washington Post* in the amount of $53,565. And the last one is to the *LA Times* in the amount of $72,000 even."

She added the numbers on a calculator on the desk, ripping the tape off when she was done. "Including fees, that will be $183,072.50."

Hobart tugged at the straps on his bag and began pulling out neatly bound stacks of hundred-dollar bills. Jennifer looked on in amazement.

"There you go. I think it's all there."

Jennifer looked around her and picked up an empty cloth bag with the bank's logo on it. She slid the money off the desk and into the bag and struggled for the door.

"I'll go get your checks. Would you like a cup of coffee? It might take a few minutes."

"No, thank you, I'll just wait."

She paused at the door. "Oh, could you please get out your driver's license and Social Security card. The bank is required by law to keep track of large cash transactions."

"Sure, I'd be happy to."

When she reappeared she was holding three cashier's checks. Hobart looked them over while she copied information from his forged driver's license.

"Look okay?"

"Perfect. Thanks a lot for your help."

She slid the license back over to him. "Now, Mr. Harrison, if you could just look over the information on this form and sign at the bottom if everything looks accurate."

He glanced briefly at the form and signed, using his left hand. The signature was completely illegible.

Jennifer stood up and offered her hand. "It was nice to meet you, Mr. Harrison. Let us know if we can be of any more help to you."

"Thanks, I will."

Back out in the parking lot, the rain had slowed to a drizzle. Hobart hurried down the street in the opposite direction of his car, the empty satchel hanging from his shoulder by its long center strap. When he was well out of sight of the bank, he began looking for a cab. It only took about five minutes to get one this time.

The cab driver watched his rearview mirror silently as Hobart piled into the back seat.

"I'm going to the Safeway up a few miles on the right, but I think I'd like to see the Arch first." The cabby started the meter and made a U-turn in the middle of the street, heading back to the freeway. Hobart relaxed and began going through a mental checklist, distracted only by the sound of western music and the overpowering scent of car air freshener.

His tour around the Arch killed about forty-five minutes, and it was almost five thirty when the cab driver let him off at the Safeway where he had parked his truck. He went in and did a little food shopping, stuffing a cooler full of ice, Pepsi, and deli sandwiches. The shopping trip took fifteen minutes—plenty of time for the cab driver to move on.

Hobart grunted as he hefted the cooler into the back seat of his car, centering it for easy access from the driver's seat. Pointing the Jeep back toward the freeway, he glanced at his watch. He wanted to get in at least five hours of driving tonight.

* * *

"How'd the bank thing go, John?" It was eight o'clock and Robert Swenson was already staring intently at his computer screen.

Hobart tossed three cashier's checks on the desk. "Went okay. File these, would you?"

Swenson took them and walked to the filing cabinet in the back corner of the office.

"You're working on the ad?" Hobart asked, motioning to the computer, though his partner's head was still stuck in a file drawer.

"Nah, playing solitaire. I finished the ad yesterday. Hang on and I'll print it out." He slammed the file drawer shut and sat down at the computer. When the whirring sound of the printer stopped, he pulled a single sheet off the top and laid it on the desk in front of him.

*****ATTENTION NARCOTICS USERS*****

In light of the seriousness of the drug problem in America and the government's inability to stem the tide of illegal narcotics, the COMMITTEE FOR A DRUG-FREE SOCIETY has voted to act unilaterally to end this threat.

Let it be known that on [date] the CDFS will begin a SYSTEMATIC POISONING OF NARCOTICS IN THE U.S.

To include all organic and manufactured illegal recreational drugs.

Anyone using narcotics after that date will run a SERIOUS RISK OF DEATH or permanent disability.

We at the CDFS regret that such drastic measures must be taken and any casualties that may result from our actions. It is our belief that the countless lives saved from drug-related health problems and violence will eclipse those lost as a result of our decision.

*****ATTENTION NARCOTICS USERS*****

"I went out and bought this software package called CorelDraw—it's like a desktop publishing thing—does graphics. But I haven't had time to figure it out. So I ended up just doing it on Word."

"Shit, looks okay to me. It gets the point across. I like what you did with making us look remorseful. It plays well."

"Hey, John, if I didn't believe that this would save lives in the end, I wouldn't be here."

Hobart backpedaled. "I know, Bob. I wouldn't, either. Hey, I talked with my friend in Mexico. You're set for next week. He offered to let you stay at the house—but I told him the hotel would be fine."

"You haven't had time to tell me anything about this guy, John. How about a little background. I'm about to bet my ass on the reliability of his information."

"His name's Richard Penna—call him Rick. We met years ago when we were both with DEA. Actually, I haven't seen him in almost ten years, but I still get a Christmas card every December. Hell, I'll bet there's one at my house now."

Hobart settled himself into the chair more comfortably and put his feet on the desk. "Could I get a Pepsi, Bob?"

Swenson dug through the small refrigerator at his feet.

"Anyway, back in '83, Rick and I were on a four-man detail to apprehend some dealers in D.C. To make a long story short, these guys somehow got tipped off and they were ready for us. Things got ugly real fast, and Rick got hit in the leg while he was in these guys' backyard. He managed to get behind a tree and stop the bleeding in his leg, but he was pretty much pinned down. I went in and dragged him out."

Hobart took the can of Pepsi offered him and continued. "The whole thing really got to him, and he ended up taking an early retirement—got some disability pay—a pretty good deal, if I remember right. But he credits me with saving his life."

"Sounds like you did."

Hobart smirked. "Not really. Like I said, he was behind a tree and he'd stopped the bleeding. The guys out front took care of the perps in about ten minutes. Truth be told, he'd have been better off sitting it out behind that tree than getting dragged across an open yard by me. Stupid move on my part, but shit, we all do stupid things when we're young."

Swenson nodded.

"So Rick retires and gets hooked up with some investors in an up-and-coming resort area in Mexico. I understand that he got in on the ground floor there and he's done really well. Word is that he's still pretty plugged into what's going on, though—kind of as a hobby. I suppose it's also helpful to be able to get whatever your customers need."

Swenson looked skeptical. "And you think Rick will let me in on what's going on with the heroin trade down there. C'mon, man, I've never met him and you haven't seen him in years."

"Rick's a guy who likes to drink a lot and talk big. And he trusts me. You're not gonna have a very hard time maneuvering him into telling you anything you want to know. Shit, you'll probably just have to sit there and take notes."

11

Near Houston, Texas, January 15

Steve Garrett smiled mischievously. "So fess up, Mark. Deep down, you're missing all that high-powered head-quarters stuff, aren't you?"

Mark Beamon sighed and adjusted his seat belt to rest more comfortably across his chest. "Oh, yeah. It's been tough, but the opportunity to work for a man of your stature doesn't come along every day."

Garrett laughed. "No, seriously, Mark. You're not getting bored are you?"

"Not a chance," he replied honestly.

Beamon had been at his new job as the number two agent in Houston for only a couple of months, but he already felt like a new man. To him, the field agents *were* the FBI and Washington was just there to make their lives easier. Unfortunately, his view wasn't a popular one with management.

The fierce loyalty and sense of belonging that had made the Bureau special was quickly fading in Washington. It was becoming just another nine-to-five government organization, run by typical social-climbing bureaucrats.

He had been overjoyed to find that his cynicism wasn't shared by the agents on the street. They were out there chasing the bad guys with the same dedication that he remembered as a young man. He felt he was back where he belonged.

"I was beginning to think those guys at headquarters just kept me around for target practice."

His new boss chuckled. "Well, you sure as hell gave them enough ammunition."

"You know how it is."

Beamon turned and stared blankly out the window, surveying the hard earth and stones as they flashed into view and then just as quickly disappeared. His mind wandered back thirty years to the last days of summer after his graduation from high school. The small concrete schoolhouse where he had spent a good deal of his childhood had long since been torn down, but it hadn't been far from where they were now.

His family had been so proud when he was accepted to Yale on a full academic scholarship. Like many of his friends from that period, he had been the first of his family to go to college. The fact that he was accepted to the Ivy League was completely lost on his father, who saw all colleges as equally regal and mysterious institutions. Until the day he died, he would brag to anyone who would listen that his son had gone to college. When they asked which one, he'd reply that it was a place "back east." Beamon never quite understood that particular mental block.

On the day before he left, he finished packing and drove out to the desert with his girlfriend. Driving the obscure desert roads with a case of warm beer had been a favorite pastime in an era of quickly disappearing drive-ins and skating rinks.

He had never seen her again. Her parents moved to Dallas about halfway through his freshman year at Yale. They had written at first but the time between letters grew longer and longer as the months passed. He could still see the way she looked with the desert sun setting behind her. Strange what the mind grabs and holds on to. It had seemed at the time to be a pivotal moment in his life, but had turned out to be nothing.

The harsh ring of a cellular phone interrupted Beamon's daydreams, and he turned his head away from the side window, not yet ready to be pulled back into reality. They still had an hour of driving before they reached their destination and what would undoubtedly be a very long and very dull meeting.

Garrett punched the button on the side of the phone, turning it to Speaker. "Steve Garrett," he announced.

"Mr. Garrett, this is Bill Michaels. We just had a report of a branch of Houston National being robbed and a guard there being killed. A single marked unit is in high-speed pursuit on Limestone Road about forty miles west of Houston, heading north. We've dispatched agents to the scene."

Beamon sat upright and looked behind him out of the back window of the car, then scanned the landscape all around.

"Keep me posted, Bill, I've got my portable with me."
"Yes, sir."

Garret punched the button one more time and the phone went silent.

"Did you know that I grew up around here, Steve?" Beamon asked.

Garrett looked at him strangely. "I think someone mentioned that to me once. It might have been you, actually."

Beamon wasn't listening. "I spent about six years here as a street agent, too." His voice was rising in volume.

"So?" Garrett replied, dragging the single syllable out longer than he needed to.

"Well, I'd swear that if we take a left onto an old dirt road about a mile up here," Beamon pointed through the windshield, "we'd get to Limestone. It's not a very long road, as I recall."

Garrett looked at him blankly.

"Are you suggesting that I get us involved in a high-speed chase on a dirt road in my wife's car?"

Beamon looked around him in disgust. "Jesus, Steve, I thought this was a Bureau car. Couldn't you have gotten her something a little more sporty?"

Garrett frowned. "You got a gun?"

"Nope. You?"

"Huh-uh."

Beamon shrugged. "Shit, Steve, they gotta be most of the way up Limestone by now. We'll just take a leisurely drive up there, pull in way behind the cops, and show up after they've got the whole thing sewn up. You know how the Director's always harping on our relationship with the locals. Lots of PR points to be had here, you know? Besides it'll be fun."

Garrett mumbled something under his breath that Beamon didn't catch. Then he spoke up in a defeated tone. "Okay, where's the turn?"

Beamon smiled broadly. "You should be able to see it up on the left in a minute or two."

A narrow dirt road appeared as they came over a rise, and Garrett swung the car onto it, slowing to under forty miles per hour. He simultaneously grabbed the phone and hit a speed-dial number.

"Bill Michaels, please."

"Bill? It's Garrett. Please advise the police that Mark Beamon and I are heading up . . ." he paused and looked to his new ASAC for help. He didn't get any.

"Shit, I don't know. Some road that goes to Limestone."

Beamon strained to hear what was being said on the other side of the phone, but it was impossible over the noise of the car. It wasn't used to being off the asphalt.

"That's right. We should hit Limestone in—" he looked at Beamon, who held up six fingers, "—six minutes. I'm driving a blue '92 Ford Taurus. Tell 'em not to shoot at me."

He hung up the receiver.

The Ford's suspension did an admirable job on the old road, though the low-slung bottom scraped the ground every few minutes. Each time metal scraped rock, Garrett winced as if he could feel the car's pain.

Beamon knew that he wasn't making points by shaming his new boss into this chase. The thought of a couple of young kids in a squad car coming up against a proven killer didn't sit well with him, though. And as an added bonus, they'd almost surely miss their meeting.

"We should be coming up on it pretty soon, so stay sharp. If I remember right, this road's gonna dead-end into it."

Garrett leaned forward slightly, squinting through the dust kicked up by the car's tires. A low ridge bobbed up and down on their left like a buoy in the ocean. The wail of a siren became barely audible from the north.

"Shit, it looks like we may be closer than we thought." Garrett touched the brakes, slowing the car to a little over thirty miles per hour.

"Sound travels funny out here—that squad car could be anywhere," Beamon said, trying to sound casual.

The crossroads appeared in front of them, following a natural gully, and marking the end of the ridge to their left. Garrett pulled the car as far to the left as he could without getting into the rocky soil that guarded the road's edge, and set up for a hard right turn.

Just as his hands tightened on the wheel, a dark green car rocketed into their field of vision, heading at a speed that was going to put the front grill of Garrett's wife's car into its passenger side door. Beamon's hands flew instinctively to the dashboard, bracing himself for an impact, as Garrett slammed on the brakes and spun the wheel hard to the right. The tires didn't bite into the loose dirt and gravel, and the car's forward momentum continued, back wheels drifting left in a lazy arc.

It turned out to be just enough to avoid a major collision, and their front bumper only lightly tapped the back of the car in front of them. The impact was enough to send the other car into an exaggerated fishtail, finally slamming its front end into a sturdy rock outcropping along the left side of the road.

The siren that had seemed to be in front of them turned out to be emanating from a police cruiser coming up quickly behind them. Beamon had been right about sound in the desert—the siren had been reflecting off the low ridge to their left, making it impossible to accurately pinpoint.

Both men jumped out as the squad car skidded to a stop behind them. Garrett had his FBI credentials held high in the air and was yelling "FBI" at the top of his lungs just in case the police hadn't gotten the message. He dropped them when a gunshot shattered his wife's front windshield.

Beamon jumped for the ditch alongside the road and began crawling toward the police cruiser.

"Mark, you okay?"

It was Garrett, yelling through a barrage of gunfire that seemed to be coming solely from the car that they'd just run off the road. Beamon hoped that it was just another acoustic trick, and that the cops hadn't forgotten their guns too.

"Yeah. You?" he shouted back.

"Yeah."

By now Beamon was directly below and to the left of the squad car. He could just see the top of its lights from the four-foot-deep ditch that he was lying in.

"Hey guys," he shouted to the men above him. "It's

Mark Beamon with the FBI. You got a call telling you we were coming, right?"

"Yes, sir, Mr. Beamon," a young voice replied. "You should be okay to come up here."

Beamon noted that the shooting had stopped. He struggled to his knees and peeked over the edge of the ditch. As luck would have it, the squad car was turned sideways in the road, and its front fender was only about five feet from his position. The shooter was nowhere in sight, probably huddled behind his car, reloading.

Beamon jumped out of the ditch and rolled to the squad car, noting sadly that it wasn't as smooth a ride as it had once been. His headquarters-bred gut caused him to bounce up once every revolution.

He ended up on his back behind the front wheel of the squad car, looking up into a frightened face.

"Are you all right, sir?"

"So far." Beamon dragged himself to his knees and began brushing himself off.

A slightly older cop was peering around the back bumper of the squad car. Beamon's eyes moved from him to the young cop's gun.

The young man followed Beamon's gaze to his right hand. "Is there something wrong, sir?"

"Three-fifty-seven with a four-inch barrel," Beamon observed in a conversational tone that sounded out of place in the eerie silence that had followed the suspect's initial barrage.

The young cop didn't seem to know how to respond to the comment.

"You know, I only brought an old .38 snubnose with

me," Beamon lied. "I don't suppose you'd consider lending me yours, and using the shotgun."

"No problem, sir," he said, handing the pistol over.

Beamon eyed carefully down the sights as the young cop slithered into the car for the shotgun. Early in his career Beamon had been a firearms instructor and one of the best shots in the Bureau. It had been years since he'd spent any meaningful amount of time practicing, but shooting was like riding a bicycle. He figured he'd probably still rank in the top five percent.

Beamon turned to the cop at the rear bumper. "Can you see anything?"

"Not really, sir. The suspect's car is sideways to us with its back wheels in a ditch. It's about thirty-five yards from us and about fifteen from your car. He must just be sitting behind it. Can't really go anywhere without walking right out into the open." The cop moved back to let Beamon take a look. The name tag on his uniform read O'ROURKE.

Peering around the back bumper, Beamon could see Garrett about forty feet in front of him, back pressed against a rock outcropping. He didn't look happy as he stared back, arms crossed in front of him.

"You okay there, Steve?"

His boss replied with an obscene gesture.

Beamon leaned back against the tire of the car and took a deep breath. The two police officers looked hopefully at him, obviously grateful to relinquish command of the situation.

"What're you hearing about backup, guys?"

"Ten or fifteen minutes," O'Rourke replied.

Beamon grimaced. The smart move, he knew, would

be to just wait for the troops. That plan of action had one rather serious flaw, though. He wasn't looking forward to being found covered in dirt and hiding behind the tire of a squad car. All in all, that would be only marginally better than being shot in the ass.

"Look, Bud," he yelled in the general direction of the suspect's car, "it's four against one now and the odds aren't gonna get any better for you. Why don't you just come out from behind the car with your hands on your head, and we'll put an end to this before they bring in those fucking SWAT prima donnas."

He peeked back around the bumper to see if his speech had any effect. For a moment there was nothing. Then a single shot rang out. Beamon whipped his head back behind the car. The two cops looked disappointed.

When his heart slowed down enough for his brain to start functioning again, Beamon realized that the suspect had never appeared from behind the car. What was he shooting at? He let that compute for a minute.

"I do believe that man just shot himself," he said finally, mostly to himself. Expressions of disappointment were replaced by expressions of hope on the faces in front of him.

"Why don't one of you guys go check it out."

O'Rourke adjusted his gun in his hand and began to make his way toward the back of the car. Beamon stuck a foot out, blocking his path.

"That was a joke, son. Geez, you guys need to lighten up."

"I'd be happy to go, sir."

Beamon believed him.

"Nah, it was my play. I'll go. You guys cover me."

He poked his head out one last time, and seeing that it was clear, ran to Garrett's position behind the rock.

"What do you think?" Garrett asked, arms still folded. He looked like he was getting ready for a siesta.

"I think the guy might have shot himself, actually."

"Great! When's our backup getting here?"

"Ten minutes or something. I think I'm gonna go around and take a look, though."

Garrett didn't seem excited about that strategy. "You really think that's smart, Mark?"

The truth was that he didn't, but he'd never let that stop him before. "No fucking way I'm gonna be found hiding from a corpse."

With that, he began moving slowly away from the rock, eyes focused intently on the car in front of him. In his peripheral vision, he could see that the two policemen had their guns out over the hood of their car.

He gave the suspect's Buick a wide berth, moving silently around it. When the area behind the car started to come into view, he wanted to have at least thirty yards between him and the shooter. He may be a touch rusty, but there still weren't that many people who could outshoot him at that distance.

The dirt road behind the suspect's car slowly came into view as Beamon continued circling to the left. He concentrated on staying relaxed and breathing evenly.

A motionless foot appeared and Beamon froze. He waited for a couple of minutes, watching for movement. Satisfied that there was none, he began edging left again, keeping his eyes locked on the leg that was slowly appearing. Even from this distance, it was obvious that the dirt next to the man was discolored and slightly reflective. Beamon quickened his pace, bringing the man into full view. He was dead.

He relaxed his grip on the .357 and walked up to the car. The top of the suspect's head was missing, and a 9mm pistol had been dropped in the dust next to a still-smoking crack pipe. Beamon ignored the pistol, focusing on the man's right leg. Everything below the knee was missing.

"He's dead!"

Garrett appeared from behind his rock. O'Rourke and his partner stood up from behind the car, still pointing their guns in the general direction of the Buick.

Beamon continued to stare at the suspect's stump of a right leg. "Uh, was there anything unusual about the description of this guy when it came over the radio?"

They two policemen looked at each other as they followed Garrett toward the car. "Not really. Male Caucasian, mid-thirties, about six feet."

"Is that it?" The front page of a newspaper appeared suddenly in Beamon's mind, complete with a large unflattering picture of his face. The headline read:

FBI CHASE CAUSES INNOCENT MAN TO COMMIT SUICIDE

"No, wait a minute. They did say he had a real bad limp."

Beamon rushed to the car and dove into the open passenger side door. The front seat was empty. He crawled in, leaning over the seat into the back. He exhaled violently enough to blow the thin layer of dust off the seat in front of him. A paper bag full of cash had been knocked onto the floor between the seats. On top of it sat a prosthetic leg.

It had been long over a week since Swenson left for Mexico. To relieve the boredom, Hobart had set to updating his financial records and reestablishing contact with his operatives. Unfortunately, after three solid days of work he'd run out of things to do. After that, the days seemed to last forever.

The fact that he couldn't go home, and felt uncomfortable going to places he had regularly frequented before, magnified his idleness. The tastefully decorated walls were beginning to close in on him as he sat in the office, watching CNN and playing chess against the computer.

When his mind wasn't fully occupied, he tended to worry. Every day, his thoughts worked through what had occurred thus far. He began with his individual operatives spread out across the U.S. Would they get caught? If they did, would they give him up? It was true that none of them knew where he was or how to contact him, but the loss of his anonymity would sure as hell give the FBI an edge. And what about the FBI? He had worked with them long enough to foster a grudging respect for their tenacity and intelligence.

Finally his thoughts would turn to Reed Corey. He

was finding it difficult not to replay Corey's escape over and over again in his head. How could he have made such a stupid mistake? He'd gone to Colombia specifically to recruit one of the best military men he'd ever known, and then after meeting with him, had dismissed him as some kind of brain-dead coke fiend.

What was the old saying? Hindsight is twenty/twenty.

On the other hand, Hobart didn't have much respect for the intelligence or professionalism of drug dealers—even the top men sitting in their fortresses in the mountains of Colombia. As far as he was concerned, they were just a bunch of children. Having said that, though, he wasn't anxious to have them gunning for him.

And then there was the future. An operation of this scale was bound to have screwups. What would they be?

Hobart turned back to the chess game glowing on the computer screen. He knew better than to sit around and run endless doomsday scenarios. Pretty soon there would be FBI agents and cartel thugs behind every telephone pole. He tried to focus on his game, but it was becoming more and more difficult.

It was almost three o'clock when the sound of the telephone broke through the drone of CNN. He snatched it off the desk before the first ring faded. "Clipper City Antiques and Oddities."

Swenson's voice cut through the static of a marginal connection. "How are things going?"

Hobart glanced at a VU meter next to the phone. It indicated that the line was free of bugs. "Question is, how are things going with you? Did you find what you were looking for?"

"I think so."

Hobart frowned deeply. "What do you mean, you think so?"

"Well, actually I'm ninety-nine percent sure, but it's all based on circumstantial evidence. Penna gave me a general location for the refinery and told me it was disguised as a private airfield. I found the strip pretty much where he said it'd be, but I can't get very close 'cause it's clear-cut. I'm working from about a hundred and fifty yards with a spotting scope—can't hear any conversations. There's a pretty big hangar on the property, bigger than they need. No planes ever go into it. Every couple of days, a plane lands. They load it up with a few boxes and off it goes again."

"Sounds like what we're looking for."

"Yeah, I'm sure it is. They also bring a lot of supplies into the hangar, though they don't seem to be on as tight a schedule as your friends in South America. Also, I can't tell how much stuff they've got stockpiled 'cause it's all stored inside."

"So are we a go?"

"Absolutely. I've tracked the, uh, items in question to their suppliers, and shouldn't have a whole lot of problems with access. Their security just doesn't anticipate this kind of thing. You'd need an army to steal a fucking peso from these bastards, though."

That was one of the things they had working for them this early in the game. Drug dealer security was set up to prevent someone from stealing finished product—not to stop someone from introducing something new into the production line.

"The problem I'm gonna have down here is with timing. I can, uh, do what we proposed within, say, four days of your go-ahead. But I don't know when it will affect America, if you know what I mean."

Hobart smiled. The doomsday scenarios that he'd been creating over the last week didn't seem to have materialized. At least not yet.

"That's not a problem. I should be able to get my timing down to somewhere between five and ten days, so we'll make the notification coincide with that. You just do the best you can to work within that time frame. If your product is a few weeks late, it's a few weeks late. Where can I reach you?"

Swenson gave him the number.

"I'll call you on the twenty-second, at three o'clock your time. Stay on top of what's going on down there."

"Don't worry," Swenson replied. "Talk to you next week."

12

Bogotá, Colombia,
January 22

Hobart tempered his need for anonymity with his need for sleep and compromised on a slightly nicer hotel this time through Bogotá. While the employees were less forgetful when it came to faces, the bed was a lump-free queen, and the bathroom wasn't down the hall. Correcting another mistake, he rented a sturdy four-wheel drive at about five times the cost of the puny economy car he had subjected himself to the month before.

It was 3:55 P.M. Bogotá time, and would be approaching three o'clock in Mexico. He picked up the phone next to the bed—another amenity he was grateful for—and dialed the number Swenson had given him. It was picked up on the second ring.

"Hello."

The combination of street noise floating through his open window and the static on the line made it difficult to hear. "How are things going over there?" he asked in a loud voice.

"Real good. Just waiting for the go-ahead."

"You've got it. I'm going tomorrow night. I should be back home sometime the day after."

It was difficult to tell if the sound coming through the line was a heavy sigh or just another wave of static.

"It'll be good to get this over with and get home. I'll see you in a couple of days."

There was a loud click as Swenson replaced the receiver.

His final words struck a chord. The tension was building in Hobart, too. The preliminaries of a mission always tied him in knots. Too much planning and not enough action.

Hobart maneuvered the powerful Range Rover through the midmorning traffic, cutting across the heart of the city. Ahead of him, the mountains seemed to float in a haze of exhaust fumes. He sucked in a deep breath of the foul-smelling air and exhaled loudly. The adrenaline pumped evenly through him as he approached the point of no return. He had almost forgotten what it felt like during his uneventful years with the church. It was a little like dying, he imagined.

The traffic eased as he moved farther from the city center toward the suburbs. By the time he turned off on the old mountain road, his was the only vehicle in sight.

The ride wasn't much more comfortable than it had been the first time, but he was covering terrain at least three times faster. He worked through the gears slowly, keeping in mind that a road like the one he was on could cripple even the Range Rover. This was not the time to get careless.

About halfway to the pullout that had been so useful on his reconnaissance missions, a cloud of dust became visible high on one of the switchbacks in front of him. A moment later, the source of the cloud appeared. He instantly recognized it as the truck used by the refinery. Right on time.

The decrepit old truck slowed to a crawl, its right tires dipping out of sight on the steeply angled shoulder of the road. Despite the distance still between them, Hobart could see the look of concentration on the driver's face as he stared intently forward. The expression was almost too intense. Happy hour must have already started.

Hobart's suspicion was confirmed when the man in the passenger seat put a clear, unlabeled bottle to his mouth and took a healthy slug. The driver maintained his focus on the road as they passed within a foot of each other. His passenger stared intently at Hobart through glassy eyes. It wasn't a look of suspicion—more one of mild interest. Not very many cars traveled this road. In fact, this was the first time Hobart had seen one, despite his frequent trips to study the refinery.

It was almost another half an hour before he found the pullout. He took a deep breath and backed the truck down the steep slope and into the jungle. At the bottom he came to a full stop for a moment, shifted into first gear, and gunned the engine. The truck came to life, shooting up the steep incline like a rocket. Satisfied that he wouldn't have any trouble getting out, he backed down again.

Hobart jumped out of the truck, and struggled back up the hill on foot. From the road, the Range Rover was completely invisible. The only problem was the tree branches that had been bent from its entry. They all pointed to the truck's position. Fifteen minutes of sweaty work in the waning light returned the branches to a more or less natural position. He walked along the road one last time, satisfying himself that everything looked as it had before his arrival.

He opened the hatch on the back of the Range Rover, and changed into the torn jeans and T-shirt that had served him so well on his first trip. A grimy poncho and weathered felt hat completed his costume. Scooping up a handful of dust from beneath his feet, he splashed it on himself and brushed it in vigorously. Finally he pulled a full bottle of tequila out of his bag, and dabbed the clear liquid on his poncho. Walking around to the passenger-side mirror, he examined the result.

It wasn't great. A close inspection would undoubtedly reveal him to be a gringo. Of course, a close inspection wouldn't be necessary if he was forced to speak. His Spanish was still weak.

The good news was that he was completely unrecognizable as the well-groomed, bespectacled man who had passed by the guard's truck only an hour ago. Not that Hobart anticipated being seen, but it paid to be cautious. Secreting the .22 in his waistband, he began backtracking on the road until he found the other feature that had prompted him to pick this as an ambush site. A little over one hundred yards from where he had pulled off, a sharp turn in the road com-

bined with a deep horizontal rut. It had been necessary to slow his Range Rover to a crawl to negotiate
these obstacles, and he imagined that the old truck
the guards were driving would have to nearly stop.

Walking down the slope to the south of the road,
Hobart picked out a comfortable-looking tree and sat
down, leaning his back against it. He estimated
another two hours before the truck came lumbering
back up the mountain.

The change in temperature as warm day turned to
cool night dispersed the clouds, and he could see the
stars twinkling through the canopy of the forest.
Other than that, it was completely black.

His estimate had been optimistic. It was almost
three hours before he heard the unmistakable sound
of the old engine struggling in the thin mountain air.
He stood, stretching his legs. The truck's headlights
weren't visible yet, and he had to feel his way up the
slope and into a thick stand of grass. The natural
sounds of the jungle stopped. The only things that
existed were the coughing of the motor and the soft
grass beneath him.

He shielded his eyes as the truck's light arced
through the night, searching for his fully dilated
pupils. Slowly he lifted his hands away from his face,
adjusting to the sudden explosion of color around
him. The smell of exhaust fumes replaced the comforting perfume of decaying leaves.

As expected, the truck slowed with a shudder as
the washed-out groove in the road became visible to
the driver. The front tires dropped in gingerly. Once
in, the driver gunned the engine and the tires obedi-

ently popped out the other side. The drums of kerosene in the back pulled apart and clanged back together, despite the ropes securing them to the bed.

When the back wheels had fully cleared the wash and the driver had peeled his eyes from his sideview mirror, Hobart jumped to his feet and circled behind the truck. The gears ground as it slowly gained speed, held back by the weight of the drums.

Hobart jogged up behind the struggling vehicle and sat down on the foot or so of empty space remaining on the back of the makeshift plywood bed. Taking a deep breath, he relaxed for a moment, knowing that the large metal drums completely hid him from view. After he had collected himself, he grabbed the rim of the drum directly behind him, using it to steady himself as he peeked over the cargo.

During his reconnaissance of the refinery, he had noted that the back window of the cab had been replaced by an old metal sign. It was still there, further blocking him from the eyes of the men up front.

The truck swayed violently as it made its way up the road, forcing Hobart to keep both hands on the barrels in front of him to keep from falling off—something he hadn't anticipated. He was going to need his hands.

Climbing carefully onto the swaying barrels, he noticed a gap where three of them hadn't been pushed completely together. He crawled over and wedged his right leg down into it, then rocked back and forth, confirming the stability of his position. The truck hit a bump, and drums shifted, biting painfully into his thigh.

With both hands now free, he pulled a pair of pliers out of his back pocket and began twisting the tops off of the drums. The smell of kerosene, combined with the rocking of the truck and the loud laughter coming from the cab, were causing the nervous lump in his stomach to evolve into full-fledged queasiness.

It took him almost ten minutes to get the tops off all of the drums and to stash them in a cloth pouch brought along for the purpose. He stuffed the pouch partially into the hole that his leg was wedged into and pulled a bundle from under his poncho. It consisted of seven lengths of white PVC pipe, each about eight inches long. One end of each pipe had been sealed with a white plastic disk, making them look like candles on a stand. The other end was sealed with only a condom stretched tightly across the opening.

Half listening to the loud conversation coming from the cab, he slid them, condom first, into the holes in the tops of the drums. The large bases kept the pipes from falling in.

The pain in his leg was becoming excruciating as the weight of the drums shifted rhythmically back and forth. The constant rubbing had torn through his jeans and was working on his skin. He could feel blood beginning to slide down his leg.

After a few more minutes of agony, Hobart began pulling each pipe back out in the same order that he'd put them in. The condoms had been dissolved by the kerosene, and the deadly powder emptied into the drums with anticlimactic silence. He threw the pipes one by one into the trees behind the truck, holding his breath against any particles that might escape into the air.

By the time he had the seventh of ten tops screwed back on, kerosene had sloshed onto the tops of the barrels and was being held in quivering pools by their raised edges. He had managed to avoid most of it, but he could feel it beginning to drip down the hole next to his leg. He shifted violently to keep the poisonous kerosene away from his widening wound.

One more.

He tightened the second to the last top with his pliers. As he pulled the last one out of the cloth pouch, the conversation that he had been half monitoring took a turn for the worse.

"Pull over here, I've got to piss," the passenger in the cab said in Spanish thick with alcohol.

Hobart began working his leg from between the barrels, cursing quietly. It came out in painful inches as the truck slowed to a stop. He threw the last stopper into the trees and positioned himself so that he could use his free leg to push against the drums. As the passenger nearly fell from the truck, Hobart's foot cleared the hole, and he dropped on his back onto the kerosene pooled on the tops of the barrels.

The quiet splash startled the man stumbling toward the trees. Hobart watched through half-closed eyes as the man spun clumsily, moving his hand from his fly to his side. It took him a few seconds, but he finally managed to get his gun clear of its holster and level it in the truck's general direction.

Hobart lay perfectly still. His body tensed as the

barrel of the gun leveled at him, praying that the man wasn't stupid or drunk enough to fire a gun at fourteen barrels of kerosene from five feet away. Apparently, he was. His hand jerked on the trigger, and Hobart's teeth clenched involuntarily as he waited for death. Nothing happened.

The safety was on.

Hobart continued to watch through half-closed eyes as the man tried to comprehend what had happened. It didn't take long. He flipped the safety off the revolver and leveled it at the back of the truck again.

"You on the truck. Get down from there!"

Hobart stirred. He sat up slowly, as though in a drunken stupor.

"What the fuck is going on out there, Carlos?" The driver yelled, opening his door.

"It looks like we have a passenger!" Carlos was speaking confidently now, but was still swaying slightly from the tequila that he'd been nursing on the drive.

Hobart jumped off the truck, falling to the ground. The fall wasn't pantomimed; his leg was completely numb. He lay there motionless on the dirt road, thankful to be off the top of the barrels. The poisoned kerosene had been soaking through his clothes.

From his position on the ground, Hobart could see the flicker of the headlights as the driver passed in front of them.

"What the fuck were you doing up there?" Carlos screamed, pushing the gun into Hobart's face as he got unsteadily to his feet. The driver stopped a few feet away and leveled a rifle at his head.

"Ceratibo," Hobart replied quietly, keeping his head down in a submissive pose. Ceratibo was a small village about twenty miles past the refinery that was the truck's destination.

Carlos pushed his .357 harder into Hobart's cheek, pressing him back against the truck. He used the barrel of the gun to force his head to the right.

"Does this look like a fucking bus to you?"

"No, señor," Hobart replied, trying to keep his answers to simple phrases that were easy to pronounce.

"Smells like one of the tops came off the kerosene, and this asshole's been sleeping in it," Carlos said to the driver, looking disgusted. "Hey, I got an idea."

He grabbed the front of Hobart's poncho and swung him away from the truck, almost falling himself. Digging in his pocket with his free hand, he produced a lighter and flicked the flame to life.

"I'll bet this prick would make a nice torch!"

The driver laughed and Hobart almost joined him. It seemed ironic that he was replaying his recent visit with Peter Manion, but on the other side of the lighter. If there was an afterlife, Manion was loving this.

Hobart fell back against the hill behind him, sliding a hand innocently under his poncho and releasing the safety on the .22 tucked into his waistband. It wasn't ideal, but if he had to he could shoot both men, take their guns and money, and the kerosene would still end up at the refinery by tomorrow night.

The driver chimed in as Hobart began to slowly pull the gun free.

"Carlos, you fucking moron. You light that asshole up, and he's gonna run right over to the truck and blow us all to Kingdom Come."

Carlos looked disappointed, but seemed to see the wisdom in his friend's words. He put the lighter back in his pocket.

"Now let's get the hell out of here—we're late as it is." The driver's tone suggested that he was Carlos's superior.

"What do you want me to do with this piece of shit?"

"You shoot off that gun an' we're gonna have trouble," he warned. "They'll be able to hear it from here." The driver walked back around the truck and began surveying the drums. Finding the one without a top, he stuffed a rag into the opening.

Carlos grunted in frustration as Hobart continued to slowly free his pistol.

When the driver's door slammed shut, Carlos finally made a decision and gave Hobart a vicious kick to the face. He could have avoided it easily, but there was no sense in pissing the man off anymore.

Through watering eyes, he watched Carlos pull out his penis and begin to relieve himself on his chest. As he felt the warm fluid seep into his clothes, he briefly considered pulling the gun. The thought passed quickly, though, and he just lay there quietly as Carlos zipped his pants up and walked back to the truck, cackling.

The moment the truck disappeared from view,

Hobart jumped up and jogged slowly across the road. He managed to make it down to the forest bed before the light from the receding truck completely disappeared. He stripped off all of his clothes and strapped on his' night vision goggles. He headed quickly away from the road, remembering a stream that ran fairly straight north to south. It took him about ten minutes to reach it, and he walked into its center and began scrubbing. The mountain water took his breath away at first, but no more than the mingling smells of kerosene and urine. The water stung the open wound in his leg, drowning out the throbbing coming from his blood-spattered nose. Finally he put his goggles on a rock at the side of the stream and washed the blood from his face, carefully feeling the bridge of his nose. Broken. Another battle scar to add to his collection.

The trip back to his truck went much faster than he had anticipated. Visibility was poor, even with the goggles, though it was sufficient to avoid large objects such as trees. They did manage to pick up one of the pipes that he had thrown from the back of the truck, giving it an eerie greenish white glow. He gave it a wide berth.

Back at the Range Rover, he quickly dressed and pulled out onto the road. The smell of kerosene hadn't been completely eradicated, so he rolled down the window to circulate the air.

He tried unsuccessfully to push the thought of the poison from his mind. It hadn't made it to the gash worn into his leg, but had it penetrated his skin? Had the poison mixed well enough to cause the fumes to be dangerous, or had it been forced to the bottom when it was dumped in?

He wished that Peter Manion were still alive. Even if the news was bad, he'd rather know now. Wondering for the next two weeks was going to be a hell of a lot worse.

13

Baltimore, Maryland,
January 30

The good news was that it had been a week since his kerosene bath in Colombia, and he felt fine except for the dull throbbing in his nose. Of course, that didn't prove anything. Manion had warned him that the effects of the mushrooms would be negligible for almost two weeks. And then you'd be dead.

The bad news was that he hadn't heard a word from Robert Swenson since he had given him the go-ahead. Hobart was struggling to keep his mind from running endless worst-case scenarios. Its current favorite was that his partner had been captured and was at this moment giving him up. He had briefly considered moving from the warehouse, but where to? Better to just sit it out and keep his eyes open. In the interim, a bullet-proof vest and extra clips for his .45 had found their way under his jacket.

He had planned to have a ballpark time frame on the arrival of the tainted heroin before putting the ads in the paper, but it didn't look like he was going to have that luxury. In the scenario currently branded

into his mind, the heroin didn't even get poisoned—
Swenson was caught going in. In any event, his best
guess was that the first wave of bad coke was going to
hit the American shore in about four days. His estimate wasn't based on scientific study or statistics—it
was really just a guess. There were too many variables
to get a reliable estimate. Shipping schedules, modes
of transportation, Coast Guard activity, final destination. The list went on.

Grabbing a handful of tissues from a box off the
desk, he walked to the open filing cabinet behind him
and pulled out three Federal Express envelopes, careful to keep the tissues between his fingertips and the
flimsy cardboard. He tossed them on the desk and sat
down. It wasn't quite the elevating moment that he
had hoped for, but the ads had to go today. He had
probably already waited too long.

The climax to all of the preparation seemed to dissolve in light of Swenson's disappearance. All Hobart
could do was hope that his partner hadn't been caught
until he had finished what he was there to do. Or better yet, that he had been shot leaving the refinery
area.

Hobart switched on the computer in front of him,
and pulled up Word.

Dear Sir or Madam:
I have enclosed an ad that I would like placed
on a full page in Section A on February 3. I have
also enclosed a cashier's check for the amount
quoted to me by your advertising department.

The amount of the check should, I hope, be
enough to convince you that this is not a hoax.

Sincerely,
CDFS

He stuffed each envelope with a copy of his letter
and a copy of the ad, careful not to touch the paper
with his fingers. He mentally thanked FedEx for its
self-sealing envelope—the FBI was doing amazing
things with saliva these days.

He opened the front door carefully, scanning the
street. Fortunately, this section of Baltimore housed
almost no Hispanics. A Mexican drug enforcer
would stand out like a man in a tuxedo. Not spotting
anyone who looked like they were from much farther south than D.C., he stepped out onto the street
and set the alarm. His eyes continued their slow
sweeps of the neighborhood. The fact that no one
had tried to knock down the warehouse with
machine guns was a good sign. Maybe Swenson was
killed after all. The thought of his old friend's bullet-
riddled corpse lying on a dilapidated airstrip in
Mexico was sad, but not as sad as the thought of his
own bullet-ridden corpse lying next to a dilapidated
warehouse in Baltimore.

He glanced at his watch as he pulled his truck out
into the quiet street.

Four thirty. Just in time for the fucking rush hour.
Maybe the aggravation of the Beltway would be
enough to get his mind off Mexico.

* * *

The traffic had been even worse than he expected because of a fender bender that left two middle-aged men fistfighting in an overgrown grass median.

Instead of getting his mind off his problems, the cramped confines of the truck and mindlessness of driving had focused his thoughts into an ever-changing and increasingly morbid collage.

It was almost eight o'clock when Hobart pulled back into his parking space in front of the warehouse. The three FedEx packages were now irretrievable, locked in a drop-off box near the Capitol building.

The street was as he had left it. The group of children playing ball in the alley alongside the warehouse were still there, though the bright winter sun had been replaced by shadowy streetlights.

The warehouse wasn't as he had left it.

The perimeter security was on, but the interior systems had been disabled. Hobart shut down the door alarm and moved quickly inside, pushing the door shut with his foot, and drawing his gun out of sight of the people on the street. Something else had changed. What was it?

He had left the lights on, as they were now. The furniture all looked untouched. Then it hit him—there was a quiet, almost imperceptible, hum coming from the office. He vividly remembered shutting off the computer after using it.

Hobart moved silently across the floor and darted into the office, his .45 held out directly in front of him and his finger already squeezing gently on the trigger.

No one. He walked quickly around the desk. The computer screen glowed a soft gray.

THE PASSWORD IS INCORRECT. WORD
CANNOT OPEN THE DOCUMENT
C:\WINWORD\ADLET.DOC

Someone had been trying to access the letter that he had just written to the newspapers. Hobart flipped the switch on the computer's side and walked back to the door of the office. The outer room was still empty and quiet. He slipped through it and down the hall toward the warehouse, peering into the empty bathroom as he passed. The door to the warehouse was open, and he heard the unmistakable scraping of furniture being moved—as though someone was searching for something.

He stood motionless for a moment, back pressed firmly to the decaying brick wall beside the open door. It couldn't be the cops—no way—he hadn't done anything yet. The Mexicans? How could they have bypassed his security?

No point speculating when the answer was fifteen feet away. He jumped through the doorway and leveled his pistol at the head of a man wearing dark sunglasses and carrying a large box. The man dropped the box while Hobart was still in motion. The sound of breaking glass was followed by the strong smell of beer.

"Jesus, John. Don't shoot," the man cried. He sounded like he had cotton balls in his mouth.

Hobart didn't instantly recognize the soft, round face before him, but the voice was unmistakable. "What the hell happened to you?" he asked, sliding the gun back into its holster under his arm.

Robert Swenson pulled off his sunglasses, revealing black circles around red eyes. His cheeks bulged comically. "Pretty nice, huh?" He bent and collected a few unbroken beer bottles from the open top of the box. "You haven't been keeping the 'fridge stocked."

"Did you do it?" Hobart said, ignoring Swenson's comment.

"Why yes, I'm fine. Thanks for asking. Yeah, it's done. Shit should hit the streets in a week or two."

Hobart sighed heavily, feeling the week's anxieties melt away and the burning in his stomach fade with them. He took the beers from his partner's hand and walked back to the office, sitting in the chair in front of the desk. Swenson took his usual place behind it.

"Doesn't look like things went too great for you, either," Swenson said, pointing to Hobart's swollen nose. "Did you get the job done?"

"Yup. And the ads went out in FedEx today."

"I figured that's what the file ADLET was." He pointed to the blank computer screen. "Couldn't get in though—didn't know what your password was."

Hobart pointed to the beers on the desk. Swenson grabbed them and put them in the refrigerator, pulling out the last two cold ones and handing one across the desk.

"So where the hell have you been?" Hobart asked.

"Fucking bad luck's all. I was too close to the airstrip and got spotted. Some guy taking a piss where he shouldn't have been, you know. Anyway, they kicked my ass good—thought I was DEA." He took a pull on his beer, shaking his head at the memory. "They kept me in a back room in the hangar I told you about for a few days. To make a long story short, they were waiting for their boss to give the okay to put a hole in my head."

"Did he?"

Swenson smiled mischievously. "You're gonna love this. So the boss shows up. We talk for a couple of minutes and I stick with my story about wanting to charter a plane. By the end of our conversation, I'm pretty sure I'm a goner. Then he quotes a Bible passage to me—kind of out of the blue, you know. I guess that was supposed to be my Christian burial. Anyway, I recognize the quote from one of Blake's sermons—you know how good my memory is for useless shit—and I cite it. So that leads to a big conversation about God and the Bible. Turns out this guy's some kind of combination murderer/dealer/Christian soldier. So we talk Jesus for about another hour and he just lets me go. Actually, he didn't only let me go, he made his soldiers apologize to me and take me back to my hotel."

His story finished, Swenson leaned back in his chair and put his feet on the desk. "So what's with the nose?"

Hobart related his adventure with the drunk guards on the truck, leaving out the part about lying in the tainted kerosene.

Swenson laughed loudly, seeming to take perverse pleasure in the image of his ever-serious partner getting pissed on. "We're a couple of sorry old farts, aren't we? All we have to do is fool a bunch of drunk dumb-shits with second grade educations, and we both get caught and beat up." His laughter faded into a quiet giggle. "Thank God, it's over."

"You said it," Hobart replied, holding his beer up. His partner leaned forward, and the bottles clinked quietly as they touched together.

The Reverend Simon Blake padded down the stairs in the new slippers that his daughter had bought him for Christmas. They were a bit small, but he could never bear the thought of taking back anything she bought him. As soon as she forgot about them, they would be relegated to the box at the top of his closet. They would make a nice addition to the ugly ties, useless electronic gadgets, and one very large belt buckle stored there. Erica insisted that the children pick out his gifts themselves.

A cold blast of air tried to blow his robe apart as he opened the front door, but the belt tied across his ample belly managed to hold. He trotted out onto the frost-covered porch, retrieved two newspapers, and rushed back to the house. The sun was peeking up over the trees at the end of his property, quickly turning the frost into gently quivering dew.

Back in the kitchen, Blake poured a healthy slug of skim milk into a bowl of low-fat granola. A look of distaste spread across his lips as he watched the individual grains bob up and down in the white liquid. This was the substitute for bacon and eggs that his wife had devised to halt the progression of his waistline. No way to start the day, as far as he was concerned.

The Baltimore Sun and Washington Post lay in front of him on the table, wrapped in damp plastic bags. The house was dead silent. He'd had the same ritual for years. Getting up a half an hour before the rest of the family to read always seemed to put his day into perspective. He knew that there wasn't much time before pandemonium struck, so he pulled the Post out of its bag and carefully stripped it of its rubber band.

As he smoothed the paper out on the damp table next to him, his hand passed over the boldface type announcing the top story of the day.

ORGANIZATION THREATENS U.S. NARCOTICS SUPPLY.

His emotions ran away from him for a moment, starting with excitement and ending, inexplicably, in despair. He had managed to put the entire situation out of his mind over the last few months and now it all came flooding back. Seeing it in black and white, sprawled across the front page of the Post, made the whole thing uncomfortably real. He smoothed out the paper one last time and began reading.

Toward the end of the article, he was feeling a little better. It seemed that the press hadn't gotten ahold of any information that his ex-security chief didn't want them to have. Blake nurtured a healthy fear of the tenacity of the press, as did all television evangelists. The story had also described how serious the drug problem was, and that this may be an effective way to correct it. Overall, a more balanced piece than he had expected.

Blake's reflections were interrupted by the sound of small feet pounding down the stairs on their way to the kitchen. He quickly folded the paper back up and pushed it to the center of the table, as if it were some girlie magazine that he was hiding from his parents. Realizing what he had just done, he shook his head silently. He just wasn't cut out for this kind of work.

14

Washington, D.C.,
February 7

Thomas Sherman gathered up a stack of folders from his desk and tucked them securely under his arm. He paused on his way out to catch the tail end of a news report on the television nestled in a bookcase next to his desk. The channel was perpetually tuned to CNN—a station that was becoming more and more a staple in the diet of FBI and CIA. When they weren't caught up in something trivial, CNN had its nose in everything. More evidence of the superiority of free enterprise over government agencies, as far as he was concerned. Profit, it seemed, was the great motivator of man.

When the screen faded into a commercial for Teflon pans, he clicked the TV off and continued for the door. He should have been running a tape on the report—it dealt directly with his top priority of the day. The problem was that he had never learned to record on the complex VCR built into the TV—despite his daughter's diligent tutelage.

Sherman rushed down the drab hall, taking a hard

right into the last office suite. He smiled at the Director's secretary as he charged through the outer office. She smiled back. "They're all in there, Tom."

Punctuality was not what had propelled his meteoric rise through the ranks of the Bureau to become its second in command. Sometimes he wondered what had propelled it. His soft voice and grandfatherly demeanor didn't fit the image of the take-charge FBI man. Mark Beamon delighted in introducing him as a hat maker, insisting that Sherman had became the associate director only by some bizarre twist of fate.

He closed the door quietly behind him, confirming uncomfortably that he indeed was the last to arrive. Director Calahan sat behind his large desk, framed by two American flags. Across from him sat Frank Richter, associate deputy director in charge of investigations, and Eric Toleman, ADD in charge of administration. The chair between them was empty, and Sherman rushed across the thick carpet to take it.

"Sorry I'm late," he said, narrowly averting dropping all of his papers on the floor as he sat.

"No problem, Tom, we know you're a busy man," the Director replied with a sarcastic edge to his voice. It was well known that he didn't like to be kept waiting.

Sherman had learned to dread these meetings. Calahan had become Director almost two years ago and liked to have his hands in everything. That, in and of itself, was not a problem. Sherman had been critical of the previous Director for his lack of involvement in day-to-day administration. The problem arose when Calahan had decided on his first day that his fifteen

years on the appellate bench, and subsequent appointment to the FBI, made him the country's number one
law enforcement expert. But he had never bothered to
learn the first thing about the operation of the organization he now commanded. That, combined with his
comically overinflated ego, made him a dangerous
man. It was common for him to ask questions that a
first-year agent could answer, but if any of his executives appeared pedantic in their reply, he would throw
one of the tantrums that had become legend at the
Bureau.

Sherman stretched his long legs out as far as they
would go without hitting the desk in front of him. The
three executive agents were seated in a straight line in
front of the Director's desk, like schoolboys in the
principal's office—a position that they had become
accustomed to over the last couple of years, and one
that was obviously designed to give Calahan the psychological edge.

"I didn't call this meeting, Frank did," Calahan
announced. "You wanted to talk about this drug poisoning business?"

"Uh, yes, sir. I was going to call a meeting last night,
but I thought it would be better to come in with a few
more facts." He shuffled the papers on his lap until he
was comfortable that they were in the proper order.

"It looks like the CDFS is going to make good on its
threat. We have reports of three suspected poisonings
from hospitals across the country. Let me stress that
these aren't confirmed victims. They do have symptoms that are consistent with poisoning, though, and
the hospital staff has established that they are drug

users. None have died yet, but all three are terminal and not expected to live through the week." He paused to see if anyone had comments.

"That's why I was late," said Sherman. "I was watching a report on this on CNN."

"Yeah, it looks like the press has picked up on one of the three, and they're all over the TV with it. It's been a slow news month."

"Do we know anything about the people poisoned?" Sherman asked.

"Not yet. I've got our guys running them down. We really just got the word last night. I should have a hell of a lot more tomorrow."

Calahan cut in. He seemed to have a formula to calculate how long he would allow a conversation to go on without his input. "Where are they from?"

Richter shuffled through his well-ordered notes. "Two from Miami, one from New York."

"And the cashier's checks?"

"We're working on it, but nothing so far," Richter replied vaguely. It had been irrefutably proven that giving Calahan too many details would set him to suggesting endless, and painfully obvious, investigative avenues.

"So have you done anything but sit around with your thumb up your ass, Frank?" Calahan's voice rose a notch.

Sherman cut in, rescuing his subordinate. "Director Calahan, there really wasn't anything to investigate until last night. Frank's as on top of it as anyone could be."

Calahan looked as though he was going to lash out, but then seemed to think better of it.

Richter continued, effectively veiling his anger. "Sir,

this is pretty high-profile and it crosses the jurisdictions between us, DEA, and the local police. I suggest that we form an interdepartmental task force to handle it."

Calahan thought for a moment, playing absently with the handle on the front drawer of his desk. "And who would you suggest that we put in charge of this task force?"

"I was thinking of Dave Schupman—he's a hell of a good investigator."

Tom Sherman squirmed in his chair and suppressed a laugh. It came out sounding like he was trying to clear his sinuses. Calahan's eyes moved to him. "I take it you disagree, Tom?"

"Uh, yes, sir." He turned to face Richter, feeling a little guilty about his lack of self-control. "Look, Frank, Dave's a great investigator but he comes off like an MIT computer nerd. Christ, last time I saw him he was wearing a pocket protector."

"Actually, I think Dave is an MIT computer nerd," Toleman said, speaking for the first time in the meeting. He looked around him for confirmation.

Sherman ignored the comment and continued. "I think we all understand why Frank suggested Dave. I think we also know who we should put in charge of the investigation."

Richter's eyes narrowed. "Good thinking, Tom. Maybe he can just beat the information out of a few dying junkies."

"That charge was bullshit, Frank, and you know it," Sherman snapped back.

The Director broke in again. "Who are we talking about?"

Sherman and Richter had locked eyes and looked like they were in telepathic communication. Toleman answered the question. "Uh, I think they're talking about Mark Beamon, sir."

A look of disbelief crept across Calahan's face. Sherman winced. He would have liked to have introduced the idea a little more gently.

"Is that true, Tom? Is that what you're suggesting?"

Sherman nodded, getting ready to speak, but Richter cut in before he could open his mouth.

"Sir, Beamon's uncontrollable—he's only been in Houston for a few weeks and he's already gotten the SAC there involved in a gunfight. A goddam gunfight! I can't be responsible for his actions if we bring him back."

"Relax, Frank, I agree with you," Calahan said smoothly. His distaste for Mark Beamon was no secret. "But I also agree that Dave is a bad choice. We need someone who plays better to the press." He turned back to his deputy. His shocked expression had melted into one of disappointment. "I'm surprised that you would bring up Beamon, Tom. Give me another recommendation."

Sherman stood abruptly and turned to the men beside him. "Could you excuse us for a few minutes?"

Toleman looked relieved and headed for the door before Calahan could change his mind. Richter rose more slowly, his body language suggesting suspicion. Sherman's powers of quiet persuasion were well documented. Even Calahan had been known to succumb.

The associate director followed them out as far as the door and closed it behind them.

"So what's so important, Tom?" There was a hint of nervousness in Calahan's voice.

"I would like to reiterate my recommendation that we put Mark in as head of this investigation," Sherman replied, taking his seat again.

Calahan laughed maliciously. "Just dying to get your old buddy back to D.C., aren't you, Tom. Having to spend too much time with your wife?"

Sherman ignored the insult. He knew that he had the power to intimidate the Director and that this was just his feeble attempt at keeping the upper hand.

Sherman stood, walking around behind his chair and grabbing the back of it to support his weight. "I sent Mark to Houston so that he could finish his career in peace. If I was really a good friend to him, I'd leave him there."

"Then leave him there. The Bureau's got to have one other guy who can handle this case. Find him." It was a direct order, but the conviction had drained from Calahan's voice.

"No, I don't think there is." Sherman walked over to a wall virtually covered in photographs. Almost all depicted Calahan with a well-connected government official.

"The recent criticism of you in the press has given us a black eye."

Sherman was referring to the widespread speculation that Calahan had been using Bureau resources for personal benefit. An allegation that everyone in the FBI knew was absolutely true.

He continued scanning the photographs but in his mind's eye he could see a flush coming over Calahan's face. The Director's inability to conjure up a good poker face when backed into a corner had been the subject of more than a little concern at the FBI.

"Go on," Calahan said coolly.

"The press loves Mark. Hell, they damn near deified him after the Coleman kidnapping. And whether it's true or not, they think he's our best man." Sherman moved to his right and began trying to find Calahan's young face in a photograph of his law school graduation.

"I've got a bad feeling that we've only seen the tip of the iceberg with these first three poisonings. If I'm right, the press is going to latch onto this thing and not let go. We'll be performing this investigation under a microscope." He turned and looked directly at his boss to drive the point home. "We damn well better look like we're pulling out all the stops to get these guys. And if this whole thing turns out to be nothing, we just send Mark back to Texas. And you know what the media says? They say that you pulled out the big guns to ensure the safety of a bunch of drug users. What a guy."

Sherman crossed his arms, signaling that he was done with his pitch. Calahan turned and looked out the window while his deputy stared intently at the back of the wide leather chair. Finally he swiveled it back, and they were once again face to face.

"Have it your way, Tom, but keep him away from me."

Sherman nodded. "I'd also like to suggest that Mark report directly to me and not Frank. I don't think that their relationship is particularly constructive."

Calahan was already shuffling through his "In" box

with feigned interest, indicating that the meeting was over. "Whatever. It's your show."

As he walked out of the Director's office, Sherman wondered whether or not he should be happy with his victory. Mark Beamon and he had been friends for almost fifteen years, and he knew that taking this job would be a risky move for Beamon. He suspected that one of the reasons Calahan had agreed so quickly was that he was looking forward to making Beamon a scapegoat for anything that went wrong.

Mark Beamon pushed an old lamp off his sofa and twisted the top of his beer. The house was a goddamn disaster. He'd been in Houston for three months and had unpacked the sum total of three boxes and two hanging bags. It was the same story every move, putting off unpacking and buying whatever he needed to survive. It was this procrastination that was responsible for his owning three ironing boards and no less than six electric razors.

The phone rang just as he was cutting into the top of box number four and cursing himself for never marrying. He gratefully tossed the old utility knife on the couch and waded through the packing material strewn across the floor. He got to the phone just before the machine picked up.

"Hello."

"Hi, Mark. How you doing?" Tom Sherman's voice.

"Still trying to settle in. What's going on with you?"

"Well, I'm knee-deep in it, I guess. Things are nuts around here."

Beamon pushed himself up onto the counter. "I'll bet. I've been watching the news. This drug thing must have the Director taking oxygen." He paused for a moment to savor that mental image.

"Any chance you and I could get together, tomorrow?" Sherman asked.

Beamon remained silent.

"You still there, Mark?"

"Yeah, but I'm thinking about hanging up. Tell me you're not about to get me involved in this fiasco."

"The media doesn't have the whole story yet, Mark. I think we could have a serious problem here."

Beamon knew better than to ask for details. This kind of case was just too tempting. "Geez, Tommy, I'd love to help you guys out, but I'm just the ASAC Houston. I don't think I'm really qualified to take on something like this."

"Don't bust my ass over that, Mark. You know I did the best I could for you."

"Yeah, I know. Besides, I kind of like it here. It's sort of a politics-free zone."

There was a long pause over the line. "The Bureau's going to get one hell of a black eye over this if we don't wrap it up quick, Mark."

Beamon tried unsuccessfully to keep the anger and frustration out of his voice. "You know what? Standing here in the middle of some piece of shit Houston suburb, demoted, with my entire life in boxes, I'm having a hard time giving a rat's ass. I think I'll let Calahan and Richter take this one."

"I thought you might say something like that, Mark. So let me put it another way. Do it for me."

Beamon sighed and jumped down to the kitchen floor, gritting his teeth. Tom Sherman was the best friend he'd ever had. "I fucking hate you."

"Oh, it's not gonna be that bad. I've gotten you pretty much a free hand here. You'll be reporting directly to me—Frank's out of the loop."

"That must have taken some doing," Beamon said, genuinely impressed.

"I think the fact that they're bringing you back tells you exactly how important this investigation is to the Director. He tells me he's already taking a lot of heat from the White House. You come out here and put an end to this thing fast, and I expect that the Director will let you have his wife".

Beamon laughed. The Director's fanatical devotion to his rather unattractive and bitchy wife was a topic of some speculation at the Bureau. Most of it was pointedly unflattering.

"Want to hear the rest of the good news?" Sherman asked.

"I don't know if I can take any more."

"I've been having trouble renting my town house on Capitol Hill, so it's yours as long as you're here. You'll clean up on per diem."

Mark nodded into the phone and smiled. Sherman's trouble in renting his vast D.C. real estate holdings stemmed from the fact that he never listed any of them. His father had owned a number of department stores when he died, and Sherman had inherited them. Apparently he had wanted to be an FBI man since he was six, and as soon as he got in, he turned the operation of the stores over to a close family friend. No one knew exactly how wealthy he was, though popular theories put his net worth in the fifteen million dollar range. Sherman's willingness to put up needy agents and their families in any number of half-million-dollar town houses across D.C. hadn't hurt his popularity.

"You owe me big for this, Tommy. I mean it. Paybacks are going to involve half-naked women, palm fronds, and grapes."

"Uh-huh. You're flying TWA tomorrow at 10:06 A.M., flight 324. Your ticket's at the desk. I'll have someone pick you up at National."

"Yeah, fine."

Beamon hung up the phone and sat quietly on the counter for a moment, looking out across the sea of boxes filling his living room. It was a no-win situation, he knew. If he wrapped the case up quickly, Calahan would take as much credit as he possibly could and send his ass back to Houston on the first plane available. And if he blew it, Calahan'd hang him out to dry.

On the bright side, though, it could be one hell of a case.

"Thanks for the ride, Todd," Beamon said, tugging mightily on a large suitcase wedged in the trunk of the Ford Taurus. The muscular young agent standing next to him grabbed a loop on the side of the bag and freed it effortlessly. Beamon frowned and took it from him, hoping that the moment Todd let go it wouldn't drop to the ground. He managed to arrest it with an inch to go.

"It's been a real honor to meet you, sir," the young man said.

"Good meeting you, too, Todd. I imagine I'll be seeing you around."

They were standing in the middle of the narrow breezeway that ran under the J. Edgar Hoover Building. The dismal gray facade of what was often referred to as the ugliest building in D.C. wrapped around them, but failed to block the cold wind. Beamon looked around as the car that had brought him pulled slowly away, heading toward the heavy traffic of Ninth Street. He had always liked the building. If it was supposed to be a monument to the man whose name was carved on the front, it was a triumph. Hoover had embodied grace and beauty about as much as a rusty jackhammer. The squat, monochrome bunker really did him justice.

He turned and hurried to the glass doors. It didn't take long to realize that the thin suit that had been serving him so well in Houston was transparent to the damp midwinter cold of the nation's capital.

"Mark!" squealed a plump black woman sitting behind the reception desk on the other side of the doors. Beamon insisted that everyone call him by his first name. "Mr. Beamon" had always made him think that his father was standing behind him. Inexplicably, he'd never grown out of the feeling.

"Victoria!" He dropped his heavy bag and leaned over the desk to give her a peck on the cheek. "So how's your son, darlin'? Is he graduating this year?"

"One more year," she answered, taking a cursory glance at the credentials that he was holding.

"Does he know what he wants to do when he gets out?"

"He tells me he wants to be a G-man."

Beamon shook his head and pulled the bag back to his shoulder. Victoria clipped a gold pass to his lapel. "Hopefully he'll grow out of it."

Beamon tiptoed into Tom Sherman's office, putting his finger to his lips when the secretary spotted his approach. Sherman was sitting with the back of his chair to them, looking out the window and dictating a letter in slow, purposeful sentences. Beamon took the pad from her hands and motioned for her to get up. She rose and gave him a quick hug, then padded quietly out of the office. Beamon had been a constant source of entertainment to the executive office staff when he had been stationed in D.C. She looked happy to have him back.

"Please feel free to call me if you have any questions or comments. Cut a copy to Calahan on this one please, Billie."

Sherman swiveled his chair back around as Beamon furiously scribbled on the pad in his lap.

"Jesus!" He slammed his feet down on the floor, bringing the chair to an abrupt halt.

"Yours Truly, or Sincerely?" Beamon grinned.

"Sincerely, you asshole." He got up from the desk and grabbed his friend's hand. Sherman's secretary reappeared with a couple of cups of coffee, trading Beamon for her note pad. He tested it and shot her an approving look. Billie made the best coffee in the Bureau. Always something exotic.

"I got your fax, Tom. Thanks. The information was kind of sketchy, though. You have anything new?"

"We'll find out in a few minutes. Frank's gathering

together everything we've got. He's giving a presentation for us and the Director in about five minutes."
Beamon followed him to a group of sofas set up for
conversation. Unlike Calahan, Sherman rarely discussed business from behind his desk.

"So how's Houston treating you—no more gun-
fights, I hope."

Beamon laughed. "You know how it is, Tommy.
Stuff like that just seems to happen to me. Bad luck."

"Yeah, right."

"So you guys got time for dinner tonight—I feel like
I haven't seen Leslie forever."

"Way ahead of you. She's promised to make you an
Indian feast."

Beamon licked his lips in an exaggerated motion.
Houston hadn't turned out to be a hotbed of fine
Indian cuisine.

A familiar voice behind him shattered the image of
shrimp vindaloo and dal that had constructed itself in
his mind.

"So, I see he's arrived."

Beamon didn't stand, but twisted around in his seat.
"How you been, Frank?"

Richter took the chair next to him and extended his
hand. "Not bad, Mark. I hear you're tearing up Houston."

Out of the corner of his eye, Beamon saw Tom
Sherman look up and begin to rise. He took a deep
breath and did the same.

"Good to see you, Mark," Bill Calahan lied, taking a
seat on the sofa against the wall and putting his feet on
the coffee table. He didn't offer his hand. "So what do
you have for us, Frank. I hope it's more than yesterday."

Richter flushed, and Beamon remembered why he liked Houston so much.

"Yes, sir." He handed out an identical blue folder to each of them, keeping one for himself. Clearing his throat quietly, he began.

"Of the three people identified as possible poisoning victims yesterday, one died early this morning and the other two are not expected to survive another forty-eight hours. We've sent our best people out to examine the corpses but we don't have any data back yet. Reports from the hospitals suggest that the victims all have severe liver and kidney damage. The three victims are Jason Scott of New York, Randall Sanchez, and Steve Platt—both from Miami. I'll run through what we know about them in that order.

"Scott was an attorney at a large law firm in Atlanta. He informed the doctors at the hospital that he was a heavy cocaine user when he was admitted. Prior liver damage from a childhood illness apparently contributed to his rapid decline. He's the one that's already dead—and he died before he could give us the name of his supplier."

He flipped the page. "According to DEA, both Sanchez and Platt are involved in the cocaine trade in Miami—call 'em midlevel managers. I expect a full report this afternoon. Our guys have tried to interview them, but they're pretty sick. Neither one is talking about where they got the drugs."

Richter closed the blue folder in front of him and watched the other men page through theirs. For the most part, the folders contained what he had told them, though the illness was described in more detail and each victim had a limited biography and photo. Beamon was the first to speak.

"So we're sure that we're dealing with poisoned drugs here, and not coincidental illnesses, or some other poisoned product."

"Pretty much," Richter replied. "Apparently this kind of organ damage isn't very common. It's definitely the result of some toxic substance. The fact that all three were confirmed coke users implies a connection."

Beamon looked skeptical.

"Those three aren't the whole story, though. What I didn't lay out in writing is that there have been more reports of similar terminal illnesses since I wrote this. When I left my office, there were twenty-two reported cases virtually identical to these. Of course, they're all unconfirmed."

Beamon let out a low whistle and tossed his folder onto the coffee table. His aim was dead on, and it bounced off the Director's feet.

"So what's happening from the cashier's check angle?"

"We've interviewed everyone working at the bank that day, except one teller who quit and we haven't been able to locate. No prints—the guy wore gloves. The woman who did the checks for him gave us a pretty good description, but it sounds kind of suspicious. Five foot eight or less, long gray hair, bright blue eyes, beard, dark tan. Except for the height, probably a good indication of what he doesn't look like. We also have his signature and driver's license number. The driver's license is from California and it's in the name of someone who died as an infant. Whoever he is, he's covered his tracks pretty well."

"I assume that they'd rotated through all their surveillance tapes?" Beamon said.

"Yeah, no pictures. We're also expecting to run into a dead end on the FedEx packages. No prints or fibers on the letters or ad copy that we can't identify. We're still tracking down the prints on the outside of the envelope, but I'm not hopeful."

Beamon leaned back in his chair and put his feet up on the coffee table in front of him, knowing full well that it would irritate the hell out of Calahan.

"So what do you think, Mark?" Sherman asked.

"I think we've got problems," he replied quietly.

"Would you care to elaborate?" Calahan didn't bother to mask his annoyance.

"Sure." He pulled his feet off the table and sat in a more upright position. "Okay, how is coke distributed? Say it gets manufactured in Colombia. It's shipped to the U.S., in this case, probably into Miami. Then it gets passed down through the chain, from the big organized crime guys to the street dealers and users. So let's say this stuff gets passed down to some middle-man somewhere who's actually one of our friends from the CDFS. He drops in a little poison and sends the shipment on through the chain. Now, depending on how much the people further down on the chain trust each other, they may or may not try the stuff. If they do, they're gonna die. If they don't they just keep passing it along. Frank said two of our victims were midlevel dealers—that tells me that someone hit a shipment fairly high in the chain, and these two unlucky bastards were the suspicious types who like to try the stuff."

The group was silent for a moment, letting his words sink in.

"So what you're saying is that we may have a large quantity of coke, possibly distributed all across the States by now, that is going to kill everyone who uses it," Sherman said.

Beamon turned to Richter. "Have we confirmed that it's only coke?"

"Not really. Three people isn't much of a basis for a good statistic."

He turned back to Sherman. "Yeah. Best case."

"And you agree with him, Frank?" Calahan asked.

"Yes, sir."

"Recommendations?"

"I recommend that I get to work catching these guys before things get out of hand," Beamon answered. "I'll need to put together a few people to help me out. Are there any empty offices around? Maybe something with a decent-sized conference room?" Beamon stood up and jammed his hands in his pockets.

"Why don't we just give Mark the SIOC," Richter suggested, using the acronym for the FBI's Strategic Information Operations Center. "He's gonna need the communications equipment and computer anyway."

"Fine." Sherman began to rise. "Mark—this is top priority—you can have anyone you want, unless they're undercover." He turned to Calahan. "The most important thing now is to get a press conference together to announce Mark's appointment and to warn people about the scope of the threat. Do you agree?"

"Absolutely," the Director replied. It was well known that he loved to see himself on television. "Perhaps we can set something up for tomorrow?"

15

Washington, D.C., February 9

Mark Beamon walked unsteadily along the center line of the street. The sun was blinding him as it reflected off the windshield of a van stopped in the middle of the road about twenty yards away. He turned slowly in circles, watching brightly colored cars skid to abrupt stops and well-dressed young men and women jump out and take cover behind their open doors.

Beamon's slow turning eventually brought him face to face with a haggard group of men peeking out from behind the van. They were further distinguished by the old gray Thompson submachine guns gripped tightly in their hands.

He was vaguely aware that he was dreaming, but he dropped to his knee and pulled his pistol anyway. He was completely exposed, standing alone in the middle of the street. At least he had backup.

The men behind the van started firing, filling the air around him with bullets. He could see individual rounds as they whipped past him and as they left the barrel of his .357. He looked behind him. The young agents crouched behind their car doors, reached into their jackets in unison, and pulled out laptop computers. As they powered up, a beeping sound drowned out the gunfire.

He swung his arm wildly at the alarm clock as the beeping turned to ringing. He hit the snooze button dead center, and silence once again reigned in the dark bedroom, though the smell of gunpowder in his nostrils was slower to dissipate as the dream slipped away. When the ringing started again only moments later, he realized that the phone, and not the alarm, was the culprit. The bright red numbers on the clock hovered in the darkness, announcing that it was just after four A.M.

Beamon fumbled for the phone, keeping his body flat on the bed. Finally finding the receiver, he pulled it to his ear.

"Beamon," he announced sleepily.

"Turn on CNN." Tom Sherman's voice.

Beamon pushed the phone back onto the nightstand and sat up. In his youth, he had loved these late-night calls—they promised an interesting morning and made him feel important. Now they just made him feel tired.

He piled his two pillows behind him and fumbled for the remote. After a moment of searching, he found it, and the room was bathed in the unsteady gray light of an old black-and-white movie. Humphrey Bogart was lighting a cigarette in the lobby of an obscenely ornate hotel.

The light in the room flickered again as Bogart disappeared and a thin young woman with a microphone took his place.

The woman's green coat glowed in the harsh light of the TV cameras, contrasting her pale skin and quickly moving red lips. Behind her the light faded, leaving about forty feet of dead space ending in a white building with heavy-looking double glass doors. As his eyes adjusted, Beamon began to focus on the dead space. Upon further examination, it appeared to be full of people at different levels of activity. Along the bottom of the television, the caption JOHNS HOPKINS HOSPITAL was spelled out in capital letters. Slightly larger was the word MUTE. Beamon had always liked TV better with no sound.

"So what the hell's going on, Tommy?"

He pressed the volume control, and the woman's voice went from a timid whisper to a self-assured shout: ". . . what you're seeing is happening at hospitals all over the country."

Beamon focused on the screen as the camera panned away from the reporter and splashed light on the activity behind her.

He had never been in a war but was a fan of war movies. What he saw reminded him of triage after a battle. The soldiers were always strewn out in the dirt, some lying quietly, others writhing and bleeding. Heroic doctors and nurses would run from litter to litter, hunched over against sniper fire and helicopter wash.

Every once in a while, a light from another source flooded the scene, bringing a new perspective. He punched the volume button one last time.

". . . it's impossible to tell how many patients there are here, because they keep moving them in and out of the hospital—I lost count at seventy-eight. Obviously the doctors have begun examining people out here in the parking lot. From where I'm standing I can see in through the glass doors of the building. It looks like the floor is covered with patients. I'm not sure how they're getting stretchers in and out—it looks impossible to walk in there." Steam billowed from her mouth as she spoke.

The camera panned right, illuminating the face of a blond man in a leather bomber jacket, lying on the ground amidst the turmoil. His face was stark white. Beads of water clung to his cheeks, shining like diamonds under the harsh camera light. He didn't acknowledge the attention, he only stared up through the rain, chewing on his lower lip with a jerky mechanical precision. Blood had begun to flow from it, mixing with the light rain to run pink down his chin.

Beamon sat silently in his bed, vaguely aware of Sherman's breathing on the other end of the phone. The reporter turned away from the camera and tried to stop a quickly moving young doctor. He shrugged her off without looking up. Her second attempt, involving actually grabbing a man's arm, met with more success. He was much older, apparently wiser about good publicity's role in saving lives.

"Could you tell us what's going on here, Dr. . . . ?"

"Mason," he replied looking into the camera with a practiced calm. "We're not entirely sure. The symptoms seem to be consistent with the victims of the suspected drug poisonings that have been getting so much press lately, but yesterday we only had six patients with those symptoms. Today . . ." His voice trailed off as he pointed to the chaos behind him.

"Doctor, the prior victims of these tainted drugs were all diagnosed as terminal. Are you saying that none of these people are going to survive?" Her professional poise began to crack as it sank in that she might be standing in the middle of a graveyard.

"I really couldn't say." He fingered the stethoscope hanging around his neck. "What I can tell you is that they're at the best hospital in the world and we're doing everything we can—now you'll have to excuse me."

Beamon hit the Mute button as the reporter began to summarize the few words that she'd been able to get.

"Shit, Tommy," he said quietly into the phone. As he spoke, the screen darkened for a moment, switching to a man standing in front of a similar scene. The caption placed it as a hospital in Phoenix.

"I sent a car for you, Mark. It should be there in less than fifteen minutes. See you at the office." There was an audible click.

Beamon sat for a moment in silence, cradling the receiver in his lap. He'd had a gut feeling that this case was going to be uglier than anyone expected. But he hadn't planned on this.

The doorbell rang just as Beamon finished the right sleeve on the shirt he was ironing. He laid the iron upright on the board and jogged to the door, wearing only a pair of gray slacks.

"Mr. Beamon, I'm Steve Adams. I was sent to pick you up." Beamon examined him carefully. He looked impossibly young.

"Come on in, Steve." Beamon eyed the crisp white collar poking up from the young man's navy topcoat. "Agent Adams—I do believe that you look like a man who knows his way around an iron."

A puzzled look came over the smooth face.

Beamon led him to the ironing board and offered him a position behind it.

"I owe you one," he called, racing up the stairs of the town house to shave.

Less than five minutes later he reappeared, still bare-chested, but now wearing shoes and holding a jacket, coat, and tie. He found his shirt hanging neatly on the end of the ironing board, and the young agent flipping through a six-month-old copy of *Newsweek*.

"I knew you wouldn't let me down . . . what's your name again?"

"Steve Adams."

"Sorry, it's early," Beamon explained, as he finished buttoning his collar and began tying his tie. "Okay, let's go."

Beamon stretched wildly as the Bureau sedan cruised slowly past Union Station. He glanced at his watch. No wonder his mind was still foggy, it had been less than twenty minutes since Sherman's call.

"Hey, Steve, you know if you take a right at this light, there's a little twenty-four-hour donut shop up about a mile on the left."

Adams looked at him incredulously. "Sir, I don't know if you've been briefed, but there are hundreds of people dying. Mr. Sherman told me to get you to headquarters as soon as possible."

"Shit, son. I'm not a doctor—there's nothing that I can do for these people now that I can't do in ten minutes. Take a right."

Adams went silent and swung the car onto a narrow side street. Beamon's memory for pastry was photographic and it was less than three minutes before a Dunkin' Donuts appeared.

He jumped out of the car before it had made a full stop, and walked briskly toward the shop. The perfume of brewing coffee masked the smell of the city.

"Here, I got you some coffee," Beamon said sliding two steaming cups into the drink holders between the seats, and dumping a handful of sugars and creams between them. "I forgot to ask how you took it."

As they pulled away, he searched through the grocery-sized bag on his lap. "Bear claw?"

"No, thank you."

Beamon could barely keep from laughing out loud. Young agents could be so unbelievably stiff. It was the academy that did it, he knew. Pumped them full of patriotic images of saving the world, and built up their confidence with constant reminders that they were the best America had to offer. He had been the same way after graduation.

"You sure? Donuts are the cornerstone of good police work—especially the creme-filled ones."

"I'm sure."

This one was a tough nut, and Beamon decided that he was too tired to crack him. Settling back into the comfortable seat, he nibbled on an eclair and lit a cigarette. He ignored the young agent as he made a show of rolling down his window.

Beamon had quit smoking the day that he arrived in Houston. Back in D.C., though, the willpower had drained from him. He hoped to have this thing wrapped up before lung cancer set in.

Perry Trent peeked around the doorjamb of the open door to the Oval Office. "Mr. President?"

Daniel Jameson sat in jeans and a red work shirt on the leather sofa centered in the office.

"Morning, Perry. Come on in. Coffee?"

"Yes, thank you." It always made Trent uncomfortable to have the President of the United States pour his coffee. He nodded a greeting to Michael Bryce, the White House chief of staff, who had taken his customary seat in a soft tapestry chair directly across from the President. As attorney general, Trent rated a less comfortable spot a few feet farther from the power.

"So what the hell's going on, Perry. Yesterday you told me some crazy had dropped rat poison in a few drugs, and this morning I get woken up out of a sound sleep and told that hospitals all across the country are filling up with dying dopers." Jameson plunked two sugars into the cup and held it out.

Trent reddened slightly. The President was already suffering from a serious ulcer and dangerously high blood pressure, though those facts had been effectively kept from the press. When he had asked for a briefing on the first victims, Trent had downplayed the situation. At the time there had been no reason to think that it was anything more than some right-wing fanatic running around with a household chemical. No reason to start the President's ulcer bleeding.

"I was wrong," he explained simply.

Trent had spent almost the entire drive to the White House on the phone with Tom Sherman at the FBI. Now that he was sitting across from the President, he wondered what they'd talked about for so long. The information he had didn't amount to much.

"It would appear that a shipment of cocaine has been tainted with an extremely deadly poison that attacks the liver and kidneys. It looks like the shipment was hit somewhere pretty far upstream—and now it's been cut up and distributed all over the country."

The President let out a sound like a leaky tire and leaned back into the sofa. Trent paused, thinking that the President was going to ask a question. When he didn't, Trent continued. "The FBI began their investigation the moment the ads appeared in the paper and are tracking a number of leads. So far none has panned out. Obviously they have made this investigation their top priority."

"And you think Bill Calahan is competent to run an investigation of this magnitude?" Bryce asked.

"No, but Tom Sherman can. And he's brought in Mark Beamon to head up the investigation."

"Isn't he the guy that found that Coleman kid?"

Trent nodded.

"Good choice," Bryce said. "The press loved him— not a lot of political savvy, though."

The President seemed deep in thought for a

moment. The two men watched his expression carefully. "So what's your recommendation, Perry?" he asked finally.

Trent's brow furrowed slightly. "I don't think that there is anything you or I can do, really. The Bureau's got its teeth into this thing, and I've directed them to use every method available to get these guys—fast. I told Sherman confidentially that if he had any ideas that might be unconventional, I wanted to hear them. And if they had any merit, I'd bring them to you."

Trent took a sip of his coffee. "I know that neither of you much cares for Bill Calahan, but I don't think he's particularly relevant to the investigation. In my opinion, we can trust Tom to get this investigation off the ground pretty quickly."

"Calahan's having a press conference tomorrow at ten, isn't he?" Jameson asked.

"Yes, sir."

"Okay, Perry. Thanks. I want to be kept up on everything that happens in this investigation. Daily reports. Nothing's insignificant, right?"

"Yes, sir."

Trent promised himself that he wouldn't make the same mistake twice. Jameson would get more detail than he could handle. Trent was painfully aware that he was getting off easy. Too easy. It gave him a queasy feeling.

"Thank you, sir," he said, putting down the nearly full cup of coffee and heading for the door.

"Close it behind you, please," Bryce called.

"So what do you think?" The President didn't look at his chief of staff, but concentrated on the stained glass lampshade next to him.

Bryce slid his feet onto the table in front of him, pushing himself farther back into the chair. "It's a difficult situation. The press is going to come out firmly against the poisoners and are going to be more and more critical of us every day these guys aren't caught. On the other hand, the public perceives your administration to be soft on crime."

The President opened his mouth to protest, but Bryce cut him off.

"I'm not saying that it's true—but you're a Democrat and you've stressed rehabilitation over punishment. The fact is that crime's gotten worse with every administration since Lincoln—you just happen to have the chair now."

"So what are you getting at, Mike?" Jameson respected Bryce's ability to see all angles of an issue, but God knew he liked to hear himself talk.

"I'm not sure that these guys—what do they call themselves? The CDFS? Are going to be all that unpopular."

"I'm not following you."

"Look, Dan, you go talk to some guy working forty hours a week in a factory in Sheridan, Wyoming, and you ask him what he thinks about the whole thing. You know what he'll say? He'll say that the druggies got what was coming to them. That it's about time someone cleaned up the cities."

Jameson flushed. "So what are you suggesting? That we tell the media that I think it's okay to go out and kill as many people as you want—just as long as they're narcotics users?"

Bryce straightened up in his chair. "No. That's what's so difficult. You have to go out there and say that the government is going to do everything in its power to stop these guys—but you have to do it in a way that doesn't make our friend in Wyoming mad. The media's on your side. They'll focus on the most horrible and unjustified deaths. You know, high school track stars with straight A's, cute twelve-year-olds from the projects—that kind of thing. You're not gonna see the guy with a murder rap and six aggravated assaults. I'll guarantee you that."

Jameson stood up and walked past his desk to face the large window behind it.

Bryce continued. "You'll have to be at that press conference tomorrow, Dan. We've got to make sure that the media sees you getting personally involved in this."

Jameson was only half listening. "Is it our fault, Mike?"

"Excuse me?"

"I don't just mean you and me. I mean the government in general. In the last, say, fifteen years, what has the U.S. government done that has really made a difference to its citizens?" He turned around and looked at Bryce. "Now things have gotten so bad, the public is forced to take action to correct the country's problems."

"This isn't the public taking action, Dan. This is some nut running around murdering people."

"Yeah, you're probably right," Jameson said, but he wasn't as certain as he made himself sound.

Bryce stood. "Of course I'm right. You've got a good record of trying to get a handle on crime. We just have to make sure we keep that in front of the public during this thing."

16

Washington, D.C., February 9

Beamon punched in the combination to the door guarding the FBI's Strategic Information Operations Center, or SIOC, and pulled the heavy door open. Inside, the space was broken into a number of sound-proof rooms. The interior walls were glass, and he could see straight through to the back.

The suite was almost empty. Beamon nodded to a young agent manning the phones as he refilled his Styrofoam cup with coffee. Calls coming into the JEH Building after hours were fielded in SIOC. It was this kid's unlucky week.

To Beamon's left was the largest of the four rooms and the space reserved for his team. Through the glass wall he could see that Laura Vilechi was already hard at work. She sat at the conference table that dominated the room, framed by a large blackboard. Her nose was stuck in a blue file folder.

On the blackboard she had written a chart.

INVESTIGATION

DRUGS	CHECKS	POISON
Tracing to Source	Bank	Identifying
?????	Description (Disguise)	
	Handwriting Sample	
	Alias/Driver's License Number	
	Lance Richardson?	
	Physical Evidence (FedEx)	

Beamon shook his head and wondered for the fiftieth time if he'd made a mistake in hiring Laura as his right-hand man—as he intended to introduce her.

They had met almost five years ago on an embezzlement case and discovered quickly that they couldn't agree on anything. Beamon was the absentminded professor—prone to flashes of brilliance that left everyone shaking their heads in amazement. Between those flashes, though, he had to struggle to keep up with the mundane details of the nuts and bolts investigation.

Laura had a completely different style—and the chalkboard told him that it hadn't changed. She had a photographic memory for details, and fanaticism for process. She left no stone unturned, and never, never made mistakes.

Their first meeting had been less than pleasant. She had already decided how she wanted the investigation run, and she wasn't about to let anyone screw it up. Beamon had his own ideas about how to get things done. She had stood there, hands on hips, staring coldly at him as he ranted and raved about her inexperience and uninspired approach to investigation. She hadn't backed down, and he respected that.

"How you doin', Laura," Beamon said, slipping

through the door and closing it quietly behind him. He couldn't believe it, but he was actually a little nervous.

She looked up at him with mild suspicion. "I'm good, Mark."

Beamon examined the blackboard more closely, finally pointing to it. "I see you haven't changed."

She pointed to the large bag of donuts dangling from his right hand. "I see you haven't, either."

Beamon laughed and set them on the table.

"I didn't know what you liked, so I got an assortment."

She opened the bag and pulled out a chocolate-covered. The topping stuck to her fingers. "Well, I'm here, but I sure can't figure out why."

"My doctor told me I didn't have enough stress in my life. Naturally, you came to mind." Beamon flashed a wide grin and reached into the bag to find another bear claw. "I think you took our last run-in too seriously, Laura. I defended my methods and you defended yours. Shit, if anybody came off that case worse for the wear it was me."

"Come on, Mark. You obviously don't agree with my methods. Why did you bring me in on this?"

Beamon frowned. "If I gave you the impression that I didn't agree with your methods, I'm sorry. The fact that you and I approach a problem from opposite sides is precisely why you're here. I'm willing to admit that my weakness is detail and procedure. And as I see it, yours is being too rigid." Laura bristled slightly at the criticism, but he ignored it. "Put both of us together, you get the perfect investigator."

"And you think we can work together?"

Beamon turned serious. "Yup. Our problem last time

was that neither one of us was really in charge. This time I'm the boss."

They stared straight at each other for almost ten seconds. Laura finally averted her eyes and reached for her donut. "Maybe next time it'll be me."

He laughed. "The thought keeps me awake at night. So when did you fly in? You look tired." Her blue skirt and white blouse looked like they had come directly from a suitcase, and her strawberry blond hair wasn't pulled back as tightly as he remembered it. It didn't matter, though, she would have been striking in old blue jeans and a dirty sweatshirt.

"I got in tonight at ten. I was up watching TV when CNN started reporting on the hospitals, and I figured I might as well come in before the phone started ringing."

Beamon nodded toward the blue folder lying next to her on the conference table.

"So what have we got?"

"Not a whole lot," she said quietly. "The Saint Louis office has interviewed everyone at the bank where the suspect got the cashier's checks—except one guy who apparently quit and is on a rock-climbing trip in parts unknown. We should be able to find him in a few days, but he didn't really have much in the way of direct contact with our guy. Anyway, not much there." She flipped the page.

"We and DEA are interviewing the victims who are still able to talk and getting the names of their suppliers. DEA's working on tracing the poisoned drugs back to where they got hit—but it's too soon to see if that'll go anywhere." She flipped another page.

"Our forensics guys haven't had much luck in figuring out what the poison is, but they're working on it round the clock. Apparently they've brought in one of the world's leading experts on toxicology. He's from Harvard, or something." Laura tossed the folder on the table, sending it spinning to the far edge.

"What about the envelope? Anything there?"

"Zip."

"So I'm safe in saying we don't have dick," Beamon said.

"An unfortunate choice of words, but that's what it boils down to."

"Any estimates on casualties?"

"Last time I looked, we were moving into four digits."

Beamon crossed his arms and stared at the blackboard. "This should be one hell of an interesting case. It's the only crime I've ever investigated that the victims don't want to talk. We're gonna hit a brick wall trying to get information out of the narcotics community."

Beamon considered his next move. No brilliant strategies flashed into his mind, and he knew from experience that he couldn't force them. They would probably have to wait for the CDFS's next move to get anything concrete. That is, if there was a next move.

The piercing ring of a phone cut off his train of thought. He looked around, spotting it on a credenza against the wall. He strolled slowly over and picked it up. "Mark Beamon."

"Mark! It's Trace."

Trace Fontain was the head of the Bureau's laboratory science group, and in charge of filtering through the blood of the victims and confiscated narcotics to isolate the poison. Beamon didn't know him well, but they had been running into each other every now and again for the last fifteen years.

"What's the good word, Trace?" Beamon found a remote control and was trying to figure out how to turn on the television anchored to the wall above him.

"Afraid there is none, Mark. Your choices are bad news and worse news."

"Jesus, I just can't seem to get a break around here. Bad news first."

"We haven't been able to figure out what they're using yet. We know it attacks the vital organs, but it's nothing we've ever seen before."

"Fuckin' hell, Trace. All you have to do is put the shit under one of those mass spectron microscope doodads and the goddam computer does your job for you."

Laura frowned deeply and stared up at him. He'd forgotten how much he hated that look.

She was right, of course. Trace had enough academic plaques to side a house. The Bureau was lucky to have him.

"Sorry, Trace. It's early, you know? Hit me with the worse news."

"You're really not gonna like this one."

"I'll try not to kill the messenger."

"We've been interviewing the victims that are still lucid, and examining the organs of the dead ones, and there is evidence that the poison has a, uh, bit of a delayed reaction."

Beamon considered that for a moment. "So, like, if I snort some coke today, I might not show symptoms till tomorrow? They have stuff like that?"

"Uh, no. It's a little worse than that. It works on kind of a bell curve. Depending on how much you take and your body chemistry, reaction times are different."

"Get to the point, Trace."

"Well, a pretty good average would be, uh, right around a week and a half for the first symptoms. Death three days after they start appearing."

Beamon started pounding his head slowly on the wall in front of him. "No more bad news today, okay?"

"You all right, Mark?" Laura asked as Beamon slammed down the phone.

"Did you know that some poisons have delayed reactions?"

"Sure, I guess. I never really thought about it."

"And how long do you think the longest delayed reaction would be?"

"Dunno. One or two days?"

"Try one or two weeks."

She was silent for a moment. "Is this another one of your dumb jokes?"

"You're not feeling any better, are you, honey?"

Erica pulled the gray and brown afghan up around her husband's shoulders and looked into his red-rimmed eyes. The Reverend Simon Blake didn't reply.

"I can't imagine that this is helping any," she said, looking at the TV where a CNN anchor was discussing casualty estimates. In the upper right-hand corner of the screen a black-and-red graphic depicted a needle and vial with the simple caption THE DRUG CRISIS. The media's ability to attractively package a tragedy like a bar of bath soap never ceased to disgust her. She took the remote control off the arm of her husband's chair to try to find something a little more upbeat. He snatched it back before she could aim it, slamming it back down on the arm of the chair.

Erica eyed him strangely. She couldn't ever remember him grabbing something from her like that. She had also expected him to have something to say about what was happening in the news, but he hadn't uttered a word on the subject. He just watched the reports, keeping any feelings about them bottled up inside. It was probably just the flu, she reasoned, as she walked angrily out of the room.

"Close the door," her husband yelled. She wanted to leave it open—he hadn't showered and it was getting a little close in his den. But she didn't want to argue, and did as he asked.

As the door clicked shut, Blake increased the volume on the TV until the sound penetrated every corner of his mind. He sat there, staring blankly at the screen in the dim light of the den.

He had stopped sleeping after the first few victims died. It had turned out that two of the first few had been drug dealers—scum of the earth, as far as he was concerned. But he'd been responsible for their deaths and that was a sensation he wasn't familiar with, and as it turned out, wasn't fond of.

Then the sky had fallen. CNN was estimating four hundred deaths and another six hundred terminally ill. A thousand people. Hobart and he had discussed the possibility of casualties, but never in his wildest dreams had he thought anything like this could happen. Why hadn't people stopped using? The ad had been clear enough—had they not read it? No, that was impossible. The media had saturated the airwaves with the story. Everyone knew, he told himself. Everyone.

Blake coughed loudly, leaning over the arm of his chair until the spasms subsided. Waves of nausea came over him, combining with the burning in his stomach. For a moment he thought he was going to throw up, but he managed to fight it off.

Mark Beamon pressed his back against the wall, narrowly avoiding a collision with a Secret Service man hustling to the other side of the room. He didn't know how those guys did it. There must have been thirty people moving frantically back and forth waiting for the President to appear; all dressed the same, all with nearly the same haircut, and all talking in the same medium-loud monotone. And these guys had to keep it all straight. No thanks.

Beamon slid a few feet to his left, giving himself a partially obstructed view of the curtain leading to the small auditorium where the President held his press conferences. He could detect movement behind the curtain, but couldn't really see anything.

He wished they'd get this show on the road. The makeup that had been slathered onto his face in preparation for the television cameras was beginning to dry in the corners of his eyes, and it was driving him crazy. He reached up to scratch at it.

"Don't do that, Mark."

Beamon turned his head toward the familiar voice

and watched Laura Vilechi weaving effortlessly through the crowd.

"Laura! What are you doing here?"

"I brought you a present."

"A present? Really? What is it?"

Laura pulled a deep maroon tie with subtle blue dots from her bag and pressed it against the frayed lapel of his jacket. She nodded approvingly. "I didn't have time to do anything about the suit, but this tie should help."

"I take it you don't like the one I have on."

Laura pursed her lips and ran her tongue across the front of her teeth. "If you're going to be on TV, you need a tie that says 'trust me, I know what I'm doing. I've got everything under control.'"

Beamon grabbed Laura by the shoulders and moved her a couple of feet to her right. A boom mike just missed her head.

"I know I'm going to regret asking this, but just what is it that my tie says?"

She pulled it out of his jacket and held the tip like it was the tail of a dead mouse. "Meet me at my trailer later, I've got a cooler full of brewskis."

"I brought a six-pack. It's a little early, but I thought we might need it," Robert Swenson said, slamming the door to the apartment and making a beeline to the refrigerator. It was 9:58 A.M., and Hobart was sitting on the sofa, watching the lead-in to the President's press conference. The subject today was near and dear to his heart.

Swenson plopped down on the sofa and put two

beers on the coffee table in front of them, unopened. The scene on the television changed from a reporter framed by the White House to a crowded room with an empty podium as its focal point. An unintelligible rumbling came from the reporters fidgeting in neatly organized chairs.

A few moments later President Daniel Jameson strode purposefully out onto the stage, followed closely by two conservatively dressed men. He took his place behind the podium and shuffled papers for a moment, a look of deep concern on his face.

"Shit," Hobart said, no louder than a whisper.

Swenson looked over at him. "They haven't said anything yet."

"See that ugly son of a bitch next to Calahan?"

"Yeah."

"That's Mark Beamon."

"Beamon. Why do I know that name?"

"He's the asshole that got me thrown out of the DEA," Hobart replied, twisting the top of a beer. Swenson was about to ask for more details, but the President began to speak.

"As all of you know, a group known as the Committee for a Drug-Free Society threatened, through advertisements in a number of major newspapers, to poison the U.S. narcotics supply. It would appear that they have made good on that threat. I understand that current estimates of dead and injured are nearing a thousand people." He paused for a moment to accentuate the point. The reporters struggled to contain themselves.

"I have directed the FBI to take the lead in this investigation, and to make it their top priority. I have further directed that all other law enforcement agencies give the FBI their full cooperation. With that, I would like to introduce Bill Calahan and Mark Beamon from the FBI."

Jameson began to turn away from the podium but was prompted back by the shouted questions of the press.

"We'll take questions at the end of the conference," he said into the microphone, and turned away again, shaking hands with the two men moving toward the podium.

Calahan spoke first, with Beamon flanking him a few feet behind.

"At the request of the President, I've formed a task force to investigate this most serious crime, and have told my people to make it their top priority. I've also appointed Mark Beamon, whom many of you know, as head of the task force. Mark should be able to bring you up to speed on where we are in the investigation. Mark?" Calahan gave up the podium and took a place alongside the President. Beamon moved forward and adjusted the mike, wondering how he was going to stretch what little he knew into a reasonable speech. There was nothing he hated more than coming out on national TV and saying he didn't know what the fuck was going on, but that he'd do his best to find out.

"Obviously the Bureau's been investigating this case since the ad requests were first made. We have a number of leads that we're aggressively pursuing, though we don't have any suspects yet."

Christ, this sounds lame.

"We haven't been able to isolate the poison used,

but we have been able to get a feel for how it works. I think you guys have already done a pretty good job of describing its effects." There was a hint of sarcasm in his voice. The press seemed to be in a bitter contest to see which network could be the most graphic.

"What we just found out this morning, though, regards the, uh, reaction time." He paused, knowing that his next words were going to send a panic through the narcotics community. He felt a little bit like he was about to yell fire in a crowded theater.

"Apparently, symptoms will not appear for between one and a half and two weeks following contact with the poison. Death can be expected within three days of the appearance of symptoms. There appears to be no antidote."

Beamon stepped back involuntarily at the force of the shouted questions from the men and women in front of him. Gathering his composure, he raised his hand, effectively quieting them.

"To date, it would appear that only cocaine has been contaminated, but let me stress that the ads did not limit their threat to coke. At this time, all illegal narcotics should be considered suspect."

Beamon leaned against the podium and, for the first time, looked directly at the camera. "If you're using illegal drugs, stop. Go to a rehab clinic, see your priest, start drinking, take up knitting—whatever it takes. Even if we catch these guys tomorrow, there's no telling how much of this stuff is floating around on the streets."

He turned his head and called to Calahan and the President to join him. The two men approached the podium, looking reluctant.

"Uh, I guess we have time for a few questions." Every hand in the hall shot up.

Neither of the men flanking him made a move, so Beamon pointed. "Stacey."

A woman who seemed too elegantly dressed to be a reporter stood up. Beamon remembered her having a little more class than most of her peers.

"If there is a two-week delay on the reaction time on this poison, is it possible that these first thousand casualties are only the tip of the iceberg? Does the FBI have an estimate of how many deaths are expected?"

Calahan didn't seem to want to get anywhere near that question, so Beamon answered it himself. "Could the first thousand only be the tip of the iceberg? Maybe, but there are way too many variables to make an accurate estimate."

All hands went from scribbling to reaching for the ceiling.

"Gill." He was quickly running out of reporters that he knew to have even a small spark of decency.

"Mr. Beamon, there have been a lot of rumors flying around that this is a covert government operation to stop the illegal narcotics trade in the U.S. Would you care to comment on that?"

"Not really. But we've got the number one expert on government operations right here. Mr. President?"

Jameson stepped up to the podium, looking angry. "That's ridiculous. If anything, my administration has been criticized for not being heavy-handed enough with the punishment of criminals, and of being too reform-oriented. These kind of rumors are bound to start when something like this happens—they are completely unfounded."

Jameson stepped back, whispering in Beamon's ear to wrap things up.

Beamon leaned into the mike. "We've got time for one more. Kim?"

"You said that you're following up a number of leads. Would you care to comment on those leads, and give us a feel for how long you expect it'll take to resolve this case?"

Beamon smiled. "No, and I don't know. But you can rest assured that we're doing everything humanly possible to find these guys. Thank you."

Hobart flipped off the TV and finished his beer.

"They don't have shit," he observed.

Swenson looked concerned. "But there's some history between you and that Beamon guy?"

"Yeah," Hobart admitted. "Must have been ten years ago—we were working on a joint investigation. Peter Manion was one of my snitches back then. He was stonewalling me and I was pushing him around a little bit. To make a long story short, Peter fell over a table and broke his arm. Beamon walks in a few minutes later and goes ballistic. Takes Manion to the hospital and comes back and presses charges against me."

"So what happened?"

Hobart smiled. "I fought back—got Peter to testify that Beamon was in on the whole thing. Goddam hearings went on for a year with both of us on unpaid leave. In the end, I got canned and he got demoted and sent to . . . Montana, I think."

Swenson nodded thoughtfully. "Is he good?"

"Sure. But not as good as he thinks he is. He doesn't have much support with management, either. Getting an official reprimand for beating up an informant is pretty tough to live down."

Hobart laughed as he stood and walked across the room to a strangely configured chess board and pulled a black king off the television. He placed it ceremoniously on the board.

"I'd been meaning to ask you about that, John," Swenson said, walking quietly up behind him. "I don't think you've got it set up quite right."

Hobart surveyed the board. "It's set up exactly right." He pointed to the right side of the board where a white king and queen sat in the first rank. Eight white pawns were spread out over the board. There were no more white pieces. "We're the white. You and I are symbolized by the king and queen. The eight pawns represent our men in the field."

He shifted his focus to the left side of the board, where two full rows of pawns stood, one blue and one black. On the first rank stood a king and queen of each color. "The black pieces represent the FBI. Beamon's the king. Tom Sherman, the associate director, and Beamon's strongest ally, is the queen."

"And the blue?"

Hobart scowled. The answer was obvious. Maybe his partner wasn't as bright as he had thought. "The narcotics cartel. I don't know who the king and queen represent yet, but my guess is that it will be Luis Colombar and his advisor—Alejandro something. Colombar's the most powerful man in Colombia now—and it was his refinery that I hit. Of course, nothing stays the same for long in that business."

17

Near Bogotá, Colombia,
February 12

Luis Colombar walked briskly through the spacious entryway of his home listening to the complex chime of his doorbell fade away.

"Roberto! How have you been?" Colombar said to the tanklike man standing on the other side of the door. The two men shook hands warmly, effectively disguising their hatred for each other. Roberto Ortega wiped his feet carefully on the mat in front of the door and entered. Colombar noticed a complex sweat stain in his white cotton shirt that accurately traced a shoulder holster. This was the first time he had seen Ortega unarmed.

It had been a difficult call. On one hand, these were all businessmen—the most powerful drug lords in Colombia—and should be able to be trusted not to start a gunfight in his living room. On the other hand, the bad blood between many of his guests was old and strong. In the end, he had personally guaranteed everyone's safety, and politely insisted that no firearms be brought into his home. A few of them had offered token resistance, but deep down they had been relieved by the directive. Colombar was a killer, drug dealer, and thief, but he was a man of his word.

"You are the last guest to arrive, Roberto," Colombar said, scanning his front yard as he slowly closed the door. The one hundred yards between the front of his house and the formidable white stucco perimeter wall was thick with carefully laid out native plants. Secreted in this foliage were no fewer than twenty men with meaningful bulges under their arms. Their dark suits looked out of place next to the explosions of color supplied by the flowering plants.

Colombar followed Ortega closely as they wound through the wide halls of his home. Light was provided solely by the endless skylights dotting the terra-cotta roof.

Colombar had hired the finest architect in Colombia to design his home, and had brought in an interior designer from New York to furnish it. It was obvious to anyone who knew him that the house didn't reflect the man. The sophistication and class that he had hoped would spring from the art-encrusted walls had only served to highlight his poor upbringing and crass sense of humor.

The hall eventually opened to an expansive room with a high, clear-glass roof supported by imported Canadian logs. Each log was draped with a large antique tapestry, their well-worn ends dangling down into space.

No less than fifteen men stood in small clusters, sat on well-coordinated leather sofas, and huddled around various tables covered with sterling silver chafing dishes. Occasionally a burst of laughter would come from one of the groups. It sounded strained.

Colombar stopped at the top of the steps leading to the sunken floor of the room, and watched Ortega stride bull-like through the men, straight to the table covered with dripping beer bottles.

He looked down over the crowd. "Gentlemen! I believe that with Mr. Ortega's arrival, we are all here. Shall we begin?" His accent had improved significantly over the last year, thanks to a voice coach who had a talent for transforming wealthy South Americans into sophisticated Europeans. All eyes turned to him as he strolled across the room, trying to look calm and in control. The men followed him to a conversation pit that had been set up specifically for this meeting. At the focal point of the grouping of furniture was a large-screen TV.

Colombar sat on a sofa directly across from the television. The other drug lords followed his example, looking less collected as they jockeyed at the last minute to sit next to an ally and not a dreaded enemy.

Unbeckoned, a young man walked quickly from a door at the side of the room and slipped a tape into the VCR under the TV. At thirty-three, he was ten years Colombar's junior, and seemed to exude the sophistication that the drug lord would never achieve. His gray Armani suit fit as if he'd been born in it. He flashed a practiced smile at the group. His teeth were white and straight.

"I think some of you know my attorney, Alejandro Perez," Colombar said. "I've asked him to give us a little presentation on this situation." With a wave of his hand he gave the floor to Perez.

"Gracias, Luis."

Perez scanned the crowd as he spoke, using all of the public-speaking skills that he had learned at Georgetown Law. "As they say, a picture is worth a thousand words, so I have prepared this videotape. It includes what I feel are significant media reports relating to this, uh, situation. It will only take a few moments to view, and I think you will find it interesting. My understanding is that all of you speak English. If not, please let me know now and I will translate as the tape runs." Perez made a show of looking from face to face. No one spoke, though he knew that at least three of the men would have a hard time ordering a hamburger in English.

"Okay, then." He pushed a button and the television came to life.

His tape began with Beamon's press conference and then ran smoothly into various CNN reports from hospitals across the country. It ended with an interview of a cocaine addict. His face was in shadows and his voice disguised, but he was clearly an educated man—probably around Perez's age.

The addict told the reporter between sobs that he had taken a leave of absence from work to put himself in a rehab clinic. He also related that he had last snorted coke five days earlier and was waiting to see if he had been poisoned. He had sworn to himself that if he survived he would never do another line.

The television faded artistically to black, and Perez punched the stop button on the VCR.

"If I can take up just a few more moments of your time, I'd like to make a few comments about what you have just seen." He paused. No objections were raised.

"Mark Beamon, the gentleman speaking at the press conference, my sources say is probably the FBI's top investigator. I have also heard that he and the Director are mortal enemies and that he had recently been demoted and sent to a field office in Texas. I think that Mr. Calahan's willingness to bring him back to head this investigation shows the American government's commitment to putting a stop to the CDFS's actions."

Perez pushed one hand in his pocket, adjusting the hang of his suit into yet another well-thought-out configuration. "Having said this, my sources, whom I consider very reliable, tell me that the FBI has no significant leads in the case. The narcotics manufacturers' and dealers' unwillingness to cooperate with the authorities is working against them. In addition, it seems reasonable to hypothesize that the individuals involved in this drug poisoning operation are quite sophisticated and probably have some knowledge of investigative procedures." Perez pulled a folder from the top of the television next to him.

"Current estimates put deaths at twenty-eight hundred, with an additional seventeen hundred showing symptoms that would suggest that death is inevitable within the week." He tossed the folder back where he'd found it. "I think that the last segment on the tape really drives home what we're seeing on the demand front. Only five days from the first death, we are already experiencing a substantial downward trend in cocaine purchases by casual users, who, as I'm sure you know, consume the lion's share of the cocaine supplied annually to the U.S."

There was a general grumbling from his audience. Perez knew that many of them wouldn't have known that. The demand for their product had always been a given—it was manufacture and transport that demanded the concentration of the men in this room.

Perez started pacing back and forth as he spoke, and all eyes in the room followed him closely. "It's impossible to tell at this early a date exactly what kind of a demand reduction we're going to see, but I performed an informal poll of some of our associates in the States this morning, and I think the problem is even more serious than we had thought. Apparently, street-level dealers' phones are silent. Some have been put in the unusual position of calling their customers and cutting prices to cost. Reports suggest that their calls have been mostly unsuccessful and that purchasers are insisting that the dealers use some of the product at the sale as an act of good faith. Many of them are unwilling to do this, unless they have a supply that was purchased well before the ads came out."

An impossibly fat man sitting next to Colombar interrupted him. "So what does that translate into in numbers."

"It's difficult to say at this point, but my survey suggests that we can expect around a sixty-five percent reduction in the casual use of cocaine in the next couple of weeks, if this threat continues. That translates into, say, a fifty-percent reduction in overall demand."

With that statistic hanging in the air like a noose, the room broke into loud conversation. The men

258 • KYLE MILLS

turned back and forth to one another, pointing and
gesturing wildly, voices fighting to be heard.

Colombar stood.

"Gentlemen . . . Gentlemen!" The din faltered and
went silent.

"I believe that Alejandro is almost finished. We have
the rest of the day for discussion." He motioned to
Perez and took his seat.

"Thank you. In the habitual users, I think it is safe to
surmise that we will see a less significant drop in use. I
have no estimate of what that will be."

"Maybe it is a government plot." The fat, loud one
again.

"I don't think so. The U.S. government has never
shown any real commitment to stopping the demand
for drugs in their country. No, the U.S. has always
concentrated on stemming supply—despite the fact
that this approach has proven to be woefully ineffec-
tive."

The room was silent. Colombar looked around to
see if any more questions were forthcoming, but the
men seemed deep in thought.

"Thank you, Alejandro."

Perez pulled the tape from the VCR and walked
briskly out of the room, nodding to the group as he
went. The sound of Italian shoe leather against stone
seemed very loud in the silence following his speech.

"Any comments?" Colombar asked, to get the conversation rolling. Roberto Ortega was the first to
speak.

"Your assistant is very smart, Luis, but as with others
of his kind, he told us our problems but didn't offer any

solution." He fairly spat out the words. Ortega hated the new generation of criminal—slick and well educated. Despite this well-known bias, his comments got a few nods from the group.

"Alejandro is here to provide information, Roberto, not to run our business for us," Colombar chided. "It is our job to find a solution."

The fat man to Colombar's left spoke again. Sweat glistened on his upper lip despite the air-conditioning. "And what do you suggest, Luis?"

Colombar felt the attention of the room focus on him. It was a position that he was finding more and more comfortable.

"As we speak, my men are tracing the tainted coke back to its source, looking for the moment that it was poisoned—information that will be very difficult for the authorities to obtain. We'll catch these people ourselves and cut their fucking heads off." Colombar stood and walked through the conversation pit, aiming himself at the elaborate wet bar in the corner of the room. He regretted the profanity at the end of his last sentence. It didn't fit with his new image.

He dropped an olive in the martini he was preparing. Grimacing slightly, he took a sip. Tequila was his drink, but it lacked a certain sophistication. He turned back to face the group.

"I would appreciate you gentlemen using your resources to do the same. If we can pinpoint exactly where the poison was put into our product, we will be quite a bit closer to finding our quarry." He returned to his seat.

"And what if Pedro is right, and this is the work of

the U.S. authorities?" a thin man sitting on the edge of the sofa asked.

Colombar smiled. "Then we simply find proof of that and leak it to the press. I'm sure that they would be very interested in a story like that. I must agree with Alejandro, though. I don't believe that the U.S. government would ever take such drastic action within their own borders. They are much more decisive in other people's countries." There was a general grumble of agreement.

Colombar spotted his butler standing motionless at the entrance to the living room.

"Gentlemen," Colombar said, standing in a single quick jerk and startling a few of the guests with whom he was not on the best terms. "I believe our luncheon is ready." He weaved through the group, hoping that none of them noticed that he had left his nearly untouched drink on the table. He decided that his image could survive a couple of beers at lunch. They were imported from England, after all.

Scott Dresden carefully placed the white cuff links in the mahogany and glass display case across from his desk. The pounding in his head was beginning to subside, succumbing to the three extra-strength Tylenols he'd chewed up fifteen minutes ago. The cuff links were a gift from the secretary general of Interpol, and took a place of honor next to various other items commemorating police forces from across Europe and Asia.

It had been almost a year since Dresden had given

up his post as the ASAC in the FBI's Portland, Oregon, office, and had accepted a transfer to Germany. He had spent the last twelve months in Bonn as the assistant legal attaché. The title called forth images of bureaucratic attorneys reviewing endless documents. Nothing could be further from the truth. In 1940, J. Edgar Hoover had decided that crime, along with the rest of the world's big business, was going international. Shortly after coming to that realization, agents known as Legats began cropping up in major embassies across the world. The plan met with some success and the program had gone through a number of expansions, adding offices to more far-flung countries across the globe.

Dresden's gift for languages and interest in European cultures made him perfect for the position. It had been a difficult call—conventional wisdom was that becoming a Legat significantly reduced one's visibility and, therefore, promotability. In the end, he'd decided that it was worth it to spend a few years in Europe and to give his children an opportunity to see the world.

He carefully closed the glass door to the case and walked back to his desk, plopping down in the tall leather chair and leaning as far back as possible. He had removed a spring from the base of the chair, making it possible to go almost horizontal. Running his fingers through his thick, dark hair, he closed his eyes and concentrated on relaxing. His headache's grip on the back of his head loosened a little more.

The morning had started as a typical one. He had been running late, practically pulling his pants on as he ran out the door. A few New York driving tricks had put him at the office one minute before eight o'clock. At eight-fifteen he was quietly reviewing the leather Franklin Day Planner at the top of his desk.

At eight-twenty Mark Beamon had called from Washington.

Beamon had related that Trace Fontain, Harvard University and the Centers for Disease Control, had finally isolated the poison used to taint the U.S. coke supply. It came from a mushroom indigenous to Eastern Europe—Poland mostly. Smack dab in the middle of Dresden's territory.

One of the things he liked best about running a Legat was the fact that you were given as free a hand as could be had in the Bureau. For the most part, headquarters just wasn't watching. They preferred to defer many decisions to the individual legal attachés based on their contacts and knowledge of the culture. Now, though, Dresden felt freedom leak away as he was drawn into one of the most visible cases the FBI had ever been involved in.

He'd spent the last five hours on the phone with every law enforcement officer he knew in Eastern Europe, calling in a number of favors that he had hoped to save for a cushy consulting job after retirement. Dresden's network in the former Soviet Union was impressive, and the wheels of the investigation were turning. The problem was coordinating with the myriad local law enforcement groups—the people who might have noticed an American running around the woods piling mushrooms into a pickup truck.

Dresden's secretary slipped into the room, her

mouth already forming the beginnings of a sentence. Recognizing his position, she caught herself and instead padded silently across the carpet and set a cup of tea down on the coaster on his desk. The man on her heels wasn't as considerate.

"Wake up, Scott—I just got off the phone with Customs," Kip Spence said, taking a seat in front of his desk.

Dresden righted himself slowly, reaching for the steaming cup on his desk.

"What did they have to say?" The pounding in his head notched higher.

"Nothing. You know Customs. Said they'd check their records and fax us any significant shipments of mushrooms over the last six months. It'll take 'em a few days, though."

Dresden frowned. His opinion of that particular government organization had never been very high. "Well, I think I've talked to damn near every person I know this morning." He touched his right ear unconsciously. It was bright red.

Spence grimaced. "Cryin' shame that Europe doesn't have *America's Most Wanted*. Why the hell don't we just commandeer a little cash from headquarters and put an ad in every local rag from here to Moscow?" He held up his hands, framing an imaginary advertisement: "If you have any information regarding an American picking a bunch of poisonous mushrooms in the last couple of months call the number below. A thousand dollar reward for information leading to the apprehension of this suspect."

Dresden took another sip of the scalding tea.

"Precisely what I suggested. Mark Beamon told me that they'd kinda lucked in to isolating the poison as fast as they did, though. Some guy at the CDC is a fungus-ologist or some such thing. He's hoping that these guys are counting on us taking a few more weeks to nail down the source. Wants to see if we can catch 'em napping."

"Long shot," Spence observed.

His boss nodded in agreement. "The scary thing is, I think it's the best we got."

The Toyota Land Cruiser slammed headlong into a deep puddle, sending thick, muddy water splashing across the windshield and drenching the men in the open Jeep a few feet in front. Luis Colombar whooped with joy and punched at the CD player that was skipping wildly as the truck's tires bounced along the rutted dirt road. Glancing in his rearview mirror, he saw another Jeep full of men approach the same mud puddle cautiously, finally forging reluctantly ahead.

"Fucking pussies!" he shouted over the engine noise and intermittent sound of Madonna coming through the vehicle's hidden speakers. He stomped on the gas one more time, nudging the Jeep in front of him. One of the men sitting in the back almost toppled out, caught at the last second by a companion. Colombar felt a slight pang of disappointment. He was curious as to how his new truck's suspension would handle a body. Probably wouldn't feel a thing.

Life had been good since the meeting with his associates. Quite a few had called later that evening to thank him for his cool head and diligent work in solving what had become known simply as "The Problem." Colombar had always felt that it was counterproductive to have so many lords and no king—as long as that king was him.

This was the perfect opportunity to show that he could rise above the petty infighting between the different Colombian factions and move into a de facto leadership position. When he had gained their trust, he would kill them. With the heads of the major families gone, Colombia's vast narcotics machine would be looking for new leadership. He would slip in as savior and give everyone raises. He suspected that most of them wouldn't mourn their prior bosses' passing for very long.

Colombar glanced again in the rearview mirror. His chase car had fallen even further behind. The Jeep in front of him was maintaining its speed only out of fear that he would ram them again if they slowed. With a flurry of expletives, he let up on the gas slightly and allowed his men to catch up. He was at the height of his popularity with Colombia's nouveau riche, but it never paid to get too far from one's more tangible protection. He had never seen good will stop a bullet.

Every week, Colombar left his fortresslike home and traveled to one of his refineries or plantations. Perez refused to join him on these field trips, insisting that it was stupid—though he didn't have the balls to actually use that word—to get physically close to any illegal operation. Colombar had berated his advisor repeatedly for his unwillingness to get his hands dirty. Perez would be surprised to know that the day he agreed to go on one of Colombar's outings would be his last day on earth. Though he would never admit it, Colombar feared Perez and those like him. Their education, level heads, and ability to hobnob with senior government officials worried him. Perez's fear of dealing one-on-one with the production and smuggling end of the business made him, in Colombar's opinion, unsuited to leading a major drug organization. But it made him the perfect second in command.

Colombar jerked the wheel right, driving by memory through the dust kicked up by the vehicle in front of him. As he came out of the thick cloud, the forest became more dense, forming a solid living wall less than a foot from the sides of his truck. He slowed further, carefully staying in the middle of the road so as to minimize any paint damage that might be caused by an errant branch scraping against his new toy. In less than five minutes he was in a clearing dominated by a small, dilapidated hut. The men in the vehicle behind him had managed to catch up, being less concerned about their paint job.

Colombar pulled slowly into a man-made hollow in the forest and set the emergency brake. The beat-up flatbed that was normally parked there had been moved out into the open and covered with camouflage netting in anticipation of his arrival.

"Buenos dias, Señor Colombar," one of the refinery's dust- and sweat-encrusted guards said, opening his car door for him. The guard's smile suggested a disdain for toothpaste.

Colombar ignored him and started for the hut. The cotton of his shirt was already starting to cling to him.

The day wasn't particularly hot but a recent rain had doused the forest, and was now evaporating, filling the air with a visible cloud of unbearable humidity.

Colombar's personal guards had already taken up positions at each end of the clearing and in front of the hut, displacing the two men who had been standing stiffly at the entrance, awaiting his arrival. They now stood in a new, less-prized station, nervously straightening their fatigues.

"What was that?" Colombar asked no one in particular, stopping short ten feet from the entrance to the hut.

One of the refinery guards fingered the strap on his rifle nervously. "What?"

Colombar stood perfectly still, his head cocked slightly, scanning the tree line.

"I heard someone in the woods—there." He pointed.

The guard sighed with relief and a sadistic smile crossed his lips. "Oh, that's just Manuel. You know him, he works with us." The man pointed to one of the rotting front teeth that he still had. "Gold tooth."

Colombar nodded, prompting the man to continue.

"He's real sick, kept throwing up all over himself. Smelled fucking awful—so we threw him out in the woods." The guard smiled again. "You can still smell him when the wind is right." His final words were met with snickers from his healthier companions.

"Motherfucker drinks too much tequila," Colombar replied angrily. "You go get him—I'm not paying him to sleep in the woods."

The man shook his head gravely, stepping back as Colombar poked him hard in the chest. "It's not the tequila, Señor Colombar—I swear. He's real sick. Think he's gonna die."

Fucking peasants. He paid off half of the law enforcement officials in Colombia to stay away from this place. All these assholes had to do is sit around and suck on bottles.

He waved to the four men who had been in the Jeep in front of him, and three of them trotted off into the jungle. The one who had almost been pulled under Colombar's tires stayed behind. He still looked a little shaky.

A few moments later the men reappeared, crashing through the jungle wall. They were dragging what looked like a corpse by its legs. It clutched a thick wool blanket in one hand, leaving most of it sliding along behind. As they broke into the clearing, the blanket caught on a tree and was pulled from the stiff hand. Only then did the body show signs of life, making a mournful sound deep in its throat. They dropped the sick man's feet onto the hard dirt surface in front of the hut.

Colombar pushed at the man's ribs with the toe of his cowboy boot. He leaned over slightly and squinted, bringing the man's face into sharp focus. His mouth was caked with dirt and vomit, and a fist-sized leaf was stuck to the side of his mouth. His skin had gone an eerie greenish white—an unusual color for a Latino who spent his days in the heavy Colombian sun. The guards were right about the smell.

"What the hell's wrong with him?" Colombar gave the man another nudge with his boot, then moved to a safer distance. "And what happened to his foot?" He pointed to the man's right foot. It was wrapped tightly in a rag heavily stained with dirt and blood. It smelled faintly of kerosene.

"I don't know what is wrong with him, señor. He was fine until a couple of days ago. Then he started puking all the time and couldn't pee. When he finally did, he pissed blood." The guard glanced nervously at Manuel. "He cut his foot week before last. We cleaned it with kerosene to keep the infection away—but I guess it didn't work."

Colombar's mouth curled into a snarl. His teeth gritted almost audibly. He spun quickly on his heel, simultaneously pulling the .45 holstered in the small of his back. The young guard moved back instinctively, catching his heel on his sick companion's torso. As he fell, the butt of Colombar's pistol slammed into his teeth, knocking out most of the top row. Colombar grabbed a handful of the man's hair. He dragged the man off of Manuel, who had begun vomiting again, and pulled him to the center of the clearing. His guards had perked up and were moving toward him, but were unsure what was happening.

Colombar stuck the barrel of his pistol in the man's face. "He's been into my coke!" he screamed.

Blood and spit gurgled from the man's mouth, forming clusters of red-hued bubbles that were beginning to flow down his cheek. He tried to speak, but his voice was muffled by the flowing blood and his inexperience at talking with no front teeth. He shook his head vigorously instead.

"Get Juan!" Colombar shouted at the men now encircling him, delighted by the interesting turn of events on what was usually a tedious day. Two of them ran to the hut and disappeared through the door.

Colombar dropped to his knees, landing one squarely on the man's stomach. Blood and detached teeth flew from his mouth.

"Don't lie to me, you fucking cockroach," he yelled, pressing the barrel of his gun into the man's cheek.

The guard shook his head again, a look of terror spreading across his swelling face.

Colombar stood and turned his attention to the two remaining refinery guards. He stared at them through his gunsight. They were completely frozen, except for their eyes, which darted from side to side looking for an escape. There was none.

"Manuel here's been into my coke." It was a statement, not a question. "And you let him have it."

"No, señor! There is no way he could have gotten to it without one of us seeing him! No way!"

The barrel of the gun moved slowly from one man to another as if it had a mind of its own and was deciding which one to shoot.

"Let go!" Juan Cortegna screamed at the guard who was pushing him roughly out of the hut. Cortegna's hand had slammed into the deceptively sturdy door on the way out, and he was squeezing it between his thighs when he saw Colombar holding two guards motionless with his pistol.

"Señor Colombar! What is going on?"

"That!" Colombar pointed in the general direction of Manuel without taking his eyes off the guards in front of him.

Cortegna looked unsure how to respond for a

moment. "Manuel? He is very sick, I am told. An infection."

"He's been into my coke," Colombar repeated for the fourth time.

A look of horror swept across Cortegna's face for a moment, followed by a look of deep thought. After a moment he spoke. His voice had calmed somewhat. "No, that is quite impossible. You know the safeguards that we use. Manuel has no access to the final product."

Colombar did understand the security measures that Cortegna had in place, but the evidence, and more important, his gut, told him that Manuel had been poisoned. The fact that he couldn't figure out how it had happened made him that much madder. Outsmarted by some piece-of-shit guard.

"Your fucking safeguards don't work then . . . unless you were involved." He turned the gun on Cortegna, who began to shrink away. The sturdy frame of one of Colombar's men blocked his retreat.

"You know I would never do that, señor. You know!"

Colombar did know. Cortegna had been with him for years—he was one of his most loyal employees.

"What makes you think that Manuel has been stealing your product, señor? He does not even like coke—says it doesn't agree with him."

Colombar began pacing the length of the clearing, the pistol hanging loosely in his right hand as it swung back and forth. The guard who had greeted him when he arrived had managed to rise to his hands and knees and was crawling around aimlessly, as though he was looking for his teeth. As Colombar passed by him, his hand tightened almost imperceptibly on the gun. The man once again fell flat. This time with a baseball-sized hole in the back of his neck.

Finally Colombar spoke. "Juan, have all of the kerosene loaded on the flatbed and brought to my house. Immediately. You," he pointed to the driver of his chase car and then the two terrified men standing with their backs to the hut. "You're going to take those two to the house."

"And him . . ." Colombar looked down at Manuel, who was now breathing in shallow gasps from all the excitement. "Tie him to my luggage rack."

The Jeeps were both overloaded, and he sure as hell didn't want this filthy piece of shit stinking up the interior of his new truck.

"Doctor! So good of you to come on such short notice." Colombar strolled across his living room and shook the soft, plump hand of the elderly man standing at the entrance. Dr. Santez, a tiny, white-haired man in his late sixties, had been Colombar's personal physician for almost seven years. Santez came when beckoned, treating his wealthy patient mainly for hangovers. And for that, Colombar paid him five times his normal fee.

The doctor looked at him strangely. Usually when he arrived, Colombar was laid out on his couch, stinking of tequila. The man in front of him was the picture of health.

"You look well, Luis," he observed suspiciously.

"Oh, I am, Doctor, I am. Actually, it's one of my men

who is seriously ill, and I want you to take a look at him."

The doctor looked mildly relieved. Colombar's violent mood swings had always made him nervous. Generally, if you were invited to Colombar's home for unknown reasons, there was a good chance that you had done something to irritate him and that you were going to end up as plant food for his orchids.

"I'd be happy to, Luis," he said, starting for the back of the house, where he knew that there was a wing for the employees who worked in the compound.

Colombar held his arm out, blocking the doctor's path. "No, no. This way." He pointed to the front door.

It was growing dark as they walked through Colombar's gardens toward a detached three-car garage next to the main house. Black clouds swirled wildly, driven by the unpredictable Andean winds. The rain was light, a mist that was imperceptible until it built up enough to trickle from hairline to chin.

As they approached the garage, Colombar slipped his hand into his pocket and activated the garage door opener. One of the three doors began creeping up.

This section of the garage was used by the full-time gardener. The walls were neatly lined with various exotic lawn tools. Heavy-looking plastic sacks of fertilizer were stacked in discrete piles according to brand and type.

At the base of a riding lawnmower that verged on being a tractor, a figure in stained green fatigues raised his head weakly.

A gust of wind blew into the garage and was blasted back into the doctor's face as he stood near the entrance.

It carried with it an odor that he was very familiar with. Impending death.

Colombar motioned the doctor in. "Here is your patient." He sat down on a stack of mulch bags, careful to wipe the dust off them first.

"What is his name?"

"Manuel." Colombar replied impatiently.

Santez walked hesitantly to the side of the man and crouched. A weak smile of recognition crossed Manuel's lips.

After pulling on a pair of thin rubber gloves fished from his black leather bag, Santez went about a quick examination of the man. He looked into his eyes and mouth, took his pulse and blood pressure, and carefully unbound his injured foot. Finally he stood, looking down at his patient's chest. It was moving quickly as he took in short shallow breaths.

"Well?" Colombar hopped from his place on the mulch.

"I do not know, Luis—he is very ill. Do you know when he contracted this sickness?"

"I'm told that he was feeling fine until about two days ago and that he deteriorated rapidly."

The doctor nodded thoughtfully. "Could he have come into contact with some toxic substance? Perhaps some pesticide you use in your garden?"

Colombar shook his head. "What I am about to tell you is highly confidential, Doctor. Do you understand?"

There was a clearly implied threat in Colombar's words. Santez nodded. "I believe that Manuel may have been deliberately poisoned . . . like the Americans."

"Are we speaking of the poison secreted in cocaine?"

"Yes."

"But how . . . ?"

Colombar cut him off. "You let me worry about that. All I need from you is to tell me whether or not I'm right."

"I cannot tell you for certain, Luis, though the symptoms seem to be similar. We must get the patient back to Bogotá—to the hospital there. I will let you know what we discover tomorrow, though if it is a similar poison to the one in the U.S., I doubt those tests will be conclusive. We will have to examine the vital organs—it is my understanding that this particular toxin attacks the liver and kidneys. This could probably be done by next week.

Colombar stared at the doctor as if he were a retarded child. "I'm sorry. Perhaps I didn't make myself clear." Colombar's politeness was well practiced, but lacked even a hint of sincerity. It was as though he was reading from a cue card. "I need to know tomorrow whether Manuel was poisoned. Please take him to Bogotá and do whatever is necessary."

A confused expression crept across the doctor's face. "I can't perform those kinds of tests on his vital organs right away, Luis."

Colombar was becoming visibly irritated. "Why not?"

"He's, uh, using them, Luis."

Colombar took a deep breath and expelled it loudly. Pushing past Santez, he reached up under the back of his thick Irish wool sweater and closed his fingers around the .45 resting in the small of his back. He aimed the pistol at Manuel's chest, and then changed his mind. The concrete floor under him could cause a dangerous ricochet.

Looking around him, his eyes fell on a nearly empty bag of mulch at the base of the stack that he had just been sitting on. He brushed past the baffled physician again and grabbed the bottom of the bag. As he walked back over to Manuel, the upended bag spilled what was left of its contents, leaving a thick brown trail behind him.

In one swift motion, Colombar grabbed the front of Manuel's fatigue shirt, jerking him upright, and pulled the bag over his head. Briefly, the dying guard came back to life. His pale hands clawed at the bag, legs kicking wildly. Concerned that Manuel would manage to rip a hole in the plastic, Colombar flipped his victim onto his stomach. Placing a knee firmly in his back, he pulled with all his might, arching Manuel's back and neck into an unnaturally bowed position.

Santez had backed all of the way out of the garage by the time Manuel's struggles had faded. Colombar kept the pressure on for another minute, just to be sure. "Doctor," he exclaimed, looking behind him. "Why, you're getting soaked! Come under the roof."

Santez did as he was told.

Colombar released the bag, and Manuel's lifeless body fell to the floor. There was a hollow smack when his head hit the concrete. "I will expect a complete report tomorrow afternoon, Doctor."

18

Washington, D.C., February 14

Laura Vilechi climbed up on a chair and stretched to reach the Volume button on the television anchored to the wall of SIOC. As usual, the remote was nowhere to be found. Not surprising with no fewer than fifteen men coming and going at all hours of the day and night. What was it about men and remotes?

She pushed the UP button, repeatedly watching the word-fragment VOL appear in green at the bottom of the screen. The television responded obediently, and CNN went from background noise to a more conversational tone. She climbed down and took a seat at the conference table, shushing two agents talking loudly on the other side of the room.

The camera was panning what seemed like endless rows of dogs in small cages set into austere concrete walls. In the right-hand corner of the screen was the telltale syringe symbol that labeled this as a report on "The Drug Crisis." The dramatic theme music that CNN had composed for the biggest story of the decade filled the room. Laura's interest was piqued.

The news media had splashed this unfortunate situation over every publication, radio broadcast, and television station in the country. They had covered it from every intelligent angle, finally slipping into the absurd. She was curious whether the casually dressed young man with the microphone was going to try to interview the house pet of a poisoning victim.

"This is the Seventeenth Street Animal Shelter in Chicago, Illinois," he started, beginning to walk the length of the narrow corridor between the individual cages. The camera panned back and forth, focusing on some of the more adorable animals. He stopped next to a cage containing a small border collie. The cameraman gave each of them half the frame.

"Until yesterday, you might have seen a young family walking through this corridor, looking for a faithful companion for a small child."

He turned and tapped the front of the cage behind him. The collie jumped excitedly at his hand, thankful for the attention. When the young reporter turned back to the camera, his face was grave. "This is Darby." The dog yipped happily when he spoke its name. "Darby is scheduled to be destroyed in three days. Until yesterday, he had a chance. It's easy to imagine a little girl coming in here with her family and falling in love with him." Darby barked in agreement.

The reporter walked away from the cage, and the collie's hopeful face slipped from the frame. It was replaced by the face of a tall, serious-looking woman.

"Yesterday," the reporter continued, "this shelter, and all other shelters in the Chicago metropolitan area, suspended their animal adoption programs." As he turned to the woman, a caption flashed identifying her as the director of the Chicago-area animal shelters.

"Ms. Kelly, may I ask you how you arrived at your decision to stop allowing animal adoptions?"

"Uh, yes." She was clearly unaccustomed to the camera. "Over the past few weeks, we had just over a thirty percent increase in people wanting to adopt dogs—and my research indicates that most animal shelters have seen about the same jump. We didn't know what was causing it at first, but later we started hearing rumors that people were using them to test their narcotics on." Her voice wavered. "At first we didn't think it was true. We couldn't believe that anyone could do something so cruel. But when we thought back on it, we knew it was true. A lot of the people coming in didn't seem to show as much interest in which dog they got. They just wanted a dog." She paused for a moment, a sad expression crossing her face. "Then yesterday we found out for sure. A vet that we work with treated a dog for massive liver and kidney failure. He confirmed that the dog had been poisoned, and that it had traces of cocaine in its blood . . ."

Laura jumped back onto the chair and slapped the On/Off button. She'd bought a yellow Lab after her divorce a couple of years ago and she didn't know what she would do if someone poisoned it.

"Pretty grim, huh?"

She hadn't noticed Beamon standing directly behind her throughout the broadcast. She spun to face him.

"Are we sure we know what we're doing? Working our butts off to save people like that?" She jerked her thumb at the now silent television. "What kind of scum gives poisoned coke to a dog?"

"They're desperate, Laura," he said, taking a chair at the conference table. "You and I will never have any idea what it's like to be addicted to something like that." Beamon's voice didn't have its usual dead-sure ring.

Laura nodded sadly. "I know you're right. Seeing stuff like that makes you wonder, though, doesn't it?" She pointed through the glass wall at the room next to them. "Looks like they're all here. You ready for our first staff meeting?"

He grimaced.

"Good afternoon, gentlemen." Beamon admired Laura as she walked through the door ahead of him. "And lady."

The small table was crowded. Dick Trevor, Laura's counterpart at DEA, sat directly across from Beamon's chair. Tom Sherman was on his right and Trace Fontain his left. There wasn't a smiling face in the room. Laura's mood seemed to be catching.

"So how goes the war?" Beamon asked hopefully.

No one seemed to want to start. Fontain actually looked away, like a kid who didn't know the answer to a question in class.

"Have you seen this, Mark?" Trevor pulled two copies of *Newsweek* out of his briefcase and slid one each to Beamon and Tom Sherman. "Just came out today."

Beamon looked at the cover. It contained a graphic picture of a corpse lying on a sofa in a cluttered apartment. It looked like the man had been dead for a few days.

"Thirty-four, Mark."

Beamon flipped through, finding the page. A slightly overexposed picture of him standing at a podium, flanked by the President and Director filled an entire page.

"Do you think this makes me look fat?" He held the picture up to Laura. She smiled and relaxed a little.

"Read the poll," Trevor prompted.

Beamon looked at the facing page as Laura stood up and leaned over his shoulder. A yellow box housed a *Newsweek*/Gallup poll. It asked whether the respondents were for or against the CDFS. Thirty-one percent were showing pro-CDFS, with another seventeen percent undecided.

Beamon closed the magazine and held it up over his head. Laura took it, returned to her seat, and began casually flipping the pages.

"What else you got, Dick?" Beamon asked pleasantly.

Trevor shrugged. "Not a whole lot to report, Mark. We've penetrated a few more layers since our last meeting, but nothing yet. Looks like these guys hit the shipment way up the line. We're talking to some pretty high level distributors now. Sorry."

Beamon knew that Trevor had a bad habit of taking every failure personally, spending nights second-guessing himself. Not a healthy trait in a DEA agent.

"I do have some interesting stats, but they're a little off the subject," Trevor added.

"Go ahead, I'm not in a hurry."

"We've compiled data from our street agents all over the country and washed it through the computer.

You'll be interested to know that, as best we can tell, cocaine use is down about sixty percent."

Laura looked up from her magazine, and an involuntary "Jesus!" escaped her lips before she could stifle it.

Sherman looked at her reproachfully and then turned back to Trevor. "Who told you to take that poll?"

"Uh, Director Calahan said he would be interested in any information we had on what effect the CDFS was having on drug use."

"Well, stop," Sherman said.

"Excuse me?"

"Stop. Under no circumstances are you to ever gather that kind of information again. You saw the poll," he tapped his copy of *Newsweek*. "If your stats leak, we'll be fighting public opinion even more than we are now."

Trevor obviously saw his point, but looked uncomfortable.

"I'll talk to Calahan," Sherman promised.

That seemed to satisfy Trevor, and he leaned back in his chair, indicating that his report was completed.

Sherman kept control of the meeting. "Laura, what's happening in your world?"

"Hang on a second," Beamon interjected. "I think Dick's math bears a little conversation."

"And what exactly would you like to discuss?"

"Hell, I don't know. I think we could start with the observation that the CDFS, with a few guys and less money than the U.S. spends on studying the mating habits of the duck-billed platypus, has accomplished something that the entire law enforcement community will never get done."

"So what's your recommendation, Mark? Do we just stop looking for these guys? Let them kill off our problem citizens?"

Beamon looked at his shoes uncomfortably. He felt like a child being reprimanded by his teacher. "No."

"Look, Mark, I understand what you're saying. I've been hearing rumblings about the decline in drug use for a couple of days now, but our job is to catch these guys. Not to make moral judgments."

Beamon turned back to Trevor. "How many people die from drug-related causes every year?"

"Dunno. Lots."

"Stop right there, Mark," Sherman cautioned. "I don't want to hear it. It's easy to punch numbers into a computer and come out with the quantitative benefits of poisoning our narcotics users, and ignore the qualitative issues. But what if it's your kid dead?"

Beamon remained silent and let Sherman change the subject. "Okay, then. Laura, I believe that you were about to report on your end of the investigation."

"Right. Well, we're still groping for solid leads at this point. The check angle has really come to nothing. The suspect bought the checks with cash and then disappeared. We're still doing some follow-up there, but I'm not hopeful." She juggled the papers in front of her and started back in. "The hotline we set up has pretty much turned into a forum for public comment—mostly people applauding the CDFS and telling us to back off. At Mark's suggestion, we've changed it from an 800 number to a toll call. Hopefully that'll cut down on the traffic. As you know, we've publicized a five hundred thousand dollar reward for information."

She stood and walked to the corner of the conference room. A large piece of posterboard leaned against
the wall. She picked it up. "We're up to roughly fifteen
thousand eight hundred casualties." She placed the
edge of the posterboard on the table, giving the rest of
the agents a closer look. It depicted a roughly bell-
shaped graph. Next to it was a much smaller red bar.

"This blue curve charts the daily deaths from
cocaine poisonings since the beginning of the out-
break." Her finger traced the length of the graph. "As
you can see, the first section, depicting the first week,
is quite steep. That's because of the unexpected
delayed reaction in the drugs. Lots of people were
using them thinking they were safe. It's starting to level
out now for a few reasons. One, because the poisoned
coke seems to be getting used up. Two, as Dick
pointed out, people are using less. And three, quite a
few users are, well, dead. The last one doesn't really
have that much of a statistical impact, though."

Sherman pointed to the center of the graph. "And
what does it mean when the line goes from blue to black?"

Beamon rolled his eyes. It wasn't enough that Laura
spent half her life drawing graphs and charts. Now
Tom was actually going to prolong the discussion of
them.

"The black line represents our projection of remaining deaths. You can see along the bottom that the
color change corresponds with today's date."

Sherman nodded. "You're assuming that no more
cocaine is poisoned, though, right?"

"That's right. It's hard to say what would happen if
they got to some more drugs. It depends on how com-

fortable people are feeling that the poisoned stuff is dwindling."

"So what's the other one?" Sherman pointed to the red bar.

"Oh, that's just deaths to date. Fifteen thousand eight hundred."

Laura leaned the posterboard against the wall and took her seat as Sherman turned back to Beamon. "What's happening in your world, Mark?"

"Turns out Customs doesn't have a record of anyone bringing in a shipment of mushrooms that couldn't be traced to a legitimate source—grocery stores, restaurants, whatever. Scott Dresden, out of Bonn, is running down the mushroom angle—where they got 'em and how they got 'em here. No luck yet—he's a good man, though."

"Pretty tall order," Laura observed sympathetically, "finding some guy running around the woods picking mushrooms in Poland."

"And he's got to do it without a single graph," Beamon added.

She kicked him hard under the table.

Beamon turned to Fontain, rubbing his shin with the top of his foot. "Trace—you want to tell everyone what you told me?"

Fontain didn't like meetings, and had protested when Beamon had asked him to come. He spoke reluctantly. "You know that we've been trying to get around and interview just about everyone who's been poisoned. We've been trying to track where people got the bad coke, to help the DEA pinpoint its origin." He shifted uncomfortably in his chair. "Well, we interviewed a young man yesterday who swears that he hasn't done a line of coke in six years. We did some tests this morning and confirmed that he was telling the truth. He's a heroin addict."

"Goddammit," Sherman exclaimed in a rare use of profanity. "Where'd he get it?"

"L.A."

Beamon jumped in to divert Sherman's attention from the frail-looking scientist. "I typed up a press release a couple of hours ago, Tom. The press should be running a story within the hour."

"Goddammit," Sherman repeated for good measure. "How many people are they gonna get this time?"

Beamon shrugged. The number of deaths was just noise to him—irrelevant to the investigation, and a subject that he found particularly depressing. The last thing he needed was a constant reminder of the lives being lost because he hadn't caught these guys yet.

Sherman's gaze turned to Laura.

"I don't know, Tom. There are so many factors . . ."

"Well, speculate then," he shot back impatiently.

"I can't. We have no idea how much product they hit—in the end, that's the most important variable."

Beamon agreed. "Yeah, but I think we can count on all the poisoned stuff getting used up. There's nothing quite as desperate as a heroin addict in need of a fix. They're gonna take a hell of a lot more chances than some guy who likes to do a few lines before he hits the clubs on Friday night."

* * *

"So good of you to come personally to give me the news!" Luis Colombar crossed his expansive living room and gave his physician a firm handshake.

Colombar was dressed impeccably in an off-white linen suit and maroon silk shirt. He showed off the thousands of dollars worth of ongoing dental work correcting years of youthful neglect.

Santez followed him to the bar, where Colombar poured him a Stolichnaya and tonic. Even there, in his beautiful home, in his expensive suit, with his practiced accent, the drug lord was surrounded by an aura of violent insanity. It wasn't just the memory of his recent experience with Colombar—it was something in the drug lord's gait. Something around his eyes.

The doctor accepted the drink gratefully, downing a good portion of it in the first gulp. It burned its way down but didn't kill the butterflies below.

"And so what news?" Colombar asked.

Santez didn't understand what he was involved in, but his churning stomach told him that it was big. Regret coursed through him—regret for the greed that had prompted him to take the job as Colombar's physician and had entangled him in the invisible web of the cocaine trade that blanketed his country.

"We have not been able to fully complete our tests on Ma—the subject's—organs." Somehow speaking Colombar's victim's name out loud seemed impossibly dangerous. "However, based on information provided by Johns Hopkins Hospital in the States and our initial review of the damaged liver, I believe that there is a ninety-five percent probability that the subject was poisoned by the same substance that is being used to poison drug users in the USA."

There, he'd said it. He watched Colombar's face carefully.

To his relief, the drug lord appeared to be unaffected by the news. He just stood there and sipped his drink. Finally he laid down his glass and clapped Santez on the shoulder.

"I really appreciate your help on this, Doctor." He took the drink from Santez's slightly trembling hand and began leading the old man out.

"Drive carefully!" he called as Santez slid behind the wheel of the Blazer that he always rented when he came into the mountains. Santez held his breath as he turned the key—sure that the car would explode into a ball of fire. The engine roared innocently to life.

"You heard?"

Alejandro Perez had appeared like magic and sunk into one of the large chairs by the entertainment center. He wore white shorts and a white Polo shirt. A tennis racquet was propped next to him.

"I heard. I think I know how it was done, too."

Colombar dropped into the chair across from him. His jaw was clenched tightly.

"One of the men you brought back goes with the truck to pick up kerosene every week. He tells me that a few weeks ago, they stopped to relieve themselves and found an old drunk hitching a ride on top of the barrels on the back of the truck."

Colombar's expression changed from sullen to hopeful.

"They let him go."

"Fuck!"

"I've doubled our guards on the refineries and told them that one man is to ride on the back of the trucks with the kerosene. We're also going to start using different suppliers on a random basis."

Colombar was still seething at the thought of just barely missing the man who'd done this to him. He took a deep breath, quelling the rage that was building up inside him. "I want the motherfucker who let this happen dead! Send the other son of a bitch back to the refinery—but give him something to remember me by." Guards weren't that easy to come by, and he seemed to be losing them fast.

Perez looked embarrassed. "He, uh, passed away during his conversation with Rico."

"Oh." Colombar stood and paced behind the sofa, a habit his interior designer had complained about on numerous occasions. A light-colored swath was becoming visible on the hand-tied Oriental.

"When do we get the analysis back on the kerosene sample that we sent out?"

"Probably not for another two weeks."

"No matter. I know what it will say." Colombar stopped pacing and leaned against the couch. "Somebody must know something—this guy must have been going around town asking questions." He stopped and turned to face Perez. "Put the word out, Alejandro. I'll pay two hundred and fifty thousand dollars for information on this son of a bitch."

* * *

The thick clouds that almost delayed his flight into Denver International had miraculously disappeared. Mark Beamon squinted his eyes almost shut as he swung his car onto a steep gravel road and headed directly into the sun.

At the crest of the hill, he slipped the gearshift into neutral and let the car's momentum fade and then reverse itself. After rolling back ten feet or so, he reluctantly yanked on the emergency brake and brought the car to a skidding stop.

Beamon hated Colorado. He hated the shining mountains, the clean air, and the annoying bicyclists who waved as he passed them in his rented subcompact. Funerals deserved more somber settings. And the funeral of a family member—a child—should, at the very least, rate a good steady rain.

Beamon put the car in gear and forced it forward without releasing the emergency brake. He stopped again when he reached his previous high mark, and surveyed the scene below.

To the left of the cemetery's imposing front gate were no fewer than four white vans, each adorned with a satellite dish and elaborate logo. The logos were illegible from this distance, but it was a safe bet that the vans represented local affiliates of national news organizations. Beamon didn't even bother to count the cars nosed up to the fence, or the people perched on their roofs, peering through camera lenses as long as his arm.

Releasing the brake, he started down the hill. On the drive from Denver, he had started to feel a little guilty about the scene he had made in the rental car agency when they had told him that they didn't stock cars with tinted windows. As he watched the enormous lenses of the press swivel toward him, though, he made a mental note to find out who ran the rental car agency and have someone shoot out his porch light.

Beamon slowed to a stop ten feet from the cemetery's gate and rolled down his window. The camera flashes went wild, but finally dissipated when a large man in dark glasses positioned himself directly in front of the car window.

"Sorry to hear about your nephew, Mark."

"They're not," Beamon said, jerking his head in the general direction of the press. "It's good to see you, Frank. I really appreciate you helping out."

Frank grunted and looked at the ground. "No problem. I just can't believe these vultures have the balls to come out here like this."

"Are you kidding? When my nephew dies from snorting bad coke, they clear their calendars."

Frank shrugged and rose to his full six and a half feet. "It's already started. You'd better get going."

Beamon pulled the car forward, keeping his bumper within two feet of another somberly dressed man slowly pushing the gate open.

Frank had always been a good friend. He hadn't offered a word of protest when Beamon called and asked him to take on the distasteful and only marginally legal job of bouncer at his nephew's funeral. Frank was the only man for the job, though. One look at his heavily pockmarked face and solid two hundred and fifty plus pounds would make even the most obnoxious reporter think twice before spouting off about the pub-lic's right to know.

Beamon pulled in too close to a blue Toyota pickup, purposefully blocking it to give himself an excuse to make a run for it at the end of the service. With some effort, he separated himself from the tiny car and weaved his way, alone, through the snowdrifts and headstones toward a small knot of black-clad mourners clinging to each other for support.

He was thankful that no one looked back as he found a strategic position behind a man whose head blocked Beamon's view of the coffin. He peered around the man's shoulder for a moment, looking briefly at his sister. Her head was lowered and her stare was fixed on the thing he couldn't bring himself to look at.

The service went on forever.

The priest alternatively mumbled and shouted, but said nothing about the guest of honor. He talked only of the pervading godlessness that had led to the boy's death. Beamon's mind wandered, and he looked around at the small group of people gathered around him. He recognized almost no one in his sister's life. That wasn't surprising though—they had never made any kind of real connection when they were children. They spoke now only on holidays, and the conversations consisted of the self-conscious prattle of complete strangers.

Beamon was interrupted from his daydreaming by the sudden silence of the priest and the brief crush of people as they moved past him. He looked up and watched his sister moving purposefully toward him.

The tear in the corner of her right eye was quickly lost in her cold stare.

"You've never been much of a brother to me, Mark."

He didn't see much point in denying it and remained silent.

"Now's the time to make up for it. Find out who did this to Kevin. Find out and kill him." She brushed past him and headed for the cars.

Kevin.

Hearing his name and looking at the dirty snow around his grave brought back the few fleeting memories Beamon had of the boy. He'd been impossibly bright and completely out of control for most of his life, much like Beamon himself had been. Fortunately, the stifling atmosphere of the early sixties had kept the young Mark Beamon from straying too far from the straight and narrow. The nineties had offered no such barriers. Until now.

"Franz—nein," Scott Dresden pleaded, performing his best tired look from behind the large desk.

Franz Gullich looked down his long straight nose at him, continuing to screw the top off of a fifth of Jack Daniels. When the cap was freed, he followed a tradition that Dresden had come to dread. He threw it in the trash can.

Gullich hadn't become the head of the German police based on sobriety. In fact, his ability to perform magical feats of deduction while half-cocked was the marvel of two continents. He and Dresden had become fast friends during Dresden's tour as an assistant legal attaché in Bonn—a friendship based on mutual respect.

Gullich's lack of political ambition made him a joy to work with. He'd started as the German equivalent of a beat cop almost twenty years ago on the streets of Munich. Today he was still just a cop. Dresden had come to miss the company of cops in his current position as FBI agent/diplomat.

Gullich pulled two large commemorative mugs from their display case and blew the dust out of them.

The glasses cleaned to his satisfaction, the German worked himself into the sofa at the opposite end of the office and placed the bottle ominously next to him. Dresden hit the intercom button on the complex-looking phone on his desk.

"Hello, Kip? Kip?"

"Hi, Scott. Finally figured out how to use the intercom, huh?"

"Yeah. Hey—Franz is here, why don't you come over for a drink?" Dresden knew that the bottle would be empty by the end of the night and figured to spread out the pain a little.

"I'd love to, Scott, but I've got an appointment that I'm already late for. Tell him I'll catch him when he gets back. I'm anxious to hear what he has to say about Quantico."

Dresden flicked off the intercom and came out from around his desk. His mind wandered to how he was going to get back at his assistant for that little white lie.

Gullich was already pouring healthy slugs of the brown liquid into the mugs, emptying almost a third of the bottle. He slipped his shoes off and put his feet on the coffee table in front of the sofa. The table top wasn't attached and it tipped wildly, almost upsetting the bottle. He didn't seem to notice.

"Cheers," he said holding up his mug.

"Cheers." Dresden settled into a love seat positioned perpendicular to the sofa.

The Austrian took a long pull from the glass. The corners of his eyes scrunched up a bit as he swallowed, accentuating the deep crow's-feet that were a relic of his years walking the streets in the harsh German winters.

The conversation moved smoothly from subject to subject, starting with general politics and economics and becoming more and more personal as the liquor took effect. An hour later they were having a heartfelt discussion of the perils of in-laws. Dresden's head felt light as a feather, a sensation that he was becoming used to, and one that he knew guaranteed a tough morning. Gullich was less affected, though his English was becoming worse and worse. Dresden was indistinguishable from a native in German and French, but Gullich's English needed work, so he insisted that all conversations between them be in that language.

Tiring of the in-law issue, Gullich fell silent and held up the nearly empty bottle. Dresden offered his cup to be topped off. The Austrian looked mildly disappointed as he tipped a splash into the nearly full mug.

"So how goes the mushroom-hunter hunting?"

Dresden scowled clumsily. His facial muscles were a bit more relaxed than he'd thought. "It's hopeless.

They've got me trying to find one lone American, running around the woods somewhere in Eastern Europe, stuffing mushrooms into a garbage bag." He put his glass to his lips, shaking his head. "I might have gotten lucky in Western Europe, but you know the condition of law enforcement in the East."

Gullich swung his feet up on the sofa and leaned his head against a pillow. Dresden thought he was preparing to pass out and watched him carefully during the long silence that ensued. Finally his friend came back to life. "I think you're approaching this whole thing wrong," Gullich said, switching to German.

Dresden leaned forward slightly. He'd known Franz long enough to know not to dismiss his drunken musings out of hand. "Care to elaborate?"

"You grew up here, didn't you?"

"Not here—Berlin," Dresden answered. "My father was in the army. But you know that."

A smile spread across Gullich's face. "It always makes me laugh—how out of touch you are with your countrymen. Let me ask you a question. What do you see when you bump into an American tourist in Bonn?"

They were getting way off the subject here, and Dresden relaxed. His friend must have had a few drinks before he had arrived. He was rambling.

Getting no response, the German answered his own question. "You see a fat, poorly dressed person with no understanding of our culture or language. Without their tour guides, most of them wouldn't be able to find their hotels and would die of starvation in the streets."

Dresden opened his mouth to defend his countrymen but closed it again when he came to the realization that his friend was ninety percent right.

"And that's Western Europe. I expect they're even more lost in the East."

Dresden waited for his friend's eyes to focus elsewhere, and dumped a good portion of his drink into the unhealthy-looking tree next to the sofa. His secretary, who prided herself on her green thumb, could never understand why the tree always looked like it was about to die.

"Okay, so we're a little ethnocentric."

"Put yourself in the shoes—sneakers—of your right-wing friend. You've been to Europe, say, three times. You've toured, oh, London, Paris, and Rome. You speak no foreign languages and have never been to the former Soviet Union. So you've got a problem—you need a bunch of mushrooms from—Poland, is it?"

"That's where they grow, primarily," Dresden confirmed.

"Okay, Poland. You've never been there, don't speak the language, and probably don't know a shiitake mushroom from a portobello. What do you do?"

Gullich drained his glass and turned his head, looking ruefully at the empty bottle on the table. Dresden reached over and poured some of his into his friend's glass.

"You," he pointed at Dresden, "get a book on mushrooms and take your four languages and intimate knowledge of Europe and pick them yourself. You wouldn't have any problem figuring out where you were going and blending in. Like you said—it would be damn near impossible to track a person like you. Joe American, though, couldn't. He'd draw lots of unwanted attention getting lost, trying to find places to eat, trying to figure out where the mushrooms grow—whatever."

"So what's he do?"

"He hires it done. He calls some farmer or something and gets him to pick the mushrooms. He sends the guy some money and has him mail the lot to him in America."

Dresden cursed under his breath, dumping what little was left in his glass into the tree. Franz was right. He had spent so much time ignoring his countrymen's embarrassing attitudes that he had missed the obvious.

Gullich reached an arm up toward the ceiling and swung it around drunkenly. The glass in his hand sloshed and the bourbon dripped down his arm. He switched to heavily accented English again. He had been working on his slang for the past few months, concentrating on the worst that American TV had to offer. "So what do you think, paesan? Am I right or am I right?"

19

Washington, D.C.,
February 18

Bill Karns scanned the street carefully as he walked back to the house he had rented in Southeast Washington. It was almost four blocks from the house to the Korean-owned grocery store that he had come to rely on over the last couple of months.

The day was cold, with a driving wind whipping through the tightly packed rows of decaying houses. The neighborhood had once housed some of Washington's wealthier families, but the last shards of its dignity had been stolen by neglect and young men with spray cans.

The stone homes on his block were distinguished by their round turrets, topped with almost Russian-looking roofs. Their large windows were now covered with boards, which were in turn covered with paint and an infinite number of peeling flyers. The flyers made a loud chattering noise as the wind tore across them. Every couple of minutes a chunk of paper would break loose and go cartwheeling down the street.

Karns turned abruptly right, glancing behind him at the empty street.

Pulling a set of keys out of his pocket with his free hand, he slipped one into the dead bolt. The door popped open and he pushed through, slamming it behind him.

Inside, the house was even less impressive. The hardwood floor had long since been ripped up and moved to a neighborhood more suitable. The artfully rounded walls were covered with graffiti and topped with a discolored strip where an expensive crown molding had been removed.

He walked to the kitchen and laid his groceries down next to a small refrigerator that shared a bright orange extension cord with an even smaller hot plate. Karns's groceries consisted of a twelve-pack of National Bohemian beer, three cans of Hormel Chili, a box of Velveeta, and two bags of generic tortilla chips. He closed the refrigerator door tightly on eleven of the twelve beers, keeping one out for himself.

He had been living in this place since John Hobart assigned him to D.C. at their meeting in his hunting lodge. The house was in a "disputed" area. To the north, the neighborhood was one hundred percent black. To the near south it was Hispanic. Farther south, it was an "up and coming" neighborhood, where Caucasian yuppies were buying relatively inexpensive homes and renovating them with window bars and high-tech security systems.

His first month had been slow. Neither the blacks nor the Hispanics were prepared to accept a fifty-year-old white man with a slight Southern accent into their respective folds. He'd worked his way in slowly—differentiating himself with top-notch product at below-market prices. He was always fair and always had merchandise to sell. Eventually many of the small-time local dealers grudgingly came around. Economic concerns, it seemed, transcended racial bigotry.

There had been problems, of course. Mainly with the dealers that he had usurped. The most vocal of these, and ostensibly the most violent, had met with an unfortunate accident at the wrong end of Karns's twelve gauge. That had quieted down the market resistance temporarily, as his competitors moved in on the dead man's turf. They were better off with Karns than their unpredictable friend. They seemed to realize this, and an uneasy truce was born.

He hadn't heard a word out of Hobart for weeks and he was getting impatient. Right now he was just another drug dealer, adding to the problem that he had hired on to eradicate.

He sat down on the floor and opened a can of Hormel, dumping it into the dirty pan sitting next to the hot plate. He cut a healthy chunk of Velveeta with his pocket knife and tossed it in with the chili. Stirring occasionally when the sides began to bubble, he polished off his beer and reached into the refrigerator for a new one.

A loud buzzing startled him as he peered into the pan to see if the cheese had completely melted. It was the doorbell that he had installed when he moved in. It was loud enough to be heard anywhere in the house.

Karns pulled his 9mm out of its holster and chambered a bullet before replacing the gun in the holster under his arm. He walked quietly to the front door and peeked through a peephole drilled in the wall. There was a much more obvious hole in the door, but it was just there as a decoy. Looking through it was a good way to get a bullet in the eye.

It took him a moment to recognize the young black boy fidgeting on the porch. Reeling through the file of local dealers in his head, he finally placed him. His street name was Tek, and he was pretty far from home, by drug dealer standards. Karns glanced out the window and spotted another fidgety youth keeping lookout on the sidewalk. He had heard that his counterpart in Tek's territory had been picked up a few nights ago, and that Tek had been having a hard time finding a new supplier. He also heard that there were some other "businessmen" interested in Tek's territory.

Karns opened the door slightly and moved away from it, being careful to stay out of sight of the young man on the sidewalk. Tek took the open door as an invitation and stepped in.

"Close the door behind you. Pretty far from home, aren't you, Tek?"

The young man looked around him, trying to see into the kitchen. He looked nervous. "Yeah."

"I hear you're having a hard time finding product—that some people are moving in on you."

Tek's attention turned from the kitchen to Karns. A sneer passed his lips.

Karns calmly registered the anger on Tek's face. His experience with the local dealers was that they couldn't hit the broad side of a barn at ten paces with a howitzer. He was confident that with his 9 mil and a few extra clips he could walk down the middle of the street and kill every dealer in Southeast without getting a scratch. Hell, they'd probably end up popping each other in crossfires. If this little nigger wanted to pull down, he'd have a bullet in his head before his hand hit his pistol grip.

"Thought you might have something to sell."

Karns nodded thoughtfully. His calm demeanor belied a racing mind. "I might. What do you need?"

"Some rock, man."

Karns nodded again, recognizing the street name for crack cocaine.

"I don't want to get pulled into this shit between you and DJ. Anybody know you're here—other than your backup?"

Tek shook his head, and Karns believed him. If he found a new supplier, he sure as hell wouldn't want his competitors finding out who it was. Besides, Tek and his friend—Twan was the name, if he remembered correctly—were both heavy users. The opportunity was just too good, Hobart or no Hobart.

"How much you need?"

"I got a grand."

"Let's see it."

Tek's hand moved slowly to his pocket. Karns tensed imperceptibly, though he knew that the jacket pocket was too small to house a Tec-9—the only weapon the young man was reputed to use. A moment later Tek produced a healthy-looking wad of bills.

Karns smiled approvingly. "Have a seat." He pointed to an old vinyl chair sitting in the corner of the room. "I'll be right back."

He rushed through the kitchen, stopping for a moment to turn off the chili that was beginning to boil over. At the back of the kitchen was a new, sturdy-looking metal door leading to a windowless basement. A perfect place to store merchandise, and a nearly impregnable fortress to retreat to, if things ever came to that.

The basement room was mostly in shadow, lighted only by a desk lamp on a small table. Along one wall, mired in gloom, stood a shelf fastened to the brick with long rusty nails. On it were at least twenty shoe boxes. Karns crouched down, his knees cracking loudly.

Pulling out three of the boxes in front, he reached back through barely perceptible cobwebs until his fingers hit crumbling brick. Moving his hand right, it fell on another box. This one was almost indistinguishable from the others, except that the masking tape label on top was printed in red, instead of the uniform blue on all the others.

Taking the top off, Karns began piling small vials into the dusty gym bag lying at his feet. He picked up the bag, weighing it, and tossed in a few more vials. He zipped it up as he walked back up the stairs.

"Here you go," he said, handing the bag to Tek, who'd just jumped up from his seat, startled by Karns's abrupt reappearance. Tek unzipped it and looked inside. His suspicious expression changed to one of approval.

Tek handed him the wad of bills and zipped up the bag. Karns decided to hedge a bit. It seemed safe to assume that Tek would rush off to his customers, supply them, and then retreat to his house to sample the product. There was no way to be sure, though. "I gave you a deal, 'cause I haven't tried that stuff yet. I'm working with a new supplier."

Tek looked up from the bag.

"It should be at least as good as what I had before—
you let me know what you think."

Tek hefted the bag to his shoulder, but made no
move for the door. Karns faced him silently. Tek
looked like he was about to say something.

Karns knew exactly what was going on.
Washington, D.C., hadn't been hit with poisoned narcotics as hard as some might have expected—or
indeed, many apparently had hoped. Death was still
there, though. It flooded their living rooms twenty-
four hours a day, in full color and stereo sound.

He would have never pegged the blacks in the
neighborhood's reaction to the poisoning. The popular theory on the street, and in the minds of the more
conspiracy-minded black leaders, was that this whole
thing was the white government's doing. That it was a
plot to wipe out black Americans. The rational reaction, then, would have been to stop using, and to foil
the government's plot. Just the opposite had happened. The false bravado that had so often been the
undoing of young urban blacks had twisted their logic.
They thought that to stop using coke was to admit fear
and defeat to the white hierarchy that they had grown
to hate. As far as he could tell, the use of cocaine
hadn't slowed in Southeast D.C.'s black community. In
fact, he knew of at least one gang that had made a
group of its inductees smoke crack that they alleged
was poisoned. It hadn't been, as it turned out, but they
hadn't known for sure.

"What—you worried that it might be mickey?" Karns
said, using the slang term that had become popular for
poisoned product. Tek's reaction was predictable.

"Hey, fuck you. I ain't afraid of none of that shit."
He reached for the door and backed out, keeping his
eyes on Karns, who stood motionless, arms crossed.

He watched as Tek joined his friend and half
walked, half jogged up the street. They swatted and
slapped at each other playfully, oblivious to the driving wind. Karns marveled at how alive they looked. An
image of their corpses lying facedown on a dirty carpet next to a smoking crack pipe superimposed itself in
his mind, and made him smile.

"You sure were in there long enough," 'Twan said
haltingly. All this running was getting him out of
breath. "You sucking on his dick?" A devious smile.

"Fuck you," Tek replied with mock severity, barely
missing his friend's head with a vicious open-handed slap.

As they ran, the bag bounced along under Tek's shoulder. The vials within made a seductive rattling sound.

"Let's stop off at my place and do a little smoke,"
'Twan suggested. He had run through his supply two
days earlier, and the embargo by Tek's competitors was
wearing him down.

"No way—business first." They slowed to a walk.
'Twan was holding his side uncomfortably.

Their first stop was a three-story brick apartment
complex, sitting like a large brick box amidst the curv-
ing architecture of the rest of the neighborhood. In the
mid-seventies, the brightly painted building had been
a flagship of urban renewal. The mayor himself had
stood barefoot in the grass and cut a wide ceremonial
ribbon. He had spoken briefly of a new day for the
city's underprivileged, before rushing off to more
pressing matters.

The colors had faded over the years, falling victim to pollution and neglect. Hope had faded with them. In the early eighties, a young girl had managed to work her way through the metal guard rails protecting the building's open-air hallways. Her life, like her body, had been abruptly halted by the asphalt below.

Following that incident, the city had covered the entire front of the building with chain-link fencing. People had joked that the cops weren't satisfied with putting the residents in jail, they wanted to imprison the building, too. In the end it had just added to the despair that quietly engulfed the neighborhood.

The two young men walked quickly through the asphalt-covered playground spread out in front of the building.

Two heavy wood doors protected the main entrance to the apartment building. One had a weblike crack emanating from its top hinge, keeping it from closing all the way. Tek pulled it open.

The air inside wasn't much different from the outside because of the broken door. As they climbed the stairwell, though, the atmosphere grew heavier. The sounds of civilization replaced the whistle of wind through the buildings. A baby's cry, a shout, a television turned up loud enough for an old lady to hear.

The numbers had long since been torn from the doors of the individual apartments—an obvious target for budding vandals. Tek knew the building well enough to make his rounds in the dark. It was a prerequisite for his job—lightbulbs were an easy target, too.

He rapped authoritatively at his first customer's

door. 'Twan was a few feet behind him, looking back
down the gloomy stairwell. His right hand rested
casually under his sweatshirt.

Mark Beamon leaned back and listened for the
cigarette lighter to pop. The street outside his window
seemed unusually silent and dark by inner-city standards. He scanned the gray-and-black landscape as if
it were an old photograph. The only movement was
his faded reflection in the windshield.

Goddam Tom Sherman, he thought, tapping the cigarette lighter as though it would speed the heating process. Right now he should have been half-sauced, sitting
in front of the TV at his borrowed Capitol Hill town
house. Instead, he was here. In the middle of D.C.'s
no-man's land, hiding in his car.

A comforting popping sound came from the dashboard, promising a quick nicotine fix. As he raised the
lighter to his mouth, the red glow lit his face slightly,
momentarily stealing his anonymity. The smoke was
barely visible as it twisted through the confines of the
car, obliterating its new smell. He concentrated on it
anyway, blocking out the dim scene outside of his
steel-and-glass cocoon and feeling the nicotine flow
through him.

Reports of a serious poisoning incident, the epicen-
ter of which was only a few miles from the J. Edgar
Hoover Building, had come flooding into the switch-
board less than an hour ago. Sherman had stormed
into SIOC only a few moments later.

Beamon had argued vehemently. He had insisted

that he was buried with paperwork and subtly implied that there were important leads that he needed to follow up on. In the end it had all been a waste of time. Sherman had listened sympathetically, as he always did. Then he had told Beamon in no uncertain terms to get his ass to the housing project that had been hit. It wouldn't look good for no one from the Bureau to show up when this kind of thing happened in their backyard.

The cigarette had burned down almost to his fingers. Beamon took one last hard drag and tossed the butt out a narrow crack in the driver's side window. A quick turn of the key brought the car to life. He swung it out onto the narrow road.

Turning the corner was like jumping off a cliff. The quiet monotony of the side street gave way to a kaleidoscope of lights and activity. As he drew slowly closer, he could see that yellow-and-black striped barriers blocked the streets leading to an ugly box of a building. Crowds of people milled around the perimeter, many wearing robes pulled hastily over pajamas. The flashing blue and red of the police cars and fire trucks was drowned out by large spotlights—the kind used to advertise circuses and auto dealership sales. They had been set up on an asphalt playground in front of the apartments. They were aimed at the top of the building, and the glare lit the area sufficiently for rescue workers to rush from victim to victim, without the risk of tripping.

The lights gave the building a malevolent feel. The chain-link fence covering its facade became teeth, and the reflective windows, lifeless eyes.

Beamon's car pushed forward. People milled lazily in the streets; knots of conversation formed and dispersed at random. They looked mildly annoyed as they moved unhurriedly from the path of his car. About fifty feet from the barricades, the crowd of haphazardly dressed spectators became too dense to drive through. Beamon pulled the car over onto the sidewalk and continued on foot. He was carefully examined as he proceeded to the barricades.

"I'm sorry, sir. There's no admittance to this area," a haggard-looking cop said. He was moving back and forth in the ten-foot gap in the barricades that allowed emergency vehicles to get in and out. The crowd carefully tested his defenses, anxious to get a closer look.

Beamon reached into his jacket, producing his credentials. When the officer's pacing brought him back, he flashed them inconspicuously. The cop waved him through.

The crowd was even worse inside the barricades. Same number of people, but instead of milling around in bathrobes, they were moving at a speed between a jog and a sprint, and carrying all kinds of gear. Children—newly orphaned—were herded like sheep toward the fire trucks.

He walked less than purposefully through the rescue workers, feeling stupider and stupider. There was nothing for him to do here except be seen. Out of the corner of his eye he saw another, more energetic, group of people than the one he had just driven through. Three more cops looked like they were barely holding the line. The Press.

Beamon altered his trajectory slightly, taking a path to the building that would get him within fifteen feet of the rabid reporters. That should make Sherman happy.

He was still almost thirty feet out when one of the reporters recognized him and shouted a question, slapping at his cameraman. The others jumped on the bandwagon and the question became an unintelligible roar.

Close enough.

He aimed his best "no comment" wave in their general direction and resumed slowly walking toward the apartment building. He felt alone and detached.

Ahead of him he saw a reporter who had managed to get through the barricades. He was interviewing a child of no more than twelve, holding her arm tightly. Probably asking her how she felt about her parents being dead. Beamon considered helping the kid out, but thought better of it. This wasn't his show.

The scene grew considerably more gruesome as he drew closer. Rushing rescue workers were replaced with grotesquely contorted victims. Directly in front of him was a man lying on a white stretcher. He was wearing only a pair of heart-covered boxer shorts. His face looked lined and old at first, but as Beamon drew closer, he realized that it was only the effect of the harsh spotlights. The man's body was smooth and well muscled.

What was remarkable, and what cemented Beamon's feet to the ground, was what was happening to the man. He had been lying relatively quietly a moment before. Then, without warning, his back began to arch.

Beamon didn't pay much attention at first, anxious to make his obligatory turn through the building and then head back home. But the quiet figure started to scream. His back continued to arch, soon coming fully off the ground. His only points of contact now were his head and heels, which were bunching up the white sheet under him as his stomach continued to rise skyward.

Just when he reached a point where Beamon was sure that he could crawl under him, the man flopped over onto the pavement. His screams died for lack of air, though his mouth still worked silently. The progression continued. Beamon had been awakened from his trance when the man had tipped, but he had no idea what to do. As the man's head and heels continued to close on one another, Beamon's body tensed. He waited to hear the inevitable crack of bone as the man's vertebrae shattered.

It didn't happen. The progression slowed, then finally reversed itself. The man's fluttering eyelids closed as he slipped into unconsciousness.

The show over, Beamon reached out and grabbed a paramedic unfortunate enough to be within his reach. "What the fuck's going on here?" He knew the symptoms of the drug poisonings backwards and forwards. He had never heard of anything like this.

The young paramedic looked at him blankly and pulled away. He was about to rush off, when the unmistakable look of recognition registered on his face. Over the last couple of weeks, Beamon had unwittingly become the most photographed man in America.

"Looks like a different poison," he said simply.

"What kind?"

He shrugged. "Dunno. Heard somebody say strychnine—but I don't know that much about poison, you know?"

Beamon watched him hurry away, then turned and

continued toward the building. Looking up, he saw that the windows had been either opened or broken out. The malevolent eyes had turned into empty sockets.

At the bottom of the steps someone caught his arm. A fireman. He looked like he was in charge.

"Mr. Beamon? I'm Shannon Calloway." He extended his hand. "Sorry to hear about your nephew."

"Call me Mark, and thanks." Beamon reached out to take the fireman's hand.

"You can't go in there without one of these." Calloway thumbed at the tank on his back. A hose attached it to a full face mask pushed up onto the top of his head.

"Is there a fire?" Beamon looked for signs of smoke.

"Oh, no—no fire. It looks like the poison was in crack cocaine. There were quite a few smoking pipes lying around. Don't want to take any chances."

Beamon backed away from the building as a burly-looking fireman ran down the stairs with another victim. There was no way in hell he was putting on a respirator and running around this brick graveyard just to please the press.

"I can get you a . . ." Calloway started. A man standing on the steps shouted at him, interrupting his train of thought.

"We're clear in here, Shannon—fully ventilated." The man jogged down the steps, pulling the heavy tank off his back with practiced ease.

"I stand corrected," Calloway said, holding his hand out toward the dark opening where the front doors had once been. "Be my guest."

It took a few moments for Beamon's eyes to adjust to the gloom of the hallway. The shouts of rescue workers and the crash of ax on door echoed through the building. He paused at the base of the steps and forced himself to take a deep breath. He had been holding it since he passed through the shattered doorjamb that was the front entrance to the building. The image of the dying contortionist seemed to superimpose itself on everything he saw.

Feeling a little more collected, he started up the stairs, idly trying to decipher the stylized graffiti adorning the walls. He was on the first landing when the shout "coming through" bounced off the walls, followed by heavy footsteps. Between two firemen was a stretcher with a heavy-looking man strapped firmly to it. The fireman on the low side had to hold the stretcher almost above his head to keep it level. Under normal circumstances, he looked more than up to the task. These weren't normal circumstances. The man on the stretcher was convulsing violently, straining against the heavy straps holding him in place. The motion was throwing the two back and forth, slamming them into the sides of the narrow staircase. Beamon flattened himself against a wall, but it was too late. The hard edge of the stretcher, backed by the full weight of the three men, slammed into his chest. They didn't seem to notice, or at least didn't acknowledge the collision. Beamon stood on the steps, slightly stooped for a moment, catching his breath. When the pain in his chest subsided to a dull throb, he continued up.

He reached the first-floor landing and began walking slowly down an interior hallway. It reminded him of a house of horrors at a cheap traveling carnival. As he walked past open doors, it seemed that the scenes behind them were being acted out for his benefit. Corpses, people in the throes of violent convulsions, crying children. Above them all hovered busy men and women in various uniforms identifying them as fire fighter, paramedic, ambulance driver, police.

Beamon felt the weight of the situation come crashing down on him. The feeling came on suddenly, adding to the pain in his chest. He came upon a closed door—the first he had seen. A large red X had been spray painted on it. Somehow the mark didn't blend with the graffiti blanketing the dank walls, and Beamon reached out and touched it. Still wet.

Two more firemen appeared from a door at the end of the hall and began rushing toward him. Beamon could see something squirming under the clean white sheet covering the stretcher between them. He pushed mightily on the door in front of him. It opened with the sound of cracking wood. He made it through just as they passed and slammed the door behind him.

Shouts could still be heard through the thin walls, and through the open window to his right, but he was grateful for the calm motionlessness of the room.

The only light was provided by the spotlights on the asphalt below, creating a rectangular beam that cut through the room. He could see dust floating lazily in the light, but the more tangible occupants of the room were obscured in shadow. They came slowly into focus.

The room was only about twenty feet square. At the far end was an open kitchen. Dishes were piled high in the sink and on the counters. In the center of a chrome and Formica table sat a box of breakfast cereal and a bowl. The living room consisted of a sofa and a couple of old chairs arranged around a high-tech–looking TV.

On the floor behind the sofa lay a woman in a floral patterned dress. She was on her side, her back arched unnaturally. Beamon walked quietly across the room and stood over the body. Her eyes stared up at him.

Next to the woman was a clear plastic crack pipe. It was lying in a puddle of water that was undoubtedly the work of the firemen who had been trying to clear the poisonous fumes from the building. Beamon looked back at the woman. Something in her expression had become accusing. He walked to the kitchen and began rifling through the drawers. It was hard to make out their contents in the semidarkness, but he didn't want to turn on the lights. The woman on the floor belonged in the dark.

Finally finding what he was looking for—a pair of scissors, he went to the table and sat, pushing the half-full bowl of Lucky Charms off to the side. He pulled a cigarette from his pocket and cut the filter off, lighting it with a cheap plastic lighter. The smoke attacked his lungs, giving him another much-needed rush of nicotine.

He had been working well with the casualty numbers that Laura put on his desk every morning. Numbers agreed with him. They could be added, subtracted, and multiplied, but they couldn't bleed or cry out in pain. Even the television reports, while certainly more graphic than Laura's charts and graphs, were only pictures. Little pixels scanned across an electronic screen at the speed of thought.

He took another drag on his modified cigarette, feeling the eyes of the woman on his back.

The ambiguities of the CDFS's actions, and their long-term effects, had disappeared from his mind. They were killing people. Real people. The obvious conclusions about lives saved in the future by lower levels of drug use, and the other coldly logical arguments for the CDFS's actions, seemed ludicrous as he looked down on the woman's frozen form.

The front door to the apartment began to open, and Beamon waved in its general direction. "FBI. It's all clear in here."

"Mark?"

"Laura?"

She moved through the door and closed it quietly behind her. Through the shadows he could just make out her slim figure and perpetually tied-back hair, as she walked across the room and sat down next to him. "Tom told me you were here." She reached out for his hand. "Are you okay?"

He remained silent and took another deep drag on his cigarette.

"I thought you didn't take cases personally." She looked around the room. "This is just noise to you. Isn't that what you told me?"

Beamon pointed to the woman lying on the floor. "They don't sound like noise this close up."

Laura walked over to the woman, took a quilt off the sofa, and covered the body with it. She looked down at the lump under the blanket for a moment and then took a seat in the chair directly in front of Beamon.

"You know, Laura, I took this case just to feed my ego. Calahan burned me, so I came back to show him and the world just how smart I am. Thousands of people are dead, and I was just playing a game."

"Come on, Mark. You had no idea that this case was going to blow up like it has. No one did." She plucked the cigarette from his mouth and tossed it in the sink. "You know, they put the filters on these things for a reason."

"Yeah, I know."

"You sure you want to do this, Tony? It makes me nervous having you this close to a buy."

Anthony DiPrizzio, head of the DiPrizzio crime family, nodded and calmly straightened his tie. He didn't like to be this close, either, but times were changing, and he needed to be there. This was no time for the hands-off management style professed by his favorite instructor at Wharton. It was time to get personally involved.

It was eleven-thirty P.M., and DiPrizzio was sitting in the small office on the second floor of one of his many New York waterfront warehouses. Across from him was Chris Panetti, an old and trusted enforcer who had worked for his father before Tony had taken over the helm. At the other end of the room sat three more men, each with a shoulder holster wrapped around his thick torso. He knew all of them too. All were men who had been with the Family for years. They were transfixed by a football game playing on a tiny black-and-white television. DiPrizzio watched the game from his side of the office with mild interest. He had never understood the appeal.

The unmistakable rolling sound of the warehouse's cargo doors going up floated up to the office. The men watching the game stood and turned off the television. Panetti stood too, touching the holster under his arm. "I don't suppose I can convince you to watch from up here, eh, Tony?"

DiPrizzio shook his head as he listened to the sound of the door going down again. "Let's go."

"Juan! It's good to see you."

The man standing in front of the rusting ice cream truck parked in the middle of the warehouse looked confused and a bit worried. He stood flanked by two of his own men, who were wearing the same surprised looks on their faces.

"Mr. DiPrizzio. What are you doing here?"

DiPrizzio stopped a few feet in front of the three, careful not to let his eyes wander to the men who were quietly positioning themselves around the truck. "Oh, you know how it is, Juan. Every once in a while they let me out of the office."

Juan's expression didn't change, and he stayed rooted to the floor.

"Why don't you show me what you've got?" DiPrizzio asked.

"Sure, Mr. DiPrizzio, sure."

Juan and his companions walked to the side door of the truck and opened it, producing a wooden crate that looked something like an old army footlocker. They carried it with some difficulty to the front of the truck.

Juan took a key from around his neck and unlocked the box. He opened it, revealing that it was completely filled with one-kilo bricks of cocaine, each individually wrapped in plastic and duct tape.

DiPrizzio bent over the box. He reached out a gloved hand and grabbed a brick, closed the trunk, and placed it on top.

"Chris?"

Panetti leaned over and handed him a pocket knife, which he used to put a small slit in the top of the package.

Juan smiled. "It's top quality stuff, Mr. DiPrizzio, you got my word on that."

DiPrizzio continued to stare at the brick, focusing on the white powder oozing out of it. "I appreciate that, Juan, but I'll tell you what would make me feel even better."

Juan was starting to look nervous again, as were his companions. They were surrounded by no less than twenty of DiPrizzio's men.

"Sure, Mr. DiPrizzio. Anything you need," Juan said.

"Why don't you just try a little." He pointed to the brick.

A look of horror flashed across the young Hispanic's face and then disappeared.

"I'd like to, Mr. DiPrizzio, but you know, I gave it up. It was fucking with me." He pinched the bridge of his nose and winced to illustrate the point.

"Do it for me, Juan. Just this one time."

Juan and his two companions began slowly backing away. DiPrizzio's easy smile disappeared. "I insist." The last syllable of the word "insist" was drowned out by the clatter of rounds being chambered.

The three men looked around them. DiPrizzio's enforcers, who had been standing so casually a moment before, now each had a gun trained on them.

"This stuff's good, Mr. DiPrizzio. I swear. I wouldn't try to sell you no product that was mickey."

"I know you wouldn't, Juan. This is just for my peace of mind." He nudged the open bag toward him. Juan looked around. He seemed uncertain about what to do for a moment. His companions were frozen.

Finally he walked up to the brick and dug a tiny amount of coke from the slit with his finger.

"No, no, don't be bashful. Get some on there," DiPrizzio said.

Juan reached back down, pulling out some more of the powder. He brought his hand to his nose and inhaled deeply.

"Get it all . . . good."

DiPrizzio put his arm around the quivering man. "Thanks Juan. I'll be able to sleep well tonight."

Juan didn't reply, he just wiped hard at his nose.

DiPrizzio turned and headed toward the office. "We'll hold on to this stuff for a while, Juan. I want you to come back here at the same time in two weeks. I'll have the money for you then. Don't send a messenger. I'll only give it to you."

One of Juan's companion's spoke up for the first time. "Hey! We delivered. We don't work on credit."

DiPrizzio stopped and turned around. "There's been a change in the way we do business. Is there a problem with that?"

The man looked around him and down the barrels of the guns trained on him. He grabbed Juan, who was still standing next to the footlocker looking dazed, and pushed him toward the truck.

20

Baltimore, Maryland,
February 19

Robert Swenson burst through the apartment door without knocking. "You watching this?"

Hobart sat silently on the sofa, fixated on the television. The muscles in his jaw rippled as he slowly ground his teeth back and forth.

Swenson took an indirect route across the room—keeping himself from getting between Hobart and the television. He sat in a chair to the right of the sofa and turned his attention to the screen.

CNN was replaying the events of last night. Mark Beamon's sad face was supernaturally pale as he walked by the cameras. He looked like the eye of the storm as he strode slowly toward a large brick building in the background. The camera pulled back and panned right, focusing on the victims splayed out across an asphalt playground. Swenson ignored the voice-over, focusing on the eerie scene captured on the screen.

Finally the images faded, replaced by a well-dressed anchorwoman. Hobart punched the MUTE button on the remote in disgust. For a moment neither of the men spoke.

"What the hell happened?"

"Karns," Hobart answered simply.

"You gave him the okay for this?"

"Fuck, no. Piece of shit did it himself. I knew he was a loose cannon—but I sure as hell didn't think he'd go off and do something like this." Hobart was rubbing his temples now. "Shit, shit, shit," he whispered. Finally he raised his head and looked squarely at his partner.

"We've gotta pull him out. The FBI'll trace that stuff back to him eventually."

With operations like the one that Karns had set up, it was a one-shot deal. Then you pulled up stakes and set up somewhere else. Unfortunately, this wasn't the one shot that he had planned on.

Swenson arched his back slightly, imitating what they had just seen on the television. "What was the deal with those reactions?"

Hobart shook his head miserably. "You know how we figured we'd use cyanide-based rat poison on the downstream stuff—save what's left of the orellanin for big hits?"

Swenson nodded.

"Well, it looks like that stupid son of a bitch used the wrong thing. I did a little reading on my own when I was researching this operation. That," he pointed at the now soundless television, "was strychnine poisoning."

"Should be good for our image," Swenson said sarcastically. They had been enjoying the positive public reaction to their activities. The heart-wrenching suffering of the people on the playground was bound to turn people away from their cause.

Hobart grunted and began dialing Bill Karns's number on the small cellular that was resting on the sofa next to him.

Luis Colombar wasn't known for his punctuality. Reed Corey had been waiting for almost fifteen minutes. He began playing nervously with his hair, twisting it back and forth and pulling until it hurt. He pulled harder, using the pain in his scalp to clear his head and to try to return to a mindset he hadn't had in years. The man who had fought bravely in Vietnam seemed to slip further away every year, the memory obscured by drugs and liquor and time.

Corey felt only fear and anticipation, sitting in the expansive living room. The guilt that he expected to wash over him never came.

John Hobart had cold eyes—like a shark in a National Geographic special. They were less windows to his soul than cameras taking in everything around him. Despite this, Corey had come to know his old friend better than anyone. And looking into his eyes the last time they had met, Corey knew that Hobart intended to kill him.

He had made the right decision, leaving the house and spending the last few weeks taking a tour of the sofas of Bogotá. He had first heard of Colombar's offer three days ago in a run-down bar not far from where he and Hobart had met. He had been in unfamiliar territory and unsure whether or not to believe the people he was sitting with. The next day he confirmed the story. Luis Colombar had put up a two hundred and fifty thousand dollar reward for information leading to the capture of the person or persons inquiring about certain aspects of his cocaine refining activities.

The memory of his first meeting with Hobart was a bit clouded, but his questions regarding refinery locations and chemical suppliers stood out in Corey's mind. He wasn't sure what this was all about, but he suspected that Hobart was the man Colombar was looking for.

Though he had been expecting them, he was startled by the footsteps coming up behind him. He turned quickly to face the sound, pulling his hand quickly away from his hair and wiping it absently on his dirty trousers. Two men appeared at the far end of the room and walked down the wide steps. Both were impeccably dressed, but the younger one was much more formal. He walked silently behind the older man in a calculated expression of his subordinate status. The older man walked around Corey, not looking at him. The younger one moved toward him.

"Mr. Corey, my name is Alejandro." He didn't offer his hand.

"Hello," Corey stammered. The act of speaking dislodged the sweat that had been collecting on his upper lip, sending a few small drops into his mouth. They tasted salty.

"We appreciate you coming here so quickly. You have information for us?" His smile was warm and calm.

"Uh, yes, sir." Corey hadn't heard the other man

coming up behind him but he knew he was there from the gentle tinkling of ice in a glass. Alejandro raised his eyebrows, signaling that he wanted Corey to continue.

"Um, a couple of months ago, a guy that I fought in 'Nam with came to town. Hadn't seen him in years. Anyway, he and I met in a bar and did a little drinking and he starts asking questions about drugs and stuff. I knew he used to be DEA but got kicked out, so I'm thinking he's just interested in talking about the old times. So we talked for a while about coke in general. You know, how big a business it's gettin' to be. That type of stuff." Corey paused and patted his forehead with his sleeve.

"Can I get you something cold?" Alejandro asked. His smile was still warm but there was something in his eyes that told Corey it was a rhetorical question.

"Uh, no thanks." The hairs on the back of his neck stood up at the sound of tinkling ice as the man behind him, who he assumed was Colombar, took another drink.

"So we're gettin' pretty drunk, and we do a little blow, and he starts asking some pretty specific questions."

"What kind of questions?"

"Well, he starts asking about where stuff is getting refined exactly. This is what I thought was weird—he asked about the chemicals that go into making coke and where you get 'em. Like he was kinda specific about that. He wanted to know names of companies that distribute stuff like kerosene."

Something flashed across his inquisitor's face at the word "kerosene" but Corey wasn't sure what it was.

"And you told him?"

"Hey, no way, man," Corey replied too loudly. His voice echoed off the walls.

"You know, he and I are old buds and I didn't mind talking with him about the general state of things, you know, but I didn't want to get into talking about any specifics. I know when to keep my mouth shut, you know."

Alejandro nodded. "I'm sure you do. Please go on."

"So, anyway, I pretty much told him that, you know, I wasn't gonna tell him anything like that. Lot of the stuff I didn't know, anyway. He got pretty pissed off and, you know, just kinda blew outta the bar. Didn't see him again, but I heard he was around for a while longer, you know, a couple of weeks or something."

More jingling ice.

"Now, who might this old friend of yours be?"

Corey was silent as he looked around the room and then finally back into Alejandro's eyes.

"Don't worry, my friend, we'll get you the money. I think you know we are good for it." His hand waved about the room, putting forth the lavish surroundings as proof of their wealth. "I hope you understand, though, we don't keep two hundred and fifty thousand dollars in cash lying around. We can either have it delivered to you in cash or deposit it into a bank account. Of course, we want to check your story out first."

Corey let this sink in, finally deciding that it seemed reasonable. He mopped his brow again.

"His name's John Hobart."

Alejandro pulled an expensive gold pen out of his breast pocket. He wrote down the name.

• "And where might we find this Mr. Hobart?"

Corey was silent for a moment. As sure as the sun •

rose tomorrow, he knew that Hobart had intended to kill him before he left Colombia. Despite that, an inexplicable twinge of guilt grabbed him in the stomach. Memories of their time together flashed jungle-green across his mind. There was no going back now, though. Besides, he wasn't so sure that his old commander wouldn't come out on top in the end, anyway. Son of a bitch could probably teach Colombar a thing or two about cold-blooded killing.

"Last I heard, he was in Baltimore, Maryland, working for some TV evangelist. Blake, I think, is his name. Hell, he's probably in the phone book."

Alejandro smiled and scribbled into his notebook. He looked up and past Corey, nodding conspiratorially. Corey stiffened. He tried to see the man behind him through sheer force of will.

Instead of a knife in his back, he got a grateful smile. "We appreciate your help on this. I hope you understand, we don't want anyone knowing about our conversation or about the information you've given us. I assume that you haven't told anybody?" Corey shook his head.

"Well, as I said, we want to check out your story. I assume that we can contact you at the same number?" Corey nodded.

The butler appeared like magic at the far end of the room. Alejandro stepped aside and motioned toward him. Corey mumbled a good-bye and headed for the door. His gait was unnatural. His entire being was focused on his back, still expecting to be attacked.

He felt a great sense of relief as he passed through the front door and into the hard Colombian sun. He decided that he had made the right decision. Two hundred and fifty thousand easy dollars. And Alejandro didn't seem like such a bad guy.

"Well, what do you think?" Colombar took another sip of his drink.

"It's our man, it must be. Did you notice that he mentioned the kerosene by name, and this guy's ex-DEA. It fits too perfectly."

Colombar walked over to one of the thick sofas and sat down, putting his feet on the table in front of him. Alejandro Perez followed, perching himself on the arm of the opposing sofa.

"And the others?" Colombar asked. Corey was the fourth man to try to claim the reward.

"I think we should start with this one. It seems to be the most promising."

"I agree," Colombar said finally. "Send some guys out to find this John Hobart, and bring him back to me."

"I don't think we should do that, Luis. Kidnapping American citizens and transporting them across the border can be . . . complicated. Actually, I would suggest simply notifying the FBI. They'll find him in short order, and things will quickly return to normal."

Colombar bared his teeth. "I don't want this motherfucker to get caught—I want him dead! Since when do we work with the fucking FBI, Alejandro? Since when?"

"We don't, Luis. I only thought that in this situation . . ."

"In this situation you're going to do what I say—just like always."

Perez took a deep breath to calm himself. He wasn't

going to win this battle. He took another approach. "Perhaps you're right, Luis. Better to get this over with quickly. Let me send Renaldo to Maryland. He can take care of the problem there. No need for you to get directly involved."

Colombar thought for a moment. "Okay, do it." He stood and started for the bar at the opposite end of the room. "That piece of shit was lying to us about not helping this guy. Little fucker'd do anything for an ounce of blow and fifty bucks. No, he gave him the information all right. Son of a bitch has cost me twenty million dollars! Call whoever's driving him back to town and tell him to dump that fucker's body by the road somewhere."

Perez had already enjoyed one minor victory in the conversation. Two was going to be pushing his luck. "I don't think we should do that, Luis."

Colombar turned away from his ice bucket and stared at him, dumbfounded.

"You're telling me that I can't kill some cockroach street addict that cost us God knows how many millions?"

"We asked for information out on the street and offered a reward. I'm concerned that if it gets out that we killed the man who brought it to us, no matter how justified, we may have a hard time collecting intelligence in the future."

Colombar slammed his drink down on the table, spilling most of it. "This isn't open for discussion. Kill him."

21

New York City,
February 23

Anthony DiPrizzio put his finger to his lips and motioned to the television, prompting his consigliere to move quietly to the sofa next to his desk. DiPrizzio leaned back in his chair and turned his attention back to the screen where Jake Crenshaw, America's voice of conservatism, was beginning his show.

The audience was on its feet—most clapping loudly, the others punching the air with balled fists. The occasional loud whistle or catcall mixed into the thunderous applause.

Crenshaw quieted the crowd, using the same gesture as a professional football player in a stadium.

Crenshaw snapped the paper in his hands loudly, signifying that he was about to speak.

"I'm a little depressed today," he told the cameras. "Oh, you probably think you know why. You think it's because I had to sit through three hours of Democratic drivel last night—geez, and I thought *I* liked to hear myself talk."

The audience giggled.

"But that's not it, ladies and gentlemen. Why am I depressed? It's because tonight's the last night of college week." He indicated to the cameraman to pan across the crowd full of young people, most advertising their respective universities in bold letters across their chests.

"As you probably know, we've flown in youngsters from different universities to sit in the audience every day this week." He turned to his producer. "Who do we have today?"

"Princeton and Yale," came the unmiked voice.

"Princeton and Yale . . . a couple of fine community colleges," Crenshaw boomed.

The audience laughed again.

He turned and struck a pose reminiscent of the Heisman Trophy. The crowd cheered in anticipation. He walked over to a large easel near his desk and flipped back the sheet covering it. On it was a vertical red bar with numbers going up one side in increments of one thousand.

He took a red indelible marker from the tray on the front of the easel and made a show of reading from the paper in his right hand.

"Says here that the death toll's reached twenty-four thousand five hundred." He drew a corresponding square on top of the red bar and colored it in.

He turned back to the audience. "It also says things are tapering off. You think these people are finally wising up?" An uncertain grumble came from the crowd. "No? Me neither."

Crenshaw walked to the end of the stage, still holding the marker. "Y'know, I'm getting a lot of garbage

for our little chart. You wouldn't believe the mail I get."
He affected a whining voice. "How can you condone
murder, Jake? How can you condone the killing of the
people in society that need our help most?" He grimaced. "Ladies and gentlemen I want to be perfectly
clear on this point. *I do not* condone murder . . . but this
just ain't murder."

The crowd cheered again—more fists in the air.
This time he let them go, pacing the stage. "Look, the
CDFS gave the druggies plenty of warning. Geez, the
liberal press had this story plastered across every TV
and newspaper in the country. Look at this . . ." A
newspaper article popped up on the screen. The headline was VIGILANTE GROUP THREATENS TO POISON U.S.
NARCOTICS.

"This was clipped from a local newspaper from a
town of less than two thousand people in South
Dakota—not exactly a hotbed of narcotics trafficking.
My point is this: Everyone knew what was going to
happen. It's like putting a gun in front of somebody
and then warning them over and over that it's loaded.
If they shoot themselves, is it murder?"

The crowd was on its feet.

"And now Jameson gets on the TV and says that this
is a crisis that compares to WW II." Crenshaw looked
straight into the camera. "I'll tell you what the crisis is,
Danny Boy, it's that you liberal Democrats let these
druggies take over our cities in the first place." He
jogged back to his desk and picked up a copy of
Newsweek.

"I guess the White House doesn't actually subscribe
to this, but it has an interesting statistic this week." He

flipped through the magazine, stopping at a page marked with a paper clip. He held it up.

"I don't know if the cameras can pull in on this . . ." The camera closed in on the article.

"If you can't read this, it says that forty percent of the U.S. public is behind what the CDFS is doing and that fourteen percent are undecided. If you were to read further in the article you'd find that it says that the undecideds are moving to pro-CDFS positions, and that quite a few of the people who were arguing against what they're doing are changing their minds."

Crenshaw turned and nodded almost imperceptibly. "Looks like it's time for a break." He mopped his brow with a pudgy hand. "It'll give me some time to cool off."

The television screen faded into a pizza commercial as Anthony DiPrizzio pulled himself upright and hit the MUTE button on the remote in front of him. "It would seem that the tide of public opinion continues to turn, eh, Randy?"

"And that ain't the worst of it," Randall Matlin said, tossing a manila folder onto DiPrizzio's desk.

DiPrizzio slid the folder toward him and began flipping through the pages it contained. "The numbers are worse than we thought."

"Yeah, I didn't expect demand to drop off as fast as it did. It was like someone turned off a fucking spigot. It's killing our cash flow, Tony."

DiPrizzio chewed idly on his lip, considering the problem. The CDFS was having more of an impact than he had expected. But he hoped to avoid restructuring the organization based on what he assumed would be a short-term problem.

"Do we have enough cash to get us through the month, Randy?"

"Yeah, but we're gonna have to pull from the offshore accounts. And it's gonna cost us to carry all this inventory. We probably should have refused delivery on that last shipment."

DiPrizzio nodded. "We only pay for it if it's good, though. Go ahead and bring in some cash. I don't want to do anything drastic until we see what's gonna shake out."

Matlin looked worried. "What if it takes a while for the Feds to catch these assholes, Tony? Hell, what if they aren't even looking that hard? Our cash reserves are gonna run out sooner or later."

DiPrizzio smiled. His counselor knew the streets better than anyone, and he was insanely loyal. But he was old school.

Matlin had been his father's counselor and had been a part of DiPrizzio's life since he was a small child. It had been Matlin who recognized young Tony's intelligence and convinced the old don to send him to Wharton for an MBA, and later to put him in charge of the Family's growing concerns.

"Times change, Randy. This could turn out to be a hell of an opportunity for us."

Matlin dug around in his pocket for a cigarette, but didn't find one. "You're a miracle worker, Tony, I'll admit that, but I sure don't know how the hell you're gonna turn this into an opportunity."

DiPrizzio stood and walked to the opposite end of the room, opening a small hutch and pouring himself a cup of coffee. He dropped in a couple of sugars and started back for his desk. "We've got it too good now, Randy. The Colombians take on the risk getting the stuff here, then we buy it, cut it, and sell it for one hell of a profit margin. Demand is unlimited, and our customers depend on us. The cops make trouble every once in a while, but that risk is built into the price. It's the perfect business."

Matlin nodded his agreement. He had a nostalgic look on his face, as though he thought that those days were gone forever.

"Think about IBM," DiPrizzio continued. "They'd been making business machines forever—stuff like typewriters and cash registers. But then computers come along. That could have driven them out of business. But it didn't. Why? Because they changed with the times.

"And what about the music industry? Do you think that the record album manufacturers were happy when they found out that albums were going to become obsolete? They had to throw out millions of dollars in manufacturing equipment and buy millions more in replacements. But now they're selling CDs—that are cheaper to produce than records—at twice the price."

"But we're not IBM, Tony."

"Sure we are. What happens if the FBI doesn't ever get these guys, and the floor drops out of our market?"

The look on his counselor's face told him that he didn't have any idea.

"We adapt, Randy. I haven't given it that much

thought—'cause I think the Feds'll come through—but off the top of my head, I think we'd start with a vertical integration."

"A what?"

"Vertical integration. Set up a partnership with the Colombians, get more involved in street-level dealing—regulate it. That way we can watch the drugs from coca leaf to when it goes up our customer's nose. Before, all you had to do was be breathing to sell the stuff. That'd be over. We'd differentiate on quality. Our customers would know that the stuff was safe, and they'd easily pay double the price for a little peace of mind. I see us packaging in those tamper-proof bottles—like Tylenol comes in now. The price increase should more than make up for higher expenses and loss in volume."

Matlin laughed and clapped his hands together. "I always said you were a goddam genius, Tony. Now I'm sure of it. Hell, you almost got me hoping that the Feds blow it."

DiPrizzio sipped at his coffee. "Yeah, we'll be okay in the long run—it's the next few months I'm worried about. It's gonna cost us a lot of money to wait around and see what happens."

"What about trying to get these guys ourselves?"

DiPrizzio shook his head. "Don't see how. We're working with the Colombians to help them figure out where the stuff was hit—but whoever's doing this knows we'd do that. No, I think we pretty much leave it to the Feds." He chuckled. "I never thought I'd be counting on the goddam Bureau's efficiency to save my ass."

22

Near Baltimore, Maryland,
February 24

The weatherman's promise of a beautiful late winter day had been broken. The Reverend Simon Blake increased the speed of the wipers as the slightly frozen raindrops splattered against his windshield like bugs.

He slowed the car slightly, bringing it back under fifty-five, and glanced nervously in the rearview mirror. His paranoia and depression had been deepening over the last few weeks, and his wife was near panic. The face that looked back at him in the mirror was almost unrecognizable. The twenty pounds he had lost looked great at his waistline, but his face had become gaunt. Combined with the red-rimmed eyes and shadow of a beard, he looked like a completely different person.

He shook his head violently, clearing his eyes of his image, but not the other image. The one that wouldn't leave him alone. The one that God himself had planted. It was hell, he knew now. In it, people writhed in agony on a cracked asphalt playground. Behind them the face of Satan laughed. Others watching the news report had only seen a dilapidated public apartment building. He knew better. It hadn't been God who had sent him down this path, it had been his age-old nemesis.

The Reverend caught a glimpse of a Days Inn in the distance and veered the car onto an off-ramp. He passed by the hotel, circling to the rear. The Mercedes splashed loudly through a large puddle as he entered the parking lot.

He slipped the car into a space between two trucks, thinking it would make his vehicle less conspicuous. Taking a deep breath, he got out and jogged through the rain toward room 115. He exhaled loudly as he stood in front of the door, realizing that he had been holding his breath. Panting slightly from the run, he rapped sharply on the door. A moment later it seemed to open itself. He stepped in. The door slammed shut behind him.

"Nice to see you, Reverend," John Hobart said. His back was pressed against the wall, so he could remain out of sight with the door ajar.

"This has to stop, John."

Hobart slipped gracefully around him, and sat at a table next to the door. He picked up a can of Coke and took a long swig. With his free hand he pointed to the seat across from him. Blake took it.

"Did anyone see you come in here?"

Blake shook his head. "The parking lot was empty. It's raining pretty hard."

"Your car?" He knew that Blake drove a rather conspicuous Cadillac with AMEN on the plates.

"Erica's."

Hobart set the can down. "This isn't such a good idea, Reverend. For you I mean. You're risking a lot."

"I know, but I had to talk to you." Blake's eyes silently scanned the room, though there wasn't anything to see. Hobart had seen him do this a hundred times. He was rehearsing a speech.

"I saw a news report a few days ago. It looked like the hand of God had reached down and was twisting people's bodies—trying to rip them apart." His eyes had become unfocused. He didn't seem to realize that Hobart was still in the room. It was as if he was talking to himself.

"Let me explain about that, Reverend . . ."

"Twenty thousand people are dead, John. I heard twenty thousand people are dead." His eyes finally came up. "It has to stop, John. Everything stops now."

Hobart pushed the half-empty Coke can around the table with his index finger.

"Little late for that now, isn't it." It was a statement, not a question. Nothing was going to get between him and the success of this operation.

"This ends now," Blake repeated.

Hobart looked up and suppressed a smile. Blake's voice was thin and he looked sick and weak. His attempt to give an order was a joke. Control of the situation had shifted.

"Have you seen the report that CNN started running today?"

Blake shook his head "Did you hear what I said, John? We've got to . . ."

Hobart cut him off. "They quote anonymous sources in the DEA. Casual use of cocaine is down seventy percent—habitual's down thirty-five. Heroin use is down forty percent. Enrollment in drug rehab programs is up nine hundred percent—hell, they got people sleeping on the floors." He took another swig of his Coke and threw the empty can into a wastebasket across the room. The clattering of the can punctuated the Reverend's words.

"Didn't you hear me, John? Twenty thousand people are dead! We've killed twenty thousand people!" Speaking the words out loud seemed to jar Blake fully back into reality. He put his head in his hands.

"Christ, Reverend. There are probably fifty drug-related deaths every day in the U.S. We'll be net ahead in two years." He looked at Blake with what passed for sympathy. "Look, the big stuff's over. People know we're serious. Now all we're going to do is hit a few shipments here and there. Keep people scared. You don't really want to stop now. If we do, all those people would have died for nothing. Drug use would go right back to where it had been before."

Blake nodded and began studying the room again. His entire demeanor had suddenly changed. Behind the pale face, a flicker of his powerful television persona appeared.

"What's this maintenance phase going to entail?"

Hobart relaxed slightly. "Not that much, really. We'll hit a shipment every month or so probably. I want to do some manufactured stuff here soon, too. Amphetamines, X—that kind of stuff. You've heard of Anthony DiPrizzio, haven't you?"

Blake nodded. "Some kind of Mafia don in New York."

"Yeah. I've got a man working in one of his warehouses on the waterfront. Word is that there's a good-sized shipment of coke that's going to be passing through there on the twenty-eighth. I've authorized my guy to hit it. Then that'll be it for another month or so."

Blake stood and moved for the door. He paused with his hand on the knob. "Where on earth did you find that poison? The papers say it takes two weeks for it to work."

"It wasn't easy. A few hours west of Warsaw."

"Poland?"

"Yeah."

Blake pulled the door open. The clouds had parted, and the sun blinded him for a moment as he walked quickly to his car. Once inside, he took a deep breath and held it for a moment. It shook as it came out. He rested his head against the steering wheel, fighting the urge to vomit. The image of hell came flooding back. Could he ever redeem himself in the eyes of the Lord?

23

Washington, D.C., February 25

Mark Beamon pulled his briefcase from the back seat of the car and made a grab for the door handle. "Here is good, Stan," he said to the young agent driving.

"This traffic'll let up just ahead, Mr. Beamon. I'll have you there in less than five minutes," he pleaded.

"Yeah. I'd just like to get some fresh air, you know?"

"Lots of people on the streets this time of morning—somebody's bound to recognize you."

The controversy regarding the effectiveness and morality of the CDFS's actions had reached a fevered pitch in the media, and Mark Beamon was right in the middle of the debate. His face had been plastered across nearly every newspaper, magazine, and TV screen in the country over the past few weeks. In fact, it was rumored that GQ was running an article on him in their next issue and would be giving him two thumbs up on his fashion sense. It appeared that his nine-year-old, too-tight suits were considered "retro."

"Don't worry about it, Stan. Nobody'll recognize me. I'm told that I look much smaller in person." He

• 343

jumped out of the car, slammed the door, and leaned in through the open window. Horns began to sound behind him. "Call Laura and tell her I'll be a few minutes late. Thanks." He slapped the windowsill and disappeared into the herd of people shuffling off to begin their workday.

Special Agent Stan Paulous frowned deeply. The party line was that Beamon had been provided a car and driver because of his well-known hatred for and lack of skill in maneuvering an automobile. Paulous had later been informed that the real reason was to impose a more predictable schedule on the investigator. His job was, in essence, to keep tabs on Beamon and make sure he was where he was supposed to be, when he was supposed to be there. He dialed the phone slowly, silently composing a report that would deflect the wrath of Laura Vilechi.

Mark Beamon jammed his free hand inside his raincoat and breathed the late winter air deeply into his lungs. It smelled of car exhaust and aftershave.

He had felt too confined lately. House to car to office to house over and over again—no doubt, exactly what Laura had in mind. What she didn't understand was that that kind of rigidity eventually imposed itself on his mind. His thoughts became confined, commonplace. Beamon's haphazard lifestyle was designed to keep the hemispheres of his brain slightly off center. Just where they should be for artists, and investigators.

Beamon took a right, escaping the thick crowd, and headed directly away from the JEH Building. He would treat himself to a quick trip around the block.

Halfway around, he ducked into a small convenience store.

"Pack of Marlboros in a box, please," he said, reaching into his back pocket and pulling out a tattered wallet.

The old man behind the counter eyed him curiously as he reached under the counter for the cigarettes. He placed them on the counter and punched the price into an ornate old cash register. One eighty popped up in the register's window on what looked like miniature tombstones.

Beamon handed him a five and watched the man's expression as he counted out the change. He could see that the clerk was desperately trying to make a connection. The face in front of him must be irritatingly familiar.

Back out in the cool air, Beamon cupped his hand against the wind and lit a cigarette. He quickened his pace slightly, beginning to feel a little guilty about ducking out on his driver. He seemed like a good kid.

As he approached headquarters, the normal D.C. morning chaos melted into the background, eclipsed by the ongoing activity around the building. Beamon paused, tapping ashes onto the sidewalk. It got worse every day.

There were two camps. Directly across the street from the building were the pro-CDFS demonstrators. Beamon counted heads and came up with roughly fifty. About a third were holding signs that poked up from the crowd like the sharp spines of a poisonous sea animal. Their organization had improved, Beamon noted. When they had first appeared, it had been just a bunch of right-wing loudmouths with a few hand-painted signs. For a day there had actually been a guy in a fucking Klan robe.

Things had changed. The group was now more uniformly dressed in dark suits and skirts. Their signs were clever and professional. The wind changed slightly, making their chant intelligible from where he stood. *You roll the dice, you pay the price.*

About fifty yards farther down the street were the anti-CDFS protesters. They were equally well dressed, with equally clever and professional signs. Beamon couldn't make out their chant.

The two groups looked well matched. The five or six policemen keeping them apart looked as though they were in danger of being swallowed up—or worse, choosing sides. Beamon tossed what was left of his cigarette on the sidewalk and ground it out with his shoe. He immediately lit another.

The country hadn't been as divided since the Vietnam War, and the U.S. government, in its infinite wisdom, had seen fit to charge him with repairing the rift. He laughed quietly to himself.

The President seemed to be doing everything in his power to ignore the issue. Sure, the papers ran quotes about his devotion to finding the people responsible, his horror at the deaths, and so on and so on. What Jameson didn't seem to realize was that something had started here, and its momentum was increasing geometrically. Beamon pictured it as a large rock rolling down a hill. If he'd been able to apprehend the members of the CDFS a week after they'd started this thing, the rock might have been stopped.

But it wasn't the first week anymore. He would catch these guys eventually, of that he had no doubt. But when he did, and he threw himself in front of that rock—it might just roll right over him. Did the issues relating to Vietnam end when the helicopters pulled the last Americans from Saigon? No, they grew to define a generation.

And this was no different. The growing problems of drugs and crime in America had been receiving lip service for years. But now somebody had offered an effective solution. America seemed to be finding that it liked the taste of blood and the changes it could bring.

Beamon held up his hands, attempting to silence Laura before her mouth was fully open. There was no chance of it working, of course, but it was worth a try.

"Out for a stroll, I hear?"

"Fresh air. Good for the little gray cells," Beamon replied, tapping his head and imitating the Belgian accent of his favorite fictional detective.

She grabbed his elbow and leaned in close to his ear. "You can't keep doing this, Mark. Every time you're late for a staff meeting, Tom and the rest of them end up running around loose, looking over people's shoulders and making them nervous. Takes me an hour to get everyone calmed down and back on track."

"I just do it so I can watch the tops of your ears turn red."

Her right hand went up to her ear and then immediately back to her side. "You just live to get under my skin, don't you."

He grinned and made an exaggerated gesture toward the conference room, where the other members of their morning meeting were already gathered.

"Out for a little stroll?"

Frank Richter and Laura had obviously been talking.

Beamon ignored him and turned to Tom Sherman. "Sorry I'm late." Sherman shrugged.

Besides Richter and Sherman, Dick Trevor and Trace Fontain were the only other people present. Beamon squeezed into his chair. The table they had chosen was a bit too small for the group.

"So what have you got for us, Mark?" Sherman asked.

"Good stuff, actually. Things are starting to look up a little." He snapped open his oversized briefcase and pulled out a complicated-looking portable stereo and a slightly crumpled piece of paper that contained his most recent notes on the investigation.

"The first good news is that poisoning deaths are way down. Coke-related deaths are almost nonexistent—not counting that recent episode in D.C. That seems to have been an isolated incident. Heroin deaths seem to be slowing down."

Laura's graphs had proven to be surprisingly accurate, and had become popular tools in estimating future deaths. The fact that estimating future deaths was a pointless exercise seemed to have been lost in the FBI's sheer love of statistics.

"What have you been able to find out about the episode here?" Richter interrupted.

"Not much. Strychnine was the poison—probably

household rat poison—we should have confirmation on that this afternoon. Obviously, we're working to track it back to its source, but as you know, that line of investigation is turning out to be a disaster."

"Why?" Sherman cut in.

"Well, three quarters of the witnesses are dead and the other quarter won't talk. It seems that the narcotics-using community has convinced itself that this is all the government's doing and that we're just pretending to investigate, when what we actually want is to collect intelligence on distribution lines . . ." He left the sentence hanging.

Tom Sherman looked at him strangely. "Is there something else?"

"Well, yeah. Laura has a theory on the strychnine poisoning. And I hate to admit it, but she might be right."

All eyes turned to her.

"Um, yes. Well, it seems like this was a pretty sloppy operation. The fact that now, two days later, we haven't seen any more of this type of poison appear, and the isolated geography—one housing project—seems to indicate that the drugs were hit pretty far downstream. Also, the poison was unsophisticated, probably something that anybody could pick up at any of a hundred stores in the D.C. area. It makes me—us—wonder if the CDFS was behind it at all."

"A copycat," Sherman proposed.

"It's a possibility. I think everybody would agree that this doesn't really jibe with what we've learned about the CDFS to date."

"I hope you're wrong," Sherman said.

The thought of copycats cropping up across the

country made everybody's head swim. A red herring in every state from here to California.

"And we may well be," Beamon said. "I mean, if it were me, I'd mix it up a little. Different drugs, different poisoning methods. It keeps us off balance and it keeps the drug users guessing. And scared."

The group nodded in general agreement, and Beamon decided to move on. He pointed at Trevor. "DEA's got some new info."

"Yeah." Trevor's voice was quiet. He sounded almost depressed. Beamon understood and sympathized.

"Luis Colombar, whom I'm sure everyone here is familiar with, has put the word out that he's looking for information regarding an American asking specific questions about his drug-manufacturing facilities. The word is that he suspects that someone poisoned his coke during the manufacturing process."

Frank Richter stood and walked over to the coffeemaker and poured himself a cup. "That makes sense—it's what I'd do. You figure that security isn't all that great at the manufacturing stage. And what security you have is aimed at people stealing stuff."

Beamon nodded gravely and continued the thought. "Right. And what better way to hit a lot of stuff with only one operation."

"Do you know if he's gotten any bites?" Sherman asked.

Trevor shrugged. "As you probably know, we've been unsuccessful at putting anybody into Colombar's operation. At this point we don't know what he's got."

A long silence ensued. Finally Sherman spoke.

"Been watching TV lately, Dick? Your statistics seem to be on every channel."

Trevor winced. "We're trying to track down the leak, but I don't see much hope. I gave the order to stop keeping statistics the day we spoke—but I can't keep the street agents from talking to each other."

"Are the numbers accurate?"

"I don't know."

Sherman's voice softened. "Are the numbers accurate?"

It was well known that the quieter Sherman got the madder he was. If you had to strain to hear him, you were on your way out.

"Yeah. They're accurate. Give or take five percent. The numbers on the drug rehab clinics I can't vouch for. At this rate of decline, we could see the complete eradication of coke and heroin within our borders in a couple of months."

Beamon reached for the briefcase that he had brought into the meeting with him. He opened it and pulled out a T-shirt. "You guys seen this? I picked it up yesterday." He shook out the shirt, presenting it to the group. The front depicted a chalk outline of a man traced on a sidewalk next to a smoking crack pipe. The caption read: "I've fallen and I can't get up."

Beamon tossed the shirt to Laura. "Souvenir."

"Let's face it, public opinion was moving away from us anyway," Beamon continued. "DEA's little leak is just gonna speed things up a little."

"Okay, enough of this," Sherman said. "What's going on in Poland?"

"I think everybody's heard that Scott over in Bonn

found the guy who collected the mushrooms. Apparently he runs a business supplying exotic produce to restaurants. Our man posed as an academic who was going to use the mushrooms to study cancer or something."

"Description?"

"Yeah," Beamon pulled his glasses from his shirt pocket and began reading from the paper in front of him. "Short—five foot eight or so—and thin. Long, light-brown hair and beard, wire-rimmed glasses and—this is interesting—he goes on to describe him as kind of cold."

Richter looked perplexed. "Why is that interesting—I could have told you this guy was one cold son of a bitch."

"If you remember, the girl who helped him at the bank said the exact same thing."

"So it's the same guy?"

"Laura and I would bet our respective asses on it."

"So where does that get us?"

"Nowhere, really. Scott's convinced that this mushroom guy—Lech something or other—was involved in smuggling them out. You'll recall that customs has no record of anything like that coming through them. Anyway, he's following up. And on that note, Trace has some information that I know is near and dear to your black hearts. Now that we know how many mushrooms were transported, we can take a shot at estimating potential deaths. Trace?"

Fontain cleared his throat. "Uh, yes. Mr. Orloski estimates that he provided our suspect with approximately one and one eighth tons of mushrooms.

Assuming that the CDFS's distilling process is reasonably efficient, that translates to around ninety-seven thousand kills."

Sherman groaned.

"Actually, it's not as bad as it sounds."

"My analysis of the tainted drugs shows that the CDFS used about half again as much poison as was necessary—which explains the limited number of nonfatal incidents. So that knocks back our kill potential pretty significantly. Also, you have to make an assumption about how many times someone is going to use the stuff. For instance, a heroin addict might buy a two-week supply and unknowingly take fourteen lethal doses. In essence, he's wasted thirteen kills."

Beamon cut the scientist off. They would be here all day if he let him start in on his assumptions. "Okay, Trace. Boil it down. How many people can they kill with what they've got?"

"Best guess. Thirty-six thousand."

Beamon nodded gravely. "Assuming that they don't branch out into other types of poisons."

Fontain shrugged and nodded.

Beamon could see from the faces around him that the scientist was in danger of an endless Q&A. He decided to put a stop to it before it started. "Thanks, Trace. We won't hold you up any longer. I know you're busy."

Fontain stood and scampered out of the room before anyone could start in on him.

"Well, there you have it, for what it's worth. Now let's get down to some real cop stuff." He reached into the pocket of his jacket and produced an unlabeled cassette tape. It took a few moments for him to figure out how to get the tape into the portable stereo on the table, but the machine finally accepted it upside-down. He pushed the door shut and hit PLAY.

"I saved the best for last."

Nothing happened.

"Do you have batteries in that thing, Mark?" Laura asked, looking smug.

"Batteries? Uh, no. Don't these things come with batteries?"

She sighed and pulled the rubber band off the tightly wound cord, running it to an outlet behind her. The recorder came to life, spewing out loud tape hiss. A moment later the hiss deadened, and Beamon managed to find the PAUSE button. "One of the operators on the deathline brought this up to me yesterday."

The hotline set up to collect anonymous tips on the case had become known as the "deathline" because of the reams of death threats that Beamon received on it every day. It seemed that there were more than a few people who were concerned about the FBI's thoughtless interference in the CDFS's solution to the national drug crisis.

"I had the tape washed through the computers. It was pretty hard to understand at first. The guy used the old towel-over-the-mouthpiece trick."

"Traced?" Richter asked.

"A pay phone between here and Baltimore." Beamon pressed the PAUSE button again, setting the tape back into motion.

The tape noise deadened and the operator's voice came on. It had a strange mechanical edge. "FBI."

The other voice on the line was clearly nervous, even through the towel and computer tampering. "Hello . . . I, uh, thought that you'd want to know that they're planning on poisoning a shipment of cocaine on the twenty-eighth. It's going to be in one of Anthony DiPrizzio's warehouses on the New York waterfront." Pause.

The operator's voice: "Sir, can you give me your name and how you came by this information?"

"No. But so you know I'm telling the truth, I'll tell you this. The poison came from mushrooms growing a few hours outside of Warsaw." Dial tone.

Beamon reached over, ejected the tape, and stuffed it back into his suit pocket.

"You all know that we've kept the source of the poison pretty quiet."

Sherman looked doubtful. "Well, we've done our best, but there are a hell of a lot of people in the health care community who have figured it out. You think this might be something?"

"You never know. I'm meeting with DiPrizzio at four this afternoon. Joe up in New York set it up."

"That ought to be an interesting get-together. Anything else?" Sherman scanned the faces at the table. No one spoke.

"Okay, let's get back to work."

The group stood, pulling jackets from chair backs and tucking notebooks under their arms.

"Not you, Mark. Have you got a few minutes?" It wasn't really a question. The others picked up their pace. Laura was the last one out, struggling to pull the door shut while holding a coffee mug in one hand and the portable stereo in the other. Sherman got up and handed her the dangling cord. He quietly closed the door.

Beamon pushed the chairs next to him away, giving himself enough room to stretch his legs out. He had an overwhelming desire to smoke, but resisted.

"So you think this DiPrizzio thing might come to something, Mark?"

"Probably not—but we've gotta cover all the angles. So what's up, Tommy? You didn't keep me after class to ask me that."

"Same shit, different day. Problems, problems." His smile was forced. Beamon waved him on with an exaggerated motion.

"Calahan and I met with the President yesterday."

"I heard—my condolences."

The weak smile again.

"The President's not happy, Mark. I'd go so far as to say he's panicking." Beamon opened his mouth to speak, but his friend cut him off.

"He's pretty surprised by the public's reaction to this thing. It's put him in an impossible political position. He's got to condemn the CDFS as radical vigilantes, but he can't speak out too forcefully without pissing off all the people who are pro-CDFS."

"I've got a crazy idea, Tommy. Why the hell doesn't he just pick a side and say how he really feels, instead of hiring a bunch of weasels to tell him what the voting majority wants to hear. It's their goddam fault. If the boys on Capitol Hill didn't spend all their time chasing girls and rounding up campaign funds, maybe these guys wouldn't have found this necessary." The frustration he felt was quickly turning to anger.

"That's not the way of the world and you know it, Mark. You like to deal in facts, so here they are. The only way for President Jameson to win is for these guys to get caught. He hopes that the issue will fade in the two years before the next election. He's serious, Mark. He actually intimated that it might be better for the country if there wasn't a drawn-out trial."

Beamon's eyes widened. "He did not! What did you say?"

"I told him we didn't do that kind of thing."

Beamon snorted. "Christ!"

"That doesn't go beyond this room, Mark. I just want to get across to you where you stand."

"Where I stand? What do you mean?" He knew perfectly well.

"This is all going to come down on your shoulders in the end." Sherman couldn't meet his eyes. "I'm sorry I got you into this."

Beamon slapped him on the shoulder.

"Jesus. Cheer up, Tommy. I knew what I was getting into." That wasn't entirely true, of course. No one could have predicted the way this case would consume the nation.

"Who was it that said there's no such thing as bad publicity? You wouldn't believe the calls I've been getting from private industry—I'm not gonna have to fill my pockets with the salmon at my retirement party, you know? I'm thinking about getting a fucking agent."

That was true. There was nothing the American public respected more than fame. Private companies were virtually beating down his door, making him various offers of employment. Each one was more spectacular than the last. And that didn't include the $1.2 million guaranteed advance on his autobiography.

Sherman perked up a bit and remained silent when his friend gave into temptation and lit a cigarette in the poorly ventilated room. At least the filter was still attached.

"You know I'm not screwing around here, that I'm doing everything I can, right, Tommy?" Beamon's tone had turned serious.

"I'm not second-guessing you, Mark. You're the best man for the job. I told Jameson that again yesterday."

"Did he buy it?"

"Good to see you, Joe," Beamon said, extending his hand. He had to raise his voice a bit to be heard over the chaotic background noise that was a constant at the FBI's largest office.

"Welcome to New York, Mark. Come on back." Joe Sheets motioned toward the open door of his office across a sea of agents and support personnel.

Beamon hadn't seen Sheets for years. Shaking hands with his old friend had brought back a flood of memories. They had been roommates at the academy and had become fast friends during their twelve weeks there—despite the fact that they were very different people. Beamon had been first in his class academically but had been less than impressive in the physical fitness category. In fact, his performance had been bad enough for Sheets to call him when women were first being accepted as agents, just to point out that Beamon's time in the mile wouldn't have passed him in the women's category, either.

Sheets hadn't shone in any one category—but had been a solid all-around performer. Fairness, reliability, and hard work had landed him an assistant director's slot and the helm of the New York office. Well deserved, as far as Beamon was concerned.

As he pushed the door shut and looked around his friend's spacious office, he pointed at a picture on the credenza. "Jesus, is that Bobby?"

Sheets sat on a slightly threadbare sofa and smiled. "It's Robert now. He's a commercial artist in Chicago. Wouldn't you know that my son would be the only artist in the world who doesn't want to be in New York."

Beamon chuckled. To say that Sheets and his son didn't see eye to eye was an understatement. If he remembered correctly, his old roommate's idea of a good painting involved dogs playing poker, and his son saw all FBI agents as fascist scum. A little distance probably wasn't an entirely bad thing.

Beamon filled a cone-shaped cup from a water cooler in the corner and sat at the other end of the sofa. "You can't keep 'em from spreading their wings, I guess."

"That you can't," Sheets agreed, looking at his watch. "You're late. Our guest should be here any time now."

Beamon nodded and took a sip of water.

"So what's this all about, Mark? With this CDFS thing going on, I wouldn't think you'd have time to worry about New York's organized crime problems."

Beamon looked behind him, confirming that the door was completely shut.

"We got a tip that they're gonna hit one of DiPrizzio's shipments."

"The CDFS? Who gave you the tip?"

"Nobody. Anonymous."

A timid knock at the door interrupted their conversation, and a round-faced woman poked her head in. "Mr. DiPrizzio is here for his three o'clock appointment." Her tone was bored, as though the most powerful man in the New York mob always dropped by around this time.

"Conference room two please, Joan." Her face barely cleared the doorjamb as she closed the door behind her.

Beamon stood and tossed the crumpled paper cup at the trash can, missing by a full three feet. "Game time."

Sheets picked up the cup and sank it.

"Mr. DiPrizzio—I'm Mark Beamon." The two men shook hands.

"I recognize you from your photos, Agent Beamon. I'm pleased to meet you. And it's nice to see you again, Agent Sheets."

"Tony." The use of the mobster's first name was less familiarity than contempt.

"I'm not sure you know my attorney, Glenn Montrose." DiPrizzio motioned to the heavyset man standing next to him. Montrose didn't offer his hand, but immediately went for a seat. His build seemed to make standing uncomfortable.

Beamon watched DiPrizzio walk smoothly across the room to take a seat with his back to the wall. Despite his relative youth—he had turned thirty-seven only a week ago—he moved with extreme self-assurance. If he was the least bit uncomfortable being summoned by the FBI for unknown reasons, he didn't show it.

"I don't want to take up any more of your time than necessary, Mr. DiPrizzio. I'll get right to the point," Beamon said.

"I'd appreciate that," DiPrizzio replied, glancing at an expensive-looking watch for added effect.

"We have information that would lead us to believe that the CDFS is planning on targeting one of your drug shipments."

DiPrizzio's expression didn't even flicker. He looked from Beamon to his attorney and then back at Beamon. Finally he spoke. "This is ridiculous. I am a *legitimate* businessman. Let me repeat that—a legitimate businessman. I am constantly amazed that the FBI continues to harass me and my family simply because we are successful Italian Americans. You have absolutely no evidence that I have ever done anything more heinous than park at a yellow curb."

DiPrizzio seemed to be warming up to his victimization speech, and Beamon was on a tight schedule. Beamon motioned to the windows lining one side of the conference room. The rain drove against them, making it look like the building was going through a carwash.

"It sure is a nice day. How would you like to show me a few sights—you did drive, didn't you?"

DiPrizzio looked surprised for a moment, but regained his composure quickly. "Of course."

"Great. Joe, why don't you give Glenn here the ten-dollar tour. Tony's gonna show me Times Square."

Montrose started to protest, beginning the long process of extricating himself from the narrow conference room chair. But his client was already up and heading for the door, with Beamon close behind.

"Jesus!" Beamon shouted, his voice echoing off the walls of the parking garage. "What the hell are you trying to do, sterilize me?" DiPrizzio's chauffeur had his testicles in a death grip.

"I'm sorry, sir. It seems a popular place to put wires." He had a sadistic smile on his face. Probably always wanted to have an FBI man by the balls.

"Well, I hope you're satisfied," Beamon said, gently rubbing his scrotum.

"Almost." The chauffeur reached into the passenger side of the limousine and pulled out a metal detector like the ones used in the airports for people who have baffled the walk-through unit. He ran it carefully over every inch of Beamon's body. It beeped on his belt buckle and watch.

DiPrizzio looked surprised. "No sidearm, Agent Beamon?"

"Ruins the hang of my suit." He tugged at a frayed lapel.

DiPrizzio laughed and opened the back door for him. Beamon climbed in.

"Just drive around, Billy." The chauffeur grunted and slammed the back door.

"Nice car. Is that a bar?" He pointed.

"That it is. Can I interest you in a cocktail?"

"Are you having one?"

DiPrizzio answered by pouring two Bushmills. The car moved smoothly out of the parking garage and into the crowded New York streets.

"So you were saying, Agent Beamon?"

"Mark, please."

"Mark."

"I was saying that I think that the CDFS is going to hit one of your shipments."

DiPrizzio nodded thoughtfully and sipped from his glass. "Well, that is a problem. What do you propose we do about it?"

Beamon didn't let show the relief he felt. For a few moments he had been sure that he was going to get nowhere. "We have a date and a general location. I propose that you give us an exact location, and we catch this guy—as they say—red-handed."

DiPrizzio laughed out loud. "Your friend Sheets has been after me for almost five years, Mark—and now you want me to just lead you to my product and say, 'Here it is, officer.'" He was dabbing at the corners of his eyes with a linen handkerchief. "I don't think so."

"Look, I hate to say this, but we're on the same side here. We both want these guys stopped—you want to see demand for your merchandise rebound, and I don't want anybody else hurt. I can guarantee that we'll forget everything we see." Beamon reached across the compartment and grabbed the bottle of Bushmills. He refilled his empty glass and topped off DiPrizzio's.

"Now that you've warned me, I don't really need you. Do I?"

"Come on, Tony. It could be anywhere, anytime. You'd have to quadruple your payroll for the next goddam six months—and it still wouldn't guarantee that you'd catch this guy."

"I have a proposal for you, Mark. I think we can solve both of our problems quickly and painlessly. With a little luck you could be sitting by your pool this time next week."

Apparently DiPrizzio had done some homework, too. "I'm listening."

"I think you'd agree that I have . . . interrogation techniques that aren't at your disposal."

Beamon nodded. He knew where this was going.

"You give me the wheres and whens, and I'll capture this gentleman. The next morning you'll have a FedEx with everything you ever wanted to know about the CDFS. I believe that solves both of our problems. I keep the FBI out of my business, and you clean up this mess faster than you could have on your own."

The car lurched sickeningly, and Beamon turned his eyes to the tinted window next to him. A group of men clad in orange coveralls talked heatedly near an open manhole. The sound didn't reach him.

"It's a tempting offer, Tony. Very tempting. But I'm not sure we're that desperate yet."

DiPrizzio smiled almost imperceptibly. "You've got to be getting damn close."

"Damn close," Beamon repeated, eyeing the cellular phone cradled next to his leg.

* * *

"I think I've got some bad news," Robert Swenson said, dropping into a chair. He tossed his damp coat out the door of the office, landing it expertly on the arm of a sofa. Hobart held up his index finger, indicating that he was concentrating, and continued to tap figures into the computer.

The initial costs of the operation had run over a bit, but he was quickly getting back on target. The contingency fund he had set up for any unpleasant surprises hadn't been touched in over a month. Hobart had made it perfectly clear that Bill Karns's relocation was to be at his own expense—and that no more unauthorized operations would be tolerated. Karns made a feeble attempt to defend himself, but in the end had apologized profusely and assured Hobart that he would be a model soldier from here on out.

Satisfied with the bottom line, Hobart saved the spreadsheet and flipped off the computer. "Beer?"

"Sure, why not."

He fished around in the small refrigerator and produced the last two bottles, making a mental note to bring another six-pack down from his apartment. "So? What's the news?"

"Looks like your friends showed up."

Hobart chewed on his lip silently and twisted the top off the bottle. Letting Reed Corey escape had been the biggest screwup of the operation—potentially a hell of a lot more damaging than putting Karns on too long a leash.

When Hobart returned from Colombia he had instructed his partner to drive by his house a few times a week. Look for loiterers.

"I saw them for the first time Tuesday and made a mental note. When I drove by today, they'd moved about half a block, but they were still there. Two Hispanic males, between twenty-five and thirty-five, driving a red Nissan Maxima. Well dressed, but they've got the look, you know. The car and the clothes fit the neighborhood, but they don't fit their faces."

The first rule of surveillance, Hobart reflected. Blend in. No small feat for two young Hispanics in Roland Park—one of Baltimore's most prestigious neighborhoods.

"Fuck," Hobart said simply. He had seen it coming, but there had always been a glimmer of hope that Corey wouldn't make the connection, or better yet, that he had stepped in front of a speeding bus.

"Well, we're gonna have to take care of that."

Swenson looked apprehensive. "Hey, I know that most of these cartel enforcers are idiots, but you never know when they're just gonna be luckier than you. Why don't we just leave 'em alone? We know they're there and you never go within ten miles of the house."

Hobart shook his head. His partner needed to learn chess. It wasn't the next move that got you, it was the one after that. "If I thought they'd just sit there with their thumbs up their asses, I would. But they're not going to."

"So what? You've altered your appearance and rented this place under an alias. Get a rental car and there's no way they'll ever track you down."

"Probably true," Hobart agreed. "But it's not them I'm worried about. When they figure out that I'm not coming back, and that they can't find me, they'll tip off the Bureau. As the de facto leader of the cartels right now,

Luis Colombar's gotta be under a lot of pressure to get this thing wrapped up quickly."

Swenson looked as though he still didn't see his point. "So what good's killing them gonna do? They'll just call the FBI that much sooner. And we expose ourselves for nothing."

Hobart took a long pull from his beer, wondering how his partner could have spent so many years in drug enforcement and still not understand the mind of his opponent.

"Trust me on this one, Bob," he said standing and heading toward the door to the office. He walked around the perimeter of the building in his shirtsleeves, ignoring the damp cold. In his apartment he walked directly to the chess board sitting next to the television and advanced two blue pawns to threaten the king. He stood over the board for a long time, mentally reconfiguring the players, conjuring elaborate attacks and defensive strategies. Finally he tore himself away and walked toward the refrigerator and another cold beer.

24

New York City,
February 28

Phil Newberry—at least that's what he'd been calling himself for the last few months—was running out of tricks. He had watered down drinks, poured them on the floor, "forgotten" them in the bathroom, and switched them with his companions' nearly empty ones. Now he was immersed in a deep personal conversation with a man big and dumb enough to be a professional wrestler.

They had met a few times at the warehouse where he had been working for what seemed like forever. Their friendship had grown stronger with every drink The Giant had put away. At last count, fourteen.

Worse yet, his new friend had just purchased him an imposing vodka shot and was leaning close enough to be heard over the noise of the jukebox and patrons of the bar.

Not much hope of getting out of this one.

The Giant—Tim Carey, if he remembered correctly—raised his beer and held it motionless above the table. The gesture was obvious. Newberry raised his shot, tapped the glass against his new friend's bottle, and tossed it back. The red-hot fluid seemed to stick about halfway down. He reached across the table and took the beer from Carey, finishing it in one gulp. He shook his head wildly, slammed a fist into his chest, and grinned.

Carey laughed and waved to the bartender for another round.

"Gimme a beer this time, man," Newberry shouted over the din. "A couple more of those and I'm gonna fall right off this fucking bar stool." Carey held up his empty bottle and two fingers.

Newberry surveyed the bar. Dark and foul smelling, just like a waterfront dive should be. He theorized that all bar scents had the same components—sweat, smoke, beer, perfume, mold, grease. What made each particular establishment unique was the combination of those universal aromas. The Rat favored mold and grease.

"I got this one, man," Newberry said, grabbing Carey's rock-hard right arm. He reached into his jeans and pulled out a wadded ball of bills, making a show of carefully peeling off a ten dollar bill and laying it on the bar.

Carey leaned close again and started back into his story. Newberry only half listened. He had too many things on his mind to give the conversation the attention necessary to hear every word over the background noise. Somebody fed a few quarters into the jukebox and it blared a distorted version of an unidentifiable country song, making the conversation even harder to follow.

Undercover operations were hard. Though he didn't know Carey well, he liked him. Despite his imposing figure, Carey was known to be about as violent as a baby seal. His story related to problems that he was having at home with his son. He was afraid that he'd fallen in with a bad crowd. It was a story that Newberry had heard hundreds of times during his years as a cop. He turned his eyes away when the concerned father speculated on the possibility that his son was using drugs—and how dangerous that could be these days.

Carey wasn't the only friend he had made in his three-plus months at the warehouse. He had been to people's homes for dinner, watched their children play in the Little League, lost money at drunken late-night poker games, and helped them move. A professional liar. His old boss used to say he had a real flair.

A woman backed into him as the bouncers continued to herd people through the door with disinterested glances at their driver's licenses. His beer sloshed over and splashed into his lap. Less he would have to drink, he reflected, taking a measured sip of what was left in the bottle.

This assignment was better than most, he remembered, still half listening to the increasingly incoherent discourse from the next bar stool. At least he wasn't setting up to arrest one of the people he had come to know so well. The thing he hated most about undercover work: the inevitable end—the arrest. Instead of a feeling of triumph, he always saw himself reflected in the eyes of the suspect. A betrayer.

"I gotta go, man," he said apologetically, leaning heavily on Carey's leg. "I'm way too fucked up."

"You all right, Phil?"

Newberry stood. "Yeah. I just need some fresh air and a bed, you know?"

Carey gave him the thumbs-up. He knew.

Newberry grabbed a small black backpack sitting at his feet and made his way across the bar with practiced unsteadiness. He waved clumsily to a knot of men playing pool and continued staggering toward the door. They shouted a few good-natured insults and turned back to their game.

He took a hard right as he left the bar, breathing in the cool New York air. It wasn't exactly the mountains, but it tasted just as sweet after six hours of nursing drinks in The Rat. He slipped the backpack on and tightened it around his waist. The illuminated dial of his watch read 12:13 A.M. as he passed through a narrow, trash-strewn alley.

The warehouse was only about a ten-minute walk from the bar, but his indirect route increased the time to almost a half an hour. As he approached it, he rolled his head on his neck, checking for any effect from the vodka shot. None was apparent—undoubtedly the liquor had been absorbed by the cheesesteak and fries he had wolfed down right after work.

He paused next to a large Dumpster overflowing with the by-products of waterfront commerce and scanned the street for almost five minutes. Satisfied that its daytime inhabitants were nestled into their beds, or propped up in a rickety bar somewhere, he

372 • KYLE MILLS

pulled off his bright blue sweatshirt and stuffed it behind the Dumpster.

Padding quietly across the dimly lit street in dark jeans, black turtleneck, and black hightop basketball shoes, he became aware that he wasn't nervous at all. When Hobart had okayed this operation, his stomach had leaped into his throat, making it difficult to finish the conversation. His head had been spinning when he replaced the receiver.

In the days since then, he had been mesmerized by the news reports. Every night he threw a bag of popcorn in the microwave, popped the top off a beer, and rested his tired body on the sofa. The rest of the night was spent surfing the channels, watching myriad reports on the CDFS's actions from every possible perspective. He had come to three conclusions.

One: If you had cable you could find some kind of related story twenty-four hours a day.

Two: The public was getting more and more behind them.

Three: *It was working.*

Fear and apprehension had given way to pride and a sense of purpose. There had been endless rhetoric from the politicians about taking back America from the drug pushers—and now *he* was doing it.

Newberry pressed his back against the warehouse and looked up. From this angle, it looked like a mile to the third-floor windows—the first ones not guarded with bars. He slipped along the wall, stopping at a squared-off alcove in the exterior wall. The warehouse wasn't just a box—it was from an era when all structures were held to a certain standard of aesthetic beauty. The incut corner, in which he now stood, was adorned with creative brickwork, leaving two-inch ledges every few feet. Newberry tightened his pack one last time, and started his ascent.

By carefully placing his feet on the small ledges and moving them up one leg at a time, he didn't expect to have any problem getting to the third-story windows. He had been practicing this technique in his garage between a couple of two-by-sixes set up specifically for this purpose. Technically, it should be much easier on the actual building. The ledges were sharper and bit into the bottom of his shoes, and the alcove was quite a bit deeper than six inches, making the balance easier. For some reason, though, it seemed much harder.

He was looking straight ahead. The dark alcove made the brickwork in front of him look blank. Finally he dared a look up—he felt like he had been climbing forever. The act of leaning his head back made a surprisingly drastic change in his equilibrium, and he jammed a foot back to keep from reeling over into space. His heart raced and his entire body tingled from the adrenaline forced into his system. He wanted to take a few moments to collect himself, but the burning in his forearms and calves made him press on.

His estimate hadn't been far off. Another five feet brought him to the foot-wide ledge under the unprotected third-floor windows. He steadied himself and carefully shed his pack, pushing it onto the ledge. Finally he pulled himself up and sat, feet dangling, on the narrow ledge. He remained there for some time, catching his breath, oblivious to his exposed position. The night was calm, and he could see the flickering lights of New Jersey in the distance. Ships moved lazily across his field of vision, looking like constellations against the black water.

Realizing that eventually someone was bound to walk by and think he was a jumper, he scooted slowly left, pushing the backpack in front of him. It was less than ten feet to the first window. He twisted precariously on his narrow seat and pushed hard on it. It didn't move. He pushed again, wondering for a moment if he had disabled the lock on the wrong window. It wouldn't be hard to do: The old warehouse's design made it difficult to judge interior versus exterior features.

He pushed one more time and it opened with a dull crack. He slid in belly first and poured out onto a metal catwalk. Pulling the pack through after him, he hurried for the stairs.

It was dark. The only significant light came from the streetlights filtering through the windows and the second-floor office, a square box perched improbably on the second-floor wall. The venetian blinds were closed, but glowed white with the interior light. The sound of muffled voices floated through the dusty air. He slowed his progress on the metal stairs, making no sound at all.

Reaching the bottom floor, he rushed expertly through the maze of towering crates to the far corner of the building. He was forced to slow his pace slightly, as the pathways became narrower and the turns sharper. Finally he was stopped by a chain-link gate. He took off the pack and pulled out a pair of bolt cutters, making short work of the lock. He stuffed it into his pocket and pulled a matching one from the pack, hanging it on the dangling chain. When they came to open the gate in the morning, their key wouldn't turn. They would be confused for a few minutes and protest that the key had worked fine the day before. Finally they would cut it off and forget all about the incident.

Newberry padded silently into the cage and weaved through its contents, stopping at a box that looked like an old army footlocker. It opened easily after a few nails were pulled. The light was too dim to see into the box, so he reached in. His hand caressed a hard rectangular plastic bag, covered with some kind of textured tape. Duct tape, he guessed, as he pulled the first brick out.

He sat down on the floor, making himself as comfortable as possible, and reached into the open backpack, pulling out a bundle of drinking straws. The ends of each straw had been carefully sealed with masking tape. He pulled his turtleneck over his nose and mouth and punched a small hole in one end of the brick lying in front of him. Then he pulled the tape off one end of a straw and forced it into the brick until it hit the plastic at the other end. Upending the brick, he pulled the tape off the exposed side of the straw and pulled it slowly out. It worked just as Hobart had promised, distributing the poison in a deadly cylinder through the middle of the brick. When the brick was divided and the cocaine cut, the orellanin would be evenly distributed.

He was into his third brick when he heard movement behind him—actually, he felt it more than heard

376 • KYLE MILLS

it—a stirring in the still air. Turning, he was blinded by a striking match. The hissing of the flame was deafening as it cut through the silence.

The match was held to the end of a cigarette, illuminating a familiar face.

"I'm Mark Beamon," the figure said, shaking out the match, leaving them once again in darkness. Newberry couldn't see a thing. His pupils had contracted violently in the face of the unexpected light. That had undoubtedly been the plan. Beamon's eyes had been closed when he lit the cigarette.

Newberry's mind raced. He once again became aware of the weight of the gun under his arm. Beamon seemed to read his mind.

"Don't do it, son. You know us FBI guys—we never fight fair. I got at least three guns aimed at your head."

Newberry carefully weighed Beamon's words. From what he knew of FBI tactics, he concluded that it wasn't a bluff. He looked one last time toward the gate, and freedom, as his eyes finally began to readjust to the gloom. Then he kneeled down and laced his fingers on top of his head.

25

The White House, Washington, D.C., March 1

"Tea?"

"Thank you, Mr. President," Tom Sherman said, holding the cup steady as Jameson poured. He took a couple of sugars from a silver tray and leaned back, stirring. The President finished his tea ceremony, pouring cups for the attorney general and FBI Director, who Sherman knew hated tea. He watched as Calahan politely took a sip and smiled approvingly.

"I thank you all for coming so early. I'm pretty booked up during the days." The antique clock on the wall read 5:05 A.M. "So I hear you're the expert on the CDFS, Tom."

"That's not entirely true, sir. Mark Beamon is more in tune with the details of the investigation."

"Yes, well, Bill apparently didn't want to subject me to your Mr. Beamon, and suggested that I be briefed by you instead. I assume that you're up to the task."

"Yes, sir."

"I hear we've had a major break in the case."

"Yes." Sherman drew the word out longer than necessary. His tone was hesitant.

"You don't sound sure," the President observed, reaching for a cookie. The others took the cue and grabbed a few for themselves.

"It's true that we did capture one of the CDFS's operatives—but he isn't talking."

"He won't talk?" The President enunciated the words carefully, as though Sherman was an idiot. Undoubtedly just the effect he was shooting for.

"I'm not sure you understand the situation, Tom," the President said. "We have to stop these people. You have my authorization to make any kind of deal you have to." He looked smug, as though this was some kind of revelation.

"We've offered him complete immunity to prosecution and a place in our witness protection program," Sherman said. "He's not interested."

A confused look came over the President's face. He leaned forward and set his empty cup on the table. "This guy's gonna go to prison when you've offered to let him walk? I don't understand what you're telling me."

I wouldn't expect you to, you political hack.

"He believes in what they're doing, sir. In his mind, he's a captured soldier. A patriot putting America back on track."

The President looked around at the other two men in the room. "A little cocky for a mass murderer, isn't he?"

"Maybe," Sherman replied, though the question clearly had been rhetorical. The President let it pass, but the look he gave Sherman would have filled most bureaucrats shoes with sweat.

Sherman couldn't bring himself to care. He had twenty years in and more money than he could possibly ever spend. The picture of him fly fishing on a quiet river surrounded by willows was destroyed when Jameson began speaking again.

"So after one day, you've decided that there's no way we can make him talk."

Sherman reached for another cookie. "You haven't asked me anything about this guy, but let me tell you about him anyway. He was a cop for ten years in Atlanta. Apparently he quit to take this on. His former supervisors have nothing but good things to say about him. Honest, smart. His record's spotless. He knows exactly what's going to happen if he ends up in prison. They're not crazy about cops, but I expect they like the CDFS less. He's a tough guy, but I doubt he'll last two days."

"You sound like you respect him," Jameson goaded.

"I don't feel one way or another. He's willing to put himself on the line for what he believes in."

Another thinly veiled insult. This time Jameson pretended he didn't hear.

"Your recommendation?"

"We throw some manpower at it. Track down everybody this guy knows and find the ones who recently dropped out of sight. It's only a matter of time."

The Director cut in, speaking for the first time. "Mr. President—Perry and I were discussing the situation earlier. We think we have a better plan."

Uh oh. Sherman looked at Calahan with apprehension. The President looked with hope.

Perry Trent started. "Bill and I feel that we should

put out a press release saying that this guy's gonna make a deal. Force the CDFS's hand."

"Force their hand to do what?" Sherman wondered aloud.

"A hit. Bring the guy in and out of the courthouse on a set schedule every day. Make it look easy."

Sherman's mouth gaped, revealing a half-chewed cookie. He slowly scanned the faces of the three men across from him. They all looked deadly serious.

Calahan continued the thought. "We can position enough men around the courthouse to guarantee catching the assassin. Maybe we'll have more luck with him."

The President nodded thoughtfully. "And what's your opinion, Tom?"

Sherman had managed to close his mouth and begin chewing again. A thousand smart-ass comments came to mind. "This is a joke, right?"

"You have a better suggestion?"

"Yes. Track down all this guy's known acquaintances. I know it's not a particularly sexy plan, but, Jesus . . ."

"Hundreds of people are dying each day," the President began. The sympathetic tone didn't play as well in person as it did on TV. "Drastic circumstances call for drastic measures, wouldn't you agree?"

"Drastic, yes. Desperate, no." The eyes of his boss and the AG bored into him. "Look, sir, there's no guarantee that they'll try a hit. And if they do, there's no guarantee that we'll get the shooter alive—at all, for that matter. And even if everything goes right, there's no guarantee that he'll talk."

Jameson buttoned the top button of his shirt and tightened the tie that had been hanging loosely around his neck. "As I see it, we've got nothing to lose here. If they don't try a hit, we've in essence taken your road." He pointed to Sherman. "If they do and you kill the would-be assassin, or he won't talk, it's still a productive operation. I assume that having two suspects will narrow down your search significantly. Won't it?" The President looked pleased with himself for that piece of detective work.

"Yes," Sherman conceded.

"Unless you have a better suggestion—and by better, I mean a faster way to stop these maniacs—I believe we've found our course of action."

Sherman shifted uncomfortably in his chair. His resignation was on the tip of his tongue, but something was stopping him from uttering it. "Yes, sir," was all he could get out.

"They want us to what?"

Beamon actually jumped from his chair as he spoke. "Sit down, Mark."

He ignored the advice and began pacing violently around the small conference room.

"You told them no way, though, right?"

Sherman's tone was sarcastic. "Yeah, Mark. I told Calahan, the President, and the AG, no. And they said, 'Hey fine, if you don't want to do it, we won't.'"

Beamon ran his hand through his hair as he marched across the room, grabbing what was left on his crown. He stopped and stood motionless in that position for a few seconds. "Why are you still here, Tommy? All you talk about is retiring. I'd have thought this would be the perfect opportunity."

"I guess that, when I was faced with it, I just wasn't ready to leave."

That was a lie and Beamon knew it. He wouldn't pull out and leave an old friend twisting in the wind. It just wasn't in him. He went for the chair across from Sherman, deciding to let the subject drop. "Got any aspirin?"

"Took my last five an hour ago," Sherman replied. They both giggled like schoolboys.

"So what do you think, Mark?"

Beamon pulled at his lower lip. "None of these young guys gets hurt." He was referring to the team of agents assigned to protect the suspect. "If you and I don't have the guts to stand up to the President, we've gotta be the ones in the line of fire."

Sherman nodded in agreement. "This is gonna blow up in our faces, you know."

"Oh, man," Beamon slurred through the unlit cigarette clenched between his lips.

26

Baltimore, Maryland,
March 2

"There they are."

John Hobart followed his partner's gaze up the street. A red Nissan Maxima sat inconspicuously between two other cars parallel parked on the quiet, tree-lined street.

"They were there yesterday," Swenson continued, pointing to a narrow side street along Hobart's east property line. "And there on Tuesday."

Hobart grunted an acknowledgment, pulled back around the corner, and walked back to his Jeep.

His house was perched on a steep, one-acre lot. The trees scattered across the property were old and plentiful, blocking the structure from view. Hobart had taken his privacy seriously, even before his recent change in profession.

He turned the key in the ignition halfway and punched a button on the CD player. A Bach concerto surged through the interior of the car as he watched Swenson stroll casually down a side street, finally turning and leaving his line of sight. Hobart leaned forward and looked at the sky through the front windshield as raindrops began to slap the glass.

The wind started to pick up, gently rocking the Jeep. Sturdy-looking trees bowed submissively as the first thunderclaps echoed down the streets. Hobart smiled. The large, well-kept houses surrounding him were almost invisible now, obscured by the coming darkness and thickening wall of water. The weather gods were smiling down on him. The street was deserted.

The shrill ring of his cellular phone interrupted his musings. His partner was on the other end.

"There's no sign that anyone's been in here—it'd take a wizard to beat your security system. I walked around the grounds. No sign of anyone there, either."

"Are you ready?"

"Whenever you are."

"I'm coming in." Hobart flipped the phone closed and laid it on the seat next to him. He started the car and moved slowly around the block, passing close to the parked Nissan and turning up his driveway. He couldn't see the expression on the faces of the Nissan's occupants, but he could detect excited movement in the car as he passed. A feeling of relief passed through him. Amateurs.

Hobart hit the garage door opener well before getting to the house and was able to pull in without pausing. He hit the button again and watched his rearview mirror to see if his admirers had followed him up the drive. They hadn't.

Climbing out of the Jeep, he pulled on a Gore-Tex jacket that had been lying in the back seat, and escaped out of the garage through the side door. The rain hadn't let up, and his boots sank in the softened earth. He struggled through his thickly landscaped backyard and alongside the house, finally stopping in a dense group of trees. In theory, his position should have given him an unobstructed view of the front door about twenty yards away. Through the storm, though, all he could see was the dim glow of the carriage lights.

Hobart crouched down and waited. The driveway was the only practical entrance to his property, due to a tall wrought-iron fence protecting the perimeter. While the fence had been installed by the previous owners for aesthetic effect, its arrowlike pinnacles effectively discouraged climbing.

He didn't have to wait long. A few minutes after he took up his position, two shadowy figures could be seen hurrying up the steep drive. About halfway to the front door, one of them broke off and positioned himself twenty-five feet to the right of the door. The man stood motionless next to a tree, melted into it by the rain.

Hobart walked carefully along the edge of the lawn, staying out of sight. He stopped ten feet behind the figure. The man's shoulders were broad, and well-defined muscles could be seen through the cheap suit plastered to his back by the downpour. A .45 dangled loosely from his left hand.

Hobart crept up behind him. His feet made an inevitable sucking noise as he moved, so he walked slowly, stopping at odd intervals to mask their rhythm. The combination of the noise from the storm and the man's focus on the door made him an easy target.

He stopped just behind the man—so close that he had to control his breathing for fear his quarry would feel it on the back of his neck. Gazing down at the man's gun, he confirmed that his finger was not on the trigger.

In one swift motion Hobart grabbed the gun, switched hands, and pressed the barrel into the man's cheek. The man stood in the same position as before, except that his eyes strained right—focused on the barrel of the gun.

Hobart grabbed his shoulder and pressed down. The man sank slowly to his knees and then lay face first in the deep mud. Hobart knelt over him, keeping the barrel behind his ear, and watched the activity at his front door with silent anticipation.

The other man, who was still only a vague form to Hobart, had moved to within a few feet of the front door and was standing on tiptoe, peeking in a large bay window. He stood like that for almost thirty seconds, despite the downpour from the overflowing gutters. From that position, he reached over and rang the doorbell, and then pressed his back against the wall next to the door.

Swenson began moving along the front of the house. He would have been in full view of the man at the door, had the man's attention not been focused in the other direction. Swenson moved smoothly, trying to keep out of the waterfall coming off the roof.

It would have been impossible to hear Swenson's approach. Hobart later theorized that the cartel enforcer had been alerted by the water splashing off his partner's body. Whatever it was, he spun to his right just as Swenson moved within three feet of him.

The struggle was short. Swenson was able to block the gun arcing toward his face and charge the man, lifting him off his feet and landing him hard on the brick porch. As his back impacted, the gun went off. Hobart tensed, inadvertently pressing the pistol harder into his captive's ear. To his surprise, the pathetic whimper floating up from beneath him was more noticeable than the gunshot, which had blended seamlessly with the crash of the storm.

Hobart grabbed his captive by the back of the hair and dragged him to his feet. They marched toward the door. A scared-looking Robert Swenson was standing over the man's companion, gun shaking slightly.

"You all right, Bob?"

Swenson swallowed hard and nodded, stepping back and inviting his prisoner to stand.

As they descended the basement stairs, Hobart came to the realization that he would never live in that house again. Nor would he ever be able to exist under the name John Hobart. The drug cartels had a nasty way of holding a grudge. In essence, the thing he prized most—his privacy—had been stripped away. The price of fame in this case would be a bullet in the head.

"Gentlemen. I always like to know who I'm talking to. What are your names?"

The two men sat under a bare bulb, wrapped in an almost comical amount of rope. Coils of white nylon twisted and turned across their bodies, pinning their arms painfully behind their backs. Swenson had gone back to the warehouse after he had finished tying them.

The basement was typical of Baltimore's older homes. Rotting overhead beams dripped water on the dirt floor. The cement walls were pockmarked and stained by a dark line running horizontally about three feet from the floor, suggesting that the basement at one time had been under water.

Hobart rarely used it, and with the exception of the large, well-equipped tool bench, most of the junk in it belonged to prior owners. Old bicycles, golf clubs, a bathtub. He had been meaning to clean it out for years, but had never received the proper inspiration.

"Fuck you, man," spat the one who had grappled with Swenson. Hobart looked at his deeply lined face for a moment. The man's stare glowed with hatred and sadism. Hobart moved his eyes to the man's partner, who didn't meet his gaze. There was weakness there. It could be seen in the curve of the mouth. The slightly flared nostrils.

Hobart stood and walked past the men toward the work bench.

"What if we just start yelling, man. Your neighbors won't like that too much," the angry one said in thickly accented English.

Hobart shouted for him. "Help! I'm being murdered!" He lowered his voice to a conversational tone. "You're in the basement of a house sitting on an acre of land in a rainstorm. Who the hell's gonna hear you?"

He selected a scratch awl from the tool bench. The angry one was straining his neck, trying to see what

Hobart was doing. The quiet one was dead still, head drooped forward.

The angry one gave up trying to see what was going on, shouting an idle threat instead. "You're dead, man. Dead." The sentence had a practiced finality to it.

"Maybe," Hobart answered, "but you first." He clamped his hand over the man's mouth and nose, and pressed the awl into the base of his skull. The bone resisted at first, but gave way with a sickening crunching sound when Hobart put his full weight behind the tool. Once inserted to the handle, he rotated it in a slow circular motion.

Hobart felt the muscles in the man's jaw go slack, and he released him.

The surviving man, who had appeared dead before, jumped as if someone had run an electric current through him. His head snapped up and every fiber in his body tried to move away from Hobart, who was busy wrapping duct tape around the corpse's neck, sealing the small, oozing wound. Despite the man's valiant effort, the chair only teetered slightly. A tribute to Swenson's overzealous rope work.

Hobart walked around the chair-bound corpse and took his seat. The quiet one stared at him, wild-eyed.

He had the look of a flunky. No doubt he had hung on his companion's every word, convinced that he was the ultimate killer. Lean, mean, fighting machine. What little strength he had, had drained from him with the blood and brains of his companion.

"So what was it you said your name was?" Hobart played with the bloody awl suggestively.

"Jesus, my name is Jesus." He barely spoke English. Hobart switched to Spanish.

"Pleased to meet you, Jesus. Now why don't you tell me who sent you here?"

The young man thought for a moment, weighing his options.

"Look, Jesus. In an hour you'll be dead—no matter what. The question is how comfortable you are during that hour."

It was a psychological trick that Hobart had always been fond of, but had found little opportunity to use. In the face of certain death, earthly loyalties and conventions held little meaning.

A brief look of despair crossed Jesus's face and he drooped as far forward in the chair as the ropes would allow. Hobart waited quietly. Finally Jesus's head rose. The expression of despair had been replaced with one of resignation.

"Luis Colombar," he said in a breathy voice that Hobart had to strain to hear.

"And his orders?"

"To kill you."

"Why?"

"He did not say."

Hobart walked back to the work bench. His captive craned his neck, as his companion had, with similar futility.

As he passed Jesus on his way back to his chair, Hobart swung a heavy hammer into the man's immobilized knee. Jesus howled in surprise and pain, eyes rolling back in his head.

"Why?" Hobart repeated, settling back in his

chair and placing the hammer next to the awl on the floor.

Jesus coughed violently, turning his head to the side as though he was going to vomit. Blood soaked through his pants where the shards of what had once been his kneecap had sliced through the skin.

"I swear, he didn't tell me!" There were tears in the corners of his eyes. "Why would he?"

Hobart had believed him the first time, but it never hurt to be thorough. Satisfied that he had the information he needed, he grabbed the awl and walked behind the young man.

Jesus jerked his head side to side and back and forth violently, grunting with every move, trying to delay the inevitable. Hobart grabbed a handful of his hair and forced his head forward, exposing the base of his neck.

Hobart eased Robert Swenson's Cadillac over the steep hill leading to his cabin. The bottom scraped loudly, as though it was intentionally reminding him that it had been made for the highway and not weed-choked dirt roads. The tires spun a bit, but he made it over the rise and began down the steep slope to the cabin.

Pulling up next to the house, he killed the engine and the lights, letting the dark quiet wrestle its way into the car. He sat for a few minutes with the door half-open, letting his eyes adjust and listening for any sign of life in the dense woods that surrounded him. He heard nothing but the wind.

Despite the cold dampness of the night, Hobart

was sweating profusely. He had one hand on the collar of Jesus's jacket and the other wrapped around the handle of a rusted shovel. It never ceased to amaze him how heavy corpses felt. Unconsciousness added a few pounds to be sure, but death . . .

He had to stop every ten feet or so to catch his breath and regain his bearings—a flashlight seemed ill advised. The work gloves weren't helping matters, either. The loose leather made gripping the rain and blood-dampened wool of Jesus's jacket nearly impossible.

A half hour's walk brought him to the edge of a small clearing less than a quarter of a mile from the cabin. He stopped a few feet from it, positioning himself where he could make the most of the moonlight while still staying under the cover of the trees. Finding a piece of ground relatively free of rocks and roots, he began to dig.

It was an hour before dawn when Hobart dropped Jesus's nameless companion in the hole on top of him. Despite the moonlight, it was inky-black in the four-foot-deep grave—something he hadn't entirely counted on. He jumped in, landing on the bodies with a muffled thud. He reached down and ran his hand up one of the men's chests until he felt the smooth duct tape wrapped around his neck. He removed his hand and replaced it with the blade of the shovel. He worked it back and forth with his heel, feeling it slowly bite into flesh and finally into bone. One last push severed the man's head. Hobart reached into the darkness and retrieved it. He stuffed it into a thick Hefty bag and tied off the top. As he walked back to the cabin, the head bounced playfully against his knee. It too seemed heavier than it should be.

The theory was simple. When Colombar found that his men had disappeared, he would get impatient. And if he got impatient, he would probably end up calling the Bureau. Hobart couldn't allow that to happen.

His years in the DEA had taught him a few things about the minds of these men. He would FedEx the head to Colombar. Boxed up nicely—possibly with a bow. More important, he would include a note, preferably with something attacking Colombar's manhood in some way. The drug lord's reaction was absurdly easy to predict. He would fly into a rage. He would send more men, ordering them to capture Hobart and bring him back to Colombia. Hobart smiled and tossed the bag over his shoulder. Some things were constant in the universe. Pi, gravity, time, and the fact that drug dealers thought with their balls and not their brains.

27

New York City,
March 5

Bill Karns pulled himself from the cab with some difficulty and hurried down the sidewalk.

The New York streets were relatively quiet. It was three o'clock—the late lunchers had all finished their martinis and returned to work, and the people contemplating sneaking home early were going to give it another hour or so.

When John Hobart had called about the strychnine poisoning in D.C., Karns had thought he was out. He had never heard Johnny like that. Hobart's calm composure under stress was a big part of his personality. Hell, it *was* his personality. The screaming, swearing person on the other end of the phone had taken Karns off guard. And scared him.

He had moved out that day and headed for Oklahoma City. Not exactly a hotbed of high-dollar narcotic traffickers, but it looked like it was where he would stay. Missionless for the rest of the operation.

The call last week had been a shock. Hobart was flying to Oklahoma City and they were to meet.

Hobart said that he had a critical mission and needed someone he could trust. One of the CDFS's men had been caught and, according to CNN, was going to talk. He hadn't yet, but unnamed FBI officials were confident that their negotiations were headed in the right direction.

Hobart had arrived the next day and charged Karns with taking care of the problem. The hit was already completely planned, right down to scale models and carefully drawn diagrams. Karns had listened silently, struggling not to let his face reveal his relief at being reinstated as one of Hobart's top men.

And now it had begun.

Karns approached the doors of the building across from the jailhouse where Phil Nelson, as his name had turned out to be, was being held. On the other side of the street, the inevitable crush of reporters and protesters ebbed and flowed across the sidewalk, barely contained by wooden barriers and police. Some had spilled into the road, and the combination of their bodies, and the interest of passing drivers, had caused a near standstill in traffic. The cars sat helpless, horns blaring, and drivers shouting inane obscenities.

He pushed through the glass doors and turned left. The entrance to the stairwell was right where Hobart said it would be. He paused, looking up at the seemingly endless flights of concrete and metal stairs as they rose into the gloom above his head. Finally he took a deep breath and started up.

Under his dirt-streaked coveralls, one hundred and fifty feet of nylon rope was coiled around his torso. A climbing harness clung to his ample waist, and a rifle hung under his right arm. On the outside of his work clothes, an overflowing tool belt hung lifelessly, full of oddly new-looking tools. The weight of these items, combined with years of inactivity, made it necessary for him to stop on each landing for increasingly long periods. The farther he ascended, the harder it was to catch his breath and clear his swimming head.

Almost there.

He could hear the unmistakable sound of power tools and hammering coming from above. Hobart had told him that the last two floors were undergoing a major renovation. No one would notice one more worker making his way up the stairs.

One more flight.

He was bent over as low as the tightly coiled rope would allow. It felt like someone was twisting a knife in his side. He ignored the pain and continued on, finally arriving at the door leading to the roof.

The old hinges had been recently oiled, and the heavy wooden door opened easily. Karns slipped through and pushed it shut behind him. He walked nonchalantly to a pile of debris stacked over eight feet high on the west side of the roof and began picking through it. Typical construction debris—pieces of drywall, insulation, and lumber, mixed with old furniture that couldn't handle the onset of the information age, and the computers that came with it.

After about twenty minutes of seemingly aimless scrounging, Karns straightened out and stretched his back. He looked around, casually scanning the roofs of the surrounding buildings. Then he bent again, squeezing himself into the insulation-lined hole that he had made for himself. He worked his body back and forth, trying to flatten out the sharp edges caused by the haphazardly stacked debris. The rope coiled around his torso was a blessing now, keeping nails and glass from cutting into him.

Satisfied that his comfort had been provided for about as much as it was going to be, he pulled a large piece of drywall in front of him. That, combined with his dull gray coveralls, would make him invisible. Unless of course someone needed something from the pile. That didn't seem likely, though. It was four-thirty, and construction was winding down for the day.

He shifted his position one last time—something was sticking into his neck. The weather was getting noticeably colder, too, cooling the sweat that had begun to soak through his coveralls. It was going to be a long night.

The last two hours had seemed as long as all the others combined. Bill Karns twisted his wrist painfully and looked at his watch for the hundredth time. Nine-thirty. Just a few more minutes.

The rubble that surrounded him like a cocoon had provided surprisingly little insulation over the last seventeen hours. The climbing rope that was such a burden on the way up the stairs had been his savior—keeping the cold night air from penetrating his torso, but not doing much for his extremities. His hands were stiff, and his legs felt completely lifeless. He could feel the warmth of the sun in the few places that it filtered through the debris.

Nine thirty-five. Hobart's plan had Karns waiting as long as possible before emerging from his hiding place, lessening the chances of him being spotted from one of the surrounding buildings. He decided to revise the plan slightly. The shot wasn't going to be particularly difficult by his standards, but it would help if he could actually make his finger squeeze the trigger.

He began pushing the large piece of drywall lying on top of him to the side. The noise startled him a bit after spending the entire night on the quiet roof, with only the drifting sound of traffic to keep him company.

His legs were in even worse shape than he had thought. He had to literally drag himself from the hole, scooting on his belly to the northwest and nestling himself in the crook of the four-foot wall that surrounded the roof. He stretched his legs out painfully and began balling and unballing his fists. When his fingers loosened up, he tucked them under his armpits to warm.

Nine forty-five. Time to move.

Karns dropped his tool belt and pulled out a hammer and two six-inch nails. Crawling quickly, he made his way to the only door opening onto the roof and drove the nails through the door and into the doorjamb. Hobart had really done his homework. He had told Karns that the large air-conditioning unit would obscure him from prying eyes as he sealed the door. And there it was, right where it had been on Hobart's elaborate cardboard model.

Karns crawled back to his corner and began unwinding the rope from his body, stacking it next to him. Pulling the covers off the scope on his rifle, he sighted carefully across the roof at a flag just visible on the top of the building next to him. Other than a small amount of condensation on the scope's optics, everything looked good. He chambered a round.

Hobart had definitely been on the roof. Karns had suggested that he bring a mirror or something to set on the wall so that he could watch for his target. But Hobart told him that he would be able to hear the commotion when they brought Nelson out. Karns had been doubtful during their conversation, but had to admit now that Hobart had been right. Some kind of acoustic anomaly seemed to quiet the traffic noise and amplify the sound of protesters and reporters. He could hear their excitement growing as he continued to flex and stretch his legs.

As he had for the last three days, Mark Beamon stopped ten feet from the glass doors leading to the steps of the building. From where he stood, he could see six or seven agents holding back the reporters and interested bystanders, cutting a twenty-five-foot-wide swath in the crowd. He couldn't see the dark blue LTD waiting for him on the street, or the one hundred and fifty other agents stationed on roofs, sitting in cars, and casually strolling through the neighborhood. A nervous sweat trickled down the back of his neck and behind his bullet-proof vest.

He had thought that the first day would be the worst. He had been dead wrong. The tension seemed to grow every day, like the crescendo at the end of a symphony.

"Are you all right, Mr. Beamon?" Philip Nelson asked, as he had every day since Beamon had replaced his original escort. Beamon nodded, but didn't move.

Finally he glanced at his watch. Ten o'clock. Time to go. He began moving forward, right hand gripped tightly around the chain on his prisoner's handcuffs. Nelson looked relieved.

Wait for it, Karns told himself. The reporters and onlookers' excitement level was rising, but Hobart had told him that they could see through the glass doors, and to wait until he could actually hear them shouting questions. Then he would have about eight seconds with a clean shot and another two with a shot partially blocked by a car. Karns took a deep breath and held it, adjusting the rifle slightly in his grip. It felt strange through the surgical gloves, as if it wasn't real.

The shouting started and he wasn't ready. He let the breath out and took another one, wasting two seconds.

His legs were sore from the previous day's exercise, but the blood was back in them. He rose smoothly to his feet and steadied the gun. No one in the crowd noticed the small figure leaning over the roof.

There was no need to adjust for drop due to the angle and distance. Nelson's head was directly in his crosshairs. He lowered the barrel a fraction, repositioning the crosshairs on Nelson's chest. Head shots were sloppy. It was astonishing what the human skull could deflect. He still hadn't been noticed by the crowd when he squeezed the trigger. The rifle cracked loudly, jerking against his shoulder. A fraction of a second later, he had dropped the rifle and was running for the back of the building, rope in hand.

The sound of the shot and the sound of the bullet as it ricocheted off the cement stairs behind him were virtually simultaneous. Beamon expected to feel his prisoner torn from his grasp and to have to watch him cartwheel away with the impact of the shot. In that split second between awareness and action, though, Nelson remained perfectly still.

Beamon dove to the left, pulling his prisoner by the chain between his handcuffs. They landed heavily on the stairs, Beamon on his stomach and Nelson on his back. With a shooter on a roof, it wasn't a much more desirable position than standing, he reflected, watching the crowd scatter. He was counting slowly to himself. It was a habit he had formed years ago. Time seemed to slip away in situations like this, and more often than not, it was helpful to know when things happened. When he reached five—an eternity in a gunfight—he sat up.

The other agents were still crouched behind the LTD parked at the base of the steps, as was Tom Sherman. They were aiming their guns in the general direction of the top of the building across the street. A couple were touching their ears, listening intently to the chatter on the FBI radio.

"Get up, you lucky bastard," Beamon said, poking Nelson's still prone form in the ribs. Nelson didn't move.

Uh-oh.

Beamon ripped open Nelson's shirt, finding a neat hole in his bullet-proof vest. Blood was just beginning to flow through the tear.

"Fucking Teflon bullets!" he shouted, standing up and dusting himself off. He had probably made it to the four count before the poor bastard even knew he was dead.

"Get down, Mark," Sherman yelled.

Beamon thrust his hands into his pockets. "Oh, shit, Tommy, that guy's burnin' a hole in his sneakers by now."

Sherman poked his head up from behind the car, looking indecisive. Finally he walked over and stood looking down at their dead prisoner. His gun hung uselessly in his hand. "Jesus."

Motherfucker didn't even know what hit him, Karns thought to himself as he secured the rope to a thick ventilation pipe on the roof. He hadn't stuck around long enough to watch his target fall, but he had a hunter's sixth sense. Dead center.

Adrenaline coursed through him as he anchored the rope into his harness and climbed to the edge of the roof. He hadn't rappelled since the army—thirty years and fifty pounds ago. And he hadn't been crazy about it then. He felt suddenly dizzy as he teetered on the edge, becoming aware for the first time of the whistle of the wind. The sight of his motorcycle, and freedom, steadied him.

The gear had improved, that was for sure. He slid smoothly down the rope, gripping and releasing rhythmically with his gloved hands. About halfway down he stopped with a vicious jerk. His head snapped back and he nearly turned upside down. Confused, he looked at the metal loop at his waist. Nothing caught. He looked at the rope below him and discovered the problem. Four men in street clothes were standing in the alley, each one with a pistol aimed up at him. A fifth man was pulling hard on the rope, effectively locking him in place. Karns looked up at the roof. Three clean-cut faces peered down at him over the sights of their sidearms. He looked at the window in front of him. Plexiglas.

He ticked off the facts: He had no gun, he was stuck fifty feet above the ground, and there were no fewer than seven guns pointed at him. Options? Surrendering seemed the only logical choice, though the thought of grabbing for an imaginary gun was pretty attractive, too. The young FBI agents had set up quite a crossfire for themselves.

He was leaning toward surrendering when his body was slammed face first into the side of the building. As he swung back out, he felt at his nose. *Fucking FBI. Couldn't they just let me sit and think for a minute?*

He looked down, expecting to see the young agent holding the rope swinging it back and forth, trying to hurry his decision. Surprisingly, he wasn't anywhere near the rope anymore. The agents had scrambled behind an overflowing Dumpster and were shouting at each other and pointing their guns at a faraway rooftop.

Then he saw it. There was no blood on his shirt, but he could see it running down the neon green rope.

First he looked up, thinking that maybe one of the agents above him had accidentally shot himself. No, they were in the same position as their cohorts.

Karns tore open the front of his shirt to find a bubbling hole in his chest. He never felt any pain. The last sensation he had was that of a gradual acceleration toward the ground.

John Hobart dropped his rifle onto the asphalt-shingled roof and walked casually toward the door to the stairs. He walked down two flights and came out on one of the posh upper floors of the hotel. Finding the elevator, he pushed the Down button and waited. A woman came up behind him and pushed the button a few more times for good measure. She was wearing a well-coordinated track suit, and her blond hair was tied back with a thick white ribbon. She pulled one of the ears on her Walkman out as she stretched a shapely leg against the marble wall. "You been outside yet?"

"Sure haven't," Hobart replied in a friendly tone.

"Hope it's not raining," she said to the wall.

Mark Beamon shielded his eyes from the sun and moved away from the Dumpster and the smell of rotting vegetables.

"So he shot from that hotel over there?" he asked the young agent standing next to him.

"Yes, sir."

"You make that three hundred yards, Tommy?"

"At least."

Sherman walked over to look at the body. The impact with the concrete had done even more damage than the bullet.

Beamon turned back to the agent. "So you're telling me that some guy hit a moving target from three hundred yards in this wind?"

"Uh. No. He was stopped about midway down."

"Still," Beamon said with a hint of admiration in his voice. "One hell of a shot."

Beamon slid behind Tom Sherman's desk and grabbed a coffee mug off the credenza behind him. Pulling a bottle of Jack Daniels from the brown bag on the desk, he filled it almost to the rim. He wanted a cigarette, too, but he knew his boss would have his ass for smoking in his office.

It had been one hell of a day. The second shooter had walked away scot-free. He'd had a hundred and fifty agents on the street, but they were only covering buildings that you could hit Nelson from. His mistake—and a pretty fucking big one at that.

He took a heavy slug from the mug.

And don't forget the guy you killed today.

He took another slug. He could still see the surprised expression frozen into Nelson's face. In many ways, Nelson was far more deserving of respect than the flip-flopping politicians who had sentenced him to death. Beamon had spent quite a bit of time with him in the interrogation room. Right or wrong, the kid had believed what he was doing, and was willing to put his ass on the line to see it through.

The liquor was starting to go to his head, just where he wanted it. He spun the chair around and looked out the window at the fading light washing the color from the nation's capital.

"Mark?"

Beamon spun back around and motioned toward the chair in front of the desk.

"Got one for me?" Laura asked.

Beamon filled a green mug with National Park Service emblazoned across it.

"Quite a day," Laura probed.

Beamon let the remaining half inch of Jack Daniels slide down his throat and poured another one to the rim. "Yup."

"So what happened out there today, Mark?"

Beamon shrugged. "I got a couple of men killed."

Laura took a long pull from the mug and leaned back in her chair. "You know, Mark, I sometimes question your methods—no, that's not true, I *usually* question your methods. What I've never questioned, though, is your judgment. What's going on? You knew damn well that Nelson's security was inadequate."

Beamon smiled. She had yelled at him for almost twenty minutes about that very subject last week while he had made stupid excuses. It was nice of her not to say 'I told you so.'"

"Maybe my judgment's not as good as you think it is."

Laura scowled and took another slug. "This is me you're talking to, Mark."

The less Laura knew the better, but Beamon couldn't bear the thought of her believing he'd planned this stunt.

"It seems the powers that be thought using Nelson as bait was just one hell of a fine idea."

RISING PHOENIX • 407

Laura let out a long sigh. "You couldn't do anything to stop it?"

"This didn't come just from Calahan, believe me." Beamon shook his head. "I thought that if I stuck it out, I could control the situation." He raised his mug. "Here's to controlling the situation."

"So where are we now?"

Beamon thought for a moment. "It sure as hell would have been a lot cleaner to have two live suspects instead of two dead ones. But—and I hate to say it—we're better off than we were yesterday. It should narrow things down a bit, having two names."

Laura held out her mug and Beamon filled it. "You gonna let me get you drunk?"

"I'm tempted. Do we have a name on the shooter yet?"

"No, but I'm sure you'll get me one tomorrow."

"So do you still think that the organization's centralized? That one general recruited all the soldiers?"

"Hoping, anyway. Figure it this way. The same guy got the mushrooms and the money. It stands to reason that he also hit the sources of the coke and heroin. Well, maybe him and one or two other guys . . ." Beamon shook his head and went for the bottle again. "Aw, hell, who knows? There could be hundreds of these guys running around—each one only knowing one other operative. You know, like the spooks do it. If so, we're screwed."

Laura raised her glass. "Well, then, here's to the General Theory."

28

Near Bend, Oregon,
March 6

Matt Fallon slowed his '72 VW microbus and turned left off Highway 97, passing briefly through Terrebonne, Oregon. The cool, dry wind blowing through the window quieted as he slowed, and he turned down the stereo to compensate. It wasn't long before he could see the volcanic spires of Smith Rock State Park rising in the distance. He smiled and breathed in the sweet, pine-tasting air. It was Friday, and he was anxious to get out of the van that had become a prison over the last three weeks.

The FBI had tried conventional means of finding Lance Richardson, the missing witness from the bank, and had failed miserably. Finally management had been forced to admit that they just couldn't fathom the rock-climbing-bum mentality.

And that's where Fallon came in. He had risen to the top of the U.S. competitive climbing circuit while getting his Ph.D. in physics from the University of Colorado. On the night of his graduation, he had hiked up to the cliffs above Boulder, Colorado. There, accompanied by a case of his favorite beer, he had carefully appraised himself and what he wanted out of life. He had a shot at the climbing thing—power, balance, drive. But where would that get him? Climbers were viewed by most people as a bunch of long-haired lunatics with death wishes. The best in the U.S. would be lucky to feed himself from sponsors.

He had also decided that while he had a real love and aptitude for physics, he wasn't brilliant enough to be a driving force. He would probably end up teaching, or worse, sitting behind a computer at some crazy defense contracting firm.

And then it had come back to him—the days spent riveted to his television as a small child, watching Efrem Zimbalist, Jr. catch the bad guys. He'd finished the case of beer, and the next day, suffering from a near-terminal hangover, he had applied to the FBI.

The funny thing was that they accepted him. The well-rounded agent was what they were looking for, they told him. His Ph.D. and dominance in a sport— even one as esoteric as rock climbing—had apparently qualified him as well rounded.

Fallon shook his head, remembering that it had almost been three years since that night in Boulder. Einstein had been wrong about time. It accelerated as you got older.

He had spent the last weeks scouring America's premier climbing areas—the New River Gorge, Hueco Tanks, Wild Iris, to name only a few—asking questions and running into way too many old friends. He figured that he had packed at least five beer pounds onto his painfully thin frame.

He turned left into a crowded pullout and hopped out. He shouldered a small pack full of climbing gear and headed down the steep trail toward the cliffs.

After only five minutes on the trail, he heard a familiar voice floating through a narrow passage in the rocks. He turned off and danced gracefully up the steep boulder field. At the top, he found a young woman watching a shaking figure fifty feet up a sheer rock face.

"Hi, Sara. Remember me?" he asked, approaching her quietly. She looked up, confused for a moment.

"Matt!" She looked up. "Scott! Matt Fallon's standing right here!"

The man on the rock face struggled a few more feet, finally reaching a bolt that he could clip into. He leaned back on the rope and jabbed his finger downward. Sara obligingly lowered him to the ground.

At the bottom he threw his arms around the agent. After a moment he pulled back, giving Fallon's arms a squeeze as he went. "Still feel pretty strong," he observed. "Three years in the CIA doesn't seem to have hurt you much."

"FBI," Fallon corrected. "There's a difference."

His friend looked like he was about to make a smart-ass comment, but before he could open his mouth Sara pushed him out of the way and ran her fingers through Fallon's closely cropped hair. A sad look came over her face. "What happened to your beautiful hair?"

"Cut it off—the Bureau doesn't take kindly to that shoulder-length look."

"So why didn't you call us and tell us you were coming?"

"I wasn't sure I was. Actually, I'm on business."

She snickered, looking at the climbing harness peeking out from the top of his backpack.

"No, seriously," he protested. "I'm looking for somebody. He's a climber. Name's Lance Richardson. Five foot ten, long blond hair. You know him?"

"Did he kill somebody?" Scott asked,

"Nah. He might have seen a guy we're looking for when he was working for a bank in Saint Louis. That's all."

"Well, you came to the right place," Sara said.

Fallon looked at her with surprise. After all this time on the road, he hadn't been prepared to actually find the guy. "You're kidding. You've seen him?"

"Yeah. He's been around for about a week. I think he's living in his van back in the National Forest somewhere."

"Do you know where, exactly?"

"No. But I think he's probably working Chain Reaction."

Chain Reaction was debatably Smith's most renowned climb. And it was less than a quarter of a mile away.

"You mean right now?" Fallon asked, still in a daze. The realization that his paid climbing trip might be nearly over was sinking in.

"Right now."

Scott was getting impatient with all the business talk. "So are we gonna do some climbs while the sun's still up, man?"

Fallon reached behind him and felt the pack, confirming that his notebook was in it. "Hell, yeah—just

let me go ask this guy a few questions. I'll be back in
less than an hour." He started back down the boulder
field. Stopping about fifty feet away, he turned back to
his friends. "Oh, can I stay at your place for a couple of
days?"

Sara sat back on the rock behind her. "We've got a
wedding to go to tonight. We'll leave the front door
open."

Fallon sat down in the dirt and pulled the notebook
from his backpack. He lay back and put on his sunglasses. The blond figure was about halfway up the
climb, and struggling. Despite his long arms, he
missed the hold he was aiming for and fell six feet or so
before the rope stopped him. Fallon looked on calmly,
silently critiquing his technique.

"Shit, man, I'm never going to get this—too late in
the day."

"You want down?" his partner asked.

"Yeah, might as well."

Fallon watched as the climber slowly lowered.
When his feet hit the ground, Fallon interrupted what
sounded like the beginning of a long conversation
about tomorrow's climbing strategy.

"Excuse me. Are you Lance Richardson?"

The young man looked up from the knot he was
untying. "Yeah. Do I know you?"

"Nope." Fallon didn't get up, but leaned forward and
pulled a pen from his pocket. "My name's Matt Fallon."

Richardson wagged his finger up and down, trying
to remember something. Finally it came to him. "Hey,

aren't you that guy from Boulder who quit climbing to join the CIA or something?"

Fallon frowned. "FBI. There's a difference."

"So how do you know me?"

"I've been trying to find you for weeks, actually."

Richardson's climbing partner was looking at him strangely. Fallon figured he was wondering if he'd hooked up with a mass murderer or something.

"We're looking for someone who was a customer of the bank you used to work for." The climbing partner relaxed a bit and began slowly coiling his rope.

Richardson sat down next to Fallon. "Seems like years ago, man—bank jobs, you know?"

The agent nodded, remembering the shit jobs he had taken to finance climbing trips. "You might actually remember this guy. It was right before you left. He brought in a suitcase full of cash to buy some cashier's checks."

"Oh, him. Yeah, I do remember him, sort of."

Fallon shook his head. This guy must not have looked at a TV or newspaper since he had left Saint Louis. It made him long for the good old days. "So what can you tell me about him?"

"Nothing really—don't remember his name or anything," Richardson began, spreading his legs wide and beginning to stretch. "He came up to the teller window where I was working—but we didn't do cashier's checks there, you know. So I sent him to one of the customer service reps. I don't remember which one."

Fallon decided to pass on asking for a description, they had twenty already. "Nothing else?"

He continued stretching. "Actually, I saw him later that day, now that I think about it."

Fallon perked up. "Where was that?" he asked, putting the list of climbs that he wanted do that afternoon out of his head.

"Up the street at a little shopping mall. I didn't talk to him or anything. I was just stopped at a light and he was getting into his car."

Fallon scribbled in the notebook. His heart was beating faster and faster. "Remember what kind of car, by any chance?"

"Sure. It's not every day somebody walks into the bank with a suitcase full of cash—we thought he was a drug dealer or something. Was he?"

"Not exactly."

Richardson looked disappointed. "It was a red Cherokee. Not one of those cool new Limiteds—just one of the old boxy ones. I remember thinking that a guy with that much cash ought to have a nicer ride, you know?"

"Do you remember anything else about the car? Things hanging from the rearview mirror, dents, bumper stickers—anything, really."

"Nothing like that—it was really clean. Looked new. It did have those Save the Chesapeake plates on it, though."

Fallon looked at him with a confused expression.

"You know—from Maryland. I went to school there. The climbing sucks."

29

Baltimore, Maryland, March 6

"What the hell's going on?" Robert Swenson demanded in a loud voice, bursting through the front door of the apartment.

Hobart looked up from a thick computer printout, annoyed at his partner's untimely entrance. He had a headache that no aspirin seemed to be able to cure.

"What's the problem, Bob?" he asked calmly, already knowing the answer.

"I just watched one of our guys get blown away on the steps of some jail in New York and now I'm hearing that the guy that shot him was shot from another building when he was getting away."

Hobart leaned back in his chair, turning the printout to face his desk. "I saw the report," he said cheerfully. "A stroke of good luck—looks like we won't have to close up shop as soon as we thought."

Swenson eyed him suspiciously. "How do you know he didn't already talk?"

"I have a well-positioned . . . friend. He confirmed it."

"Is he reliable?"

Hobart nodded. He had caught his "friend" stuffing his pockets full of cash at a drug bust almost ten years ago. He could have turned him in but decided against it. Better to hold out for a favor if he ever really needed one.

After confirming Nelson's silence, this particular friend had made it clear that all debts were repaid. He had slammed the phone down before Hobart could threaten him again. There had been no answer since.

"They haven't released the name of the shooter, but they're broadcasting a picture. You wouldn't be acquainted, would you?" Swenson asked.

"Karns," Hobart said, feigning disgust. "I was wrong to have let him back on board. Loose cannon. He must have heard the report that Nelson was talking and figured he'd try to make up for the strychnine thing."

"And who do you figure got him?"

"Oh, hell, probably the Bureau. They fucked up and now they're covering up. Doesn't look too good, them blowing away their star witness." Hobart could tell from his partner's expression that he wasn't buying it.

"And where were you yesterday at ten o'clock?" Swenson asked, an edge of nervousness in his voice. Hobart smiled. He could tell that his partner desperately wanted to believe that he hadn't been involved. People with that kind of bias were easily convinced.

"I was in the office working on our budget."

He knew that Swenson had been in D.C. the entire day of the shooting and had no way of knowing whether that was true or not. He would undoubtedly check the time and date of the budget file on the computer the minute he got the opportunity. Hobart had temporarily reset the internal time clock on the system when he had saved it. It would read 10:35 A.M., roughly a half hour after the incident. Not proof positive, of course, but it should ease his partner's mind long enough to finish this thing.

"They're gonna trace Nelson and Karns back to you sooner or later," Swenson said. "We've still gotta get out of here."

"Yeah, but I didn't know them that well. Even with a couple a hundred agents on it, they won't get back to me for at least four weeks. So I figure we've got two weeks to wrap things up and get a little more work done."

Swenson looked doubtful.

"I've got some stuff I've really got to finish up, Bob. You mind?"

Swenson stood. "So what's your plan for today?"

"I'm heading out in about an hour or so. Be back tonight."

"Maybe we can get together and talk about how we're gonna wrap this thing up," Swenson said hopefully. On his way out, he paused and looked down at the chess board sitting next to the television. Two white pawns, representing Nelson and Karns, were lying on their sides. Two blue pawns representing the dead cartel enforcers were in a similar position.

Alone again, Hobart flipped the printout on his desk over and continued running down the endless columns of numbers with the aid of a ruler.

The list had been provided by an old acquaintance who worked for C&P Telephone. Phil Nelson's capture had jolted him like a bolt of lightning. He'd spent hours running through the operation in his mind, trying to find where he might have screwed up.

In the end, he had decided that Nelson had blown it somewhere. That was a risk you ran in this type of operation—it was impossible to do everything yourself.

He had gone to bed that night chalking up Nelson's capture to the fortunes of war—confident that in the next two weeks he could continue to turn public opinion, and then slip silently out of the country.

It had been almost three in the morning when he had bolted upright in his bed. He had mentioned the DiPrizzio operation to Blake at the hotel. Could the Reverend have called the Bureau? Hobart dismissed the idea at first, but had been unable to get back to sleep. In the end, it had nagged at him enough to spend an entire day on a tour of the pay phones of the greater Baltimore metro area. He had pulled off every freeway exit ramp between Blake's office and home, and between the hotel where they had met and Blake's home, copying down the numbers of the first pay phones that he saw.

His acquaintance at the phone company had almost choked on the list of numbers, but Hobart had explained that the Reverend was getting death threats and that this was an integral part of the investigation. A devout follower of Blake, his acquaintance had called in some favors and retrieved a list of the long-distance numbers called from those phones on the dates that Hobart had supplied him.

He rubbed his eyes, painfully aware that the phone company could have had their computer search specifically for the FBI hotline number and saved him hours of tedium and a migraine headache. Everyone in the country knew that number, though. It had been running along the bottom of every TV screen in America for the past two months.

He was on the second-to-the-last page when he found it. Leaning back in his chair, he tossed the thick stack of paper in the garbage. He had underestimated his former employer. Blake was a consummate actor. He had left the hotel with just the right mix of nervousness, sadness, and growing calm. Not overacted, not underacted.

So now he knew. The question was, what could he do with the information?

Mark Beamon paused in the open door to the SIOC. The normally fast pace of the agents inside had been accelerated to a fevered pitch. People talked loudly on phones, typed furiously on laptop computers, televisions blared CNN. The increased activity further tightened the hand that gripped the back of his head every time he walk into the JEH Building.

Laura was leaning over a man's shoulder, reading off his computer screen. Beamon threaded his way toward her, nodding to the hustling agents who bid him a good morning.

"Jesus, Laura—do you live here?" It was seven-thirty A.M. He had hoped to beat her to the office for once, but as usual he felt like he was strolling in at ten.

"Just like to put in a full day at the office," she said, walking around the table.

Beamon grunted and made his way to the coffeemaker. "Want one?" he asked her.

She shook her head. "Had two already this morning. I'm wired."

"Well then, why don't you step into my parlor," Beamon said, heading toward an empty conference room. "Tell me what's going on."

Holding a manila folder under her arm, Laura closed the door behind her and began in as excited a voice as he'd ever heard from her. "We've got guys waiting at the front door of the MVA—Maryland Motor Vehicles Administration. They'll start running down Cherokee registrations this morning."

"What's our time frame on getting a list cross-referenced with the driver's licenses of people who fit our guy's description."

She shrugged. "I have no idea. State motor vehicle departments have different database capabilities. I should be able to give you a pretty good idea later today."

She took a seat at the small table across from Beamon. "Our dead shooter's name is William Karns." She slid the manila folder across the conference table. Beamon picked it up and began reading.

"His prints were on file 'cause he was an ex-cop."

"Seems to be a pattern emerging."

"It gets better. We have three witnesses who place Karns living in an abandoned house only a few blocks from the site of that strychnine poisoning."

"So he's probably not just some crazy—and it looks like you were wrong about the strychnine poisoning being a copycat."

"It looks like we were wrong," Laura corrected in a slightly annoyed tone. "We've got agents digging into his background and known acquaintances right now."

"I didn't catch the morning paper. What's the press got?"

"Wild speculation, mostly. They don't have his name, obviously, and they're running theories from suicide, to the FBI killing him, to one of his own getting him . . ." Her voice trailed off.

"Come on, what else?"

Laura looked down at the table. "You're taking a lot of criticism for letting Nelson get shot."

"Yeah, I seem to be developing kind of a love/hate thing with the press."

"I don't know how you can joke about this, Mark. The thing with Nelson wasn't even your idea and now you're going to be left holding the bag while everyone runs for cover."

Beamon nodded thoughtfully. "It's just politics, Laura. I hope you're taking notes. Always make sure you've scoped out a comfortable chair before the music stops."

"Well, you're setting one hell of an example."

Beamon laughed. "This is one of those 'do as I say and not as I do' situations. You'll find there are a lot of those where I'm concerned."

Laura leaned back in her chair and relaxed a little. "Well, I hope you know that I'm behind you, Mark."

"No, you're not. You'll run for cover too if you have to."

An expression of deep hurt crossed Laura's face. "How can you say . . ."

Beamon held up his hands, silencing her. "I know

you're willing to go down with me in this thing, Laura, and that means a lot. But there's no point to it. Besides, I'm counting on you being Director someday and giving me a big promotion."

Laura forced a smile. "And maybe I just will."

Beamon pushed his chair back on two legs and balanced precariously with his feet on the edge of the table. "Enough of this political crap. Chasing criminals is supposed to be fun. Are you ready for our field trip?"

"What do you mean?"

"What do you mean, what do I mean? I mean, let's get out there, have a greasy breakfast at Denny's, and do detective stuff. You and me—the whole day. It'll be just like Starsky and Hutch." He dropped the front of the chair back to the floor and stood.

"Mark, I can't just leave . . ."

He waved his hand dismissively. "The Bureau can survive without you in the office for one day, Laura. Delegate. We're leaving in a half hour."

He slugged down the last of his coffee and headed for the door. Laura scrambled out ahead of him to try to get a day's worth of work done in thirty minutes.

"Don't get me wrong, Laura. Eggs fried at a mom and pop diner have a certain subtlety that just can't be achieved in a chain restaurant." Beamon was gesturing wildly with his right hand, paying little attention to his left, which was steering the car. A toothpick hung loosely from his lips. "But to me, Denny's had the best quality/price/quantity ratio."

Laura was feeling sick from the Grand Slam breakfast lodged in her stomach and Beamon's wild driving. His dissertation on the history of the greasy Southern breakfast wasn't helping any, either. She decided to change the subject.

"You still haven't told me where we're going."

"Baltimore."

"Baltimore. Okay. Why?"

"I told you already—to do detective stuff." He dug a wad of yellow paper from his shirt pocket and handed it to her.

She unfolded the pages. They were from the phone book. The word "Theaters" was in the top right-hand corner of the first page.

"We're going to see a movie?"

He gave her an exaggerated look of disgust. "No, we're not going to see a goddam movie. Flip the page."

She turned it over. The heading THEATRICAL MAKEUP was highlighted in green.

"We've theorized that the guy in Poland and the guy at the bank were one and the same and that he was wearing sophisticated makeup. A wig, fake beard, that kind of stuff, right? Now, if he is from Baltimore, it stands to reason that he got the disguises around there. So, all we have to do is find a shopkeeper who remembers a short, thin guy buying those particular items about two months ago. Show him the driver's license pictures we're gonna get from the MVA, and budda bing. We're done."

"Why Baltimore?" Laura asked, concentrating on keeping her voice even. *Why hadn't she thought of that?*

"Well, what do we know about this guy? We know

he's not from D.C. or Saint Louis, 'cause both those cities were implicated with the cashier's checks—the FedEx place was in D.C., and the bank was in Saint Louis. Now we find out he has Maryland plates. D.C.'s an easy drive from Baltimore, and you can make it to Saint Louis in a day—I looked it up. Also, our anonymous informant called from a pay phone near Baltimore. My gut's never failed me in almost twenty years—and it's screaming Baltimore."

"Are you sure it's not the three eggs, bacon, ham, hash browns, and biscuits and gravy?"

Beamon chuckled. "Stop—you're making me hungry."

"What about somewhere else in Maryland—say Rockville? It fits the facts, too."

Beamon shrugged. "Yeah, you could be right. If we don't get what we want today, we'll get some guys to expand the search."

Laura leaned forward and flipped on the radio. She had grown accustomed to having the news blaring in her ear twenty-four hours a day. "It's a long shot . . ."

"Hey, at least it got us out of the office."

Laura juggled her legal pad and the large map of Baltimore that they had picked up at a gas station on the way there. Map reading was just not her forte.

"Turn right here," she ordered at the last minute. Beamon turned the wheel hard, squealing the tires.

"Jesus, Laura. A little advance warning would be nice."

"Why don't you let me drive and you navigate," she asked hopefully. The words 'suicide seat' had taken on real meaning in the last couple of hours.

"Nah. Reading maps in the car makes me sick."

* * *

They were on their last costume shop in the Baltimore area. No luck so far, though Laura had a list of names to follow up on the next day. People who may have been working on the dates in question, but either weren't in today or had changed jobs.

"There it is." She pointed across Beamon's nose and out the driver's side window. He wheeled the car around unexpectedly, making a U-turn in the middle of the street, and pulled up in front of the shop. Laura gripped the dash.

"Everybody out," Beamon announced unnecessarily. Laura had the door opened and was hopping from the car before it had entirely stopped.

"Hi, I'm Mark Beamon from the FBI and this is my associate, Laura Vilechi." There was no need to flash his credentials, the man behind the counter recognized him as soon as he said his name.

"Wow, nice to meet you, Mr. Beamon. I've seen you on television." He nodded a greeting to Laura. "What brings you to my store?"

"This is your place?" Beamon asked, carefully examining a luxurious blond wig on a white Styrofoam head.

"Yes, sir."

Beamon nodded and wandered off to look around.

Seeing that Beamon was beginning to lose interest in this investigative avenue, Laura decided to start questioning the shopkeeper without him. "We thought you might have some information that we need."

"Sure, anything I can do to help."

She smiled engagingly and sat down in an antique barber's chair in the center of the room. "What we're looking for is a man approximately five foot eight or less, thin, between thirty-five and forty-five, who might have come in here about two months ago and purchased, at the least, a long gray wig and beard and a long brown wig and beard, as well as makeup to perhaps make his features look different and darken his skin. He probably wouldn't have known much about using the stuff—might have asked for some advice . . ."

The man leaned against the counter behind him, a thoughtful look on his face.

"Is this about the CDFS?"

She nodded.

"Does he have short dark hair—kind of a crew cut?"

"Maybe, we're not sure."

"Yeah, I remember a guy like that. Wanted only the best. Must have spent a small fortune."

Beamon, who until a minute ago had seemed completely oblivious to the conversation, was suddenly at the man's side.

"Excuse me, Mr. . . ."

"Reasor. But call me Chris."

"Chris. You say you might remember this guy?"

"Yeah, sure. He kind of stuck in my mind, you know. Most of my business is kinda regular—so it's pretty unusual for a guy I've never seen to come in and make a big purchase like that. He also didn't really seem like the acting type."

"Did you ask him what he was going to use it for?" Laura asked.

Reasor thought for a moment. "Now that you mention it, I don't think I did. He wasn't really very friendly—hard to warm up to. He was in here a long time, too—didn't know the first thing about makeup."

"Chris, would you mind coming back to D.C. with us for the evening? We'll be happy to put you up in a nice hotel and compensate you for the time your shop's closed. I'd like to have you get together with one of our sketch artists."

"Hell, yes, I'll go. Those CDFS guys are crazy. Let me go grab my coat."

Beamon watched the store owner hurry to the back of the store. When he was out of sight, Beamon turned and gave Laura a hard spin in the barber chair. She gripped the handles tightly and laughed. "Looks like we might just save your butt after all, Mark."

Alejandro Perez hurried through the plush gardens surrounding Luis Colombar's estate, nodding to the guards as he passed them. Spring was fully upon them, and the cool evenings had turned sticky. The sun had just set on the horizon and its light was bouncing off the humid air with a spectacular effect. The sunset, combined with the quiet beauty of the garden this time of year, cast a false peace. Perez knew better.

He left the well-tended brick walkway, turning onto a narrow dirt trail. Through the trees he could see the glimmering lights of a greenhouse in the distance.

He stepped through its door, quickly closing it behind him so as not to release the warm air into the quickly cooling Colombian night. He felt his brow break out in a sweat from a combination of the heat and Colombar's tone when he had summoned him.

"Alejandro. I'm over here."

Perez caught a glimpse of his boss behind a table covered with tall and colorful flowers. He walked quickly across the wet concrete, noticing a strange and foul odor that gained strength as he approached the table. He wondered why Colombar would keep flowers that smelled so noxious, even if they were beautiful to look at. "I came as quickly as I could, Luis," he said, trying to look slightly out of breath.

"I suppose you haven't yet seen the package that I received today." Colombar wasn't looking at him, but was concentrating on the bright pink bulb in front of him.

"What package?"

Colombar gestured toward the back of the greenhouse with his shears. Perez looked at him strangely, then set off in the direction his boss had pointed. On a table in the back, next to a group of half-full sacks of fertilizer and soil, sat a box with a Federal Express sticker on the top. The tape had been torn off, but the flaps were closed. The odor continued to grow.

Perez reached out and pulled back the flaps. He gasped, the smell of the rotting head choking him. He pushed the flaps closed and stumbled backward, bumping into Colombar, who had crept up silently behind him.

"Read the card," he invited, pointing back to the box.

Perez swallowed hard, and moving forward, reopened the box. There was a blood-smeared envelope lying across the head's mouth. One yellow eye stared up at him as he snatched it and retreated to the other side of the greenhouse.

NEVER SEND A SPIC TO DO A MAN'S WORK, YOU DICKLESS FOOL.
SINCERELY,
JOHN

"I hoped that you might translate the note for me, Alejandro. As you know, my English is less than perfect."

Perez considered softening the language a bit, but thought better of it. Colombar's English was undoubtedly good enough to have read the note. The question was why Colombar wanted to hear it from his mouth?

He translated the note verbatim.

Colombar leaned against an empty table, motionless except for his right hand that twirled his shears ominously. "Do you know who that was?"

Perez answered quietly, trying to hide his nervousness. "I can only assume that it is one of the men that you sent after John Hobart."

"Our little plan didn't work very well, did it?" Colombar observed.

Our little plan?

Perez mopped the sweat from his forehead, thinking before answering. He decided against correcting his boss's faulty memory. "I guess not."

It seemed to be what Colombar wanted to hear. He turned and went back to working on the sick bulb. "I want you to go find this John Hobart. When you do, call me, and I will take care of the arrangements."

Perez winced. "Luis, this is just the reaction our Mr. Hobart was trying to provoke. We must inform the FBI. They are much better equipped to find him than I am. Especially now that he knows we're looking."

"No," Colombar replied calmly. "You'll go and find him. I want to hold this man's eyes in my hand."

Perez shuffled uncomfortably. He had seen Colombar in this mood only twice in the years he had known him. The cartel leader's levels of rage went from shouting in his practiced European Spanish, to screaming in the Spanish of his youth, to killing people with his bare hands, to dead calm. Dead calm was the worst. That's when he had someone pick you and your family up for a long, slow appointment with death.

"I'll leave immediately, Luis. Should we inform the others of this development?"

"No."

30

Near Baltimore, Maryland,
March 8

The Reverend Simon Blake watched his wife over his pool cue as she walked across the spacious basement. She was carrying a silver tray with a single mug on it.

"I was making hot chocolate for the kids and thought you might like some," she said, setting the mug on a long table behind a leather sofa.

Blake eyed her sadly, wondering how his actions would affect her. Things were out of control, and for the first time in his life, he wasn't sure what he was going to do. God's voice had been silenced.

"Thanks, honey," he said, missing the side pocket with the two ball.

"Are you having fun?"

The pool table had been a gift from her and the kids for his birthday. Erica had read somewhere that pool was an especially therapeutic and relaxing pastime. He could feel her eyes on him, and made an effort to look happier and more energetic than he felt.

"Sure am. I'm starting to get pretty good, too." The statement was accentuated with another miss. He was having trouble concentrating on anything these days.

She nodded, and padded silently out of the room. As he watched her go, he felt tears well up in his eyes.

His plan hadn't worked. In retrospect, it had been a stupid and desperate move. The man he had informed on was dead, as was his killer. And John Hobart was still a shadowy figure perched at the edge of every news report. Why hadn't he just told the FBI Hobart was behind it? He had asked himself that question a hundred times a day since Nelson's death. In the end, he discovered that the answer wasn't complicated. Fear. He had always been afraid of John Hobart—his cold demeanor, the eyes devoid of passion and morality. That twinge of fear had been a small price to pay to have Hobart's ruthless efficiency behind the workings of the church. But now control had shifted. Hobart was clearly in charge. Unhampered by Blake's values and religious sensibilities, he had no limitations.

Blake leaned his cue against the table and reached for the hot chocolate. Steam rose around the whipped cream piled on top. He sipped the hot fluid loudly, knowing he would regret it later. These past few months he had suffered from a constant sense of anxiety. It was an indescribable sensation—as if he was always on the verge of hyperventilating. As if something dreadful waited for him just around the next corner. Sugar and caffeine were definitely contraindicated.

He was nestled into the sofa, finishing his drink, when his cellular phone rang. It was always with him, used to transact business that his parishioners might not fully understand.

"Hello?"

"Hello, Reverend."

Blake's breath caught in his chest. Hobart.

"What can I do for you?"

"I know it was you."

"What are you talking about, John. I fired you months ago. What are you doing calling me at my home?"

He had devised this plan over the past week. There was no real evidence connecting him with the CDFS. He had never really been involved, beyond letting Hobart drain some insignificant dollars from the church's accounts.

There was silence on the other end of the phone. Blake waited anxiously to see if his plan had worked.

"If you want out, Reverend—fine. But you better stay out. If the Bureau gets another tip, I'm coming for your family."

Blake's jaw dropped.

"I'll make you watch while I cut them to pieces. And if I'm caught, I'll have someone else do it for me. Do you understand?"

Blake's mind churned uselessly, words not able to escape his throat. How could he have put his family in the middle of something like this?

"Do you understand?" Hobart's voice repeated. There was no hint of annoyance or threat in his voice. It was cold and matter-of-fact.

"Yes."

"That's good, Reverend. Good-bye."

The phone clicked, but Blake didn't move. When the dial tone started, he put the phone on the table next to him and wept.

Fifty miles away, John Hobart flipped on his computer. Things were going to have to be wound up pretty quickly. He still had the number to the church's computer, and the passwords necessary to access all of its accounts. It looked like he was going to have to get out of Dodge, but there was no reason to take off without a little extra pocket money.

"Reverend Blake? There's a man here to see you. He says it's urgent," Blake's secretary said quietly.

"Does he have an appointment?" Blake asked, peering at the calendar at the top of his desk. It was blank.

She stepped through the door and closed it quietly behind her. "No sir, but he's from the FBI."

Blake's expression didn't change. The adrenaline that had been coursing through him for the past two months had finally dried up. He didn't care what happened anymore. He just wanted release from the pressure.

"Please show him in."

"Reverend Blake, I'm sorry to disturb you without an appointment, but it is an urgent matter."

Blake took the agent's hand. It was cool and dry. "Don't think anything of it." He pointed toward the conference table in the corner of the office.

The FBI must be paying pretty well, Blake thought, watching the sheen of the man's expensive suit as he walked toward the table. The watch on his wrist looked like a Rolex.

"I am special agent Alejandro Martinez," the man said, flashing his credentials. His speech had more than a hint of accent. It reminded Blake of Ricardo Montalban in *Fantasy Island.*

"What can I do for you, Agent Martinez?"

"I believe that a man named John Hobart once worked for you. I'd be interested in any information that you could provide me on him. Especially in regards to his whereabouts."

The last of his adrenaline was squeezed out into his bloodstream at the mention of Hobart's name. "I really have no idea where he is, I haven't seen him in some time. Have you tried his home? I can get my secretary to get you the address."

"We've been by his home, yes. It would appear that he hasn't been there in quite a while." Martinez smiled engagingly. "And I already took the liberty of asking your secretary to copy Mr. Hobart's personnel file."

Blake shrugged noncommittally. "May I ask you why you're looking for John?"

"I apologize, but I am not at liberty to say," he answered gravely. "But it is a matter of the utmost importance, I assure you. I would also like to stress how important it is that you do not mention my visit here."

"Of course. Sorry I can't be of more help, but as you probably know, John's employment here was terminated a couple of months ago."

"Yes, we were aware of that." The agent pulled out a small notebook from his jacket pocket. "If you have a couple of minutes, I would like to ask you a few general questions about Mr. Hobart. Things that might make it easier for us to locate him."

Blake adjusted to a slightly more comfortable position in the chair.

"Sure, go ahead."

31

Washington, D.C.,
March 9

Mark Beamon nimbly sidestepped a young man with a box-filled handcart and walked through the door to SIOC.

The place was a mess. The conference table had been pushed against the wall, and a stack of large cardboard boxes had taken its place as the focal point of the room. Around the boxes were endless piles of car registrations, each with a copy of a driver's license attached with a paper clip.

Laura saw him come in and strode over with a wide grin. "We're just getting rid of some of the low priority stuff. It's getting hard to move in here."

Beamon nodded in agreement. "So you've got registrations to every red Cherokee in Maryland?"

"Actually, we have registrations for every Cherokee, period. Maryland doesn't put the color on the registration. Laura beamed. She was in her element now. As much as Beamon hated details, she loved them.

"How many?"

"Let's see . . ." She chewed the end of her pen

thoughtfully. "I think it ended up being almost seven thousand."

Beamon let out a long breath. Thank God she was here to sort through all this crap.

"So where are we?" he asked through a yawn.

"We started investigating our top thirty this morning."

The suspects were being prioritized by matching the pictures, height, and weight on the license with the descriptions obtained by eyewitnesses, and the rather vague drawing obtained from the costume store shopkeeper.

"Already?" Mark replied "Now how the hell did you manage to go through seven thousand documents that fast?"

"Only about fifteen hundred, actually. We started with the red ones."

"But you said that the color wasn't on the registration."

"It's not, but the VIN numbers have color information in them. We got Chrysler to cross-reference for us."

He bowed deeply at the waist, almost dropping his old trench coat. "As always, my dear, your efficiency leaves me speechless."

She smiled. "The thirty in process are over there if you want to take a look." She pointed to a blackboard that was covered with neat rows of driver's licenses. In the top right-hand corner of the board was the artist's sketch of their suspect.

"Why not? Let's grab a couple of cups of coffee and take a look."

Beamon looked ruefully at the nearly empty coffee

pot, and glanced back over his shoulder. "Who drank all the coffee and didn't make more?"

The agents in the room suddenly got busier, redoubling their efforts on whatever they were working on.

"So what have you been doing all morning?" Laura asked. It was almost ten o'clock.

Beamon made a face like he had just bitten into a lemon. "You know that senator whose son died from bad coke a couple of weeks ago?"

"James Mirth?"

Beamon nodded. "I just spent the morning with him. He wanted me to come by personally and tell him why I hadn't caught the people who murdered his son yet."

"Oh," Laura said sympathetically. "And how did that go?"

"Shitty. Now let's see what you've got." He headed for the blackboard, patting his pockets for his reading glasses. Tom Sherman gave him a wave from the corner of the room, where he was talking quietly into a phone.

"Here they are," Laura said, gesturing to thirty color copies of driver's license pictures taped onto the blackboard. Each had a name and brief description of the subject next to it. The description at this point consisted of little more than basic driver's license information. Finding his glasses, Beamon began inspecting each picture, starting at the top left. Somewhere into the fourth row, his face went blank for a moment.

"Son of a bitch!" he shouted loudly enough that Laura sloshed a good portion of her coffee on her blouse. "I know this asshole!"

Beamon ripped the picture off the blackboard and moved past Laura, who was walking in circles pulling her shirt in and out, trying to cool the dark stain spattered across her chest. He slapped the picture down on the conference table. "Christ, Laura, quit playing with yourself and come over here. This is him!"

The agents in the room suddenly finished the tasks that a moment ago were so important, and began crowding around him, looking at the picture that was now stuck in the middle of the conference table. Sherman hung up his phone and took a seat at the end of the table.

"I worked an investigation in Baltimore with this guy—must have been ten years ago," Beamon started. "He was working for DEA at the time. I was impressed with him at first—he was quiet, but really bright and insanely dedicated. So he's got this informant that he wants me to meet. I get there a little late and he's beat the shit out of him. Broke his arm. Lying son of a bitch almost got me thrown out of the Bureau."

He turned away from the table and went through a rather elaborate pantomime of a football player spiking a ball.

"Call up the guys investigating him. Tell 'em he's damned dangerous." He was grinning from ear to ear and seriously considering breaking into song.

"Sorry to ruin the mood, Mark," Sherman cut in, "but aren't you forgetting something?"

Beamon thought for a moment. "Let's see, find out the identity of the criminal, catch the criminal. Nope, I got it covered."

Sherman pointed to a phone anchored to one of the room's glass walls. "Call Calahan."

"Don't suppose you'd like to do it for me."

Sherman shook his head. "You did the work, Mark. Can't hurt for you to take the credit."

Beamon sighed and dialed the direct line to the Director's office. It was picked up on the first ring.

"Calahan."

"Mark Beamon, sir—I think we've identified our man. We believe he's an ex-DEA agent named John . . ."

"When can you pick him up?" came the Director's excited reply. He sounded like he was already planning his press conference.

"I don't really know, sir. We believe he's in the Baltimore area. Hell, we may just be able to pick him up at his house—but I doubt it. If he hasn't been seen there in a while, we'll have to assume that he's relocated somewhere else in the city. In that case, I figure we bring in a bunch of guys from New York and Philly to help out. With that kind of manpower, and assuming we're right about him still being in the Baltimore area, we should have him in a couple of weeks at the outside."

There was a long pause on the other end of the phone. "If he isn't at his house, bring the Baltimore Police in on this. They've got far more manpower than we can muster."

In the back of his mind, Beamon had known that the Director would make that suggestion. He had been hoping that the back of his mind would be wrong this time.

"I don't think that that's such a good idea right now.

I wouldn't want to do anything that could tip this guy off."

Beamon knew he was treading on thin ice here. The Director had been a street cop early in his career. It had only been for about a year, but he never let his subordinates forget that he had once "walked the beat."

"I've had it with this us-and-them attitude between the FBI and police." The volume of Calahan's voice had risen a notch.

Beamon interrupted before Calahan could get both feet firmly planted on his FBI/local police relations soapbox. "Sir, with all due respect to the Baltimore Police Department, I think we can count on the fact that a man like John Hobart is going to be keeping an eye on what's going on there."

Calahan was yelling now in that high-pitched whine that Beamon remembered so well. "If I want the Baltimore Police Force brought in on this, you'll goddam well bring them in on it."

Beamon tried to imitate the calm, humble tone Tom Sherman used when trying to placate the Director. "Sir, you agreed to let me head this investigation because of my experience and track record. Please, just let me do my job and I'll get this guy."

Calahan laughed bitterly. "Your experience and track record? My, we do have a high opinion of ourselves, don't we? I let Sherman bring you in on this because you're expendable. Don't ever kid yourself that it was anything more than that."

Beamon felt control slipping away from him. Thousands of people were dead, and Calahan was off on another one of his personal power trips. "Sir, I don't think that even you can be this fucking dense. Is there another agenda here that I'm not aware of?"

The room behind him went completely silent. For a moment, Beamon thought that the CNN commentator on the TV above him had even stopped talking. As he leaned back to check, Tom Sherman snatched the phone out of his hand.

"Sir, this is Tom Sherman."

Beamon noticed how effectively the plush carpet muffled his footsteps as he walked back to the conference table and fell into one of the chairs. The unintelligible high-pitched shouting coming over the phone was audible even over the sound of the television sets.

Everyone was still silent, and they were all now looking at him with faint smiles of admiration. Beamon figured that every one of them went to bed at night fantasizing about doing what he just did. He turned his attention back to Sherman as he replaced the receiver.

"Could you give us a few minutes, please?" Sherman said to the agents grouped at the other end of the room. As they filed quietly out, Beamon felt a pang of guilt. Sherman had blocked a number of vicious political blows meant for him over the years. He also knew that Sherman had put his reputation on the line in giving him this job.

"Not you, Laura," Sherman said, taking the seat across from Beamon. Laura sat down as far from them as the conference table would allow.

"What the hell are you doing, Mark? Couldn't you just finish the job and add another chapter in your legend? I could have turned this case into a real leg up for you."

"Bullshit, Tommy. It's not that I don't appreciate your effort, you know I do. But let's face it, my condition's terminal here. I never thought I'd say it, but I'm ready to put this case to bed and get back to my little life in Houston."

Sherman shook his head and let out a long sigh. "It's not your case to put to bed anymore. It's Laura's show now."

Both men turned toward her. She looked like she wanted to crawl under the table.

Beamon stood and stretched his arms wildly. "Well then, it looks like I've got a plane to catch."

"No you don't. You're staying on the team. Calahan seems to think that working for a woman might teach you a little humility."

Beamon resisted the urge to look over at Laura as he sat back down. She wasn't going to take that insult lightly. "I don't know, Tommy, has working for a moron taught you humility?"

Sherman stood and headed for the exit. "I don't care how you delegate the authority here, but I will tell you this. If we don't have this guy by tonight, get on the phone to the commissioner and get the police in on this. That's not a request."

Sherman stopped at the door. "Oh, and Laura. That woman comment came from Calahan, not from me. When Mark asked that you be brought in on this, he told me you were one of the best investigators in the Bureau. I haven't seen anything to suggest he's wrong."

* * *

"Nice job, Mark," Laura said after Sherman had pulled the door fully closed. "What were you thinking, talking to the Director like that?"

Beamon pushed violently on the table, rolling his chair back a couple of feet. "Why the hell shouldn't I? Calahan spends a few years as a judge and plays golf with a couple of political hacks, and that qualifies him to tell me how to run my investigation? It'd be funny if there weren't fucking twenty thousand people dead."

Laura moved to the chair that Sherman had vacated. "Okay, so Calahan's an idiot. That's no reason for you to push your personal self-destruct button. It's starting to get a little worn out, Mark."

"So am I."

Laura bounced her fist playfully against his knee. "Well, we better catch this guy and get you back to Houston before Calahan puts you in charge of the janitorial staff. What's the plan?"

"I'm thinking that we have to count on the general APB going out. Hobart's one smart son of a bitch. I can pretty much guarantee we won't get him by tonight."

"We'll have them announce the APB at roll call. At least we can keep it from going out over the radio."

Beamon nodded. "May I make a couple of suggestions?"

Laura smiled almost imperceptibly. "I don't think I've ever heard you suggest anything before. Maybe working for a little ol' girl is going to improve your social graces."

"Don't count on it."

"Believe me, I'm not. So what are your suggestions?"

"Well, if we find out that Hobart isn't living at his house—and I think we will—he must be living somewhere else, probably a rental. Get some guys to run down all the houses rented from around the time the neighbors said they stopped seeing him. They should be able to get a handle on that through the local realtors and old newspapers."

"Anything else?"

"Yeah. As soon as he hears that we're onto him, he's gonna have to get rid of his car—if he hasn't already. I want the car rental agencies around Baltimore faxing us copies of the driver's licenses of everyone who rents a car. We should probably try to get that going tomorrow."

Laura nodded as she scribbled on the legal pad in front of her. Finally she looked up. "So did you really say that about me?"

"What?"

"You know. About being one of the best investigators."

Beamon smiled. "Nah. Tom's a little senile—gets things confused. I've been covering for him for years."

Officer Larry McFee pulled his cruiser up behind another just like it on the crowded West Baltimore street. He turned on his lights and got out of the car, slipping his nightstick into his belt.

A small crowd had gathered and was milling around lazily in front of a crumbling row home. Domestic disputes were commonplace in this neighborhood, but could still be an interesting diversion. A brief respite from the boredom of the unusually hot March afternoon.

McFee pushed silently through the crowd. It offered token resistance, the people displaying their lack of respect for the law. He hated domestic disputes more than any other kind of bust. They were dangerous and generally pointless—charges were almost never pressed. All in all, one big waste of time.

The row home had been divided into four small apartments. The door to the apartment at the end of the hall on the right was wide open, and the shouting that had been muffled outside was now clear as a bell. He put his hand on his nightstick and walked quickly toward the noise.

He stood for a moment in the open doorway. A heavyset black male, approximately forty-five years of age, was brandishing a rolling pin threateningly. His bare chest was spattered with blood. Less than ten feet from him, a young cop was pointing a .38 at his head. The yelling was coming from the cop, as he urged the man to put down the rolling pin and lie down on the floor. McFee grimaced and scanned the rest of the room. Behind the sofa, a burly woman cop was helping a severely battered woman to her feet. Her face looked to be the source of the blood on the man's chest.

McFee shook his head, feeling a familiar hatred rising in him. A friend of his had been killed in a situation not unlike this one.

"So what the fuck's going on in here?"

The young cop shifted his eyes slightly to the right,

spotting McFee. A look of relief crossed his face. He nodded toward the man in the center of the room.

"He won't put down the rolling pin."

McFee grunted and pulled his nightstick from its place in his belt and began walking toward the man.

His eyes were glassy, and McFee noted that his body was swaying slightly.

When he got within striking distance, the man backed up half a step instead of swinging, just as McFee had expected. Fifteen years on the beat had taught him a few things about people.

McFee didn't make the same mistake. He jabbed the nightstick hard into the man's stomach, doubling him over with a loud rush of air from his lungs. He then brought the nightstick down hard across his back, dropping the man to the floor with a loud thud.

Breathing hard, McFee pulled out his cuffs, and closed them around the man's thick wrists. Behind him he heard the battered woman, who had presumably called them, go from whimpering to screaming and clawing at the cop holding her. Her partner rushed over to help.

McFee stood, hauled the dazed man to his feet, and began walking toward the door.

As he started down the steps with his prisoner, the noise from the bystanders increased. The crowd parted even more slowly than when he had arrived. He was almost to his car when he was hit hard from behind, almost knocking him off his feet.

The woman who had been half beaten to death by the man he now had in custody had apparently changed her mind about the arrest. She was now firmly attached to McFee's back, making every attempt to sink her teeth into his neck. He spun wildly, releasing his grip on his prisoner's arm, and managed to grab the woman's hair before she could get her teeth into him. The fear of AIDS was firmly planted in the mind of every cop who worked in the inner city. He slammed her hard into the side of the cruiser, and hearing the wind go out of her, managed to flip her over his head onto the sidewalk.

The crowd's volume had grown another notch, and they looked energized by the spectacle. McFee knew how important it was to regain control immediately, and he pulled his gun. The two young officers, now at the top of the stairs, followed his lead.

"Now, why doesn't everybody just calm down and go home," McFee suggested. No one moved. The two cops pushed their way toward him and handcuffed the woman writhing on the sidewalk.

McFee kept an eye on the crowd as he pushed the squabbling couple into the squad car. He walked back to his own unit and pulled into the street, watching the happy couple beginning once again to scream at each other in the back seat of the car in front of him. Something bounced off the trunk of his car. It sounded like a can.

Fucking niggers, he thought, pulling his car onto Pratt Street and heading east.

He glanced at his watch. Eleven forty-five.

When he reached Canton, he turned right and headed for the warehouse district. There was a dive pub on the water that served a cheesesteak, fries, and a Coke for four dollars. As he crossed Boston Street, a red Jeep Cherokee appeared in front of him.

At morning roll call, their Captain had told them to be

on the lookout for a similar vehicle and had given them the license number. He had gone on to say, to the amusement of everyone in the room, that the man's capture was a top priority but that he was extremely dangerous and that they were not to try to apprehend him without the FBI. An anonymous voice had spoken for everyone. "Oooh, that makes me feel a lot safer." Laughter had drowned out the rest of the Captain's speech. While he hadn't seen fit to tell them just who this desperado was, it had taken less than an hour for everyone to figure it out.

McFee shuffled through the papers on his passenger seat, finally finding the yellow Post-it note that he had jotted the license number down on. He glanced down at it and squinted through the glare of his dirty windshield.

The numbers matched.

He felt adrenaline surge through him. Taking a few deep breaths, he pulled within ten feet of the Jeep and flipped on his lights.

John Hobart had noticed the police car behind him the minute it pulled across Boston. He had checked his speed—he was going just under the thirty-five mile an hour limit—and continued to flick his eyes periodically to the rearview mirror. He swore quietly when the lights went on.

His hair had been dyed a sandy brown, and he was wearing a matching false mustache. It was the same disguise he had been wearing around Baltimore for two months now, but it didn't match his driver's license picture. And he didn't feel like explaining his change in appearance to some dumb-ass Baltimore street cop.

He eased the Cherokee to the side of the road, trying to figure out why he was being pulled over, finally deciding that it must be a brake light or something equally trivial. Even the widely heralded Mark Beamon couldn't have identified him that fast. And even if he had, he wouldn't send one lone cop to pick him up.

Hobart examined the police officer as he stepped from his cruiser and began walking toward his car. *Too slow*, he thought watching the man's gait. He also noticed the fact that his right hand wasn't swinging as he walked. It was being held unnaturally close to his gun.

That just wasn't normal. He was a middle-aged white male in an expensive automobile. This guy should be cool as a cucumber.

Shit.

He reached between the driver's seat and console and pulled out a .45. He slid the lever back and switched it to his left hand, where it would be out of sight. The cop was close enough now that he could see his nervous expression reflected in the Jeep's side mirror. His grip tightened around the gun as the cop came abreast of his open window and crouched down, bringing his face level with Hobart's.

"FBI's on to you Mr. Hobart. A lot of us are behind what you're doing."

With that, he stood and walked back to his cruiser. Hobart sat silently, watching the cop's stiff stride. He looked like he wasn't entirely sure if he was going to get a bullet in the back or not.

The cop slid back into his car. His engine roared loudly as he pulled into the street. Hobart sat and watched the car as it grew smaller and smaller, finally turning off onto a side street and disappearing into a landscape of mountainous piles of black coal.

32

Baltimore, Maryland, March 10

"Looks like he does okay," Mark Beamon commented as the elevator door slid open. The decor in the hallway that stretched before them was understated, but reeked of wealth. It didn't seem to reflect the man that they had come to see.

"Nice vase." Beamon stopped to admire it further. "My mom used to love this stuff. Had a house full of it when I was a kid."

"I don't think that one's in your price range," Laura said, continuing down the hall. They were already five minutes late for their appointment.

"Hello, can I help you?" the receptionist asked as they approached.

"Yes, I'm Laura Vilechi, and this is Mark Beamon. We're here to see Reverend Blake."

She nodded, appearing not to recognize Beamon's name. She looked like she was used to powerful people dropping by. "Go right in."

They walked through a beautifully etched glass doorway and into a large waiting area dominated by flowering trees. The air smelled fresh and sweet.

"Hello, I'm Terry, the Reverend's personal secretary. You can go right in. Can I get you some coffee or perhaps some tea?"

They politely declined.

"It's nice to meet you, Reverend," Laura said graciously, extending her hand. "I've seen your show." Beamon knew both statements to be lies.

"It's nice to see that our law enforcement officials know the Lord. I imagine it's difficult not to become cynical and hard—the things you must see." He turned to Beamon. "And you're Mark Beamon. I recognize you from your photos." They shook hands.

Beamon examined the Reverend carefully. Blake's expression was the serene mask required of men in his profession.

"Please sit down. So what can I do for you today?"

"We'd like to get some information on a former employee of yours. A John Hobart," Laura said.

Blake laced his fingers together and laid his hands on the table. He seemed to be deep in thought. "No, I can't think of a single thing that I haven't told you."

The two agents looked at each other, confused. Blake elaborated. "In my meeting with Agent ... Martinez, is it?"

"Let me get this straight," Beamon started slowly. "You've had an FBI agent in here recently asking about Hobart?"

"That's right. You didn't send him?"

"When did you meet with him?"

"Just yesterday, actually."

Laura broke in. "Could you describe him."

"Sure." He paused. "About thirty-five, I think. Very

well dressed. Slight Spanish accent. Not Hispanic—Spanish. I'd peg him as a European. He said his name was, uh, Alejandro I think. Alejandro Martinez."

Beamon shook his head, a thin smile on his lips. *The cartels are smarter than the whole goddam FBI.*

"Do you know where Mr. Hobart is?" Laura asked.

"No. As I told Mr. Martinez, he's probably at his house. I can have Terry pull his personnel file if you like."

"We'd appreciate it. "

Blake leaned back in his chair, looking around Laura. "Terry!"

She peeked in the door.

"Could you copy John Hobart's personnel file for me please." She disappeared without a word.

"Just a few more questions, Reverend," Beamon said. "We'll try not to take up too much of your time."

The questions took less than a half an hour but had still been a complete waste of time. Like Hobart's neighbors, Blake knew very little about his old employee. Personal interests, friends, hobbies. No one seemed to know the first thing about John Hobart.

"We really appreciate your time, Reverend. We know how busy you are." Beamon shook his hand. Laura was already out the door.

"Anytime, Mr. Beamon. I'm sorry I couldn't be of more help."

Beamon strode purposefully across the office. In the doorway he stopped and turned around.

"Oh, I almost forgot, Reverend."

"Yes?"

"Did this Martinez tell you why the FBI was looking for John?"

Blake's jaw clenched slightly. "No. No he didn't."

"Thanks, Reverend. It was nice meeting you." He hurried off to catch Laura, who was standing at the elevator, jabbing at the DOWN button.

Laura maneuvered the car through the thick traffic, leaning down over the steering wheel so that she could read the street signs hanging from the traffic light wires. She seemed to never be able to remember which street took them back to D.C.

"Oh, he's in on it all right." There was a note of happiness in her voice.

"Why?"

"Too cool. Not curious enough. Did you notice he didn't even ask why we were looking for Hobart? Besides, it would take some serious cash to get an operation like this off the ground."

"What if our mystery agent—Martinez—told him why we were looking?" Beamon tested.

"He still would have asked something about the case. Especially when we didn't know who Martinez was. I mean, come on. He's got the infamous Mark Beamon sitting in his office, and he doesn't even bring up the CDFS. Please."

"Yeah, you're probably right. It'll be hell to prove, though."

Laura flipped on the radio to a news station. It was playing the tail end of a report on the President diverting millions of dollars to drug rehab clinics and away from enforcement programs. Beamon ignored it. It was the same story they'd been running all morning.

"He really did it, though," she observed. There was

something in her voice that made Beamon a little uneasy.

"What?"

She looked over at him. "What do you mean, what? He's damn near killed the coke and heroin trade in the U.S. And the few people who are still using are trying to get help." She pointed to the radio to punctuate her remark. "How much have we spent over the last ten years—and never gotten close to what he's accomplished?"

"I'm embarrassed to say that I don't even know . . ."

Laura's voice softened a bit. "Yeah, me neither, but I'll bet it's a hell of a lot. Time and money that could have been spent better somewhere else."

It was something that he had been struggling with for months. The pro-CDFS arguments, hawked by the media for their sensational, audience-grabbing effect, rang true more often than he liked to admit.

The constant media coverage, with its thoughtful sound tracks and high-tech graphics, had been very effective in desensitizing the public to the carnage associated with the CDFS's actions. In his opinion, the coverage was more to blame for the public's increasing support of the CDFS than the DEA's leak of drug-use statistics.

And now the number of deaths had dropped dramatically. All that was left was fear. But when he captured Hobart, that fear would disappear. He would go back to Houston and the drug users and dealers would let out a collective sigh of relief. The lines at the rehab clinics would disappear, and twenty thousand people would have died for nothing.

There were only two things keeping his heart in the investigation, Beamon knew. The thought of his nephew rotting in the ground, and the fact that he couldn't bear letting John Hobart get the better of him again.

It was just barely enough.

His thoughts were interrupted by a breaking news story. Laura leaned forward and turned up the radio.

"We have a report that the FBI has put out a statewide APB in Maryland for John Hobart in connection with CDFS activity. He is described as a forty-year-old Caucasian male with short dark hair. He stands five foot eight and weighs approximately one hundred and fifty pounds."

Beamon reached to the dash and turned the radio off.

"Man, that was fast," Laura observed.

He just shook his head and dialed the cellular phone anchored to the floor. He put it on speaker.

"FBI."

"Carol? Hi, it's Mark."

"How are you, Mr. Beamon."

"Oh, you know. Could you patch me through to Tom Sherman?"

The phone went dead for a moment, then began ringing.

"Tom Sherman."

"Hey, Tommy, you watching the news?"

"Yup."

"Who won the pool?"

There was a pause and the sound of shuffling paper.

"Looks like Laura did. Six hundred and thirty-five dollars."

Beamon looked over at her and scowled. She flashed a wide smile and gave him the thumbs-up sign.

"Do we have that press release ready?"

"It went out an hour ago. Hobart's picture will be on every TV in the world in a few hours."

"And we've got our men in place."

"Yeah. A mouse couldn't get out of the country without our knowing it. The SAC's aren't too happy about it, though. We're draining off a lot of their manpower."

"Fuck 'em. Let 'em complain to the President if they don't like it. See you in an hour." He reached over and disconnected the phone.

"So you're sure he's going to skip the country?"

"Probably. Too many people looking for him here. And it's not just us, it's every drug dealer and addict, too. Europe's the way to go. Nobody's too mad at him there."

"Getting him at the airport's going to be tough. He'll spot our guys the minute he walks through the doors," Laura said.

Beamon shrugged. "I'm sure you're right. Hobart didn't get drummed out of the DEA 'cause he was stupid. He's not going to just waltz into an airport when he knows we've got guys crawling all over 'em."

He leaned the seat in the car all the way back. Staring up through the skylight, he pulled out a cigarette. "If I was in his position, what would I do?"

He didn't light the cigarette but just let it perch between his lips. Laura had made it clear that if he ever lit another one in the car, she'd put it out on his scalp. They remained silent for almost a half an hour. A few minutes from the J. Edgar Hoover Building, Beamon sat upright so fast that the seat belt caught, snapping him back. "Jesus, how much more stupid could I be?"

"What?" Laura asked anxiously.

"The question isn't what I would do in John Hobart's position. It's what would I do if I were John Hobart."

She failed to see the difference.

"That's the ball game," Robert Swenson said with a hint of relief in his voice. He and Hobart were sitting in his apartment above the warehouse that they had been using as a base of operations for the past two months. Both were intently watching the news report on the television in front of them. On the screen, a computer-generated image of Hobart's head was slowly rotating. After each full revolution, minor changes were made—hair, eye color, facial hair. They matched his elaborate makeup jobs surprisingly well.

"Looks like it," Hobart agreed. "I'll call our guys in the field and tell them it's time to pack it in."

"Where are you going to go?"

Hobart shrugged. "Don't know. Somewhere where I'm getting a little less press. Can you stick around for a day or two? I can't imagine they have anything on you—and I could use the help wrapping things up."

"They're looking for me, though. I doubt that they missed that I quit the church right after you did."

"Oh, they're looking all right. But what will they charge you with when they find you? Getting tired of your job?"

Swenson let that sink in for a moment. In the end, he decided that staying on would be less dangerous than leaving Hobart in the lurch. He knew better than to cross him. "Okay. I'll stick around and help you wrap things up—then I'm out of here."

"Good. Why don't you call our people and tell them to go home. I'll figure out a way to get rid of the orellanin."

"That ought to be a trick."

They were both driving rentals now, having dumped their cars in a manufacturing plant's expansive parking lot. Swenson was trying to picture how Hobart would get the large metal storage drum into the trunk of a Subaru.

"I'll figure something out," Hobart said, rising. "With a little luck, we'll be out of here tomorrow."

Those were the words that Swenson had been waiting to hear. It seemed they'd been at this for years. He turned back to the television and watched Hobart's disembodied head spin slowly around. It was somehow entrancing.

Less than two miles away, Alejandro Perez was watching the same program while he carefully tucked his clothes back into his suitcase. Luis wasn't going to be happy, but he would just have to take it like a man. With Hobart's identity public, the chances of finding him before the FBI were a million to one.

He pressed hard on the top of the suitcase and latched it. His first-class flight to Bogotá left in an hour, and at this time of evening, the traffic was unpredictable. He didn't want to be stuck in Baltimore for another night.

* * *

The Reverend Simon Blake took another pull from the vodka bottle and went into an inevitable coughing fit. He had once experimented with alcohol as a college freshman, and it was an episode that he didn't look fondly back on. Since then—almost twenty years—he hadn't touched a drop. Until today.

He laughed bitterly when his throat loosened enough to allow it. Quite a pickle he had managed to get himself into. He thought back to his meeting with John Hobart, how sure he had been that they were on the righteous path. How he was going to single-handedly bring America back on track. He laughed again and took another pull. The alcohol in his empty stomach felt like the fire of hell.

Events had conspired against him in the last few days. His clumsy attempt to put an end to the CDFS through snitching on Nelson had backfired. Now Hobart's face was plastered across every TV in America. Blake could hear the threats Hobart had made against his family as clearly as if the phone were still pressed to his ear. Threats he knew that his ex–security chief was fully capable of carrying out.

And then there was Mark Beamon—who Blake was convinced knew of his involvement. Finally, there were the countless thousands dead because of him.

Blake put the bottle down on the floor next to him and listened to the silence reigning in the house. He had sent his wife and children away for a few days. Erica had been needing to see her mother for some time.

He closed his eyes and reflected on the brief

moments in life that so easily turned into milestones. His agreement to finance Hobart's eradication of narcotics. His forgetting to ask Mark Beamon why they were looking for Hobart when he'd been so careful to ask Martinez. His call to the FBI about the DiPrizzio episode. All in all, these three events made up less than twenty seconds of his long life. But those seconds would define him, and overshadow everything he had built.

He reached for the phone and dialed 911.

"Hello," he said into the mouthpiece when the police operator answered. "I heard gunshots at the Reverend Simon Blake's home." He could hear the operator asking for details as he let the receiver fall between his chair and the table next to it. He picked up the revolver sitting on the floor next to the nearly empty fifth of vodka and put the barrel in his mouth. The taste of steel almost gagged him. "I love you, Mary," he slurred over the barrel.

The good thing about having your picture all over the TV is that you know what not to look like.

Hobart tossed his backpack on the bench next to him and watched a tugboat struggling into its slip. Pigeons flapped around his feet, waiting to be fed.

His hair was long and blond, the color that suggests years of surfing in Hawaii, or birth in Southern California. A large earring dangled from his left ear— he'd pierced it himself only an hour ago. Torn canvas pants, a turtleneck, and a brightly colored vest completed the effect. He nodded a silent greeting as a group of skateboarders strolled by. Normally they wouldn't have given him a second look, but they seemed to identify with Hobart's new image, and returned his greeting.

Satisfied that he was drawing no attention whatsoever, Hobart grabbed the army surplus knapsack next to him and headed for a pay phone perched on the side of the ice cream shop across the street. He shoved a quarter in the slot and dialed the warehouse.

"Clipper City Antiques and Oddities." Swenson's voice.

"Could you do me a favor, Bob?"

"Sure, what do you need?"

"Look something up on the computer for me."

The skateboarders began to do tricks on the steps of the large brick square in front of him. He watched with mild interest, listening to his partner walking and finally sitting down.

"How many times have I told you that you don't have to turn the computer off every time you leave, John. It's got a screen saver. You're gonna have to wait till it warms up."

"No problem."

A skateboarder took a hard fall into a steel railing. His friends laughed.

Being almost a mile from the warehouse, Hobart hadn't expected the explosion to be quite so loud. The skateboarders ducked involuntarily, then straightened up and looked around with confused expressions. Everyone else on the street did the same. Cars stopped, drivers leaned out their windows.

Hobart replaced the receiver and strolled casually to his rental car. Once inside, he retrieved a small chess board from the pocket in the passenger side door. The board had been designed for travel, and the pieces had been replaced by small magnetic discs that allowed the player to fold the board up midgame and continue later. The position of the pieces matched the board that until a few minutes ago had rested next to his television. Hobart pulled the white queen—Robert Swenson—off the board and threw it on the floor of the car.

The driver of the car behind him was still looking around, trying to figure out what had happened. Hobart gave a short honk on the horn and began backing out onto the cobblestone street.

Hobart had planned on shutting down the CDFS before his identity was discovered. That had been plan A. Mark Beamon's artful meddling had forced him to switch to plan B.

He had been careful in diverting the funds from Blake's accounts, but he wasn't so conceited as to believe he was smart enough to fool the army of CPAs the Bureau would throw at the church's books. At least he hoped he wasn't. He had used Robert Swenson's terminal number and password.

He slowed slightly as he passed within a few blocks of the warehouse. Smoke curled into the steel gray sky. The wailing of sirens echoed through the narrow streets.

Beamon was clever—he had to admit that. But what did the Bureau actually have on him? Sure, they could prove that he knew both Nelson and Karns, but so what? He could produce at least four other DEA agents who had also been acquainted with the two men. And with his death, Swenson had gone from partner to reasonable doubt. Dead men could be very useful that way.

Hobart eased the Subaru onto I95 North, careful to constantly monitor his speed. The Jeep protested at speeds much over sixty-five, but this one could get him in trouble.

Hobart was almost halfway to his destination when a police car passed him going south. He followed it in his side mirror. It was almost out of sight when it slowed abruptly and bounced across the grass. He switched to the rearview mirror and watched it overtake him. Three cars back it slowed and matched his speed.

Coincidence?

He pulled into the right lane and touched his brakes. The cars behind him began to pass by. The cruiser stayed in the left lane, but again matched his speed, staying about fifty yards behind. Hobart checked his speed. Sixty mph. Cars were beginning to pile up behind the squad car, afraid to pass.

They continued like that for almost five miles, with no cars between them. Hobart spotted another state police car driving too slowly on the overpass ahead of him. This one was unmarked, but its ugly brown color and bristling antennae announced it just as loudly. He shifted his rearview mirror so that he could see the top of the overpass as he came out from under it. The car gained speed and turned sharply onto the on-ramp. It fell in about twenty-five yards behind the black and white.

Goddam Mark Beamon, Hobart thought, slamming his

hands into the steering wheel. *He must have the cops chasing every fucking rental car in Maryland.*

To his right, Hobart saw the enormous structure of White Marsh Mall and the brightly colored IKEA store that shared its parking lot. He flipped on his blinker, and eased the car onto the off-ramp, keeping one eye on the squad car behind him. The driver slowed slightly, then regained his speed, trying to decide what to do.

As soon as he was around the corner and out of sight of the trailing cars, he slammed his foot to the floor. The Subaru jumped satisfyingly as he accelerated into the gently bending road, tires protesting with a low, constant scream. As he curved left through a stand of trees, he caught a glimpse of the two police cars speeding toward him.

He slammed on the brakes and skidded into the vast parking lot of the shopping complex. Pulling into oncoming traffic, he took his first left and sped toward one of the many entrances to the mall. He skidded to a stop in front of the bank of glass doors, and, leaving the car running, walked briskly into the building. Once through the doors, he looked back. The people behind him looked interested, but not enough to follow.

He worked his way into the crowd, turning abruptly onto a down escalator, and bumping hard into a woman with an armful of bags. She didn't drop them, but gave him a dirty look anyway. At the bottom of the escalator, he hurried for the nearest exit.

He burst out the doors, and walked purposefully toward a white Mercedes illegally parked in front of

him. Inside, a bored-looking woman examined her fin-
gernails over the steering wheel. He grabbed the handle of the passenger door and jumped in.

"Sorry I'm late, hon, let's go," he said to the woman,
pushing the barrel of his .45 into her ribs. A look of
terror spread across her face. She froze.

"Smile and press the accelerator or I'm going to kill
you." His tone and message woke her from her trance
and she pulled out into the parking lot.

"Very good. Now just take it easy, and get us going
south on 95."

"What do you want?" she stammered.

"I just want to get back to Baltimore, that's all."

She pulled out onto the freeway, her knuckles white
against the steering wheel. Hobart settled back into
the soft leather seat and flipped on the radio. The
announcer was talking about him. He flipped it off,
and began going through the woman's purse.

"I have money—credit cards, too—take it all," she
begged.

He laughed. "Thanks, but you can keep them. He
pulled out a worn leather wallet held together with a
rubber band. Pulling the rubber band off, he began
going through it.

"Your kids?" he asked, holding up a picture of two
blond boys of early grade school age. She nodded. A
tear was running down her cheek. He pulled the picture out of the wallet and dropped it and her driver's
license onto his lap. He picked up the cellular phone
nestled between the seats. "You mind? It's a local
call."

He dialed the number of the warehouse, getting a

recording that the number was temporarily out of service.

"Charley? It's me. I'm in a car with one Carol Lundan. That's spelled L-U-N-D-A-N. She lives at 506 Pullman Street. Yeah. She's got two kids—look to be six and eight. Blond. If I don't make it back tonight I want you to kill 'em all. Got that? No, 'Lundan' with an 'A.' Yeah. Okay."

Hobart hopped out of the car near Baltimore's Inner Harbor, studying Carol Lundan's face as he slammed the door shut. She wouldn't say a word. Probably not even to her husband. The terror etched across her face was as good a guarantee as a bullet in her head.

33

Baltimore, Maryland,
March 11

John Hobart pulled his new rental car into a nearly empty public parking lot and climbed out. He glanced briefly at his watch as he locked the door, calculating that he had at least two hours before the FBI sent word to start looking for the car. In fact, he probably had much more time than that, but where Mark Beamon was concerned, it didn't pay to take chances.

He jogged across the quiet street and began walking along the storefronts. Many were vacant, their large front windows cracked and duct-taped. Street numbers weren't plentiful, either. He glanced down at the section of Yellow Pages in his hand and stuffed it back into his pocket. He probably should have just gone back to the same store. Despite his elaborate disguise, he was feeling exposed on the empty sidewalk.

There was no sign on the shop, but the mannequins in the window were dressed in outrageous wigs and period costumes. A flyer taped to the door announced that it was Scarlett O'Hara week—whatever that was.

The bells on the door chimed as he opened it, and the man sitting behind the counter tossed his magazine on the floor and jumped up.

"Can I help you?" he asked, sounding elated to have a customer.

"I think you can," Hobart replied, flipping the dead bolt on the door.

"Uh, we're still open . . ."

Hobart pulled his gun from the knapsack slung over his right shoulder. "This'll only take a little while."

The man started to raise his hands but Hobart discouraged it.

"It's been a slow day," the shopkeeper explained as Hobart marched him into the back room. "There's not much cash in the register, but you're welcome to it. I've got a few bucks in my wallet, too."

Hobart grimaced. It was the second time in as many hours that he had been mistaken for a common thief.

The back room of the shop was piled high with costumes in no apparent order. One of the walls was completely covered with floor-to-ceiling mirrors. On the far side of the room sat an old makeup table. Two halogen desk lamps looked out of place on its weathered wooden top.

"Turn around," Hobart ordered, pulling off his wig. "I want to leave here a woman."

He almost laughed out loud at the absurdity of his statement. His plan to solve America's most devastating problem had fallen apart. And now, not only was he being forced to flee the country that had been his home for his entire life, he was being forced to do it in drag. Goddam Mark Beamon.

The shopkeeper looked at him blankly. Hobart raised the gun again and made a move toward him. The implied threat had the desired effect, and he began milling around the room, grabbing clothes, makeup, wigs, and elaborate-looking pads. Every few moments, he would look back thoughtfully, sizing up his customer.

It may not be the most dignified way to get out of the country, Hobart thought, but it seemed the safest. The FBI had sewn up the airports tight, but were looking for a Caucasian male. His friend in the forgery business could have him a fake passport and driver's license in an hour. With a little luck, he would be on a plane tonight.

"If you could just come out here for a moment where the light's better."

Hobart stepped back out into the front of the store and allowed the shopkeeper to walk slowly around him.

He was surprised when he felt a strong hand wrap tightly around his wrist.

Christ—a fucking hero.

He raised his free arm, preparing to slam his elbow into the man's head, when he felt the unmistakable coldness of the barrel of a gun on the back of his neck.

"FBI, Mr. Hobart. You're under arrest." The nervousness had drained from the shopkeeper's voice. In front of him, another man walked slowly from the bathroom, holding a lighter to a cigarette.

"Yeah, I liked this store best, too, John," Mark

Beamon said, taking a drag on the cigarette. "Quiet part of town. Lots of empty storefronts."

Hobart relaxed and dropped the gun. He allowed himself to be pushed face down on the floor and his arms to be pulled painfully behind his back. From his position on the floor he could only see to Beamon's knees.

It took a full two seconds for Hobart's mind to process what had happened.

The young agent, who a moment before had been pushing a pair of handcuffs to his wrists, was lying face down on the dirty shop floor next to a blackened mannequin. Both man and model bristled with countless shards of glass, brick, and wood.

Hobart scanned the room, finally spotting Mark Beamon through the quickly dispersing smoke and swirling dust. Beamon was struggling to sit up, apparently oblivious to the bullets flying overhead. He looked a little groggy, but hadn't sustained any obvious injuries. The brunt of the blast had been taken by his partner.

Hobart rolled carefully onto his back, ignoring the sharp debris beneath him. Most of the front of the store was gone. There was no sign of the large picture window that a few moments before had displayed the shop's costumes, except on the floor around him. What was left of the window's wood frame was burning.

The ringing in Hobart's ears was beginning to subside as he rolled back onto his stomach and began slithering toward a sturdy-looking island of cabinets in the center of the room. He kept his chin close to the floor, lifting his eyes occasionally to watch reddish explosions erupt from the back wall as bullets slammed into the old brick. At least one per second he estimated—standing and making a break for it wasn't an option.

Beamon was on his stomach now, moving across the room toward his partner, the human pin cushion. He passed within a few feet of Hobart, still too dazed to realize the young agent was dead.

Hobart stopped for a moment, laying his cheek on the floor and watching Beamon struggle across the room. He remained motionless for a few moments, waiting for a bullet to catch Beamon in his ample side and flip him over.

He sighed quietly when Beamon began splashing through the puddle of blood that was starting to flow across the uneven floor, finally reaching the man and beginning a futile search for a pulse on what was left of his neck. Hobart started back for the cabinets, astounded at Beamon's charmed existence.

It seemed to take forever, but Hobart finally managed to slip behind the island. Remaining on his back for a moment, he examined the cabinets carefully. When he was satisfied that no bullets were penetrating, he sat up and cradled the gun that he had found on the trip across the floor. It was a .45 automatic, not unlike the one he usually carried. He pulled the lever back and examined it for damage and debris. It looked good.

Mark Beamon's faculties were beginning to return

to him as he reached his partner, though he wasn't entirely grateful. If there was ever a situation where ignorance was bliss, this was it. The front of the store was missing, and it seemed as if half the population of North Baltimore had picked up machine guns and were now busying themselves trying to knock a similar hole in the back of the building. And to make matters worse, Bobby had definitely seen better days. The young agent's unblinking eyes had gone a pinkish white from blood and the thick dust in the building.

Number thirty-five.

In less than a second, he'd gone from husband and father to the thirty-fifth name on the plaque commemorating agents killed in the line of duty. Bad trade.

Beamon turned and began crawling toward the heavy group of cabinets in the middle of the room. He put the image of his partner's broken body out of his mind and began dealing with the problem at hand. Who the fuck had blown off the front of the building—and more important, who was shooting? And another interesting question—where was Hobart?

As Beamon came around the corner of the island, he felt a pistol barrel press against his cheek. Question number three answered.

He pushed himself into a sitting position and pressed his back against the cabinets. The gun barrel stayed with him.

"I saw a wet spot on the floor back there. I was hoping it was you," Beamon shouted over the gunfire and the ringing in his ears.

Hobart shook his head "Thanks to you, I had the best seat in the house when the front blew."

Beamon sighed and slumped further against the cabinets, reminded of the corpse in the middle of the room. He reached into the breast pocket of his suit, ignoring the increased pressure of the gun barrel on his cheek, and pulled out a small cellular phone.

"Do you mind?" he said pushing the pistol away from his face. "We can settle our differences later."

Hobart looked at him suspiciously for a moment and then lowered the gun.

Beamon flipped open the cell phone and dialed Laura, who was coordinating the SWAT team that was supposedly backing him up. She picked up on the first ring.

"Laura! Guess who? Why are you letting people shoot at me?"

The answer was unintelligible.

"You're gonna have to speak up, hon. I can't hear too well," Beamon yelled, pressing the phone to his right ear until it hurt, and sticking a finger in his left one.

"Mark! Are you okay? Most of the front of the building's gone!"

"Yeah, I'm fine, but that's not gonna last."

"We've got twenty or thirty mostly Hispanic males out here, Mark. They're armed to the teeth. Looks like at least one of them's got a grenade launcher."

Beamon looked over at Hobart, who was trying to get a glimpse of what was happening out front. "My male ego wouldn't be bruised if you were to come in here and rescue me."

"I'm sorry, Mark, but there's no way I can approach your position—it's too wide open. The good news is that our Hispanic friends can't, either. Looks like they're planning to just stay put and wait to get lucky."

Beamon watched a particularly large chunk of the cabinet island that they were hiding behind fly over his head and bounce off the brick wall in front of him. "At the rate my cover is disintegrating, they're gonna get lucky sooner rather than later, Laura. I'm open to suggestions."

"They probably have orders to see John Hobart dead. If you can, toss his body out where they can see it—they'll probably take off."

Beamon scowled. "Easier said than done. Is the alley in back of the building clear?"

"Last time I heard."

"You're a real confidence builder."

Beamon flipped the phone shut and stuffed it back into his jacket. "It seems that there are some South American gentlemen out there who'd like to speak with you."

Hobart pulled back against the cabinets. "Can't really see anything. Doesn't look like anyone's on the street, though." He looked up. "What do you think about a truce until we get out of here?"

Beamon chewed his lip. He had been about to suggest the same thing. John Hobart was a sadistic sociopath—of that there was no doubt. But, while you wouldn't want someone with those failings to marry your daughter, they weren't bad allies in a gunfight. Beamon nodded almost imperceptibly. "Truce."

Hobart seemed satisfied with that, and popped the clip out of his gun for one last inspection. "You got any ideas, Mark?"

"Going out the front ain't gonna happen."

Beamon motioned with his head to the archway that led to the back of the store. It was fifteen long feet away.

"If we can make it through there, there's a back door that opens out onto an alley."

Hobart nodded slowly. "If they've got guys on the roof, we won't last very long in an alley."

Beamon shrugged. "We won't last long here."

Hobart considered this for a moment, a thin smile spreading across his face. "You first."

Reluctantly, Beamon rose to a crouched position and backed far enough away from the edge of the cabinets to give himself room to build up some speed before leaving his cover. Hobart edged to the other side. "On three, Mark. One. Two. Three."

As he sprinted toward the back room, Beamon heard Hobart's gun begin to fire.

He landed rolling, finally coming to a stop when he hit a mannequin dressed like a turn-of-the-century Southern belle. It took him a few seconds of thrashing to untangle himself from the elaborate hoop skirt.

He walked back to the archway and pressed himself against the wall. Hobart was already up and crouched, ready to spring.

Beamon held up his hand and extended his index finger. One. He put up his middle finger. Two. Ring finger. Three.

As Hobart shot across the room, Beamon fired through the gaping hole that used to be the front of the building, deliberately aiming low to prevent injuring any of his own men. Hobart moved like lightning, making it through the archway in half the time it had taken Beamon. He also had managed to stay on his feet and come to a graceful stop at the back door.

"You first this time," Beamon said, taking a position to the right of the door. Hobart gave a short nod, grabbed the knob, and threw the door open.

Beamon tensed and pressed himself harder against the wall, expecting a flurry of bullets to come bursting into the room. Nothing. He peered out into the alley as Hobart moved silently through the doorway. It was empty except for a cat lying in the middle of a discarded toilet lid. The animal looked at them through bored, city-bred eyes, oblivious to the sound of gunfire echoing eerily off the weathered brick walls of the alley.

Hobart signaled "all clear" and began running lightly through the puddle-strewn alley. Beamon loped after him.

They broke out onto a wider, though equally deserted, road, crossing it quickly and slipping into another narrow back street.

They crossed three more streets that way, putting a reasonable distance between them and what Beamon guessed was a group of Luis Colombar's attack dogs. Despite their slow, careful pace, Beamon felt as though his heart was going to dislodge itself from his chest and skitter off to find a more sedentary home. The image was almost enough to make him laugh.

Hobart, who was about twenty-five yards ahead, slowed to a walk and then turned. Beamon stopped short, keeping the distance between them.

"Sounds like your boys are cleaning things up,

Mark," Hobart said in a conversational tone. The acoustics of the alley made it sound like he was only a few feet away.

Beamon cocked his head to the side, listening intently. He hadn't noticed that the gunfire had slowed almost to nonexistence. It sounded like microwave popcorn right before you pulled the bag out of the oven.

"Looks like our truce is about over," Hobart said.

Beamon slowly brought his gun to waist level and stuffed it in the front of his pants. He hoped that the nonaggressive gesture would keep things from getting out of hand until he had time to think the situation through.

"Looks that way."

He pulled a cigarette from a pack in his jacket and lit it, surprised that his hands didn't shake. "Why'd you do it, John?"

"Why do you think?" Hobart said, following Beamon's lead and stuffing his .45 in his belt.

Beamon relaxed a little. "God and country?"

Hobart laughed. "No, I guess I just wanted to see if I could."

Beamon exhaled, watching the slight breeze dissolve the cigarette smoke.

"So how do you want to play it, Mark?"

"I guess I'd like you to throw that pistol on the ground and put your hands on top of your head."

Hobart shook his head. "I don't think so. Tell you what. Why don't you just turn around and walk away. No one would blame you for letting me get away, with all that shit going on."

Beamon took another drag from his cigarette. "I'd blame myself."

Hobart shook his head again, looking at the ground. "Then I'll ask you again. How do you want to play it?"

Beamon looked around him. The alley was only about ten feet across—barely wide enough to drive a car through. There were a few windows in the brick buildings that lined the little street, but they were all at least six feet off the ground and covered with chicken wire. A Dumpster overflowed with boxes of rotting vegetables eight feet in front of him and three feet to the side.

There weren't a hell of a lot of choices. A running gunfight was out of the question—too athletic. Hobart moved with the speed and grace of a college track star and he didn't even look winded from their cross-town run. Beamon's knees felt like they were full of gravel, and his heart was still considering vacating his chest cavity.

The Dumpster was interesting. He could dive behind it, leaving Hobart out in the open. But what would be the point of that? Hobart was only about thirty feet from the mouth of the alley and would be long gone by the time Beamon finished pulling the lettuce out of his ears.

That didn't leave much.

Beamon dropped his cigarette on the ground and crushed it with the toe of his shoe. Hobart was standing with his arms hanging loosely at his sides. Beamon hoped he didn't feel as relaxed as he looked.

"If you won't surrender, I guess we'll just have to end it now."

The bend in Hobart's arm tightened slightly, bringing his right hand an inch closer to his pistol. "Come on, Mark, why do this? Look at you."

Beamon glanced down at his protruding stomach and then to his yellowed fingertips. Finally he looked back up at Hobart. "I remember you being a real trick shot with a rifle, John. But handguns were always more my territory."

"I've been practicing."

Beamon hoped to hell that wasn't true. "One more chance, John."

Hobart stared back at him. His eyes were as lifeless as glass. Windows to his soul.

Hobart was the first to move, bringing his hand up in a lightning-quick motion. Beamon's breath caught as he grabbed for his own gun. He was slower, as he knew he would be, and he saw the flash of Hobart's pistol a split second before he himself fired.

Beamon felt a flare of pain in his chest and then numbness as he watched Hobart jerk backwards and fall onto his back.

Beamon dropped his gun and desperately clawed open his shirt to examine what he had already decided was a fatal wound.

Nothing. Not a scratch. He marveled at the power of the human mind to play tricks as he quickly bent to retrieve his gun.

Hobart was still alive, though most of the flesh between his right pectoral and shoulder was missing.

"Let go of the gun, John," Beamon shouted as he slowly advanced. Hobart was still clinging loosely to the .45, though he didn't look like he had the strength to pull the back of his hand off the pavement. He rocked his head toward Beamon, causing a thin line of blood to flow from his mouth and make swirling patterns in the puddle he was lying in.

He shook his head weakly and began to slowly raise his gun hand.

Beamon stopped short and aimed his .357 directly at Hobart's heart. "Stop it, John. That wound doesn't look fatal. Let me get you to a hospital."

"Won't need one," Hobart croaked.

Beamon estimated that he had two more seconds before it was aimed directly at his chest."

"Drop the fucking gun, John."

There was no more time. Beamon squeezed the trigger and watched his gun and John Hobart buck simultaneously. Hobart's hand dropped back to the cobblestones, still clutching the pistol.

"Mark! Jesus, are you all right?"

Beamon continued unsteadily up the middle of the street, his gun dangling from his hand. Laura ran up to him and threw an arm around his shoulders. "Come over here and sit down."

She led him to the sidewalk and sat him down against the wall of an empty auto parts building.

"What happened, Mark. Where's Hobart?" she asked, crouching down beside him.

"Dead."

"Did the blast get him?"

"Nope. I did."

Beamon tilted his face toward the sky as a light mist

started. He still couldn't believe he was going to walk away from this. "So what's the situation?"

Laura sat down next to him. "Looks like we got almost all of them. A couple probably slipped through the cracks—took off when the tide started to turn."

"Any casualties on our side?"

"Bobby didn't make it. You probably know that."

Beamon nodded.

"Other than that, we had a guy catch some shrapnel in his leg—nothing serious. Oh, and another guy ran through a glass door. Broken nose and a few cuts. Overall, we were lucky."

Beamon looked over at her. She was wearing fatigues, a bullet-proof vest and a metal helmet with a face shield. He began to laugh.

"What's so funny?"

Beamon patted her on the knee. "I'm sorry. It's just that you look ridiculous."

Laura grabbed his hand and slapped it back down on his thigh.

"I'm sorry Laura, I can't help it," Beamon said, trying to stifle his laughter.

She stood up and put her hands on her hips, starting him laughing even louder. Her boots almost reached her knees.

"You know, I don't have to take this, Mark. You work for me."

Alejandro Perez squeezed himself through the window and onto the roof of the abandoned North Baltimore row home. The distant sound of gunfire had nearly stopped, reduced to an occasional pop carried by the cold wind.

Perez pulled a pair of compact binoculars out of his breast pocket and peered down the street toward the billowing smoke that he knew was coming from what was left of Samuel's Theatrical Supply. He sighed quietly as he watched a body-armored FBI man drag the corpse of one of Luis Colombar's enforcers to a lengthening line of similar bodies lying motionless in the middle of the street.

Perez had been on his way to the airport when the call had come. Colombar had managed to discover where and when the FBI would attempt to apprehend Hobart and was sending a hit team on the next flight to Baltimore. Perez was to meet them at the airport and wait with them until the appointed hour.

It had been another serious error in judgment. Colombar had indebted himself to two very powerful and very ruthless men in order to get the likely location of Hobart's capture. And for what? To kill a man who could have been taken so much more easily in jail. Perez could not even confirm that Hobart had been killed, though it seemed unlikely that he would have survived a blast that had been powerful enough to rip the front off the store.

Frustrated, Perez slipped the binoculars back in his jacket and turned to the open window he had come through. He would wait to confirm Hobart's death before getting on a plane back to Colombia. If Hobart had survived, it might be wise to wait a few days before leaving. Give Colombar some time to cool off.

34

Houston, Texas,
March 15

"Can't tell you how happy I am to be back," Beamon said.

Laura Vilechi grunted from behind a smoking grill. When Mark had invited her to barbecue by the pool she hadn't actually thought she would be doing the cooking herself.

Beamon was flopped over a lawn chair that looked too small for him, sipping a drink with an umbrella in it. It was a Scotch, but he had decided when he'd pulled the tarp off the pool that everyone should have an umbrella, no matter what they were drinking. It had taken no small effort on Laura's part to convince him that it was impossible to drink a beer with an umbrella stuck in the neck of the bottle.

"How're those steaks coming—I'd like mine bloody. Really, really rare."

"You'll get it the way I make it."

Beamon jumped out of his chair as the sound of the doorbell floated out to the pool. "I'll get it."

Laura watched him disappear through the sliding glass door and turned the grill up on his steak.

Beamon reappeared in less than a minute with a package under his arm. "UPS guy."

"What'd you get?"

"Dunno." He tore open the box and pulled out a beautiful gray pinstripe suit. Laura came from around the grill, wiping her hands on her apron.

"Nice," she commented, opening the jacket and looking at the label. "Hugo Boss? Geez, this is probably a three-thousand-dollar suit."

Beamon took her word for it and shuffled through the tissue paper, finally finding a small envelope. He pulled out the card. The message was written in a flowery but masculine scrawl.

> *Please accept this as a small token of my gratitude. Have your tailor bill me for any alterations.*
>
> *Anthony DiPrizzio*

Beamon laughed until tears streamed down his face.

"What is it? Who's it from?" Laura asked.

Beamon handed her the note. "A gift from Anthony DiPrizzio. Thanking me for putting him back in business." Saying it out loud got him chuckling again. "They should put this one in the dictionary as the definition of irony."

Laura frowned, apparently not fully appreciating the humor.

"Don't be mad, Laura. I'm sure your gift's on its way."

Beamon picked up the phone sitting next to him and hit the speed dialer for the JEH Building. "Tommy's gonna love this."

"Tom Sherman, please," he said to an unfamiliar operator. Sherman's secretary picked up. "Hey, darlin'. Is Tommy around?"

"Hi Mark. No, I think he's in his car. Let me patch you through." There was an audible click and pause, then Sherman picked up.

"Hey Tommy! I got a story you're gonna love. DiPrizzio just sent me a three-thousand-dollar suit as a gift for putting him back in business! He'll probably start paying his taxes if we keep helping him out like this."

There was silence on the other end of the phone.

"You still there?" Beamon asked, shaking the phone.

"Yeah. Sorry, Mark. I just got some bad news."

Beamon stood and walked over to the pool, sitting down and dangling his legs in the cool water. "What?"

"We've just gotten reports of narcotics poisonings in San Francisco and Atlanta."

"Bullshit! Hobart's organization's going on without him?"

"I don't think so. The poisons were household items—nothing sophisticated. I don't think it's organized."

"They probably won't be too tough to catch, Tommy. Get 'em and make an example out of 'em. That'll put a stop to it." He wasn't as sure as he was forcing himself to sound.

"I don't suppose that I can convince you to come back and head up the investigation?"

"Not a chance."

"Somehow I knew you'd say that."

The sun had completely dropped behind the horizon, and the automatic lights by the pool switched on. Laura walked over and sat next to him, dropping her feet in the pool. She was holding a long fork with a charred steak on the end. Part of it was still on fire.

"Looks like my steak's done, Tommy. Gotta go. And hey, good luck."

Storming Heaven

Science without religion is lame.
Religion without science is blind.
—Albert Einstein

Acknowledgments

In no particular order, I'd like to thank Elaine Mills for her increasingly professional editing work and for keeping an eye on the competition for me. Darrell Mills, for lending me his technical expertise and in anticipation of his continued marketing effort. My wife, Kim, for all her insight and effort, but mostly for tolerating the occasional panic attacks that I think grip all novelists on their second try. Laura Liner, for providing the soundtrack. Robert Gottlieb and Matt Bialer at William Morris, for their enthusiasm and hard work. And finally, John Silbersack, Caitlin Blasdell, and the rest of the gang at HarperCollins, for all the amazing things they've done for me.

I

A TRAGIC HEART ATTACK AT THE TENDER YOUNG age of fifteen and a half, Jennifer Davis thought. That's what the headlines would say tomorrow.

She stood up on her pedals, but had to sit down again when the back wheel of her mountain bike lost traction. Less than halfway up the last climb of the race, her lungs already felt like they were full of hot tar. Worse, she could hear the unmistakable crunch of tires closing in on her from behind.

Jennifer glanced back over her shoulder, ignoring the flaring color of the sunset as the light filtered through the Phoenix smog, and focused on the face of the rider behind her.

The good news was that he looked like he was in bad shape. His mouth was wide open and, despite the dry cold of the desert, the sweat was literally streaming off his nose.

The bad news was that she felt like he looked.

The angle of the hill eased off a bit and Jennifer stood up again. This time her tire held and she was able to accelerate slightly, struggling to stay out front.

The panting behind her grew louder as the rider began to close the distance between them. Jennifer grudgingly eased her bike right to allow a lane for him to pass, and then dropped her head and pedaled with everything she had.

About twenty-five yards from the crest of the hill, when he was only inches behind, he gave up. She heard a gasped obscenity and the unmistakable click of gears as he downshifted.

Jennifer remained standing, in case it was a trick or he got a second wind, but when she looked back again, he was off his bike, pushing it slowly up the hill.

At the top of the climb, Jennifer leaned forward and rested her arms against her handlebars. A small but enthusiastic crowd lined the narrow trail, and she coasted carefully through them.

She could see her parents threading their way through the throng as she passed under the checkered banner that announced the finish line. When her father jogged up alongside her, she draped an arm around his shoulders and used him as a crutch as she slid off her bike and fell to the ground.

"Great job, Jen! I thought that guy was going to get you on the hill!" She closed her eyes and listened as her father picked up her bike and rolled it off the track.

"Honey? Are you all right?"

Jennifer opened her eyes and looked into the plump face of her mother hovering over her. "Fine, Mom. No problem." She turned to her father. "How'd I do, Dad?"

"Fourth place, looks like to me. Just out of the money."

Jennifer let out a low groan as she stood and began pushing her way through the crowd, shaking various hands and stopping briefly to talk and laugh with friends and other racers.

"We've got a surprise for you, honey," her father

said as they broke free of the crowd and headed for the parking lot. Jennifer slowed and then stopped. Her father just wasn't the no-specific-occasion gift-giving type. Surprises were usually a bad thing. Her eyes followed his outstretched index finger to a white Ford Explorer in the parking lot. Three people stood next to it. Two of the three were waving.

"Oh Dad. You didn't."

"What? The Taylors have really been looking forward to seeing you race."

Her mother smiled. "They really have, honey."

The Taylors had lived two doors down from them for as long as Jennifer could remember. And for as long as she could remember, they and her parents had been conspiring to get her together with Billy, the Taylors' football-playing, cheerleader-chasing, Budweiser-swilling moron of a son.

As they neared the parking lot, Mrs. Taylor rushed up to Jennifer with her arms flung wide. She thought better of the big hug she had undoubtedly been planning when she saw the amount of mud caked on Jennifer's jersey. Instead, she adjusted an imaginary flaw in her rather tall hair and opted for a distant peck on the cheek. "Wow, that was really impressive, Jennifer. Very exciting." She turned to her semicatatonic son. "Wasn't it, Billy?" He snapped out of his stupor long enough to generate a weak smile.

There was a short lull in the conversation while everyone waited to see if he would actually speak. When it became obvious that he wouldn't, her father said, "We thought we'd go out and grab some dinner before we drive back to Flagstaff. What do you think, Jen?"

"Are you kidding? Look at me!" Jennifer took off her helmet and held her arms out to give him a better view. She was spattered head to toe in mud. A gash above her knee, suffered on the first downhill of the race, was still oozing blood. And to top it off, her hair had taken on the shape of her helmet.

Her father didn't look impressed. "We'll just tell them you were in a mountain bike race. They'll understand."

She assumed that "they" referred to the maitre d' of a really, really snooty restaurant, who would look at her like she was a homeless person and then grudgingly get them a table because her father was the largest car dealer in Arizona.

Jennifer sighed and walked over to her parents' Cadillac. Leaning into the open window, she pulled out a small backpack containing a change of underwear, a pair of shorts, and a sweatshirt.

"I'll be back in a minute," she said, walking toward a white van with SPECIALIZED painted in red across the side.

"That work?" Jennifer asked the young man sitting on a lawn chair in front of the van. He put down the hopelessly misshapen wheel he had been contemplating and picked up the end of the hose lying next to him.

"Sure, Jen. You want to spray off your bike?"

"My parents want to go out for dinner."

He examined her carefully and fished a beer out of the cooler next to his chair. "It's gonna be pretty cold."

She tossed her pack through the window of his van and waved him on. "Do it."

"Okay, now I'm ready," Jennifer said, wearing her clean clothes and drying her hair with a heavily stained towel her friend with the van had loaned her. She bent forward and shook out her damp, unnaturally blonde hair. "Hey, Billy. None of this grease is coming off in my hair, is it?"

Her question had the desired effect. Billy looked appalled.

"Well, I thought it was a very nice dinner."

Jennifer rolled her eyes.

"Watch the road, honey," her mother cautioned. "They'll deduct points on your driver's test."

Jennifer reached over and turned the volume of the radio all the way down. "Mom, Billy and I have known each other our whole lives. He's a jerk. And he thinks I'm a jerk. My history teacher says that most people faced with a common enemy, in this case you guys, develop at least a teeny bit of a friendship. You'll notice we haven't."

Her mother's chins drooped. "They're such a nice family, I don't see why you're so resistant . . ."

Jennifer craned her neck and looked at her father, who had retreated to the far corner of the back seat. "Help me out here, Dad."

He ignored her and continued to peruse the road map lying in his lap, apparently oblivious to the fact that they were half a mile from home.

Jennifer turned back before her mother could get on her about her driving again. "Try to follow me here, Mom. Billy likes the cheerleader type. Girls with long red nails who can squeal at just the right pitch when he makes a touchdown. Besides, I *have* a boyfriend. And he hasn't been lobotomized."

Jennifer flipped on the blinker and turned the car into their driveway. She sped along the winding drive and escaped the car before her mother could start in again.

As she pulled her bike off the top of the car, she tried to ignore the cold and her mother's pouting form walking toward the house. It looked like the guilt was going to get pretty thick tonight.

Jennifer wheeled her bike into the open garage and leaned it against the wall. "You want me to pull the car in, Mom?" she yelled at the open door that led to the kitchen.

No answer. Yeah, this was going to be one serious guilt trip, she thought, jogging up a short flight of stairs and stopping at the door. The lights inside the house were still off. "Did we blow another fuse? Dad? Do you want me to check the box?"

"Run, Jennifer!"

She froze at the sound of her father's strangled voice. The rhythm and force of her heartbeat increased until she could almost hear it in the silence following his shout.

She took the last step into the house hesitantly and edged up to the washing machine so she could see into the kitchen. "Dad?"

It took a moment for her eyes to adjust from the glare of the bare bulbs in the garage to the gloom of the kitchen, but the moonlight streaming though the windows above the sink created enough colorless contrast to see what was happening.

A man in a dark suit was dragging her mother toward the living room. His hand was clamped over her mouth and his thumb and index finger pinched her nose shut.

Jennifer resisted the urge to run to her mother and pry the man's hands from her face. Instead, she retreated, almost falling backward down the steps. When she reached out to steady herself, her eyes finally found her father. He was pinned against the kitchen counter by a similarly dressed man. The combination of a thick forearm pressed against his throat and a gun pushed into his cheek had silenced him.

Everything in her told her to stay and fight, but she knew that would be stupid. There was nothing she could do. She had to go for help.

She spun around and cleared the stairs leading into the garage in one jump. The keys were still in the car.

She didn't see the hand as it reached out from behind her father's tool bench and grabbed her by the back of her sweatshirt; she only felt the shirt go tight across her chest and her feet skid out from under her. She would have fallen on her back, except a powerful arm had snaked around her waist. An instant later, the hand that had been tangled in her sweatshirt moved to her face and clamped over her mouth and nose.

She thrashed wildly when her air was cut off, surprising her captor with her strength and throwing them both against the wall. She grabbed at his arm, finally getting her fingers behind something that felt like a thick metal bracelet.

It was hopeless. Panic and lack of air were making her groggy, and she felt herself weakening as she fought back the blank whiteness encroaching on her peripheral vision. It took only a moment for the man to regain his balance and lift her off her feet, robbing her of what little leverage she had.

Making one last effort, she grabbed for the doorjamb as she was carried into the house. Her strength had left her, though, and her sweaty fingers slid ineffectually along the wall.

"Stop!"

Jennifer heard the shout—a woman's voice—but had no idea where it came from. The fingers around her nose loosened and she felt her feet connect with the ground, though the man's arm remained tight around her waist and his hand was still clamped on her mouth. She took in a deep breath through her nose and felt the oxygenated blood begin to clear her head.

A woman stepped out from behind the shadow of the refrigerator, prompting the man holding her to loosen his grip a bit more and allow her to take another deep breath as she watched the woman approach.

She was probably three inches shorter than Jennifer's five-nine, with a boyish haircut—short and parted on the side. Her skin must have been very pale, because it just glowed the color of the moonlight bathing the room.

The woman stopped about a foot away and reached out. Jennifer jerked her head back, but it just bounced off the chest of the man holding her.

"You must be very still and very quiet," the woman said, running a hand through Jennifer's hair.

Jennifer let out a quiet squeal, muffled by the hand still clamped over her mouth. She tried to look into the woman's eyes to see if there was anything there that could tell her what was happening, but they just looked black.

The woman moved to her right slightly, letting the moonlight hit her fully in the face. "Look at me, Jennifer. You will be quiet, won't you?"

Her voice was smooth and soft, but her newly illuminated eyes looked cold and cruel. Jennifer wanted to scream when the man's hand slid from her mouth, but she found herself transfixed by the woman's stare.

"That's better," the woman said, letting her fingers fall from Jennifer's hair and slide down her arm, finally closing them around Jennifer's wrist. "Come with me. There's something I want you to see."

She pulled Jennifer from the arms holding her and toward the living room. Jennifer wanted to break away, to run for help, but she was afraid. Not of the man who had captured her or the ones who had subdued her parents, but of this small, pale woman and what her eyes told Jennifer she was capable of.

She allowed herself to be led to a small loveseat situated on the far wall of the living room. The light was better there, thanks to two skylights and the large windows that surrounded the room.

Jennifer sat down on the sofa that she had spent so many nights on—watching TV, doing homework, talking on the phone. But now her eyes were locked on her parents and the men holding them at gunpoint at the other end of the room. The woman's hand slid from her wrist and Jennifer watched her walk through the moonlight to her parents and begin speaking quietly to them. Jennifer leaned forward to try and hear what was being said, but a strong hand grasped her shoulder and pulled her back.

She watched them for what seemed like forever. The shadows made it difficult to read their expressions, but she could see the tension slowly falling from her parents' bodies. Her father was the first to peel his back off the wall, followed closely by her mother, who stepped forward, put her arms around the small woman, and began to sob. The muffled sound coming from her throat was a strange combination of deep sorrow and joy that Jennifer had only heard once before—when a close family friend had died after a long and painful bout with bone cancer.

Jennifer relaxed slightly. The cruelty she had seen in the woman and that had caused a nauseous feeling of hopelessness to form in the pit of her stomach must have been a trick of light and darkness. Her parents recognized her. Maybe they'd known her for years. Perhaps the woman was afraid, too. Perhaps she was here because she needed their help.

When the man standing next to her father reached out and offered him his gun, Jennifer let out a deep sigh of relief. Certainly killers and rapists weren't in the habit of arming their victims. Maybe she and her family were in some kind of danger and these people were here to protect them?

Her father wiped at his eyes with his sleeve as he took the gun. Jennifer watched as he weighed it uncomfortably, then pointed it at the back of her mother's head and pulled the trigger.

For a moment she felt like she was sitting in a dark theater watching a movie. The crack of the pistol, her mother's body jerking forward, the black fluid momentarily backlit and then silently painting the wall.

Jennifer threw herself forward, trying to escape the sofa, but the man behind her had anticipated this and jerked her back again. The room started to spin and she felt her stomach tighten into a sickening knot as she struggled against the hands that held her in place.

"Daddy!" she screamed as her father tucked the gun under his chin.

Her shout seemed to pull him from his trance, and he hesitated for a moment. "I know this is hard, honey. But you don't belong just to us. You never belonged just to us."

The gun sounded again and the window behind her father cracked from top to bottom, leaving a spiderweb prism as he collapsed to the ground.

She felt all the strength go out of her. She slumped forward and turned away from the scene in front of her. For a moment, it felt as though she had forgotten how to breathe. Her mind seemed to shut down everything as it tried to process what had just happened.

Her parents had both been only children and her grandparents had been dead for years. In an instant she had gone from being one-third of a happy family to being completely alone. It must be a dream. A nightmare. It must be.

She didn't see the woman approach, and barely noticed when she knelt in front of her. Jennifer saw the dull flash of the syringe in the woman's hand and felt herself being pushed face down into the soft cushions. A hand slid beneath her stomach, unbuttoned her shorts, and pulled them and her underwear down. There was the sharp jab of the needle and an unnatural heat flooding her body. Then there was nothing.

2

"PUTTING'S NOT GOLF," MARK BEAMON SAID, finally nudging his ball the last three inches to the hole. "Guess that'd be, uh, seven?"

"Try eight," the man with the scorecard said. "If you didn't swing so hard, you wouldn't have to try to improve your game with creative math."

Beamon hiked up his red-and-green-checked pants and dunked his hand into the cup. "I don't think you appreciate the subtle genius of my game, Dave."

"Oh, but I do, Mark. That genius is the reason I haven't had to pay for a drink at the clubhouse since you moved to Arizona." He nodded toward a tall, squarely built man standing at the edge of the green. "You're up, Jake."

Beamon slid his putter into his bag and dropped into the driver's seat of the cart to watch Jacob Layman, his new boss, putt. It was an easy shot and Beamon tried to will it in, but the ball broke right and missed by a good three inches.

Another brilliant plan shot to hell, he thought as he watched a flush grow slowly out of the man's polo shirt.

Layman was apparently from a "good" Virginia family—whatever that meant. He'd attended the right prep schools and had enjoyed a successful, if not exceptional, career in the FBI.

Because of this, and despite the fact that he wasn't exactly a barrel of laughs, Layman had risen to a respectable height in Arizona's social circles. It was a position that, through incessant name-dropping, he never let anyone forget.

Enter Mark Beamon, an overweight and poorly dressed product of the Texas public school system. Favorite pastime: drinking and eating too much at parties, then insulting the guests.

But Beamon had spent his career riding herd over some of the FBI's most complicated and visible cases. His face had been on TV, in magazines, and all over local newspapers. It was the kind of career that made you powerful friends.

Despite his somewhat intentional lack of social graces and the fact that he'd only moved to Arizona a month ago, Beamon had already been befriended by some of the most powerful people in the state. Suddenly he was what his secretary called an "A" party guest.

Initially, Beamon had accepted his new stature with good humor. Why not? Sure, the people could be a little phony and dangerously boring, but the food was good and the booze was free. He'd started to rethink things, though, when he'd noticed a rapid cooling in Layman's attitude toward him.

At first he'd thought his new boss had found out that some of his people were bypassing him and coming to directly to Beamon for advice on tough cases—a practice Beamon strongly discouraged. But then it became clear that it didn't have anything to do with the job. He just felt that Beamon had over-stepped his natural-born social status.

And so here they were.

A few years ago, he would have ignored the situation and eventually paid for his refusal to play the game. But now he was the new, improved Mark Beamon. He'd cut his smoking in half, taken up a sport, made a valiant and modestly successful attempt to replace bourbon with beer, and promised himself that he would suffer no more concussions from beating his head against the Bureau's political brick wall.

Today's golf excursion included the mayor of Flagstaff and the star of a Fox crime drama filmed in Tucson, neither of whom had been particularly excited by Beamon's insistence that his new boss round out the foursome.

And now Layman was having what was probably the worst game of his life.

Beamon twisted around and tossed his empty beer can in the cooler bungee-corded to the back of the cart, then pulled out a full one and popped the top. "Make it up on the next one, Jake," he said as his boss slammed his putter into his bag and slumped into the seat next to him.

Somehow it didn't look like Layman was going to remember this as the peace offering he had intended.

Beamon jumped on the accelerator and hurtled down the cart path, ignoring the cold wind penetrating his golf shirt and trying to forget that the man sitting next to him was probably trying to figure out a way to work the word "asshole" into his next performance appraisal.

When they arrived at the next hole, Beamon

grabbed his driver and went to stand at the tee, leaving Layman to sulk in the cart. As their partners pulled up, the unmistakable chirping of a beeper started in earnest. Layman looked down at his hip and the mayor toward his bag, but Beamon was already holding his up like a trophy. "Mine."

He dropped his driver, walked back to the cart, and began digging through his bag for his cell phone. With a little luck, terrorists had taken a stadium full of college students hostage. Otherwise, he was probably going to have to shoot himself in the foot to get out of the last six holes.

3

EXCEPT FOR THE ODD GOLF TRIP TO PHOENIX, the reality of Arizona just wasn't living up to the fantasy.

Mark Beamon unconsciously lifted his feet as his car plowed through a six-inch-deep snowdrift that washed up under the chassis and lifted the vehicle off the ground. Fortunately, the drift wasn't much wider than it was deep, and he managed to correct a minor fishtail and keep control.

"Goddammit!" he said to the empty car. "It's not supposed to snow in Arizona!"

He had been the Assistant Special Agent in Charge, ASAC, of the FBI's Flagstaff office for about a month. And in that month he'd learned something. It *did* snow in Arizona. Hell, it blizzarded in Arizona. The pictures he'd seen on TV of a guy sipping a margarita in the shade of a twenty-foot-high cactus had probably been taken in California. Or maybe the southern tip of Saudi Arabia. Still, all in all, he had to admit that it wasn't a bad gig—he finally had his own office to run and he had some good kids working for him. Now if he could just keep from screwing it up.

Beamon slowed the car to a crawl and flipped on the interior light. The high-end houses in this Flagstaff neighborhood weren't visible from the road, hidden by dense pine forests and the four-foot snowbanks piled up on either side of the quiet street. According to the directions he'd scribbled on the back of a blank scorecard, though, he wanted to take the next turn.

He aimed the car at a narrow break in the snowbank to his right and started up a long winding drive. He knew he was in the right place when he crested a small hill and saw the tops of the snow-covered trees fading from red to blue and then back again.

It took only a few moments to come upon the source of the light show—two police cruisers wedged between three unmarked cars in the driveway of a large log home.

He grabbed a piece of gum from the package sitting next to him on the passenger seat and shoved it in his mouth next to the two in there already. He'd read somewhere that your sense of smell was supposed to go as you got older, but he hadn't been so lucky. There was something about the stench of day-old blood that made him more nauseous every year. Gum was his latest attempt at a remedy.

Beamon slid his vehicle to a stop and stepped out, feeling the cold air penetrate his sweater and thin golf pants. He'd come directly from the course, a two-and-a-half-hour drive that rose thousands of feet from the mild red desert of Phoenix to the snow-covered forests of Flagstaff.

Beamon waved at two approaching policemen and ducked into the back seat of his car. He pulled out his newly purchased goose-down parka and slipped it on.

At the party celebrating his promotion and transfer to Arizona—and after no less than eight bourbons—he had donned all of his winter clothes at once and performed an elaborate striptease on his friend's dining room table. His wool overcoat had been the first article to be thrown into the cheering crowd. In retrospect, probably not such a great idea.

"Can we help you, sir?" one of the two troopers said, taking a sip from a styrofoam cup. His next breath came out like thick steam.

"Maybe." Beamon held up his right arm, displaying a large price tag hanging from the bright red sleeve of his new jacket. "Either of you guys have scissors?"

The cop with the coffee pointed back down the half-mile-long driveway. "Sir, this is a police matter. I suggest you get back in your—"

"Mark!"

Chet Michaels danced through a tangle of police line tape and deep snow as he made his way down from the house. "It's okay, guys. This is my boss."

The two cops mumbled an apology and started back toward their squad car.

"Sorry to drag you away from your golf game, Mark, but I thought you'd want to see this."

At twenty-five, Chet Michaels had come into the Bureau as one of its youngest agents—an honor he'd earned by graduating from college at nineteen and passing his CPA test on the first try. By all reports, he'd also been one hell of an athlete—a wrestler—but it was a tough mental image to conjure up. The combination of his carrot-red hair and the bumper crop of freckles across the bridge of his nose made him look about as threatening as a cantaloupe.

Beamon took off his plaid golf cap and was going to toss it back into the car, but thought better of it. The sun had dropped behind the mountains and the stars were starting to appear in the deep blue of the sky. It was going to be another cold one.

"Believe me when I tell you that this is the bright spot in my day, Chet," Beamon said, motioning toward the house and letting the young agent lead.

A yellow rope cordoned off the steps climbing to the front door, forcing them to skirt around through a deep snowbank. Beamon was still wearing his golf spikes—great for traction but a little weak in the warmth department.

"Don't think you're gonna get much in the way of footprints, Chet," Beamon observed, trying unsuccessfully to stay in the depressions made by the feet of the people who had gone before him. "It hasn't snowed for a couple of days and it looks like a football team's run up and down these steps ten times."

"You're probably right, but we thought we'd bring in some people to look at it anyway."

Beamon shrugged as he stepped through the front door and into the house. It wasn't much warmer inside than out, so he tucked the price tag into his sleeve and watched Michaels cross the entryway at a slow run and disappear through a set of hand-carved double doors to the left.

All that energy, Beamon thought, shaking his head. He tried to remember the excitement that had gripped him on his first big case, but the feeling was gone. He could recall the details like it was yesterday, filed away in his mind for future reference, but the emotional charge of being twenty-odd years old and out to save the world had shorted out a long time ago.

Beamon reached into the collar of his sweater and pulled out a pair of reading glasses from his shirt pocket. They fogged up instantly, so he let them dangle from his hand as he looked around the entryway.

The walls were constructed of large logs, probably almost a foot and a half in diameter. They'd been haphazardly stained a deep natural brown, giving them a casual worn look that complimented the flagstone floor. An elk-antler chandelier provided a soft light from above that was periodically overpowered by camera flashes emanating from the next room.

Beamon walked across a faded Navajo rug and stopped in front of a small antique table. It was covered with photographs of every size and shape conceivable, each with a simple frame of either gold or silver.

His glasses still hadn't quite cleared, so he hung them around his neck and bent forward, bringing his nose to within a few inches of the pictures.

It looked like sort of a family history. The photos in back were all faded black-and-whites, their subjects uniformly dressed in well-starched suits or dresses with petticoats, and all staring out from the frames with the same stern expression.

Beamon took a step back and jumped forward in time. He picked up the eight-by-ten photo on the edge of the table and brought it up close to his face.

He recognized the man in the tan sweater as Eric Davis. They'd met briefly at a cocktail party a few weeks ago. Beamon didn't remember meeting the tall, heavyset woman standing at his side but guessed that she was his wife.

Beamon's eyes wandered down to the girl sitting in the leaves in front of the couple. The blonde of her hair was the product of a calculatedly obvious dye job, contrasting with the dark, uneven tan of an athlete. There was a slight glint on her left nostril that Beamon guessed was a nose ring.

She was a pretty little thing, probably sixteen or seventeen—though that was really just a wild guess. By design, he really hadn't spent much time around children.

"Mark, I keep losing you. They're in here!" Michaels said, reappearing suddenly in the doorway to the living room.

"All right, all right," Beamon said, putting the picture back on the table. He turned toward the young agent. "Lead on. I'll stay with you this time. Promise."

He followed Michaels into a large, roughly octagonal room surrounded by windows that must have been fifteen feet high. The ceiling rose and disappeared into shadow at the top of an enormous log pillar that, until tonight, would have been the focal point of the room. Beamon shoved his hands into the pockets of his parka and looked down at the new focal point.

Michaels stood next to the two bodies with the proud expression of a sculptor showing off his most recent work. "We assume that these are the remains of Eric and Patricia Davis. The maid who found them IDed them from their build and clothes. Obviously, she can't be a hundred percent sure, though."

Beamon nodded, letting his gaze linger for a moment on the shattered head loosely connected to the body of a plump woman in a thick off-white sweater. He crouched down, careful not to dip the end of his new coat in the puddle of curdling blood at his feet.

It didn't look like their faces had been damaged by the bullet impacts, but the dried blood and brain tissue clinging to their skin had subtly distorted their features. Beamon wouldn't swear to the fact that they were the couple in the picture, but it was probably a pretty good guess.

"Mr. Davis was forty-four years old, Mrs. Davis was forty," Michaels started, reading off a small pad of paper he had pulled from his pocket. "Apparently Mr. Davis owned a number of car dealerships."

"Biggest dealer in Arizona," Beamon said.

"Excuse me?"

"Someone told me he was the biggest dealer in Arizona. I met him at a party a couple of weeks ago. Briefly." Beamon stood and carefully stepped over the puddle of blood at his feet. The plastic spikes on the bottoms of his golf shoes that had served him so well in the snow were proving to be a little treacherous on the polished oak floor. He crouched down again and examined the scene from a slightly different angle.

The Mrs. looked like she'd gotten it in the back of the head. The blood had pooled and dried, leaving something that looked like a large scab over her hair. Beamon couldn't see if there was an exit wound because of the body's position.

Eric Davis's body was a little more perplexing. Based on its condition and the pattern of the splattered blood, it looked like he'd taken his bullet right under the chin. Beamon pointed to the broken window. "Did the bullet break that window? It looks like it should have gone straight up."

"Oh, I think it did. Looks like a piece of Mr. Davis's skull broke the window."

"Lovely," Beamon said, standing up and shoving another piece of gum in his mouth. "What about the girl?"

"Jennifer Davis is fifteen years old. Blonde. Tall—about five-eight or -nine. According to one of the neighbors we talked to, she was competing in a bike race near Phoenix yesterday afternoon. They— the neighbors—were down there watching the race and went out to dinner with them afterward. The Davises would have returned here around ten o'clock."

Beamon flopped down on the sofa and stuffed a fifth stick of gum in his mouth. "So what happened here, Chet?" he slurred.

The young agent looked confident. He'd obviously learned enough about Beamon in their month working together to know the question was coming and to prepare an answer.

"They were waiting for them."

"Who?"

"The perpetrators."

"Why?"

"The garage door's still open and the Davises' car is outside. I figure it this way. The perpetrators get dropped off by an accomplice who takes the car they came in and drives around the neighborhood."

"Why doesn't he just park it?" Beamon broke in.

"The Davises would have been suspicious if there was a strange car in their driveway. And you can't park on the street 'cause of the snow."

Beamon raised his eyebrows and rocked his head back and forth in a calculated effort to make the young agent nervous. Michaels was probably right, but he needed to learn to work under pressure. Besides, what was the fun of being king if you couldn't torture your subjects occasionally?

"Okay, Chet. Go on."

His body language had its intended effect, and Michaels started to sound a little hesitant. "Uh, yeah. So, anyway, they—the Davises—come in through the garage and are ambushed in the kitchen."

"I see." Beamon stood up and walked through the open French doors that led to the kitchen. There was a light haze of fingerprint dust in the air and a man in a blue suit was hunched over the sink, working furiously with a soft brush.

Beamon pointed to a picture lying in a halo of glass on the floor, then rapped on the kitchen table, which had been pushed haphazardly against the wall. A broken dish lay at the base of the refrigerator.

"I'd say the hypothesis that the Davises met our friends in here is a reasonable one," Beamon agreed.

Michaels picked up where he had left off, looking relieved. "Okay, so they all reconvene to the living room, where the perpetrators line Mr. and Mrs. Davis up against the wall and execute them. Then they call their accomplice on their cell phone and have him pick them up."

Beamon peeked through the pantry/mudroom and out through the open door to the garage. "What if it was a car they recognized? Someone they knew?"

"Excuse me?"

"The Davises pull up and someone they know is in their driveway. They all chat while Jennifer takes her bike off the top of the car and then one of them pulls a gun. They come through the garage into the kitchen, and Mr. Davis makes a grab for the gun. There's a struggle that he ultimately loses. They drag them into the living room and shoot them."

The young agent's face fell and he stared at his shoes. "I guess that's possible . . ."

"How 'bout this?" Beamon continued. "Mr. and Mrs. Davis come inside while Jennifer takes her bike off the car. She's too young to drive, so she can't pull the car in, and her mom and pop aren't anxious to go back out in the cold, so they put it off for a while. In the meantime, our perpetrators just drive up and knock on the front door."

Michaels looked up from his shoes. "But then why would the struggle have taken place in the kitchen? It's not between the front door and the living room."

"Maybe they were being forced to prepare omelets against their will." Beamon broke into a smile and backhanded Michaels in the chest. "Your theory's best, bud. You just shouldn't be so damn sure about it. Keep an open mind." Beamon paused. "But not so open your brain falls out, right?"

The bright beam of headlights washed through the windows of the living room, prompting Michaels to lean through the kitchen door. "That must be the coroner."

Beamon nodded. "Go ahead and give him the tour. Oh, one more thing. Get someone to walk around the outside of the house with a flashlight and look for footprints. This could be nothing more than a botched robbery attempt, and if the little girl was an athlete she might have made a break for the woods. She'll freeze her ass off if she's out there lost."

The huge wad of gum in Beamon's mouth was starting to make his jaw ache and he could feel that the smell of the bodies was about to break through his makeshift spearmint barrier. Time for plan B.

He stepped over the latent print guy, who had sunk from the counter to the lower cabinets, and pushed hard on the door at the back of the kitchen. It scraped against the snow and ice on the deck, stopping dead after moving about a foot. Beamon looked dejectedly at the small gap, then down at his bulging waistline. It wouldn't be easy, but then, what in his life ever was? He grabbed the edge of the counter and the doorjamb and forced himself through the opening.

It was a beautiful spot. Large pines filtered the starlight, giving the clean white snow an ethereal glow. There was no wind, and the muffled sounds of the investigation that managed to filter through the broken window in the living room were almost completely swallowed up by the forest.

Beamon retrieved a bag of tobacco and papers from his jacket and began rolling a cigarette. The cold numbed his fingertips, making the process even more arduous than normal.

"What are you doing?"

Beamon jumped, dropping the half-rolled cigarette in the snow and almost losing his balance. Steadying himself against the house, he looked in the direction of the voice.

Less than ten feet away, a small Hispanic woman, wrapped in a thick wool blanket, sat in a lawn chair. She leaned forward and pulled her knees closer to her chest. "What were you doing there? Aren't you a policeman?"

He looked down at himself and chuckled. With the green and red pants and the new parka, he must look like a giant Christmas ornament rolling a joint. "My doctor told me I have to give up cigarettes, so I started rolling my own. It's such a pain, I smoke half as much."

The woman's hand appeared from behind the blanket and pointed toward the scattered tobacco at Beamon's feet. "But those don't have a filter. They're probably twice as bad."

Beamon thought about that for a moment. "No such thing as a perfect plan."

He walked toward her and held out his hand. "I'm Mark Beamon. I work with the FBI. I didn't know anyone was out here."

She took his hand. "Carlotta Juarez. I am the Davises' maid . . . was the Davises' maid."

"Your hand feels like ice, Carlotta. Would you like to go inside?"

She shook her head.

"How about a car? You could go sit in my car and run the heater."

"No, I like it out here."

Beamon leaned against the house and followed her gaze toward a grove of aspen glowing pink in the starlight. "Are you all right?"

Out of the corner of his eye, he could see her turn back toward him. "I came here from Bogotá. I've seen so many horrible things."

Beamon nodded and was silent for almost a minute.

"How long have you worked for the Davises?" he said finally.

"Eight years."

"Do you live here at the house?"

"No. In town with my husband and five sons. I come every day, though."

Beamon slipped his hands under his armpits. "Five sons? That must be a handful."

"Sometimes."

"Have you had a chance to walk through the house, Carlotta? Does it look like anything's missing?"

"Nothing that I could see." She paused. "Only Jennifer."

Beamon looked up at the stars. "Tell me about her."

"She's a wonderful girl. Bright, kind, thoughtful." Her voice trailed away. "How could someone do this?"

He ignored the question, having asked himself that same thing at crime scenes all over the country and never coming up with a good answer. "Does she have a boyfriend?"

"Jamie Dolan. He's a senior at Jennifer's high school."

"Anything unusual going on lately, Carlotta? Strange phone calls? People you didn't know coming over?"

She shook her head.

"How about between Jennifer and her parents? Were they angry at her for something? Maybe they didn't like her boyfriend?"

"Mrs. Davis always wanted Jennifer to see their neighbor's son Bill. But I don't think she disliked Jamie."

Beamon peeled his back from the frozen side of the house. "I appreciate your help, Carlotta. Oh, and I apologize in advance for the people who are going to ask you all the same questions." He turned and began tugging at the door to the kitchen. "Don't freeze out here, okay?"

A couple of brief, but harrowing, expeditions into his sister's room decades ago had given Beamon his only image of a teenage girl's natural habitat. Apparently it was hopelessly outdated.

The wall of dolls and full-sized poster of Shaun Cassidy that he halfway expected to find had been replaced by bicycle parts hanging from the ceiling and posters of what looked like young homeless men. A closer inspection of the posters revealed that they were music groups with names like Gas Huffer and Mudhoney.

Beamon wandered across the room, stepping over the clothes and towels strewn across the floor, occasionally pausing to look into a drawer or box. Nothing leapt out at him as particularly significant so he ducked into the attached bathroom. The counter was covered with various tubes and vials that, as a lifelong bachelor, he found completely baffling. He stepped over the cord of a blow dryer and pulled a few blonde hairs out of the sink. Wrapping them up in a length of toilet paper, he headed back downstairs.

"I'm out of here, Chet!" Beamon yelled from the front door.

Michaels jogged out of the living room and caught Beamon shuffling around the roped-off area on the front porch.

"You're not staying?" He sounded shocked that anyone would choose to spend an evening at home when presented with the opportunity to hang around a house full of blood and death.

Beamon waved his hand dismissively as he cleared the cordoned-off area and made a beeline for his car. "You seem to have it under control, Chet. Call me at home if you run into any really earth-shattering problems. I'm not available for little glitches and snafus 'til tomorrow morning, though. Right?"

4

BEAMON MADE IT THROUGH THE DOOR OF THE
FBI's Flagstaff office just as the wall fell.

He saw the expressions of the young agents
crammed into the small room converge on resigned
annoyance as they covered their coffee cups and
computer keyboards. A white cloud of plaster dust
enveloped two men in coveralls and billowed slowly
across the room.

Beamon stepped over a pile of acoustic tiles and
headed for his office, shaking his head. Director Calahan didn't take defeat lightly. When he had finally
been shamed into giving Beamon a management
position, he'd been overcome with another one of
the flashes of complete idiocy that had become the
hallmark of his tenure at the Bureau.

He'd decided to take a small resident agency,
expand it enough to make it look good to the press, and
put Beamon in charge. In the director's mind, giving
Beamon the somewhat imaginary title of ASAC-
Flagstaff would make him a laughingstock. And as an
added benefit, it would separate Beamon from his old
cohort Laura Vilechi before he could bring her over to
the dark side.

Unfortunately, the expansion of the office was
going to cost taxpayers hundreds of thousands of
dollars and leave quite a few agents who owned

homes in Phoenix with a long and utterly pointless commute. Welcome to the FBI.

"Think we should rename the office Jericho, D.?" Beamon said, ignoring the door to his outer office and walking through a gap in the newly framed wall.

His secretary stood and followed him as he passed by her and went straight for the coffeemaker next to his desk.

"You need one, D.?" Beamon asked, dumping a couple of teaspoons of sugar into his cup.

"No thanks. How went the golf game?"

Beamon flopped into the worn leather chair behind his desk. "Jake shot like a four hundred or something."

His secretary grimaced.

"And that was for twelve holes. I took off before they teed up the thirteenth."

"You know what they say, Mark. The best-laid plans . . ."

He threw his hands up in a gesture of frustration and grabbed the neatly folded newspaper off his desk.

"Two things, Mark. First, you still need to review and sign off on this year's pro forma budget. It's past due."

Beamon pretended not to hear. He hadn't yet built up the willpower to wade through that ocean of paper.

"Second, Chet Michaels has been walking by every five minutes or so for the last hour. He looks like he's going to burst. Should I send him in?"

"Ten minutes, D. Hold him off for ten minutes.

Give me a chance to at least skim the newspaper and get a little caffeine into my system. And I promise I'll go through your budget at home tonight."

She nodded and started back for her desk.

"Hey, D.?"

She stopped and turned back toward him, her sharp, youthful features melting into a sly smile.

Since Beamon's first day in Flagstaff, his secretary had steadfastly refused to tell him her given first name, preferring to be called by her first initial. Of course, he could have looked in her personnel file, but what would be the fun of that?

"I was listening to this Johnny Cash song on the way to work today . . ."

She shook her head sadly. "Good try, Mark. But it's not Delia."

"The old saying is wrong," Beamon said, poking an index finger into the open newspaper spread across his desk. "Kill all the journalists."

From his position at the door to the office, Chet Michaels took it that his boss's sacred and absolutely inviolable ten minutes were up.

"Look at this headline," Beamon said. "'FBI Baffled by Double Murder/Kidnapping.' Shit."

"You aren't?" Michaels said as he sat down in one of the three chairs lined up in front of Beamon's desk.

"There are a few things that baffle me, Chet. Serial killers? Occasionally. Women? More often than not." Beamon looked down at the stained concrete floor of his office. "Why they ripped up my old carpet when the new one isn't due for another couple of weeks? Definitely haven't figured that one out.

But kidnappings? No way. At worst I'm briefly per-plexed."

Michaels laced his hands across his stomach and leaned back in his chair. "Well, they were prob-ably talking about me, then. If you've got this thing figured out, I could really use some help."

Beamon spun the paper around so Michaels could see it and slapped his palm on a picture of Jennifer Davis. "Voilà."

"What?"

"What do you mean, 'What?' She did it."

Michaels' bright red eyebrows rose. "The little girl?"

"Honestly, Chet. Sometimes your lack of cyni-cism disgusts me. Answer me this: Why do people kidnap?"

"I dunno. Lots of reasons, I guess."

"No. There are only three. Financial benefit, blackmail, or you want the kid. Of course, each of those categories has a subheading or two."

Michaels remained silent as Beamon took a slug from his coffee cup. "Okay, Chet, let's start with number three—you want the kid. Why?"

"Uh, ransom?"

Beamon shook his head. "Ransom fits in under financial benefit. No, most often you want the kid because you're a parent that didn't get legal custody. Now, Jennifer's a little old for that kind of nonsense—no one wants to steal a kid they're going to have to put through college in a couple of years. Besides, weren't the Davises still on their first marriage?"

Michaels glanced at the blue file lying in his lap, but didn't open it. "I think so."

"That brings us to subheading number two. You're some crazy pervert. What do you think? Pervert?"

Michaels's eyes scrunched up for a moment. "I doubt it. The facts don't support the theory that one lone person did this. Sex offenders don't usually work in teams."

"I'll buy that," Beamon agreed. "Besides, you told me that this girl races bikes. If I were your garden-variety weirdo, I'd just snag her when she's all alone on some trail in the woods."

Beamon batted away a thick cable hanging from his ceiling and put his feet on his desk. "So, moving right along. Category number two— blackmail. What do you think of that theory."

"Can't blackmail a dead person."

"'Nuff said. Number one, then. Financial benefit. Ransom?"

"Not very practical at this point."

Beamon grinned. "To say the least. So who benefits from this thing?"

Michaels leaned forward in his chair and braced his elbows against his knees. "I know what you want me to say, Mark. That Jennifer lined her parents up and shot them so she'd inherit all their money. That she's gonna show up in a few days with some crazy story about the whole thing." He shook his head. "Doesn't feel right to me."

Beamon pointed again to the picture of Jennifer in the paper. "Are you kidding? Look at her!"

Michaels laughed and picked up the paper for a closer inspection. "Come on, Mark. My girlfriend's got a nose ring. Couple of tattoos, too. Doesn't mean anything. It's just, you know, fashion." A wide grin spread across the young agent's face. "Your parents probably said you looked subversive when you came in with a bunch of grease in your hair and your cigarettes rolled up in the sleeve of your T-shirt."

Beamon rolled his eyes. "I'm only forty-three, you little bastard." He paused for a moment and watched two men in the outer office trying to lift a scaffold over a group of file cabinets. "Okay, it's not a great theory," he admitted. "But it's the best one I can come up with. Could be that this was a botched robbery. The perps had just arrived—didn't have time to take anything—and the Davises came home. They shoot them, then decide to take the girl for some fun and games."

Michaels perked up a bit. "That sounds possible."

"I don't know. A house that you can't see from the street—you'd have to be watching it. No sign of forced entry would suggest they're pros. If the Davises had gone to this race and five miles into their trip remembered they left the iron on and come back, I'd say we've got a great theory. But they were gone all fucking day. All our friends had to do was slip in after the maid left at five and they'd have had time to clean the place out and watch a ball game on the Davises' big-screen TV."

Somewhere in the office, a table saw started.

"When are we gonna get a report on the physical evidence and autopsy?" Beamon shouted over the roar of the saw.

"Should start trickling in tomorrow," Michaels yelled back.

"Okay. Keep thinking about it, Chet. We've missed something, and I'm briefly perplexed as to what it is."

Michaels stood and turned to leave.

"Oh, and Chet! Tell that guy out there that if he doesn't shut that saw off, I'm gonna use it to remove his foot."

5

A WAVE OF HEAT WASHED ACROSS JENNIFER Davis, instantly covering her in tiny beads of sweat. She kicked the covers off the bed, and for a moment the cool air meeting her damp skin eased the nausea that had gripped her since she woke up.

And how long ago had that been? An hour? Two?

The comforting glow of the clock on her nightstand and the gentle creaking of her house as the immense logs dried and settled were gone. Everything was gone. There was no blue-white glow from the snowdrifts beneath her window, no light filtering in from under the door. Just a dizzying blackness.

Jennifer felt another surge of heat overtake her and she rolled on her side, clenching her teeth and struggling to not throw up.

The memories returned slowly, retracing themselves in her mind over and over again until she could see faceless black-and-white outlines moving purposefully across the background of her home. She could feel the strong arms holding her and the adrenaline-surge panic as her air was cut off by a hand damp with perspiration.

It didn't take long for the outlines to sharpen and collect color and sound. The pale woman with dark eyes kneeling in front of her. The shadows crisscrossing her father's face as he raised the gun to his wife's head. The crack of the pistol and the strangely insignificant jerk of her mother's head before she fell, doll-like, to the ground.

No. It couldn't have happened. It was just bad dreams. She must have been coming down with a bug before the race and the effort and dehydration had played tricks on her in her sleep.

She reached out for the lamp beside her bed, but her hand just hung uselessly in the empty air, confirming what she already knew but hadn't been able to fully face. She wasn't in her room. She had no idea where she was.

She tried to stifle it, but the long mournful cry still escaped as she tried to stem the tide of memories projecting themselves onto the darkness that surrounded her.

Her father's image appeared a few feet away, pressing the barrel of the gun under his chin and speaking his final, meaningless words to her. Then her mind replayed the sting of the syringe as it broke her skin and turned the room to quivering mush and then finally to nothing. She felt a tear make its way across the bridge of her nose and down her cheek. Then another. And another. Once she started to cry, her sobbing just grew in intensity, melding with her nausea and leaving her choking and coughing uncontrollably.

She went on like that until the muscles in her stomach and sides exhausted themselves and her mind decided it had had enough and let her drift off into unconsciousness.

When she awoke again, her head still hurt and her throat was painfully dry, but the nausea was gone. The image of her parents' death began creeping back into her mind, but she pushed it off into the emotional numbness that was quickly overtaking her.

"Hello?"

Her voice was little more than a harsh whisper, but it seemed impossibly loud in the darkness and silence that surrounded her.

She waited for some reply, some indication that she wasn't completely alone in the world, but there was nothing.

She cleared her throat painfully. "Is anyone there?"

Louder this time, but still weak. She sounded like a frightened little girl, even to herself.

She sat up slowly and swung her feet onto the cold floor. The blood rushed from her head and she had to bend forward at the waist for a moment to keep from passing out. After a few seconds, she raised her head and slid off the bed.

She tried to crawl but the bruises and cuts on her knees were too painful against the hard floor and she was forced to turn over and slide on her butt until her back reached a wall.

Feeling along it, she finally came to the smooth wood of a doorjamb. She used the doorknob to steady herself and struggled to her feet. It took only a few moments to find the light switch.

She covered her eyes with one hand and flipped the switch with the other. The flare of light worked its way between her fingers as she pulled them slowly away from her face.

When she finally opened her eyes, she fell against the wall and screamed.

A black-clad woman sat motionless in a chair less than a foot from where Jennifer had slept. The woman's head turned slowly toward her as Jennifer backed into the far corner of the room and sank to the floor. The brief surge of adrenaline overloaded her weakened system and her breath came in short, useless gasps as the woman stood and moved across the room.

The pounding of her heart seemed to be robbing her of her strength. Her arms felt impossibly heavy as she raised them in front of her face.

The woman paused and looked down at her, then opened the door and disappeared through it without a word.

Jennifer listened to the latch on the door click shut as she crumpled to her side on the hard tile and struggled to even out her breathing.

It had been the same woman. The one who had driven her parents crazy. The one who had drugged her.

Why had she been sitting there in the darkness? Why hadn't she answered?

Jennifer crawled sobbing toward the door and flipped the light switch. It was better that way, she thought as the darkness closed in on her. Better to see nothing.

6

"YOU ALL RIGHT?" MARK BEAMON YELLED. The brand-new window at the front of his office had gone almost completely opaque with white paint. A smear the size of the painter's back was transparent enough to allow him to see the collapsed scaffold and two slightly dazed construction workers on the other side.

Beamon crossed his office and stood in the open door. The men involved in this latest of a recent string of construction disasters looked more or less unharmed. Unfortunately, that wasn't true of the two freshly painted PCs and three freshly painted FBI agents that had been sitting a little too close.

He sighed quietly, remembering that it was now *his* job to get the Three Stooges Contracting Company to pay up for the damaged computers and business suits.

He pointed at Chet Michaels and reminded himself that he'd been bucking to get into management for years. In the future, he'd be more careful what he wished for.

"I've got the new stuff on the Davis case," Michaels said, walking carefully across the paint-splattered floor with a large box in his hands and a blue folder under his arm. "I take it you're ready?"

Beamon settled back into his chair as one of the

painters attacked the floor in front of his office with a mop. "Yeah. Have a seat."

The young agent dropped the box next to his chair and flipped the file folder open on his lap. "We got the initial background stuff on the Davises."

"And?"

"They're actually not Jennifer's real parents. She was adopted."

"Shit, really?" Beamon snapped his fingers. "That's it, then. Reason number three, subcategory one."

"Huh?"

"Come on, Chet, we talked about this yesterday. What's reason number three for kidnapping someone?"

"Uh, ransom?"

Beamon frowned. "That's reason one. Try again."

"Oh, wait a minute. It's 'cause you want the girl."

"Or whoever. And *why* do you want the girl?"

"Uh, I thought that one was 'cause you were divorced and didn't get custody."

"Precisely. Adoption's just a variation on that theme. Find the biological parents and you find the girl." Beamon lifted his mug in a salute to his own deductive genius and took a sip of the hot coffee.

"We already found the parents, Mark. They're dead. Died in a fire years ago."

Beamon tried not to let his disappointment show. "Oh. Back to Jennifer, then."

Michaels flipped a page in the file. "So far, we're not finding any real problems at the Davises.

The neighbors and friends we've talked to have told us that Jennifer was pretty well adjusted and that there were no significant problems in her relationship with her parents. She's an excellent student, athletic, and well liked—if not exactly popular. As you mentioned, she's a little alternative. Oh, and a pretty good mountain bike racer."

Beamon tapped his front teeth with the nail of his index finger. "The maid told me that maybe Jennifer's mother wasn't crazy about her boyfriend. Was she putting pressure on Jennifer to get rid of him? Love tends to rank right up there with money as a motive for murder."

"Don't think so in this case, Mark. I did get that Mrs. Davis would have liked her to get together with their best friends' son, but that had been going on for a long time and I think she probably knew it was never going to go anywhere."

Beamon interrupted him. "Why not? What makes you say that?"

"I met the kid—Billy's his name. Not a match made in heaven, believe me."

Beamon remained silent, prompting him to continue.

"I went through Jennifer's room with a fine-toothed comb, Mark. She listens to Naked Raygun, reads Kerouac and Burroughs. Rebuilds suspension forks. This guy her mother liked for her was dumb as a post. Pure generic high school football player."

Beamon gave a short laugh and shook his head. "God, you make me feel old, Chet. I have absolutely no idea what you just said."

"Would you care for a translation?"

Beamon held up his hand. "How about I just take your word for it. What about the boyfriend she *did* like?"

"Jamie Dolan. Haven't talked to him yet; I'm going this afternoon. Preliminarily, though, he doesn't look great as a suspect. He's a drummer in a band and was apparently playing that night. I think there are going to be a lot of witnesses nailing him down between way before ten P.M. 'til about three A.M. I don't think there was any way he could have sneaked out between sets, but maybe he could have slipped out of his house early in the morning. I'll know more later."

Beamon looked across his office at the man smearing paint around on his window with a rag. "I have to wonder about that. The Davises were attacked in the living room in the same clothes they'd been seen in at dinner, right? He'd have had to roust them out of bed, get them to put on their clothes, and bring them downstairs before he shot them. Maybe he's that clever, I don't know. Does he have access to a gun?"

"No gun registered to his mother, but who knows?"

"What about the Davises?"

"No gun registered and none of their friends we talked to know of any."

"Shit," Beamon said, tapping out a complex rhythm on his desk with his knuckles. "You're not going to make this easy on me, are you, Chet? Physical evidence?"

"So far, we don't have anything in the way of prints or fibers and the autopsy report's still pending. Didn't get anything from phone records. There was no sign of forced entry or robbery. Oh, and Jennifer had a credit card. Last used . . ." He flipped a couple of pages in the folder. "Middle of last month. We're watching for any new usage."

Beamon leaned across his desk. "What's in the box?"

"Oh, we finally got into the Davises' safe." He dropped the folder and hefted the box onto his lap.

"So, what have we won?"

Michaels grabbed a red velvet bag with a ribbon tied around the top and let it dangle from his hand. "A bag of gold and diamond jewelry. Good for evening, or feeding a thousand homeless people for a month."

"Commie."

The young agent affected a hurt expression and dropped the bag on Beamon's desk. "Passports for all three of them, roughly four thousand dollars in cash, a few stock certificates, Mr. Davis's college transcript, the financial statements of the corporation that owns Mr. Davis's car dealerships . . ."

"How do those look? Maybe he was borrowing from the wrong sort?"

"They look pretty strong, actually. Of course they could be bogus."

Beamon screwed up his face. "Maybe. But why keep fakes in your own safe? Partners?"

Michaels shook his head. "He owned the whole thing, one hundred percent."

"Uh-huh. Go on."

"Lessee. Birth certificates for all three, and a copy of the Davises' irrevocable trust."

"What's that say?"

"We've got a lawyer going over it, but I read a lot of these when I was an accountant. It pretty much says that Jennifer gets it all. She's got to attain a certain age and there are provisions for her living and school expenses until that time, as well as some other stuff, but that's the gist of it."

"What if she dies?"

"The whole estate turns into a charitable foundation. No specific charities or people are named."

Beamon leaned back in his chair and folded his hands across his stomach. He sat there for almost a minute, with Michaels watching his face carefully.

"I don't know, Chet. I keep coming back to Jennifer and Jamie. We've got a young couple in love, a mother who doesn't like the boyfriend, and a pretty favorable trust here. What time are you leaving to meet with this kid?"

"Around noon. I'm going to the high school to talk to him and all her friends."

"Set Jamie up for the first interview. I assume you don't mind if I join you."

"Not at all."

7

BEAMON GAZED DEJECTEDLY AT THE LOW-slung yellow brick building as Michaels eased into a parking space next to an overflowing bike rack.

If memory served, the seventies was not one of the most economically sound periods in American history. And if that was true, it must be one of the great mysteries why all public buildings looked like they were built during that decade.

". . . So this kid's pretty bright . . ."

The flat roof of the school had gotten piled with snow and Beamon watched a tall black man walk carefully to the edge and begin to stab at a particularly large cornice with a shovel.

"Mark! Are you listening to me?"

Beamon pressed the release on his seatbelt and let it snap back toward the door. "Sorry, Chet. I was somewhere else. What were you saying?"

"Jamie Dolan. He's seventeen, a senior this year. Extremely intelligent—fifteen eighty on his SATs . . ."

"Is that good?"

"Uh, yeah. To put it in perspective, eight hundred is average. Sixteen hundred's perfect."

"Uh huh."

"So anyway, Jamie's parents split up when he was ten. Apparently his father had a drinking problem and was pretty abusive. Now Jamie lives with his mother in a trailer park about ten miles from here. He works at a local video club to help make ends meet. His mother's a waitress."

Beamon sighed. Sounded like an okay kid. Strong enough to rise above the less than full deck life had dealt him. Had he become impatient? Wanted it all now?

"You okay, Mark?"

"Yeah."

"I talked on the phone with a couple of his teachers and they pretty much all described him the same way. Very bright. Mature beyond his years. Not crazy about authority figures."

Beamon pushed the car door open and grabbed hold of the luggage rack to keep his feet from skidding out from under him as he got out. He knew how he was going to have to play this and was already starting to feel the guilt and regret creeping up on him. Despite the large neon sign in his head pointing to Jennifer and Jamie as the Davises' murderers, his intuition was telling him that that sign might be pointing in the wrong direction.

The problem was that he couldn't figure out if that gut reaction was the result of their innocence, or the fact that he just didn't want to believe they were guilty. There was just no satisfaction in nailing two love-crazed teenagers. Instead of making you feel like you'd won, it just made it feel like everyone had lost.

"Okay, Chet. Let's get this over with," Beamon said as he half-walked, half-slid across a wide puddle of ice to a patch of snow that would get him to the door.

The school didn't look a hell of a lot better inside than out. The walls were painted a uniform faded orange, broken only by an occasional mural, painted with a childlike sensibility that pegged it as the work of the student body. The halls were empty and the doors lining them were all closed. Prompted by a sign that read OFFICE, Beamon turned down a hall to his right and walked through the first door he came to.

The woman behind the tall counter jumped up from behind her desk and looked at Beamon with mild expectation. "Can I help you?"

"I hope so," Beamon said, digging into his jacket and pulling out his credentials. "I'm Special Agent Mark Beamon and this is Special Agent Chet Michaels. We were told we could use one of your conference rooms to talk with a few of your students?"

She looked down at the counter sadly. "I read all about it, but I still can't believe it. Mr. and Mrs. Davis were such nice people. And Jennifer . . . Do you have any leads?"

"We're doing everything we can," Beamon answered, anxious to get this over with and escape the vaguely musty-smelling building before he started having high school flashbacks. "I'm sorry, but I'm running a little tight on time . . ."

She spun on her heel and disappeared through a door behind her. A moment later she reappeared with a sturdy-looking gray-haired woman in a tweed suit.

"Mr. Beamon. I'm the principal here. Louise Darren."

"Nice to meet you, Ms. Darren. This is my associate, Chet Michaels."

As they shook hands, she motioned toward the door behind her. "Jamie and his mother are already in my office. You're welcome to use it to talk to them."

Beamon looked at the cheap hollow-core door that she had indicated, and its proximity to the outer office. "I appreciate that, but I wouldn't want to put you out of your office. Also, it might be more convenient if we could find something with a bit more privacy?"

She thought for a moment and then pointed down a narrow hall with walls papered in various announcements and lists. "There's a room we don't really use anymore down at the end of the hall. It's kind of full of junk, though."

Beamon smiled. "No problem. You should see my office."

"Right though here, Jamie," Beamon said, opening the door to the abandoned office and stepping aside. There was a dusty old desk piled high with papers and old books centered in the room. Chairs were plentiful, but most had been stacked against the walls.

"Why don't you and Chet grab us a few chairs and I'll be back in a minute." Beamon put his hand lightly on Jamie's mother's shoulder before she could enter. He closed the door quietly, leaving Chet and Jamie to rearrange the office.

"I'd like to speak with you for just a moment, if I could . . . Ms. Dolan is it?"

She shook her head. "Rodrigues. I went back to my maiden name when I was divorced."

"Excuse me—Ms. Rodrigues."

She looked up at him with deep concern that bordered on fear. It didn't seem to be an expression specific to the situation—just the generic powerlessness many poor Hispanics seemed to feel when faced with white male law enforcement officials.

And he was about to use that unfortunate feeling of powerlessness to the absolute hilt. What a guy.

"Would you mind terribly if we spoke to Jamie alone? Sometimes having a parent in the room makes kids nervous. You know how they are. It's really important that Jamie be relaxed so that he doesn't forget anything that might allow us to help Jennifer. I've been doing this for a lot of years and I can tell you that the smallest detail can be critical." He spoke—lied—slowly. Ms. Rodrigues's English was less than perfect.

Beamon pointed back down the hall toward the outer office. "Why don't you have a seat out there? We won't be long."

As she walked slowly away from him, Beamon told himself for the thousandth time that sometimes the end justified the means. He actually did believe that, it was just that he'd never run into a situation that he was dead sure qualified.

"Sorry about the wait, Jamie," he said, striding through the door and closing it tightly behind him. "Your mom's decided to wait for you outside."

"Okay."

Beamon took the chair across from the boy and looked him over carefully. His features were generally Caucasian, though he'd obviously inherited his skin and hair color from his mother. His eyes were a light brown that seemed to fade to dark green and then back again as he moved. His clothes were mostly black or dark gray and had that secondhand look that kids seemed to strive for these days— though based on what Chet had told him earlier, it was probably more of an economic necessity for him than an obsession with fashion.

"I guess you haven't found Jennifer yet," the boy said in a tired voice that carried an emotional maturity that should have been impossible at his age.

Beamon shook his head but didn't answer.

"Uh, do you know who did it?"

Beamon's silent stare was having the desired effect. What little calm the boy had entered with was starting to fray.

"Other than you? Nope."

The boy's eyes widened for a moment and he opened his mouth to say something, but checked himself. It was a moment before he finally spoke. "Why would I want to kidnap Jennifer? She was already my girlfriend. Ask anyone. We never even fought, hardly."

Beamon cocked his head. "I don't think you kidnapped her, Jamie. I think you and Jennifer were in this together. I think you finished your little concert and went home. Then I think you sneaked out of the house and took the car to Jennifer's, where you blew her parents' brains all over the living room. Then you took Jennifer somewhere where it would be a pain in the ass for me to find her and went home."

Beamon watched his young opponent carefully. The boy was trembling, but his eyes were clear and he was obviously carefully considering Beamon's words. He had to admire the kid—he'd had grown men face down on the table sobbing for less.

Jamie took a deep, shaky breath. "I read that Mr. and Mrs. Davis were found in the clothes they'd had on that day. No way I could have made it to their house before four in the morning—I got a hundred people I don't even know that'd swear to that. They'd have to sleep in their clothes."

Beamon shrugged. "I hear you got fifteen-eighty on your SATs, Jamie. I have to say I'd be a little disappointed if you'd just shot 'em in bed. No, Jennifer would have known exactly what they were wearing and you'd force them to get dressed and come downstairs. My compliments. Not terribly creative, but not bad for a minor. I mean, at least you didn't shoot the clock to establish a phony time of death, you know?"

Jamie ran a hand through his long black hair, dislodging the sweat from his hairline. Beamon watched as it ran down his face.

"Maybe this wasn't such a good idea. Maybe my mom should—"

Beamon cut him off. "If you're old enough to shoot two human beings in the face, I think you're old enough to talk to us without your mommy, don't you?"

"Why? Why would I kill them?" Jamie said in a pleading voice. "I didn't have anything against the Davises. I mean, what good would it do me that it'd be worth risking my whole life?"

Beamon leaned back in his chair and scraped an imaginary speck of dirt from under his thumbnail. "Oh, come on, Jamie. Don't insult my intelligence. Patricia Davis was not exactly shot in the ass with you. In fact, I think she had someone else in mind for Jennifer. Seems to me like a win-win proposition for you. You get rid of Patty and Jennifer miraculously escapes from her kidnappers a few weeks later. Just in time to pick up her inheritance."

"No!" Jamie protested. "Mrs. Davis liked me. That thing with Billy had been going on for years. Jennifer wasn't interested."

"That's not what I hear, son. What I hear is that she was putting a lot of pressure on Jennifer. That she hated you. She apparently thought that Jennifer could do better than a . . ." Beamon paused imperceptibly, choking a bit on the phrase, "half-spic living in a trailer park."

Jaime's face flashed with anger. "Fuck you, man." He jumped to his feet and pushed a book lying on the desk in front of him as hard as he could, but Beamon stopped it easily before it hit him in the chest.

"Sit down," Beamon ordered, raising his voice for the first time in the "interview." The boy glared at him, his breath coming like he'd just run a race.

"I won't tell you again. Sit."

Jamie looked over at Michaels, whose wide-eyed stare seemed frozen to his face, and then sank back into the chair.

"Look, Jamie. You're underage. You love Jennifer. Maybe she even talked you into this? Been

STORMING HEAVEN — 57

there. It's hard to say no to the woman you love. You start talking to me right now and I'll do everything I can to make things go easy for you. At this point, I think we can keep this in Juvenile—keep you from being tried as an adult." Beamon dropped the front legs of his chair to the floor loudly. "You keep fucking with me, though, and I'm going to make it my mission to get you. You're a smart kid. You go look up some articles on me in the library. You'll find that the people who come up against me end up in prison for the rest of their lives. Or dead."

Tears clouded the boy's eyes for the first time. "I didn't do it, man. Don't you think I want her back? Don't you?"

He ran past them and out the door, slamming it behind him. Beamon didn't bother to stop him.

"Jesus, Mark." Michaels said in a loud whisper that sounded a bit panicked. "You just threatened to kill that kid!"

"Did I?" Beamon pinched the bridge of his nose and tried to shake the feeling that he'd have made a hell of a Gestapo agent. Ripping into a seventeen-year-old kid with a history of abuse—and who was probably lying awake at night imagining his girl-friend being raped in the back of a van or some-thing—was right up there with clubbing baby seals on the fun meter. There were times when he really hated this job.

"So what do you think, Mark?"

Beamon sighed. "I got a bad feeling about that kid."

"Really? You think he did it?"

Beamon shook his head. "No, that would be a good feeling. It'd mean I found our man—boy— and was on the verge of finding Jennifer. I'm afraid that he didn't do it. And if that's true, I don't have a fucking clue where that little girl is."

8

MARK BEAMON SLAMMED HIS FOOT AGAINST the brake pedal and slid into a stand of snow-covered pines. The impact, slow as it was, knocked the snow off the trees and buried the front of his car. Apparently the snow-driving learning curve wasn't real steep for Texans. At least not this one.

The condominium complex that had been his home for the past month sparkled as the beams of widely spaced floodlights bounced off ice clinging to the sides of the buildings. It had been the first place his realtor had taken him. The FBI had relocated him more times than he could remember—in fact, someone had recently pointed out that he might be closing in on the record. And with that many moves under his belt, the monotonous chore of looking for housing had become almost physically painful.

Of course, he had no one to blame for his career as the FBI's itinerant lawman but himself. There was always some new office anxious to take on the man heralded as the best investigative mind in the Bureau. And there was always an office just as anxious to get rid of the man heralded as the biggest pain in the ass in the Bureau.

But that was the old Mark Beamon. He was the new, vastly improved Mark Beamon. He stepped from the car and kicked his front tire. Satisfied that he'd be able to get out the next morning, he started along one of the meticulously shoveled brick walkways that connected the forty units with the main office, frozen swimming pool, and each other.

Each building was configured with two units upstairs and two downstairs, and all faced out onto expanses of grass, trees, and flowers—or at least that's what he'd been told. Any landscaping that existed had been long buried when he'd arrived in January.

He slowed his pace a bit as his building came into view. As expected, Chet Michaels was sitting at the bottom of the stairs that led up to Beamon's condo. He had undoubtedly been there for exactly fifty minutes—Beamon was supposed to have met him there forty-five minutes ago and Michaels was always precisely five minutes early for every appointment. That wasn't the problem. The problem was the little girl who was unsuccessfully trying to catch the snowballs he was gently tossing to her. And the disaster was the auburn-haired woman in electric blue mittens handing him a steaming cup of something or other.

"Chet! You're early," Beamon called. "I said seven o'clock."

Michaels stood and brushed the snow off the back of his jeans as he approached. "You said six, Mark." He pointed to Beamon's right hand. "You wrote it on the back of your hand."

"Oh, yeah. So I did. Sorry." He turned to the woman standing next to Michaels. "Thanks for keeping him from freezing."

Carrie Johnstone smiled slyly and crouched down next to her daughter. "What do we do when Mr. Beamon gets home, Emory?"

The little girl ran at him and latched onto his leg. "Hi, Mr. Beamon," she slurred through a less than full complement of teeth.

"I'm trying to get Mark to relate to children," Carrie explained as Beamon tried to extract his leg from Emory's grip. "It's shaping up to be one of the greatest challenges of my career, but I think I'm wearing him down."

"What do you do, Carrie?" Michaels said.

"I'm a psychiatrist."

"Really? A psychiatrist? Wow." Michaels handed her back the barely touched cup of coffee and started up the steps toward Beamon's condo. About halfway up he paused and turned around. "You know, Doc, those of us who work for Mark would appreciate anything you could do for him. I'm sure I could take up a collection at the office to cover any fee."

Beamon glared at the young agent, who said, "Thanks for the coffee," and disappeared up the steps.

"Before you go up, Mark, could I talk to you?" Carrie said, suddenly looking a little nervous.

"Uh, sure. CHET!"

The young agent peeked over the railing at him and narrowly avoided being hit in the face by Beamon's keys. "Go on in. I'll be up in a second."

Carrie looked at him with a hint of disapproval registering in her expression. "You know, you really shouldn't leave your employees out on the steps to freeze, Mark. I tried to get him to come inside, but he wouldn't. Thought you'd be mad."

Beamon frowned. Michaels had obviously been busy using that Howdy Doody face to drum up sympathy from Carrie and make him look like an ogre. He'd have to remember to make his life a living hell for the next week or so.

"Couldn't be helped."

There was a brief lull in the conversation as Carrie reached one of her mitten-covered hands into her coat and pulled out an envelope. "I, uh, got this invitation to go to a wedding on Saturday and it says Carrie Johnstone and guest." She held it out as though he'd require proof. "Anyway, it's probably going to be pretty nice. I was wondering if you might want to go?"

He felt his eyebrows start to rise, but managed to stop them before they got too far from their normal resting position. He had met Carrie the day he'd moved in and had been instantly taken with her. She was intelligent, funny, and had a sarcastic edge that, while admittedly underdeveloped, showed real potential. He'd spent the last month trying to figure out a clever excuse to spend some time with her, but so far his normally devious mind had been a blank.

"Are you asking me on a date?" he said, a hint of a smile playing at his lips.

"Uh, I don't know if I'd call it a date. I just thought it'd be . . . fun."

He nodded thoughtfully and crouched down to bring himself eye-level with her daughter. "What do you think, Emory? Should I go on a non-date with your mother? Or should I insist on full date status?"

Emory looked at him blankly and then giggled and squealed. "Date!"

Beamon looked back up at Carrie. "Your daughter seems to think I deserve all the rights and privileges afforded a full-blooded date."

Carrie's expression turned severe, but he could tell she was trying not to laugh. "We'll have to talk about what you consider 'full rights and privileges,' but I'm willing to compromise. I'd consider an honorary title."

"I can live with that."

Beamon knocked the snow off his boots with a couple of violent kicks to the doorjamb and dropped his coat on the floor. Things were starting to look up. Of course, he still had no idea as to the whereabouts of the elusive Jennifer Davis, but he had managed to get a date with Carrie without having to go through the torture of actually asking. Not every day you got something for nothing.

"Okay, Chet, what've you got for me?"

Michaels leaned back into the sofa and put his feet on the large box that contained Beamon's coffee table. "She's really cool. Pretty, too. And a doctor." He rubbed at his bright red chin. "I think she likes you."

Beamon opened his refrigerator and pulled out two beers. "You'd better be talking about Jennifer Davis." He popped the tops off the bottles and walked around to Michaels.

"I was talking about Carrie."

Beamon sat down in a chair facing the sofa and

took a long pull from his beer. "So what I'm hearing you saying, Chet, is that you don't actually want to keep your job."

The young agent smirked and pulled two folders out of the open knapsack at his feet. He pointed to one of them. "Autopsy." Then the other. "Jennifer's real parents. Which one do you want to start with?"

Beamon polished off his beer with one more healthy gulp and started toward the kitchen for a refill. "I'm pretty sure the cause of death was their brains leaving their heads at the speed of sound, so why don't we start with the parents."

"Good choice. We've started to get in the info you wanted on Jennifer's real parents. James and Carol Passal. James was a grocery store manager in Portland, Oregon—Carol was a full-time mother, as near as we can tell. Both were killed in a fire that destroyed their home when Jennifer was two years old."

"Where was Jennifer?"

"They found her wandering around on the lawn."

"She was outside playing when the fire started?"

Michaels shook his head. "The fire started around midnight."

"Midnight, huh. What caused it?"

"The report's pretty cryptic. They ruled out foul play, but I'm not sure how, since they don't give a cause. Also, no one seems to have ever figured out how Jennifer got onto the lawn."

"Interesting."

"Oh, it gets way better than that. James had a

brother. He lived in Salem 'til he left town under a black cloud."

"And that cloud was . . ."

"Kidnapping category number three. Suspicion of child molestation."

Beamon fell back into the chair with his fresh beer. "Now that really *is* interesting. Was Jennifer involved?"

"It's possible, but I can't say for sure. The police investigated briefly, but when David took off, I guess they never got anything concrete enough to warrant bringing him back."

"Where is he now?"

"I think near Kanab, Utah."

"Where?"

"It's on the southern border of the state. Not that far from here, actually. I'm still trying to get a specific address, but the sheriff there said that Passal just lives up in the hills—pretty much keeps to himself."

"We need to find him, Chet. Now."

"I've called the guys that cover that area, they—"

Beamon pointed at the young agent, cutting him off. "That's fine, Chet, but the buck stops here. I expect to be face to face with this guy, like, tomorrow. Understood?"

Michaels looked down at the floor and nodded.

"Okay," Beamon said. "If you run into any problems, call me here or beep me. I'm available twenty-four hours a day for this. Now what else do you have for me?"

Michaels didn't seem to want to speak.

"Come on, Chet. Out with it."

"We can't seem to figure out who Carol Passal was."

"What, did Social Security lose her maiden name?"

Michaels grabbed his beer off the box/coffee table in front of him. "No, we found her maiden name no problem. We also found another identity prior to that. We're still trying peel back the layers and get at the original."

"Really? You're telling me that she purposefully changed her identity?"

He nodded.

"Only one reason to do that—you don't want to be found," Beamon said. "Check the database for any outstanding warrants on someone fitting her description. Maybe she was running from the law. Check with the IRS, too. People just hate paying their taxes. Otherwise, keep after it. Could be she was trying to get away from a psycho ex-husband or something. Anything else?"

Michaels shook his head and scribbled Beamon's instructions on the back of the folder.

"Okay, then. Hit me with the autopsy report. Just the highlights—it's getting late."

"Both Mr. and Mrs. Davis were shot with the same forty-five, Mrs. Davis in the right side of the back of her head and Mr. Davis under the chin. There were minor contusions around Mrs. Davis's mouth and nose that would suggest that someone pretty strong had grabbed her." He put his hand over his mouth and pinched his nose shut with his thumb and index finger to illustrate the point.

"Various contusions and a few fresh cuts were found on Mr. Davis, also suggesting a struggle."

Beamon nodded. "We saw the aftermath of all that in the kitchen."

"Yeah. Uh, no evidence that either of them was tied at any time, no evidence that either body was moved postmortem."

"Time of death?"

"They're putting it between eight P.M. and three A.M."

"That's kind of broad. The window?"

"Yeah. They had to make some assumptions about how fast the room cooled off after the window was broken."

Beamon nodded. "So based on what we have from the neighbors, between ten and three."

"Yeah. It would have been tight, but I don't think we can completely rule out the boyfriend based on the physical evidence."

"Yeah," Beamon sighed. "But I have to admit that I'm having a hard time creating a scenario that includes the kind of struggle you're describing if it was just him and Jennifer. That would mean, what? Jennifer held her mother while Jamie fought with her father? The struggle took place at two different times? There were more kids involved? I don't know." Beamon jumped up out of his chair and clapped his hands, startling the young agent a bit. "Okay, Chet. Get out of here. It's Friday night and that girl with the tattoos you like so much probably wants to be taken to dinner."

"I'm okay, Mark. If you want to, you know, drink a few beers and bat around some ideas . . ."

Beamon ignored the hopeful look on Michaels's face and pointed at the door as he made his way back to the refrigerator. He still had three more beers to put away before he reached his recently self-imposed limit of five per day. "Thanks, Chet, but you should go out and have a good time tonight, because this weekend you're going to be doing what?"

"Finding David Passal," Michaels mumbled as he gathered up his folders and headed for the door. "Oh, Mark. I took a message for you this afternoon from the lab. It's on your desk, but it said something like, 'A year's worth of hair, no drugs.' Does that make any sense?"

"Yeah, thanks," Beamon said, dropping onto the sofa as Michaels pulled the door shut behind him.

With his foot, Beamon snagged the coat he'd thrown on the floor and retrieved a tobacco pouch from the breast pocket. The message meant that the hair he'd retrieved from Jennifer Davis's sink—a year's growth—showed no narcotic residue. She was clean.

What was he missing? he wondered as he tapped tobacco into a paper wrapper.

What would someone want with Jennifer Davis? What good was she with her parents dead? Every time he came up with a plausible answer, there were two or three facts to refute it.

He finished rolling the cigarette and looked at it longingly for a few moments. No smoking in the house. It was another one of his new and ironclad rules. That rule, combined with the rather majestic local weather, had been instrumental in reducing his smoking from a two packs a day to five or six of these hand-rolled jobs.

He looked over at his front door. It was rattling slightly as the frigid wind outside battered it. Beamon laid the cigarette on his stomach and decided that gazing at it and drinking a few more beers would have to satisfy his vices for the night.

9

BEAMON SHUFFLED THROUGH THE TEETER-
ing stack of personnel files on his sofa, finally
finding the one he was looking for in the middle.
He gave it a quick jerk and watched the rest of the
pile destabilize and topple onto the floor of his living room.

He kicked them over toward the wall and wondered for the hundredth time if he really had what
it took to run an office. He'd spent the last weeks
trying to get around to familiarizing himself with
the backgrounds of his new staff—something that
should have been a simple task. D. gave him the
files and he just had to flip through them. Why
then, two weeks later, were they strewn across his
floor, unread?

The answer was as obvious as it was unsettling:
He owed a great deal of his success to date to his
ability to ignore the noise around him and focus all
his attention on one task. A wonderful quality in an
investigator. A shitty quality in a manager.

As he saw it, he'd already proven that he made
an impossible subordinate. So it was time to get his
ass in gear and prove that he made one hell of a
good boss. Otherwise, he had serious problems.

Beamon leaned forward and picked up his
glasses. Perching them on his nose, he flipped open

the folder in his lap and tried to concentrate on the picture of the young man stapled to the inside cover.

He was a second office agent—talented, diligent, hard-working. That is, until about a month ago when his wife ran off with the pool guy. Beamon had initially thought that this was an elaborate joke, created to welcome him to the world of management. But it turned out that she actually did. The goddamn pool guy.

And now, as the new Assistant Special Agent in Charge–Flagstaff, this was *his* problem. He had to figure out a way to straighten this kid out before he did or didn't do something that would permanently fuck up his career. The question was, how? Tell him to cowboy up? Walk it off? No, wait—how about, "There are a lot of fish in the sea?"

Christ.

Beamon dropped the folder on the couch and let the Jennifer Davis problem creep back into his mind. While he was sitting around worrying about the sexual trysts of his staff's spouses, her clock was ticking. The statistics on this kind of disappearance were clear—every day she was missing, his chances of finding her alive got cut in half.

— — —

"I'm sorry, I was expecting Mark Beamon. What can I do for you?" Carrie Johnstone said, stepping back to better take in the full impact of what stood before her.

Beamon tugged uncomfortably at the lapel of his suit. The silky-smooth wool felt strange beneath his fingers. "C'mon, Carrie. Give me a break. I feel weird enough as it is."

"Weird?" she said, motioning for him to come inside. "Why would you feel weird? You look fantastic! I don't think I've ever seen you in a suit that fit you and didn't have holes in it."

Beamon nodded self-consciously. "It was a gift. I mean, it's a great suit, but it makes me look like I mugged a European tourist."

She reached around the back of his neck and yanked his collar up. "Hugo Boss? Someone gave you a Hugo Boss suit?"

"Yeah. A mob boss in New York, actually."

"I see," Carrie said as she sat down at a small writing desk in the living room and started scribbling on a Post-it note. "Should I be concerned that my tax dollars are paying the salary of an FBI agent who receives expensive gifts from organized crime?"

"Probably."

Her dress was a deep maroon that seemed to change color magically as she moved. High-quality silk, Beamon knew—he'd become something of an expert at identifying different fabrics on an investigation involving a bomb planted in a clothing-filled suitcase.

What was important, though, was that it clung to her body perfectly. Not too tight, but suggestive in all the right places. Her auburn hair swayed slightly as she wrote, revealing brief glimpses of the smooth skin of her back.

She looked much younger than she did in the business suits and heavy sweaters Beamon normally saw her in. He made a mental note to try to devise a clever way of ferreting out her age over the course of the evening.

"When did you start wearing glasses, Mark?" Carrie asked without looking up.

"I got them a few months ago, but I don't wear them much. Having kind of a hard time getting used to them."

Carrie finished what she was writing and looked down a hall to her left. "Stacey! We're leaving now. I left some instructions on the stuff in the oven and my cell phone number in case there are any problems. Don't call me unless it's an emergency, okay, hon? I'm going to be in a church."

Beamon heard a muffled reply and Carrie, apparently satisfied, grabbed her purse and slid an arm into his.

"Why?"

"Why what?" Beamon said, having a little trouble holding onto coherent thoughts as she brushed against him.

"Why are you having a hard time getting used to them? I think they look very distinguished."

"Oh, it's not the glasses per se, it's more the clarity. I'm not sure I didn't like the world better with softer edges." Beamon reached out and opened the door for her. "By the way, have I mentioned how incredibly beautiful you look tonight?"

"No, you hadn't, actually."

"Well, it's because I was trying to find a more artistic way of phrasing it."

She smiled as they walked out into the silence of the snow-covered courtyard. "I think most women would settle for 'incredibly beautiful.'"

Beamon had read somewhere that the construction of a church pew was actually an art of some subtlety. The craftsman had to strike a perfect balance between intense discomfort—so your less fervent worshippers wouldn't fall asleep—and ergonomics, so the truly devout wouldn't suffer crippling back and neck injuries.

Fully an hour into a ceremony that didn't seem to be in any danger of wrapping up, Beamon managed to find a position that briefly relieved the pressure on his spine. Permanent damage might yet be avoided.

His chiropractic distress momentarily eased, Beamon was able to turn his attention back to the ceremony, which he had to admit had been very educational.

He knew criminally little about the fledgling Church of the Evolution and its leader Albert Kneiss, especially considering that it was headquartered right in the middle of his new back yard. It was the fastest-growing religion in the world and it was unpopular with the German government. Other than that, his knowledge consisted of a bunch of unconnected factoids.

There was really no excuse for his ignorance. The Kneissians had brought countless jobs to the area, built hospitals, schools, and museums. Beamon seemed to remember reading somewhere that their numbers had swelled to over eleven million members worldwide, and their influence over the Flagstaff area, and Arizona in general, continued to expand.

He turned to Carrie to ask her a question about the progress of the ceremony, or more accurately when the hell it would be over, but she seemed to be lost in the thoughts she was scribbling into the notebook on her lap. He sighed quietly and looked around him.

The cathedral surrounding them had been only recently completed, but the architecture and carefully chosen materials gave it a look of permanence usually reserved for buildings hundreds of years old. The complex grid of arches supporting the ceiling were hewn of a light wood and tipped with ornate geometric carvings that dangled into space like stalactites. That touch of vaguely Scandinavian informality was countered by the heavy stone of the walls—a few of which had water running down their mossy faces into marble pools.

Despite its size, the church was packed. With few exceptions, the congregation had that well turned out but unimaginative way of dressing and impeccable grooming that the world had come to associate with followers of Kneiss.

At the altar, the bride and groom were passing their hands ceremoniously through the flame of an ornate candle held by a pious-looking man spouting some mumbo-jumbo about purification.

Beamon looked over at Carrie, who was still scribbling furiously, and decided to interrupt her. He had never been much for long religious spectacles. By now, even God had to be about ready for a couple of stiff drinks and a cocktail weenie.

"Nice ceremony," he whispered.

She looked up from her pad and smiled.

"Uh, about how much longer do they generally go on?"

"Don't really know, Mark. I've never been to one of these."

"Really? You mean you're not . . ."

"A Kneissian? No."

Beamon nodded silently but decided to exercise a little more of his curiosity while he had her talking. "What's that you keep writing?"

She looked around conspiratorially and leaned so close that he could feel her lips brush against his ear. "I'm doing a study on how religious affiliation can influence various psychoses. I don't really know that much about this faith, and I thought this would be helpful."

Beamon let that process for a moment.

"Lucky you knew a Kneissian who happened to be getting married this weekend," he said hopefully.

Her expression went blank for a moment.

"We're crashing this wedding, aren't we, Carrie?"

"'Crashing' is such an ugly w—"

The congregation stood and the sound of rustling clothes and dropping Bibles drowned out the rest of Carrie's sentence.

Beamon smiled politely and waved at the young couple as they walked elatedly down the aisle, followed by their attendants. He leaned over to Carrie again. "They make such a nice couple. And what a beautiful wedding. I can't wait for the reception."

"I wasn't really planning on going to the reception," Carrie said. "I think that might be pushing it."

"Are you kidding? There's no way I'm sitting through an," he looked at his watch, "hour-and-twenty-minute wedding ceremony and not going to the reception."

"I thought maybe I'd take you out to dinner instead," she said, starting to sound a bit apprehensive.

Beamon shook his head. "Wouldn't be much of a substitute, would it?"

Now this *was* fun. Already it had completely made up for that endless ceremony.

The conference room of the Radisson, lined with balloons and paper streamers for the occasion, had been set up with countless small round tables, each surrounded by tipsy wedding revelers. The band at the other end of the room had just started and the table where he and Carrie sat had been abandoned at the first chords of "Louie Louie."

Beamon swirled a shrimp in a blob of cream cheese and popped it in his mouth. One thing he had to say about the Kneissians—they could really throw a party. Great food, and enormous open bar with only top-shelf stuff, and man, were they friendly. At a minimum, twenty-five people had approached them and struck up a conversation. And thankfully, due either to the nice suit and glasses he was wearing, or the dim light and booze, not a single person had recognized him as the man who had been recently besieged by the press over Jennifer Davis's disappearance.

Of course, his anonymity had been helped along by the fact that he told everyone who approached him that he was hard of hearing and really only Carrie's date. She was the one intimately acquainted with the bride.

Thus had started a rather long and painful

STORMING HEAVEN — 79

evening for Carrie Johnstone. She'd delighted Beamon for the last hour with a string of confused lies
and brief outbursts of nervous laughter as she discussed the bride from childhood to present.

The blue-haired woman who had been chatting
with Carrie through a smile that looked like it was
held in place by fishhooks finally straightened up,
waved a good-bye to Beamon, and began weaving
though the crowd toward the bar.

"Shrimp?" Beamon said, holding a cream-
cheese-doused shellfish in Carrie's general direction.

"I'm going to get you for this, Mark. I don't
know how. And I'm not sure when. But I will."

Beamon slipped into his most innocent smile.
"You've just spent an hour conversing with your test
subjects, Carrie. I thought you'd be thanking me."

She held out her hand and scowled. "Give me
the shrimp."

She popped it in her mouth, then sucked down
half the glass of wine in front of her.

"C'mon, Carrie. You can't tell me this hasn't
been even more productive than the ceremony. I've
learned volumes just sitting here. As venues for peo-
ple-watching, wedding receptions are right up there
with . . ." He was about to say "strip bars," but
caught himself. "Uh, public parks."

She took another gulp of her wine. "Well, what
I've learned is that *you* can't be trusted. I assume
from my conversations that you've been telling people that you're just my date and that you don't
know anybody here."

"Uh, I think I used the words toy boy, actually.
Oh, and there was that deafness thing."

"Right, a few people mentioned your little hearing problem. You'll be happy to know that I told them it was the result of untreated syphilis."

That probably explained the strange looks on the faces of a few of the people Carrie had spoken to and their furtive glances in his direction.

"Touché," he said, surprised at the depth of the relief he felt when her face broke into a beautiful smile. He'd had no idea how she would take his little prank. Some women seemed so perfect, but then you found out that they couldn't laugh at themselves.

Beamon scooted his chair closer to her and looked around to make sure no one was within earshot. "Serves you right. Getting the head of the FBI's local office to aid and abet you in crashing a wedding. At least tell me what the paper you're writing is about."

"It's about the way religion affects people's mental health." Beamon could hear the excitement creep into her voice as she started to explain her work. Another mark in the Carrie Johnston plus column. He loved people who were passionate about something. Didn't really matter what.

"How do you mean?"

"Well, if you believe very strongly in any particular religion, that dogma is going to affect your perceptions and therefore your mental outlook. Let's compare a very devout Muslim woman with a devout Kneissian woman. Now, many Muslims have very strong beliefs that keep women as sort of second-class citizens. This might create, for instance, problems with self-esteem."

Beamon thought about that for a moment.

Seemed to make sense. "And the Kneissian woman?"

"Well, the Kneissians are at the other end of the spectrum. They are almost completely lacking in institutional chauvinism. On the other hand, they are very focused on financial and political success. So a Kneissian woman might have self-esteem problems just as severe, but they would relate to, say, a lack of success in her job."

"I'll buy that."

"Obviously, that's an oversimplified example. Here's a better one. How old do you think the bride and groom are?"

Beamon shrugged. "I have no idea. They looked like kids to me, but then, so does half my staff."

"I'd guess that they were just out of high school. For some reason, Kneissians get married very young and have an extremely high divorce rate."

Beamon nodded thoughtfully. "Recruitment."

"Excuse me?"

"That's why they marry early and get divorced," he said. "Recruitment."

"I don't think I follow you."

Beamon grabbed another shrimp. "What's the purpose of religion?"

"That's a pretty complicated question. To make people feel less alone?"

Beamon scowled. "No. That's the purpose of God. The purpose of a religion is simply to force everyone into its way of thinking."

"Why, Mark. You're a cynic. I never would have guessed."

Beamon ignored the jibe. "Seriously. The Church of the Evolution doesn't miss many opportunities to tell you it's the fastest-growing religion in the world. How do you think they achieved that?"

She pushed a dirty plate out of her way and leaned against the table. "I think they've created a pretty attractive belief system that fills a lot—" The expression on Beamon's face made her stop. "You're going to tell me that I'm overthinking again, aren't you?"

He smiled and nodded furiously. "They're growing faster than any other religion 'cause they've been more scientific about recruitment. Take our young couple today. Let's assume a perfect scenario for the church. The boy was, I don't know . . . Buddhist. He converted in order to marry the girl, who was Kneissian. They have a couple of kids and get divorced, say five years from now. Our groom likes the church and decides to stay. They're both single for a few years, then he finds a nice Baptist he wants to marry and she converts. Same thing happens to our bride, but maybe she converts a Protestant. Both new couples have two more kids. How many new Kneissians have we just created?"

Carrie counted on her fingers. "Uh, nine?"

"Sounds about right."

She held her glass up in salute and took another sip of her wine. "I have to say, Mark, that's got to be the most malignant piece of deductive reasoning I've ever heard."

"Thank you. Are you ready to take me to dinner?"

She folded her arms across her chest and gave him a stern look. "That offer was *instead* of the reception, not in addition to. Besides—you have to have eaten a hundred shrimp already."

The way her eyes crinkled at the edges when she smiled really was dazzling. The truth was, he really wasn't hungry—and the shrimp and cream cheese he'd eaten had definitely not been on the new and improved Mark Beamon diet—but he didn't want the evening to end just yet. "Yeah, but they weren't very good."

The silk of her dress gathered and dispersed the dim light of the room hypnotically as she stood. "Okay, Mark. You win. Since you seem to have elevated cynicism to the level of a religion, I think I might be able to write the check off on my taxes."

10

"HELLO?" BEAMON CALLED INTO THE EMPTY reception area of the Kane County, Utah, sheriff's office. No answer.

He leaned his head into the half-open window centered in the wall. "Hello! Anyone home? I'm Mark Beamon from the FBI."

There was a moment of silence, then a disembodied voice. "Wait in the conference room."

Beamon stepped back and scanned the missing persons posters taped haphazardly to the glass. Jennifer Davis smiled out from one of them, posing self-consciously alongside a bicycle with a big red bow on the seat. The other lost souls had similarly cheerful expressions and stood with jumping dogs, new motorcycles, and loved ones, oblivious to their current plights.

Those frozen images were all that was left of most of them, Beamon knew. Few would ever be found, and most of the ones who were would be discovered because some lost hiker tripped over one of their sun-bleached bones.

"This is it," Chet Michaels said, pointing to an open door in the hall to Beamon's left and breaking him out of his trance.

They waited in the large conference room for almost twenty minutes before the sheriff finally strutted in, flanked by two deputies.

That was probably a bad sign. It was Sunday afternoon and all he needed was directions to David Passal's place. He could have just taken them over the phone, but it was his practice to meet the locals before he started prowling around their jurisdiction.

One of the deputies hopped up on the counter running along the edge of the room and tapped his hand rhythmically on the edge of the sink next to him. The other just leaned against the wall next to the door and tried to look as imposing as possible.

"You Beamon?" the sheriff said, standing near the end of the conference table and looking them over carefully.

Beamon had decided to make this trip a casual-dress affair. He was wearing an old pair of jeans and a pair of cowboy boots that hadn't seen his feet since his days as a firearms instructor to the Nevada police. No point rushing into Kanab looking like a cross between an IRS agent and a funeral director. Made people uncomfortable.

"Yeah. Call me Mark." Beamon considered standing and offering his hand but instead just motioned to his right. "I think you spoke to Chet yesterday."

The sheriff nodded curtly. He had that impossible build that seemed so common in rural America. His face, arms, and legs were lean—thin, almost—but he had a great expanse of a belly that had wrestled his gray-tan shirttail out of his pants and was now covering up the ornate tooling on his leather gunbelt.

"What do you FBI boys want with Dave Passal?"

Beamon wasn't anxious to stand around posturing with the locals, but he didn't really have a choice.

He had no idea how to find Passal, and you never knew when you'd be desperately in need of some quick firepower.

"Would you know where we could find him?"

"Nope. He don't come into town much. Could be anywhere."

His backup snorted quietly.

"David's Jennifer Davis's uncle. Her only living blood relative," Beamon said. "I thought he might know something that could help me."

The sheriff—who still hadn't introduced him-self—tried not to let his surprise show. "You think maybe Dave might have been involved?"

Beamon put on a bored expression. "Drive all that way to kidnap a girl he hadn't seen or spoken to in twelve years? I doubt it." Not exactly the truth, but he had no idea if the sheriff was Passal's hunting partner, brother-in-law, or best friend.

"We had a bank robbery here awhile back," the sheriff started. "Teller got killed. Nice kid. Bunch of your boys came up from Salt Lake. Started givin' half the town the rubber hose treatment. You know what they found in the end?

"Actually, I have no idea," Beamon said.

"Nothin'. Turned my town upside down and inside out, then they just packed up their stuff and left."

"Look, Sheriff . . . ?"

"Parkinson."

"Sheriff Parkinson. It's just me and Chet here. We want to see if this guy knows anything, then we plan to ride off into the sunset. With a little luck, we're talking *tonight's* sunset."

Parkinson nodded silently. Suspicion was still etched clearly across his face, but the hostility seemed to be fading a bit.

"Don't see much of Dave, but I reckon he's still up there."

"Up there?" Michaels prompted excitedly.

The sheriff raised his hand lazily and pointed in a generally eastward direction. "Got a place up in the hills about an hour outside of town. Doesn't come down much. Just to get supplies every now and again."

"Could you give us directions on how to get there?"

"Why don't I just send a couple of my boys up there with you." He looked into the innocent face of Chet Michaels. "I'd hate to see the paperwork if I let a couple of you FBI boys get your asses shot off."

Michaels leaned forward over the table. "So you think he's armed?"

Beamon winced and Parkinson's deputies giggled.

"Hell yeah, he's armed, son. Probably kills most of what he eats. That and he always struck me as one of those paranoid types. You know, thinks there's a Russian behind every tree. I doubt he gets many visitors and I reckon he likes it that way."

Beamon sighed quietly. If Passal was involved, the last thing he needed was a couple of the sheriff's lackeys standing around siding with the man. They'd be there all week. "I appreciate the offer, Sheriff, but I don't really think it's necessary. We aren't after Passal, we just want to talk to him for a few minutes and then we're gone."

The sheriff looked strangely pleased that Beamon had declined his offer. Probably curious to see what Passal would do to the city slickers from Flagstaff. "Your call," he said with a condescending shrug of his shoulders.

Beamon managed to open the car door about a foot before the wind blew it shut again. Chet Michaels's quiet laughter was silenced when his door was torn from his hand with the sound of bending metal.

"You mind? I'm still making payments on this thing," Beamon said, putting his shoulder into the door and successfully escaping the car before the wind blew it shut again.

They'd stopped just as the road crested a hill and disappeared into the darkening sky. In the near distance Beamon could see a column of smoke rise above the dense pine forest and then suddenly disperse in the swirling wind.

Better to finish this trip on foot, try to get close to Passal before he had a chance to dust off his grenade launcher.

"Okay, Chet, here we go. Why don't you walk up the road and knock on the door. See if anyone's home."

The young agent looked apprehensive. "What're you going to be doing?"

"I was going to sit in the car and have a smoke. It's freezing out here." Beamon smiled. "Relax. I'll be right behind you. I'm going to walk up through the trees here. Just in case."

Michaels reached for his gun, but Beamon stopped him. "Think friendly, Chet. Just going up there to borrow a cup of venison jerky, right? No need for anyone to get upset."

Michaels reluctantly flipped his sweater back over the butt of his gun and looked up at the road, trying to gauge the distance to the fading column of smoke.

"Wait about three minutes, then get moving, okay, Chet?" Beamon could feel the cold penetrating his parka and wanted to get moving before he started to get sluggish. "No, on second thought, give me about ten minutes. I think I'm going to take it easy." Michaels nodded as Beamon slid his new glasses onto his nose and pulled out his .357.

It was slow going. Utah's drought year and constant sun had kept the roads and endless miles of sagebrush relatively clear, but in the shadows of the trees, the snow and ice had accumulated. Beamon concentrated on every step, scanning the ground carefully and occasionally bypassing an area where the shadows had grown too deep to see well. He guessed he was about halfway to the source of the smoke they'd seen earlier when he saw the fading sun glint off something he'd hoped not to find.

A thin piece of fishing line about three inches from the ground blocked his path. It spanned about four feet between a small sapling and a dense tangle of sagebrush.

Beamon knelt down, ignoring the jagged edges of frozen pine needles beneath his knees, and leaned forward until his ear was almost to the ground. He gently pushed away a dead branch and exposed a simple but undoubtedly efficient mechanism involving a gas can and a road flare.

He stood and stepped carefully over the fishing line, scanning the ground for secondary trip wires.

The darkness was coming fast as the sun dipped behind a butte to the west. Beamon knew he was moving too quickly, but according to his watch, Michaels had been making his way up the road for almost a minute now. And sending him in alone to face down a man who obviously had no qualms about setting trespassers on fire would definitely take him out of the running for manager of the year.

Two minutes and one more trip wire later, Beamon could see the faded white of a trailer through the woods. He stopped just before the edge of the clearing and hovered behind a deformed pine.

It was about what he'd expected. The single-wide looked like it had been patched together with plywood and duct tape, and the only thing holding the roof on was a mismatched collection of old tires piled two high across the front edge.

The only other building visible was about twenty-five yards away and looked to be entirely constructed of old wooden signs. The low hum emanating from it and the cable snaking between it and the trailer suggested that it housed a generator. No way to get power run this far north of the middle of nowhere.

Beamon scanned the clearing as Michaels walked stiffly around the corner and started toward the trailer. Nothing. Just the wind blowing half-frozen dust and intermittent snowflakes through the air.

Michaels was almost to the door when Beamon saw one of the tires on top of the trailer move out of sync with the wind. He raised his gun too late and watched helplessly as a man in camouflage pants and a black sweatshirt jumped from the roof and landed on a very surprised Chet Michaels.

The force of the impact upended the makeshift staircase that Michaels had been standing on, and both men went down hard. Beamon jumped up from his crouched position and was about to run to Michaels's aid when the man he assumed was David Passal dragged the young agent to his feet and pushed a pistol into his neck.

Outstanding.

"What do you want?" Passal yelled, jerking back and forth on the back of Michael's sweater for no apparent reason.

Beamon was still one of the best pistol shots in the FBI, but this one just wasn't doable. It was a good twenty yards in a stiff wind. Couple that with the fact that Michaels was flopping around like a rag doll and it would have been fifty-fifty for Annie Oakley.

"I haven't told nobody nothing! You said you'd leave me alone!" Passal pulled his pistol from Michaels's neck and used the sight to scan the treeline.

With the gun no longer trained on Michaels, Beamon felt his heart rate notch higher. It was time to do something. Walking out of the trees probably wasn't a great call. Passal looked pretty agitated and would almost certainly shoot him.

Beamon turned his gaze from Passal and focused on Michaels. The fear he expected to find on the young agent's face hadn't materialized. As near as Beamon could tell from this distance, his young associate's current mood was hovering somewhere between irritated and mildly pissed off.

Passal's eyes were darting back and forth wildly. "Come out. Do it! Come out where I can see you. I'll kill him before you can do me!"

The situation wasn't improving and it didn't look like it was going to. Beamon aimed his gun a couple of feet wide of Passal's ear, took a deep breath. Hopefully this was where he was going to find out how a guy who looked like Howdy Doody became a champion collegiate wrestler.

He squeezed the trigger and the bullet smashed through the front window of the trailer, prompting Passal to duck away from the shower of glass.

And that was all the time Michaels needed. With one hand he grabbed the gun and with the other he lifted Passal's right leg off the ground and tipped him over onto his back.

When Beamon finally ran up to them, Passal's pistol was lying in the dirt and Michaels had the man's limbs so twisted and tangled up that he looked like a contortionist. A contortionist in considerable pain.

Beamon picked up the gun, flipped the safety, and stuck it in his waistband. "You had me worried there for a second, Chet."

Michaels gave one last subtle twist of his hips that made Passal cry out in pain and then pulled him to his feet. "Sorry. I wasn't looking for him on the roof."

"It was my fault. I had the wide view."

Passal tried to back away, but Beamon grabbed him by the front of his shirt.

"What do you want?" the man said in a terrified voice. "I did what you asked! Leave me alone!"

Beamon moved his hand to Passal's throat and slammed him against the trailer. "That's not what we hear, David. We hear you've been talking to people you shouldn't."

Out of the corner of his eye, Beamon could see Michaels's confused expression. Not exactly an FBI-approved interrogation technique, but he had no idea who Passal thought they were and his curiosity was getting the better of him.

Beamon squeezed the man's neck a little harder. Just enough to make his point, but not so hard that the man couldn't answer him. Passal grabbed his wrist and Beamon tensed his arm to keep the man under control. Instead of trying to pull his hand away, though, Passal became momentarily confused, finally pushing the sleeve of Beamon's parka up to the middle of his forearm.

"Who the fuck are you guys?" Passal said, the fear draining from his face in a matter of seconds.

Beamon released him and stepped back, wondering what the hell had just happened. He produced his credentials from the inside pocket of his coat.

"FBI!?" Passal said. "What the fuck do you want? Get off my property!"

"We just want to talk to you for a few minutes. We'd already be gone if you hadn't decided to do your Superman impression from the roof."

Passal grunted and looked over at Michaels.

"Who did you think we were?" Beamon asked.

"I don't have to say anything to you, man," Passal said, starting to shiver. The wind was obviously cutting through his sweatshirt as if it weren't there.

Beamon kicked the stairs back upright and took a step toward Passal's trailer. "It's been a good five minutes since I felt my toes, Dave. Why don't you invite us in?" He balanced his way up the rickety steps and through the front door of the trailer. It wasn't much warmer inside than it was out. The cold wind streaming through the window Beamon's bullet had shattered was starting to overpower the old iron wood-burning stove in the corner.

Beamon walked the length of the small trailer examining the makeshift shelves lining the walls and the large cans of fruits and vegetables stacked on them. Other than that, there were some skins drying on 2x4s and a bed in the corner. The only weapon he found was an unloaded shotgun, unless he counted the hatchet lying on an empty paint can.

"Come on up, Dave. It's cold out there," Beamon said, sliding both the shotgun and the hatchet under the bed and out of reach

Passal walked up to the door and paused as though he was entering a house he'd never seen before. Beamon motioned to one of two chairs around a formica-covered card table and stuffed a couple of split logs into the stove. When the flames reached a more satisfying height and intensity, he turned back to Michaels, who was standing in the doorway. "Why don't you go have a look around while we talk. Stay out of the woods, though— booby traps. Just around the trailer and generator house. Carefully."

"Hey, he can't do that!" Passal said as Michaels disappeared through the door.

Beamon sat down across the table from him. "He just did."

While the trailer was just about what Beamon had imagined, Passal himself wasn't. Despite his threadbare clothes and less than cosmopolitan surroundings, he was alert, and his hair was reasonably well kept—not the long scraggly locks or military cut that people who chose this type of life normally favored. The eyes that had a few minutes ago flashed with paranoia and fear had settled into the calm apprehension of a thinking man.

Beamon considered his plan of attack carefully. "I'd like to talk to you about your niece."

"My what?"

"Your niece. Jennifer?"

Passal's expression softened for a moment. "Haven't thought about her in a long time. She was two last time I saw her. Couldn't be much more than fourteen now."

"Almost sixteen, actually."

Passal nodded thoughtfully. "What's the FBI want with a fifteen-year-old girl?"

"To find her. She was kidnapped a few days back. The couple who adopted her were both shot in the head. Hell of a mess."

The muscles in the man's jaw rippled subtly as his teeth clenched. "So you thought maybe the child molester did it. Fuck you."

"Don't know who did it, Dave. Thought you might be able to help me. Maybe your brother or your sister-in-law might have had some enemies. Any ideas?"

"They're both dead," Passal said. "Any enemies they had ought to be satisfied with that, don't you think?"

"You tell me."

Passal's quiet apprehension seemed to be slowly evolving into full-fledged nervousness. "No. No enemies."

"You're sure."

"Yeah. I'm sure."

"What can you tell me about your sister-in-law?"

"What do you mean?"

"It sounds kind of strange, but we're having a hard time figuring out who she was. Looks like she might have changed her name a few times, moved around a bit. Would you know anything about that?"

"No."

Beamon pulled a pouch of tobacco from his pocket and began slowly rolling a cigarette. "Maybe you remember where she was from? Did she ever mention any family?"

"No."

Passal knew something, but his fixed stare and the set of his jaw told Beamon that he wasn't going to succumb to any classroom interrogation techniques. Beamon considered taking him in, but decided that it would be pointless and possibly dangerous. If the man did have Jennifer stashed around here somewhere, she'd likely die without him tending her. Goddamn cold in Utah at night.

Beamon lit the cigarette and mulled over his options. They were all bad. All he could do was move as quickly as possible and hope that luck was with him. He stood abruptly, prompting Passal to scoot back in his chair.

"Okay, then, sorry to have bothered you. Is there any way we can reach you if we come up with something that might jog your memory?"

Passal looked down at the table. "You won't."

Beamon paused for a moment just outside the door. "Must get kind of lonely up here sometimes. Don't know if I could do it."

Passal turned a tired face toward him. "Maybe you'll get a chance to find out. There's an empty lot about a mile down the creek. I'll save it for you."

Beamon cocked his head and opened his mouth to speak, but then thought better of it. He'd get what Passal knew. He just needed a little leverage.

"Okay, Chet, we're out of here," Beamon called.

Michaels was walking with comic slowness through the sagebrush west of Passal's trailer, his eyes locked on the ground.

"Anything?" Beamon asked as Michaels retraced his steps and came alongside him on the road.

"That shack over there is the only other building. There's a snowmobile and a generator in it and that's about it. I looked under the trailer—it's up on a bunch of cinderblocks cemented together. Nothing but some old lumber. How 'bout you?"

"He knows something, but he sure doesn't want to tell me what it is."

"So you think he's involved?"

"Either that or he has an idea who is. I don't know. This one's throwing me."

Beamon looked up at the stars coming to life in the darkening sky and pulled his parka close around his neck. "You hear the weather forecast for tonight?"

"Yeah. The wind's supposed to die down. Other than that, clear and cold."

"Good flying weather."

"You're going to fly back to Flagstaff?"

The sound of pounding drifted up behind them on the wind. Michaels jerked around, but Beamon just kept walking. Passal patching his broken window. "No, we're going to stick around."

"And watch Passal?"

"And improve our relationship with the sheriff."

"But what if he's got her? He might be planning on getting rid of her right now!"

"It's possible," Beamon said hesitantly, trying to fight back the memories of his most spectacular failure. "But if we bring in a bunch of people to watch him, he'd know it. Hell, we couldn't even sneak up on him today."

It had been years ago in the heat of a southern Texas summer. He had brought in no less than ten agents to watch and occasionally harass Bill Meyers, his primary suspect in the kidnapping of a ten-year-old girl from El Paso.

A few weeks later he'd found the girl tied up in a pit about a mile from Meyers's house. The memory of how she looked, staring up at him, her skin turning black and her swollen tongue prying her mouth open, was still painfully vivid.

It seemed that Meyers had stopped bringing the girl food and water when Beamon's men started watching him. According to the local coroner, the little girl's death had been extremely unpleasant.

II

"OKAY, SO I'M STILL BEHIND THE TREE. I thought I caught the guy solid through his car window, but I'm not sure, right? And I'm not too happy about having to stick my head out 'cause the tree next to me doesn't have any bark left from this asshole's machine gun."

Beamon kicked an empty chair across the floor to demonstrate the tree's relative position. "I had to do something, though, you know?"

The man was an artist, there was just no denying it. Sheriff John Parkinson and three of his deputies sat literally on the edges of the seats surrounding the torn-up old wood table, transfixed by Mark Beamon's manic way of telling a story.

Chet Michaels leaned back, took another sip from the Budweiser he'd been nursing for the last hour, and watched his boss's face intently. There was nothing in his expression or tone that would indicate that he was anything more than some good-old-boy cop from Texas. No trace of the reportedly off-the-scale IQ, the pressure of the press's impossible expectations and constant scrutiny, the endless distractions that came hand-in-hand with running an office. The little girl who was most likely dead or dying somewhere.

But those things were there—he'd seen them. Sometimes when Beamon didn't think anyone was looking, he'd suck the right side of his lower lip between his teeth and fix his eyes on the nearest wall. In those brief moments, he seemed like a completely different person.

Michaels took another tiny sip of his beer and continued to study Beamon's performance. In the two days that they'd been in Kanab, local law enforcement's attitude toward them had gone from mild suspicion to near-worship. He would never be able to pull that off. You just had to be born with that kind of charisma.

"I must have waited there for five minutes," Beamon continued, barely pausing to breathe. "Listening for the guy to get out of the car. Nothing. Finally I take a quick look. Shit, you can't even see into the goddamn car anymore 'cause of the blood all over the windows. Looks like he exploded in there, you know?"

The glassy-eyed cops grinned in unison.

"So I go up to it. No mistaking it, the guy's dead. I open the door and he kind of flops down face first on the back seat. Anyway, I grab him by the hair— he's got this really long hair—to pull the body out." Beamon paused dramatically. "Pulled his head clean off. Shotgun blast had caught him right in the neck."

The cops were silent for a moment and then burst out laughing. Sheriff Parkinson pounded drunkenly on the table with a closed fist.

"True story," Beamon said, leaning back and polishing off his beer. "Puked all over my shoes. Had to write a full report to get the Bureau to buy me a new—"

The sound of his beeper going off stopped Beamon in mid-sentence. "Whoops, that's us, John. I think our fax is coming through."

Parkinson pointed to the empty beers in front of Beamon. "One more quick one for the road?"

"Thanks, but no," Beamon said. "We've got to move."

"You boys still coming by the house for dinner?"

Michaels grimaced. He'd hoped Parkinson's invitation had been hypothetical.

"Hell yeah," Beamon said. "It isn't often I get a home-cooked meal. Six o'clock, right?"

"What *is* this?" Chet Michaels said, spreading the slick fax paper out on the bedspread in the hotel room he and Beamon had been sharing for the last two nights.

Beamon double-checked that his gun was loaded and began digging through his suitcase for a heavier sweater. "Think about it, Chet. Try to understand the psyche of your average backwoods paranoid."

Michaels looked down again at what seemed to be a bad fax of a photograph that hadn't turned out. He flipped it upside down. Still nothing. "I think it must have gotten screwed up in the fax, Mark. It's just dark with a few light splotches."

Beamon ignored him. "As I was saying, the psyche of the backwoods paranoid. When the Red hordes—or more likely the ATF—come over the hills and surround 'em, their trailer sure as hell isn't going to save them. What do they do?"

"Head for the hills?"

"Hell, no. That'd be un-American. They go for their bomb shelters."

Beamon slid an arm though the sleeve of the sweater he'd turned up and pointed to the photograph. "I got turned on to these things years ago when I was looking for another girl, a little younger than Jennifer. What you're looking at is an aerial photo of Passal's spread taken with heat-sensitive cameras. Tell me what you see."

Michaels studied the fax for a few more moments, then pointed to a roughly rectangular off-white splotch centered on it. "That must be the trailer. You can see the stove here in the middle."

"That'd be my take on it."

"This little thing here must be that shack where the generator was running."

"Uh-huh."

Michael's finger traced along the edge of the photo, stopping on another anomaly in the dark gray background of the photograph. "What's that?"

"That's where the ground isn't being heated by the sun. It would seem to indicate that there's something under there that's not under the rest of the area."

Michaels brought the fax up close to his face. "What do you think it is?" he said excitedly.

"I'm hoping for Jennifer Davis, but I doubt I'm that lucky."

12

JENNIFER STIRRED, BUT DIDN'T OPEN HER eyes. She rolled to her back, kicked the sheets off, and breathed deeply. Bright light filtered through her eyelids, and for a moment she imagined that they had become transparent. Through them she could see the pine ceiling of her home and the enormous wrought-iron chandelier that hung above her bed.

This was it. It had to be. Today she would finally wake up from the nightmare. Today she'd be home. Jennifer took a final deep breath and opened her eyes.

The glare off the stark white ceiling blinded her, just as it had the last five times she had played out this elaborate ritual. She threw her forearm over her eyes, rolled on her side, and began to cry quietly.

Why was this happening? Had she done something wrong? Maybe she was sick—and this was a hospital. The horrible dreams were just part of the illness. High fever could cause those things—she'd seen it on TV. And that's why she was alone. She was contagious. Quarantined.

She would think about that for a time, as she did every "morning" in the windowless room. When she had once again convinced herself of the plausibility of this explanation, she would rise and walk slowly to the doorless bathroom at the other side of the room, splash water on her face, and stare at the empty wall above the sink.

Finally, she would look down at herself. At the short white T-shirt and cotton panties that were the only clothes provided for her. At the unnaturally pale hue her skin had taken on.

She would let her fingers trace the outlines of the fading green-brown bruises that had adorned her body in various configurations since she had taken up mountain biking. Then she would return to the twin bed and sit with her back against the wall and stare at the empty room, eventually sinking to the mattress and into something that felt more like a trance than sleep. When she awoke, there would be a plate of food, a towel, and a clean T-shirt and pair of underpants by the door.

She had no idea how long she'd been alone in this room. The difference between day and night was just a flick of a light switch and there had been no sounds emanating from behind the heavy wooden door that led to . . . where?

Sometimes the feeling that she was caught in a cube in the middle of an empty desert plain overwhelmed her. She would become panicked that one day the person silently depositing her meals would lose interest and she would die alone and hungry, never knowing what had happened to her and to her family. Or worse, that the meals would continue to silently appear forever, leaving her to drown in loneliness and confusion.

At first the quiet clink of metal against metal didn't sound real. Just another trick played by her mind. When it came again, though, she struggled back to a sitting position. The heavy knob on the door jiggled almost imperceptibly.

It was real.

She pressed her back against the wall and drew her knees to her chest, feeling the numbness and despair that had become oddly comforting in their familiarity wash away in a flood of adrenaline.

Could it be her father? Of course, it must be. He'd finally come for her. It had all been a fever-induced dream. And now she was better.

The door opened slowly as Jennifer slid to the edge of the bed and began to stand, wanting nothing more than to be folded in her dad's arms and to be told that she was okay now and going home.

"Jennifer."

She fell back onto the bed, legs pedaling desperately in the tangle of sheets until her back slammed against the wall. It was her. The woman who had made her father go crazy. The woman who had been sitting at the edge of her bed staring into the dark while she slept.

Jennifer kicked at the air weakly in an effort to keep the woman away, to no effect. She easily caught one of Jennifer's ankles and threw her legs to the side.

"Be still," the woman said, grabbing the back of her hair. Out of the corner of her eye, Jennifer saw a man with a thick black mustache pull the door closed, leaving them alone.

Jennifer could feel the woman's eyes boring into her and tried to turn away, but the woman's grip on her hair kept her head immobile. "No, you look at me, Jennifer. Look at me."

Jennifer wanted to push her away, but she felt

weak, confused. Like she was floating in a current that was impossible to fight.

"Do you know what's happened?" the woman said.

Jennifer opened her mouth, but she hadn't spoken in so long and she was so afraid, her throat felt paralyzed.

"Do you know what's happened?"

"I don't know," Jennifer got out.

"Yes you do. Tell me."

The images of her parents' death that seemed to have finally begun to fade suddenly returned to her with devastating clarity. "My parents," she stammered. "They're . . . gone."

"That's right, Jennifer. They're dead. And you know how, don't you. Tell me how."

Jennifer threw her arms over her face and felt the tears begin to flow down her temples. "No," she sobbed. "No, don't make me."

The woman pulled Jennifer's arms away from her face and tightened her grip on her hair.

"How did it happen, Jennifer?"

"He killed her . . . then he killed himself. What did you do to them? What did you do to my parents?"

She felt the woman slide her hand under her T-shirt and gently caress the skin on her stomach from her navel to just beneath her breasts. Jennifer tried to move away, but the powerful hand tangled in her hair held her fast. "They weren't your parents, dear. You know that. Don't you?"

"They were," Jennifer heard herself say. "They loved me just as much as if I was their real daughter."

"That's what you were supposed to think, Jennifer," the woman said, shaking her head with something that looked like sadness. "It's what I told them to make you believe."

"You're lying!"

The edges of the woman's mouth curled up almost imperceptibly. "Then why didn't your father use the gun I gave him to save you?"

Jennifer closed her eyes so tight she could see dull streaks of imaginary light streaking across the insides of her eyelids. "He would have . . . he wanted . . ." Her voice trailed off. Why hadn't he? Why hadn't he saved her?"

"He didn't save you because you weren't really his child. I gave you to them and told them to take care of you until it was time for you to come back to me. That's all."

The woman's hand slid from underneath her shirt and into her hand. Jennifer heard her stand and felt a gentle pull. She allowed herself to be led into the bathroom.

"I'm the only one who loves you now, Jennifer. I'm the one who takes care of you," the woman said, reaching into the small shower and turning on the water. She tested the temperature and then turned back to Jennifer, who was standing immobile on the cold tile floor. Jennifer didn't resist as the woman pulled her T-shirt over her head and then dropped to her knees and slid her panties down her legs.

She stepped silently into the hot shower, trying to fight off the distorted image of her parents' shattered bodies swirling around her in the thick steam. She closed her eyes again as she felt the woman begin to run a soapy washcloth along her wet skin, trying to let her mind retreat into the past. She surrounded herself with the memory of her last race, her friend spraying the mud off her with a hose, the look on her parents' faces as she toweled her hair with the old grease rag.

"I want to go home," she said so quietly that the sound was almost completely swallowed up by the running water.

The woman dropped the washrag into the bottom of the shower and ran a soapy hand slowly down Jennifer's back. "You are home, dear."

13

THE STOVE WAS PRETTY MUCH COLD.

Beamon stuck his hands into the open grate and tried to warm them on the few remaining coals glowing dimly through a blanket of ash. The cans lining the walls around him had gone pale white with a thin layer of frost. The door had been wide open when they'd arrived.

Beamon dropped to his knees and looked under the bed. The shotgun and hatchet he'd put under it were gone.

"You got anything, Chet?" Beamon yelled, walking down the steps and back into the blinding light of a heatless sun.

Michaels threw open the door to the generator house, gun stretched out in front of him. He poked his head into it, lowered his gun, and turned back toward Beamon. "Nothing."

"Now, where the hell did he get off to?" Beamon said.

Michaels walked slowly toward him, scanning the clearing. "Do you think he just headed into the hills? His truck's still here."

Beamon shook his head. It had been a bad call. He should have been watching. "I don't know. Let's see that fax again."

Despite the clarity of the heat signature on the photograph, it was difficult to judge distances with any real precision. Beamon made his best guess as to the location of the possible underground chamber and he and Michaels began kicking through debris-scattered underbrush in a less than scientific pattern to find the entrance.

"Are you sure that blob on the picture is something underground?" Michaels said, dropping to his knees and peering under an unusually thick stand of thistles.

"I'm starting to wonder." Beamon kicked a rotted piece of plywood. It flew into the air and was sent careening across the clearing by a strong gust of wind. "It feels right."

Beamon tried to jam his toe under an old sign lying flat on the ground in front of him, but it wouldn't budge. Thinking that it was perhaps stuck in the ground frost, he crouched down and felt around the edges. Along the back, the rough surface of peeling paint was broken intermittently by the oily metal of hinges.

"Chet. Over here."

Michaels jogged up and looked down at the old sign. "You think this is it?"

Beamon nodded.

"You think he might be in there?"

"Don't know. His truck's still here, and it looks like most of his stuff's still in the trailer. But then, why let the stove die down and leave the door open?"

Beamon took a step back and pulled his gun from his jacket. "Mr. Passal! David!" he yelled at the plywood sign at his feet. "It's Mark Beamon with the FBI. I have a few more questions for you. Why don't you come on up and we can talk."

Michaels scanned the treeline nervously. Out in the open like this he couldn't shake the feeling that there was a set of crosshairs tickling the back of his neck.

"Dave! Come on! Let's go!" Beamon shouted, giving the makeshift trapdoor a hard kick.

Nothing. Why couldn't anything ever be simple?

"You ready, Chet?"

Michaels jerked his head in the affirmative and aimed his gun at the sign.

"Don't shoot my foot off, now," Beamon said, finding a place where he could work the toe of his boot under the edge of the plywood.

"Okay, Dave. Come on out," Beamon said, kicking the trapdoor open and inching forward with his gun aimed into the hole.

No answer.

Beamon lay down on his stomach and slid slowly forward until his head was almost even with the edge. He shook off the mental picture of Passal sitting down there with that damn shotgun and burst forward, shoving his gun hand into the hole. It wasn't shot off, so he poked his head in and swept his eyes back and forth, scanning for movement.

"You okay, Mark?" Michaels said nervously. "Is he in there?"

Beamon pulled back, letting a little more light into the hole and slowing the rush of blood to his head. "Yeah, he's in here. But he's seen better days."

One of David Passal's legs was resting on the bottom of the ladder that led into the hole, bent at an unnatural angle. It looked as though it had been snapped when he'd fallen, caught between the 2x4s that made up the rungs.

Passal's head was resting in a wide puddle of blood that was beginning to form little white ice crystals across the top. Beamon adjusted himself so that the sunlight could fall directly on the man's face. His skin was a less than healthy shade of blue and his eyes were frozen wide open.

"What've you got, Mark?"

"He doesn't look like he's got much to say."

"What?"

"Looks like he fell down the ladder, hit his head, and froze," Beamon said, pulling his lighter from his pocket. He flicked the wheel and the flame sparked to life, improving visibility only marginally.

The hole was probably only about ten feet square and maybe six and a half feet deep. The clay walls still showed the marks of the shovel that had created them behind wooden shelves.

Beamon got to his knees and slid into the hole, careful not to disturb Passal's snapped leg.

The shelves were a sturdier version of the ones in Passal's trailer, probably providing structural support as well as storage space. They were covered with neatly stacked cans of meat and vegetables. Large bags of sugar and flour were propped in the corner.

Beamon leaned over and confirmed his diagnosis. Passal was definitely dead.

The stack of old lumber he'd landed on had a number of nails sticking out of it. Unfortunately, one of them had lined up nicely with the back of his head.

The guns Beamon knew he would find were piled on a wide shelf to his left. He stepped closer and examined the black body of an M-16 through the thick, clear plastic bag it was stored in.

This was all he'd been looking for—he'd never really believed that Passal had the girl, only that he knew something that could help. The threat of being brought up on an illegal weapons charge would have gone a long way toward convincing him to open up.

"You all right in there, Mark?" Michaels called into the hole.

"Yeah, fine," Beamon said, sitting down next to the corpse.

"You coming up?"

"In a minute. I need to think."

He sat with his back against the cold dirt wall for almost ten, his eyes wandering from Passal to the ladder and back again. The man must have come down it a thousand times—he stored food down here. Why did he decide to fall today? What was different about today than all those other days? Only one thing he could think of. The FBI was poking around asking questions.

Sheriff John Parkinson pulled his head from the hole and rocked to his feet using his vast stomach as a fulcrum. "Yeah, that's dead, all right. You say he hit a nail?"

Beamon nodded and looked around him. The sheriff's men had cordoned off the clearing—not that this was exactly a high-traffic area—and were all standing around shifting their weight from one foot to the other in an effort to stave off the cold of the approaching night.

"Right in the back of the head," Beamon said. "Bad goddamn luck."

"Accidents happen out here, Mark. You get a little ice on the ladder. Or maybe you have a few too many snorts before you come out here. And then you're dead."

"You're probably right." Beamon clapped him on the back as they started toward the line of cars blocking the narrow dirt road. "But to be sure, I'm going to have a few guys come up and take a look."

Parkinson didn't look excited by the prospect.

"Me and Chet, though, we've got to get out of here," Beamon continued. "I'd appreciate it if you and your boys'd look after things till my guys get here."

"Sure, Mark, whatever you need."

"Okay, then. You've got my card. If any of our people start being a pain in your ass, use it."

14

JENNIFER DAVIS STOOD IN THE MIDDLE OF THE room, bunching the light cotton of the pants she'd been given in her still-damp fists. She was strangely transfixed by the sight of the open door and the simple hallway on the other side of it. Transfixed and terrified.

All the little things that made up her life had disappeared overnight. Everything she knew—all that was familiar now—was in this room. What would she find outside of it?

"I . . . I can't," Jennifer said, her voice quivering slightly.

The woman's eyes flared as she strode across the room and put her hand on the back of Jennifer's neck. "There are people who want to hurt you, Jennifer. I'm going to do everything I can to stop them, but you have to help me."

"Yes, but I'm afraid. I . . ."

The woman was behind her now. She couldn't see her anymore, but felt an arm slide around her stomach and pull her close. "I'm taking you to someone, Jennifer. He's going to talk to you, ask you questions. When he does, you will answer simply and directly. Before you speak, though, I want you to look at him very carefully. To see how weak he is. He can't protect you, Jennifer, only I can. But only if you follow my instructions very carefully. Do you understand?"

She didn't understand. She didn't understand anything anymore. Was this woman telling the truth? Every time Jennifer felt her touch or looked into her eyes, she felt hopeless and afraid.

Her head began to throb dully, making thought even more impossible. "I . . ."

The pressure around her stomach increased, silencing her.

"Do you understand?" the woman repeated quietly.

Jennifer fought back the tears that she felt coming and nodded.

Unlike hers, the room she was taken to was enormous—so far across that you'd have to shout to be heard by someone on the other side. The ceiling was more than thirty feet high, with heavy-looking moldings around the top. Three of the walls were blank, but the fourth had tall, heavily tinted windows that filtered the light from outside into long, jagged shadows.

It was daytime, Jennifer realized as the woman steered her toward the far wall, where there was a small bed surrounded by light gray medical machines. They stopped a few feet from the side of the bed and Jennifer looked down at its occupant.

Was he dead? His closed eyes had sunk so deep that she could see the outline of the round holes in his skull. The color of his skin wasn't much different from the color of the machines humming around him, except that it was occasionally broken by bright

red sores or the spidery tracks of broken blood ves-
sels. Long tufts of white hair still clung at random to
the rice-paper-thin skin of his scalp.

The woman's hand dropped from the back of
Jennifer's neck, and she took a syringe from a stain-
less steel tray next to the bed. Jennifer took an involuntary step backward but realized it wasn't for her as
the woman inserted it into an IV tube taped to the
man's forearm.

Jennifer watched the man's face as the sound resonating from the heart monitor turned erratic and
then fell back into a livelier pattern. His eyelids flut-
tered slightly and then opened into a blank stare. He
stayed that way for almost a minute until, finally, his
head lolled over and his gaze settled on Jennifer.

"Don't be afraid," he breathed through cracked
and peeling lips. "Come."

His left hand turned palm up and edged to the
side of the bed, but she didn't move. A moment
later, the woman's hand took its place on the back of
her neck again, and she felt herself being pushed
forward.

"Please. I won't hurt you," he said. His voice had
strengthened a bit, but was still almost completely
lost in the expanse of the room and the humming of
the machines surrounding them.

The pressure on her neck increased, and she
reached out and placed her hand in his. It felt like a
cold bag full of chicken bones.

"I'm so glad you're here."

Jennifer struggled to overcome her fear and
forced herself to look into the old man's eyes. She
was surprised at what she found there. A strange

spark, dimmed by time for sure, but still there. An incredible depth of emotion. Kindness. Strength. Suffering.

"This must be so hard for you," he said. "To have to leave your parents and come here; everything so unfamiliar. You'll understand soon, though. You'll understand everything." He looked at the woman standing behind her. "Listen to Sara and the others. They have so much to teach you. I wish I could do more, but I'm so tired."

His voice was losing what little strength it had had a few moments before. Jennifer leaned forward, unconsciously squeezing his hand.

"Sara," the old man said, turning his head toward the woman behind him. "I want to talk to you and the others. It must be soon."

Jennifer tried to move away as the woman— Sara, he'd called her—stepped closer to the bed, but the old man's hand tightened around hers and she was afraid she'd hurt him if she pulled away.

"Of course," Sara said. "As soon as I can."

"She's your responsibility now, Sara. You have to teach her."

15

MARK BEAMON TURNED THE KEY IN THE LOCK and pushed the icy door to his condo with his shoulder. It flexed slightly but held fast as a faint ringing on the other side became audible.

He stepped back and gave it a short kick. Not the full-on door kick that had made his Quantico instructor so proud, but enough to shatter the thin film of ice gleaming in the complex's floodlights and allow him to throw open the door and run for the phone.

"Beamon," he said, mouth not yet within optimal range of the handset.

"Mark? It's Trace."

Trace Fontain ran the FBI's lab and had reluctantly agreed, as a personal favor, to go to Utah and supervise the extraction of Passal's body.

"Trace! How are you feeling?" The Utah winter probably had Fontain's bronchitis well on its way to full-blown pneumonia by now, Beamon thought with a pang of guilt.

"Not so good. I think this could be turning into pneumonia." He coughed loudly into the phone, and Beamon felt the pang turn into a twinge at the sound of Fontain's inhaler.

"I'm really sorry, Trace. Couldn't be helped. I've got this little girl missing out here and I can't seem to put the facts together so they make any sense. I needed the best."

Another fit of coughing. The rattle in his lungs sounded like static over the phone. "I'd hold off on the flattery till you hear what I've got to say."

"What've you got?"

"You're going to be pissed."

"Come on, Trace. You have to have something."

"I don't know what happened here."

Beamon pried off his snow-covered boots and grabbed a beer out of the fridge. "What is it exactly that you don't know?"

"Well, I don't know whether your Mr. Passal was murdered or whether it was an accident. And I don't know for sure whether Jennifer Davis was ever here."

"Let's start with the first one. Why isn't it murder?"

"I didn't say it wasn't. I put a couple of mattresses on the ground and pushed one of the local cops down the ladder about twenty times. Figured out how you could do it—one guy behind the ladder grabs his foot and pulls it through the rungs, the other grabs his face and the shoulder of his jacket and pulls him down onto the nail. Once you got the technique down, it wasn't too hard."

"Wouldn't there be contusions on Passal's face or stretched material on his jacket, then?"

"Don't think so." Cough. "The victim is in the air, so the attacker's got all the leverage. Wouldn't really have to exert much force. Besides, Passal was wearing one of those heavy wool hunting jackets. I don't think it would be possible to stretch it with your hand."

"So it's possible that it was murder, but likely it was an accident."

"That's the way my report's going to look."

"Moving on, then. What about Jennifer?"

"We've gone over the trailer, the generator house, and the pit with a fine-toothed comb and we've got nothing."

"Nothing?"

"Well, we'll run it up more thoroughly when we get back, but I brought some equipment along and I doubt the main lab's gonna tell me anything different. No blonde hairs at all. Hell, we haven't found *any* that don't look like they came directly from Passal's head. Or some game animal."

"He was apparently kind of a hermit," Beamon said.

"That would explain it. With very few exceptions, we've eyeballed all fibers as belonging to stuff in his closet."

"And the exceptions?"

"They look old. Probably stuff he got rid of. In any event, I seriously doubt we're going to find any matches in the wardrobe of a fifteen-year-old girl."

"Prints?"

"We found two sets that weren't his on the formica table in the trailer and one set on the doorknob. They're in pretty good shape, and . . ."

Beamon finished his thought. "They're mine and Chet's."

"That'd be my guess. We'll confirm when we get back."

A knock at the door startled Beamon, breaking his concentration. "Trace, could you hold that thought for a minute? Someone's here."

Beamon walked through the snow melting on

his carpet in his stocking feet and pulled the door open. Carrie Johnstone stood on the other side, haphazardly dressed in a down jacket, boots, and light cotton pants. Emory stood next to her, similarly dressed, except pajama bottoms substituted for the cotton pants.

Carrie looked at the phone in Beamon's hand and then at the cord stretched out across the room. "I'm sorry, Mark," she whispered. "I didn't know you were on the phone."

"No problem. I won't be much longer. Come on in."

A strained look crossed her normally cheerful face. "Actually, I came to ask a favor. One of my patients called and is having . . . some problems. There's no one to stay with Emory and I was wondering . . . well, could you watch her for a while?"

Beamon looked down at the little girl, whose face was turned up toward him. She smiled and waved at him.

He pulled the phone off his chest and up to his mouth. "One more second, Trace. I'll be right with you."

He took it as a positive sign that Carrie was willing to trust him with her daughter, but what the hell did he know about children? "Uh, Carrie, I'd be happy to in theory, but I really don't know much about taking care of a four-year-old girl."

"I'm almost five," Emory reminded him.

He looked down at her and laughed. Hell, how hard could it be? You feed them, let them watch a little TV, then put them to bed. Right?

"Almost five?" he said, stepping out of the way

and providing her a clear path into the condo. "In that case, come on in." Emory ran past him and dove onto his couch.

"It's an hour 'til her bedtime, Mark," Carrie said, looking relieved. "She's already eaten and brushed her teeth—won't be any trouble at all." She gave her daughter a stern, motherly look. "Will you, honey?"

"Uh-uh," Emory replied convincingly, punching buttons at random on the TV remote control.

"Thanks, Mark. I'll be back as soon as I can," Carrie said, already heading for the snow-covered steps.

He leaned out the door. "Take your time. No problem."

By the time Beamon had closed the door and walked back to the kitchen, Emory had found the ON button and was surfing through the channels at breakneck speed.

"Sorry, Trace. Minor emergency. Where were we?"

"Nowhere."

"Oh, yeah. Right."

"Anyway," Fontain continued, "I examined Passal's body to see if there were any scratches or injuries that might suggest he participated in a rape. Nothing."

"He could have tied her up before he r—" Beamon looked over at Emory, who was bouncing up and down on her rear in the soft cushions of the sofa. "Before he, you know . . ."

There was a confused silence over the phone for a moment. "Before he raped her, Mark?"

"Yeah. Before that."

"The only comfortable place to do that looks

like the bed in the trailer. No marks on the bedposts or fibers that might have been left by a rope. We did find a rope in the generator shed that had a lot of blood on it, but my guess is that we're going to find out it was deer or elk or something. The good news is, it doesn't look like this guy's taken a shower in weeks, so if he has come into contact with Jennifer, we'll be able to tell you."

"But you're not hopeful."

"I just don't think she was here, Mark."

"Yeah. Shit. Listen, Trace. I want you to get the locals to widen the search of the area. And bring in that heat photography plane to go over the area again. Passal's been running around the backcountry there for years. He could have her stashed a ways out from his property. I think you're right, but let's be sure, okay?"

"Then can I go home?"

"Then you can come home."

Beamon hung up the phone and leaned over the counter. "Hey, Emory. Give you a cookie if you flip it to channel seven for a while."

She craned her neck around and pushed herself up high enough to see over the back of the sofa. "What's seven?"

"The news."

"Yechy," she said, crinkling up her nose.

Damn. He figured the cookie ploy would be foolproof. What was he going to do now?

"*The Tick*'s on," she said hopefully.

"I'd, uh, kind of rather watch the news for a few minutes."

She shrugged and flipped the channel to seven without another word.

Beamon smiled. That wasn't so hard. This could be fun. One cookie for the news, one for going to bed, and he'd still have enough to put him in a sugar coma while he awaited Carrie's speedy return.

"You want milk, too?" he asked.

Emory flipped over on the sofa so all he could see was her feet sticking up over the back. "Mom says I can't eat cookies."

"Can't eat cookies?" He lowered his voice. "A food Nazi, huh? I should have guessed." Beamon grabbed his beer and took a seat in the chair next to the sofa. The newscast was just starting.

"What's a Nazi?"

He stopped the beer a few inches from his mouth. It probably wouldn't take Carrie long to figure out who had been working on her daughter's vocabulary. "Nazi? I didn't say Nazi."

Emory was about to continue her line of questioning when the local news anchor saved him.

"Mark Beamon refused to comment on the FBI's ongoing investigation into the kidnapping of Jennifer Davis . . ."

Emory, her attention momentarily diverted, flipped over and scooted forward so that she was half on the box containing his coffee table and half on the sofa. She squealed excitedly when the screen went from the newsroom to a group of reporters mobbing Beamon as he fought to get through the front door of his office building.

"That's you! You're on TV!"

"That's me."

"Mommy was on TV once, too, but it was really boring," she said excitedly.

The screen cut back to the anchor, framed by a large photograph of the building housing the FBI's Flagstaff office. Beamon's head sank into his hands as the man began quoting an unnamed source regarding the possibility of a white slavery ring operating in the Flagstaff area. The office building background faded artistically into a picture of Jennifer Davis's young body stuffed into a black halter top and skin-tight biking shorts as the newscaster related a sordid tale of wealthy Arabs and their penchant for spunky young blondes.

Beamon groaned quietly. It wasn't enough for them that a fifteen-year-old girl was missing and possibly dead. No, there had to be some sex in there somewhere to loosen up the advertisers' check-writing hands.

He looked over at Emory and pointed to the TV. "You don't believe anything you see on this thing, do you?"

She looked at him like he was crazy. "Sure."

16

"Hey, D. how are you this ungodly morning?" Beamon said, knocking his umbrella on the floor and leaving a ring of slush in front of his secretary's desk.

"I'm fine. How was Utah?" Her voice sounded tentative.

"Weird. Something wrong?"

"Well, I've got good news and I've got bad news."

Beamon grimaced. D. hated to deliver bad news, so she always dreamed up something inconsequentially positive to try to cheer him up. "Bad news first, please."

"I couldn't hold her off anymore."

Beamon leaned over and peeked through the open door of his office. There was a tall blonde hairdo growing from the back of one of the chairs in front of his desk.

"I assume that the hair belongs to Nell Taylor."

She nodded. "Sorry."

Nell and her husband Tom owned the house two doors down from the now defunct Davis family. She had taken it upon herself to use her considerable financial resources to lead a civilian search for the missing girl and her kidnappers.

She seemed to have made it her life's pursuit to see that Jennifer's face was plastered across nearly every city, town, and crossroad in the U.S. She'd hired a virtual army of private investigators that were at this minute running around Flagstaff like the Keystone Kops. And man, did she like to talk to the press.

"I gotta know, D.," Beamon said. "What's the good news?"

His secretary flipped his calendar around on her desk and jabbed at it. "You had two hours open this morning. I told her you had fifteen minutes."

Beamon entered his office with a wide smile. "Mrs. Taylor! I'm so glad we're finally able to get our schedules to dovetail."

The hair turned and rose from behind the high-backed chair. When the pudgy face supporting it appeared, Beamon held out his hand.

"I appreciate you taking the time to meet with me, Mr. Beamon." Her tone was cold.

Beamon dropped his coat and umbrella next to his desk and walked to the percolating coffee pot at the other end of the office. "Can I tempt you with a cup, Mrs. Taylor?"

"No, thank you."

"I was in a small town in Utah a couple of days ago and there was a poster with Jennifer's picture on it in the window of the sheriff's office," Beamon said, sitting down in the chair next to her. He took a tentative sip from the steaming cup in his hand. "I assume it was one of yours. Quite an accomplishment to get that kind of coverage so quickly."

The compliment seemed to go unnoticed. Or at least unacknowledged.

"What is it that I can do for you, ma'am?"

She smoothed an imaginary wrinkle from her gray business suit and then folded her hands neatly on the manila envelope in her lap. "I wanted to discuss the direction you're taking in this investigation, Mr. Beamon."

"Mark, please."

She ignored him. "We have some concerns."

"We?"

"The Jennifer Davis Recovery Foundation."

"The Jennifer Davis Recovery Foundation," Beamon repeated. "Of course you do. And what exactly are they?"

She cleared her throat. "Did you see the local news broadcast last night? Channel seven?"

Beamon thought for a moment. "I did, actually, yes."

"What are we going to do about it?"

Beamon tried his most winning smile. "Well, Mrs. Taylor, as much as I'd like to, I can't just go around shooting reporters."

The look of impatience etched across her face deepened. "Mr. Beamon, you may think this is all very funny, but I know Jennifer Davis. She's a wonderful girl . . ." She paused for a moment and seemed to be switching back to her mental script. "We are very disturbed that Jennifer, right now, may be suffering the worst kind of . . . abuse at the hands of Arab terrorists while the FBI is harassing and threatening an innocent seventeen-year-old boy."

Could this case get any worse? Beamon wondered. It wasn't bad enough that he didn't have a single reasonable suspect and hadn't been able to dream up even a farfetched motive that fit the facts, but now a woman with a beehive was telling him how to conduct an investigation. There used to be some goddamn dignity in being an FBI agent.

"I assume you're speaking of Jamie Dolan," he said.

She nodded in a single jerky motion. Her hairdo flexed perilously.

"You have to understand, Mrs. Taylor, that the FBI doesn't just follow one line of investigation. Just because we talked with Jamie doesn't mean that we aren't pursuing many other leads. We have to cover all the bases."

She looked like she had something to say, but Beamon continued before she could get anything out.

"I have to tell you, though, for the record, that I've seen nothing to suggest that there is anything even remotely resembling a white slavery ring operating in the Flagstaff area. In fact, if you look at the data, there have been relatively few unsolved abductions of girls and women who would be . . ." He was going to say "salable," but thought better of it. "That would fit the profile. Frankly, I don't know where they got that story. I'm guessing that it's a complete fabrication."

She picked up the envelope from her lap and handed it to Beamon. "I hired a psychic to look into this matter, Mr. Beamon. She's one of the best in the field. It was she who uncovered the Arab connection."

The Arab connection. It sounded so terribly official. Beamon shook off the image of a woman with a handkerchief on her head looking into a crystal ball. "I appreciate the information, Mrs. Taylor. I'll have my people review it right away."

Beamon waved to Michaels, who had been hovering outside his window for the last five minutes. "Before you leave, Mrs. Taylor, there is someone I'd like you to meet. This is Chet Michaels. He's working with me on this investigation."

She stood and took his hand.

"Nice to meet you, Mrs. Taylor," Michaels said with a hint of recognition in his voice.

"My pleasure."

"Mrs. Taylor is the head of the Jennifer Davis Recovery Fund."

"Foundation," she corrected.

"I'm sorry, foundation. Chet here's up on all the details of the case, Mrs. Taylor. And he's probably much easier to get in touch with than I am. If you have any questions or concerns, please feel free to give him a call."

She granted them one more of her jerky little nods and the two FBI agents watched her walk proudly from the room.

"Thanks a lot, Mark. I have a feeling I'm going to be spending a lot of time on the phone with that woman."

Beamon handed Michaels the envelope she'd given him and settled into the chair behind his desk. "Better you than me, son. When you get a few minutes, look over the stuff in that envelope. My guess is she's going to quiz you on it when she calls this afternoon. Now, what have you got for me on Passal?"

"I haven't talked with the guys in Utah yet . . ." Michaels said.

"I have. Inconclusive on all counts. No evidence that Jennifer was there and nothing pointing in any particular direction on his death."

"We had a mechanic go over Passal's truck," Michaels said. "The thing looks like it has a top speed of thirty miles an hour and it gushes black smoke."

"Any record of him renting a car?"

"None. We circulated his name and description to all the agencies in the area. Nothing. Preliminarily, a check of signatures on rental contracts for the time period we're looking at doesn't match his handwriting. The guy didn't even have a credit card."

"Figure out what roads he could have taken to Flagstaff and call the state cops. See if anyone remembers seeing a pickup like his crawling along the highway billowing smoke," Beamon said, then leaned back in his chair and began tapping out a rhythm on the desk with his pen.

"What're you thinking, Mark?"

"Wondering. Based on my conversation with Passal, I'd be willing to bet that he knew more than he was telling us. But what did he know? Who did he think we were when we got there and how did he suddenly figure out that we weren't them? And last, why the hell did he pick this week to go to that big trailer park in the sky?"

"You think maybe he wasn't involved directly, but knew something and was killed for it?"

Beamon shrugged. "I think it's possible. I mean, we go and talk to him and suddenly he falls off a ladder he's been down a thousand times before? You see, Chet, there are only a few reasons people die—"

"Wait a minute. Let me write this down. I can't keep up with all your lists."

"What lists?"

"Why you kidnap, why you die . . ."

Beamon chuckled. "I didn't realize I had so many. Tell you what, though. This one's easy. You give it to me. There are four."

Michaels chewed on his eraser. "Okay. Murder, accident, natural causes." Pause. "And, uh, um . . ."

"Suicide."

"Right. Suicide."

"For the sake of argument, let's rule out natural causes. It's possible, of course, but kind of boring."

"Uh, he had a nail in the back of his head, Mark. Doesn't that kind of automatically rule out natural causes?"

"No. What if the autopsy finds that he had a heart attack on the way down that ladder? Dead before he hit the ground?"

Michaels looked at his shoes. "You're right."

"Where was I? . . . Oh, yeah. Suicide. I like suicide from a motivational standpoint—FBI's on to him, so he kills himself. But the logistics of throwing yourself backward off a ladder onto a nail are pretty complex. You'd probably die of tetanus before you hit the thing right. So that leaves accident and murder. And accident seems like just too much of a goddamn coincidence to me."

Beamon stopped tapping his pencil and pointed to the blue folder that Michaels had put on the desk when he'd come in. "Okay, enough mental masturbation. What's in the folder?"

Michaels grinned and picked it up. "This is really going to destroy your day, Mark. We finally tracked down Jennifer's mother's real identity. She'd changed her name illegally four times before she was married—each time relocating geographically."

"Did you check to see if she was wanted?"

"Yup. But she wasn't."

"So who was she?"

Michaels paused dramatically. "Her name was Carol Kneiss."

Beamon raised his eyebrows. "As in nice day or as in our local messiah?"

"As in our local messiah. You're going to love this—Carol was his daughter. Jennifer's his granddaughter."

Beamon stared over the young agent's shoulder and watched through his window as two workmen sorted through a thick stalk of brightly colored wires dangling from the ceiling.

"So, what do you think, Mark? Is there a connection?"

Beamon let out a deep breath and turned his palms up. "Shit, I have no idea. Don't know that much about the Kneissians. They serve good food at weddings." Beamon pointed across the desk at Michaels. "You're from Tucson. You must know something."

Michaels pursed his lips thoughtfully. "I remember all the publicity when they chose Flagstaff as a base—I was in junior high or something. There was a real uproar from the born-agains. Blasphemous cult. Satanists—you know, same thing they say about everyone. But it seems like as soon as the Christians got on a roll, they suddenly shut up. Decided that keeping Kneiss out of Arizona would be un-Christian, I guess. Since then, the Kneissians have bought up half of Arizona and three-quarters of Flagstaff. And then, I suppose you know about Kneiss's ascension."

Beamon rolled his eyes. There was no way to live in Flagstaff and not hear about that at least once a day. "This is the year that Kneiss is going to take his seat at the right hand of God. On Good Friday, right? Translation: They can't keep the old fart alive any longer. He must be, what? About a hundred and fifty?"

Michaels shrugged. "He's pretty old. I don't think he's been seen in public for years."

"Does Kneiss have any living relatives other than Jennifer?"

"Not as far as I can tell."

Beamon downed the last of the lukewarm coffee in his cup and walked across the office to get a refill. "I don't know, Chet. It's worth following up on, though. What if some Kneissian zealot found out about Jennifer? Kneiss has scheduled his own death for a month from now and this guy goes nuts. Can't handle it. Figures Jennifer's the next best thing."

"You never know," Michaels said enthusiastically. "Religion can get people to do things they'd never normally do."

"Tell you what, Chet. Why don't you *quietly* gather some information on the church? Just stuff available publicly, no inquiries. See if we can put a scenario together that makes sense." Beamon wiped up a small spill with his last paper towel as Michaels stood and gathered up his folders. "Oh, and Chet? Let's not talk about this with anyone just yet. If the papers get hold of this I'll have every weirdo in Arizona camped out on my front lawn."

17

BEAMON SWUNG HIS CAR INTO A LOVINGLY shoveled driveway next to an old but well-maintained Ford Explorer. Almost a half-hour late, he hurried toward the small white house, patting his pockets to confirm that he had brought his pad and pen. The door opened before he had a chance to knock.

"Mark Beamon. How was it that I knew you'd be late?"

He'd only met Marjorie Dunham once, years ago—at a retirement party for a mutual friend—but she hadn't changed a bit. Her light brown hair was still cut straight and off the shoulder and her face was almost completely unlined. If he remembered her right, the smooth skin was probably the result of breaking into a smile only about once a year.

"I'm from Texas," Beamon said, trying to sound apologetic. "Haven't learned to maneuver in the Arizona arctic zone yet."

"Uh-huh. Well, come in before you freeze."

Beamon used a boulder next to the door to kick the snow off his boots and stepped into the modest entryway of her home. A moment later, two labradors pounced on him.

"They like you," Marjorie said. "Most guests, they just rip their throats out."

Beamon rubbed the two dogs' heads vigorously

and padded off behind the woman in stocking feet. The labs followed along right behind him, having identified him as an easy mark for a good head scratch.

"Have a seat," Marjorie said, pointing to a worn sofa against the wall and pulling a rather uncomfortable-looking chair up to face him.

The dogs curled up at his feet as he sank into the old couch and looked around the cluttered but obviously well-organized den.

"So I hear you've already managed to turn my old office completely upside down," she said.

Beamon sighed and shook his head. Until about a month and a half ago, Marjorie had been the supervisor of the FBI's Flagstaff office. When she'd retired, they'd turned it into a bogus ASAC position and thrown it to him as a bone. "Not me. Layman and the director are behind that. At first I thought they were just trying to make my getting an office look respectable—but now I think they're trying to kill me with paint fumes."

"I wouldn't put it past them," she said humorlessly. "So what can I do for you? I know you can't be having problems figuring out my filing system."

"No, D. seems to be pretty much on top of things. Actually, I wanted to talk to you about the Church of the Evolution."

"Really. What are you doing with the Church?"

Beamon had thought long and hard about how to answer that question on the drive over. "Nothing very interesting. We've got a lead on a guy who might be embezzling from them. When I started digging into it I found out how completely ignorant

I am about the church and I figured you could help me out. You were here, what? Five years?"

"Six. I would have thought you'd be wrapped up in this Jennifer Davis thing," she said, obviously probing for gossip.

"Oh, I am. But with the church as politically connected as they are around here, I can't exactly ignore their problems."

"Well, that's probably wise. What *do* you know about the church?"

"I'm embarrassed to say almost nothing."

"Do you know any of the church's followers?"

"Don't think so."

Beamon didn't really see that he had much in common with the Kneissians. He found their fresh-scrubbed optimism and well-pressed look a little irritating, if the truth were to be known. The human equivalent of Wonder Bread.

"So you don't even know what its members believe?"

He shrugged. "That this Kneiss guy is God and he's going to die next month and rule over heaven or something?"

"Hardly," Marjorie said. "The premise of the religion is that every two thousand years God sends a messenger to earth to teach humanity about Him and His will."

"And Albert Kneiss is that messenger?"

She nodded. "Each messenger was at one time human and is chosen to serve God for some period of time before he or she is sent to his or her reward. The—call him an archangel if you like—that appears to us now as Albert Kneiss also appeared two thousand years ago as Jesus. Before that he had other names, but no record has survived of his prior incarnations beyond a few mentions in the Kneissian Bible."

Beamon rubbed the back of one of her dogs with his foot, trying to digest what Marjorie had told him. "So God sends Kneiss down here and he writes another Bible. Isn't that redundant? What's wrong with the one he wrote two thousand years ago?"

"That's a little more complicated." She looked thoughtful for a moment. "Let me see how I can explain this clearly . . . okay. It's really just a matter of context. We," she pointed to herself and then Beamon, "as humans are still too limited to truly understand the mind of God."

"I'll buy that."

"But we're not as limited as the people Jesus taught two thousand years ago," she continued. "That is to say, as a group, we're more enlightened than they were."

"I'd argue that point," Beamon said.

"Let me rephrase. We know more than they did—about ourselves and the world around us."

"Okay, you've got me hooked again."

"So when the archangel that we now know as Kneiss appeared as Jesus, he had to put the teachings of God into the current context. And that, uh, dumbing down of God's message is what has created all the paradoxes and inaccuracies in the regular version of the Bible."

Beamon's rubbed his chin. "Okay, yeah. It works on the principle that you can't explain the Big Bang

to people who think flatulence is caused by evil spir-
its crawling up their behinds."

Marjorie let a rare smile pass her lips, but it disappeared too quickly to cause wrinkles. "I've never
heard it expressed quite that way, but you're exactly
right."

"And so now Jesus has reappeared as Albert
Kneiss," Beamon started. "And he's rewritten the
Bible to take into account what we've learned in the
last two thousand years."

"Precisely. The spirit of Kneiss's version of the
Bible isn't that different from the traditional Bible.
But the way it's laid out and the way it embraces current scientific, psychological and sociological thinking is radically different."

"It's pretty far flung now, isn't it?" Beamon said.

"The church? Very much so. It's increased its
membership geometrically in the last decade or so.
It's up to around eleven million members now. Something like that."

"Pretty impressive," Beamon said.

She leaned forward in her chair. "Unprece-
dented, really. It seems that there are a lot of Christians out there who are having trouble with the obvious inaccuracies in the traditional Bible. Kneiss's
message—that God wasn't wrong, we were just too
dumb for Him to tell us the whole truth—has proved
to be very attractive."

"And are we watching them?" Beamon asked.

"We meaning the FBI? No. Why would we?"

There was no reason, Beamon knew. It was just
that he had always been a little suspicious of large religious machines. Organizations bigoted by definition

and full of millions of people whose motivations were very strong and, to him, very murky. "Remember a few years back when we busted those people at the IRS for browsing through people's returns?" Beamon said. "Weren't they Kneissians? Did we ever follow up?"

She shook her head. "Three of the four convicted were members of the church. But what if three of the four had been Catholic? Would we have gone after the Vatican?"

"I might have," Beamon responded.

"Well, *we* didn't. Very dangerous politically in a country that was founded on the principle of religious freedom."

"What about the Germans?" Beamon asked. He'd read numerous articles about Germany's persecution of the Kneissians. It seemed that having an organization as rich and powerful as the CotE operating independently within its borders wasn't sitting well with its government.

"The Germans, for some reason, have become very paranoid about the church and blatantly persecute its members. It's very disturbing—the parallels between their treatment of the Jews during the war and the Kneissians now."

"Would you know anyone, maybe at the German embassy, that I could call? I'd be interested in what they have to say."

She shook her head. "I don't know. Obviously, the Germans' treatment of the church has been a public relations nightmare for them in the States. I doubt you'd find many of their officials interested in talking."

"You're probably right." Beamon glanced at his

watch and wrestled himself out of the sofa. "I've got to run, Marjorie. I really appreciate your time." He breathed in deeply. "It smells like your dinner's about ready."

She rose from her seat and took his hand. "I was going to ask you to stay for dinner. My husband makes a wonderful veal parmesan."

"I'd love to, but I can't. You won't be surprised to hear that I'm already late for my next meeting."

"No, I guess I wouldn't be. Be careful driving now."

Beamon started out of the den but paused at the door, suddenly realizing that in their entire conversation, she had never used the word "they" when speaking about the church. He turned back to face her. "One other thing, Marjorie. Are you a member of the Church of the Evolution?"

She hesitated, crouching down and stroking her two dogs simultaneously. "Yes. Yes, I am."

18

IT WAS NIGHTTIME. THE TALL WINDOWS surrounding the room looked dead. Black streaks against the stark white of the walls.

Just inside the door, Sara stopped and knelt down beside her. "There's something I have to tell you, Jennifer. Are you listening?"

Jennifer nodded silently, her eyes moving to the machines grouped around the small bed and then to the old man lying motionless there.

"Do you know who he is?" Sara asked.

"No."

"His name is Albert Kneiss. You recognize the name, don't you?"

She did, but hearing it just added to the confusion that had continued to weaken her. She tried to concentrate, to process what she knew about Kneiss and his church. She'd lived in Flagstaff for most of her life; many of her friends—some of her best friends—were Kneissians.

"Yes," she said finally.

"Good. That's good, Jennifer." Sara took her hand and gently caressed it. Jennifer's mind told her that this woman was a liar—that she wanted to hurt her—but she couldn't pull away. She was so lonely and Sara was all she had. In the little room that had become her universe, Jennifer was beginning to have trouble distinguishing minutes from hours and hours from days. Sara's visits were becoming one of the only things that reminded her that time moved on and that there was a world outside.

"I know it's hard for you, staying in that room all alone," Sara said, seeming to read her mind. "But it's very dangerous for you right now and it's the best way for me to protect you. You understand that, don't you? You understand that I just want to keep you safe?"

"Yes," Jennifer mumbled, still trying to overcome the effects of her captivity and think clearly. What did this woman want? And why was she about to speak again with a man many people she knew thought was God?

Sara stood and steered Jennifer to the bedside of the old man. His breathing was even more labored than she remembered, each gasp punctuated by the quiet click of a machine next to him, making it obvious it was no longer a completely biological act.

Jennifer stood immobile as Sara inserted a syringe into the clear tube running into his arm. She watched the operation for a moment and then let her eyes wander from machine to machine, finally letting them fall on the papers taped to the back of the heart monitor. They were calendar pages.

Jennifer felt a weak rush of adrenaline as she shuffled silently to her right. Sara was completely absorbed in what she was doing, all her concentration locked on the old man's face. The two pages of the calendar became readable as she took one more small step. They were for February and March.

She leaned forward at the waist, afraid to move

any closer, and scanned the writing in the small squares, searching for anything that would tell her where she was and why. But it was only medication and cleaning schedules.

Jennifer took a step closer to the heart monitor as it stuttered and began to increase in tempo. The small clock built into the display read Thursday, February 27, 7:32 P.M.

Jennifer moved back to her original position, feeling a brief sense of elation at her small triumph, followed closely by a deadening sensation of despair. She had been there a week and a half.

The random fluttering of the old man's eyes became more purposeful and Jennifer turned her full attention to him, watching the gray mask come to life as his eyes opened and cleared.

He took a few shallow but conscious breaths and once again reached out to offer his hand.

"Jennifer. You don't know the peace the sight of you brings me."

This time she moved toward him without prompting and slid her hand into his. Despite everything— the memories of her parents' death, her loneliness and confusion—Jennifer felt a sense of calm spread through her as she looked into the ancient face.

The old man's head rose almost imperceptibly from the pillow as he looked around the room. "Where are the others?"

Sara knelt next to the bed and put a hand gently on his shoulder. "There was a storm, Albert. No one can travel."

The deep lines in the old man's face rearranged themselves into an expression of deep thought for a moment. "Perhaps it would be best to wait, then. They all must hear. They all must understand."

Sara's hand moved from the old man's shoulder to his nearly bare scalp. "I don't think we can wait any longer. You're becoming so weak. If what you have to say is important, you should say it now."

"Sara. My Sara," he said, smiling weakly and then looking back at Jennifer, who was standing transfixed, waiting for him to speak. She was finally going to find out what had happened to her. She could feel it.

"You're right, of course," he said. "It doesn't matter. You've done more to deliver my message than I ever could have hoped. I'll ask you to help me one more time."

She kissed his cheek and moved away from them. As she passed by, though, she brushed against Jennifer in a way that suggested that she would be watching her closely.

"You know who I am, don't you, Jennifer?"

She nodded slowly. "You're Albert Kneiss. People think you were sent here by God."

Another weak smile. "That's right. God did send me here. To teach and make people better understand Him. And themselves."

She concentrated on the face of the old man in front of her, breathing in the strong scent of dust and antiseptic cleaner that seemed to emanate from him. "You don't look like an angel," she heard herself say.

He breathed out audibly. The laugh of a man too weak to laugh. "No, I don't suppose I do."

Kneiss moved his free hand to a worn leather

book lying next to him. "Take this. It's yours now."

Jennifer sat down on the edge of the bed and leaned across the old man, gently sliding the book from under his hand. She'd seen it many times before. On TV, in local bookstores, in the hands of her friends and neighbors. The gold letters on the front had been almost completely worn away by time but were still legible.

THE HOLY BIBLE
Kneiss Edition

Jennifer opened it and turned a few of the cracked and yellowed pages. Each was cluttered with notes scrawled through the margins in an elegant hand that must have been his.

"You probably didn't know that I had a daughter, did you, Jennifer?"

She looked up from the book.

"Her name was Carol."

"Carol," Jennifer repeated quietly, as she carefully closed his Bible.

"And she, in turn, had a daughter," the old man continued. "That daughter is you."

Jennifer stood and backed slowly away from the bed, pulling her hand from his and letting the book fall to the floor.

Kneiss reached out to her again, but she just moved farther away. She had always been told that her real parents were dead and that she had no blood relatives. But she could see now that it had just been another lie. Her whole life was just one stacked on another. And now it was all coming down around her.

"When my daughter and her husband died— you were very young then—I wanted to bring you here. To raise you myself, in the church. To prepare you." He looked past her at Sara. "Sara convinced me that it would be a mistake. That trying to bring you up surrounded by people who knew who you were and what you would become would be impossible. Seeing you now, I know she was right. She so often is."

Jennifer glanced back at Sara as the old man continued. "Eric and Patricia Davis were two of my most devoted followers. And they were childless. We decided that it would be best for you to develop naturally on your own. Without my influence or the influence of the church."

"Why?" Jennifer stammered. "Why did you do this to me?"

"I know this is hard, Jennifer, but my time here is almost over. You understand that, don't you? That I have only a short time left here?"

She nodded dumbly. He was supposed to die on Good Friday, just like Jesus. Everyone knew that.

"Well, when I'm gone, the church will be yours to lead."

19

"YOU'RE EITHER GOING TO HAVE TO START getting here on time or give me a key," Chet Michaels said. "I'm numb from the waist down."

Beamon adjusted the gym bag thrown over his shoulder into a marginally more comfortable position as the young agent peeled himself from the steps.

Today had been his first session with the personal trainer he had hired, and his first attempt at real exercise since his unheralded but pivotal bench-warming position on his high school football team.

This regime of self-improvement was starting to get to him. Nicotine withdrawal, booze with no burn, and now a set of quivering leg muscles that probably wouldn't propel him the rest of the way to his front door. He wondered if all healthy people felt like crap and were just good liars.

"You been working out?" Michaels said. "Feels great, doesn't it? Get out of the office and sweat off your stress?"

Beamon threw his gym bag at the young agent. "Shut up and carry that up the stairs for me."

Michaels grinned and bounded up the icy stairs two at a time as Beamon tested the first step with his foot and grabbed the handrail.

"You all right, Mark?" Michaels said, his head appearing over the railing above him

God, how he hated that kid.

Beamon could feel Michaels's eyes on him as he waddled across the living room to the fridge.

"I forgot it was your first day with that personal trainer. How'd it go? I love—"

Beamon looked up from the two beers he was hovering over and gave Michaels a glare that prompted him to change the subject.

"Man, I could have used a hot cup of coffee tonight. Your neighbor decided not to take pity on me, I guess."

Beamon dropped into the sofa and pushed one of the bottles toward Michaels, who was pulling a folder out of the small backpack that had been slung over his shoulder.

"She's visiting her mother."

Michaels' eyebrows rose slightly. "Really? When's she coming back?"

"Don't know," Beamon lied. In truth, he knew she'd be back the day after tomorrow. And if he'd regained full use of his legs by then, he intended to take his newly buffed physique over to her door and ask her out on a proper date. "Let's go, Chet. I just want to have a couple of beers and go to bed."

"If you're tired, I could just—"

"Nah, you're here and I'm going to D.C. Sunday. Won't be back till Monday afternoon."

"What're you doing there?"

"Budget meeting," Beamon lied.

The truth was that he was scheduled for another in a string of pointless hearings relating to a case he'd wrapped up almost six months ago. When a group of well-organized vigilantes had decided to end America's drug problem by poisoning the narcotics supply, one of their early victims had, unfortunately, been the son of a powerful senator. The hearings, ostensibly begun to ensure that America's hospitals would never again be flooded with thousands of dying addicts, had now degenerated into a forum for Senator James Mirth to allocate the blame for his son's death. Blame that, by all reports, rested firmly on his shoulders.

Michaels looked a little uncomfortable as he held out a thin stack of paper.

Beamon eased himself forward and took it. The pages consisted of a few copied articles on the Church of the Evolution from various newspapers and magazines.

"I'm underwhelmed," Beamon said. "Where's the rest of it?"

"There is no rest right now. I *am* working on getting some more, though."

Beamon scanned a copy of a *Wall Street Journal* story describing the phenomenal investment performance and financial strength of the church, then flipped through the remaining articles. Most related to the persecution of the church by the German government.

"Come on, Chet. You're telling me that an organization with eleven million members," he flipped back to the *Journal* article, "bringing in ten billion dollars a year, has had a whopping seven articles written about it—five of which are about its activities abroad? I don't think so."

Michaels seemed to have anticipated Beamon's skepticism. "I went through the academic index at the library and searched for the Church of the Evo-lution, Albert Kneiss, God, organized religion, cults, you name it."

"And this is all you found?"

Michaels shook his head. "Not exactly. It's true that there hasn't been much written on the church considering its size . . ." He pulled out another piece of printer paper from his bag and laid it in front of Beamon. "But this is probably why."

The page was full of titles of articles printed directly off an index. Most related to libel suits filed against various media companies. The list included such names as ABC, the *New York Times,* and *Newsweek.*

"Okay," Beamon said. "This is more the type of thing I was looking for. Where's the text to those articles?"

"Gone."

"Gone?"

"I went to three different libraries. When you go back into the old newspaper and magazine issues, the pages that these articles appear on are missing. If it's on microfilm, the microfilm is missing. I've ordered copies directly from the publishers, but it's going to take some time to get them."

Beamon took a long pull from his beer. "I guess when you have eleven million devoted followers, there isn't much reason to leave negative articles lying around where the public might stumble onto them."

Michaels nodded. "Yeah. Notice how most of the articles I *could* find relate to the Germans?"

"Makes perfect sense," Beamon said. "America

was founded on the concept of free religion. The hatred of religious persecution is in our genes. If I was running the church, I'd milk this Germany thing for everything it's worth."

The phone rang as Beamon drained the last of his beer. He held the empty bottle out toward Michaels and motioned toward the kitchen.

Michaels took the empty, walked over to the phone and picked it up.

"Hold on a second," he said and handed it to Beamon, who pointed to the refrigerator in an effort to get another beer without having to make an attempt at getting out of the chair.

"Hello?"

"Mark? Jake Layman."

"What can I do for you, Jake?" Beamon said tentatively. His new boss had certainly never called him at home. Hell, they hadn't even spoken since that unfortunate round of golf.

"I wanted to talk to you about the Jennifer Davis case, Mark. A very disturbing memo came across my desk today."

Beamon heard the unmistakable sound of air escaping from the neck of a beer bottle and he held his hand up over his head.

"Disturbing how, Jake?"

"It says that you've been looking into the Church of the Evolution in relation to the case."

Beamon was a bit surprised. "Who wrote the memo?"

"I don't think that's important, Mark. What is important is whether or not it's accurate."

Beamon felt the cold glass of a beer bottle hit

his hand and watched Michaels walk around him and sit down. "I am following up on Jennifer's family connections. As near as I can tell, Albert Kneiss is her only surviving biological relative—her grandfather."

There was silence over the phone for a few moments. "I'm not sure how that's relevant to the investigation, Mark."

That didn't surprise him. Layman probably didn't understand how gasoline was relevant to his car starting in the morning.

"Probably isn't," Beamon said. "But on the other hand, you never know. With Kneiss scheduled to bop off to heaven next month, maybe some nut wants his own personal messiah. Maybe Kneiss has made enemies in his business dealings. Hell, maybe the church—"

"Look, Mark," Layman interrupted. "I know it's got to be tough for you going from D.C. to a little post in Flagstaff, but this is where you landed and you're going to have to adjust. We're dealing with a pedophile or a botched robbery here. Not a religious conspiracy. Are you going to be able to keep your eye on the ball? Because there's a lot of media coverage on this thing and we can't afford a fumble."

Beamon covered the receiver and took a deep breath. The old Mark Beamon would point out that his conviction rate in kidnapping cases was the best in the Bureau and at least three times Layman's. But the new Mark Beamon was going to handle this situation with the well-balanced mix of calm dignity and bald-faced lies that it demanded. "Just trying to be thorough, Jake."

"Hey, and I appreciate that, Mark. I know you're doing the best you can out there. But we have to look at the big picture. After Waco and Ruby Ridge, we're not ready for the press to start in on us again. Don't embarrass the Bureau, right, buddy?"

"Yeah. You're right, Jake. Sure."

"So you're on the team, then?" Layman said.

Beamon frowned. One more sports cliché and he was going to drive down to Phoenix and beat Layman to death with a hockey stick. "Yeah, Jake. I'm on the team."

"All right. Good. I knew I could count on you."

Beamon hung up the phone and turned to Michaels. "What else you got for me?"

"Was that Layman?"

"Mmm-hmmm."

"He doesn't like the church angle?"

"Not excited about it, no."

"Are we going to get off it?"

"As far as I'm concerned, we're really not on it. Just following up all the angles." Beamon paused. "Having said that, when we're looking into stuff that's church-related, we probably shouldn't wave flags and blow horns. Okay?"

Michaels nodded.

"Now where were we?"

"The fact that there isn't much info on the church."

Beamon leaned forward in the chair, ignoring the pain in his lower back. "What about an exposé? Some ex-Kneissian who was pissed off about not getting God's personal phone number or something and wrote a book?"

Michaels flipped another piece of paper from his knapsack and let it spin through the air and onto the cardboard box serving as a coffee table. "*The Betrayal of a Messiah: Albert Kneiss and His Church*. By Ernest Willard."

"I knew you wouldn't let me down, Chet. Where is it?"

"What?"

"The book."

"It's been out of print for years. Publisher's out of business. I called over a hundred libraries and probably fifty stores dealing in rare books and came up empty-handed. Even the Library of Congress has managed to lose their copy."

"Great. What about the author?"

"Looked in all the regular places. Nothing. I managed to track down his agent, but she says she hasn't heard from him in years. I'll keep digging."

Michaels stood and began slipping on his jacket. "Beyond that, we're still following up Passal's known acquaintances and anyone who might have had an infatuation with Jennifer, and we've expanded our investigation of local sex offenders to neighboring states."

"You in a hurry?"

"Told my girlfriend I'd meet her at the brewpub for a beer at eight-thirty. You want to come? It's a really fun place." He pointed at the bottle in Beamon's hand. "And their beer beats the hell out of that swill."

Beamon shook his head. "I like this swill. Thanks anyway, but I think I'm just going to spend some time with my couch tonight." His legs had continued to stiffen during their conversation. Hopefully, a few beers would loosen them up enough to get him to the bedroom.

"I'll see you in the morning, Mark."

"Right," Beamon said, punching the ON button on the TV remote and then surfing through the channels until he landed on the Church of the Evolution's cable access channel.

Albert Kneiss was wandering benignly across a gloomy stage talking about God's plan for humanity. "August 1969" was printed in the bottom corner of the screen.

Despite the poor quality of the tape, the image of Kneiss moving smoothly along the elevated stage and the sound of his powerful voice resonating through the static was strangely hypnotic. Even to an old agnostic like him.

20

NONE OF THIS WOULD EXIST WITHOUT HER. None of it.

Sara Renslier stood silently in the middle of the small chapel that had been built into the expansive compound housing the room where Albert Kneiss was spending his final days on earth.

She stared through the moonlight penetrating the large skylights overhead and at the ten-foot-high cross glowing dully above the altar. Even that was hers. A symbol she had created for people to rally around. Its design, with its stylized head and footboard, was close enough to the standard cross to be comfortable to the world's powerful Christian population, but different enough not to alienate the more significant number of non-Christians. She ran her hands down the bottom of the cross and over the smooth stone of the altar, thinking back to her earliest memories of God.

She had been immersed in the Catholic Church almost from the day she was born—Catholic schools, mass two days a week, confession once a month. She could still remember how she'd felt at her first communion, awed by the ancient ritual and air of the supernatural that had swirled around her in the cold of the cathedral.

She'd chosen a college close to home, unwilling to leave her parish for the four years it would take to complete a business degree—instead becoming even more involved in the church. By the end of her first year, she had joined most of the local Catholic organizations and was attending mass almost daily.

It was during that time that she'd begun to see weaknesses in the Catholic machine. Much of the dogma that ruled the actions of the church seemed hopelessly mired in civilization's distant and superstitious past. The aging priests whom she had always seen as spiritually superior to the rest of humanity began to look out of touch and reckless in the direction they'd chosen for their church.

As her studies progressed, she'd become fascinated with the idea of adapting the increasingly scientific theories of business and marketing to the management of a religious organization. She chose that as the subject of her senior thesis, writing an elaborate analysis of the mistakes made by the world's major religions and creating a blueprint—in hindsight, more of a rough sketch—of how to steer a church to a position of dominance. Her professor, a young man whose ponytail and round wire-rimmed glasses made him almost indistinguishable from the student body, had given her an A⁺. Next to the grade, written in a bold scrawl, was one word. *"Terrifying."*

Shortly after her graduation, she had gathered up the courage to meet with her priest and present her ideas. She'd argued that the Catholic Church was allowing itself to be slowly stripped of its power—that it had become self-indulgent and no longer provided a service that people needed or wanted.

He had listened politely for almost an hour but had heard nothing. Sara remembered falling silent as he began a passionless and disjointed speech about God's will and the wisdom of the Vatican. Later, when she'd defended her position, he had accused her of vanity and a lack of faith.

Vanity and a lack of faith! Had it been vanity to want to save her church from the backward-thinking old men destroying it? Had it been a lack of faith to want to use the gifts God had given humanity to effectively carry out His will?

Sara sat down on the cold marble steps leading to the altar, remembering the pain she had felt as she walked from the priest's office, and her single-minded determination to have her ideas heard. Over the next few months, she sent literally hundreds of letters to the church's leadership and lay organizations. Each contained a clear explanation of her ideas and a plea for reform.

She'd received very few letters back, mostly from people she knew or had met briefly at church functions. Their responses were all the same—full of carefully chosen words, caution, and fear.

Finally, almost a year after she had met with her local priest, a different kind of letter arrived at her small apartment. It was handwritten on the elegant stationery of the bishop and granted her an audience.

She'd gone prepared to make her argument for change, but when she'd arrived, she discovered that the intimate exchange of ideas she had hoped for was not what had been planned. There were five of them, dressed in the formal robes that hadn't changed in six hundred years. In front of each man was a copy of her senior thesis—a document that she had enclosed with many of the letters she had sent.

It didn't take long for it to become obvious that they weren't there to listen. They were there to punish. They'd spoken angrily, reading highlighted lines from her thesis out of context and accusing her of atheism. In the end, they had made vague intimations about excommunication and implied that if she were to confess her sins then and there, God would forgive her.

She'd walked out without a word. A few weeks later, she had moved across the country and taken a job in a small accounting firm in upstate New York. It was there that she had become obsessed with the study of religion, and it was there that she had lost her faith. Contemporary religions, she had found, were nothing more than a collage of earlier and more primitive beliefs pieced together by the ruling class as a convenient way to control its subjects. The considered infliction of fear and hope, it turned out, was infinitely more effective than the infliction of pain and death.

As time went on, she had become entrenched in her atheism, beginning to look down on the faithful as desperate and weak. They knew that the childish concept of God was a lie created to keep them docile but hadn't the courage to accept that and go out into the world alone. No, they found it easier to wrap themselves in the ridiculous paradoxes of the Bible and books like it, and to ignore the truth.

She had moved quickly through the ranks of her firm, spending impossibly long hours in the office and continuing her education through courses at night. The owner, a small, weak man of limited ability, had continued to heap more and more responsibility on her.

It had been a little after seven o'clock, in the summer of 1975, when he had dragged a box full of loose notebook paper and receipts to her desk and sat down with the grave expression that he always seemed to wear at the office.

They had never spoken about religion, but it was common knowledge that he was involved with an esoteric little cult centered near Lake Placid. At the time, she hadn't known much about the fledgling church or its leader, Albert Kneiss, beyond the fact that he claimed to be a reincarnation of Jesus.

She had reluctantly accepted her boss's invitation to a "presentation" that Kneiss was making at a small auditorium nearby, as well as his request that she take over as shepherd of the church's paltry accounts.

That night had changed everything.

The less than half-full auditorium had smelled vaguely of marijuana when they walked through the curtains at the back. She and her boss—she couldn't remember his name, though she thought she'd read that he'd died recently—settled into a couple of folding chairs just as the lights dimmed and Albert Kneiss wandered onto the stage.

His long white hair had seemed to move on its own as he slowly paced in front of them, speaking in a low, patient tone. Despite the poor acoustics of the auditorium, his voice didn't fade as it floated to the back where they sat.

It had been far from the bizarre and pointless evening she had steeled herself for. The self-absorbed megalomaniac that she had expected to appear and ramble incoherently instead delivered a message that stripped away the superstition and compromise from Christianity, leaving a simple and elegant melding of God and science.

This man, with his penetrating charisma and beautifully constructed theology, seemed to have created something with almost unlimited appeal. His ideas had the potential to spread like wildfire through the hearts of the myriad people who wanted desperately to believe in something but also wanted that something to reflect the world they lived in and not the world of their distant ancestors.

She remembered taking a paperback copy of Kneiss's Bible from a poorly groomed young man at the auditorium's exit and walking out into the cold night somewhat dazed. Albert Kneiss had done something that she had never considered. He had taken the philosophy she had applied to religious organizations and used it to reinvent God.

Over the following year, her boss had happily diverted her non-church-related clients to other accountants at the firm until she was, in essence, working for Kneiss's organization full-time. As she dug deeper and deeper into the workings of the church, she began to tailor the ideas she had developed to fit the infinitely more flexible and forward-thinking Church of the Evolution.

When she had finally presented her ideas to the seven Elders who controlled the church, she'd found their minds just as closed as the priests who had threatened her with excommunication. At first she'd thought that their disinterest stemmed from the fact that she was not actually a follower of Kneiss, so in 1976 she joined his church. Her conversion, though, did nothing to penetrate the wall the Elders had built around themselves.

She could still remember, down to the last smell and sound, the day almost twenty years ago when she had opened the door to her apartment and found herself face-to-face with Albert Kneiss—the man some believed to be the returned Jesus.

He accepted a cup of tea and told her that he had been instructed by God to come to her and hear her ideas on the future of His church. She remembered how still he sat and the passive expression on his face as she described her theories on building a contemporary church. But, like her priest, he didn't really seem to be listening. When she finally fell silent, he stood and walked toward the door of her apartment. He didn't close it behind him, and she heard him speak as he disappeared down the hall. "You'll lead my church into the next century, Sara."

It had taken months to break down the barriers the Elders created to try to make her look incompetent. What she had found when she finally penetrated the deepest layers of the church's management had horrified her. The financial reports the Elders had been providing her were completely fictitious. It was an organization teetering on the brink of bankruptcy, led by a group of ineffectual, bickering asses, all jockeying for the attention of their messiah.

When she reported to Albert what she had

found, he had just smiled calmly and told her that he would no longer be involved in the management of the church. That his God had directed him to focus on making people understand. The church was hers to run as she saw fit.

She hadn't believed him at first, but when he sat passively by as she disbanded the existing group of Elders and replaced them with volunteers experienced in practical areas such as finance, psychology, and marketing, she'd begun to feel the power and potential of her position. That had been the true first day of the Church of the Evolution.

At that time, the church had been made up of about twenty-five thousand loosely connected members, largely confined to the northeastern U.S. And now, as the sun continued to set on Catholicism, her church had swelled to millions of members and was growing faster than any other in the world. The priests should have listened.

Sara stood and turned back toward the altar. She had created this church from nothing and now Albert was trying to take it from her. She had always known that this day would come, that before he died he would make one last desperately sentimental act. And she had been preparing for that act ever since she'd become aware of Jennifer's existence.

Over the years, she had systematically isolated Albert until his wishes and hers were indistinguishable to the church's members and leadership. It had been a simple matter, really. Albert preferred quiet reflection and needed time alone to exercise his genius for devising ever-new ways to enthrall the public with his message.

What she hadn't anticipated was that he would, for the first time in a decade, call a meeting of all the Elders instead of passing along his wishes through her. It was at that meeting that he had announced Jennifer's existence to the others and ordered Sara to bring her to the compound.

At that point she'd had no choice but to comply. Her power at the church was nearly absolute, but not so unshakeable that she could ignore Albert's wishes with impunity.

She had come here that night full of rage and panic. Slowly, though, she'd come upon a way to keep control of the church that she had built. She had set her plan in motion when she convinced Eric and Patricia Davis that it was Albert's wish that they ascend to heaven before him. She had chosen them for their blind fanaticism and she had chosen well.

Witnessing her parents' death had thrown Jennifer into a state of confusion and pain that Sara had been able to amplify and use to keep control of the girl. With that control, the problem of Jennifer's existence and Albert's ambiguous speech about her to the Elders could be solved simply and finally. When Albert and his granddaughter were gone, the church would be free to grow in size and influence. And she would grow with it.

"YOUR TIMING WAS MOST FORTUITOUS, MARK," Hans Volker said, slowing his boat of a BMW to a crawl and slipping it expertly through the thick crowd of people milling about in the street. "The Church of the Evolution is expecting over half a million people to attend this rally. Quite extraordinary, really—they only began planning it three weeks ago."

Despite the dreary skies and intermittent rain, it looked like that estimate would prove low. From their position near the Capitol Building, only occasional flashes of asphalt and grass were visible beneath the flowing carpet of well-dressed humanity.

Beamon had sicced his secretary on the German embassy last week, figuring it would take her at least a few days to coax someone into meeting with him while he was in D.C. subjecting himself to another fiery Senate inquisition. He'd been more than a little surprised when, two minutes into her first attempt, she'd connected him with Volker—the German government's U.S. watchdog in all things church-related. He'd been even more surprised when Volker not only agreed to meet with him, but also offered to personally pick him up from the airport.

"I really appreciate you taking the time to meet with me on such short notice, Hans."

Volker waved his hand dismissively. "It is I who should thank you. I have been meaning to contact you since you took your post in Flagstaff. I had hoped to cultivate a better relationship with you than with your predecessor, Ms. Dunham."

"You knew Marjorie?"

"Oh, yes, I'm afraid so. I had a number of conversations and meetings with her relating to our concerns about the church. This was a number of years ago, of course, before I discovered that she was a member and just using me to gather intelligence for Albert Kneiss. As I'm sure you can imagine, our relationship cooled after that."

"I guess I can see how it would," Beamon said, remembering his conversation with Marjorie Dunham and her insistence that the German would be unwilling to talk with him. He turned and looked through the tinted windows, noting the glares that they were getting from the people around them. He wasn't sure if the problem was that theirs was the only car moving on the pedestrian-choked street or if it was that they were driving a car manufactured in Germany.

"So all this is for you, Hans? I mean, I'd read that Kneiss was upset about your government's policies, but this looks more like pissed off than upset." Beamon said.

"Pissed off? Oh, yes, absolutely. The church has been very vocal in their criticism of Germany's treatment of the church's followers and I'm afraid they've found a willing audience in the American public." He paused for a moment. "I assume that you are aware of our disagreements with Kneiss's church?"

"Aware, yes. Knowledgeable about, no. I understand that Kneissians can't hold public office and are barred from a bunch of other sensitive positions in the German government. I think someone told me that they're denied positions that might allow them to influence young people, too—teachers, day care workers, that kind of thing."

"That's all true," Volker said.

"Seems like I also heard that if a church member owns a business, the fact that they're Kneissian has to be disclosed on their letterhead and business cards."

Volker tapped his brake to avoid bumping a man who had lifted the car's windshield wiper and shoved a bright yellow flyer under it. The text of the flyer was impossible to read, but the heading GESTAPO TACTICS was clearly legible through the windshield.

"And how do you feel about those policies, Mark?"

"I don't see any reason to lie to you. I think it all sounds very familiar."

Volker nodded. "The church has been very efficient in distributing propaganda comparing our policies to the Nazis' treatment of the Jews during the war. It's ironic, really. Our actions have been fueled by a fear of what happened to the Jews in our country. That the Kneissians' organization could incite their German followers."

Volker slowed the car again, this time rolling to a stop in front of an angry-looking group of young people who were obviously blocking their path on purpose.

Beamon watched as they talked urgently amongst themselves, building their courage and finally directing their shouts toward the car. It was impossible to hear exactly what they were saying through the two-ton piece of German engineering, but Beamon wasn't having a hard time catching the gist. "You know, Hans, I appreciate the tour, but it might be time we backed on out of here. I thought the dirty looks we were getting were about your car, but it may go beyond that."

"Hm?" Volker said, apparently completely unconcerned. "No, you're quite right, Mark. I'm sure they recognize my car. The church keeps its members very well informed."

Beamon twisted around and looked out the rear window at the crowd that had closed in behind them. "I've got to tell you, Hans, I've been an FBI agent long enough to learn more than I ever wanted to about this kind of group dynamics. If one of those kids gets fired up enough to so much as throw a spitball at us, the others are going to tear this car apart and then do the same thing to us."

Volker laughed quietly and inched the car forward. Miraculously, the crowd parted. "I'm afraid that you don't understand the Kneissians, Mark. They would never perpetrate any kind of overt public act against me—or against anyone, for that matter. That could generate negative publicity. No, they prefer to work in the dark. To use intimidation."

Volker took his diplomatic immunity out for a spin, jumping two wheels up on the sidewalk and heading toward the center of activity. "Let me give you an example. A few years ago, my son was being consistently singled out for harassment at his school by a particular instructor—to the point that the woman was warned and finally let go. Prior to this, her credentials were spotless. Her superiors apologized profusely to me, but were baffled by her behavior."

"I take it you weren't."

Volker shook his head. "It's my understanding that she took a position in a private school owned by the Kneissians within a few weeks. At first it surprised me that a woman who clearly loved children would attack my child to get at me, but as I learned more about the Kneissians I began to understand how dangerous their beliefs and organization really are."

"I don't know, Hans," Beamon said, rolling down the window and pulling the flyer from under the wiper. "This just isn't all that new. How long has religion been prompting people to attack non-believers? 'I can see into the mind of God and you—Hindu, Muslim, Jew, whoever—can't. Therefore, I am good and you are evil, irrelevant, or damned.'"

"Do you have a copy of Kneiss's Bible, Mark?"

Beamon shook his head.

"I suggest you read it. You'll see that the Kneissians look to the future—not to the past, as do most religions. This is what makes them so dangerous. By discarding many of the traditions of older faiths, they've been able to gain a great deal of power too quickly. And that forced us—the German government—to slow down their growth before they were able to begin imposing their bigotry on others."

Beamon frowned deeply. He'd heard a saying once—that you could tell a bad man from a good one not by his actions but only his intent. He'd thought long and hard about it and wasn't sure if he agreed. Religious persecution was just too easy to justify.

Volker stopped the car and set the brake. "The Kneissians are starting to use their great membership and wealth to indulge their organizational paranoia. To crush those they perceive to be their enemies and to spy on those who might exert some control over them. I suspect that they are very interested in you, Mark. They are quite concerned with America's enforcement agencies—FBI, CIA, IRS, NSA—and you, as the head of the FBI's Flagstaff office, probably top their list. I assure you that they are quite ruthless. But clever at keeping themselves from the media."

Volker opened his door a few inches, letting in the buzz of the enormous crowd and the sound of intermittent feedback as a PA system was tested. "It might surprise you to know that we have to sweep the phones at the embassy and my home on a daily basis. On three separate occasions we have found listening devices. Once the police apprehended a man placing one of them. He was a member of Kneiss's church."

"Are we getting out?" Beamon said, as Volker pushed the door the rest of the way open and stepped from the car. The German poked his head back in and pointed behind him at a large stage set up at the end of the Mall. "I thought it would be easier for you to hear the speaker. And that perhaps you would like to, uh, mingle a bit. I assure you there's no danger."

Somehow the assurance of one slightly effeminate European surrounded by half a million people who thought he was spitting in the face of their god didn't make Beamon feel all that warm and fuzzy. But what the hell—he hadn't incited a riot since college. "I guess whatever happens to me happens to you first," he said, stepping from the car.

Volker smiled and began to talk loudly over the drone of the crowd, ignoring the hostile looks of the people within earshot. "I and my wife are routinely followed—the church makes no effort to hide it, hoping, I imagine, to intimidate me. Men I've worked with in Germany have suffered even more. One had a number of rather graphic photographs of him and his mistress sent to his wife, another was elaborately framed for a crime which he had nothing to do with."

Beamon had heard quiet whisperings of the church wielding their power a bit unethically, but he'd never seen any proof. As much as he liked to believe the worst of organized religion, without corroboration, he'd always assumed that it was just mudslinging by rival faiths jealous of the Kneissians' success.

Beamon let Volker hook an arm though his but didn't move when the German tried to pull him away from the car and toward the stage. "I'd rather not have to shoot my way out of here, Hans. As much as I appreciate the effort, I'd be just as happy finishing this conversation over a cup of coffee at your office."

Volker tugged insistently on his arm. "Please don't worry, Mark. I personally guarantee your safety."

Beamon stood his ground for a moment and then gave up and allowed himself to be led through the crush of people. "What can you tell me about Albert Kneiss?"

"A fascinating figure," Volker shouted over a deafening round of applause. A man in a dark suit had just walked on the stage and everyone seemed happy to see him. "Born Christmas Day 1913 to a devout Christian preacher. You're aware that it is believed that Kneiss will ascend to heaven—die— on Good Friday this year?"

"Yeah. Born on Christmas, dead on Good Friday. Just like Jesus."

Volker nodded. "Interestingly, Kneiss did not immediately follow his father into the spiritual, but studied anthropology and later became a professor at the University of Chicago. He was quite brilliant, but his theories were extremely radical for the time. One—that a number of different species of humans inhabited the earth at the same time—has only recently been adopted. Unfortunately, his approach to anthropology was too much for the university, and he was eventually let go—a laughingstock in the world of science."

Volker stopped next to a small knot of people in blue polo shirts identifying their home parish as Spokane, Washington. Between them, they held a large banner reading FREEDOM TO WORSHIP.

"This should do, don't you think?" Volker said, looking up at the man on the stage and gauging their distance. "You probably recognize Senator Tompkins from Massachusetts."

Now that he looked more carefully, Beamon

did recognize him. Tompkins had taken a leadership role in criticizing Germany's policies toward the church. It was impossible not to see him posturing in the media for the benefit of religious freedom at least once a week.

"Now what was it you were saying about Kneiss?"

"Oh, I'm sorry. Soon after his removal from the university, his wife succumbed to cancer, leaving him with an infant daughter. He disappeared from the eyes of history for a number of years around this time. Eventually he reappeared in upstate New York with his Bible, transformed into God's messenger on earth."

"So he just combined his two areas of expertise—theology, which he learned from his father, and science, which was his chosen profession."

"One would assume."

"If he was born in 1913 he's in his late eighties now. Is he still in control of the church?"

Volker shrugged. "I think it's unlikely. There's a group of seven Elders who operate the church. A woman named Sara Renslier controls the group." He pointed toward the stage. "See the rather petite woman with short dark hair sitting at the back?"

Beamon nodded.

"That's her. It was her appointment some twenty-five years ago that was the turning point for Kneiss and his followers. A formidable woman. She will certainly become the unequivocal head of the organization when Kneiss dies."

Beamon pulled a pad from his pocket and struggled to overcome the jostling of the people around him and write the name down. "But if he dies on Good Friday, shouldn't he be resurrected on Easter like he was last time?"

Volker chuckled. "That would be quite a trick, wouldn't it? But the answer, of course, is no. The Kneissians do not believe that the resurrection of Jesus had any real significance. Nothing more than the last in a long list of what they consider banal parlor tricks that Jesus—Kneiss—was forced to perform to gain credibility in a hopelessly superstitious time."

"And he's been doing this since the dawn of humanity—popping in every two thousand years to update the current thinking?"

Volker rose onto his toes to get a better view as two men shook hands on stage. "You really should make it a point to read their Bible, Mark. But the answer to your question is no. They believe that at some time in the distant past, the entity we now know as Kneiss was chosen by God to take the place of the prior messenger, who had gone on to his reward. And one day another messenger will be chosen to replace Kneiss."

The booming voice of Senator Joseph Tompkins resonated over the PA system, and Volker had to raise his voice another notch to be heard. "This issue has become quite a boon for the senator, don't you think? The church strongly encourages its members to contribute to his campaign fund every year, and what American doesn't hold the issue of religious freedom close to his heart?"

22

BEAMON PULLED THE NOTEPAD OUT OF ITS paper sack and stuck it to the inside of his windshield with the suction cup on the back. Damn Volker was making him paranoid.

He groaned quietly as he forced his still-sore legs to jog through the snow toward the office of his condo complex. The light was still on, and Beamon could see that the property manager was stuffing papers into a large leather briefcase in preparation for calling it a day. He tossed a half-smoked cigarette—his first of the day—into a snowbank and slipped through the door.

"Tina! How goes it?"

She flashed him that broad smile full of straight white teeth that always seemed to take the chill off. She was such a cute little thing, just out of college and surrounded by the healthy glow that seemed specific to the inhabitants of America's mountainous middle section.

"Mr. Beamon! What brings you out in this weather?"

"I was wondering if you could help me with a little information."

"Have you been smoking?" she said, sniffing at the air.

"Just one," Beamon said proudly, electing not to volunteer that he'd been in either Hans Volker's car, the J. Edgar Hoover Building, or an airplane since eight that morning. All locales under the ruthless control of the smoking Nazis.

She looked at him with mock severity. "I'll let it go. But just this once. You absolutely must quit. Okay?"

He gave a noncommittal nod.

"Okay. Now, what can I do for you?"

"I need some information on a few of the renters here."

"Which ones?"

Beamon ran his finger along the full-color map of the complex taped to the counter. "Anyone from buildings A, C, F, or H."

"That's a lot of people," she said, obviously anxious to leave for the day.

"Let me narrow it down. I'm not interested in any leases signed before I got here, so just people who moved in January fifteenth or later. And I'm not interested in anything shorter-term than, say, a month."

"Well, you're in luck," she said, turning and crouching down next to a cardboard box on the floor. "I hate filing and tend to put it off forever." She pulled out a stack of folders and began sorting through them, tossing a few on the counter but dropping most back in the box. When she was finished, she neatened the stack of five folders lying on the counter and centered them in front of her. "These are all the ones signed in January and February for those buildings." She flipped open each folder and threw three of them back in the box. "These two are the only ones that aren't short-term."

Beamon opened the first one. A family of four had signed a one-year lease. The second was a single male. Robert Andrews. Also a year. Beamon ran his finger down to the "employment" line. It simply read "self."

"Could I get copies of these, Tina?"

"Sure." She looked at him slyly. "Fugitives from the law?"

Beamon laughed. "Nah. Just haven't hit them up for the FBI raffle yet."

As usual, the phone was ringing when he stepped through the door, leaving him no time to take off his shoes. There was a visible trail of mud and water emerging on his carpet.

"Yeah. Hello," he said, grabbing the phone

"Mark! It's Chet. Man, I've been trying to reach you all day! I thought you were supposed to be back at two."

"It was a more elaborate trip than I bargained for. What's up?"

"Hey, have I ever told you about that friend I have at the coroner's office? Susan Moorland? You know, the girl I went to school with."

Beamon thought for a moment, but his brain was already in shutdown mode. He just wanted to get into his beer rations and then into bed. "Sure," he lied. "Seems like you've mentioned her."

"Well, she called me this morning. Apparently she helped do the work on Jennifer Davis's parents when they came in. She wants to talk to us about it."

Beamon peeled off his parka and cradled the phone with his shoulder. "I've read the report, Chet—

and we both saw the bodies. If she wants to make an amendment, that's what fax machines are for."

"She didn't do the report, Mark. Her boss did. And she disagrees with his conclusions—strongly, judging from her phone call. I guess he's normally pretty receptive to what she has to say, but this time he freaked out when she contradicted him. I can pretty much guarantee she isn't going to put anything in writing."

Beamon sighed. "Let me guess. She wants me to haul my ass out there in the middle of the night and stand around in a refrigerator with a bunch of corpses."

"Uh, yeah. Tonight, actually. I know how you feel about morgues, but she's got the bodies there still and she can't keep losing their paperwork forever. Come on, Mark—meet you at the back door at nine? Please?"

Beamon rubbed at his eyes. He was dying to say no. Michaels and his little friend had undoubtedly tripped over a molehill and built it into a mountain while he was in D.C. But he knew that the kid would be devastated if he passed. "All right. You win. Nine o'clock. Anything else?"

"Uh, I don't think so. No, wait. I got the stuff you wanted on Jennifer's adoption. Nothing very interesting—quick and easy. She was only at the foster home for a couple of days when the Davises started paperwork."

Beamon perked up a bit. "Really? Now, how does that work? Is it like buying a car? When the foster home gets in something they think you'd like they give you a call?"

Michaels laughed. "You make it sound so . . . cheap. I don't know if that's how it usually works, but it's not the way it went in this case. The Davises hadn't ever tried to adopt before."

Beamon nodded into the phone. "The ever-present impulse purchaser."

"You're a sick man, Mark. I don't know why I hang out with you."

"I sign your paychecks."

23

BEAMON STAMPED HIS FEET LOUDLY ON the icy concrete and thrust his hands deeper into the pockets of his parka. The mercury was down around zero, but on the bright side, the cold was keeping any strange smells from escaping the dumpster they were using as a windblock. No telling what those creepy coroners threw in there.

"Jesus Christ, Chet," Beamon said, staring at the firmly locked side door to the newly constructed Flagstaff morgue. "If I knew we were going to spend a couple of hours out here I would have brought along a couple of Huskies and some firewood."

Michaels put his finger to his lips, but Beamon refused to take the hint. He'd lost the feeling in his toes five minutes ago. "You know, Chet, they might let us in the front door, since I am, well, *the goddamn head of the FBI here.*"

"I told you, Mark," Michaels said in an exaggerated whisper. "Susan's really going out on a limb here. She already wrote a contradictory report and her boss went nuts and threw it in the shredder. If he knew she'd called us she'd probably lose her job."

"Uh-huh," Beamon growled as he dug Robert Andrews's lease agreement out of his pocket and handed it to Michaels. "Get me what you can on this guy, Chet. Nothing fancy, just a quickie."

Michaels tried to read it, but the dim glow provided by the ice-covered lamp above the door made it impossible. He stuffed it in his coat. "What is it?"

"Probably nothing. A guy leasing a condo near mine. Oh, see if you can get some background on a Sara Renslier. Apparently she runs Kneiss's church. Again, nothing fa—"

The metal on metal sound of a deadbolt sliding back, followed by a blast of warm air, interrupted him. He squeezed past a slightly startled young woman without a word and into the relative warmth of the building.

"Mark Beamon," he said quietly, holding out his hand. She took it as Michaels slipped through the doorway and closed it behind him.

"I'm sorry you had to wait out there," she said, already starting down the hall. "Some of the people in the office decided to stay late. Follow me, and please be as quiet as possible."

The initial warmth Beamon had felt seemed to fade as they hurried deeper into the building—though he assumed it was just his imagination. With all the cigarettes, straight bourbons, and chili dogs he'd consumed in his lifetime, morgues tended to put a little too much perspective on things.

The woman in front of him stopped short as the hall came to a T, and Beamon watched as she poked her head around the corner and peered down the hall. She was small—no more than five-three—with long dark hair tied in a ponytail that was pinned under the top strap of the green apron she wore. Something about her reminded him of Carrie. Maybe it was the purposeful stride, or . . .

"We're going to go left here, Mr. Beamon. It's possible that the night watchman could come by. If you hear him, just duck into one of the rooms."

As she moved out into the hall, Beamon leaned in close to Michaels. "I'm having real dignity problems with this, Chet."

The young agent grinned silently back at him and tiptoed out into the hall at Susan's "all clear" signal. He looked like he was having the time of his life. Real cops-and-robbers stuff.

Fortunately, the rest of their journey was a bit less cloak-and-dagger, and in three minutes Susan was locking the door to the examination room behind them.

"All right. We made it!" Michaels gushed.

Susan took a deep breath and let it out loudly. "Sorry about the melodrama, guys. But this could get me in a lot of trouble."

Beamon hopped up onto the hard slab of the examining table and scanned the grid of metal doors covering the wall to his left. "We appreciate the risk you took, Susan," he said without enthusiasm. She couldn't possibly have been more than a year out of college. This was starting to look like an exhausting waste of time. "What have you got for us?"

She walked over to the wall of drawers and pulled out two of them, then unzipped the bags containing the bodies of Eric and Patricia Davis. From his position on the table, Beamon could see the blood-matted hair dried to their scalps and black stitching left by the coroner.

He stuffed a piece of gum in his mouth as Michaels approached the bodies and looked down at them. To his credit, the young agent managed to look somber and to stifle the cry of "cool!" that Beamon could tell was trying to bubble to the surface.

"I believe that the autopsy report you read was colored by the facts of the case," Susan said.

"How so?" Michaels said, still struggling to sound the calm professional. Beamon picked up a styrofoam head off the table next to him. It had what looked a bit like a shish kebab skewer stuck all the way through it, beginning under the chin.

"I think we should just have the bodies dropped off and be left to our own conclusions," Susan explained. "Having the facts of the case just creates preconceived ideas about cause of death."

Beamon looked back at the two pieced-together corpses, then at the young professionals hovering over them. "Are you going to tell me that the cause of death wasn't gunshot wounds, Susan?"

She shook her head. "No, it was definitely gunshot. But I think there are some pretty surprising indications about the gunman that didn't make it to the report."

"You have my undivided attention, my dear," Beamon said, hoping she'd move things along. He had just realized that he'd been going nonstop for almost twenty-two hours.

Susan walked over to a large chalkboard on the wall and pointed to a drawing depicting two stick figures. One was aiming a crudely rendered handgun at the other. There was a dotted line drawn from the gun through the victim's head.

"From what I can piece together," she tapped

the board, "this is what happened to Patricia Davis." Beamon shrugged and nodded.

"Now, as you probably noticed from the autopsy report, Mr. Davis was only five-eight, and Mrs. Davis was taller—five-ten. Now, judging from the powder burns on the side of Mrs. Davis's head, we can infer that the gun was approximately one foot three inches from her head when it was fired. Based on this and the angle of the bullet's trajectory, we can calculate that the killer had a shoulder height of four feet eight inches."

Beamon scowled and jumped off the table. He picked up a piece of chalk and continued the dotted line through the killer depicted on the board and drew another stick figure, shorter and farther away. "Come on, Susan, that powder burn stuff is voodoo. You could be off six inches one way or another. It could have been a shorter guy farther away, or a taller guy closer."

She looked indignant. "I believe that my calculations are quite precise, Mr. Beamon. But even if I'm off your six inches, I think we can be fairly confident that the perpetrator was shorter than Mrs. Davis."

Beamon looked into her face and, seeing the steady stare and the set of her jaw, sat back down on the table, scratching the back of his head. "Okay, Susan. I'll give you that one. Why? Because I have no idea where you're going with this."

She gave him a polite smile and picked up the styrofoam head that he had been playing with earlier. "This shows the angle of the bullet that killed Mr. Davis."

She pulled a rather realistic-looking plastic pistol out of one of the pockets of her apron and handed it to Michaels. "Okay, Chet. I want you to shoot me, just like this." She pulled a matching skewer out of her apron pocket and held it up to her head, mimicking the angle of the one in the styrofoam facsimile.

Michaels stood in front of her and stuck the plastic gun under her chin. Because of their height differential, he couldn't get anywhere close to the almost vertical bullet trajectory. Instead, the gun was aimed at a severe angle that would have sent the bullet out of the back of her head.

She stepped up on a small overturned crate that she had obviously put there for the purpose. "This makes me roughly Mr. Davis's height." The angle moved closer, but was still significantly off.

Normally, Beamon would have had to laugh at the sight of a tiny young woman holding a shish-kebab skewer to her head and being held at plastic gunpoint by a guy who looked like Richie Cunningham from *Happy Days*. But he was starting to get interested despite himself.

Michaels bent his wrist unnaturally but still wasn't able to get the angle right before the butt of the gun hit Susan in the chest. He stepped back for a moment and circled around her. Holding the gun under her chin from behind put it at the correct angle.

Susan jumped down from the box. "Exactly what I came up with, Chet. It seems to me that the killer would have had to be standing behind Mr. Davis in order to produce the correct bullet trajectory. I think you'll agree that you wouldn't want to be standing that close behind him when the top of his head came off."

Michaels nodded vigorously.

"Are you starting to get interested yet, Mr. Beamon?"

"Mark, please." He shrugged. "Interested might be too strong a word. Intrigued, maybe. For now, call me mildly attentive."

She gave him a sly look and walked over to the two corpses protruding from the wall. "Come on over, Mark. I'd like you to look at something."

Beamon jumped off his perch and walked slowly toward the corpses as Susan picked up Mr. Davis's right hand and held it out toward him. She pointed to the pale skin between the dead man's thumb and index finger. "See these parallel scratches here?"

Beamon pulled his glasses from his pocket and put them on. The scratches were small, but obvious when pointed out. He nodded.

"They precisely match the slide on a forty-five."

She pulled out a tape measure from the seemingly inexhaustible pocket of her apron and ran it from Mr. Davis's feet to his shoulder. The tape read four feet eight inches.

Beamon smiled. "Uh-huh."

"Hold on, I've got one more thing." She rushed into the attached office and came back with a diagram of a man standing slightly sideways aiming a gun directly out of the picture. There were various splotches drawn onto the man's body in red. Each had a line going from it to some writing at the edge of the sheet. Beamon had no idea what it meant.

"I did some tests on the bloodstains on Mr. Davis. Many of them matched Mrs. Davis's blood type. This diagram shows those findings. I think you'll agree that the pattern is intriguing. Her blood is most prevalent on Mr. Davis's right hand in the pattern that's shown there."

"Now we're getting into some serious voodoo," Beamon said.

She nodded her agreement. "There are other explanations. I really just did this test to see if it refuted the overall hypothesis."

Michaels looked at the diagram with a confused expression. "I guess I'm just dumb, you guys. What overall hypothesis are we talking about?"

Beamon took a deep breath of stale, antiseptic air. "It seems that your friend here thinks Mr. Davis killed his wife and then committed suicide."

"What? No way!"

"Why not?" Susan said confidently.

"Because it's nuts, Susan. It doesn't even come close to fitting into what we know."

Beamon ignored the heated debate that started between them and picked up Eric Davis's cold hand again. He hoped that on further inspection he could come up with a more plausible explanation for the marks. He couldn't.

24

SARA RENSLIER LOOKED DOWN AT THE shriveled form of Albert Kneiss and then to the tank that fed his nearly paralyzed lungs oxygen. The room was almost completely dark. The large windows had turned to mirrors, vibrating with the low howl of the storm battering the world outside. Only the light from the heart monitor made it possible to see, casting a flickering glow over the bed and the man lying in it.

She watched silently as the shadows cast across his face shifted and his eyes opened. "Sara?"

She reached out and touched the old man's cool, dry forehead. He looked so small now, the charisma that had made him such a powerful tool almost completely lost in his withered body.

"Don't speak, Albert," she said, running her hand along his scalp and through the few remaining tufts of hair clinging to it. She felt Kneiss's eyes on her as she pulled a syringe from her pocket and removed the plastic cap covering the tip of the needle.

"What is it, Sara?" he whispered as she slid the needle into his IV tube.

In the semidarkness, she couldn't see the fluid from the syringe make its way down the tube toward his arm, but she knew that it had reached his bloodstream when the slow rhythm of the heart monitor began to shudder and the old man began to jerk weakly. His right arm came to life, reaching for the IV needle taped into his veins, but Sara held it firmly in place.

"What . . . what are you doing?" he said, clawing pathetically against the back of her hand.

She knelt down and leaned in close to him. "The church has outgrown its living prophet, Albert. I need one now who can appear to its children in times of trouble. One that can appear to them on their deathbeds."

The stimulant she had injected into Kneiss cleared his eyes as it began to overload what was left of the systems in his broken body. "What are you doing to me?" he repeated in a stronger voice.

"You've never understood, have you, Albert? You've never been able to grasp what the church has become. What I've made it." A thin smile crossed her lips as she watched the old man struggle to control his ragged breathing enough to speak. "What could have possibly made you think I'd let you take it away from me?"

"What are you saying, Sara? You . . . you've been my most devoted pupil. You helped Jennifer. After my daughter died. You knew that she—"

"How can you be so naïve, Albert? Your daughter didn't die. I killed her. She would have poisoned Jennifer against the church—made her useless to me."

Kneiss's heart rate notched higher. "No. No, you couldn't have. You believe. I gave you my trust. My love."

Sara gripped his arm tighter until she could feel

the slight movement of the IV needle as it vibrated with the old man's heartbeat. "I know you did, Albert. And I gave you what you most wanted—an audience." A tear ran down his nearly paralyzed cheek and she wiped it away with her thumb. "I thought I needed Jennifer—that someday I might have to use her to help me maintain control of the church. But I already have control, don't I? You gave it to me. She can only cause problems now, Albert. Confuse my followers."

Kneiss was finding it increasingly difficult to speak. "You can't. The others—they know about her. They won't let you harm . . ."

"You still don't understand, do you, Albert? You're dying. Right now. Not on Good Friday. Now. What does that mean?"

He just stared up at her with that supernatural expression of pain and despair that had sucked in so many. The rock she'd built her church on.

"You know, don't you, Albert? It's in your Bible. Your brilliant Bible. If you die before Good Friday, your time as God's Messenger is done." She smiled. "And I've helped Him choose your successor."

Kneiss's hand closed on hers again, but she couldn't tell if it was intentional or just the final random firing of his dying nerve endings. "No. Sara, you don't know what you're doing. There's still time for you to stop this."

"It's your fault, Albert. If you had just slipped away quietly like you were supposed to, none of this would have to happen. But you didn't, did you?"

"Not her, Sara," he gasped. "Please."

She felt his hand fall away from hers and his

eyes fix on the ceiling above him. "There's nothing that can stop it now, Albert. Your granddaughter *will* take your place on Good Friday—God's new Messenger. I have a beautiful ceremony planned for her ascension. I think you'd approve."

Sara released his arm and turned away, staring into the darkness of the room and listening to the increasingly erratic tone of the heart monitor. The church was hers now. Hers.

She heard a low moan from behind her and turned to see Albert Kneiss struggling to lift his head one last time.

"I prayed for you, Sara. Just like I prayed for all the others." He began to sink back onto the pillow. "But every time must have its Judas."

The pulse of the heart monitor slowed, finally fading to the steady tone that signaled the end of the Messenger's time on earth and a new era for her church.

25

MARK BEAMON TOOK ANOTHER SIP OF HIS coffee and continued to watch the young man through the window of the cafe. He was impeccably dressed—blue topcoat, white shirt, red-and-green-striped tie. And he had the look of clean-cut optimism Beamon had come to expect in the followers of Albert Kneiss. That confident but solicitous carriage that proclaimed, "I know something that you don't."

Beamon scraped up the last of the cream cheese that had dribbled from the bagel he had just wolfed down and popped it in his mouth. It wasn't biscuits and gravy, but he was actually starting to get used to the things.

The young man's pattern hadn't changed since he'd taken his position on the sidewalk across the street almost an hour ago. Eye contact, a confident sentence or two, hand the pedestrian a pamphlet, then attempt to shake hands and engage them in conversation.

From the looks of it, he worked that corner regularly. He'd received and returned at least a hundred silent nods from the early-morning foot commuters, bantering with some he knew well, thanking those who refused a flyer, and giving an occasional impassioned speech to anyone who stopped and expressed interest.

He wasn't doing too badly, either. In the last hour or so, three people had been interested enough to let him lead them through the stained-glass door of the Church of the Evolution bookstore/office behind him. Within a few minutes, he would reappear out front, but without the interested party.

Perhaps they had already been sacrificed in some hedonistic ritual that involved snakes and naked virgins? Only one way to find out. Beamon tossed back the rest of his coffee and went out through the doors of the cafe and into the cold Flagstaff morning. The clouds had parted and the sunlight was beaming through the thin mountain air with an almost tangible force. Beamon slipped on his sunglasses as he jogged across the street and began walking up the sidewalk toward the despicably enthusiastic young man.

"Have you read the latest on human evolution, sir?" he asked, establishing forcible eye contact.

Beamon stopped and took the proffered flyer. The first page was a glossy reproduction of the cover of a recent *National Geographic* containing a story relating to the anthropological discovery that many years ago, various species of humans shared the earth. Across the bottom a quote had been artistically superimposed on the cover:

> *Humanity's path had become confused, with many species competing for the eye of the Lord. But it was only one, Sapiens, that had begun the journey toward enlightenment. God*

*sent his Messenger to them, to teach them to
see as He did.*

NATURE 3:14
THE HOLY BIBLE/KNEISS EDITION

Beamon flipped through the pamphlet's reproduction of the *National Geographic* article, now
modified with occasional italicized passages from
Kneiss's Bible corroborating the theories described
there.

"People laughed when they first read the New
Bible, just like they mocked Jesus and his teachings.
But now science is catching up with us, proving that
our truth is the universal truth."

The boy's voice carried a deep sincerity, but Beamon suspected that if he were at a Kneissian recruiting station in New Zealand instead of Flagstaff, he'd
be getting precisely the same well-thought-out spiel.
It wasn't cocky or condescending, it stayed cozy
with the science that people had come to trust and
rely on, and finally, it smoothly worked in Jesus so
as not to scare off America's devout Christian con-
tingent.

"You know, I read something about this awhile
back," Beamon said in as earnest a tone as he could
conjure up.

"Then you're familiar with our beliefs, sir?"

Beamon shook his head. "Not really. I'm just
visiting Flagstaff. I'm from Kansas City. I wish I
could remember where I read . . ."

The boy stroked his chin thoughtfully. "There's
been a lot of publicity about this lately. Could have
been almost anywhere. The fact that science has

turned a hundred and eighty degrees to agree with the Bible isn't a common occurrence." He gave a short, self-assured laugh that made Beamon feel like he was in on the joke.

"So, Albert Kneiss wrote this stuff over fifty years ago?" Beamon said, looking down at the pamphlet.

"I'm really not as much of an expert as some of the people inside. If you've got a few minutes for a cup of coffee, I'm sure I can dig up someone who could answer your questions with a lot more authority than I can."

Beamon shrugged. "Sure, I guess I have a minute."

The boy grinned and led Beamon through a set of double doors and into the tastefully decorated outer office. "This gentleman would like to speak with someone about the article," he said to the woman behind the counter and then turned back to Beamon. "I'm sorry, I forgot to ask your name."

"Mark."

He offered his hand. "Todd."

Todd hung around and chatted until a woman came out and politely stood off to the side until Beamon finished what he was saying.

"Mark, this is Cynthia," Todd said. "Cynthia, Mark."

Beamon turned to the woman and took her hand. "Very nice to meet you, Cynthia."

She was quite striking, with a long, straight nose and blonde hair covering her shoulders in a tumble that somehow didn't look random. Just by looking at her, Beamon would have put her in her early thirties, but the way she carried herself made him adjust upward a bit.

She led him through the door of a spacious but cozy room full of antique furniture and pleasantly worn rugs and offered him a chair next to a roaring fire. As he settled into the soft leather, she slid a tray with two steaming mugs on it toward him. He ignored the cream and sugar on the platter as he reached for one of them.

"Me too," she said. "I'd go intravenous if I could."

Beamon smiled and took a sip. He expected it to be good, and it was. He pulled out a cigarette he had rolled at the bagel shop, more to see her reaction than anything else. "Do you mind?"

"Not at all."

As he lit it, she opened a thick leather book and laid it on the table between them. "Would you care to sign our guest book?"

He hesitated, once again to judge her reaction. "I'd rather not. Not just yet."

"That's fine," she said with an easygoing flair, closing the book and sliding it down next to her chair. "So, Mark, how familiar are you with our church?"

"Not very, Cynthia. I mean, I know the basics. That you believe Albert Kneiss is a messenger from God who comes down to earth every couple of thousand years to teach."

"That about covers it. Want to join?"

They both laughed. Beamon was confident that if he had actually been there for the reason she thought, the remark would have done exactly what it had been designed to do—relieve any tension he might have felt.

"Seriously, you're right," she continued. "But in order for someone to teach, he or she has to take into consideration the abilities of the students. You don't try to teach a toddler calculus."

Beamon nodded his understanding, prompting her to go on.

"So when God's word was first written down in a coherent way—in the original Bible—a lot of parables and analogies were used. God revealed of himself only what the people of that time could digest."

The woman was starting to look a little peaked from his smoke, so Beamon tossed the cigarette into the fireplace. "Just can't seem to completely kick the habit."

"We have wonderful programs for that," she said. "I'm told they have the best success rate of any in the world."

Beamon took a sip from his mug, washing the taste of tobacco from his mouth. "So the new Bible—your version—tells the whole truth. Throws out the superstition and cuts right to the chase. The nature of God, what He wants from us, why we're here."

She smiled engagingly and shook her head. "Oh, no. We've come a long way in the last two thousand years, but unfortunately not that far. We still aren't prepared to fully understand God. Albert has simply given us God's teachings in the current context, so that we can understand more about Him. In another two thousand years, Albert will be back, under another name, to explain as much as he can based on what we've learned over the next two thousand years."

She was good. She exuded the calm confidence and sense of belonging that everyone was after. On another level, she was very attractive and roughly the right age for Beamon. He wondered if his spirit guide would have been some dashing hunk if he were a woman.

"I've read a few articles about your church in Germany. That they seem to think you're breaking the law—some kind of threat."

She looked sadly into the fire for a moment. "Obviously, the Germans have a poor history of accepting diverse faiths. Our followers have had to struggle there, it's true. We're giving them all the help we can, but as you know, not all countries put the same premium on freedom that we do."

A perfect answer, Beamon concluded. It attacked the attacker instead of defending the victim and it brought up the rather intangible concept of freedom that was guaranteed to get any American's red blood pumping.

"I have to admit, though," she continued, "we are a pretty close-knit group. The church provides business networking, counseling if you need it, help for the needy, health care, and hundreds of other things. Do you have children?"

Beamon shook his head.

"Too bad. We've built some of the finest schools in the country. We're really dedicated to educa-tion—probably more than anything else, we cherish that."

"I hear it's pretty expensive to be a member of the church," Beamon interjected.

A look of mild suspicion crossed her face and

then was gone. "Not particularly. Obviously, with all the services we like to provide and our commitment to charities, we do ask for some support from our members."

"Does Albert Kneiss ever appear in public?"

The look of suspicion stayed a little longer this time. "Are you a reporter?"

Beamon was a little surprised by the abruptness of the question, but then remembered Chet Michaels's difficulty in dredging up press articles on the church.

"A reporter? No. No, I'm not."

There was a long pause and Beamon began to wonder if the interview was over.

"Albert meditates," she said finally. "As I'm sure you've heard, his time with us is nearly over."

Beamon stood and pulled another cigarette from his pocket. "I really appreciate your time, Cynthia. I learned a lot." He pointed to a stack of Kneissian Bibles by her chair. "I'd love to have one of those if you can spare it."

She handed him one, somewhat reluctantly. "I hope it touches you as much as it did me."

Beamon flipped through the book and smiled. "I have no doubt that it will."

26

BEAMON COASTED INTO HIS SPACE, MANAGING for once to avoid sliding into the trees in front of it. He left the car running as he lit a cigarette and pulled his new notepad off the windshield. Turning on the interior light, he began flipping through the pages.

Reluctant to dismiss Hans Volker's views on the church, Beamon had begun to watch for cars that could be tailing him. Every time he saw one that might be popping up behind him more often than probability dictated, he jotted down the color, make, model, license number, time, and approximate location. Then, every night when he arrived home, he'd check to see if there were any matches.

So far there had been nothing exciting—other than the fact that he'd almost run over two pedestrians and a border collie while trying to juggle a cigarette, a cup of coffee, and the pad of paper.

Beamon ran his finger down the list of four cars he'd entered that day, memorizing their make and model, then shuffled back through the prior pages. He stopped at an entry on a red Taurus and flipped back to that day's record.

The license numbers matched, but that didn't mean anything. Could be just a neighbor who left for work at the same time. He compared the time of day. Nine A.M. and 3:45 P.M. Location: One between his home and the office, the other nowhere near either.

Beamon leaned back and blew a smoke ring at his rearview mirror. It could be a coincidence, of course, but that seemed unlikely. The real question was whether or not it was the church and if it was, whether it had anything to do with Jennifer Davis. If Hans Volker was right and the Kneissians were generally paranoid about the government's enforcement machine, it seemed likely that they would keep an eye on the head of the FBI's Flagstaff office on principle alone.

Beamon kicked his feet up onto one arm of his sofa and worked his head into the soft pillow covering the other.

The Kneissian Bible that the church had been kind enough to provide him appeared to be separated into four books—Nature, Old Testament, Jesus, and The Future. Each book had at least twenty subheadings.

Beamon flipped to the last page. Number 1,212. Probably better just to skim.

It took him about an hour to figure out the significance of each book. Nature took the place of Genesis, describing the creation of the universe, as well as the evolution of man and the "lesser species," from a significantly more scientific standpoint than the original Bible. In the universe according to Kneiss, God breathed life into the primordial soup that existed on Earth—as well as on an undisclosed number of other planets in the universe—and then waited to see what happened.

Actually, that wasn't entirely true. He occasionally saw fit to muck around with the evolutionary process, creating the more intricate structures of life such as wings and the complex organs that created a spider's web, among other things that had baffled anthropologists since Darwin.

Of course, he had taken a special interest in humanity, sending the first Messenger many years ago to stack the deck for homo sapiens against the protohumans who had turned out not to be the sharpest knives in His drawer.

The Old Testament section tended to debunk sections of the original Bible more than anything else. It provided insight into the characters of the original Old Testament, making them much more human and therefore much more believable. David became a murderous and somewhat vain man necessary to God's plan. The black-and-white treatment of the Romans melted to a gunmetal gray, and God's motivations became clearer and more ambiguous at the same time.

The Jesus section seemed to serve much the same function as the Old Testament chapters. It covered many of His most pivotal moments on earth, told from His point of view. The squalor and superstition that ruled the lives of the people of that time was rendered so artfully that Beamon could almost feel Jesus's frustration as he tried to impart the mind of God to a population that understood nothing and feared everything.

The section entitled The Future replaced Revelation, and was the book most starkly different from its predecessor. It stated that the end of humanity was not yet etched in stone. God's hope for mankind was that it would evolve to a state of complete enlightenment. That was to be the criteria on which it would be judged. Would humanity be able to leave behind superstition, fear, and hate? To develop fully those things that set it apart from the other species that shared the earth?

Beamon yawned and laid the book down on his chest. Four-thirty in the morning. He looked over at the coffee table and counted the empty beer bottles on it. Eight. Three more than his daily allowance.

He picked up Kneiss's Bible again and stared at the black cover.

As a work of literature, it was truly amazing. The prose style was a seemingly impossible mix of passion and reason, formality and accessibility. It stripped the wings off the angels and the horns and teeth from the devil, offering humanity a glimpse of its potential and a clear path to achieving that potential. It provided answers to a world trying so desperately to find meaning and clinging to gods that had stood still while their flocks had moved on.

27

"IT'S A MIRACLE!"

Beamon surveyed his office with a sense of satisfaction. True, the cables were still hanging from the ceiling and there was still that unavoidable layer of white dust over everything, but by God, the concrete floor had disappeared beneath a layer of utilitarian tan carpet.

His secretary walked up next to him and leaned against the doorjamb as though she hadn't noticed until he pointed it out. "A miracle, huh? From what I hear, you had a conversation with the general contractor about his continued ability to—how did he put it—travel America's highways and byways? I understand his people were in here all night."

"Morning, Mark."

Beamon didn't look out from behind his paper. "Have a seat, Chet. Your shoes aren't dirty, are they?"

"Nope. Nice carpet."

"Clearly a floor covering befitting a man of my stature," Beamon said, finishing the article he was reading and tossing the paper on the desk.

Michaels chuckled quietly. "Clearly."

"What did you think of your friend's theory, Chet?"

Michaels's expression turned serious. "At first, I was really embarrassed to have dragged you out there. But then I couldn't sleep that night, you know? The angle of the bullet, the scratches on his hand. I don't know, Susan's really smart."

"Attractive, too," Beamon said. "How'd you ever let her get away?"

"Lesbian."

"No."

"Yup."

"Well, a good woman's hard to find. Sometimes you just have to overlook their little imperfections." Beamon looked at the blue folders his young protégé never seemed to be without. "So what have you got for me?"

"Wait a minute, Mark. You can't leave me hanging like that. What do *you* think of Susan's theory?"

"We'll get to that, but first things first," Beamon answered, shaking his finger again toward the folders.

Michaels reluctantly tossed one of them onto Beamon's desk. "That's a bunch of articles on the church that have come in from the publishers. Some are pretty old—actually most are. Objective media coverage seems to be less every year."

"I'll read'm tonight. I've got a meeting starting in an hour that's going to take all day. Is there anything in here that I need to know right now?"

"Not really. There's some stuff criticizing the church's business tactics and the fact that they use nuisance suits to beat down their detractors. Some stuff on how it's really expensive to belong . . . oh, and there's a really interesting *Psychology Today* article about the pressure the church puts on its people to recruit new members and the toll it takes on them emotionally. That one was pretty cool. Now, what about Susan's theory?"

"We're going to work on that in a few minutes," Beamon said, pointing to the remaining folder lying in the young agent's lap. "What's that one?"

"Information I put together on your neighbor and Sara Renslier."

Beamon waved him on. "Give me the *Reader's Digest* version."

"Robert T. Andrews. Thirty-five years old, originally from Louisiana—Baton Rouge. Career military: 82nd Airborne. Honorably discharged a sergeant June 1995. As near as I can tell, he's been unemployed since then. I tried to check out his prior address—it's a property up in the mountains. Couldn't get there, though—the road leading to it was snowed in." He looked up at Beamon. "You think this guy's watching you?"

Beamon shrugged. "Probably not. Just a feeling."

"I can dig deeper."

Beamon shook his head. If the church *was* watching him, best not to jump up and down with his pants around his ankles. "Do me this, though. See if you can quietly find out if anyone else is living at his prior address and if so, get me some general information on them, too. Now what about Renslier?"

"Sara Renslier is fifty-one. Lists the church as her employer and Kneiss's compound as her permanent residence. It looks like she was an accountant for a few years after school, then went to work for the church. No criminal record; nothing specific about what she does for the church. Time to talk about the suicide theory yet?"

Beamon stood up from behind his desk. "It's

time. Go get me Theresa and James," he said, naming the two agents in his office, besides Chet, who seemed the most flexible and imaginative. "And let's not mention the church angle, okay?"

Michaels looked confused, but complied. Beamon followed him to the door. "Hey, D., you were a drama major, weren't you?"

"I *do* have a public administration minor," she said a little defensively.

"Don't need an administrator. Need an actress. Are you any good?"

She looked at him suspiciously, obviously waiting for the punch line. When none came, she said, "There are worse."

"Shut the door behind you, Chet," Beamon said as Michaels walked in with the two agents Beamon had sent him for.

"Okay, here's what's happening. Chet and I have a theory about the Davis case and we need some help working it out. Now, what I'm going to tell you doesn't leave this room. I mean that. If I hear anything that leads me to believe it has, I will make it my life's work to track down the leak and see him or her thrown out of the Bureau. Anybody have a problem with that?"

Beamon surveyed the young agents' faces and the face of his secretary as they all mumbled their assent.

"Okay then. We have physical evidence that leads us to believe that Mr. Davis may have shot his wife and then committed suicide."

With the exception of Michaels, the expressions worn by the people in the room turned to shock. There was some low murmuring, but no one spoke up clearly. Probably still intimidated by his little speech.

"Now, my problem is that I can't figure out a motivation for Mr. Davis that fits the rest of the facts. And that's where you all come in."

Beamon grabbed some note cards from his desk drawer and began writing on them. "D., you're Patricia Davis." He handed her a nametag that she taped to her chest.

"Theresa—you're Jennifer, I'm Eric Davis. And Chet and James—you guys are our hypothetical perpetrators." He handed them nametags reading "Thing 1" and "Thing 2," then leaned back to examine his cast. Something was missing. He handed Michaels a stapler and James a ruler. "Those are your guns."

Something was still wrong. He looked at Theresa's neatly trimmed hair and conservative blue business suit, then down at his desk. He unwound a paper clip and broke a third of it off. Fashioning the remaining wire into a loop, he held it out to her. "Put this on your nose."

She looked doubtful.

"Jennifer has a nose ring," he said impatiently. "Come on, let's get with the program."

She reluctantly stuck it to her nose, then looked down at it cross-eyed.

"That's what I was looking for," Beamon said. "Okay. Chet, would you like to give us our first scenario?"

"Wait a minute, Mark," D. broke in. "You know all there is to know about Mr. Davis, and Jennifer's life story has been plastered across the newspapers since she disappeared. But I don't know anything about my character."

Beamon pointed at D. but looked at the others. "Now that's what I'm talking about. A little enthusiasm."

He stood and took a position with his back against the wall, inviting D. to do the same. "Patricia Davis put her husband through college and supported him in his various business ventures, but hasn't worked since adopting Jennifer thirteen years ago. She's active in the PTA, an apparently devoted mother—though Jennifer considers her kind of, uh, square? She's also involved in numerous charities and belongs to a bridge club. Jennifer is her only child. Never had one of her own."

D. held up her hand. "That should do it."

"Okay, then. Chet, I believe you were about to convince me to kill my wife and commit suicide."

Michaels reached out, grabbed Theresa, and held the stapler to her head. "Okay, Mr. Davis. Shoot your wife and kill yourself or your daughter gets it."

Silence.

"Uh, I don't have a gun, son," Beamon said.

Chet turned to James. "Give him your gun."

James looked doubtful. "No way. There's no telling what a guy would do in this situation if he were armed. I'll shoot him for you if you want, though."

"Yeah, you're right," Michaels said, releasing his grip on Theresa.

"That's okay. That's what we're here for. To eliminate possibilities," Beamon said. "How about this. Jennifer never made it home. Her dad went nuts and killed her on the way."

Beamon took Michaels's stapler and aimed it at Jennifer. He was about to pull the "trigger" when his secretary grabbed him from behind and started choking him.

As he peeled her arm from his throat, Theresa ran to the door. Beamon corrected his scenario. "D.'s right on that one, there was evidence of a struggle." He grabbed her and "shot" Jennifer. D. played the distraught mother beautifully, throwing herself to her knees next to her fallen daughter—obviously having the time of her life.

"Okay, okay," Beamon said. "You're right. Super-unlikely that he could have killed Jennifer and then controlled the mother long enough to get her home. Hell, why bring Mom back at all?"

Theresa lifted her head from the carpet. "What if she was in on it and then you—Mr. Davis—started feeling really guilty when you got home?"

Beamon was skeptical. "What do you think, D.? Do you feel like you were in on it?"

She shook her head.

"Me neither. No indication of this type of tendency at all in either of them. And then there's the Big Question—where the hell's the gun?"

They all grumbled as they wrestled with the problem.

"Okay," Beamon said, ignoring the crowd forming on the other side of the window to his office. "Let's try the obvious one on for size. Dad goes nuts, Jennifer gets away."

He turned to D. "Patricia, you've left the cap off the toothpaste one too many times. Bang."

D. fell to the floor and Theresa ran to the edge of the room. Beamon pointed the deadly stapler at himself, "bang," and fell to the floor.

His eyes were closed, but he could hear Theresa walking toward him. "I'm sorry, Mark, but I can't think of any reason in this world why I'd take that gun."

Beamon sat up. "Shit. Me neither. Eliminate that one."

"What if Jennifer was involved?"

Beamon shrugged. "Takes us back to the first scenario. Even if she had an accomplice holding a gun to her head and she was pleading with her father to kill her mom and shoot himself, I don't think he'd have done it. Besides, what would be the point of taking the gun and making it look like murder after going through all that trouble? And why hasn't she reappeared to collect her inheritance? And where the hell is . . . Shit, I don't know . . ."

"What if they walked in on a robbery?" Chet began. "And the robbers take Jennifer and tell the parents that they're going to rape and kill her. That she'll be dead in a half-hour. Dad gets despondent—kills himself and his wife."

Beamon shook his head. "No way. He'd at least call the cops. Try to save his daughter in the next half-hour. And once again, where's the gun?"

"What if Jennifer was killed early on?"

"What, with the robbery scenario? Why the hell would they take the body? Necrophilia? I think we're reaching."

Beamon stood and helped his secretary to her feet. "Okay, guys, thanks. You've helped a lot."

They filed out through the door, discussing further possibilities in quiet whispers. Michaels closed the door behind D. as Beamon sat down at his desk and took a sip of cold coffee from his mug. "What are we going to do about this one, Chet?"

Michaels frowned. "I just can't think of anything we've missed. I mean, there's the church angle, but I sure don't see how that fits in with Eric Davis shooting his wife and killing himself."

Beamon rubbed his temples, feeling the beginnings of a throbbing that was likely to last until this thing was over. "Unfortunately, I can."

Michaels looked hopelessly frustrated. "Please, Mark. This thing's killing me."

"I'm gonna say it again, Chet. None of this leaves the room, right?"

Michaels nodded his assent.

"I've talked to a few people about the Church of the Evolution and done a little research myself," Beamon said. "They've created quite a religious machine for themselves—and their followers are incredibly devoted. Let's consider the facts in chronological order." Beamon held up his index finger. "One: Jennifer's real mother changes her name and place of residence numerous times, though for no reason we can find.

"Two: Jennifer's real mother and father are killed in a mysterious fire in the middle of the night, but their two-year-old daughter manages to escape and is found wandering around in the yard.

"Three: The Davises, a couple who moved to Flagstaff around the same time as the church did and who'd never tried to adopt before, pop in and take Jennifer right after she gets to the foster home."

Michaels had a strangely bemused look on his face.

"You okay, Chet?"

"Huh? Yeah. It's just that I do all this work gathering information for you—spend a ton of time writing it out, give it to you every morning, and, well, you always seem to be only half paying attention. I never thought you actually remembered any of it."

Beamon laughed. His mother used to get on him for the same thing. "Where was I?"

"Four."

"Four: Albert Kneiss decides he's going to die this year, leaving a leadership void at the church."

"Five: Kneiss's granddaughter suddenly disappears, and her adoptive parents, in essence, kill themselves."

Beamon stood up and grabbed his mug. "Process those five facts while I get another cup of coffee.

When Beamon sat back down, the young agent was scribbling furiously on a yellow legal pad. He finally laid it down on the desk, and Beamon could see that he'd written down the five points almost verbatim. Michaels looked up at him. "I'm still thinking."

Beamon put his feet on the desk and blew gently across the top of the mug. "Thinking is good. No hurry."

Michaels sat motionless for almost five minutes, elbows on his knees, staring at the pad. Finally his head rose and he leaned back in the chair. "Okay. I've got something, but it doesn't seem right."

"Go ahead."

"Jennifer's biological mother was running from the church. Kneiss wanted Jennifer to eventually succeed him, but his daughter didn't want anything to do with him and his followers. People from the church burned down her house with her and her husband in it, but made sure Jennifer wasn't injured."

He paused, looking a bit uncertain.

"Doing okay so far, keep going," Beamon prodded.

"The church sends two devoted members to adopt her right away. They keep her, pretending not to be part of the church, because they don't want any appearance of wrongdoing that could get into the press that they fear so much, and they wait. Finally, Kneiss announces that it's time for him to ascend. The church takes Jennifer and orders her adoptive parents to commit suicide. Religion is probably as good a motivation for suicide as any—history's proven that."

Beamon nodded thoughtfully.

"There's just one problem, though, Mark. Why the suicide?"

"It would be the only option. Think about it, Chet. They have to get rid of her folks—they'd be the first people I went after when she disappeared. And their backgrounds wouldn't have taken heavy scrutiny with all the church connections."

"Okay, I see your point. But why not just kill them? It's like you always say, the simplest answer is usually the right answer."

"You *could* just kill them, but consider the problems. Jennifer would hate her captors for killing her folks and would probably be reluctant to get involved with the Church. The second, better option would be to take Jennifer and then kill them. The problem there is twofold: Jennifer would think she had a family to get back to, making her conversion even more problematic. And, of course, when she did eventually find out they were dead, the shock could undo all their careful brainwashing."

Beamon sipped at his coffee. "If it were me, I'd

have the Davises commit suicide right in front of her. That would convince her of their devotion to the church and cut her off from any family support. I mean, can you imagine what something like that would do to a fifteen-year-old kid?"

28

JENNIFER DAVIS LOOKED DOWN AT THE
dripping faucet and estimated the time at between
2:30 and 3:30 in the afternoon, March 6.

The design was simple. She had counted endlessly—one Mississippi, two Mississippi—while the
dripping of the faucet filled the cup she had been
provided. Then, by filling the sink with the cup and
carefully scratching lines in the porcelain with a
fork, she had built a clock.

Regaining her sense of time had gone miles
toward helping her get her balance back. She'd used
it to establish a routine: go to sleep at ten, wake up
around eight. During the day, study the Bible the
old man had given her; early afternoon, try to get
some exercise. Then more study in the evening.

Her first impression had been right. Her meals
were being served at erratic intervals, sometimes as
little as an hour apart, sometimes as much as eight
hours apart.

She hadn't seen or spoken to anyone in seven
days and she'd used that time to think. Sara was a
liar. She told herself that at least ten times a day, trying to get the message to penetrate her fear and
loneliness.

The old man she had been taken to—her grandfather—knew nothing of how she was being treated.

That she was sure of. Sara was going to try her best to break her, she knew. Sara wasn't going to hand over her position as head of the church easily.

At the sound of the key hitting the lock, Jennifer ran out of the bathroom, afraid that her makeshift timepiece might be discovered. She stood in the middle of the room and watched the door open and Sara walk through.

"I'm so sorry, Jennifer. So sorry to have left you alone for so long."

Jennifer jerked back when Sara brought her hand up to touch her hair. The woman's face transformed into an expression of concern. "Oh, honey. I know how lonely you must be, but you have to trust me. There's no other way."

Jennifer looked past her and saw the man who always seemed to accompany Sara on her visits standing in the doorway. She'd only caught brief glimpses of him before today—identifying him by his thick black mustache. But now she could see the scar running from it to his expressionless right eye and his thin, powerful build.

"What do you want from me?" Jennifer said, having trouble keeping control of the jumble of emotions trying to take hold of her. Sara was the only person who came to see her, the only person who really spoke to her. And while she knew that it was Sara who had imprisoned her, it was so hard to distrust the only voice in her life. Late at night she found herself trying to reinvent Sara as someone who cared about her. To convince herself that the only human being she had any real contact with was good.

"You know what I want, Jennifer. I want to keep you safe from the others. This is very complicated, you—"

"I don't believe you," Jennifer said. She'd rehearsed this conversation at least a hundred times over the past few days, but was still having trouble getting the words out.

"What did you say?"

Jennifer could hear the edge of anger in Sara's voice and felt a sickening twinge in her stomach. She felt her resolve faltering, suddenly feeling like a small child who had angered her mother. She bit the inside of her mouth and concentrated on the pain, a trick she used to focus her mind when she raced. "I don't believe you."

"Jennifer. Listen very carefully. It's important that you fully understand what I'm going to tell you. Are you listening?"

Jennifer nodded.

"You've been alone in here too long and I know that what happened to your parents has affected you very deeply. You're not thinking clearly right now. You have to trust me. I'm going to take you to see your grandfather now, but there will be others there. It's very important that you say absolutely nothing unless it's in answer to a direct question posed by me. Okay?" She reached out again, but Jennifer caught her by the wrist.

"No. It's not okay."

Sara withdrew her hand and looked down at the floor for a moment. When she raised her head again, her eyes had turned cold. Jennifer took an involuntary step backward when she saw the man at the door coming toward her. She dodged right, but wasn't quick enough and felt herself being lifted off the ground and then slammed face first down onto the bed.

"Let me go!" she screamed as the man pinned

her arms behind her. She thrashed wildly, feeling the rage building in her. They had no right! No right to hold her here. No right to have taken her life away. She kicked out hard when the pressure on her back eased for a moment, but only connected with air.

She struggled even harder when she felt the cold metal against the back of her hands and then heard the ratcheting sound as a pair of handcuffs closed around her wrists. She twisted around as Sara came toward her and then fell back onto the mattress, exhausted and helpless. There was nothing she could do.

The man holding her moved away when Sara reached for the chain between the handcuffs binding her wrists. Jennifer cried out in pain when the woman forcefully twisted the chain, but something in her kept her from fighting back.

"Don't make another sound," Sara said quietly. Jennifer complied, lying motionless on the bed as the man returned to his position outside the open door.

Her wrists felt like they were going to break, and the combination of the pain, fear, and frustration was bringing tears to her eyes. She pressed her face into the tangle of sheets beneath her and wiped them away.

"That's better." The pressure on the handcuffs eased. "See what happens? If you do what I tell you, everything will be all right."

Sara didn't speak again for what seemed like forever, and Jennifer just lay motionless on the bed listening to the woman's breathing.

"I told you that I was taking you to see Albert and that some other people were going to be there.

What else did I tell you?" the woman finally said.

Jennifer's throat had gone completely dry and was making it a struggle to speak. "You . . . you told me just to answer your questions," she managed to say in what sounded like a loud whisper.

"That's right, Jennifer." There was another long pause before the woman spoke again. "There's no one else, you know. Your parents gave you to me. I cause your meals to brought to you, provide you with clean clothes, water. You've been orphaned for a second time, Jennifer. There's no one left who cares what happens to you. No one but me."

Jennifer pressed her face into the pillow again and began to sob quietly. Why was this happening to her?

"Don't cry, dear," Sara said, running her fingers gently up the inside of Jennifer's bare leg and over the back of her panties. "Don't cry. Everything's going to be all right."

Jennifer could feel the lines of sweat that Sara's fingers had left on her thigh. It made her feel cold.

The old man's room was different now. The windows seemed to have lost their tint, and the heatless light of the afternoon sun painted the floor in wide strips.

The elaborate array of medical machines was gone and the old man's bed had been moved into the middle of the room. Around it stood five conservatively dressed people. Two women and three men.

Jennifer's breath came out as steam as Sara led her through the frigid room. She pulled back when they came within about fifteen feet of the bed, but Sara put a hand on the back of her neck and forced her forward. As they moved closer, she could see that the old man was completely motionless and that his limbs had been arranged in a configuration too neat to be natural. She felt the tears begin again as she was forced to accept the fact that the old man, whose eyes had carried away some of her loneliness and fear, was gone. And now there really was only Sara.

The people turned slowly from the old man's body and locked their eyes on her as she and Sara stopped a few feet from them. The man who had handcuffed and later released her continued past them and joined the small group.

"Jennifer," Sara said in a clear voice obviously meant for the others in the room. "Your grandfather told you that you were the one that God had named to take his place. Do you remember?"

Jennifer continued to stare down at the old man, the image of his lifeless body filling her mind.

"Jennifer?" Sara prodded in a gentle tone that carried a hint of menace in its timbre. "Do you remember?"

What she remembered was the biting steel of

the handcuffs against the bones of her wrists and Sara's quiet threats.

"Yes."

"Then you accept your place in the church?"

Jennifer took a deep breath and looked away from her grandfather, trying unsuccessfully to clear her head. What else could she do?

"Yes."

The people began walking up to her one at a time, each silently leaning over and kissing her on the cheek with eyes full of awe. All except the man who had come in with them. The man with the mustache. He kissed her as the others had, but his expression was one of quiet triumph.

In a moment they were all gone and she was alone in the room with Sara, her nameless companion, and the shell of what was once her grandfather and God's messenger on earth. Jennifer looked around her and then back down at her grandfather's body, feeling a small glimmer of hope in her chest. Sara didn't want her there, she knew that. And she wanted nothing to do with her church. Jamie's mom would take her in. It would be less than two years until she went to college and then she could build her own life. One that had nothing to do with Albert Kneiss or Sara, or her parents.

"I don't want any of this," Jennifer said. "Bring the others back in and I'll tell them. You can have the church. It's yours."

Sara's mouth curled into a smile devoid of warmth. "I don't think you understand, Jennifer."

"I do understand. My grandfather wanted me to take over for him as the head of the church."

Sara shook her head. "He wanted much more than that for you."

Jennifer was confused for a moment. She knew what he had said.

"Albert has served God for many years," Sara said. "And God has taken him to his reward." She reached out and took Jennifer's hand. "You haven't been chosen to lead the church, Jennifer. You've been chosen as God's new Messenger."

Jennifer tried to step back, but Sara tightened her grip on her hand. She looked down at her grandfather's body, Sara's words penetrating her mind. Good Friday was still a few weeks away. He wasn't supposed to be dead yet.

"It will be time for you to take your place with God soon, Jennifer."

"No!" Jennifer screamed, pulling away and trying to run. The man at Sara's side caught hold of her before she could make it even a few feet. "That's not what he said! It's not and you know it. My grandfather wanted to give the church to me!"

"Your grandfather is dead, Jennifer," Sara said smoothly. "You have no idea what he wanted. How could you?"

Jennifer squeezed her eyes shut and bit the inside of her cheek again, harder this time. How could she have been so stupid? She'd let Sara trick her into telling those people that she wanted to die.

She pushed at the man holding her, knowing that she had no hope of escaping his grip, and then sunk to the floor. There was no one left to help her. No one cared if she lived anymore. And Sara only cared that she died.

29

BEAMON TOOK THE PLASTIC BAG OFF HIS frozen doorknob and pushed through the door into his living room. He leaned back outside for a moment to shake the snow off his parka and briefcase, then pulled the door tightly shut.

They were rotating, he thought as he sat down on one of the stools at the edge of his kitchen counter and began to flip through the pad he'd brought with him from the car. And they liked Fords.

He grabbed a Hi-Liter and put a green stripe over his notes relating to a red Taurus that had been popping up behind him more often than it should. That was two cars. It was possible that there were more, but he hadn't been watching long enough to be sure of the pattern. What he was sure of, though, was that he was being followed. And worse, he was about seventy-five percent sure that his new neighbor's decision to rent in that particular location had been influenced by the view. Of his condo.

He reached into the plastic bag that had been hanging on his door and pulled a damp envelope from it. The envelope contained a single yellow Post-it note.

Never got a chance
to thank you for
watching Emory.
Dinner at seven?

Carrie

Beamon glanced at his watch and then looked at the briefcase bulging with administrative bullshit. It had been backing up for weeks—what harm would one more day do? He walked over and opened the fridge but found nothing more than a few cans of beer. Showing up on Carrie's doorstep with the dregs of a twelve-pack of Busch probably presented a little too realistic an image for this early in their relationship. Probably better to go empty-handed.

But then, what did he know? His history with women was less than impressive. If you didn't count the logistically impossible attraction between him and his old partner, Laura Vilechi, his last date had been almost two years ago. A friend had set it up, describing the woman as intelligent and attractive, but a witch. Beamon hadn't seen any serious problem with that—he himself had been known to be an occasional pain in the ass. What he hadn't understood was that "witch" hadn't been an evaluation of her personality; it had been a statement of religious affiliation.

It had been torture. A black cat had wandered in front of them on the way to the restaurant, then a woman who had something that looked like an enormous wart on her nose sat down in booth next to them. He'd bravely resisted temptation, though, and managed to make not a single comment through the appetizers and most of the main course. Then she had to go and start telling a story that somehow involved a broom. He'd ended up alone with a lap full of red wine.

Since then, there had never seemed to be time. Always some life-or-death case tempting him from the sidelines or some administrative snafu that promised to make his life miserable if he didn't deal with it yesterday.

Until recently, his plan had been to continue with his former lifestyle and drop dead of a heart attack a few years before he reached mandatory retirement. But he finally realized that was stupid. There was more out there than the quickly waning adrenaline rush of a good case.

Beamon went into the bathroom and smoothed down a curl in what was left of his hair. At least the weight he'd lost had thinned out his face. A significant improvement, though he still wasn't in any real danger of being described as good looking. But what the hell—he had other endearing qualities.

Beamon rapped on Carrie's door and glanced at his watch. Only ten minutes late. She came to the door almost immediately, accompanied by her daughter and the smell of garlic.

"Will you accept me empty-handed, Carrie? I just walked in from work."

"Absolutely. Come on in."

Emory attached herself briefly to his leg as he stepped into the house, a credit to her mother's exhaustive training.

"You're dealing with that better and better, Mark," Carrie said as she walked back to the kitchen.

"I think my conditioning experiment is working."

Beamon picked Emory up almost to the ceiling and spun her around. "I remember my first autopsy, Carrie. It's amazing what you can get used to." He swung the little girl back to the floor, ignoring the smirk on Carrie's face. "Right, Emory?"

"Right!" she agreed and threw herself onto the sofa in front of the TV. "Your show's over."

Beamon walked into the kitchen with a questioning look on his face.

"Emory seems to think you have your own show. Every evening at the same time she switches the TV to the local news and watches for you." Carrie poured him a rather full glass of red wine. "She's very impressed."

Beamon smiled and sipped at the wine. He'd never really acquired a taste for it. "It's nice to know I have a fan."

"How are you doing on that case, Mark?" she said as she turned to check the oven. "I saw the thing about the white slavery ring. It's so horrifying."

"There *is* no godda—" Beamon cleared his throat and lowered his voice. "There is no white slavery ring."

"No?"

"No. That came from some psychic. The press printed it like it was gospel 'cause they consider violence without sex kind of dry."

She slid a bubbling casserole out of the oven using a pair of garish oven mitts and then reached back in for a tray of muffins. "I think we're about ready."

The meal was indescribable. Despite the rich garlic smell and the satisfying bubbling of the deep red sauce, Carrie's eggplant parmesan tasted like, well, like his fork. Its blandness was matched only by that of the almost dressing-free salad.

"You know, Mark, someday I'm going to write a cookbook," Carrie said, right on cue. "I swear, the cookbooks you get today are so full of things like sour cream and butter that the dishes could kill you if you just look at them." She pointed at his plate. "I just leave all that stuff out. You can't even tell the difference."

"I sure can't," he lied through a mouthful of muffin that seemed to be soaking up saliva faster than his body could produce it. "How's that thesis you're working on going?"

"Really well, thanks for asking. It's almost done. It looks like it's going to get published next month."

"That's great. Congratulations. I trust you didn't have to crash any more weddings to finish it."

She affected a seductive pout that seemed to transform her into an entirely different woman. "You're not still mad about that, are you? You did get two free dinners out of it, for God's sake."

"No, no. Not mad," Beamon said, laying down his fork and hoping that dessert wasn't on the menu. "Intrigued. I actually find the Kneissians fascinating."

That turn in the conversation was the last straw for Emory, who asked to be excused from the table and rushed off to her room before her mother could answer.

"Me too. You know, it's really the first religion to embrace science. Most faiths in one way or another are at odds with technology. I mean, God has to make statements, and those statements remain static while the world continues to move forward. Causes friction. The other thing I find interesting is that the Kneissians' belief system isn't built around a lot of set-in-stone—if you'll excuse the pun—rules like many other Western religions. Right and wrong is a little more of a gray area. They're more interested in being all they can be."

Beamon nodded thoughtfully and reached over to refill her wineglass. "Does that make them dangerous?"

She thought about that for a moment. "I don't mean to say that they don't have a strong sense of morality—all you have to do is look at them to see that they do. All I'm saying is that their Bible allows for more flexibility. That in turn should keep it from becoming obsolete as we continue rushing toward . . . whatever it is we're rushing toward."

She stood and stacked Beamon's plate on top of hers.

"Let me help you with that," Beamon said.

"Oh, I'm not cleaning up—just getting these out of the way. Back in a sec."

She was wearing a pair of brown wool slacks and a loose-fitting white blouse that, once again, draped along the curves of her body beautifully. Beamon watched her with admiration as she glided off to the kitchen and then reappeared a moment later.

"Let me ask you a related question," he said.

"Am I being interrogated?"

"Absolutely not—I'm just trying to distract you while I get you drunk."

"Oh, that's okay, then," she said, sitting down and picking up her wineglass. "What's your question?"

"From a psychological point of view, why isn't religion as important now as it was, say, a thousand years ago?"

She swirled her glass and stared into the deep red liquid contained there for a few moments. "What you expect me to say is that we just don't need it as much. That we used it to explain things we didn't understand and we understand more now. That we don't suffer as much during our lives now, so we don't need an afterlife as desperately." She took another sip of her wine. "But I don't know if that's it. With the speed that our lives go by now, we don't have as much time for real companionship. We're losing the ability to reach out to people around us. Maybe we need God more now than we ever did."

"God, yes. But religion?"

She shrugged. "I don't think the answer to your question is as psychological as it is political. You're a historian, aren't you?"

Beamon chuckled. "I squeezed in a history degree between benders at Yale, yes. But I don't think anybody would confuse me with a historian."

She looked at him with what might have been affection; his senses in that arena were hopelessly dull. "Somehow I think you're being modest. You tell me, Mark. You don't seem to be in the habit of asking questions you don't know the answers to. Why is religion less dominant today than it was a thousand years ago?"

Beamon took a deep breath and tapped his nail against his glass, producing a clear, unwavering tone. "Maybe it's not the worshipers, but that religions limit themselves."

"How so?"

"It seems to me that all organized religions have some factor that keeps them from gaining power. The most obvious is what we were talking about—

the backward thinking. Some of the older religions of the world have customs and dogma that worked well when they were first implemented, but now, hundreds or thousands of years later, they create barriers to progress—to meeting the needs of today's worshiper. The Catholic church in the United States might be a good example of that. Their views on the marriage of priests, women, abortion, divorce—all reflect a time that's long gone."

He paused for a moment to examine her expression and make sure she wasn't finding this offensive. So far so good. "Another limiting factor, particularly for newer religions, would be a very unusual belief system. The Mormons and Scientologists—right or wrong—run into trouble there. What they have to say is perhaps too new. It doesn't tie back to a concept that people grew up with and therefore don't question."

"What about some of the Eastern religions? What's their 'limiting factor'?"

"A lot of them are more philosophies than religions. They lack a central deity to order them around and really don't seem to have developed political agendas. Too inward-looking."

"Okay, then. Here's one for you. What's the Kneissians' 'limiting factor'?"

Beamon picked up the wine bottle in front of him and poured some into his glass. "That's just it. I can't think of one."

30

THE PATTERN HAD COME CLEAR OVER THE weekend. Three cars. All Ford Tauruses—one blue, one green, and one red—rotating daily.

Beamon had dropped the red one in town almost an hour ago. It really wasn't difficult to lose a tail; the problem was making it look like an accident. They'd find out he knew they were watching eventually, but he preferred to put that off for as long as possible.

Beamon checked his rearview mirror one more time, looking back over the empty road and flat, snow-dusted desert behind him. Satisfied that he was the only thing moving for miles, he decided to cover the last quarter-mile or so on foot and pulled his car to the curb.

Despite the fact that all the houses in this oasis of a neighborhood looked the same, Beamon found the one he was looking for with little difficulty. After almost a minute of pounding on the door, though, there was still no answer. He stepped back and double-checked the numbers between the garage and front door. They were the ones given to him that morning when Ernest Willard's former book agent had called him out of the blue and told him that the man who had written the now-unavailable exposé on the church had agreed to a meeting.

Beamon thought he heard a dull scraping sound coming from inside the house and stepped back onto the porch. "Hello?"

"May I see your ID?" came a muffled voice on the other side of the closed door.

Beamon pulled out his credentials, but the door didn't open. He stepped back and, finding a peep-hole oddly located about halfway up the door, held them up to it.

A moment later, the door swung open and he was faced with what looked a little like a small tank in a sunflower print muumuu.

The woman backing up to give him a clear path into the house seemed impossibly fat. The garish tent/dress she wore went from her thick neck to her knees in what looked like a perfectly straight line. Her legs, where they appeared under the dress, resembled gigantic sausages in tan nylon casings. What gave her that true tanklike feel, though, was the wheelchair she had, by some strange anomaly of physics, managed to stuff her rear end into.

"I'm sorry, Mr. Beamon. I was in the back." She diverted her gaze to the chair for a moment. "It takes me a little longer to make it across the house than it used to."

"I'm the one who should apologize, I didn't mean to attack your door like that. I thought maybe you couldn't hear me," Beamon said, closing the door and following her as she wheeled through the hallway toward the back of the house. "Is Ernest Willard in?"

She pulled to a stop in a small room overflowing with computer equipment, newsmagazines, and reference books. There wasn't a single surface that hadn't been used to haphazardly route cables or wasn't covered with some piece of high-tech machinery or phone book–thick document.

"About Ernest Willard," Beamon prompted again, "I think he agreed to see me?"

"I did," the woman said, turning her wheelchair to face him. "I'm Ernest Willard. Well, actually I'm Ernestine Waverly. But I wrote the book you're interested in."

"A nom de plume," Beamon said, moving a stack of computer disks from a chair and taking an uninvited seat.

"At the time, it seemed like a good idea."

"Well, I'm glad we have the opportunity to talk. When my associate called your agent a while back, he was told that she hadn't heard from you in years."

She smiled. "I provide her with books—computer tech manuals now—and in turn, she protects me."

"Protects you? From what?"

"The church has . . . held a grudge. They can be very difficult. I don't see anyone anymore."

"You're seeing me."

She used her thick arms to propel herself toward him, stopping a few feet from where he sat. "I dream about you, Mr. Beamon."

Beamon shifted uncomfortably in the chair as the woman stared at him. "I'm not quite sure how to respond to that."

"It started a few months ago," she explained. "I couldn't see you clearly at first, but every night your face became a little sharper. Of course, I didn't know who you were, until I saw you on TV."

"And what am I doing in these dreams?" Beamon asked, not sure he really wanted to know.

"Different things. Tell me, Mr. Beamon, do you believe in God?"

"That's a complicated question."

"No, it's not."

"Let's say I have an open mind."

His answer seemed to satisfy her. "That's more than most people can say. Now what is it I can do for the FBI?"

Beamon let out a quiet sigh of relief. He wasn't really looking to spend the day debating theology with a woman who seemed to have a less than iron grip on reality. "I'm interested in the Church of the Evolution and I'm told you're probably the most knowledgeable resource in the world."

"May I ask what this is about?" she said, though there was something strange in her voice that made Beamon think she already knew.

"Nothing in particular. I'm just looking for general background information."

"I'm sorry, Mr. Beamon," she said, suddenly sounding like a surgeon telling someone that they had a week to live. "I did do a significant amount of research into the church before I wrote *Betrayal*. But that was in 1986—more than a decade ago." She looked down at the floor and shook her head sadly. "I don't know if I can help you anymore . . ."

"Hey, it's okay, Ernie," Beamon said, reaching out and patting her soft shoulder. She looked like she was about to start crying for some reason. "I'm sure you're going to be a lot of help."

Beamon picked up an old copy of the *Wall Street Journal* lying on the table next to him. He recognized the issue as one containing an article on the church's business dealings. "It looks like you still keep up."

"Only superficially. I've let myself get distracted by work." She punched herself in the leg. "And by my own stupid problems. If only I'd known earlier that you were coming . . ."

Beamon looked over at a wood-framed photograph propped on the table next to him. It depicted a pleasantly plump woman with what looked like a touch football team. "You?" he said, trying to distract her before her mind wandered so far it got lost.

"In happier times."

"When you were with the church?"

She nodded slowly. "When I was an official member of the church."

"What was it that drew you in, Ernie?"

She cocked her head for a moment and then waved a thick arm around at the computer systems that surrounded her. "I'm a programmer, Mr. Beamon. A mathematician and formerly a Baptist. Like many people, I suppose, I had a hard time devoting six days a week to the study of science and technology and then forgetting everything I'd learned on the seventh so that I could be with my God."

"So it was the church's mix of science and theology that appealed to you."

"Initially, yes. Then I read Albert's Bible." Beamon noted the reverent drop in her voice at the use of Kneiss's name.

"I've read it," Beamon said. "Brilliant. He even had me going there a couple of times. And that's not easy."

"Have you ever seen him speak, Mr. Beamon?"

"Please call me Mark. On TV."

She shook her head sadly. "It's not the same. I can't imagine anyone seeing him in person and still doubting that he is who he says he is."

"God?"

"God's messenger. But then, you know that."

"So it was seeing him that hooked you."

"There's so much more, Mark," she said, struggling into a more comfortable position. "It's hard to explain to someone who's never been involved. After you show initial interest, they barrage you. Invitations to dinners, picnics, promises of important business connections, as well as more personal introductions. If you have children, they're invited on camping trips and other activities. I guess they gave me a sense of belonging that I wanted but had never had."

Beamon looked down at the picture again and at the other faces staring out of it. They all had that clean-cut look of optimism that stamped them as Kneissians. "How long were you involved with the church?"

"As a member? Four years."

"Really?"

"You sound surprised."

Beamon laid the picture down. "I guess I expected you to say six months or something. I understand that you wrote a pretty scathing exposé. I assumed you joined, hated it, and left."

She shook her head. "As efficient as the Kneissians are at getting you into the church, they're even better at keeping you there. You have to understand that your entire life is wrapped up with them. I worked as a freelance computer consultant at the time. After a few years, probably eighty percent of my customers were members of the church. I met my boyfriend at a church function. You become too intertwined. And then, of course, there are the psychological factors . . ."

"Psychological factors?"

She looked at him with a strange intensity that was really starting to make him feel uncomfortable. "Are you aware that the Kneissian Bible you buy publicly is only a portion of Albert's writings? That more books exist?"

Beamon took off his jacket and pulled a pad and pen from the pocket. "If by more books, you mean other sections to the Bible, no, I'd never heard that. What's in them?"

"I don't know. You see, it's all a matter of levels. When you enter the church you go in as a Novice or Level One. You're encouraged to take classes and go to counseling sessions in order to improve your standing—your level. Of course, they're quite expensive and you rarely pass the first time."

"How many levels are there?" Beamon asked.

"Eleven last time I counted. I was a Three when I left the church."

"So you're learning what's in these secret books in order to move up?"

"Not exactly. Actually, getting to Level Two has nothing to do with God or religion. The class you have to pass is on—how would you describe it? Manners? General conduct?"

Beamon raised his eyebrows. "Come again?"

"You've got to understand the philosophy of the church, Mark. They're very interested in growth, but they're also interested in quality membership. I guess you could call their first class 'communications.' You learn how to dress, firm handshakes, looking people in the eye when you talk, what fork to eat with at a nice restaurant. That kind of thing. I know it sounds ridiculous, but it works. You've probably noticed that Kneissians project a pretty uniform image."

Beamon nodded and she continued.

"So getting to Level Two isn't very hard. Moving up through the later levels involves more theological training and very strenuous counseling sessions. Those are a lot like the Catholic confession. But, of course, there are other factors."

"Other factors?"

"I started getting a bit disillusioned when I was working on my Four. Level Four, that is. I flunked twice. That's twelve thousand dollars' worth of classes for nothing. I should tell you that at the time, I was making about forty-five thousand dollars a year and living in a one-bedroom apartment with two other women because all my money was going to the church. Despite that, though, it wasn't the money or the time that bothered me, it was the people who were passing. Many of them had done much worse than me in the class."

"Politics," Beamon said knowingly. "It always comes down to politics."

"You're exactly right. I found out later that some of these people were doctors and lawyers and politicians. I was just a lowly programming consultant. In the scheme of things, not that useful to the church."

"And for you, moving through the levels was important?"

"Oh, yes. It is to everyone. I really can't stress how important. Your level and how long you've been a church member are public knowledge, so it's really embarrassing if you're not doing well. The flip side of that is, if you are doing well, there are all kinds of bragging rights. There's a pervasive obsession with levels that the church really encourages."

"What about these other books to the Bible?"

"You don't start getting to look at those until you're a Seven. The rumor is that they're sections from the Bible that will be given to humanity when the Messenger returns."

"Two thousand years from now?"

She nodded. "Obviously, you must be very evolved to understand them. People who are Sevens and higher are treated like royalty. Everyone wants to learn what's in those books."

"The meaning of life," Beamon said.

"Perhaps. I've met very few people who have reached above Six. The 'counseling' sessions become increasingly strenuous and expensive. I've even heard rumors of the use of psychoactive drugs in high-level sessions."

"I find it hard to believe that anyone would submit to that."

"I would have."

Beamon leaned back in his chair and chewed the end of his pen for a moment. "I went to one of the recruiting stations a few days ago. The woman they set me up with must have gone through your 'communications' training. She was very good. Not very taken with me, though, I'm afraid."

Ernie smiled and reached into the small fridge she had parked her chair next to. "Diet Coke?"

Beamon held a hand out and caught the ice-cold can.

"I'm sure you're right on both counts," she said, popping the top on her can and taking a quick sip. "You can't work a potential recruit unless you're at least a Two. And I can almost guarantee that she wasn't, as you say, very taken with you."

Beamon held his hands out innocently. "How can you say that? People love me."

The thick folds in Ernie's face rearranged themselves into a nervous smile. "I'm sure they do, but, again, it's all about levels. Let me guess: you didn't want to sign the register—what they call the guest book."

"Uh, I think I did pass on that."

"You just got a One there. Ask a few tough questions? Tell her you'd heard some negative things about the church?"

"Yeah, probably. A few."

"Well, the first negative question you asked got you a Two. The second, a Three. When you hit Four she'd have asked if you were a reporter."

"She did!" Beamon said, impressed. "She did ask me that."

"They hate reporters. Afraid the press might shine too bright a light into their organization."

"You shined a pretty bright light into it, Ernie. What did you find?"

"Paranoia. When I started getting upset about the politics in the levels, I started talking with people—both active members and people who had quit for one reason or another. I started to get a picture of an organization trying to control everything. Its members, its image, and more and more, the secular world." She sighed deeply. "It didn't take long for me to find out that some of the ex-Kneissians I was talking to were plants. Put there to ferret out anyone who wasn't toeing the party line. I had to go before a council of elders from my parish and they stripped me of my levels. Later I was thrown out."

"Then what?"

"I continued to dig. I must have gone through ten thousand pages of documents and talked to two hundred people. I figured they'd already excommunicated me, what more could they do?" She laughed bitterly.

"I take it there was more."

"At first it was just threatening phone calls. I kept changing my number, but it never did any good. Then the lawsuits started. I've been sued for just about everything you can imagine. I was once sued for sexual harassment by a man I had never met."

"But you won the suits."

"Oh, sure, I won. Every one of them. But I had to declare bankruptcy from all the legal bills. They also made available, to anyone who wanted them, some of the more personal aspects of my counseling sessions—confessionals—which are taped as a matter of routine."

"This is all before the book came out, though, right?"

She nodded. "When the book came out, things went crazy. A man came to my door and threatened me with a knife; I was being constantly followed. Later, I found out that a woman who had befriended me while I was at a really low point was a member of the church and had been directed to subtly drive me to suicide. It almost worked."

She took another sip of her Coke. "I've moved twelve times since I wrote that book. I've been here eight months. They'll find me soon. Then it will all start again—the cars driving by the house too slow, the calls . . ." She suddenly looked deflated.

"What happened with the book?"

"It never went anywhere. The initial print run was twenty-five hundred and they were instantly bought up and destroyed by church members. Then the publisher was purchased by a church-owned corporation set up specifically for that purpose. So then they had the rights to the book and they used those rights to keep it out of the stores."

"Do you think that when Albert Kneiss is gone the church will come back in line?"

Her head jerked as though he had struck her. "Why would you say something like that?"

"Well, Albert—"

"Albert doesn't know about any of this! I wrote the book for him. He knows nothing about what's happening, what they're doing."

"But he must know," Beamon said. "It's his church."

"You're wrong," Ernie spat out. "*She* keeps it from him, relies on his goodness to keep him from suspecting what she's done."

"She?"

"Sara. Sara Renslier. She's the one who's twisted the church into what it is now."

"Tell me about her."

"She's evil."

Beamon frowned. "Could you be more specific?"

"She took over the leadership of the Seven Elders probably twenty-five years ago . . ."

"When the church's membership started to take off?"

Ernie reluctantly conceded the point with a short nod. "She's systematically isolated Albert and now hides behind him and uses his name to control everything. Her and a man named Sines."

"Sines? You got a first name?"

She shook her head. "Just Sines. I know he came to the church from the military. He's the head of security." She ran a finger from her lip to her right eye. "He has a scar here. Hides part of it with a mustache. Rumor has it that he's put together a group of ex-policemen and military people fanatically devoted to Albert."

"Meaning they answer to Sara," Beamon said.

She nodded. "Sara uses the fear of this group to keep the high-level members in line."

"Have you ever met one of them?"

"No. There are probably fewer than ten in total." She pointed to her wrist. "I was told by someone who once met one of them that they have an iron bracelet welded to their right arm. A sign of their devotion to Albert—who probably doesn't even know they exist."

Beamon started gnawing on his pen again, replaying in his mind his struggle with David Passal. He remembered the man's fear and how he'd mistaken them for someone else. During the struggle he had grabbed Beamon's right wrist, and suddenly that fear had disappeared. Passal had immediately stopped fighting and demanded to know who he was.

"Mark? Are you all right?"

Beamon looked up. "Sorry, I was just thinking. What was it you were saying?"

"I was saying that the church has become more sophisticated and efficient now. They pay people not to publish books about them. They don't have to buy publishers anymore. Through their members they control companies that you would never expect. They influence politicians with contributions. Companies owned by church members control a huge number of government contracts that the Elders find interesting—they just make the lowest bid or put a minority in as the head of the company."

Beamon glanced at his watch. He had about a hundred more questions that he'd like to ask, but he was running late. Again. "I'd love to read your book, Ernie. Would you have a copy I could borrow?"

He followed her unbidden as she wheeled her chair down the hall to a narrow set of stairs. She unwedged herself from the chair and began struggling down the steps to the basement, scraping both walls as she descended.

Beamon followed, shaking his head in disbelief. She wasn't crippled at all, just a whale. Couldn't entirely support her body weight out of the water.

The basement was stacked with still more documents, books, and old computer equipment. Except for the poor lighting, it didn't look much different from her office. Beamon flipped through a stack of old computer paper almost three feet high. "This stuff's all on the church?"

"Most of it," Ernie said, struggling to reach a high shelf and pull down a dusty book with a dark green jacket.

"I may want to borrow some of it, if you don't mind."

She waddled over and handed him the book. "It's just primary source material. I've summarized pretty much all of it in the book."

He pointed to the teetering stack of paper at his feet. "What's this?"

"It's a list of the church's membership from 1981."

Beamon kicked at it, trying to make a guess at its weight. "Can I borrow it?"

She walked over to an old computer resting on a card table and turned it on. Beamon winced when she sat down in the metal folding chair in front of it, but the chair managed to hold her with only a slight creak.

"I don't think you really want a hard copy, Mark. There are almost a million names on that printout. Let me put it on disk for you."

She punched a few keys as Beamon approached, and he saw the list of names and other personal information come up in alphabetical order.

"Can you search for specific names?" Beamon asked as she slid a new diskette into the computer.

"Of course."

"Could you do a couple for me? Try Jacob Layman."

She typed in the name of his boss and searched the screen. "No match."

"Would members' children be in there?"

"They should be."

"Try Chet Michaels."

She typed in the name. "I've got a hit on that one."

Beamon frowned and looked over her shoulder.

"Born 1943, joined in 1980," she said, running a plump finger along the screen. Beamon let out a sigh of relief. That would put Michaels in his mid-fifties.

It took almost a half-hour to save all of the names to the stack of disks now stuffed in the various pockets of Beamon's coat.

"Thanks, Ernie. I'm sorry to take these and run, but I'm real late."

"So what is your open mind telling you now, Mark?"

He stopped with one foot on the staircase. "Excuse me?"

"You said you had an open mind where God was concerned. What is it telling you?"

"Nothing. I guess I'm still a devoted skeptic."

Her smile held a trace of irony. Beamon was amazed at how subtly expressive her face was, considering the deep folds of fat surrounding it. "What?" he said.

Ernie struggled out of the chair and across the basement, stopping next to him and supporting herself on the banister. "What are you going to do with what you've learned here today, Mark? Do you know?"

Beamon shrugged. "Same thing I always do, I suppose. Try to use it to find the truth."

"The truth about the church?"

"Maybe."

"Have you ever thought you were being directed by God? That your goals are really His goals? Is it a coincidence that you are here talking to me three weeks before Albert is to take his place with the Lord and Sara is to become the unchallenged leader of the church?"

Beamon suddenly understood the strange looks and the stuff about the dreams. He looked down at her and shook his head slowly. "I'll tell you, Ernie, if I'm the Chosen One, we've got problems. God's really scraping the bottom of the barrel."

31

"WHAT'RE YOU LOOKING FOR?" CHET Michaels said.

Beamon pushed the box onto his new carpet in frustration and began digging through the green folders that had been stacked beneath it.

"I'm trying to find the stuff we got out of Eric and Patricia Davis's safe." He pointed down at the haphazardly stacked boxes that were beginning to take over his office. "It's just not here. I don't even know what half this shit is."

Michaels leaned over one of the boxes that Beamon had already searched and carefully emptied its contents. "Voilà," he said, pulling three unmarked manila envelopes from the bottom.

"You know, those kinds of envelopes do take ink. You could label them," Beamon said, stalking back to his chair.

Michaels looked a little hurt when he sat down and began emptying the contents of the envelopes onto Beamon's desk. "You never try to find stuff yourself, Mark. I figured if you wanted anything, you'd ask me or D."

Beamon scowled. Michaels was right, of course, but he was in no mood to have his tendency toward absentmindedness pointed out to him.

"How'd your meeting with Willard go?" Michaels said, wisely changing the subject.

"Fine."

"Productive?"

"Yeah, it was," Beamon said, finding it impossible to stay mad. "We've got confirmation that Sara Renslier runs the church. As far as Ernie's concerned, Kneiss isn't really aware of what's going on anymore. That could be a biased view, though."

"It'd make sense," Michaels said, looking at the calendar on his watch. "The guy's pretty old and he's said in no uncertain terms that he's planning to die in about three weeks. I would think he'd have pretty much turned over the church to someone by now."

"I suppose so," Beamon said.

"What else did he have to say?"

"Who?"

"Willard."

"It's *she*, actually. And it's Waverly. Willard was a pen name. She painted a pretty vivid picture. Not a very attractive one, though."

"How so?"

"In her mind the church is paranoid and bent on control. Of their members, people they perceive to be their enemies, whoever."

"Maybe *she's* the one who's paranoid. She's the only person who's ever written an exposé-type book about the church. Maybe she had an ax to grind. How'd she come off? Did she seem grounded?"

Beamon shrugged. "I don't know if I'd use the word 'grounded.' 'Wacko' might be more descriptive. But I'll tell you, every time I thought what she was saying was getting a little farfetched, she'd come up with something I could corroborate with what we've already dug up. I also skimmed the copy of her book she gave me and it seems well researched and, well, pretty credible. My gut feeling is that she gave it to me straight."

Michaels gave the thumbs up sign. "So we've found a great resource. All right."

"Maybe," Beamon said in a wavering tone.

"What? She doesn't want to talk to us anymore?"

Beamon shook his head. "No, I reckon she'll give us anything we need. I'm just a little concerned about her motivation."

The young agent's eyes widened. "You think she's a church plant? Like they set her up to feed people misinformation? Wow . . ."

"Ho, Chet. Come on back to reality with me here. All I meant was that she's still loyal to Kneiss—I think she believes he's who he says he is. In her mind, it's this Renslier woman who's causing problems."

Beamon leaned forward and began digging through the pile of documents Michaels had spread across his desk. "She also may think that I've been chosen by God to put the church back on track."

Michaels made a sound like a strangling cat as he stifled a laugh.

"Go ahead," Beamon said. "Laugh."

"Sorry, Mark," Michaels said through a loud guffaw. "It's not that I don't think you'd be a good choice, it's just that I think if God needed someone to do his work on Earth, he wouldn't pick a guy who refers to Christ and His disciples as 'JC and the boys.'"

Beamon found what he was looking for and threw it at Michaels, who was wiping a tear from the corner of his eye. "That's pretty much what I told her—though not in so many words."

Michaels looked at the stock certificates that Beamon had thrown at him, still smiling. "What's up with these?"

"I want you to look into those two companies."

"These are just stock certificates from closely held corporations that Davis had bought into. His investment here is really pretty insignificant. Certainly nothing to kill him over."

Beamon began stuffing the rest of the safe's contents back into the manila envelopes lying on his desk. "According to Ernie, one of the things the church has gotten into is buying up companies that might provide them with information or control over areas they think are important. Apparently they don't do this directly, they do it through various members buying stock."

Michaels's eyebrows rose. "So then it looks like a bunch of unrelated people own the company, but it's actually run by the church. Cool."

Beamon pointed to the certificates. "I don't think the Davises were killed or Jennifer was kidnapped over Eric's ownership in those two companies, but let's see if we can learn something about how the church operates. Might be useful."

Michaels laid the certificates out flat on the desk. "Vericomm, I can already tell you, is a long-distance provider and Internet service."

"Maybe you can pull some information from the FCC? Do it quietly, though."

"I can do better than that—and quieter, too. There are at least two annual reports on Vericomm in one of the filing cabinets in Mr. Davis's home office. I'll go grab 'em and see what I can figure out."

"What about TarroSoft?"

Michaels shrugged. "I don't remember seeing anything on them in any of Mr. Davis's stuff."

"Ever hear of them?"

"Nope."

Beamon stood and began walking toward the door to his office. "Okay, Chet. Run with that and get me what you can on a guy named Sines—he's the head of the church's security. I don't have a first name on him, but I think he's ex-military and he's got a mustache and an obvious scar on his face." He paused with his hand on the doorknob. "I don't want it to get back to him that I'm looking. Not quite ready for that headache yet, okay?"

He didn't wait for Michaels's answer, but pulled the door open and began threading himself through the tightly packed desks and construction equipment that filled the office. The workmen seemed to be less obvious now that the heavy work was done. With a little luck they'd be history in a few weeks.

He made his way to a small cubicle along the far wall, pausing to chat briefly with the young agents who inhabited this part of the office and answer the myriad questions that always seemed to be on the tips of their tongues. He hadn't been doing much of a job on the management end of things lately. Once he got on top of this Jennifer Davis thing, he promised himself, he'd turn over a new leaf.

Beamon poked his head into the cubicle next to him and looked at the back of Craig Skinner, the young man who managed the office's information systems.

"Craig! How're you doing with those disks?"

The young man started and swiveled around in his chair to face Beamon.

He didn't look like he belonged in an FBI office. His hair went well past his shoulders and his inter-pretation of the dress code was that anything was acceptable as long as you wore a tie with it. But the kid knew his way around a computer, and Beamon wasn't about to lose him over the FBI's obsession with throwing a three-piece suit on everything that came through the door.

"Jeez, Mark. What is this? A copy of the D.C. phone book?"

"Don't worry about it. Are you done?"

"Yeah, I've loaded it into a database. What now?"

"How would I go about searching for a name?"

The young man did some magic with his mouse and a prompt appeared on the screen. "You'd just type it in here. Last name, comma, space, then the first name."

"And what if I wanted to check another name when I was done with that one?"

Skinner pointed to the top of the screen. "Just click here and the prompt will come up again."

Beamon motioned for him to stand. "Why don't you go grab yourself a cup of coffee for a minute."

"Uh, sure," Skinner said, looking a little con-fused.

Once he was gone, Beamon sat down in his chair and typed in "Davis, Eric."

The cursor turned to an hourglass for a moment and then the name appeared with Davis's birthdate and "August 1968" in the field reserved for the date the person joined the church.

Beamon didn't feel the elation that normally

overtook him when one of his off-the-wall theories started to come together. The prospect of going up against the Church of the Evolution and its eleven million followers wasn't a pleasant one. He was getting too old and too wise for this kind of crap.

He cleared the screen the way Skinner had showed him and typed in the name "Davis, Patricia." It, too, was positive, showing a membership date of January 1968.

The dates indicated that both had been children when they joined. Their parents must have been among Kneiss's original followers. Great.

"Can I come in yet?" Skinner's voice called from the other side of the cubicle wall.

"One second," Beamon said, his fingers hovering nervously over the keyboard. He hated himself for being such a suspicious sonofabitch, but he couldn't help it. Beautiful women with advanced degrees just didn't normally knock down his door.

He typed in "Johnstone, Carrie" and held his breath as the computer searched.

NO MATCH FOUND.

PLEASE REVIEW

SEARCH PARAMETERS.

"Come on in, Craig," he said, abandoning the chair and swiveling it toward Skinner, who took a seat.

"Thanks, Mark."

"Okay, here's the deal," Beamon said. "I want you to run this list against the FBI's personnel list. See if you get any matches. Is that possible?"

"Sure, but it might take some time."

"Okay, but let's keep it quiet. Don't tell anyone anything about this."

Skinner grinned. "I couldn't if I wanted to. I don't know anything."

"You'll be happier that way in the end, Craig. Believe me."

"Come on, Mark. Just give me a little hint. You looking for spies?"

32

"THAT CAN'T BE GOOD," BEAMON SAID, stepping to his right and setting a large box of doughnuts on his secretary's desk.

She covered the mouthpiece of the phone she was talking into and said, "Sorry, Mark. I wanted to warn you."

Beamon leaned out so he could see through the window of his office. Jacob Layman had planted himself in his chair and was staring intently into a folder that Beamon had left his desk.

"What's his mood look like, D.?" Beamon asked as she hung up the phone.

"I don't think it's good, Mark. He didn't even look at me when he came in. Just walked over to your desk and sat down."

Beamon sighed and began slowly walking toward his door. "You know, D., I was reading a play by Shakespeare yesterday . . ."

She shook her head sadly. "It's not Desdemona."

"Okay, I'll leave you in charge of the doughnuts," he said, pointing at the grease-stained box he'd left on her desk. "If I'm not back in an hour, organize a rescue."

"Jake, how're you doing? What brings you to my neck of the woods?"

Layman closed the folder in front of him and laid it down on the desk. He spent a few seconds tapping at the edges so that none of the paper peeked out. "What are you doing, Mark?" he said without looking up.

Beamon rolled his eyes at Layman's tone. That private school headmaster shit hadn't worked on him when he was kid and it hadn't become any more effective over the last thirty-five years. "I'm walking across the office to get a cup of coffee. You want one?"

Layman pushed a stack of computer disks across the desk. "What are these?"

Beamon looked back over his shoulder, recognizing the disks that contained the Kneissian membership list. Getting the morning off to a pleasant start.

He took a chair across from his desk and tried to make eye contact with his boss. Layman, who looked like he was struggling to maintain control, continued to stare at the folder in front of him.

"Look, Jake, we're both busy men," Beamon said. "You know what's on those disks or you wouldn't have hauled your ass up here from Phoenix. What do you want?"

Beamon regretted his word choice the second they were out of his mouth. Layman looked like he was about to explode all over his new carpet.

"Last time we talked, what did we talk about?"

Beamon took a sip of his coffee. "We talked about the Davis case. That you didn't think the church lead was worth pursuing."

"I don't think that's quite what I said. I told you to *stay away* from the Kneissians on this. That the FBI's taken enough flak already over Waco. And you agreed."

"I agreed that the FBI had already taken enough flak over Waco. Not that the church angle wasn't relevant in this situation."

That did it. Layman jumped up from the desk. "I don't give a shit what you did or didn't agree to. I gave you a direct order and I expect you to carry it out!"

Beamon looked at him calmly in the silence following his outburst. "Look, Jake. I've got a missing fifteen-year-old girl and two adults with their brains painting the walls of their house. I've got the press up my ass twenty-four hours a day wondering why I haven't lived up to my reputation and figured this thing out yet. It's easy for you to shut down lines of inquiry, 'cause the buck stops in my office. If I miss something, it's my ass, not yours."

"Who the hell do you think you are, Beamon?" Layman leaned farther over the desk, making sure his voice was loud enough to carry through the open door of the office to the young agents outside. "You know why you're in Flagstaff? The director had to promote you and give you an office so he'd look good in the papers. There were only three open offices small enough that you couldn't do any real damage. Do you know why you ended up in this one?"

Beamon took another sip from his coffee. The cream tasted like it might be going off. "I guess you're going to tell me."

"Shut up!"

Layman's train of thought got lost in his anger for a moment. Unfortunately, it only took him a moment to find it again. "You're here because I was on vacation. That's it—I was on vacation. The other two SACs were around to threaten to quit if they got you. I wasn't."

He sat stiffly back down in Beamon's chair. "And as for your reputation? It's for being a pain-in-the-ass drunk who stumbled over the solutions to a few high-profile cases. I wouldn't worry too much about protecting that image." Layman paused for a moment, but Beamon kept his mouth shut.

"Your career is pretty much finished, Mark. You know that as well as I do—it has been for years," Layman said, the volume of his voice dropping off. "Mine's not. I still have places to go in this organization and I'm not going to let a glorified supervisor dead-ended in Flagstaff fuck that up for me. Do you understand?"

"Okay, I think I'm ready to talk now," Beamon said, slamming his cup down on the edge of his desk hard enough that coffee sloshed over onto the papers strewn across it. "Am I finished at the FBI? Sure, probably. I've been the Bureau's dirty little secret for years. But you can't always get the job done by kissing the right asses and spouting off a bunch of politically correct bullshit. Sometimes you just got to go out there and get the sonofabitch you're after. And I'm sorry if things get a little politically inconvenient for you, but this seems to be one of those times. So why don't you let me do my job, and maybe, with a little luck, I'll stumble over little Jennifer Davis and we'll both be heroes."

Layman stood and grabbed the disks off the desk. "This is your last chance, Mark. If it wouldn't cause too much speculation in the press, you'd be off this case. I suggest you take the rest of the day off and give some serious thought to your future here."

Beamon leaned back in his chair as Layman stormed out, already starting to replay the conversation in his head. He probably could have handled that better. After a few more moments of contemplation, he decided that he couldn't have handled it much worse. So much for the new, improved Mark Beamon.

He sighed loudly, walked across the office, and leaned out the door. Layman was gone, but his presence was still palpable in the hush that had fallen over the office. Beamon waved at Chet Michaels and then turned to his secretary. "D., I've got a job for you, but you're going to hate me for it." He thumbed behind him to the wall of boxes containing the data on the Davis case. "See those boxes?"

She nodded hesitantly.

"I need one copy of everything in there."

"When do you need them by?" she said, wincing slightly.

"Top priority. I want you to lock yourself in the copy room and try to get it done by midday tomorrow. If anyone else needs the copier, tell 'em to go to Kinko's and save the receipts. Okay?"

She nodded. "I'll get started right after lunch."

"Thanks, I appreciate it." He stepped aside and let a nervous-looking Chet Michaels walk by him and into his office. "Get some of the guys to carry the boxes to the copier for you. They're pretty heavy."

Beamon walked back to his desk and settled into his chair. It was still a bit damp from Layman's back. "How're you coming on Vericomm and TarroSoft, Chet?"

"So-so, Mark."

"So-so?"

"I've got some stuff on Vericomm, but I haven't been able to find anything on Tarro."

"Okay, then. Vericomm."

"Like I told you, they're a holding company for long-distance carriers and a few Internet access providers. Their business is concentrated in small long-distance carriers in about twenty states. They're those ones that you call an 800 number and then punch in your personal ID number before you dial and you get a good rate. Kind of like having a really cheap calling card that you use at home, too."

Michaels pulled an envelope and some glossy papers from his coat pocket and laid them on the desk. "This is the Arizona-based Vericomm subsidiary. I got one of their solicitations about a week ago. Fortunately for us, I'm a procrastinator and haven't sent it in yet."

Beamon reached over and picked it up. The cover letter had NICKELINEAZ in glossy red letters across the top.

"It's a really good deal, actually," Michaels continued. "Five cents a minute, twenty-four hours a day, seven days a week. I have no idea how they stay in business, though. I looked at their financial statements. They're kind of strange."

"Strange?" Beamon said, finishing the solicitation letter and flipping through a stack of NICKELINE stickers and application material.

"Well, they're not a very large company—under thirty million in annual sales."

"Is that unusual?"

"Well, considering they cover, like, twenty states. That's not very many customers per state."

Beamon pursed his lips and shrugged. He was the first to admit that this financial stuff just wasn't his bag. Thank God the Bureau was infested with CPAs.

"It gets more interesting," Michaels promised.

"They lose a lot of money—every year I looked at, so the last three. There isn't a lot of financial data on this type of long distance company, but when you compare them to RMA and some other data I was able to dig up, they're really out of whack."

"Huh?"

"RMA gets financial statements from all kinds of companies and creates a database for financial statistics on different types of businesses. So you can take the statements of any given company and compare them to an average for that industry."

"And they don't line up?"

Michaels shook his head. "For one thing, Vericomm has absolutely no debt. They fund everything—including their losses—through the sale of stock."

"I don't know much about this stuff, but it seems like if you lost money every year, people would stop investing."

"Normally they would. The other thing that's funky is that they have too many fixed assets."

"Come again?"

"They have too much, uh, stuff. All companies have a different makeup of assets and liabilities. Take, say, a consulting firm. You wouldn't expect them to have, oh, I don't know, inventory, say, as high as a grocery store's. A grocery store has tens of thousands of dollars' worth of food and a consultant has, like, a computer and some reference materials."

"Makes sense."

"Well, Vericomm has way too many fixed assets. It's like they have enough equipment to run a company five times as big."

"Maybe they're setting up for a growth spurt?"

"Maybe, but I doubt it. It looks like they've had about the same number of customers for the last three years."

"Okay, good job, Chet. I wouldn't have gotten any of that. Do me a favor; put it in writing. Give me the numbers and details—so I can understand them, though, okay?"

Beamon watched Michaels walk from the office and pulled out his wallet. He searched through his credit cards and the other junk that had accumulated, finally coming up with a bright yellow laminated card. His name and a ten-digit number were emblazoned across it, beneath an orange box with bright red letters spelling out "NICKELINEAZ."

33

THE SNOW-COVERED HILLS STRETCHED OUT as far as Beamon could see, broken only occasionally by a thick stand of pines. He eased the car to a stop in front of a tall iron gate, reluctantly rolling down the window and letting the wind whip the inevitable fine mist of snow through the opening.

The guard who stepped from the small wooden booth to greet him was dressed in the standard garb—blue pants with a stripe running down the length of each leg, solid blue tie, and a down parka with an official-looking patch on the shoulder. The man himself, though, was a little less typical. The way the heaviness in his arms and shoulders tapered to a minute waist was obvious even through his bulky coat. He walked with a relaxed, businesslike stride that said he was more than an eight-dollar-an-hour rent-a-cop. A hell of a lot more.

"I'm sorry, sir. Albert is not available to take visitors right now. If you give me your name and e-mail address, I'll be happy to have him contact you as soon as possible," the man said, putting his hands on the car's windowsill and flashing a courteous smile.

Beamon examined the guard's right wrist, wondering if this might be one of the phantom protectors of the faith that Ernie had told him about.

Unfortunately, if there was an iron bracelet welded there, it was hidden by his sleeve.

The guard's polite speech had a practiced air, suggesting he'd repeated it at least a thousand times before. Obviously, there was a problem with Albert Kneiss's awestruck followers coming to his compound to try to get an audience. Beamon had to admit to being a little impressed by the reaction to his uninvited visit. It wasn't every church that offered timely e-mail access to the Messiah.

Beamon reached into his jacket, noting the slight tensing of the guard's body.

"I'm Mark Beamon with the FBI," he said, pulling his credentials from his pocket and flipping them open. "I'd like to speak with Mr. Kneiss on an official matter."

The guard examined Beamon's ID carefully. "Just a moment, please, sir." He walked back to the guardhouse and picked up a phone. Beamon rolled up his window and dusted off the snow that had accumulated on his dashboard while he waited. It didn't take long.

"Sir, if you continue up this road, you'll come to the main house. Just park right under the portico. There'll be someone waiting for you there."

The man stepped away from the car, and Beamon accelerated through the gate. It was almost a half-mile on the narrow road before he crested a hill that afforded a spectacular view of a small valley dominated by an enormous Tudor-style mansion. The house was beautifully constructed and meticulously maintained, but it sprawled out a bit unnaturally, suggesting that the expansive wings on either side had been an afterthought.

The car skidded a bit as Beamon maneuvered it

down the other side of the hill and pulled up beneath the wide portico at the front of the building.

"Mr. Beamon. Please come in," the woman standing at the front door said as he stepped from the car and started up the steps. "My name is Sara Renslier." She walked through the door and motioned to a beautifully wrought antique coat rack. Beamon hung his jacket on one of the brass pegs and stretched out his hand. "Mark Beamon."

The strength of her grip belied her small stature. "Very nice to meet you, Mr. Beamon. Please follow me."

The mansion was spectacular. It was decorated with an unlikely combination of artifacts from all over the world that seemed to melt into an odd harmony. The pieces all looked fantastically expensive, but they were laid out sparsely enough to maintain a vaguely monastic atmosphere.

Beamon followed the woman obediently as they progressed into the heart of the house. There was nothing that looked even remotely suspicious, but he couldn't help wondering what the chances were that he was within two hundred yards of Jennifer Davis. By the time they entered the small room at the end of the hall, he'd decided they were probably better than fifty-fifty.

"Please take a seat," Sara said, pointing to a heavy-looking leather chair in front of a roaring fire. "Warm yourself."

Beamon sat down and looked around him as Sara made coffee in an ornate press. The room was perhaps a bit more opulent, but beyond that, it differed very little from the one he'd been taken to at the recruiting station. Obviously, the church had figured out the formula that worked, and then didn't deviate from it.

Beamon took the offered coffee and watched Sara settle into the chair across from him. Her short dark hair was not unstylish, but screamed utilitarian. She was perfectly groomed and neatly dressed, as he would have expected from the leader of the perfectly groomed and neatly dressed hordes that had taken over Flagstaff. What he hadn't expected was the air of power and self-control she exuded. He'd met more than a handful of the most powerful men in the world, and there weren't many who sucked the air out of a room like she did. Now that he had met her, he didn't find it the least bit surprising that this woman had been able to take an esoteric cult and turn it into the fastest-growing religion in the world.

What did surprise him was the fact that she was there meeting with him. Undoubtedly she was about to provide a perfectly logical reason why it was going to be impossible for him to speak to Kneiss. The question was, why would a woman who controlled debatably the most efficient religious machine in history meet personally with a lowly ASAC?

She seemed to be waiting for him to speak, so he took a sip of his coffee and started. "As I told the man at the gate, I'd like a few minutes of Mr. Kneiss's time."

"May I ask what about?"

"It's a private matter relating to a case I'm working on."

"Jennifer Davis?"

"Excuse me?" Beamon said, slipping into a suitably coy expression.

"The disappearance of that little girl," Sara said. "I read about it in the papers almost every day."

He considered lying—telling her that it was a

different case—but it was obvious that she knew exactly why he was there. And it was even more obvious that she didn't really care. There was something in her posture, the way she sipped at her cup, that was infinitely condescending.

"Jennifer Davis, yes," he said, pulling a pad from his pocket and flipping though it, purely for show. "Sara Renslier. You pretty much run the church. Is that right?"

She smiled at him as though he was a child who had just added two and two and come up with five. "No. No, it's not. Albert is in control of all parts of his church. I just carry out his wishes as best I can."

"And what are those wishes?"

"That's a fairly broad question," she said, laying her cup down on the leather insert in the table next to her. "Albert is obviously very committed to world charities and the purity of the faith he started. I help translate his ideas into reality. I watch after the mundane details."

"And will you take over the church when he dies?"

"Ascends," she corrected.

"Right. Just a little more than two weeks now, isn't it?"

She nodded politely. "He'll rejoin God on Good Friday, as he has in the past. Who will lead the church when he's gone? That's entirely up to him."

It seemed a bit unlikely that she wouldn't have given that matter a little more thought, but Beamon decided not to press the issue. "May I speak to him?"

"I'm afraid not. He's in Turkey meditating."

"Really? Turkey? How long's he been there?"

"He left in January. He has a great deal to prepare for."

"Yeah, I guess so."

Sara crossed her legs and leaned back into the chair. "If you have a message you want to get to him, I will do my best to pass it along. I can't promise anything, though."

Beamon nodded absently, watching the writhing of the flames next to him. It was pretty much the answer he'd expected. "Does Mr. Kneiss have any living relatives?"

"None that I'm aware of. He's certainly never spoken of any." Her answer was too easy. She'd been ready for that question.

It was time to make a decision on how to play this. There was the smart way, of course—stand up, thank her for her time, and leave. But that seemed kind of boring. The other option was to shoot himself in the foot and see if he could make the ice princess sweat a little.

"I'm afraid I have to insist on speaking with Mr. Kneiss," he said, deciding that the low road had always worked for him before.

Sara's eyebrows rose slightly. "I don't know what you want me to do. He's incommunicado. I already told you that."

"Then make him communicado," Beamon said, wondering idly if Jake Layman was going to put him in front of a firing squad for this or opt for the more traditional hanging. "I have to admit I'm finding it a little hard to believe that you've misplaced your messiah. I suggest you take a couple of thousand bucks from the ten billion you make every year and rent a helicopter. Fly it to whatever mountaintop he's sitting on and hand him a cell phone."

He had to give her credit. For a woman who had probably never been spoken to like that, she

STORMING HEAVEN — 275

retained her self-control admirably. The slight quiver in her jaw and a nearly imperceptible crinkling around her eyes, though, told Beamon he'd just crossed the line. There would be no going back now.

"I'll be back to check on your progress in a couple of days," he said, standing and offering his hand.

That same irritating smile he'd seen earlier reappeared on her lips. "Oh, you will, will you?"

"Yeah. I will."

Beamon dialed his cell phone with one hand and tried to maneuver the car around a slick corner with the other, all while trying to calculate how long it would take for his meeting with Sara Renslier to get back to Layman.

"Mark Beamon's office."

"D.! I want you to get Ken Hirayami on the phone for me. He's our guy in Athens."

"Greece?"

"Yeah. You may have to get him on his home number—it's probably the middle of the night there."

"Okay. That's going to take a few minutes, though."

"No problem. Put me through to Chet while you work on it."

The phone went dead for a few seconds.

"Chet Michaels, can I help you?" came the earnest voice.

"Jesus, Chet, you sound like the guy at the McDonald's drive-through."

"Thanks, Mark."

"Here's what I need you to do for me. Check the

passenger manifests on all flights going to Turkey last month. You're looking for the name Albert Kneiss."

"You think he's fled the country?"

"Hardly. Also, find out if the church has a private jet. If they do, call our guys in Oklahoma City and get 'em to find out if they registered a flight plan for Turkey—you'll need the numbers off the plane's tail."

"How do you suggest I find out if they have a plane?"

"I don't know, be resourceful. Tell them you're from *Corporate Jet* magazine and you heard they've got the biggest cockpit in town. I don't care—"

"Hey, Mark," Michaels said, cutting him off. "D.'s waving at me. I think I have to transfer you back."

"Drop everything and get on this, Chet. I want it tomorrow morning. Understand?"

The phone clicked again and his secretary's voice came on. "Mark. I've got Ken."

"Great. Hey, D.—How're you coming on those copies?"

"You'll have them, Mark."

"You're a goddess."

"Uh-huh. Here he is."

"Ken!" Nothing. "Hey, Ken!"

"Mark? Yeah, I'm here. Do you know what time it is?"

Beamon looked at his watch. "Four-thirty in the afternoon."

"—hole." There was a slight delay on the line that cut off the first part of Hirayami's reply, but Beamon could guess at it.

"Ken, I need a favor. Actually, I need two."

"What?"

"I need you to get the cops in Turkey to find out if there's any record of Albert Kneiss coming in there in January."

"You got a date?"

"Nope."

"Shouldn't be a problem. Everyone has to get a visa when they come in. They either get it here or at one of the consulates. When do you need it by?"

"Yesterday."

"Why did I ask?"

"Look, this is important, Ken. Get me this by tomorrow and I will literally get down on my knees and kiss your ass next time I see you."

"I'll have to give that offer some thought. What's the second favor?"

"I'll get back to you on that."

"Uh-uh. I'm going back to bed, Mark. I'll call you tomorrow."

34

MARK BEAMON PUT HIS HANDS ON HIS LOWER back and bent backward, trying to stretch the muscles that were twisting his spine. Feeling guilty about blowing off his new personal trainer last week, he'd unwisely decided to haul the mountain of boxes containing the Davis file copies to his car by himself.

Satisfied that he wasn't permanently crippled, Beamon began threading his way through the sea of desks toward Craig Skinner's cubicle. His young computer clerk saw him coming, though, and made a dash for the bathroom.

"Freeze, Skinner."

The young man stopped a few feet short of the men's room. Beamon grabbed him by the collar and led him back to his cubicle. "Sit. What the hell happened, Craig? Do you not understand the word 'quietly'? Let me translate: The use of subtlety. Wanton sneaking. The overzealous practice of stealth. What did you do, call personnel and ask them if you could download their files?"

Skinner twisted a lock of his hair around his index finger. "Well, do you know how long it would take me to scan in the entire FBI personnel list? I figured it would be easier that way."

Beamon pushed his glasses up and pinched the bridge of his nose between his thumb and index finger. "Okay, I've got something else for you, Craig. But this time we're going to keep it between us. And by us, I mean just you and me, right?"

Skinner looked doubtful. "They thought I was a spy or something, man. I got in a lot of trouble, you know? Layman made me delete the whole file."

Beamon ignored his protest. "There's a software company—TarroSoft. I want you to find out what you can about them."

Skinner thought about it for a moment. Finally he turned toward his computer and began working with his mouse. At a screen with Yahoo! written across it, he typed in the word TarroSoft.

"That's weird."

"What?"

"No hits. You sure it's a software company?"

Beamon shrugged. "Not dead sure. But with a name like that I figure it's either software or toilet paper—and I'm guessing it's not toilet paper."

Skinner chewed the end of his pencil, obviously intrigued by the problem. "Let me do some digging and I'll let you know."

Beamon looked at him sternly.

"Subtle digging," Skinner corrected.

Satisfied, Beamon turned, walked to the middle of the office, and jumped up on a chair, opting for a less subtle approach to solving his next problem. "May I have everybody's attention, please? Hello?"

The low buzz of voices that made up the background noise in the office faded and the agents all looked up from what they were doing.

"Thank you. I'd like everyone here—everyone—to write down on a piece of paper what long-distance company they use." He pointed to Michaels. "Then bring them to me at Chet's desk."

Beamon jumped down, feeling another twinge in his back, and then dragged the chair over to Michaels's desk. "Where have you been all day, Chet?" The young agent still had snowflakes clinging to his red hair.

"Workin' for you, Mark."

Beamon dumped out Michaels's inbox and pointed to the empty container as the first people began walking up with scraps of paper in hand. "And what is it you've been doing for me?"

"Freezing to death at a private airport before six this morning."

Beamon didn't let the fact that he was impressed show. He hadn't been at all sure that Michaels could run down the church's plane this fast. "Kind of waited till the last minute, didn't you? What did you find?"

"They do have one private jet capable of making it to Turkey. I got the numbers and called them into the Oklahoma office this morning. They're checking with the FAA."

"What's the time frame?"

"Real fast. I told them it was top priority," Michaels said, taking a manila envelope off the edge of his desk and handing it to Beamon. "I ran some computer checks on the previous address of your new neighbor—Robert Andrews. Kind of interesting. There are seven other people who list that address as their permanent residence. All men. All between the ages of thirty and forty. All ex-military or ex-cops, now self-employed. But then you knew what I'd find, didn't you?"

Beamon looked over his shoulder. The inbox was full of paper, and everyone appeared to have sat back down and gone back to work. "I didn't *know*—it was just a hunch. Ernie told me that Sara Renslier had put together a specialized security group at the church. Fanatics who'll do anything she says. I think you found them."

Michaels looked a little worried. "Based on the records I was able to pull, Mark, these aren't people you want to mess with . . ."

"And you should remember that. What about Sines?"

"Sines sounds like he's probably part of this group. Ex-military—resigned for no apparent reason shortly after being promoted to major. He's forty-one. Lists the church as his employer and Kneiss's compound as his permanent residence. No criminal record. I couldn't find anything relating to what he does for the church—just that he works there. Same as Renslier."

Beamon opened the manila envelope in front of him and wrote each of the names it contained on a piece of legal paper, adding the name of the man watching his condo to the bottom. "I'll be back in a second."

He walked across the office and stuck his head into Skinner's cubicle. "Hey, Craig."

"It's only been a few minutes, Mark!"

"Calm down, son," Beamon said, holding out the paper in his hand. "I just want you to run these names against that list I gave you."

"I told you, Mark. Layman made me delete that file."

Beamon rolled his eyes. Skinner had a hacker's heart. There was just no goddamn way he'd deleted that file. "Run the fucking names, Craig."

"Well, uh, maybe there is a way to reconstruct the file," Skinner said, reaching hesitantly for the sheet.

"Uh-huh," Beamon said, starting back toward Michaels's desk.

"What else you got, Chet?"

Michaels turned his palms upward. "I'm sorry, Mark. Nothing. David Passal's known acquaintances are a dead end—and I don't mean that I couldn't find anybody he knew who might fit the profile—I mean I can't find anybody he knew. The guy was a freaking hermit. Otherwise, there are no local sex offenders with MOs even close, or for that matter the opportunity. Our national search of people who have been involved in this kind of thing so far is a big zero. Recent parolees? Another big fat zero. And we've got nothing on the physical evidence side."

Beamon looked blankly at the young agent. "That's quite a laundry list of things you don't know. So what do you think happened here?"

Michaels let out a loud breath. "Maybe it does have something to do with the church. Or maybe the whole thing was a big coincidence. A fluke."

"How so?"

"What if Jennifer's dad just went nuts? Killed her mom, then himself? Jennifer saw it all. She panics. Runs out into the street where she flags down a passing car. Turns out that the guy who picks her up is a bad seed. Things get out of hand and he kills her. I'm starting to think that one way or another, we're gonna find her when the snow thaws."

"Why didn't she just use the phone? Call for an ambulance?"

"Couldn't stay in the same house with what was left of her folks."

"Reasonable. Why'd she take the gun?"

Michaels shrugged. "I've been thinking about that. She's completely freaked out. She falls to her knees and cries for a while beside her parents' bodies. She's got no relatives living, so she's totally alone. She can't take it. Picks up the gun, puts it to her head, then chickens out. Forgets to drop it when she runs out of the house."

"Why wouldn't she just go to a neighbor's?"

"Maybe the guy in the car saw her running without a jacket toward a neighbor's house and offered her a ride. She'd have probably taken it."

The phone on the desk started to ring, but Michaels ignored it.

"I don't think so, Chet," Beamon said, speaking slowly. "It's good piece of reasoning, but my gut just says its wrong."

"Mine too, actually. That leaves us with the church, but Layman's pretty much shut us down there."

Beamon had purposely kept many of the individual components of the investigation—his visit to Sara, much of the information he'd gotten from Ernestine Waverly—from the young agent. He had a feeling that the less Michaels knew, the better off he'd be in the end.

"Chet!" D. yelled, holding her phone in one hand and waving with the other. "There's a guy from the Oklahoma City office on the line. Says you'll want to take the call."

"Could you put it through, please?" He picked it up on the first ring.

"Hi, Terry. Nothing, huh? Nothing on the commercial flights, either? Hey, thanks for doing this so quick. Yeah, I'll tell him . . ."

Beamon reached out and plucked the phone

from Michaels's hand. "Terry. Mark Beamon."

"Mr. Beamon. How are you, sir?"

"I'm good. Hey, I just wanted to tell you myself how much I appreciate you jumping on this like you did."

"If there's anything else I can do, Mr. Beamon, please let me know."

"Actually, there is, Terry. Tomorrow afternoon I want you to try to pull that flight plan again."

"We've never had problems with the FAA before, Mr. Beamon. I think the information is accurate . . ."

"I'm going to have to ask you to humor me on this one. It's important."

"Of course. I'll call you tomorrow evening."

"Thanks, Terry. I owe you one."

Beamon replaced the handset and looked into the confused face of Chet Michaels. "Another hunch," he explained. "Chet, keep going where you're going on this case. Make sure we didn't miss anything and I'll concentrate on the church. Stay away from that. Okay?"

Beamon grabbed the scraps of papers that had accumulated in Michaels's IN box and walked back to his office.

After going through them, all but two were in his garbage can. He took out a Post-it, wrote his name on it and put it in between the one with his secretary's and Michaels's names.

"D.!" he yelled at the open door to his office. She leaned around the corner.

"When did you sign up for NickeLine?"

"I don't know exactly. It was probably around the same time I took this job. So about a year and a half ago." Beamon heard the phone on her desk start to ring and she disappeared to answer it. Her head reappeared in his doorway a moment later. "It's Ken Hirayami from Athens."

"Put him through, please," Beamon said, picking up his phone.

"Ken! What'd you find out?"

"No record, Mark. As far as Turkey's concerned, he's not in the country." There was a pause over the phone. "Now are you going to tell me what the second favor is?"

"Yup," Beamon said. "Tomorrow afternoon I want you to run the same check again."

"The same check?"

"Yeah."

"I don't know if I want to do that, Mark. I think the Turks would find it a little insulting. It'd look like I was saying they didn't know how to do their jobs. And they do."

"Ken, I got fifty bucks that says they find a record of Kneiss's visa this time through."

"What've you got cooking over there, Mark?"

"Will you do it?"

"I guess I can find someone else to run the search and hope it doesn't get back to the first guy. Yeah, I'll do it."

"Thanks, Ken. Oh, and Ken?"

"Yeah."

"I want my fifty in American." Beamon pushed the lever on the phone down with his index finder and stared at it like it was the enemy. He had to do it, he knew. He had to make the call. But he knew he was going to live to regret it.

He pawed through his Rolodex and dialed one of the numbers he found there, grimacing as it started to ring.

"You've reached Goldman Communications Consultants, leave a message at the beep," a mechanical voice told him.

Goldman Communications Consultants. It sounded so benign. The Goldman part was Jack Goldman. They had worked together years ago when Beamon was just starting with the Bureau and Goldman was just getting ready to retire.

Goldman had started as a telephone repairman when he was still in his early teens and when phones in private homes were probably more the exception than the rule. After he got busted placing bugs for Al Capone's organization, J. Edgar Hoover had taken him under his wing and Goldman had become the king of the FBI's "black bag men."

When Beamon first met him, Goldman was already older than God. And about as cantankerous a sonofabitch as had ever walked the earth. That little personality flaw aside, though, he was the best. Always had been, always would be. The man could bug the incisor teeth of a rabid Doberman.

Despite his undeniable skill, the government wouldn't work with him anymore. His corporate clients, though, were more than happy to put up with his colorful demeanor in return for his ruthless efficiency at finding—and most likely placing—any eavesdropping device ever invented.

"Mr. Goldman, this is Mark Beamon. I have a question that might be up your—"

There was a momentary screech of feedback and then, "Mark! Goddamn, boy, I can't remember the last time I heard from you. Someone told me that you'd screwed the pooch one too many times at headquarters and they sent you off to pasture!" His voice shook with age.

"Uh, hello, Mr. Goldman," Beamon said slowly into the phone, already starting to regret the call. "I'm in Flagstaff now."

"Jesus, son. They did put you in a one-horse town. What do you do there, investigate shoplifting?"

"It's actually a pretty good size—"

"Uh-huh. So what do you want? I'm a busy man, you know."

"Yes, sir. I have a theoretical question. If I bought one of those phone companies where you dial an 800 number and enter your PIN before you call long distance, could I listen in on all the calls that went over those lines?"

"No."

Beamon was momentarily confused by Goldman's answer. Could he have been wrong? "You couldn't? It's impossible?"

"Shit, I don't know if it's possible or not. But why the hell would you want to? Think for once in your life, boy! Why buy a goddamn phone company for millions of dollars when you could hire one of my more unscrupulous colleagues for a few thousand? And then you'd get the goddamn local calls, too."

"But what if you wanted to spy on a group, Mr. Goldman? Let's say you hated, I don't know, Jews. You could offer a great long-distance rate to influential Jews through the mail and get a feel for what they were doing though their long-distance conversa—"

"You saying that we kikes'll do anything to save a few cents a minute on long distance?"

"No, sir. I was just using it as an example—"

"Think we're stupid?"

"No, I—"

"That's an interesting theory you got there, Marko. It's clean—almost no chance of detection. Elegant—except for the part about not getting local calls. I'd have to research it, but off the top of my head I can't think of a reason it wouldn't be technologically possible. Of course, you'd have to have serious computer power to monitor the number of lines you're probably talking about. And a hell of a lot of storage space, too, it wouldn't be practical to have people listening in real-time."

"So, it's possible?"

"What did I tell you? I'm going to have to look into it. It's an interesting concept, though. Interesting. Maybe I should come out there. Get the lay of the land. Yeah, get a feel for what you're into."

Beamon bolted upright in his chair. "No! Uh, thanks anyway, Mr. Goldman, but there's no way I can get authorization for your fee . . ."

"We could work that out, Mark. I'll tell you that I'm getting good and goddamn sick of sweeping the offices of a bunch of fatcats for bugs. Not one of them's got a damn thing to say that anybody would want to listen to, let alone record. Yeah. Maybe I'll come out and give you a hand . . ."

Beamon desperately switched gears and tried another approach. "You know, Mr. Goldman, it's really not much of a case. Embezzlement. I've spent the last three weeks reading through a ten-foot-high stack of paper filled with about a million numbers. Starting to go blind." He paused to see if his words had any effect and then added, "It's not even about that much money," for good measure.

Goldman didn't seem to have even been listening. "Yep. Sounds like you're in over your head again." The phone went dead.

Beamon began banging his head slowly and repeatedly on the blotter that covered his desk. How could this day get any worse?

When he sat back up and looked through the window into the outer office, he saw Jake Layman, flanked by two rather serious-looking men in dark suits. The speed at which they were moving his way seemed to answer his question.

"That's them over there," Layman said, pointing to the boxes stacked along the wall. He looked up at Beamon. "Are those all the Davis files?"

"Afternoon, Jake. I'd ask you to sit down, but my chair is otherwise occupied."

"Are those all the files?" he repeated angrily.

Beamon watched the two men who'd burst through his door alongside his boss struggling to lift the overflowing boxes. "That's all of them."

Layman balled his fists and pressed them against Beamon's desk as he leaned toward him. "I got a call from Travis Macon today." Beamon recognized the name of one of Arizona's senators. "You know what he said?"

Beamon shrugged.

"He said that he got a call from one of his constituents at the Church of the Evolution yesterday. That you went to one of their most sacred buildings and started throwing around threats."

Beamon smiled weakly. He didn't regret the way he'd handled his meeting with Sara Renslier—he needed to shake this case loose. What he *was* starting to regret was the way he'd handled Layman. His boss probably wasn't a bad guy. Just trying to play it smart and not suffer the repeated screwings that Beamon had brought upon himself. That was fair.

"Look, Jake. I'm sorry. I shouldn't have gone in there without talking to you first; sometimes I can be kind of an . . . asshole. Tell your guys to go get a cup of coffee and we'll shut the door and I'll lay out what I've got on this case. I think once you've heard—"

"I didn't ask you what you think," Layman yelled. "I just spent two hours on the phone getting a lecture on the meaning of religious freedom from one of the most powerful senators in the country! You are off this case, Beamon. I told you twice—clear enough for even you to understand—to back off. I've written a full report to headquarters about your conduct and I'm telling you that you don't have many fuckups left. You're lucky to still have a job."

Beamon suddenly came to the realization that every time he tried to be reasonable and maybe even lightly kiss an ass or two, it was like throwing gas on a wildfire. It was time to face the fact that he just didn't have the gift.

"I don't feel lucky, Jake."

Layman stormed over to the remaining boxes, picked up one that was too heavy for him, and refused to put it back down. He looked a little like a penguin as he teetered out of the office toward the elevator.

35

BEAMON HAMMERED ON THE DOOR OF THE small house again, this time harder. "Ernie! It's Mark! Open up."

He knew she was home. There were no tire marks in the driveway and little chance that she could negotiate the snow-covered walk on foot or in her thin-tired wheelchair.

Beamon bent at the waist and put his face close to the peephole so that she could see him. A moment later he heard a chain rattling on the other side of the door.

"Ernie! Damn, I was starting to get worried."

"I'm sorry. I was downstairs," she said, backing her wheelchair away from the door.

He followed her as she glided down the hallway, trying to decide what he was going to do. "I lied to you, Ernie."

She stopped for a moment but didn't turn around. "The difference between a saint and a hypocrite is that one lies for his religion, the other by it." She gave the wheels another push and they passed through the door to the cluttered office at the back of the house.

"Albert Kneiss?"

"Minna Antrim. But it was one of Albert's favorite quotes." She picked up a piece of pizza from her desk and slid the steaming end of it into her mouth.

"I told you that the questions I was asking about the church didn't relate to the Jennifer Davis case. That isn't entirely true."

She peered out at him through the folds of flesh on her forehead but seemed to be seeing something else. "I know," she said finally.

There was a casual thoughtfulness in her voice that for some reason made Beamon believe her. "How did you know?"

"Because I dream about *her*, too."

Beamon questioned his strategy for the fiftieth time since leaving the office. Spilling everything he'd learned and suspected about Jennifer and the church to a morbidly obese woman prone to ecstatic visions seemed a little stupid. But what choice did he have? Layman would make damn sure he wouldn't have access to the Bureau's resources to run down the church. And he wasn't going to get this done alone.

He took a deep breath, forcing his doubts from his mind. At this point there were no other options. But if she started showing any signs of stigmata, he was history. "Do you understand the connection between Jennifer and the church, Ernie?"

She shook her head. "God hasn't seen fit to reveal that to me. I assume that's why He sent you."

"This is just between us, right, Ernie? You, me, and God. I'm about to tell you some things even the guys at my office don't know."

"Of course."

Beamon hesitated. Getting her involved in this wasn't fair. It wasn't her job. What the hell was he doing here?

"Are you all right, Mark?"

"Look, Ernie. You've come up against the church before and look what happened. Maybe this isn't such a good idea." He started to stand. "I've changed my mind. You don't need to be involved in this."

"Please sit down, Mark." Ernie said. "I already am involved in this. I have been for years. I thought that God had directed me to write my book—to warn Albert about what was happening to his church—and for all these years I thought I'd failed Him. Now I know that my real purpose was to be here for you."

Beamon hesitated and finally sat back down. He was feeling increasingly uncomfortable and dishonest—like he was a fraud playing to this woman's faith.

"Okay, Ernie," he said slowly. "You're in, but I feel like I should tell you again that I don't for one minute believe that I'm being directed by God. I just want to find this girl so I can look like a hero and twist the knife in my boss. If, as a by-product, Sara Renslier takes a beating and your church gets the overhaul you think it needs, then fine—but in the end, I don't really care. It's not my job to save people from themselves."

She smiled. "It doesn't really matter what you believe. What either one of us believes. God will do what He will do."

Beamon took off his parka and threw it on the floor after extracting his copy of the Kneissian bible. He pulled a couple of legal-sized sheets of yellow paper from the book and smoothed them out on his lap. On the sheets, he'd sketched out the theory that had woken him up at 2:00 A.M. that

294 — KYLE MILLS

morning. What he needed from Ernie was for her to tell him he was wrong.

"What's that?" Ernie asked, wheeling her chair around and handing Beamon a slice of pizza. He accepted it gratefully.

"It's something I want you to help me think about."

She craned her thick neck and looked at the unintelligible writing connected by undecipherable arrows and grids.

"I think better in pictures," Beamon explained. "Let me translate." He took a bite of pizza and slurred through a mouth full of cheese and dough. "Fact number one: Jennifer is Albert Kneiss's grand-daughter."

Ernie shook her head. "Carol Kneiss died child-less."

"Actually, your research wasn't entirely accu-rate with regard to her death. Carol Kneiss died Carol Passal in a fire in the early eighties after changing her name and moving a number of times. I'm guessing that she knew she was being watched by the church and that she was afraid for her daughter."

"I didn't know . . ." Ernie said sadly.

"Fact two. Well, actually, this is more of a strongly supported hypothesis, but let's raise it to the exalted status of fact. Eric Davis killed his wife and committed suicide. Both had been members of the Church of the Evolution since the late sixties."

"What? Why?" Ernie stuttered.

"They adopted Jennifer shortly after her biolog-ical parents' death—I'm guessing at the direction of the church."

"But why would they . . ."

Beamon held his hand up and silenced her. "I thought it was to cut Jennifer off from her support system. The church couldn't kill them without alienating Jennifer and they couldn't leave them alive because she'd have a home and family to get back to. And what better way to show Jennifer their strong belief and dedication to the church?"

"So you think they're trying to brainwash her to replace Albert?"

"I did. Until last night, I was convinced that when Kneiss died, the church would tell the world they had her. They'd have her say that she knew Albert was her grandfather all along. That her father went nuts, killed her mother and himself, and she ran to granddad—her only living relative. The church elders would swear they didn't know anything about it till Albert told them on his deathbed." Beamon took another bite of the quickly cooling pizza. "Then Jennifer is inserted as head of the church. Easy as pie."

Ernie shook her head. "Except one thing. Sara Renslier will never give up her power over the church. She gives God and Albert almost no credit in building it—she believes that it's hers." The hatred in her voice cut through the air.

"I met Sara," Beamon said. "And I got the same feeling. That, combined with the fact that Albert's already dead, is what woke me up last night."

Ernie jerked back in her wheelchair so hard that it drifted back a foot. "Albert isn't dead. He can't be. Not until Good Friday."

"I know this is hard for you, Ernie, but let me finish. I tried to get in to see Albert the day before yesterday. Sara told me he was in Turkey meditating."

Ernie looked like she was about to say something, but Beamon ignored her and continued. "There's no record of him entering Turkey, nor is there a record of him taking a commercial or private flight to Turkey. Why would Sara keep me from talking to him? The best reason I can come up with is that he's dead. He must have ordered Jennifer's retrieval before he died. Sara wouldn't have wanted to, but she would have had to obey. So we can hypothesize he was still alive as of the day Jennifer was kidnapped—give or take. Then, at some point since then, he's died. I mean, the guy was pushing ninety and hadn't been seen in public for years. He had to have been on his last legs."

"But he can't die until Good Friday. That's God's will!" Ernie repeated in a voice tinged with desperation. "What if Sara has isolated him completely? Taken over . . ."

Beamon shrugged. "Maybe, but we know he wasn't isolated before Jennifer was kidnapped—he must have given Sara the order in front of a group of people, probably the Elders, or else she could have just ignored it. And I think it would have been difficult for Sara to suddenly isolate him in his final days when everyone is wondering what exactly to do with their new leader, don't you? No, the simplest answer is the best in most cases. He's dead."

Beamon doubted he was ever going to win Ernie over with the dazzling logic of his argument. Logic was oil to religion's water—always had been. She'd need more.

He opened his copy of the Kneissian Bible to a page marked with a Post-it note. "There is a way that he could be dead, Ernie."

She looked at him blankly, obviously still strug-

gling with what he'd told her and the credibility
she thought God had bestowed on him.

"It says here that Kneiss hasn't always been the
Messenger, right?" Beamon said, trying to coax her
out of her stupor. She didn't respond.

"Right?" he prompted.

"Yes. Yes, that's right. Our Bible specifically
names three of his incarnations. Kneiss, Jesus, and
before that Persiah. Eventually God will take him to
his reward and he'll be replaced by another, like he
replaced the one before him."

Beamon flipped to another marked page and
began reading. "I was once flesh like you . . ."

Ernie finished the passage in a voice so quiet
that Beamon had to lean closer to hear. ". . . full of
fear, doubt, and hatred . . ." She looked up at him.
"It's central to our belief. That the Messenger was
once human and became more. An example to all
of us."

Beamon closed the book slowly, feeling the
tightness at the bottom of his stomach cinch down
a bit more. He *was* right. Somehow he'd known he
would be. "Follow me now, Ernie. Kneiss is dead,
but he didn't ascend on Good Friday. That can only
mean one thing, right? That he's served God long
enough. That he has been accepted into heaven."

She still didn't seem to be fully tracking on
what he was saying, but she nodded with enough
authority for him to continue. "To replace Albert,
God will choose a worthy human being, right?"

Ernie nodded again.

"We know that Sara isn't going to be happy
about turning over the church she spent a quarter
of a century building to an adolescent girl with a
ring in her nose, so she needs to get rid of her,"

Beamon paused. "The question is, how far would Sara go?"

He could see from Ernie's expression that his words were beginning to sink in. She reached out and grabbed his arm in her soft hand. "Of course, it's the only way she can protect her position. If Albert is dead, she could tell the other elders anything. And if she told them that Jennifer had been chosen . . ."

Her voice faded away and Beamon finished her thought. "Then Jennifer has to ascend on Good Friday."

Ernie's hand tightened around his arm. "And then there will be no one. No one but her!"

Beamon chewed on his lip, wishing for once that his instincts had failed him. He'd come hoping that he'd missed something. Hoping that Ernie's intimate knowledge of the church would point him in another direction. He looked at the calendar on his watch. Fifteen days until Good Friday. If he was right, and his gut told him he was, he had to find Jennifer in the next two weeks or he never would.

Beamon stood and patted Ernie on the back, trying to comfort her as her sniffling turned into sobbing. He wondered if it was for Jennifer or if it was the final realization that the church she loved had turned so far from God.

"Ernie. Ernie? Come back to me now. We can still turn this thing around if we work together." She sobbed louder. "Come on, Ernie. The Bureau's left me hanging on this one. You and I are all Jennifer's got. We're all the church has."

She wiped at her eyes with her sleeve and her sobbing faded back into sniffles.

"I want you to do something for me, Ernie. I

want you to run your old Kneissian membership list against lists of influential people. Give me an idea of who we might be coming up against."

She looked up at him. "What . . . what kind of lists?"

"I don't know exactly. Politicians. *Who's Who.* World's richest people. That kind of thing. Whatever you can think of. Are you up to it?"

She nodded. "But I want you to do something for me in return."

"Sure."

"Pray with me."

She pulled at his sleeve and he sank to his knees next to her wheelchair. She squeezed her eyes shut and began moving her lips soundlessly. Not really knowing what to do, he bowed his head and waited for her to snap out of it.

36

BEAMON ADJUSTED HIS READING GLASSES TO a more comfortable position on his nose and slid a withdrawal slip and his driver's license through the teller window. "I'd like to get five thousand dollars from my savings account, please."

The teller looked the two documents over briefly and then punched a few keys on the terminal next to her. "Just a moment, please, sir."

Beamon felt a nervous twinge as the young woman hurried off and disappeared through a door at the back of the teller line. His fears were dispelled, though, when she reappeared a few moments later and started counting hundreds onto the counter. When she was finished she slid an envelope to him and he stuffed the cash into it.

"Come and see us again, sir."

Beamon smiled and walked back out onto the sidewalk, pausing to watch the flare of orange on the horizon slowly deepen and cast a red glow over the mountains. He stood there for a few minutes, filling his lungs with the cold dry air and trying to focus his mind on the most urgent problems facing him. There were so many to choose from—the fight he'd purposefully started with the eleven million members of the Church of the Evolution, the tenuous grip he had on his job, the fact that there was a good chance that Jennifer Davis had only two weeks before Sara sacrificed her on the altar of power and influence.

Beamon sunk his hands into the deep pockets of his parka and jogged down the sidewalk toward a dully flickering PACKAGE LIQUOR sign a block and a half away.

In his two months in Flagstaff, he'd been into that particular liquor store more times than he'd like to admit, but this was the first time he'd set foot in the attached bar. It was about what he imagined. Dark and worn, with the strangely comforting smell of age and countless spilled drinks.

It was almost completely empty, he saw as his eyes adjusted to the gloom. There was a woman in a dark coat to his right, speaking to the bartender as though she knew him well. Across the room, in the booth next to a dead jukebox, he could see the thick brown hair of his favorite computer nerd, Craig Skinner.

Skinner had become a little paranoid after the unfortunate incident with the Kneissian membership list and Jake Layman. He'd taken Beamon's lecture on keeping things quiet a little too seriously, insisting that they meet away from the office in order to give him what would undoubtedly be a rather mundane report on TarroSoft.

Beamon had picked the place. Figured he might as well kill two birds with one stone—his beer inventory was getting dangerously low.

Beamon sneaked up behind the young man and leaned in close to his ear. "The blue moose howls at the moon," he whispered.

Skinner jumped and almost spilled his drink. He was still clutching at his chest as Beamon slid onto the bench across from him.

"Jesus, Mark! You almost gave me a heart attack!"

"If you don't give the countersign, I'm going to have to kill you."

"You said be subtle!"

Beamon nodded and lit a pre-rolled cigarette. He had said subtle.

"So what have you got for me, Craig?"

"I talked to some friends . . ."

Beamon stopped in mid-drag and raised his eyebrows.

The young man held his hands out. "Subtly. I talked to them subtly. TarroSoft is a holding company—they don't actually produce software themselves. They own BiblioNet and apparently do software design work for the telecommunications industry. Mostly for a company called Vericomm."

"Vericomm I've heard of, but what's BiblioNet?"

"You know, the company that created the software for the national interlibrary loan system?"

Beamon looked at him blankly.

"You know. Have you ever tried to check out a library book and they didn't have it, so they ordered it from another library?"

"Yeah, I guess."

"That's the interlibrary loan system. It used to be state by state, but now it's nationwide. BiblioNet created the software for the system and now they manage it under a government contract."

Beamon took another deep drag on his cigarette and blew the smoke out through a thin smile, appreciating the irony of Skinner's report. The FBI had tried for years to get the right to track what books people were buying and checking out. There was a pretty strong argument that keeping tabs on books

STORMING HEAVEN — 303

relating to poisoning, bombs, murder, and so on could be a powerful tool in the right hands.

Unfortunately, there was just no way that kind of a Big Brother tactic was going to fly in the U.S. of A. Not for a government agency, anyway. But what about a private organization? Chet Michaels had received his NickeLine solicitation about a week after Beamon had sent him crawling through the local libraries looking for information on the church. He'd assumed that Michaels had simply run into an astute Kneissian librarian. He took another drag on his cigarette. It was that kind of small thinking that was going to make Jennifer Davis dead.

"I can probably get more, if you need it," Skinner continued. "But I won't be able to be as quiet about it . . . I don't need any more trouble from Layman, Mark. I don't know if you noticed, but I don't really fit in at the Bureau. You're, like, my only ally."

"No, that's what I needed, Craig. Thanks." Beamon tossed a few bills on the table for Skinner's drink and slid out of the booth.

"What about the names I asked you to run against that database?"

"All positive but one."

"Okay, thanks. I'll see you at the office tomorrow."

Beamon walked through a door next to the bar and into the attached liquor store. He grabbed a twelve-pack of Pabst Blue Ribbon out of the cooler, then walked along the rack of red wine against the wall. He examined a few labels, but they meant nothing to him. Finally, he decided to follow the theory of "you get what you pay for." He pulled the most expensive bottle out of the rack and took a place in line behind a man in a tall cowboy hat who

304 — KYLE MILLS

was making a less than persuasive argument about the Communists' and Democrats' involvement in raising the price of chewing tobacco. Losing interest in the debate, Beamon let his mind wander back to Sara Renslier and her church.

He'd underestimated her, he knew now. He'd read Ernie's book and talked to Volker at the German Embassy, but in the back of his mind he'd considered both of their reports a bit suspect. Some people just had conspiracy on the brain—anyone who'd been with the Bureau for as long as him knew that. How many times had he been surrounded at a party by people wanting the inside scoop on the space aliens that had really killed Kennedy or the CIA/KGB team that had developed the AIDS virus?

But now here he was, tilting at an organization with millions of followers and a yearly income that would give it a respectable position on the Fortune 500 if it were a corporation. They were watching what people read and—though he hadn't gotten Goldman's confirmation yet—they were probably listening in on the long-distance phone conversations of some of the country's most influential people. And then there was the small matter of that group of ex-military nutcases fanatical enough to weld bracelets to their wrists.

Beamon pulled his credit card from his wallet and laid the beer and wine on the counter as the cowboy walked away, still grumbling.

"How are you today, Mr. Beamon?" the man at the register said.

"I've been better, Barry. You?" He was in this store regularly enough to have become a favored customer. He would probably put braces on Barry's kids' teeth before he got transferred out or canned.

"I'm good, Mr. Beamon. Thanks for asking."

"The kids?"

Barry frowned and ran Beamon's credit card through the machine again. "They're good, too. Taking them to their mother's house for the weekend."

The skin above Barry's nose creased as he looked down at the little black keypad next to the cash register.

"Problem?" Beamon said.

"It doesn't seem to want to accept your card. Could you be maxed out?"

Beamon shook his head and handed the man his other card, though he didn't have much hope for it.

"How you doing on that little Jennifer Davis girl?" Barry asked as the machine decided how it felt about Beamon's second credit card.

"Working on it. See what happens."

The man nodded knowingly and looked down at the keypad again, obviously a little embarrassed. "It doesn't like this one either, Mr. Beamon. There must be something wrong with the machine. Let me put it on your account."

Beamon took a deep breath and let it out slowly. "Thanks, Barry. And while you're at it, could you throw in a carton of Marlboros?"

"I thought you rolled your own," he said, pulling down the carton and laying it on top of the beers.

"Oh, I did. But I think I might be needing them faster than I can roll 'em for a while."

Beamon sat in his car and ceremoniously bent his credit cards back and forth until the pieces littered the floorboard. He stared at the brightly colored shards of plastic lying at his feet and thought about what they represented.

What could the church hope to gain by getting their lackeys to screw with the credit of an FBI executive? In the long run, nothing but trouble. So why expose themselves and their tactics so blatantly? He could only come up with one answer—that he was right about their plans for Jennifer.

They just needed to distract him for the next two weeks. At the end of that time, when Jennifer's body was being used to help prop up one of their new cathedrals, the church would use its money and influence to silence any report of their attacks on him. At worst they would make a quiet statement apologizing for their overzealous members' treatment of him, knowing full well that at that point he wouldn't have a prayer of connecting them to Jennifer or her parents.

37

BEAMON STOOD OUTSIDE THE DOOR OF HIS condo and gently twisted the doorknob again. He vividly remembered locking it when he'd left that morning and now there it was, unlocked.

He looked over his shoulder at the front windows of the condo occupied by the guardian angel the church had so thoughtfully provided him. As usual, it was dark. There was just enough light reflecting off the snow, though, to see that the curtain was propped back enough for someone to see out. He could almost feel the crosshairs tickling his forehead.

Beamon pulled his gun from its holster and slipped into his living room as quietly as the ice-encrusted door would allow. The battalions of well-armed Holy Rollers that he expected to find weren't there. The room was empty.

As he worked his way across the living room, he noticed a strange hum coming from his bedroom and froze. The sound was undoubtedly mechanical in origin. Some kind of a booby trap?

He considered backing his way out of the condo and calling for backup, but decided against it. What if it was nothing? He didn't need to give Layman any more ammunition regarding his alleged paranoia.

He paused for a moment with his back a couple of inches from the wall next to the door to his bed-

308 — KYLE MILLS

room and then spun smoothly into the opening.

The man standing by his bed didn't seem to notice Beamon's arrival and continued examining pieces of his disassembled phone, looking up at the screen of an open laptop computer every few seconds.

"You're clear here, Mark," the man said as Beamon holstered his sidearm.

He hadn't laid eyes on Jack Goldman in more than five years. The decade hadn't been kind to the old man. His white hair had thinned considerably, revealing wrinkles across his scalp that made it look like it was a size too big for his skull. The thickness of his glasses seemed to have more than doubled and now looked too heavy to be propped up by the gnarled nose beneath them. The lenses distorted light so badly that the middle of Goldman's head seemed to flow like liquid when he moved.

"Mr. Goldman," Beamon groaned. "What're you doing here?"

The old man turned away and began collecting the parts of the phone scattered across the bed. "What the hell's it look like I'm doing, boy? I'm sweeping your house. And I'd thank you to use a more grateful tone with me. I normally charge two thousand dollars." He paused. "Plus expenses."

The phone was about ninety percent reassembled when it started to ring, but Goldman was having trouble timing the tremors in his hands efficiently enough to plug the cord back in. Beamon walked over to him and tried to offer a hand, but was stopped short when Goldman grabbed his cane and hit him across the shins with it.

"Jesus Christ," Beamon howled, bending over and grabbing the leg that had taken the brunt of the impact. "What the hell did you do that for?"

"Don't think I can put a phone back together? I've been taking phones apart and putting them back together since . . ."

Beamon hobbled back out into the living room and out of range of Goldman's voice in time to grab the phone in the kitchen. "Yeah, hello," he said, sitting down on a stool and continuing to rub his shin.

"Is this Mark Beamon?" The voice was lightly accented. "This is Hans Volker at the German Embassy."

"Hans! An unexpected pleasure. How are you?"

"Mark. Thank God. I'm fine, but how are you? I've been hearing some very disturbing things."

"I've been getting a lot of that lately. What exactly are you hearing?"

Volker's voice was a bit hesitant. "I have to have your word that what I'm about to tell you is just between us, Mark."

"Sure, Hans. Just between us."

"We have a few well-placed . . . informants inside the Church of the Evolution. You suspected as much, I'm sure, but you can see how this kind of, uh, monitoring, if it became public, could be very embarrassing to us."

"Like I said, Hans. Just between us."

"Your investigation of the church is generating quite a lot of interest, Mark. Quite a lot. My sources tell me that the church is convinced that you believe they're involved in the kidnapping of Jennifer Davis. They are very concerned about this, and about your continued efforts to penetrate the outer layers of their organization."

Beamon grunted into the phone. He wasn't

happy about how public this all seemed to be getting, but there wasn't a hell of a lot he could do about it now.

"Frankly, Mark, I'm becoming concerned about your safety."

"How so? "

Volker cleared his throat nervously. "The church has a significant number of weapons in its arsenal to deter this kind of inquiry. They've made quite an art of keeping their business private. But you probably already know that."

"Sticks and stones, Hans."

"It goes further than that, Mark. It's come to our attention that the church may have formed a security force that could be used for violence against people who aren't persuaded by their normal methods."

"Are you sure about that?"

"I'm not," Volker admitted. "It's hearsay, really. I'm concerned that if they've already guessed that you won't succumb to their normal techniques, and if this group actually exists, you could be in physical danger."

Beamon walked over to the refrigerator and pulled out a beer. "I appreciate the warning, Hans. Believe me, I'm doing everything I can to protect myself . . ."

"One more thing, Mark. I believe you know a man named Jacob Layman?"

"He's my boss. The SAC Phoenix."

"There's some very circumstantial evidence that the church may have influenced Mr. Layman's appointment to that position."

Beamon gave the beer bottle's cap a hard twist and tossed it in the sink. He'd already considered that possibility. Layman had final authority over the office covering the Kneissians' back yard. And it was Layman who was so desperately against the investigation into the church.

"I appreciate the heads-up, Hans. Anything else you can tell me?" Beamon said, watching the stooped form of his latest problem as it hobbled into the living room.

"To get out of town for a while?"

"Can't do that."

"Well, then I'll tell you to be careful. And that I'll do whatever I can for you. Do you still have my number?"

"I keep it right here, close to my heart."

"Good luck, Mark."

Beamon caught him before he hung up. "Hey! Hans!"

"Yes?"

"Answer a question for me. What long-distance service do you use?"

There was a pause over the phone. "Um, AT&T, I think. I'm honestly not sure."

"So you just pick up the phone and dial—no codes or anything."

"I just pick up the phone and dial. Why do you ask?"

"Just something I've been working on. Nothing important. Thanks again, Hans."

Beamon hung up the phone and chewed at his lower lip. This was going to get ugly. He could feel it coming.

"What's with the cane, Mr. Goldman? You actually need it or is it just a weapon?"

"Sprained my ankle skydiving," the old man grumbled.

Beamon laughed. As best as he could remember, he'd never heard Goldman say something funny. At least not on purpose.

"What're you laughing about, boy?"

Beamon looked down at the old man's ankle and then at his cold expression. "You're serious? What the hell were you doing skydiving?"

Goldman shrugged, causing the hump growing between his shoulders to rise and fall. "Never did it before. It was stupid, though."

"Stupid?"

"They jump right on either side of you," Goldman said in a disgusted tone. "Don't let you make your own decisions."

"When to pull the cord?"

Goldman shook his head. "I just turned ninety, Mark. It's whether to pull the cord now."

Beamon almost laughed again, but something told him that the old man was serious. He decided to change the subject. "What'd you come up with on Vericomm?"

"Is that the long-distance company you were asking about? Never heard of them."

"It's a holding company. They're called Nicke-LineAZ around here."

Goldman hobbled over to the sofa and leaned against the arm. "Okay, sure. They're NickeLineNY in New York."

"Do you use them?" Beamon asked. He'd never really considered it, but Goldman—the top man in corporate eavesdropping countermeasures—would be an obvious target.

"I get offers every now and again, but I ain't never found a good reason to actually *pay* for long-distance service."

"So have you had time to research my question? Is it possible?"

"For a small carrier to listen in on long distance? Probably not for a standard company. They rent phone lines from the big boys, like AT&T, but calls just go through whatever line is available at the time. But the kind of company you describe is IP based—IP stands for Internet Protocol. That type of system compresses analog signals and routes them through the Internet. It'd be expensive and hardware-intensive as all hell, but a company like that *could* listen in on calls."

Beamon remembered the devastating losses taken by NickeLine and the fact that they owned far more equipment than they should. It looked like he was right again, but he was having a hard time getting his arm around exactly what that meant.

What did Sara know? Goddamn near everything about everything, he guessed. And another interesting question—who could he trust? Even if Jake Layman wasn't a Kneissian, what had he said over a long-distance line that they could use to persuade him of the righteousness of Kneiss's God? He *was* starting to get a clearer picture of the Church's vaunted investment record, though. Half the corporate executives in the U.S. were probably NickeLine patrons.

Beamon looked down at the old man and took another pull from the beer bottle. What was he going to do with him? Trying to cut loose from him was pointless. Jack Goldman did whatever the hell he wanted. And right now, he wanted to be involved in this case.

"Who we after, anyway?" Goldman said.

Beamon figured there was no way he was going to get rid of him, so he might as well make the best of it. He really *was* the best in the world. "The Church of the Evolution, Mr. Goldman. I think they're involved in the Jennifer Davis kidnapping."

"The Kneissians? Those goddamn weirdos? Christ. I say we return the favor."

"The favor?" Beamon said.

"I'll show those assholes a thing or two about bugging phones. We'll be able to hear 'em taking a dump when I get through with 'em."

Beamon held his hand up. "There's no way I'm going to get a court order for a tap, Mr. Goldman. So we're gonna have to forget that."

"Court order? What the hell's wrong with you? Show a little initiative."

There was a knock at the door, and Beamon slid off the stool and started across the living room. "I'm still an FBI agent, sir. No illegal wiretaps."

Beamon started opening the door but stopped halfway and squeezed through the opening. "Carrie!" he said loudly, trying to drown out Goldman's voice.

"If Hoover was still alive, I'd have wires so far up those guys' asses, they'd chip a tooth on 'em when they ate!"

"How are you?"

She looked at the door. "What was that?"

"What? Oh, my uncle. He's up for a visit. A brief visit. He's a little crazy—excuse me, I didn't mean to say 'crazy.' Older'n God, you know? Worked on the construction of the Roman aqueducts."

She smiled. Beautifully. "Can I meet him?"

Beamon shook his head a little too violently.

"Not decent. Never wears pants. Something about letting his legs breathe."

She smirked and took one last suspicious look at the door. "I haven't seen you since we had dinner. Are you avoiding me?"

"No," Beamon said firmly. "I am definitely not avoiding you. In fact, I was planning on coming over to see you tonight, but . . ." He thumbed at the door. "Hadn't really expected company."

He reached behind him for the knob. "I'm going to take Uncle Jack to where he's staying and then I'll be back. You'll be up for a few hours, won't you?"

"He's not staying with you?"

"Uh, doesn't want to. Hates my place. And he's not really that crazy about me, either."

She turned and began walking toward the stairs. "If it's past eight, don't ring the bell. Emory'll be asleep."

38

THAT HAD BEEN UNPLEASANT.

For a few minutes there, Beamon had thought
he was going to have to pry those bony old fingers
off his sofa with a crowbar. But if it had come to
that, he would have. He had enough problems
without that crotchety old SOB limping around his
apartment. There was just so much he could take.

Goldman had given him the silent treatment
through their entire search for an apartment complex that offered furnished units by the day. He
hadn't spoken a single word when Beamon had
lugged his equipment into the dingy interior of the
only place they could find. Goldman had barely
perked up when Beamon, overwhelmed by guilt,
had invited him to be in on his meeting with Ernie
Waverly tomorrow.

Beamon hung his parka next to the door and
walked across the living room to his answering
machine. He grabbed the bottle of wine he'd purchased earlier that evening while the tape rewound.

"Mr. Beamon. This is Terry Bland calling from
the Oklahoma office." The hiss of the tape couldn't
disguise the nervousness in Bland's voice. "I
checked on that flight plan to Turkey again like
you asked. There is, I repeat, *is* a record of that
flight plan being filed last month—for January

fifteenth . . . I'm really sorry, Mr. Beamon. I don't know how we made that error. Normally we get it right the first time. Let me know if you need anything else . . . Again, I apologize for the error and hope it doesn't cause you any problems."

Beamon made a mental note to call that kid when all this was over and tell him it wasn't his fault.

The machine beeped loudly and a somewhat garbled voice faded in. "Mark! Ken Hirayami here. I don't know how you called it, but you were right, goddamn you. There *is* a record of Albert Kneiss's visa in Turkey. He arrived January sixteenth and is apparently still there. I'll send you your fifty goddamn bucks when you call me and tell me what's going on. I've got some Turkish friends who would love to know how you found a glitch in what they thought was a pretty good system."

Beamon sighed loudly and headed for the front door, bottle of wine tucked securely under his arm. In forty-eight hours, the church was two for two on Kneiss's imaginary trip to Turkey. Beamon had hoped they wouldn't have the juice to falsify the records at all, but had reasonably expected they'd get to the FAA and fail in Turkey. The arms of the church seemed to be looking longer and longer, he reflected as he walked down the stairs outside his condo and rapped quietly on Carrie Johnstone's door.

She opened it a crack and then slipped outside. "Emory fell asleep on the couch," she explained.

Beamon handed her the wine, and she looked at the label with an expression somewhere between gratitude and surprise. Obviously, she'd expected less from a Pabst Blue Ribbon drinker.

"How about Tuesday?" Beamon said, realizing

that the question didn't make much sense after it had already escaped from his mouth.

"Tuesday, what?"

"Dinner. I thought we could go out."

Beamon felt the knot in his stomach, started by his theory on Jennifer Davis's impending doom, tighten at the thought of his dinner with Carrie. He had to distance himself from her until he got this church thing straightened out—there was just no other way. The tough part was doing it without: A) making it sound like a blowoff, B) making it sound like he was the kind of guy who couldn't commit to a goldfish, or C) making it seem that FBI agents were just too much trouble to seriously consider having a relationship with.

"Sounds great. Pick me up at seven." She leaned forward and kissed him lightly on the mouth, then disappeared back into her apartment.

Beamon stood there for a moment, stunned by the kiss. The clean, vaguely tropical scent of her hair still hung in the air, cinching down the knot a little tighter.

He cursed the church under his breath for their timing as he started back to his apartment. Couldn't Kneiss have done his messiah act and died last year? Before he'd moved in above the most spectacular woman he'd ever met?

Spectacular or not, though, he had to figure out a way to get rid of her for a while and hope she'd come back to him when all this was over. That is, if Sara Renslier saw fit to leave anything for her to come back to.

39

MAKING IT LOOK LIKE AN ACCIDENT when he dropped the church's tails was getting more and more complicated. The blue Taurus had been a little more tenacious today, forcing Beamon into a combination car wash/playacted road rage scenario that probably looked pretty thin.

He slowed a bit as he passed Ernestine Waverly's house, noting the unfamiliar car parked in the driveway, and then eased to a stop against the curb about a block away.

The muffled shouting from inside her house was audible by the time Beamon made it halfway up the walk. He slid his hand around the handle of his revolver and put his ear against the door.

"Don't do it, for Christ's sake! Put that pizza down!"

"You have no right to judge me! That's for God to do."

"A few more slices and He's going to be the only one that's going to be able to haul your ass out of that chair!"

Beamon peeled his ear off the door and opened it. The car in the driveway and the voice inside belonged to Jack Goldman. He'd apparently arrived early—before Beamon had had a chance to prepare Ernie for his colorful disposition.

"Decided to sleep in? Whole morning's gone," Goldman said as Beamon walked into the cluttered room.

Ernie glared at Goldman as he struggled over to a small table and leaned against it, breathing sporadically. She looked like she was trying to stroke him out by sheer force of will as she tore into a piece of cold pizza with spiteful abandon.

"Morning, Ernie," Beamon said. "Am I in time for breakfast?

"Don't encourage her, Mark," Goldman croaked.

"You be quiet," Ernie shot back through a half-full mouth of pizza.

This was just perfect. He was up against an organization with millions of fanatical followers, nearly unlimited capital, and apparently unparalleled information-gathering capabilities. Even with the FBI behind him, he'd probably lose this one. But he didn't have the FBI behind him. What he had was a man who had probably bought a Model T new from the showroom and a morbidly obese shut-in who thought he was some kind of avenging angel.

Ernie shoved the rest of the pizza into her mouth with a final Herculean push and reached over to pull a piece of paper from under her keyboard. She wadded it up and threw it at Beamon. Hard. "That's what you asked for. I ran the church's old membership list against every database I could find."

"Hmmff," Goldman let out as Beamon unraveled the paper. He ignored the old man and ran a finger down the list of names. It was about what he'd expected. The presidents of two mortgage companies—one of which was probably getting ready to foreclose on his condo—the head of a medium-sized health/life insurance company, the heads of Vericomm and its sister company, Verinet. On the political side, three senators—one of whom chaired Ways and Means—and eleven representatives, not to mention more than a handful of high-level bureaucrats. Interestingly, though, no credit card companies. Of course, any lowly clerk probably had the juice to completely unravel his credit for all time.

"You done screwing around yet?" Goldman said.

"Look, *Jack*," Ernie said. "Mark is looking at the information *I* got for him. Maybe you should be quiet for once."

Goldman glared back at her and pulled a stack of papers out of a briefcase that looked as old as he was. He caned his way across the room and spread them out on the table next to Beamon. They seemed to consist of wiring schematics and maps, though Beamon could only guess at their significance.

"The church's compound, where that Kneiss guy lives, is here," Goldman said, jabbing a gnarled finger at a colorful map. "They've got eight phone lines running out to an aboveground pedestal, here." He flipped to a wiring schematic. "And then into a cross-connect box about a mile away. We can hit 'em at the box. There are four lines coming into Ernie's house, so we can terminate the taps here— use cell phone service. Then we can run a redundant site into the apartment I'm staying in. I've got three additional lines being installed this afternoon."

"Where the hell do you get this stuff, Mr. Goldman?" Beamon said, shaking his head. "You just got here yesterday, for God's sake."

"You don't think I have contacts?"

Beamon rolled up the maps and handed them back to Goldman. "Contacts or not. I may not have the support of my organization, but I'm still an FBI agent. No illegal wiretaps. That's the final word."

"Jesus Christ, boy! You know what you're up against here? They aren't playing by your rules—"

Ernie cut off his tirade before it gained too much momentum. "As much as I hate to say it, Mark, he's right. God doesn't follow man's law. We have to ask ourselves what He wants of us. The Lord gave us the ability to see beyond black and white."

Beamon leaned his head forward and rubbed his temples. "Ernie, darlin', you've got to give me a break on the religious stuff. I'm just an FBI agent, not Martin Luther."

Goldman looked smug. "Well, for whatever the reason, I'd say it's two against one."

Beamon looked up at him. "Fortunately, my decision is the only one that counts."

40

JENNIFER DAVIS LAY MOTIONLESS ON THE COLD floor with her heels resting on the bed that had become the focus of her life over the past month. The burning in her stomach had just about subsided, so she lifted her back up off the floor and began a second set of situps.

After forty repetitions, her muscles felt like they'd caught fire, but she just pushed herself harder, trying to burn her anger, loneliness, and fear in the flame spreading across her abdomen. After fifty-five, the fuel for the fire was gone and she struggled to her feet and walked over to the remains of her breakfast lying on a plastic tray by the door.

She took the spoon off the plate and turned it over and over again in her fingers. Always a spoon now. The knife and fork had never reappeared since the day she had been taken to see her grandfather's body. That pale bitch Sara must think she was going to kill herself and rob her of the pleasure.

Jennifer stuffed the spoon in the waistband of her underpants and lifted the heavy bed away from the wall. Using the end of the utensil, she scraped a small line in the plaster next to a group of similar lines. March 15. She moved the bed back, trying to force herself not to calculate how much time she had left. She was unsuccessful, though, just like she was every morning. Twelve days, her mind told her as she dropped the spoon back onto the tray. The metallic clang seemed to echo through the room before being swallowed up by the silence that had swallowed her up. Two weeks.

"It doesn't matter," she said aloud.

She was going to get out of here. She'd done the hardest part, gotten control of her fear and managed to turn her loneliness and the memory of her parents' death into a fierce sense of self-reliance. She'd figure out a way to get out of here. She had to.

And when she finally did escape, she *would* have a place to go. Sara wanted her to think she was alone, but she wasn't. Jamie and his mother would take her in until it was time for her to go to college. With the money her parents must have left her, she could buy them a new house. Mrs. Rodrigues didn't deserve to be stuck in that horrible trailer park.

The key hitting the lock startled her, as it always did, but she managed to fight the urge to back against the wall, instead standing in the middle of the room and facing the door defiantly.

Sara came in alone, but Jennifer could see the man who always accompanied her as he took a position outside the door. She'd never get past him. She had to think of another way.

"The elders would like to see you again, Jennifer," Sara said, stopping a few feet away from where she stood. "You're very important to them now."

Jennifer struggled to control her rage. She couldn't tear her eyes away from the woman's throat and couldn't stop wondering if she could choke the life out of her before Mustache Man made it through the door and dragged her off.

"You tricked them. They don't know what my grandfather really wanted," Jennifer said.

Sara made a move toward her but then stopped when Jennifer didn't shrink away. The woman glanced behind her at the open door, confirming her companion's presence, and then turned back. "Think, Jennifer. If you do, I think you'll remember things differently. You'll understand what you are and what you'll become."

"You're a liar," Jennifer said. "He gave the church to me. He wanted *me* to have it."

Sara smiled. "There's nothing you can do to stop this, Jennifer, it's God's will. Deep down you know that's true, don't you? Your parents believed—enough to die for you."

"It's not true!" Jennifer said. Sara was just trying to confuse her.

An expression of anger crossed Sara's face and then disappeared. "I thought you might like to leave this room one more time. But now I see that it's impossible." She walked out into the hallway and began pulling the door closed behind her. "Good-bye, Jennifer."

"No! Wait!" Jennifer heard herself say. But Sara was gone.

She stood alone in the middle of the room for a long time, quivering with rage and frustration. She had to get out. In less than two weeks they were going to kill her. This wasn't a game—it was real. She fell onto the bed and pulled her knees to her chest, feeling the tears well up in her eyes for the first time in a week.

She stared at the heavy wood door for a long time and thought back over the month she'd been there. There wasn't any reason for them to let her out again. And even if they did, what could she do? The strength and will she'd managed to piece together over the last few weeks wouldn't do anything against the Mustache Man.

She was lying to herself. They would never let her escape. In twelve days Sara and the Mustache Man would come through the door for the last time. She'd struggle uselessly as they plunged the syringe into her. And that would be the end.

41

A HUNDRED AND FIFTY MILES BETWEEN THEIR offices and he just couldn't keep that man's ass out of his chair.

Beamon looked through the window to his office at Jake Layman, who was, once again, flipping though the paperwork he'd found on Beamon's desk. He didn't look as angry as he had the last time Beamon had seen him, but he wasn't sure if that was good or bad.

"Morning, Jake," Beamon said, opting to skip the trip to the coffee pot in an effort to get Layman back on the road ASAP. "To what do I owe this visit?"

Layman looked almost happy as he slid a two-page fax across the desk.

It was copied from a newspaper article, Beamon saw when he picked it up. The headline, in bold capital letters, read: MARK BEAMON—FIT FOR DUTY?

"I have a friend at the *Chronicle*," Layman explained. "He was courteous enough to send this to me before it hits the paper tomorrow."

Beamon scanned the article, hoping that the headline was just a teaser and that the rest would get better.

It didn't. The focus of the piece seemed to be his drinking habits and was heavily slanted toward the negative. It failed to mention his uncanny convic-

Beamon almost managed a bitter smile as he remembered piecing the Hose together out of an old cooler and a bilge pump during exams his junior year. It had been a simple yet inspired device. You filled the cooler to the top with beer from a keg, stuck the hose emanating from the front into your mouth, and pushed the doorbell on the side. The bilge pump would fire up, a siren on top would start, and, well, you'd get filled full of beer in about a second and a half. As far as he knew, the original Hop Hose was still enshrined in a specially constructed glass case at his old fraternity house.

The article moved on to outline his inauspicious first meeting with the born-again director of the FBI, which, in hindsight, probably *had* involved about ten ounces too much bourbon and about a pound too much sarcasm.

The rest was more mundane, but equally damaging. Anonymous, but despicably accurate, stories of late-night party excesses and bloodshot mornings. It concluded with the same tired old crap about the vaunted FBI old-boy network protecting his "secret," yada, yada, yada.

Beamon threw the fax back onto the desk. "Interesting timing."

"Excuse me?"

"Nothing."

Beamon sat silently, eyes locked on Layman, waiting to hear exactly what his boss was planning to do about this unfortunate little essay. He didn't have to wait long.

"I've tried to protect you, Mark. But I just can't anymore."

Beamon would have liked to know exactly how Layman had tried to protect him, but decided this probably wasn't the time to ask.

"What they don't have here, thank God," Layman said, stabbing a finger at the fax, "is the report that you'd been drinking when you examined the scene of the Jennifer Davis kidnapping, and the fact that you were drunk when your primary suspect was somehow killed."

Beamon couldn't seem to work up anything that felt even remotely like anger. He just felt tired. He should have seen this coming, and now he was getting exactly what he deserved for not staying awake. "Come on, Jake. I had a few beers while we were playing golf—you were there, for God's sake."

Layman opened his arms and shrugged. "I wasn't watching. I have no idea how much you drank that day. But I do have a report from two cops who were at the scene that you smelled like a brewery when you arrived."

Beamon seriously doubted that, since, as he recalled, he had about six pieces of gum in his mouth by the time he got out of the car. "I don't suppose it matters that David Passal fell down a ladder while I was twenty miles away, trying to mend some fences with the local cops . . ." He let his voice trail off. Of course it didn't matter. He could see from his boss's expression that he was wasting his breath. No point in making this any more fun for Layman than it had to be. "Okay, Jake. Cut to the chase. What's this to me?"

"I spoke at length with the director this morning."

Beamon closed his eyes and took a deep breath. That couldn't be good.

"We went over the issues I just spoke about, and your recent lapses in judgment . . ."

"Lapses in judgment?" Beamon said, opening his eyes.

"Your investigation of the Church of the Evolution. The fact that you've become obsessed with the Kneissians and that you've ignored my repeated attempts to put you back on track."

"Come on, Jake, you weren't even keeping up with the facts of the case. Who are you to question my investigative judgment?"

Layman just smiled calmly. "I'm your boss, Mark. Maybe if you could remember that, you wouldn't be in the position you're in today."

Beamon grabbed the fax and held it up. "Hasn't it occurred to you that this is pretty typical for the church? They probably own the fucking *Flagstaff Chronicle*."

"Typical? Are you talking about the organization that's built hospitals and schools all over Arizona, and feeds the homeless during the holidays? The organization that gives hundreds of millions of dollars to charity every year? This is what I'm talking about, Mark. You've become paranoid. And we think it's from the drinking."

He leaned back in Beamon's chair and began picking at one of his nails. "You're a competent agent, Mark, and we don't want to lose you. Whatever help you need, you're going to get. You might even be able to come back from this if you really focus on getting your problems ironed out."

Beamon looked up at the ceiling and took a deep breath, fighting to keep some kind of emotional distance between himself and what was happening.

"You're being put on immediate paid leave until we can get this straightened out."

Portraying as much outward calm as he could, Beamon reached into his pocket and pulled out his FBI credentials. To Layman's credit, he was almost successful in suppressing his smile when Beamon handed them over.

"We've scheduled a physical for you on March twenty-fifth. You're to report to headquarters on that date. Any questions?"

Beamon managed to push his suspension and the irreparable damage that was going to be done to his reputation tomorrow to an unused corner of his mind. Sara Renslier was going to find that he wasn't as easily handled as some others.

"What long-distance carrier do you use?"

Layman looked at him strangely and shook his head as he walked around the desk to leave. Beamon grabbed his arm. "You asked if I had any questions. That's my question. What long-distance carrier do you use?"

"What the hell are you talking about, Mark? Are you drunk now?" Layman said, trying to pull free. Beamon squeezed harder, sinking his fingers into the flesh of Layman's forearm.

"I don't know," Layman said finally. "You dial a code. It's five cents a minute."

"Mark, have you seen this?" Chet Michaels said, running into the office without his customary nervous pause at the door. "A friend of mine just sent it to me." He slapped a bad fax copy of the offending article on the desk.

Beamon nodded and continued picking through his drawers, occasionally dropping an item or two into the box at his feet. He hadn't been there long enough to accumulate much junk. Usually this operation took days.

"It's the church, isn't it? What do you want to bet the guy who wrote that article is a member?"

Beamon shrugged.

"So what are we going to do about it?"

Beamon looked up from the drawer and into the innocent face of Chet Michaels. "Nothing. I've been suspended. It's over."

"Suspended? No way! They can't do that! You're the best we've got. Everybody knows that."

"Thanks, Chet. I appreciate that. I really do," Beamon said, standing and pulling his coat off the back of his chair. "I guess I'll see you around."

"Come on, Mark, you know the church is involved. We can't give up now."

"Finding Jennifer isn't my job anymore, Chet. And it's not yours, either—Layman's going to take this one."

"But he won't—"

"Chet! Let it go. There'll be other cases. If you don't screw up here, you'll still be around to solve them."

"It's not just a case, Mark. Have you forgotten Jennifer? What about her?"

Beamon shrugged and picked the box up off the floor. "What about her? Wake up, Chet. I'm just in this for the game. And I lost."

42

BEAMON PINNED THE BOX FULL OF HIS PER-
sonal effects against the wall and struggled to get
his keys out of his pocket. He glanced back over his
shoulder at the condo inhabited by Robert Andrews,
his church-appointed spy. The window looked the
same as it always did, curtains pulled to within a
couple of inches of being fully closed, interior dark.

There *was* one change worth noting, however.
Andrews was standing on the walkway that ran
along the front of his building, leaning casually
against the railing and staring right at him.

Beamon was too far away to read the man's
expression, but his stance spoke volumes. The
church was letting him know that they were responsible for his current situation. That they had filed
down his teeth to the point that they didn't even
need to hide their presence anymore.

Beamon turned his key in the lock and threw
the door open, sending a shower of snow and ice
onto his carpet when it slammed against the wall.
He dropped the box on top of the Davis case files
covering his sofa and pulled an unopened bottle of
bourbon from the top of it.

The familiar weight of it wasn't as comforting as
he thought it would be, but he still pulled what was
left of his beer stash from his refrigerator and

dumped it ceremoniously into the trash.

He grabbed the carton of cigarettes lying on the counter and dropped into a chair, unscrewing the top of the bottle with one hand and punching the remote next to him with the other. The church's channel came to life on the screen with a young woman professing how Kneiss's bible had changed her life. He lit the first of what he hoped would be many cigarettes and watched the smoke curl through the virgin air of his condo.

It had changed his life, too.

He'd always pushed the envelope at work and it had hurt him—personally and professionally. But that had been his choice—to never move very far up in the ranks, to work for men and women whose abilities were inferior to his, to be bounced around from office to office, state to state.

He'd managed to find a delicate but generally durable balance between his often self-destructive impulses and his ability to get the job done faster and more efficiently than anyone else. It was that balance that had allowed him to keep his job. And it was that balance that Sara Renslier had managed to disrupt.

She'd done a hell of a job, too. Not only was he most likely facing early retirement, but he was going to leave the Bureau under a black cloud that would follow him for the rest of his life. It seemed reasonable to expect that the lucrative private-sector job he'd need to feed himself in retirement wouldn't be forthcoming.

"You want fries with that?" he said to the empty room, raising his glass in salute to nothing in particular. Never too early to start training for a new career.

His thoughts turned to Jennifer Davis as he took his first slug of bourbon since arriving in Arizona. He was dead sure now that the theory that had seemed so farfetched to him at first was correct. Sara Renslier was not going to allow a fifteen-year-old orphan to take her church from her, to strip her of the power that she had spent twenty-five years acquiring and seemed to wield so effortlessly. And if he accepted that fact, then Jennifer had a real problem. Either she was already dead—the granddaddy of all problems, and one historically difficult to fix—or Sara had managed to convince the Elders of the church that Jennifer was the next Messenger. If that was the case, she was going to get rid of the kid in some kind of bullshit religious ceremony that would assure Sara continued control over the church for life.

Beamon downed another slug, feeling the alcohol begin to work its way into his mind. The beer-only diet he'd been adhering to seemed to have wreaked havoc on his tolerance. But then, it was probably good to be a cheap drunk when your career prospects were looking this bleak.

He decided that if Jennifer was already dead, the church would have stuffed her body in a chuckhole somewhere in Outer Mongolia by now and Sara would be making a real show of cooperating with him, knowing that without a body, he couldn't do shit.

But she wasn't cooperating. She was aiming the church's entire arsenal at him—a senior FBI man—and in doing that, taking a hell of a risk. No, they were playing for time. He looked at the calendar on his watch. Eleven more days.

And that brought up another interesting, but ultimately depressing point. When Good Friday—

and Jennifer—had come and gone, Sara sure as hell wasn't going to wait around for him to gather his notes and write a book. No, once that little girl's body was safely stowed, it would be time for him to slip on the ice and crack his skull or to have some equally mundane, yet fatal, accident.

There was a knock at the door, but Beamon ignored it and worked on the solution to his problem. How the hell was he going to find Jennifer in the next eleven days? He took another gulp from his glass and felt the liquid burn down to his stomach, then reverse its course and go straight to his head.

His front door opened a crack, creating a bright swath of light that illuminated the curling smoke drifting through the gloom.

"Mark?" Carrie's reddish-brown head snaked into the room. "There you are. Why didn't you answer?"

Beamon lit another cigarette with the embers of the old one. "What're you doing home in the middle of the day, Carrie?"

He turned back to the TV as Carrie closed the door quietly behind her. A well-dressed young man was asking for donations to buy food for the starving children from one of those starving-children countries.

"Chet called me and told me what happened. He's really worried about you, Mark."

Beamon let his head loll back on the chair as he remembered the look on Michaels's face when he'd left him standing in his office. What he'd said to him about only being in it for the game had been pretty harsh, but what choice did he have? The kid was too damned ready to get dragged down with him.

"Are you all right?"

"It's not as grim as it sounds, Carrie," he lied. "Just politics, you know."

She moved the box containing most of his life and sat down on the arm of the sofa. "Switching from beer to liquor isn't going to help your case any," she said, nodding toward the bottle in his hand.

He laughed bitterly. "My strict program of self-improvement doesn't seem to have done a whole hell of a lot of good. I figure, why close the gate after the horse has bolted?"

She was silent for a moment and then said, "You didn't answer my question."

"I don't remember you asking one."

"Are you *all right*?"

"Sure. I'm fine. Things like this happen."

She looked at him compassionately. "You've never married, have you, Mark?"

"Excuse me?"

"Married. You never married. Why?"

Beamon shrugged, wondering if that was kind of a bizarre change of subject or if he was just more buzzed than he thought. "I guess I never found the right woman. I've had a career that's pretty much been one crisis after the other. There just hasn't been much time."

"You've given a lot to the Bureau. What is it now? Fifteen or twenty years of putting it before everything else. And now the Bureau's turned its back on you. That must be hard."

Beamon grinned and shook his head. "Jesus, Carrie. Now I *am* depressed, do you have a rope on you? I thought psychiatrists were supposed to make you feel better."

"That's a myth, I'm afraid. We help people

identify their problems and then we force them to confront them."

Beamon's slightly fogged mind conjured up the pale, expressionless face of Sara Renslier. "Oh, I've identified my problem, Carrie. I just haven't figured out a way to confront it and come away with my skin."

She walked over and knelt by his chair. "Do you want to tell me about it?"

He put down the bottle and ran his hand gently through her hair. "Not right now. I just need to sit here and think for a while. We're still going out tomorrow, though, right? We definitely need to talk."

She pressed his hand against her cheek. "I guess you're going to want me to pay for dinner now, huh?"

43

"WE'RE GOING TO GET THOSE SONSOFBITCHES for you, boy," Jack Goldman shouted, swinging his cane wildly to punctuate his point and inadvertently knocking over a stack of books next to him.

"Would you be careful with that thing! I've got expensive equipment here!" Ernie hollered back at him.

"Come on, guys. Calm down," Beamon said, trying to bring the noise in the room to a level that wouldn't split his head open. He adjusted his sunglasses on his nose and began restacking the books at Goldman's feet, trying to ignore the nausea gripping him and the fact that he was the only member of his "team" who was capable of completing this simple task.

"If this is your new FBI," Goldman continued in a quieter voice, "you can have it. When Hoover was alive, they wouldn't begrudge a man a drink! Now all they want to do is hire a bunch of pansies who aren't afraid to cry and then send 'em to sensitivity training. No one would've dared—"

"Where's your bathroom?" Beamon asked, cutting Goldman off before he got too warmed up to his subject.

Ernie pointed behind him. "Down there, your first right."

She looked a bit confused as he sat down and dug a handful of Advils from his pocket. His stomach rolled over at the prospect of sending anything down to it, but he forced a couple of tablets anyway. "Don't need it now," Beamon explained to her. "Just wanted to get a fix on it."

"Drinking never solved anything, Mark."

Beamon let out a short, painful laugh. "I said the same thing to Mr. Goldman here nearly twenty years ago." He looked up at the old man. "You remember what you told me?"

"I told you that sobriety never solved anything, either."

"That's right."

Goldman waved his cane around again, but this time in a more controlled pattern. "It's time to get off our asses, Mark. We're letting ourselves get screwed here."

"The suspension's done," Beamon said. "It is what it is. They're trying to get me to take my eye off the ball."

"Jennifer," Ernie said.

Beamon nodded. "The FBI won't be pursuing the church angle, so they have no chance of getting her back before her time's up. We've got to do it. I'm open to suggestions as to how."

Ernie leaned forward in her wheelchair as far as her bulk and the straining banana-print fabric containing it would allow. "The church doesn't have that many places where they could be holding someone against their will, Mark. Maybe you could search them."

Beamon shook his head. "I can pretty much guarantee you that Jennifer's being held at Kneiss's ompound, Ernie. I don't think we need to look any further than that."

"Then why don't we—"

"How?" Goldman cut in. "I looked at that place. It'd take an army to get in there with all that security."

"Mr. Goldman's right, Ernie. There's no way in there. Do you think they might move her? If we're right, don't you think Sara would have to invent some kind of ceremony for her death? Where would they do something like that?"

Ernie shook her head. "There's no one place, Mark. The chapel in the compound would be as good a place as any."

"I doubt they'd dispose of the body on Kneiss's property," Goldman said. "Ground's frozen anyway. Maybe we could get them red-handed when they bring her body out Easter weekend?"

Beamon stood and began pacing back and forth across the room, the motion settling his stomach a bit. "No. No way. I refuse to be responsible for this girl's death. We're going to get her before anything happens to her."

"Then we're back to Jack's wiretap," Ernie said.

That was exactly where they were, Beamon knew. He'd spent most of his career at the FBI being a pain in the ass, completely unconventional, and occasionally even sneaky. But he'd never done anything illegal. "How long, Mr. Goldman?"

"Now you're talkin', son. You and me, tomorrow night. It'll be fun."

Beamon unbuckled his seatbelt and leaned out the car window to get a better look at the screen of the cash machine. It was heavily overcast, but he was still unwilling to take off his sunglasses and that was making it even more difficult to read the small letters.

UNABLE TO PROCESS TRANSACTION

He tried again, with the same result.

Beamon pulled his car into a space close to the door of the bank and went inside. He walked down the long line of teller windows and slid his ATM card to a young girl with bright pink barrettes in her hair. "I seem to be having some trouble making a withdrawal from your machine. Could you check my account for me?"

"Of course." She held the card up and examined it carefully. "Sometimes the magnetic strip on the back of these things gets messed up. Do you keep it in the little sleeve?"

He shook his head as she punched his account number into her terminal. An expression of mild confusion spread across her face as she looked at the screen, giving Beamon a not-so-unexpected sinking feeling.

"This is kind of weird," she explained. "You're showing a zero balance. Could you hold on a second?"

She hopped off her stool and hurried to an older woman standing at the end of the counter. The woman returned with her and, with a brief smile acknowledging Beamon's presence, began punching buttons on the keyboard.

"Could I speak to you over here, please, sir?" she said after less than a minute. Beamon followed her to a deserted area at the edge of counter.

"Mr. Beamon, your accounts have been liened by the IRS. They've ordered us not to accept any further transactions on any of your accounts."

Beamon felt his jaw tighten and he closed his eyes for a moment. When he opened them again, the woman had stepped back a couple of feet.

"I'm afraid there's nothing I can do," she said nervously. "Except give you the number of the local IRS office so you can get this straightened out."

Beamon walked out of the building to his car, looking carefully around him at the people in the parking lot. He was sure he hadn't been followed to Ernie's house, but now, in this busy part of town, it was possible that they could have reacquired him.

Satisfied that he wasn't the subject of any undue attention, he reached under the seat and ran his fingers along the envelope containing the five thousand dollars he'd withdrawn last week. All the money he had in the world now.

He wondered if he'd get a chance to spend it.

44

BEAMON STRAIGHTENED HIS TIE NERVOUSLY and then forced his hands to his sides and tried to look casual. If someone had bet him that he'd one day dread a date with Carrie Johnstone more than any he'd ever had, he'd have lost a lot of money.

Despite a substantial effort on his part, Beamon hadn't been able to come up with a single credible lie as to why he had to stop seeing her for a while. It looked like he was going to have to fall back on a rough approximation of the truth and hope he didn't scare her off. That is, if this morning's newspaper article hadn't already done that for him.

Beamon knocked again, this time a bit harder. Emory wouldn't be asleep this early—Carrie was probably in the back with a blow dryer running or something.

"Come on, Carrie," he said to himself. It was starting to get cold, and he was getting more nervous by the minute.

Carrie finally answered the door dressed in an old pair of jeans and a sweatshirt, just as he raised his hand to knock again.

Beamon pointed to a splotch of faded paint on the sweatshirt. "I was suspended *with* pay, Carrie. I was actually planning on springing for a nice restaurant."

She remained silent and took a step back in a way that was clearly not an invitation.

Beamon noticed that her eyes were tinged slightly pink. The aftermath of tears that had recently dried up. "Carrie. Are you all right? Did something happen to Emory?"

His words seemed to sting her. More than that, actually. They seemed to stagger her. She reached down to the small table next to the door and picked up something that looked like a business card.

"Carrie, what's wrong with you?"

In answer to his question, she held the card out to him at arm's length, tensing visibly when he reached for it.

"What is this?" Beamon asked, looking down at the clean white card with the words *Child Safety Administration* printed on it in authoritative black letters.

"Two men came here today," she said in a voice so strange that Beamon had to look up to make sure she was actually the one speaking. "They told me that you're being investigated for child molestation."

Beamon felt his heart twitch as a quick burst of adrenaline surged through him. He started to take a step toward her, but stopped when she moved back again. "Carrie, this is bullshit. Look, I'm investigating a very powerful organization and they're doing everything they can to discredit me. I was going to tell you about it tonight." He held up the card. "I mean, Jesus Christ, there's not even a phone number on this . . ." He let his voice trail off. She wasn't listening. The tears he had thought were exhausted earlier started to shimmer in her eyes again and he remembered. *She'd left her daughter with him.*

He looked into her face and saw horror, guilt,

and betrayal there. For a moment he was enraged. That the church would stoop to something like this. That Carrie would believe it. But then he remembered Jennifer's uncle. David Passal had been run out of Oregon for similar unsubstantiated charges. And Beamon hadn't for a moment questioned his guilt, only his motivation and ability to get at Jennifer.

What was it that Passal had said when Beamon had last seen him alive? Something about there being a plot of land down the hill—that he'd save it for him.

Beamon closed his eyes to block out Carrie's face and the card that seemed to be burning in his hand. Passal had probably been a good guy. More than likely, he'd tried to help out his brother and sister-in-law, and for that he'd been condemned to dying alone in the bitter cold of the Utah mountains.

Beamon opened his eyes again, realizing there was nothing left to be said. He slipped the card into his pocket and turned away without looking up. "Good-bye, Carrie." He walked slowly out onto the snow-covered walk and across the courtyard. Halfway to the parking area, he finally heard Carrie's door push shut. A moment later, the laughing started.

Beamon stopped and watched Robert Andrews lean over the rail outside his second-floor condo for a moment and then walk inside his unit, still laughing. The small gap in the drapes, there since Andrews had moved in, disappeared. A clear message that the church no longer saw him as a threat.

Beamon felt the anger build in him until it was at the edge of his control. He'd spent the last month screwing around, treating this like any other kidnapping case. And that had kept him from seeing the big picture—from believing that the church could actually mount an effective attack on him. He'd concentrated everything on offense, ignoring defense. And now Carrie, his job, his reputation were all gone—probably never to be recovered. He had no family to stand behind him and most of his friends would run hard and fast at this kind of trouble. They had their own lives and careers to worry about.

Beamon jumped over a small hedge and ran up the steps toward Andrews's apartment, taking them two at a time. When he burst through the man's front door, he was sitting calmly on his sofa. Waiting.

"What a surprise," Andrews said, not rising from his position on the couch.

Beamon yanked his pistol from its holster and aimed it at the man's face. He could feel the blood throbbing from his heart to his head to his gun hand.

"Oh, my!" Andrew said, mocking Beamon by throwing his hands up in a cartoonish display of terror. "A desperate man with a gun."

"Shut the fuck up!" Beamon screamed, rushing forward and stopping with the barrel of the pistol only a few inches from the man's nose. In his mind, he saw Andrews walking up to Carrie's door and handing her that business card. He could see the expression on her face as she went back inside her home, knelt down, and looked into the eyes of her daughter.

"What is it you want exactly?" Andrews said, casually lowering his hands. Beamon followed their progress with his eyes, focusing on the band around the man's wrist. It was made of black iron, probably three-quarters of an inch wide and a quarter of an inch thick. A deep white scar had been carved into the man's skin beneath the heavy bracelet. A souvenir from the torch that had been used to weld it in place.

Andrews moved his arm to better display the symbol of his devotion. "Well? What do you want?"

"I want to cut your heart out with a fucking spoon," Beamon said through clenched teeth. "That's what I want."

Andrews rolled his eyes. "I'd heard that you were given to fits of melodrama. Now why don't you run on home before you get yourself in any more trouble."

Beamon pushed the gun closer until it was almost brushing the skin of the man's forehead. "Get Sara Renslier on the phone. Now!"

Andrews ran his tongue slowly over the front of his teeth. "I'm not sure why she'd want to talk to you."

Beamon flicked his wrist and caught Andrews in the mouth with the barrel of his pistol. The blow split the man's lower lip and at the sight of the blood, Beamon's control slipped a little farther away from him. He grabbed the handset of the phone from the table next to the sofa and slammed it into the side of the man's head. "Do it now!"

Andrews's mouth tightened into a thin slit, increasing the flow of blood from his lip. He began to rise, but when Beamon cocked the hammer on his pistol back, he sank back into the cushions and sat motionless.

"You better start dialing that phone, boy."

Andrews thought about it for a few seconds and then picked up the handset and began punching angrily at the buttons.

"Ms. Renslier? This is Robert Andrews." Pause. "He's standing right here pointing a gun at me . . ." He looked directly into Beamon's eyes. "No, I'm in no danger. I don't think he can do much harm to anyone anymore."

Beamon snatched the phone from Andrews's hand and raised it to his ear. "What the fuck do you think you're doing?"

Silence.

"Answer me!"

"I'm not sure I understand your question, Mr. Beamon," Sara Renslier said, speaking slowly and clipping her words as though Beamon was a child who had difficulty understanding adult speech.

"I'm not through with you, *Sara*. Do a little research. I always get who I'm after."

"Oh, yes. Special Agent Beamon *was* impressive. But you're not Special Agent Beamon anymore, are you? You're just a drunk, out-of-work pedophile."

"Fuck you!"

He couldn't tell if the mechanical edge to the laughter coming over the phone was the result of the line or the woman. Beamon suddenly realized that she was enjoying this immensely.

He let the phone drop a few inches and looked around him. At Andrews sitting on the couch, at the sparsely furnished condominium that was a mirror reflection of his own. The pounding in his head was starting to subside, leaving him feeling disoriented—like he'd just woken up from an intense dream.

What the hell was he doing? Running up there all rage and no reason. Throwing around a bunch of threats that everyone knew had no teeth. He was looking like a complete idiot, even to himself.

"Do you have anything of interest to say, Mr. Beamon?" he heard Sara say. "I'm rather busy."

The pathetic thing was, he really didn't. Suddenly he just wanted to be out of there.

"Your God must be very proud, Sara—" He almost finished the sentence with, "plotting the death of Kneiss's granddaughter so soon after his death," but he realized that it would have been his bruised ego talking. Tipping his hand like that would be stupid. There might still be time to do something. That is, if he could manage to pull his head out of his ass.

"Did you ever consider, Mr. Beamon, that if you had accepted God and followed His path, you wouldn't have been so easy to break?"

Beamon looked up at Andrews, who was still sitting calmly on the couch, and holstered his gun. "Oh, I'm not broken yet. I'm just really bent out of shape."

— — —

352 — KYLE MILLS

The liquor store was nearly deserted when Beamon walked in. He went straight to the back, picked up a half-gallon of bourbon, and returned to the counter.

"Better throw in a carton of Marlboros, too. I'm having a really bad day."

The girl smiled and grabbed a carton off the wall behind her.

"Put it on my account. The name's Mark Beamon."

At the mention of his name, she started to look a little nervous.

Beamon rolled his eyes and sighed. What now? Had the church bought the fucking liquor store and cut off his credit? He figured they'd want him drunk.

"Could you hold on a second?" she said and then scurried out from behind the counter, returning shortly with the store's manager.

"Barry. What's the problem?" Beamon said.

The man held out a white business card, but Beamon didn't bother taking it. He knew what it was.

"Some men came around today asking questions about you," Barry said angrily.

Beamon remembered that he always made a point of asking after the man's seven-year-old daughter when he came in.

"I'd appreciate it if you didn't come in here anymore, Mr. Beamon. We don't need your kind of business."

Beamon tapped the top of the bourbon bottle on the counter. "Let me pass along a piece of advice my dad gave me years ago, Barry. Never refuse a bottle and cigarettes to a heavily armed out-of-work child molester."

Barry took a step back but managed to regain his composure quickly. Apparently seeing the wisdom in Beamon's words, he walked behind the counter and pulled out an index card that Beamon assumed was his tab.

Barry nodded toward the items on the counter as he ripped up the card. "They're on the house. So's your account. Now there's no reason for you to ever come back."

Beamon slammed his hands against the steering wheel of his car. It felt good, so he did it again. And then again.

If the church's lackeys had gone so far as to visit his liquor store of choice, they'd probably talked to every goddamn person he'd ever known. He was screwed. Thoroughly and completely screwed.

It was unlikely now that he'd ever get his job back. And he probably had a better chance of marrying Christie Brinkley than getting Carrie to speak to him again. Or for that matter, getting any of the few friends he had to speak to him again.

Not that it really mattered, he reminded himself. When Sara had completed her little plot, she'd turn her attention back to him. Most likely, he and Jennifer would be sharing that chuckhole in Outer Mongolia.

He slammed his hand into the steering wheel one last time and felt the pain vibrate up his arms.

Enough. He had ten days and very little left to lose—nothing but his life, really. And from where he was sitting, that just didn't seem all that valuable anymore.

Beamon started the car and pointed it toward Jack Goldman's apartment. After making an ass out of himself in front of Andrews and with Carrie thinking he'd felt up her daughter, home just didn't seem that inviting.

45

"SLOW DOWN, BOY. CAN'T SEE A GODDAMN thing if you drive like a bat out of hell."

Beamon let his foot off the gas and flipped on the high beams. When the speedometer had drifted down to twenty miles an hour, he returned his foot to the accelerator.

Back at Goldman's apartment, there were only a few sad inches left in the bottle of bourbon Beamon had taken over last night. As for what was left in the carton of cigarettes, he was trying not to think about that. It was hard not to, though, with his lungs feeling like someone had poured a quart of motor oil into them right after they'd emptied their old car battery into his stomach. And then, of course, there was the crowbar prying apart his skull.

"I think you should talk to her," Goldman repeated for what must have been the hundredth time. Despite the fact that the old man had kept up with him shot for shot, smoke for smoke all night, he seemed miraculously unaffected. It must be the excitement—that or all of the old SOB's nerve endings had preceded him into the grave.

Beamon groaned. The bourbon had loosened him up enough to mention his unfortunate position with Carrie last night. "Let's concentrate on what we're doing, okay, Mr. Goldman?"

The old man looked over at him. "Son, I don't need you to tell me how much to concentrate to set a phone tap."

Beamon backpedaled. In his current condition there was no way he could take one of Goldman's tirades. "*I* need to concentrate. I've never done this before."

"And you're not going to do it today. You're just going to stand there and let me do my job." Goldman gazed out the window. "Yeah, I'd march right over there and talk to her. Make her listen. Get this thing straightened out once and for all."

The pounding in Beamon's head rose in tempo from a polka to more of a disco beat. "I appreciate the advice, Mr. Goldman, but you've never even been married. So—"

"Not because there weren't plenty of women willing, that I didn't get married. Hell, when I first started in this business, I could just walk into people's houses in the middle of the day and wire their phones while I ate lunch. That's before women got all hot and bothered about careers and trying to compete with men. No, those little housewives used to be damned happy to see me . . ."

"So why didn't you ever make an honest woman out of one of them?" Beamon said, hoping desperately to change the subject before Goldman started relating details of his sexual prowess. His stomach was just barely hanging on as it was.

"Why buy the cow when you can get the milk for free? Turn left here." He looked over at Beamon. "But son, you aren't me. Let's face it, you ain't the best-looking guy in the world. You're a sloppy dresser, and, well, you're a little obnoxious. No offense."

"None taken."

Goldman reached over and smacked Beamon on the stomach. "Hey, at least you took care of that weight problem. Now what was I saying . . ."

"That I'm not you," Beamon sighed

"You're not me, right. Son, if you've got an intelligent, attractive woman interested in you, I say you should get your ass in gear before she changes her mind. May not be anybody around the next corner, you know?"

"I think she already has changed her mind, Mr. Goldman."

"Boy, you just don't know anything about women, do you? They change their minds like the weather."

Beamon wasn't sure, but he suspected Goldman hadn't ever been in quite his situation. A woman who initially thought you dressed funny and watched too much football might come around, it was true. A woman who thought you were keeping compromising Polaroids of her four-year-old daughter in your wallet would probably be a little more difficult to win over.

"I'll try flowers," Beamon said.

"That's the spirit, boy. Broads love flow—There it is! The cross-connect box is right there."

Beamon tapped the brake and started easing the car toward the curb. "Jesus, son, don't slow down! Drive past it and park around the corner there."

Goldman was out of the car before it had completely stopped, walking without his cane and with very little difficulty. In the harsh glare of headlights reflecting off the snow, he still looked like he'd been dead for a couple of days, but when he turned his back and began digging in the back seat for his gear, he could have been forty years younger. His movements were decisive, quick, and smooth. He was back in his element.

Beamon took a position behind Goldman, hefting the large duffel the old man passed back and following him as he hurried up the sidewalk with a bright red toolbox dangling from his hand.

Beamon didn't see the large metal cabinet half-buried in the snow until Goldman slipped a head-lamp over his thick knit cap and shined it off to their right. It was about ten feet back from the road amidst a widely spaced stand of pines that were casting long shadows across it, blending it into its background.

"You're going to have to dig, Mark," Goldman said, struggling through the snow toward the box.

Beamon sighed, pulled a collapsible Army-issue shovel out of the duffel, and started to work on the snow blocking the doors.

The nausea hit him full force on about the fifth shovelfull of icy snow. He did his best to ignore it but ended up having to stop. He unzipped the vaguely official-looking overalls Goldman had provided him and felt the cold wind dry the sweat covering his chest.

"No time for a coffee break, boy."

Beamon looked down at the shovel and then at the old man's head, then went back to chopping at the ice blocking the doors. Ten miserable minutes later, they were clear.

Goldman inserted a key into the box and opened it as Beamon stepped back into the shadows and fell onto a snowbank. The cold against his back felt like it might bring him back to life, given enough time.

The old man looked like a surgeon as his twisted

fingers danced over the bundles of wires with dexterity that should have been impossible. He stopped his work every ten seconds or so to look at a complex schematic that he had stuck to the inside of one of the open doors.

A car's headlights suddenly illuminated them as it turned the corner and started down the street in their direction. Beamon tensed and sat up, but Goldman seemed to read his mind.

"Relax, son. Just a couple of repairmen working late. Everyone expects their phones to work perfectly but they don't give a second thought to the people who keep them working. In five minutes, the guy in that car won't even remember he saw us."

Beamon had no reason to think Goldman was wrong, so he settled back into the snowbank and breathed in the scent of the pine tree behind him. He tried to let his mind go blank, to focus only on the quiet rustling as Goldman did his magic and the sweet smell of frozen pine needles, but it didn't work. Thoughts of the women in his life kept pushing out any momentary peace he might be able to steal.

The women in his life.

His mother had been dead for years and his sister pretty much hated him, leaving only three women of any importance. Jennifer Davis, a fifteen-year-old girl whom he'd never met and who he would probably get to remember as the other girl he couldn't save. Carrie Johnstone, a woman who now saw him as a psychotic pervert with eyes for her daughter. And Sara Renslier, who would do everything in her considerable power to destroy his life, and who, when he was rendered completely helpless, would undoubtedly swoop in for the kill.

God. How sad was that?

"Drill, Mark! Quit daydreaming and give me the drill!"

Beamon fished around in the duffel lying next to him and pulled out a beefy-looking battery-operated model, which Goldman used to cut a small hole in the side of the metal cabinet. He ran a wire through it and then went back to whatever it was he'd been doing before.

"Mark, there's a white fiberglass box in that duffel. About a foot square." He pointed in the general direction of a crooked pine tree behind the cross-connect box. "Bury it in the snow over there somewhere. One side of the box has two cables coming out of it. That's the top. Make sure the shorter of the two cables is sticking out of the snow so I can get at it."

"What about the long one?"

"Run it under the snow to the base of the tree behind you."

Beamon grabbed the box and the shovel and walked over to the spot Goldman had pointed to. "How deep?"

"Deep as you can. But make it look natural."

Beamon was just finishing—smoothing out the surface to match the unturned snow around it—when he heard the cabinet close. Goldman took the shovel from him and began digging a trench between the box Beamon had just buried and the cross-connect box, then spliced the wires together and buried them neatly in the trench.

"Is that it?" Beamon asked.

Goldman turned off his headlamp. "Nope." He reached into the duffel and pulled out another fiberglass device, this one smaller than the one Beamon just buried and painted in a brown and gray camouflage.

Goldman connected a thin brown cable to it and handed it to Beamon along with a pair of bungee cords colored in a similar camouflage. "Climb as high in that tree as you can and tie this to the trunk."

Beamon looked at the snow-covered tree behind him. "You've got to be kidding."

"You want it to work, don't you, boy?" Goldman pointed at the ground where Beamon had buried the other box. "Whenever a call comes into or goes out of the church's compound, that box will dial us on a cell and we'll get the call real-time. It'll run into Ernie's computer and a computer at my apartment, in case of a problem." He pointed at the unit in Beamon's hand. "That's the booster."

Beamon sighed and pushed his way through the lower branches of the tree, feeling snow invade every unsealed opening in his suit. He put a foot up on a sturdy-looking limb and turned to Goldman. "Who's paying for all this cell service?"

Goldman rolled his eyes. Kind of a surreal gesture given the uneven magnification of his glasses and the moonlight.

Beamon started his struggle up the tree. "I know, I know. What kind of idiot pays for cell phone service?"

46

BEAMON STEPPED FROM HIS CAR AND TRIED unsuccessfully to ignore the sad drama playing out before him in the courtyard in front of his condo.

A woman and her young son were having a playful snowball fight in the intermittent glare provided by the common area floodlights. When she saw Beamon, she jogged through the snow to the boy and began speaking quietly into his ear. Beamon couldn't help watching as the boy's attention turned from the snowball in his hands to him.

The scene confirmed what he already knew. He had to get the hell out of there before the homeowners' association started burning crosses on his lawn. He'd just draw too much attention if he stayed.

Beamon moved quickly across the courtyard and stepped up his pace even more as he walked past Carrie Johnstone's front door. Murphy's Law stated clearly that she would pick that precise moment to go to the store, take out the garbage, or whatever. He just couldn't take another confrontation right now.

For the first time in weeks, Murphy wasn't in control of his life and he reached the relative safety of his living room unscathed.

The warmth of his condo started to make him

sweat almost immediately, amplifying the hangover that was showing no sign of weakening in its twelfth hour. Remembering the beer he'd thrown away, he flipped the top of the garbage can open and dug around until he came up with a couple of bottles.

He felt pretty pathetic as he washed a now-unidentifiable leafy vegetable off them, but drastic hangovers called for drastic remedies. He slid one bottle into the freezer, punched the play button on his answering machine, and unscrewed the cap from the bottle in his hand.

"Mark, it's Chet. Pick up if you're there." Pause. "Look, I don't know what you're doing, but it's really starting to hit the fan here. I just spent most of my day getting grilled by Jake Layman and a couple of his ASACs. I knew you wouldn't give up on this thing. Call me. I want to help."

Beamon reached out for the phone, hesitated, and erased the message instead. He had to keep Chet out of this. At least for now.

After a warm beer and a cold shower, he was feeling marginally better. The shakes that had come close to knocking him out of that goddamn pine tree had subsided and his mind was starting to flash pictures of Denny's breakfast menu. A sure sign that the healing process had begun.

The phone rang as Beamon was toweling himself off. Probably Goldman, hopefully calling to tell him that the taps he'd wired were receiving five by five.

"Mark. Jake Layman."

Great.

"What can I do for you, Jake?" Beamon said as he finished drying himself and began rummaging though his drawers for a pair of jeans.

"I'd like you to come down to Phoenix. Tonight. We need to talk."

Beamon cradled the phone in the crook of his shoulder as he pulled on his pants. "I'd love to, Jake, but I'm afraid I just don't have the time right now."

"Look, Mark, I've been hearing rumors. About you. We—"

"Rumors about what, Jake? I'm already on suspension, why don't you just call the Office of Professional Responsibility and add whatever it is that's bothering you to their laundry list."

"Look, Mark. The FBI doesn't need—"

"What, Jake? Another black eye? Someone said that to me once and I stuck my ass out about a mile for the 'good of the organization.' Look where it got me."

"I know you're upset, Mark, but try to look at the big picture—"

Beamon cut him off again as he zipped his pants. "With all due respect, Jake—fuck you. I've got enough problems right now. I just don't have time to solve yours."

He leaned over the bed and replaced the phone's handset. The doorbell rang less than a minute later.

"If you work for the FBI, come on in," he yelled. "If not, I'll be right there."

He heard the door open and leaned out into the living room, still bare-chested. The two young agents self-consciously wiping their feet were from his office. Fucking Layman didn't even have the decency to send up a couple of his boys.

"What took you guys so long?" Beamon kept his tone light, but in reality he had no idea what he was going to do. "I'm still getting dressed. Hold on for a second."

Poor kids looked like they were about to die of embarrassment.

"Mr. Layman asked us to, uh, give you a ride down to Phoenix," Kate Spelling said. Her cohort pretended to be fascinated by a poorly framed print hanging on the wall.

Beamon disappeared back into his bedroom but left the door open. "I just got off the phone with him, Kate. Let me get my stuff."

"Sure. Take your time." He could hear the relief in her voice as he walked into the bathroom and began throwing toiletries with unerring accuracy into an open suitcase on the bed.

After stuffing a week's worth of clothes into the same suitcase, he got down on his knees and poked his head into the mess that was his closet. It took some digging, but he finally found the shoebox where he kept memorabilia from the cases he'd worked over the years. He dug through the old newspaper clipping and photographs, finally finding a fake driver's license he had used on an undercover assignment a few years back. He stuffed it in his pocket, then slid a shirt off a hanger and pulled it over his head.

The shotgun wasn't as easy—he had to pry it out from under a stack of unpacked boxes. He peeked out of the closet for a moment to make sure he wasn't drawing undue attention and then slowly pulled back the slide to make sure the gun wasn't loaded.

It took another minute to find the box of shells. He tossed them over his shoulder, hitting the suitcase dead center, and then crawled back out of the closet, leaving the shotgun just out of sight.

He closed up the suitcase and once again donned his bright red parka. Looking at himself in the mirror across the room, he took a deep breath. There wasn't going to be any turning back after this. If he didn't come up with the goods—Jennifer—he might as well just walk up to Sara Renslier and hand her a loaded gun.

Beamon grabbed the suitcase in one hand and the shotgun in the other and walked out into the living room. The two young agents' eyes widened when they saw the gun.

"It just occurred to me that I have a prior engagement. Tell Jake I'll have to catch up with him later."

They watched him as he walked into the kitchen and grabbed a steak knife.

"Uh, Mark. Mr. Layman was pretty clear about this. You really have to come with us."

Beamon started across the living room. "No, I don't, Kate. I'm the one with the shotgun." He opened the door and looked back at the two kids standing hapless in his living room. "Look, Layman isn't going to blame you for losing me. Tell him I went nuts. Pulled a gun. What were you supposed to do, shoot it out with me in a heavily populated condo complex?" He stepped outside. "You guys stay in here for about five minutes, okay? There's a beer in the freezer. Split it."

He closed the door behind him, knowing from their expressions that they'd do exactly what he'd told them. In hindsight, he'd have to thank Layman for not sending his own people. He'd have never gotten away with that bullshit if they'd been a couple of experienced agents Beamon didn't know.

He'd have had to crawl out of the goddamned window or something equally undignified.

He spotted their Bureau car and shoved the steak knife in the passenger-side tires before jumping in his car and spinning out of the parking lot. He adjusted his mirror and watched his home for the last two months recede into the distance. Another minor adjustment brought into focus the church's increasingly tenacious chase car. It was going to take some fancy driving, but it was time for him to permanently disappear.

His cell phone started to ring as he sped around the corner and toward the highway. As soon as he regained control of the car, he reached over and turned it off.

47

"YOU'RE SURE THERE'S NOTHING," BEAMON said, continuing to scan the nearly empty parking lot.

Jack Goldman shoved yet another piece of mysterious equipment into the back seat of his car. "Damn right I'm sure. I've checked the entire spectrum—twice. Your car ain't transmitting. It's clean."

They were alone, then. With the insane driving he'd done getting there, it was inconceivable that anyone could have followed him without his knowing it. Even multiple cars with drivers connected by cell phone couldn't have stayed with him.

Beamon looked up at the sky and felt the heavy snowflakes falling against his skin. Visibility was horrible. No way to track him by air.

"Okay, then, Mr. Goldman. We abandon it here." He opened the passenger side door and pulled what was left of his five thousand dollars from the glove box and his suitcase off the seat. "I'll need you to rent me a car."

"Where's your coffee pot? I'm fading fast," Beamon said, straightening a precarious stack of dishes before they teetered into the sink.

Ernestine Waverly wheeled to the edge of the kitchen. "I don't drink coffee, Mark. Bothers my stomach. There are Cokes in the fridge."

Beamon ducked his head into the refrigerator and grabbed one. His first swig emptied half the can. It wasn't exactly what the doctor ordered, but it was better than nothing. His return to binge drinking had had the desired effect—made it almost impossible for his mind to focus on the fact that he'd lost everything meaningful in his life in the course of seventy-two hours. The problem was that it was making it impossible to focus on anything else, either.

"You okay, Mark?"

"I'm better, thanks," he said as he followed her back to the office, where Jack Goldman was doing his best to pace back and forth. "I think it's safe to run that by me again. If the phone taps are working like a dream, what's the problem?"

"E-mail," Goldman said, continuing to shuffle back and forth.

"Never had much use for it."

"You know how it works though, right?" Ernie said.

"I guess. You type something into your computer and send it to someone else's computer. It's just a fax without the paper."

"Essentially, that's right. We're picking up phone conversations clear as a bell on all six lines coming out of the compound." She nodded a brief acknowledgment toward Goldman.

"I thought you said there were eight lines."

"There are. One is dedicated to the security system, so there're no calls coming through on it. The other is dedicated to a computer. E-mail is going out over that one."

"So?"

"So, it's encrypted. We can't read it."

"Encrypted? You mean in code?" Beamon fell onto a chair and set his half-empty Coke can on the table next to him. "What the hell are they up to?"

"It doesn't really mean anything," Ernie said. "Encryption's not that uncommon. In fact, the program they're using is very common—it actually comes with the e-mail software when you buy it. I use the same system."

"Why?"

"I don't want half the people on the Internet to be able to read my letters."

Beamon chewed at his lower lip for a moment. "I've got a friend at the NSA. We go pretty far back. He might still be willing to help me. I don't know."

Ernie adjusted her muumuu nervously. Apples and pears today. "I don't think that would do us any good, Mark. Even with their resources it would take them years to crack the Church's encryption code . . ."

"What are you telling me, Ernie? That the National Security Agency can't crack an encryption program that I can buy at Toys "Я" Us? They—"

Goldman stopped pacing. "Forget it. We're talking about an encryption code that encompasses thousands of characters. Literally trillions of possible combinations. There's no way."

Ernie nodded her agreement and looked hopefully at Beamon. Waiting for divine inspiration to strike, no doubt. Unfortunately, he wasn't feeling very inspired.

"Come on, Mr. Goldman," Beamon said. "You could record a conversation between dead people."

Goldman started his pacing again. "You get me in there and give me some time with their computer, maybe I could do something . . ."

Beamon let his head loll onto the back of the chair and stared at the ceiling. "You mean I almost got myself killed climbing a goddamn ice-covered tree in a blizzard and it isn't going to do me any good?"

"Blizzard, my ass," Goldman said. "And we got the phones."

"Screw the phones! I doubt they use them for anything more sensitive than ordering takeout. Whatever they have to say that's of interest to us is going to go out over that e-mail system. Shit . . ."

What the hell was he going to do now? Rent a tank and drive it through the front gate of Kneiss's compound? Shit, they'd probably have a newer, faster tank with more firepower waiting for him on the other side.

"There is something we could try," Ernie started.

"Oh, come on, woman!" Goldman said. "Don't waste my time!" He turned to Beamon. "Vericomm's the answer, son. That's where we need to concentrate our resources."

Beamon ignored him. "Go ahead, Ernie. What're you thinking."

"We could send the church an encryption software update."

"Come again?"

"I used to play a game with a friend of mine— he's a programmer, too. We'd try to break into each other's computers. Leave messages, move files around, that kind of thing. Well, once I had the idea of breaking the encryption to his e-mail—the same system the church is using."

"But you said that it would take years."

"If you took a conventional approach, it would. What I did was went out and bought a copy of the encryption software and reprogrammed it a bit."

"Reprogrammed it?"

She nodded. "I rewrote it so that when he sent an encrypted e-mail, he sent his encryption key along with it. Then I printed a big official-looking sticker that said there was a bug in the version he had purchased that was causing computer crashes. I re-shrink-wrapped the whole thing so it would look official and then mailed it to him."

"And it worked?"

"Uh, no."

Beamon sighed and crushed the Coke can in his hand. "It didn't work."

"Uh-uh. But I know why. Like I said, Rick—my friend—is a programmer. Even though I put on the sticker that there was an encryption problem with his version, he wanted to know the details of what was wrong. He called the software company and, you know, found out that there was no glitch."

Beamon thought about that for a moment and then turned to Goldman. "Couldn't you set up an eight-hundred line and run it in here? We could just put that number on the label—a special help line dedicated to this little problem."

The old man was looking more and more irritated. "I could, if it wasn't a complete waste of time. What did you tell us when we came in this morning? We've only got a week left! Even if the church bought this bullshit, it would probably take them a couple of weeks to get around to installing the goddamn update. By then the girl's dead, and you're not far behind."

"They've been pretty efficient at completely screwing up my life," Beamon said. "No reason to think they don't maintain their computers with the same diligence. Go ahead, Ernie. Nothing to lose."

"Jesus Christ, Mark! Wake up!" Goldman shouted. "We have to concentrate on Vericomm. Get something we can use against them."

Beamon shrugged. "I'm with you, Mr. Goldman, but I'm not hearing you give me a realistic course of action. You told me yourself that it'd take an army of people like you to figure out how they're doing it. And I doubt they're going to invite us over to their headquarters and show us their tapes. No, unless you can give me a concrete action plan, we're going to go with Ernie's suggestion. Set up the eight hundred line. Ernie, can you get that thing out in the mail tomorrow?"

"I've still got it. I can get it out today if you can take it to town and get it shrink-wrapped."

Goldman grabbed a half-full drinking glass from the table next to him and threw it across the room. Beamon ducked involuntarily as it smashed against the wall. "We can't afford to waste time like this! That little girl is going to die while you two are screwing around! We've got to get to Vericomm!"

"What the hell, Mr. Goldman! What do you want me to do? Blow the place up? I would, but it wouldn't even do us any good!"

Goldman grabbed his coat and headed for the door. "Somebody's got to get off their ass and do something," Beamon heard him grumble as he passed by.

"Jack, wait," Ernie said, but Goldman had already disappeared down the hall.

"Jesus," Beamon said when he heard the front door slam. Ernie wheeled her chair to face him and looked at him sternly

"What?"

"Don't you think you're being a little hard on him, Mark?"

"Don't bust my ass, Ernie. The guy was throwing shit around the room and cussing us out for no reason."

"He's having a tough time, Mark. I think you could try to be a little more compassionate."

Beamon couldn't believe what he was hearing. He was the one whose life had been completely trashed. It'd be dumb luck if he didn't find himself in jail or lining a shallow grave somewhere by this time next month. And now, on top of all that, now he was expected to coddle Jack Goldman, one of the most difficult SOBs to ever take a breath.

"Mark, you've got to understand that for the first time in his life, Jack's being beaten at his own game. The church has created a bugging system that he can't dismantle, expose, or subvert. He's feeling old."

"He *is* old," Beamon said, completely exasperated now.

"He's doing the best he can, Mark, but he's feeling like a dinosaur. He wants so desperately to do one more thing that really matters. And he wants to protect you. I don't think you realize how much he admires you. How much he cares about you."

Beamon was about to come to his own defense, but she held her hand up before he could open his mouth. "He can also save Jennifer. It's hard to explain. He didn't have children and he almost feels like if he can save the two of you, that you'll be a little piece of immortality for him."

"Where do you get this stuff, Ernie?"

"He tells me things."

Beamon had never heard Jack Goldman tell anybody anything other than how incompetent they were. "Look, in my own way, I love the old guy. I really do. But I don't know what he wants from me."

"Not that much, Mark. Your respect. Maybe a little friendship."

48

VERICOMM'S HEADQUARTERS BUILDING LOOKED
like a ghost. Most of the lights in its glass facade
had gone out over the last hour and now it just
reflected the darkness and the swirling of snow
though the thin mountain air.

Jack Goldman adjusted himself into a more
comfortable position in the cramped car seat and let
his mind wander into the past, as it seemed to want
to do more and more every day. Back to the simple
elegance of analog phone lines. Before digital transfer, encryption, and computer systems that were a
thousand times as fast as he was and ten times as
smart. Back to the time of closet-sized listening
posts that reeked of coffee, tobacco, and sweat, and
the reel-to-reel tapes filled with voices of glamorous
hoods bragging endlessly about women, money,
and death.

The building in front of him was a testament to
the new age that he didn't want to be part of. It
housed a system so grand in its scale that his ancient
mind could have never dreamed it up. A system that
stole the art from his vocation and turned it into
pure digital science.

He was buried too deep in his own thoughts to
notice the security guard's approach, but wasn't
startled when he heard a knock on the window. He

rolled it down about halfway and treated the guard to his most grandfatherly smile. "Hello, young man."

He saw the man's expression change from stoicism to mild concern. Goldman's age had turned into an increasingly effective tool over the last twenty years, but it was one he detested using.

"Uh, this is reserved parking, sir. You'll need to move your car."

"I'm so sorry. I was driving by and started feeling a bit ill. I just pulled in to rest for a few minutes." He reached for the key dangling from the ignition. "I didn't realize I was illegally parked."

"You're not really illegally parked," the guard said, starting to sound a little uncertain. "It's just that it's reserved. It's actually not a problem if you stay for a while. The guy who's assigned this space won't be back till tomorrow."

"I don't want to cause you any problems," Goldman said, holding his hand far enough from the keys so that the guard could see it shake.

"Not a problem. Really. Is there someone I could call? Maybe you'd like someone to pick you up? You're welcome to leave your car overnight in one of the unassigned spaces."

Goldman shook his head. "That's kind of you, but I'll be fine. At my age, you just have to rest every now and again."

The guard straightened and tapped the top of the car. "Okay, then. If you change your mind or if you need any help, I'll be just inside the front doors."

Goldman watched the man walk back toward the building as a wave of pain and nausea seized him. He leaned forward onto the wheel, his breath coming in short gasps. The attacks were getting longer and the time between them shorter as the cancer digested what was left of his stomach and continued its march through his other vital organs.

Two years ago, he'd ignored his doctor's gloomy six-month prediction, but now he felt it coming in the brief flashes of peace and numbness that overwhelmed him after the pain had, for the moment, stopped. He couldn't be sure, but he guessed that was death working to get a grip that he wouldn't be able to break.

There wasn't much time now. Just long enough to get Mark out of the quicksand he'd trapped himself in. And to save the girl.

Goldman smiled as he remembered Beamon as a first office agent. Smart. Jesus, he'd been smart. But even back then he'd had a gift for taking careful aim at his foot and shooting himself in it. Goddamned miracle he could still walk.

Goldman snapped himself back into the present and focused on a small man with a briefcase walking from the glass doors at the front of the building. He'd never laid eyes on Eugene Marino, Vericomm's tech manager, but this could be him.

Goldman had parked next to one of the few remaining cars in Vericomm's expansive parking area. The curb in front of it had "MARINO" stenciled in bright yellow letters, partially obscured by the snow.

"Mr. Marino?" Goldman said, opening his door and relying heavily on his cane as he eased himself out into the cold.

The man looked up and pulled his keys from his pocket as Goldman struggled across the icy asphalt toward him. "Yes, I'm Eugene Marino. Can I help you?"

Goldman stopped three feet from the man, ignoring the pain in his legs and another attack building in his stomach. "Yes, I think you can." He pulled a gun from his jacket and, holding it low enough that it couldn't be seen from a distance, aimed it at the man's stomach.

Marino's eyes widened, but it was clear that he didn't know what to make of the situation. "Is this . . . is this a mugging?" he said in a disbelieving voice.

Goldman could barely keep himself from laughing. He hadn't mugged anyone in over seventy years.

49

JENNIFER DAVIS LOOKED DOWN AT THE plate of food in her lap and forced herself to take another bite. She chewed purposefully, but had to concentrate not to gag when she swallowed. It had been getting harder and harder to eat. Harder and harder to sleep. To exercise. To do anything.

Her entire body quivered now, from the time she woke up to the time she finally turned out the lights and prayed for sleep to overtake her. It seemed like her brain was slowly leaking adrenaline—just enough to keep her constantly on edge but not enough to give her any strength.

Days and nights came and went—she knew that only because of her makeshift clock in the sink. As Good Friday got closer and closer, her own internal clock—the intuition that told her when she was tired, when she was hungry—had failed her.

Only seven days left.

The hope of escape that had kept her going had slowly died in her. She had seen no one since that day Sara had come and asked her to meet with the Elders. The plate of food appeared only once every twenty-four hours now—every night when she was asleep.

She fell back onto the bed and closed her eyes, trying to quiet the butterflies that flew tirelessly in her stomach all the time now. How could this be happening to her? She was only fifteen and she'd never done anything to hurt anyone.

In the last week, she'd spent her waking hours trying to live an entire life in the time she had left. She created elaborate fantasies about a future she would never see, infusing them with such intricate detail that sometimes they almost seemed real. She imagined her high school graduation: the sound of the principal's voice as it echoed across the auditorium, the bright pink high-top tennis shoes peeking out from beneath her black gown. She could feel the late-summer sun on her face as she watched herself packing her car and driving to college. She saw what her dorm room would look like. The silly arguments she'd have with her roommates. What it would be like the first time she made love.

Then her mind would wander forward. To her wedding. The pain of the birth of her first child. Finding her first gray hairs.

And one night, far in the future, she would walk, slightly stooped, to her bed. She would have just talked to her daughter and son-in-law on the phone. Their son—her grandson—was expecting his first child. She'd turn off the light that night and lie down. Then, smiling into the dark, she would close her eyes for the last time.

50

"YOU'RE DRIVING ME CRAZY WITH THAT thing, Mark," Ernie said, turning her chair away from him and covering her ears.

Beamon pulled his cell phone from his pocket. He'd finally turned it back on a few hours ago—worried that he'd miss something important. It had been pretty much ringing off the hook ever since.

"You're either going to have to answer it or turn it back off," Ernie said, hands still over her ears.

Beamon sighed and punched the button to pick up. "Yeah."

"What the fuck are you doing!"

He moved the phone to a more reasonable distance from his ear. "Jake. What can I do for you?"

"Kate Spelling told me you pulled a gun on them!"

"Melodramatic, but accurate."

"Look, Mark—I know you like to play the maverick, but you've gone too far this time. We're not just talking about your job now. We're talking about putting out an APB and making this thing public. The director's getting fucking hourly reports on this, and I'm not going to be able to keep him out of it for much longer. Let me help you."

Beamon rolled his eyes. "You want to help me."

"Okay, Mark. You say you like plain talk, so I'm

going to give it to you. I could give a shit about you. The thought of you getting run over by a bus gives me a hard-on. But despite all that, I'm probably the best friend you've got."

Sad, but possibly true, Beamon knew.

"Look, neither one of us wants this thing with you to blow up in the papers. Me because I've got a shot at an assistant directorship and this isn't going to help me; you because it's your life. Now, get your ass in here, and let's try to get control of this thing before it goes too far."

"I appreciate the honesty, Jake, but it's already gone too far."

"No it hasn't, Mark. Just—"

"Relax, Jake. Life as a fugitive doesn't suit me."

"When are you coming in?"

"I don't know yet. Soon. I've got some loose ends that need to be tied up."

"That's not good enough, Mark. The director is flying in to meet with me on the first, and you can be goddamn sure I'm going to have something for him. The gloves are coming off."

"You do what you've gotta do, Jake. I understand. The gloves are off."

Beamon pushed the button cutting off the connection and looked down at Ernie. "This just keeps getting worse, hon. I think it's time for you and me to part ways."

She looked horrified. "No! How can you say that? I'm as much a part of this as you are—you can't do it without me. I *have* to stay with you."

"Because God told you to?"

"You laugh at me behind my back, I know it. You and Jack both. But it's what I believe. How can you be sure there's no God? And that He hasn't brought us together to save His church? How can you?"

"I can't," Beamon said honestly. "I'm not sure. I'm never sure about anything. Look, I appreciate everything you've done for me and I admit that I wouldn't be anywhere with this investigation if it weren't for you. But things are going to start to escalate and I don't want to put you in harm's way." Beamon pointed at the computers behind her. "We've got a phone feed going into Mr. Goldman's apartment where I'm staying. We can monitor things from there—"

She shook her head violently and pushed her wheelchair forward until they were as close together as they could be, considering her chosen mode of transportation. "What more can they do to me, Mark? Look at me! Look around you! I haven't left this house since I moved in. And look what I've done to myself—I can barely walk. You and Jack are probably the best friends I have in the world—and I just met you. What more can they do?"

"They could kill you, Ernie. As long as you're breathing, you can change things. Take back what they took from you."

"You think I'm afraid to die?" she said indignantly.

"I hope you are, Ernie. I am."

Her face broke into a slow smile. "Thank you. Thank you for caring about what happens to me. But you really shouldn't worry. That dream I keep having, the one I told you about in the beginning. It goes on a little longer every night. Albert's in it now. He's waiting for me."

Beamon's eyes widened. "Ernie, you're starting to scare me now. You're not going to die."

She seemed so serene, sitting there in her chair.

"It doesn't matter. I know what I have to do, and I know why. For the first time, really. You can't imagine what it feels like to know—to be absolutely sure—that there is a God. And to know that you're important to Him. That you've been chosen by Him." She pointed at Beamon. "He's chosen you, too, Mark. But you'll never believe it, will you?"

"I guess I've never had much use for God, Ernie."

"But he's got use for you."

She turned her chair and wheeled it to a table that had been recently cleared of its normal complement of computer-related debris and pointed to a new blue phone. "The eight-hundred number comes in here."

"The bogus helpline on that e-mail update you sent?" Beamon said, consciously letting her change the subject.

She nodded. "They haven't called yet. But I've been praying."

Beamon smiled politely. What the hell was he going to do with her? He'd always made a practice of trying to do what he thought was right—no matter how much of an ass it made him look like or how disastrous the consequences. But what was the right thing here? He could walk out right now, have Goldman cut off the phone patch to her and never see her again. She'd probably be safe then, but without her help would he be able to find Jennifer? And how much danger was Ernie really in? He'd been so careful to keep her involvement from the church . . .

A phone started ringing, and Beamon's eyes darted to the blue one on the table.

"Sorry, Mark," Ernie said, picking up the green one next to her computer. "Hello? Oh, hold on, let me put you on speaker."

She laid the handset down on the table and punched at her keyboard. "Jack, can you hear me? Mark's here."

"Loud and clear, Ernie. How you doing, Mark?"

He sounded very strange—happy. Giddy might be a better word. Maybe it was just the reverberation of the computer's speakers.

"I'm okay, Mr. Goldman. How about you? You sound a little funny."

"I'm great. Having a wonderful evening. Ernie, I'm downloading something into your system on the seven-three-four-two number. Could you confirm that you're receiving?"

Ernie wheeled to another computer and tapped the mouse with her index finger, lighting up the monitor. "Yes, I'm receiving."

"FAN-tastic."

Beamon shifted uncomfortably in his chair. He'd never heard Goldman sound anything like this. Could he be finally losing it? At his age, senility was definitely starting to look overdue. "What is it you're sending, Mr. Goldman?"

"We were right about Vericomm, boy. I'm sending audio files of some of their more interesting tapes."

Beamon stood and walked hesitantly to Ernie's side. Leaning close in to the microphone next to her computer, he said, "Come again?"

"Vericomm *has* been taping the NickeLine long-distance calls—we were right. I'm dumping their archive to Ernie's computer."

"Are you screwing with me?"

"Of course not."

Beamon grabbed one of the speakers on the table and spoke directly at it. "You are a fucking genius, Mr. Goldman. I always knew you were. The best there ever was."

"I'm starting with the One-A-A stuff," Goldman said. "If I can get it all sent, I'll work on the lower-priority tapes."

"One-A-A?"

"Oh, Mark, this system is a thing of beauty. You wouldn't believe it." His tone had changed from giddiness to something between admiration and awe. "All calls made on NickeLine come through the computer system here at the central office. They're instantly given a number code based on who's calling. They know 'cause of the PIN you dial. Priority one means the person is important. You, for instance, as the head of the Flagstaff office, would be a priority one. A senator might be another example."

"What are the letters for?"

"The first one relates to keywords. The computer has some really spectacular voice recognition software. It listens for interesting words. *Bribe, sex, kill, Kneiss, Evolution,* and *money* are a few. Various swear words, too. It also measures volume, on the premise that if people are shouting, they're probably saying something interesting. If an important person hits on the right keywords, the conversation is given the code of one-A and it's sent down to a group of listeners who get right on it."

"Have I mentioned that you're a genius?" Beamon said, feeling for the first time in a week that he might just weasel his way out of this thing with his skin still wrapped around him. "What's the last letter for?"

"Oh, that signifies that it's been listened to and tells you how interesting it actually turned out to be."

"So we're getting the good stuff."

"Oh, yeah. I think you'll find it to be interesting listening. Could you hold on for a second?"

Beamon and Ernie both jumped at the loud crack that came over the speakers. It was followed by a muffled whimpering.

"Would you please shut up already? Try to be a man, for God's sake." Goldman's voice, but it was clear that he wasn't speaking to them.

"Mr. Goldman! Hello? Mr. Goldman? What the hell was that?"

"Huh? Oh, sorry, Mark. Just giving 'em something to think about."

Beamon realized that he'd been so elated by Goldman's coup that he hadn't really considered how he'd pulled it off. "Where are you, exactly?"

"Vericomm's tech center. Hold on for just one more second."

There was another crack that Beamon now knew was a gunshot.

"Yeah, you want some of that? Put your head out there again!" Goldman's voice taunted over the speakers.

"What's happening, Mark?" Ernie said, an expression of fear and confusion playing across her distorted features.

He held up his hand as Goldman's voice started, giddy again. "Their security boys are looking pretty upset, I'll tell you. Don't think it's going to be long before they figure out how to get that door the rest of the way open, though."

"Jesus Christ, Jack, get the hell out of there," Beamon said.

"Only one door out, Mark, and you can believe me when I tell you that they've got it covered."

The gunfire that sounded over the speakers this time was fully automatic.

"Damn!" he heard Goldman shout. There was rustling and the sound of things being knocked over as the old man took cover.

"What the fuck, Jack! You must have had a plan when you went in there," Beamon shouted desperately.

"I did. I planned on it being a one-way trip. I'll keep the feed going as long as I can. Been good knowing you, boy. Good-bye, Ernie. Oh, and Ernie? Lose some weight and find a man, for God's sake."

The phone went dead and Ernie wheeled to the screen behind her. Tears began running down her round face as she stared at it.

After a little less than a minute she made a quiet choking sound. "The feed's down."

51

SARA RENSLIER DIDN'T TURN WHEN THE footsteps began echoing off the walls behind her, but continued to concentrate on the large cross hanging above the altar on invisible wires. A symbol of everything she had built. "Was there any . . . damage?" she said when the footsteps stopped.

"Yes. A substantial amount of audio material was transmitted. All recent. All highly sensitive."

Sara took a deep breath and felt the burn of bile rise in her throat. "Were you able to trace the phone number it went to?"

Silence.

She turned and faced Gregory Sines, the head of the church's security force. His face was sunken and pale, accentuating the narrow pink scar that ran from his mustache to his right eye.

"Did you trace it?" she repeated.

"The call went to a hotel room, where it was connected to another number."

"What number?"

"There's no way to tell. Whoever set up the transfer knew what he was doing."

"Who was he?" she said.

"The man who got into Vericomm? We don't know yet. White male. Probably well into his eighties . . ."

"His eighties!" Her breath was coming short now. She closed her eyes and forced herself to calm down.

"He wasn't carrying any identification. We found the car he was driving, but it had been rented under an alias. We've fingerprinted his body and sent copies to one of our people at the FBI. We should know more soon."

"It doesn't matter," she said. "Beamon's behind this. That man was working for him."

Their private investigators hadn't been able to dig up anything substantial to use against Beamon—he was unmarried so no affairs, he wasn't a closet homosexual, no history of drug use or any other illegal activity. What they did find, though, was his drinking, his self-destructive behavior, and his lack of close friends or family—suggesting that he was a weak man with no foundation. A man the church's psychologists insisted would be easily diverted.

It was clear now that they had underestimated him. And she knew that she had accepted their analysis too easily, considering Beamon a relatively small player in another one of the government's hopeless bureaucracies.

Over the last decade, as the church's power had grown, she had begun to discount the power of the world's governments. Organizations led by men and women of shockingly limited intelligence who could be bought and sold with little more than glass beads. Beamon didn't seem to fit into that category.

She backed away from Sines and sat down on the steps leading to the altar. There was no turning back. She had created a nearly perfect plan to maintain her power over the church. But the plan didn't include a way out. When she had spoken her version of Kneiss's dying wishes to the Elders, she had set something in motion that couldn't be stopped. Jennifer had to die on the appointed date with all the Elders present. If she died before her time, the Elders—many of whom were already silently suspicious of her—would begin to put things together.

Until now, she had kept them weak by creating conflicts and jealousy between them—showing occasional favor toward one or another in Kneiss's name, passing out generous monetary rewards and severe penalties. But if they began to suspect what she had done, they would band together. Even Sines and his Guardians would be powerless in the face of that.

She considered for a moment the possibility of keeping Jennifer alive, telling the Elders that she had misinterpreted Kneiss's words. Isolating his granddaughter as she had him.

But that was impossible. Eventually they would gain access to her. And then they would learn the truth. No. There was only one way.

"We can't afford the luxury of keeping Mark Beamon alive anymore. We'll deal with whatever problems his death causes when they arise."

Sines remained silent.

"That's all, Gregory," she said, waving him away. "See to it. Now."

"We don't know where he is."

"What are you talking about?" she said, rising slowly to her feet. "He was being watched . . ."

"Our people lost him in the storm yesterday. He hasn't returned to his apartment and I don't think he will." Sines's expression turned indignant. "You've left him very little to come back to."

Sara swung an arm across the altar, sending a crystal urn and a set of elegant candlesticks crashing to the floor. "Don't you dare speak to me like that! I assumed that you would be competent enough to watch one broken man. Perhaps it was my fault for trusting in your abilities."

"It was a mistake to have him suspended. It freed him. Before, he was easy to watch and bound by the rules of the Bureau. Now—"

"I didn't ask for your analysis!" she shouted. "I only asked that you follow my instructions."

She stepped back and tried to calm down. This was not going to fall apart now. It couldn't. Not because of an overweight low-level bureaucrat.

"He's alone now," she said aloud. "The man who helped him is dead. He's alone. Homeless. He's lost everything. He can't possibly care about the girl anymore."

Beamon was controllable, she told herself. He had to be.

52

FIVE SHOTS OF BOURBON HAD SLOWED THE shaking in Beamon's hands enough for him to hold a lighter to the tip of his cigarette. He took a deep drag and felt the smoke fill his lungs. The instant lightheadedness and heaviness in his chest that he had been experiencing since he abandoned his new health regime seemed to be gone. A sign that the healing process, started when he moved to Arizona, had been completely reversed. Hallelujah.

A cockroach scurrying across the linoleum floor caught Beamon's eye. He followed it as it found its way through the maze of boxes, cables, and computer equipment that were strewn across the room, finally disappearing beneath the overalls Goldman had worn when he'd wired the church's phones. Draped over the empty box in front of Beamon, they looked like the old man's goddamned ghost.

Relying heavily on the worn arm of the chair he was sitting in, Beamon pushed himself to his feet and stuffed the still-damp overalls into the box. He began to close the cardboard flaps but stopped himself midway, realizing that this was the closest thing Goldman would ever get to a burial.

He had known the man for almost twenty years. He'd never counted it up before, but that was how long it had been.

Goldman's hair had been a little darker and fuller when they'd first met, and his skin had fit him a little better, but overall he'd been pretty much the same. People who had worked with him since the beginning—all dead now—swore he'd been a cantankerous old bastard at the tender age of nineteen.

Beamon wanted to call someone, but who? Goldman's family was long gone. As far as he knew, the old man didn't even have a secretary—having given up on them when they started objecting to being patted on the ass and called honey, and insisting that his battery of answering machines and mountains of software were more efficient and less flighty. But whenever he made that familiar speech, it was always with a tinge of loneliness in his voice.

Goldman had probably called him four or five times in the last three years. Beamon would pick up the phone and the old man would start into a tirade about something or other—the FBI, the CIA, politics, television. That was just the old man's way—he'd always known it. Goldman didn't know what else to say. But he had used Goldman's harmless badgering as an excuse to avoid him. Avoid the man who had just given his life to save a little girl and to get him out of the trap he'd sprung on himself.

Closing the flaps on the box was like throwing dirt on a coffin. Beamon raised his glass in salute, sloshing about a quarter of it down his arm. "You were right, Jack. I am a worthless sonofabitch." Words he'd have to remember for his own tombstone.

He scooted a chair up to the nearest computer terminal and unwrapped the computer disks containing the Vericomm audio from a piece of legal-sized paper that contained the instructions on how to listen to them.

He was having a little trouble bringing the instructions into full focus, but after a few minor wrong turns, he was faced with a screen full of file names. Each started with the surnames of the people on the line, then gave a date and time.

He slipped a pair of headphones over his ears and clicked twice on the first file. He recognized the name of one of the callers, but he couldn't place it exactly. A governor or senator or something.

Two hours later, halfway through the last file on the list, he tore the headphones from his ears and threw them to the floor in disgust.

"Jesus Christ!" he said to the empty room.

He'd always been a pretty hard-boiled cynic when it came to the people who chose to crawl around in the muck of politics, but never in his darkest alcohol-induced imaginings would he have ever come up with the contents of those tapes. Prepubescent prostitutes, bribes, blackmail, unholy alliances, and borderline treason. And all in glorious digital stereo.

The really worrisome thing, though, wasn't that the men running the government were into things that would make Caligula blush, it was that they weren't bright enough not to talk about those things over the phone. No, Beamon reminded himself, actually, that wasn't the most worrisome thing. The worst part of the whole thing was that the people whose voices were immortalized on his hard drive would slit their own mothers' throats to keep their extracurricular activities quiet.

As he leaned back and lit another cigarette, the cell phone in his pocket started up again. He flipped it open and put it up to his ear. "Hello, Sara."

The caller on the other end was silent for a moment. "Mr. Beamon."

"Somehow I knew you'd reconsider," Beamon said. "Real Christian of you."

"I assume that you're still interested in a meeting," Sara said.

The fury and frustration clogging her throat would normally have given Beamon at least a little bit of satisfaction. But sitting there in Goldman's empty apartment, he just felt numb. "Love one."

"Where?"

"There's a little restaurant called Antonio's. It's—"

"I know where it is."

"There, then. I'll let you buy me dinner. Tomorrow night. Seven o'clock."

Beamon flipped the phone shut and let out a long breath. Antonio's would be crowded. He'd be safe. Probably.

He looked at the calendar on his watch. He—Jennifer—had six days. Sara would try to play him for time. He was going to have to make this bargaining chip count.

The phone rang again and he picked it up on its third ring. "Let me guess. You don't like Italian."

"Mark?"

The accent was a little thicker and the voice a little higher-pitched than he remembered it, but there was still no mistaking who it was.

"Hans? It's good to hear your voice. How are you?"

"I am not well, Mark. Not well at all." He spoke quickly. "I have word from our people in the church."

"Yeah?"

"The church's leadership has recognized that you cannot be deterred by the normal means. Mark, I believe they mean to kill you."

Beamon lit another cigarette and blew the smoke into the phone. "I think you may be right, Hans."

"You must get out of there! I assure you that they not only have the will but also the means. Come here, to the embassy. I can offer you protection while we talk. Perhaps together we have enough information to expose them for what they are."

The offer was tempting. There was only one little problem. "What are your sources telling you about Jennifer Davis?"

"Nothing, I'm afraid. If the church does have her—and I know you believe that they do—they're keeping it very quiet. Knowledge at the highest levels only."

Beamon nodded and stared at the file names on the computer screen. "Well, when it's all over, if I'm still standing, I'll have an interesting story to tell you."

"Make sure you're still standing, then, Mark. A man with your reputation coming out against the church could do much to end the friction between our two governments."

"And I want to help you do that, Hans. But the girl's what I'm after. If I can do both, I will. If not, I'll have to leave politics to the politicians."

"Fair enough. But, Mark . . ."

"Yeah?"

"You must be careful. *Very* careful."

53

"DO YOU KNOW WHAT YOU'VE DONE?" Sara screamed as the door flew open and slammed into the wall.

Jennifer rolled off the bed, where she'd been lying in the half-sleep that seemed to have overtaken her in the last few days. The jolt of the cold floor cleared away some of the cobwebs, but she was still too groggy to dodge when Sara ran at her and pushed her back onto the bed.

Jennifer raised her hands too late to deflect a vicious open-handed slap that hit her full in the face. The stinging pain in her cheek cleared her mind a little more as Sara jerked her head back. The face she found herself staring into was unfamiliar—it was Sara, but the woman's eyes had gone wild and her pale complexion had turned bright red with rage.

"You think I'm going to lose everything because of you?"

She heard more than felt Sara's second strike across her face.

"Albert would still be preaching on a street corner if it weren't for me."

Jennifer tried to push her away, but she was too weak. Sara brought her face close and tightened her grip on Jennifer's hair. "No one's coming for you, Jennifer. No one."

"Why are you doing this to me?" Jennifer felt the tears coming and choked off a sob. "I just want to go home! I just want to go home."

The desperation and hate in Sara's face began to fade into the now-familiar expression of cruel superiority. "You'll never go home, Jennifer. You know that, don't you? You should have never come here."

"I didn't come here," Jennifer said, letting her body relax and her mind begin to drift away again. "You took me."

Sara was talking in a voice so low that she could almost feel it in her chest, but the words were meaningless to her. She looked away and let her eyes wander across the blank wall, trying desperately to return to the make-believe world that had taken away some of her loneliness and fear. Her gaze lingered for a moment on the door to the room. It was still open, and the poorly lit hallway was visible through it. For a moment the image confused her. Something was different. It took a few seconds for her to grasp why she could see straight through to the far wall of the hallway. The man who always stood silently at the door wasn't there.

He wasn't there.

Jennifer could feel her heart rate slowly increasing. After a few more seconds, she could almost hear it. The blood began to push through to her limbs, clearing away the lethargy that had overwhelmed her as she'd slowly lost hope.

The meaningless drone coming from Sara stopped short when Jennifer turned back to face the woman.

Closing her mouth was probably the only thing that saved Sara's front teeth.

None of the elaborate fantasies Jennifer had constructed over the last week could compare to the feeling of her fist connecting with the face that had tormented her and twisted everything in her life around. The face that had caused her father to go crazy and her mother to die. The face that she saw in the dark when she bolted awake at night.

Sara's hand fell from her hair and she watched the woman stumble backward, finally falling hard in the middle of the room. She was on all fours trying to get back to her feet when Jennifer reached her at as full a run as the short distance between them would allow.

Sara tried to cry out, but it was strangled in her throat when she was nearly lifted off the ground by Jennifer's bare foot.

A second kick, aimed at her head, glanced off her jaw.

Jennifer started to line up for another blow, feeling an indescribable sense of release as the burning in her stomach and the shaking in her limbs stopped. She wanted to kill this woman. She'd never wanted to hurt anyone before in her life, but now all she wanted was to feel this woman's skull cave in beneath her foot.

There wasn't time, though.

Instead of continuing the attack, Jennifer forced herself to use the momentum in her leg to jump over the woman and run from the room, slamming the door behind her and hoping desperately that it locked. Or, better yet, that she'd done too much damage for Sara to get up.

Which way?

To her left, the hall seemed to get darker, to her right, brighter. She picked right and began sprinting down the corridor, hoping the light was coming from the sun. She had to get out.

When the hall came to a T, she had to make another decision. *Come on, Jennifer,* she thought. *This is your chance. Don't go off half-cocked. What are you going to do?*

The possibility of her walking out of there was most likely less than zero, she realized. She had no idea where she was, it was the dead of winter, and she was in her underwear. A phone. She had to find a phone.

She moved as quietly as she could to the first door she saw, trying to get control of her breathing before someone heard her. It was a bathroom. She ducked back out of it and padded down the hall to the next door.

An office.

She went in and closed the door quietly behind her. The phone was on an antique desk, neatly stacked with official-looking papers. She picked it up and dialed 911.

A recording started, prompting her to stay on the line.

"No," she said quietly, hanging up the phone. She could already hear people in the hall.

She tried her boyfriend's number. He had an answering machine—so even if no one was home, she could tell him enough for the police to find her.

A voice over the phone told her that she had to dial a one to reach that number.

The noises in the hall were getting louder as she depressed the hang-up button on the phone and redialed Jamie's number as a long-distance call.

"Please enter your access code," came a mechanical-sounding voice.

"Oh, God, please, no." Tears began to run down her face as she punched in numbers at random.

"I don't recognize that code. Please reenter it now."

She depressed the hang-up button again, finding it impossible to catch her breath. The sounds in the hall were close now, clearly audible over her own panting.

She looked out the window. The brightness in the hall had been artificial—it was dark outside and she could hear the quiet whine of the wind. She leaned closer to the glass, reducing the glare, and saw that there was nothing out there, only low snow-covered hills and a pine forest in the distance. She'd freeze for sure. Probably in only a few minutes.

Jennifer looked over her shoulder at the closed door behind her and then back at the window. She couldn't go back to that room. She couldn't.

She was about to replace the handset and unlock the window when one last idea came to her. She crossed her fingers for a moment and then dialed another number, trying to ignore the increasing commotion outside.

It started to ring and was almost immediately picked up by a recording.

"Thank you for calling the Colorado Cyclist. If you have a touch tone phone, press one for sales, catalog requests, or product registration . . ."

It was the only eight hundred number she knew by heart. There was an access code for long distance, but why would there be one for toll-free calls? She pressed the key for the sales department just as the door flew open.

Holding the phone with both hands, she backed

against the wall and screamed as the Mustache Man ran at her. When he got hold of her, she let her knees go limp and sank to the ground, protecting the phone with her body. He tried to reach around her and pry it from her hand, but there was no way for him to get a grip.

She felt his weight come off her for a moment and she twisted around, trying to grab him as he went for the cord.

It was too late. She saw the wire ripped from the wall and heard the connection go dead, but couldn't bring herself to release the phone. It had been her only hope.

She struggled violently as he pulled her arms out from under her and pinned them behind her back, knowing that it was her last chance to fight before they threw her back into that empty room.

Jennifer heard the uneven clatter of running footsteps and craned her neck to try to see the person approaching, but she knew who it was. A splatter of blood hit the carpet in front of her as Sara dropped to her knees and swung a clawlike hand at her face. Jennifer braced for the blow, but the man holding her caught Sara's hand before it connected.

"Sara, stop! She can't be marked," Jennifer heard him say.

Sara's breath was coming in short gasps as she pulled away from the man and raised her hand again.

"Sara!"

Reason began to creep back into her eyes and she reached down and dug her fingers into Jennifer's cheeks, pulling her head up farther. "You don't ever touch me! Ever!"

Jennifer jerked her head to the left and got her teeth around Sara's thumb. She felt the warm blood starting to flow into her mouth and heard Sara scream before everything went black.

54

"TURN HERE," BEAMON SAID, LEANING OVER the front seat and pointing out the windshield.

"It'd be a lot faster to go up a couple of blocks. Your way would take us through a neighborhood."

"It's my dime."

The cab driver apparently saw that as sound reasoning and swung the cab right. He slowed to under twenty-five miles an hour as the commercial area they had been driving through gave way to a quiet neighborhood of small, well-kept homes.

Beamon twisted around in his seat and stared out the back window. Other than the occasional middle-aged man turning his snowblower for another pass at his driveway, the street was pretty much deserted. Not that he really thought he was being followed. What would be the point? The church knew where he was going. Of course, they would do everything they could to reacquire him when he left the restaurant, but better to worry about that later.

When his cell phone started ringing, he sank back into the seat and dug it out of his pocket. "Hello?"

"Mark! It's me!"

Ernie's voice. She sounded like she'd shaken off the depression that had gripped her since Goldman's death.

"If I didn't know better, I'd say you had some good news for me. Tell me I'm right."

"You're right! In fact, not only do I have good news, but I have good news and better news. Which do you want first?"

"Give me the good."

"The eight hundred number rang today."

"You're kidding," Beamon said, jolting upright in the seat. He had pretty much agreed with Goldman that the chances of her software-update scheme working were about the same as G. Gordon Liddy voting Democrat. "What did they say?"

"They wanted to confirm that there were no problems with the actual encryption."

"I trust you were very reassuring."

"Very. They're loading tonight!"

Beamon pumped a fist in the air, startling the cab driver, who had been looking in the rearview mirror. "That's gonna be hard to beat, Ernie. What's the better news?"

"I've got a recording of a call that went out from Albert's compound. I think you'll be interested. Let me try to patch it through."

There was some clicking on the line, and then a woman's voice announcing that he had reached the Colorado Cyclist and had some options. A tone sounded, then there was a loud crash, a scream that sounded like it came from a young girl, and an abrupt end to the call.

Beamon sat silently for a moment listening to his heartbeat. "That had to be her, Ernie. It had to be."

"I read in the papers that Jennifer was a mountain bike racer. I called the Colorado Cyclist. They sell mountain bike accessories."

"Fifty bucks says that if I hadn't left all the files

on this case in my condo, I could find all kinds of charges from that place on Jennifer's credit card."

"I don't think I'd take that bet," Ernie said excitedly.

"One thing bothers me, though . . ."

"Why would she call them?"

"Yeah."

"I've been thinking about that and I'm pretty sure I have an answer. If that is her, we know they're holding her at the compound, right?"

"Right." Beamon saw that they were only a few blocks from the restaurant. He put his hand over the mouthpiece of the phone and told the driver to circle the block.

"The compound is a long-distance call from where Jennifer lived," Ernie continued.

"So?"

"The place I used to work at had a phone system that made you dial a code before you could call long distance—that way they knew if you were charging personal calls to the company. What if the church has a similar system?"

"So she called an eight hundred number," Beamon said. "Clever girl. But why not just call nine-one-one?"

"I tried. Kept getting a recording. When I called the Colorado Cyclist, though, they got right on the line."

It made sense. She somehow got past Sara and her lackeys and made it to a phone. She'd have limited time before they found her. She'd try 911 first and get a recording. She'd probably call a family friend next—maybe that lady with the beehive. But she'd find out that she needed a code. Then it would occur to her that she probably wouldn't need one for an eight hundred number and she'd call the only one she could remember. Or if she knew a few, the one that had the fastest patch through to a human.

"It's like I told you, Mark. God is on our side."

"If that's true, I hope He comes up with something a little better."

"What? Better than this?"

"I already assumed that Jennifer was being held at the compound, Ernie. I just didn't know what to do with the information. If the call was more concrete, I'd send it to someone I trust at the Bureau." He paused for a moment, trying to think if there was anyone anymore. "But as it is, they'd never get a warrant—even if they bought into the theory."

Beamon tapped the driver on the shoulder and waved his hand in the general direction of the restaurant.

"Then this is all for nothing," Ernie said, sounding a little dejected again

"Hell no, Ernie! Things are starting to go our way. Shit, God's probably just warming up."

"Do you think so?"

"Sure. It's been my experience that investigations are all about momentum, and we're finally starting to get some. The only problem is, we don't have much time to let it build."

"Were you able to play the audio I sent you?"

"Yeah."

"What did you think?"

"It was something, that's for sure. We'll know if it's gonna do us any good within the hour."

"I listened to it. I can't believe the godless whores we've chosen to run this country."

"Who'd you think ran it?" Beamon said as the cab eased to a stop in front of the brightly lit façade of Antonio's Italian Ristorante.

"Look, I gotta go, Ernie," Beamon said, digging in his pocket for the quickly thinning envelope of cash. "Great work, hon. We're gonna win this thing. Don't worry."

"How are you, sir," the host said, holding a hand out for Beamon's coat. "Do you have a reservation?"

"I'm meeting someone. Last name's Renslier."

He ran his finger down the book in front of him for a moment. "Ms. Renslier arrived a few minutes ago. If you'll wait for just one moment, I'll take you to her table."

Beamon watched him as he opened a closet and picked out a hanger for the red parka that had been serving him so well. "There aren't any private parties or anything going on tonight, are there?"

The host looked a bit confused. "Private parties?"

Beamon knew he was being paranoid, but he couldn't help himself. "Yeah. Like, no one called and rented the whole place out for tonight, did they?"

"No, not tonight. We do parties like that occasionally. We also have private rooms available. Make sure you give us a call at least a week ahead of time if you want one, though."

Despite the host's assurances, Beamon couldn't help studying the faces of the diners as he weaved through them on the way to the back of the restaurant.

There were definitely Kneissians there. The annoying, fresh-scrubbed optimism that oozed from every pore all over their well-coordinated outfits gave them away. Most were couples, though, and many had tediously well-behaved children with them.

Beamon nodded his thanks to the host and slid into the booth across from Sara Renslier and a man he'd never seen before. The scar emanating from his mustache was exactly as Ernie had described it, though. Beamon reached across the table. "Greg Sines, isn't it? I don't think we've met."

The man's eyes bored into him as he put a death grip on Beamon's hand. He'd seen that look more than a few times before. It said, "One day I'm going to tear your heart out with whatever blunt instrument happens to be handy." With few exceptions, every man who had ever looked at him that way was either dead or in jail. Hopefully that record would continue with this asshole.

Sines tucked some kind of hand-held device— probably a rig that checked for wires—into his pocket and left without a word. Beamon looked around him and, confirming that he was in the smoking section, lit a cigarette. "Nice to see you again, Sara."

She looked different. The light in this part of the restaurant was set at a level more conducive to mood than discerning detail, but the heavy makeup was an obvious departure from the look required of Kneiss's minions. The other thing, less apparent and possibly a trick of shadow, was the slightly lopsided look to her face.

"Hurt your hand?" Beamon said, leaning a bit to the side to get a better angle on the line of her jaw. If he didn't know better, he'd say she had been punched in the mouth.

Sara looked down at the new white bandage wound around her thumb. "An accident."

Beamon tried unsuccessfully to stifle a smile. Now he knew how Jennifer had made it to the phone. He really *had* to meet that girl one day.

"So, Sara," he said, letting cigarette smoke roll from his mouth as he spoke. "What do we talk about?"

"We could start with the fact that we both have something the other wants."

Beamon was surprised at her directness. "I know what I have that you want, but what do you have to give me?"

"Your life back."

He'd hoped for a different answer. "My life?"

She nodded and took a piece of bread from the basket on the table. "I've heard rumors that the molestation allegations against you may be false, and I could probably find proof of that if I were to put some of my people to work on it. I also may have access to information regarding your credit and some friends at the IRS who could be helpful to you."

"And my job?"

She took a small bite of the bread, more as a nervous gesture than from hunger. "Of course that's in the FBI's hands now. I do have friends who might be able to help. Friends who have some weight."

Beamon nodded but didn't say anything.

"I would also be happy to make a donation to your legal defense fund—you may need attorneys, and they can be expensive. Of course, if you were to simply choose to take early retirement, whatever was left in that fund would be yours."

He couldn't resist. "How much are we talking about?"

"What do you think you would need to mount an adequate defense?"

"Uh, five million," he said, pulling a number out of the air.

To his surprise, nothing at all registered on her face. "I think that sounds reasonable."

Beamon leaned back in his chair and waved down a waiter. "Jim Beam on the rocks, please." He pointed to Sara, but she just shook her head.

He had to admit, the woman knew how to put a tempting offer on the table. Of course, it would take him a while to adjust to retirement, but he figured he could get used to being a wealthy man of leisure. And with his reputation dusted off a bit, Carrie would probably be back in the picture. Maybe he could try his hand at being a househusband/full-time stepfather? Learn to bake.

Nah.

"I want the girl."

"The girl?" Sara looked mildly amused. "Oh, yes. Jennifer Davis. The girl you think Albert for some reason kidnapped and is holding in his dungeon."

"Kneiss is dead."

"Excuse me?"

"Don't talk to me like I'm an idiot, Sara. It pisses me off. Kneiss is dead. We both know it. Obviously, it's not in the best interests of the church—that is, your best interests—to let that little tidbit leak until Good Friday. Got to keep that collection plate full."

"I understand now," Sara said, starting a smile but stopping its progress across her face with a slight wince. "You believe that Albert died and I needed a new messenger. I've heard that you believe that Jennifer Davis is Albert's granddaughter. If that's true, she'd be the perfect replacement, wouldn't she?"

Sara shook her head. "I'm disappointed, Mr.

Beamon. I would have thought you'd understand us better by now. There's no need for a new messenger. And for that matter, no expectation that there would be one for another two thousand years."

"I know that. I was thinking more along the lines that Kneiss wanted someone to replace him as head of the church instead of putting you in the job. I think Albert understood what you were doing and didn't like it."

"What I was doing?" she said, suddenly angry. "What do you think it is that Albert doesn't like? The fact that I've devoted my entire life to spreading his message and building his church?"

"I don't think it was your results, Sara. I think it was your methods." Beamon jerked his head toward the bar. "Men like Gregory Sines don't exactly fit into most people's idea of a church elder."

"What I've done, I've done for God."

Beamon smiled. "I believe that most of the war, torture, and cruelty in our history were started by men with those same words on their lips."

"I don't think you have any idea what it is to have faith, Mr. Beamon. God directs me in all things. He tells me what is right and wrong. He has given me the strength to accomplish what I have."

"And the strength to protect the church when it's threatened."

"That too," she said, looking directly at him.

"And Jennifer's a threat now, isn't she? You built the church, not Albert. He had the message, but you had the means." Beamon took a sip of his drink. "And then, right before he dies—the old sonofabitch gives it away. Gives away *your* church. To a fifteen-year-old girl with dyed blonde hair and a ring in her nose, no less. That had to be a kick in the ass."

"I have no idea—"

Beamon cut her off. "But then Albert goes and dies—not ascends, just dies like the rest of us. Or maybe you helped him along? Either way, it would leave you in quite a pickle, wouldn't it? The only way you'd be able to explain it is that his time as the Messenger was over. That someone is being chosen to take his place."

Sara sat perfectly still. The heavy makeup and dim lighting would have made her look like a mannequin if it hadn't been for the reflection of her eyes.

"Seems to me that Jennifer would be a good choice," Beamon continued. "Fixes your little theological glitch and has the added benefit of getting her out of your way."

Beamon put his cigarette out in the ashtray on the table. "Because somebody has to take Kneiss's place next week. Don't they?"

Sara's eyes darted left. Toward Sines, Beamon guessed.

"That's quite a theory, Mr. Beamon. I'm not sure how to respond."

"Then let me make a suggestion. Give me Jennifer. You religious leaders are masters at dredging up obscure Bible passages to justify whatever it is you want to do. Hell, tell your people that God appeared to you in a box of Cracker Jacks and told you that it was Jennifer's destiny to be a Protestant. I don't really give a shit."

"Do you think your position is strong enough to be making threats, Mr. Beamon? What do you have? A few illegally obtained recordings of conversations between—who? Can you prove these people's identities? I doubt it. And I doubt even more that you can prove how the recordings were originally obtained."

"Oh, I think you're probably right. From a letter-of-the-law standpoint, I'd have a real uphill battle. But if those recordings were sent to the FBI anonymously—or maybe better, to some of my contacts in the press—with a detailed explanation of what they were and how they were obtained, I imagine that I could generate some real interest in the way you operate your church. Hell, I probably wouldn't even have to go through all that trouble. I could just give them to your biggest fan—the German government—and trust them to use them to do the absolute maximum damage."

Gregory Sines slid silently into the booth next to Sara, prompting Beamon to move his hand a little closer to his gun. "Look, Sara. I don't care about the people on the tapes. And I care even less about the people who vote those idiots in. It's not my job to save the public from themselves. But the girl, well, as I see it, she's gotten a raw deal."

"I don't understand you, Mr. Beamon. You've lost nearly everything of value to you in the span of a few weeks. And for what? If I had the girl, I certainly wouldn't let you find her." She shook her head in sadly. "Take what I'm offering you. Marry that psychiatrist. Move away from Flagstaff."

Beamon grimaced and finished his drink. "Can you imagine what it would be like being married to a psychiatrist? Her always knowing what you're thinking? Besides, I'm considering learning to ski."

"Is this just stupid male pride? No matter what happens, you lose." Her voice lowered. "If you think what you've suffered so far has been difficult, I can assure you that you won't like what your future holds. God will not let you stand in the way of His work."

Beamon smiled. "God's work." He reached out and squeezed her hand, coming suggestively close to her injured thumb. "My guess is that you're about as religious as I am. But if I'm wrong and there is a God, I'm starting to think He's on my side."

55

"ARE YOU OKAY?" ERNIE SAID, A LOOK OF concern spreading across her face.

Beamon hung up his cell phone in disgust, promising himself that that was the last time he was going to succumb to curiosity and retrieve his phone messages. "What? Oh, yeah, fine."

"Anything interesting?"

He shook his head. "A kind of nasty call from the IRS and some woman from an AIDS counseling outfit who wants to discuss my recent diagnosis."

Ernie's hands went to her cheeks. "I'm so sorry, Mark, I had no idea . . . But I've read that there are some new medical—"

Beamon laughed easily. "Relax, Ernie. I don't have AIDS. Sadly, I can't even remember the last time I had sex."

"The church?"

He nodded. "I guess I won't be applying for a new life insurance policy anytime soon. So what's so important that I had to haul my butt down here like it was on fire?"

Ernie grabbed a few sheets of paper from her desk and held them up proudly. "E-mail."

"You actually got it working?"

She handed him the papers. "The Lord pro-

vides. We've received six e-mails in total, but most
of them relate to financial matters, things I don't
think you'd be interested in."

"And the others?"

She nodded toward the papers in his lap. "Read
the top two."

To: tara@retreat5346.com
From: ak@compound6758.com

Members currently studying are
absolved. Clear all students and
personnel from the Retreat by
midnight tonight.
God Bless

"The Retreat?" Beamon said

"It's a ranch in eastern Oregon. Kneissians
who've done something to anger the church go
there."

"Oh, yeah, right. There was something about
that in your book. It's the place they go and pay
an arm and a leg to eat bread and water and get
marched around in the mountains till they
drop."

"Till they're forgiven," Ernie corrected.

Beamon flipped to the second page.

To: Nolan@Guardians5278.com
From: ak@compound6758.com

Sara will arrive at the retreat by
seven a.m. tomorrow morning. You
and two of your men will be waiting
for her there. She will instruct when
she arrives.

God Bless

Beamon rubbed at the bottom of his jaw and read the two e-mails again.

"What do you think, Mark?"

"I forgot to tell you that I figured out how Jennifer made it to the phone."

"Really? How?"

"Sara's mouth was swelled up pretty good. In an area about the size of a fist." He pointed to his right hand. "And she had a fresh bandage on her thumb."

Beamon watched Ernie's eyes turn distant for a moment as she imagined what it would feel like to beat the crap out of Sara Renslier.

"This is it, Ernie," Beamon said, bringing her back from her ecstatic vision before he lost her entirely. "Sara is injured right around the same time as Jennifer makes it to a phone and damn near gets a call out. Suddenly they're clearing out the closest thing the church has to a prison and sending three of the wristband brigade there to meet Sara."

"I think they're going to move her, Mark."

Beamon nodded. "The question is, how? If they've left already, they could maybe drive straight through, but that would be tough. Timing-wise and risk-wise. They'd have to drug her and put her in the back of a van or something . . ."

"They're not going to drive."

"They're not?"

"No. There's no road leading to the Retreat. They have a landing strip that's kept open year-round."

56

BEAMON EASED HIS CAR THROUGH THE OPEN chain-link fence and rolled to a stop in the middle of a random grouping of vehicles near the tower building. The lights from the runway were just an undefined halo, not really penetrating the dark, just changing its color. Even the light seeping from the windows of the building next to him barely managed to filter through to his car. According to the disembodied voice coming over the radio, a warm front had crashed into a mass of cold air above Flagstaff, resulting in the torrential rain that was flowing across his windshield and over the backs of the overwhelmed wipers.

Beamon stepped out of the car and began across the tarmac, hunched uselessly against the rain. His jeans and sweatshirt were completely soaked through in less than a minute, and the clammy material against his skin reminded him that in Flagstaff, "warm front" meant low forties.

He straightened up and slowed to a normal pace as the glow from the buildings behind him faded to nothing and a light source, roughly in front of him, strengthened. He adjusted his course slightly and headed straight for it.

Two red dots seemed to float in space for a while, but as he moved closer, the unbroken white of a plane's wings began to appear, illuminated by light pouring through its open door and the small windows in its side.

Beamon circled to his right and stopped near the tail. He pulled a damp piece of paper from his back pocket and read the numbers off it before the rain smeared them into an illegible blob.

They matched. This was the plane. Thank God for Chet Michaels.

He could barely see through the haze created by the heavy raindrops exploding against the stairs leading into the plane, but as he edged closer, he could see that there was no movement inside.

Sliding his gun from the holster beneath his sweatshirt, he put his foot on the first step and gently weighted it. He'd never been on an aircraft this small and wasn't sure if his weight would rock it and telegraph his approach.

Whether it was the mass of the plane or his recent diet, the steps didn't budge under his feet, and he crept slowly up them and into the dry cabin.

The pilot in the cockpit to his left seemed to be engrossed in whatever was contained on the clipboard in his hand. He seemed completely oblivious to the sound of water dripping from Beamon onto the thick carpet, and continued running his finger down a column of switches in front of him.

There were nine seats in all, each half again as wide as the ones in an airliner's first-class cabin and each lovingly covered in soft tan leather. At the back, there was a small storage area that Beamon could see was empty.

"Excuse me," Beamon said, taking a step toward the cockpit.

The pilot tensed, bouncing a few inches out of

his chair, and then twisted around to look behind him. He gasped quietly when he saw Beamon. Or, more precisely, when he saw down the barrel of Beamon's gun.

Unbidden, the pilot raised his hands above his head. "What do you want? This is a small plane—Mexico's as far as I could get you."

Beamon wrung out the bottom of his sweatshirt and smiled. He'd never considered hijacking as a career choice, but in the current context it was looking pretty attractive. Fly down south of the border, sell the plane for a few mill to a drug runner, and spend the rest of his life on the beach with a drink in one hand and a taco in the other.

"Take it easy," Beamon said. "I was told to meet some people from the church here—that there might be some trouble . . ."

The pilot relaxed a bit. "Look, man. I just fly this thing, you know? Nobody ever tells me what's going on—I just get people where they're going."

He was a rather puffy-looking man, Beamon noted. Not really fat, just kind of formless, with a round face that was strangely pale and hairless in a way that made it difficult to guess his age.

"Okay, then. Why don't you step out of there—without touching any more of those buttons and switches, please—and have a seat back here."

The pilot looked more than happy to oblige and moved slowly but efficiently from the cramped space of the cockpit and past Beamon, all the while keeping his hands as high as the low ceiling would allow. He took a seat in one of the plush leather seats facing Beamon and looked up to see if there were any more instructions for him to follow.

Beamon couldn't think of any, unless there was

a coffee pot somewhere, and there didn't seem to be.
He leaned his back against the uncomfortably
curved wall next to the door leading outside and
looked down at his hands. They'd turned bright
white from the cold and felt completely lifeless. He
pressed his index finger gently against the trigger of
his revolver. The finger still worked, but the frozen
skin covering it didn't register the increased pressure. He'd have to be careful of that.

"Isn't there a heater in here?"

The pilot shook his head. "Not until I start the
plane."

Beamon frowned and tucked his left hand into
his armpit, accomplishing nothing but to wring a
little more water from the sweatshirt and start it
running down his side.

The rain had died down a bit, but the wind was
still gusting through the door and sending a cold
mist washing over him every few seconds. He struggled to keep his teeth from chattering and hoped
things would move quickly. Of course, they didn't.

He ended up spending the next hour trying to
fight off the effects of the cold and wondering what
the hell he was going to do if he was wrong and a
bunch of church executives showed up with their
wives and kids for a quick beach trip.

Beamon pressed himself a little closer to the
wall when the dim red glow coming through the
door wavered and then began to fade into a set of
approaching headlights. He gave the pilot a quick
glance that said "stay quiet" and poked his head
around the corner of the door. Another Taurus. The
church must get a bulk discount on those things.

The car stopped maybe twenty feet from the
plane and both driver and passenger immediately

jumped out. They had their backs to him, so he stepped fully into the doorway and watched as they opened the back door of the Ford and began to pull something out.

Even from behind, they were both easily recognizable. The small woman by her severe haircut and the bandage wound around her right thumb, and the man by the thick mustache, the tips of which were visible when his head moved. Beamon had hoped Gregory Sines wouldn't make an appearance tonight. He looked like the kind of man who would be hard to control in a situation like this.

Beamon smiled and let out a long, quiet breath as the headlights reflecting off the plane illuminated a white-blonde head of hair.

He realized that he really hadn't expected this moment to ever come. The slow burn he'd been feeling in his stomach had been the unfamiliar sensation of defeat, and he recognized now that his recent actions had been governed more by the desire to go down swinging than anything else. He had to admit, though, that it made this moment that much sweeter.

Sara and Sines draped the arms of their cargo across their necks and turned toward the plane heads down, searching for any remaining patches of ice on the asphalt.

From where he was standing, Jennifer looked to be completely unconscious; her body was limp and the toes of her bare feet dragged across the tarmac as she was carried across it. He couldn't see her face, but the skin on her arms looked as white as his—no trace remained of the athletic glow so evident in her photographs.

"Shit!" Beamon said in surprise as he threw a

hand out to keep himself from rolling down the stairs. He twisted hard to the right, keeping his eyes on Sines, who had looked up just as Beamon was hit from behind by the pilot.

The man managed to get an arm around Beamon's neck but wasn't able to lock it off. Beamon twisted again and threw an elbow as Sines reached behind him for what no doubt was going to be a really big gun.

The pilot's arm slid off the wet skin of his neck and he stuck a foot out just in time to trip the man and send him pitching out the door head first.

"Stop!" Beamon yelled over the sound of the rain and the pilot's head connecting with the ground.

Despite his warning and the fact that his gun was already at waist-level, Sines's hand disappeared beneath his jacket and was now starting to come back out. Fast.

Beamon waited as long as he dared, but when the butt of Sines's gun became visible, he squeezed the trigger.

The round hit Sines dead center, as Beamon knew it would—hell, there was probably only fifteen feet between them. Sines jerked back and fell, but somehow managed to land in a sitting position and retain control of his gun hand. Sara dove to the ground, leaving Jennifer to fall face first to the asphalt.

Beamon fired another round, this time without giving it much thought. Sines was already dead. It just hadn't registered with him yet.

Beamon ran down the stairs as Sines fell to his back for the last time and caught Sara by the collar before she could make it to her feet.

"Let go of me, you sonofabitch!" she screamed as he dragged her toward the plane and handcuffed her to the bar that supported the stairs.

Beamon stepped away from her and looked down at the pilot's motionless body. "Stupid ass-hole," he said, quietly reprimanding himself. Watching his life come crashing down around his ears was fucking up his judgment. Eleven million members and what, the church is going to use a Mormon to transport a kidnapped girl?

The pilot looked like he'd probably wake up with nothing more than a baseball-sized knot on his head, but he couldn't say the same for Sines—he was just going to lie there staring up into the rain. Beamon didn't feel a great deal of remorse over Sines's demise; what concerned him was *why* the man was dead. It was because he was allowing lapses in his concentration and getting sloppy.

Sara lunged at him, her unwounded hand twisting into something that resembled a claw. The motion brought Beamon back to the present and he watched her body jerk to a stop as the handcuff around her wrist went taut.

"Be careful you don't hurt yourself now," Beamon said, scooping Jennifer up from the puddle she'd landed in and cradling her in his arms. He could feel the warmth of her body seeping into his chest as he pulled her to him.

"Take these off me!" Sara screamed. "You *will not* do this!"

"Looks like I already did."

She grabbed the chain between the handcuffs and pulled mightily but pointlessly against them. Blood had started to flow from her wrist and was mixing with the rain to run pale pink down her hand.

"It's just you and me now, Sara. None of your lackeys are around to accuse me of child molestation or alcoholism. No computers to fuck up my credit cards. It looks like your God's abandoned you and come over to my side, doesn't it?"

She suddenly froze and looked up at him, a forced calm registering on her face. "Put her down, Mr. Beamon. It isn't worth it. If you take her I'll destroy you and everyone you've ever known."

Beamon flipped Jennifer over his shoulder, drew his gun, and aimed it at Sara's head.

"No!" she cried, throwing her hands in front of her face and shrinking back as far as the handcuffs would allow. Beamon kept the gun trained on her as she crouched down and averted her eyes toward the pavement, stoking his anger until he couldn't feel anything else—not the cold, not the weight of Jennifer on his shoulder. Nothing.

He knew he should do it—she would come after him and the girl with everything she had. He should do it for Jennifer, for Goldman, for himself.

But he'd already gone far enough across the line. He took a deep breath and holstered his gun. "You don't look like much when you're not surrounded by your church." Beamon patted the unconscious girl on the backs of her legs. "Thanks for screwing up and letting me get Jennifer back. I reckon she'll go a long way to straightening out my life."

The desperation in Sara's voice warmed Beamon's heart as he started walking back to his car. "You talked about five million dollars last time we met, Mr. Beamon. What if it was ten? Twenty?"

Beamon paused and turned around so he could enjoy the full effect of Sara's panic.

"Twenty million? Is that the number?" She pointed to Sines's body. "No one has to ever know about this."

She smoothed the damp folds in her dark suit and raised herself to her full height. "You don't have anywhere to take her anyway, do you? Who can you trust? The FBI? I think you know better than that."

He took a backward step away from her.

"Wait," she said in a tone that would have been appropriate for talking a jumper out of leaping from a tall building. "You've proven what you can do—I have a hundred times the resources you do and you beat me. You beat me. Now put her down and unlock these handcuffs. Do that, and whatever you want is yours."

Flattery, no less. He really would have liked to stick around and let her kiss his ass some more, but it was about time to get the hell out of there. The pilot was starting to twitch and somebody at the tower had to have heard the shots. They were probably up there trying to decide which one of them would get to brave the rain.

Beamon turned and started for his car.

"Stop! Wait!"

He quickened his pace.

"You'll never get out of this," Sara screamed. The calm, persuasive tone she'd been trying to ply him with was gone. "You're alone now—we put the old man out of his misery and that little fanatic can't help you anymore."

Beamon slowed and finally stopped, still within earshot.

"How could you have left her alone like that? A helpless woman in a wheelchair. How was she supposed to defend herself?"

57

THERE WAS NOTHING THE FIREFIGHTERS could do at this point—other than make sure the blaze didn't spread to the other homes in the neighborhood. Even the sheets of rain lashing the house could do little to contain the jets of flame gusting from the broken windows and into the dark night.

Beamon parked almost a block and a half away from the bonfire that a few hours ago had been Ernestine Waverly's house, not wanting to be spotted by the men who had set it. He looked over at Jennifer, whose only movement for the last hour had been prompted by the rocking of the car. Her head was propped against the window and her mouth was open, though Beamon had to concentrate to hear her breathe.

He checked her seatbelt again for no particular reason, then leaned forward and rested his head against the steering wheel. "We got her, Ernie," he said quietly. "We won."

When he looked out the windshield again, the chance of the fire spreading seemed pretty remote. The firefighters had abandoned their vigil over the other houses in the neighborhood and were moving through the small knot of rain-slickered people who had braved the elements to see the little house consumed.

He flipped his headlights back on—not that they were necessary, the glow from the fire had lit up the entire neighborhood—and put the car in reverse.

She was dead, he knew; all he could hope for now was that it had been quick. He tried to convince himself of it, but he knew that he was lying to himself. Sara's Guardians would have undoubtedly wanted to know were he was and what he was up to.

Either she hadn't told them at all or she'd held out long enough that they hadn't had time to make it to the airport. Thank God there had never been a reason to tell her where Goldman's apartment was.

That was it. The last of his patched-together team was dead. And once again, it was his fault. He'd been able to stave off the feeling of guilt about Goldman—at least temporarily. The old man had known what he was doing. Hell, he'd probably been breathing longer than he should have or wanted to.

Ernie was another story. He should have cut loose from her a long time ago. But he hadn't. He'd been blinded, as he had been a hundred times before, by the problem. Solving it, beating his opponent, proving management wrong. Those things had become everything to him. He'd used her and left her to the wolves.

As the glow in his rearview mirror faded, Beamon couldn't help thinking about Ernie's God and her unshakable faith. He'd never believed. He'd never really wanted to. There was something about the concept of a Supreme Being that made him uncomfortable. It robbed the universe of the free will and chaos that made it so interesting. And for that, all you got was an eternity of peace and tranquility. He'd always thought it was a bad trade, making life just a pointless, painful blink of an eye in an eternity of bliss.

For the first time, though, he actually hoped he was wrong and Ernie and the others like her were right. He hoped that in death Ernie would find what she had been looking for in life.

58

BEAMON PULLED HIS SHOTGUN OUT OF THE
back seat and leaned it against the side of the car.
He looked around him at the rundown apartment
complex that had become his new home, but didn't
see any movement. Other than the muffled sound
of yet another pre-coitus spat coming from the
apartment next to his, the complex was silent.

Fortunately, it was also pretty dark. Most of the
bulbs in the parking area's floodlights were burned
out and none of the residents seemed interested in
paying for the power necessary to keep their carriage lights on.

Beamon pulled Jennifer's limp body from the
car and slung her over his shoulder. He looked
around him one more time before picking up the
shotgun and beginning across the icy walkway
toward Goldman's apartment.

The snow in front of his door had been washed
away by the rain, making it impossible to look for
telltale footprints. The curtains were still closed and
it looked to be dark inside the apartment, but that
didn't mean a hell of a lot. He unlocked the door,
took a deep breath, and pushed it open with the barrel of the shotgun.

Empty.

No doubt thanks to the seemingly endless supply of phony IDs under which Jack Goldman had transacted nearly all his business.

Beamon kicked a couple of boxes off the sofa and dropped Jennifer onto it, then fell into a chair and turned on the TV. Unscrewing the cap from what was left of the bottle of bourbon next to him with one hand, he flipped to a local station with the other. Ten more minutes until the eleven o'clock news.

He'd gotten what he wanted so badly, he reflected, taking a long pull directly from the bottle. The infamous Jennifer Davis was now gracing his sofa at the low, low cost of three lives. Three and a half, if he counted what was left of his own.

Beamon took another shot from the bottle and then screwed the cap back on. It wasn't over yet. Four more days until Jennifer was scheduled for her promotion to godhood. Four days for Sara to correct her mistake. And with the FBI after him and Ernie and Goldman dead, holding onto the girl might prove more challenging than finding her had been. By now there were probably a thousand Kneissians scouring every apartment complex and hotel for three hundred miles looking for him. Not good.

He looked over at Jennifer. Except for the bare feet, she was dressed in the same clothes that she was reported last seen in—the pair of shorts and sweatshirt she'd donned after her fourth-place finish in Phoenix. She looked thinner than she had in her photographs and the calculatedly obvious dye job that kids seemed to favor these days had grown out a bit, revealing an infinitely prettier natural brown. The ring was gone from her slightly swollen nose, and dark circles had painted themselves under her eyes. All in all, she looked like the only person on earth who had had a worse month than him.

The local news opened with dramatic scenes of the blaze at Ernie's house. Interviews with firefighters suggested that they hadn't yet investigated the cause of the fire or whether anyone was inside when it started. They said they were just going to let it burn out and would know more tomorrow.

Beamon watched the rest of the program, his eyes darting nervously to the door every few seconds. There was still no mention of Goldman's death and nothing on the shooting at the air terminal. He suspected there never would be.

When the weather came on, Beamon turned the old TV off and lit a cigarette.

What now?

If he could keep Jennifer alive for the next four days and get her story on record, she should be safe. Sara struck him as vindictive but certainly not stupid.

Staying at the apartment was out of the question. It was possible that the church's people would never find this place—the threads leading to it were pretty thin—but he couldn't risk it. And that left very few options.

One: Dump the car and hole up in a motel somewhere.

Not exactly ideal. It still left him alone against the combined forces of the church and the way his luck was running, he'd end up in a Kneissian-owned hotel. But even if he didn't, they'd sure as hell be looking for him at all the hotels in the area and would be watching all the roads out of town.

Two: Take her to the press.

But who in the press? Obviously, the church

436 — KYLE MILLS

had contacts there or he'd still have a job. Besides, they'd be watching for him there, too. And that didn't solve his problem of keeping Jennifer's head off the chopping block until the Easter season was safely over.

Three: Take her to the FBI.

Probably his best option, but still less than ideal. He wasn't really ready to go in yet—there were some loose ends that he wanted to tie up before he condemned himself to six months in endless conduct hearings, and probably three to five in any number of conveniently located local penitentiaries.

Chet Michaels was the answer. Or at least the lesser of the evils. They could meet somewhere a few miles from the Phoenix office and Michaels could drive them in, with Jennifer, Beamon, and his shotgun keeping out of sight.

Even if Layman was involved with, or being blackmailed by, the church, what could he do? Jennifer would be standing in the middle of a crowded office and would become public property. From then on, the whole thing would be someone else's responsibility.

59

BEAMON JERKED AWAKE AT THE QUIET creak of the sofa. He was confused for a few moments—by the weight of the shotgun lying across his lap, by the young girl unconscious on the couch.

The events of the prior week started replaying themselves before his mind was completely back on line. His suspension, Carrie, Jack's and Ernie's deaths, and finally, the girl he'd taken possession of last night. Along with a whole host of other problems.

Jennifer was still more or less in the position he'd left her in, Beamon noted as he stood and stretched his back. The apartment was silent, except for the low drone of the computers that surrounded him. The only thing that had changed was the sun filtering through the dusty blinds.

Beamon leaned the shotgun against his chair and walked over to the sofa. He reached down and gave Jennifer a gentle shake. Her muscles tensed for an instant and then went slack again. Faker.

He shook her again, this time a bit harder. "Come on, Jennifer. Rise and shine. I know you're awake."

No reaction at all this time.

He went into the kitchen and filled a rusty pan halfway with ice from the freezer. "Wake up, Jen-

438 — KYLE MILLS

nifer. Last chance," he warned as he filled the pan the rest of the way with water.

Humming quietly, he put a lid over the pan and walked back to the sofa, slowly swirling the mixture. He could see Jennifer's neck stiffen almost imperceptibly as she tried to decipher the unfamiliar sound of ice rolling against metal. Beamon moved the lid so that there was about a three-quarters-inch gap and began pouring the contents of the pan on her face.

The first splash of water had barely reached her before she was off the couch and diving over the old coffee table toward the chair Beamon had slept in that night.

It was quite a show, really. By the time Beamon had tilted the pan back up to check the water's flow onto the now-empty sofa, he had a very scared-looking fifteen-year-old girl pointing a loaded shotgun at him.

Beamon screwed up his face and closed his eyes hard. Nearly two decades of putting some of the most notorious criminals in the world behind bars and an adolescent girl was the first person to ever get ahold of his gun. In the unlikely event he survived long enough to write a report on this investigation, he'd probably leave this part out.

Beamon slowly opened one eye. "Looks like you got the drop on me, Tex." He opened the other. "Jesus, I don't remember ever being young enough to move that fast."

"Freeze!"

"How 'bout I sit instead?" He placed the pan on the coffee table and plopped down on the sofa.

"I'll shoot!" Jennifer said as Beamon reached into his pocket. He slowed the motion of his hand

and pulled out a pack of cigarettes. Tapping one out into his hand, he said, "I believe you, kid. But let's make sure that if you *do* shoot me, it's because you want to." He held his lighter to the end of the cigarette. "What would you say about moving your finger off that trigger a little bit?"

He patted what remained of the stubborn roll of fat that wouldn't release his waistline. "I think you'll agree that I'm in no condition to get all the way across the room before you can move your finger half an inch."

She looked at him suspiciously but finally moved her quivering finger off the trigger. "Who . . . who are you?"

"Mark Beamon. I'm with the FBI."

"You don't look like an FBI agent."

He assumed she meant his casual clothing. People seemed to think FBI agents slept in their suits. "Thank you."

"Let me see your ID."

Beamon frowned. "Actually, saying that I'm with the FBI is a bit of an exaggeration. I *was* with the FBI until I got suspended last week. That's your fault, actually."

"I don't believe you."

Beamon shrugged. "What're you going to do, then?"

Jennifer chewed her lip for a moment, then moved toward a haggard-looking sideboard and began pulling open the drawers. She found a phone book in the third one she looked in and flipped through the first few pages, keeping one eye trained on him.

"Oh. I'd rather you didn't do that," Beamon said as she reached for the phone on the sideboard.

"Could be traced here. Use this one." He slid his cell phone off the coffee table and rolled it across the floor to her.

She looked at it like it might explode but eventually picked it up and dialed.

"Hello? Hi. Uh, I'd like to speak to Mark Beamon, please." She looked him up and down while she waited to be connected. The gun was shaking less now and the barrel had dipped a bit from its previous position pointing directly at his face. Not that it really mattered.

"Hello? I'm trying to reach Mark Beamon . . . No, I don't want to leave a message, it's pretty important . . . Oh. Really? Could you hold on for a second?"

Beamon caught the phone she tossed him and put it to his ear. "Hello? You still there?"

"Mark! I've been trying to reach you! Where have you been? And who was that?"

"I've been around, D. Enjoying my time off, you know?"

"Have you heard what's been happening here?" she said. Her voice echoed slightly. Because she had cupped a hand around the mouthpiece of her phone, Beamon guessed.

"No, what?"

Jennifer looked like she was getting impatient and Beamon flashed her a quick smile.

"Mark, they're talking about going public with the fact that they're looking for you. We're talking APB. The director's flying down personally to meet with Layman."

D. really was the ultimate secretary. If a clerk at headquarters got a paper cut, she knew about it the same day.

"When?"

"The APB? There's no decision yet, just talk. The director's coming in on the first, though. I think if Layman doesn't have something by then, you can count on this thing going public that day. What did you do? You wouldn't believe some of the things I've been hearing."

"Oh, I probably would. What time are Layman and the director meeting?"

"I don't know. Morning. Mark, what's going on? Are you all right?"

"Sure, fine. Hang on a sec, would you? Someone wants to talk to you."

Beamon tossed the cell phone back to Jennifer.

"Hello? Yes, ma'am. I just wanted to ask you, is that Mark Beamon? Uh-huh. You're sure. Okay. And what's his job there exactly? He is? Thanks. 'Bye."

She turned off the phone and slumped into the chair behind her, laying the gun carefully on the floor.

Beamon leaned forward. "Smart, Jennifer. Very smart. I take it I've checked out to your satisfaction?"

She seemed to have used up the last of her strength and bravery to grab the gun and confirm his identity. Her head went forward to her knees and her entire body shook as she began quietly sobbing.

Beamon wasn't sure what to do. He got up and knelt down in front of her. "It's okay, Jen. You're okay now. You're out of there."

She threw her arms around his neck and pulled him to her.

"Uh, hey, come on. Don't cry. I'm depressed

442 — KYLE MILLS

enough already," he said, patting her on the back tentatively.

"They were going to kill me, Mr. Beamon!" The words came out in jumbles when she momentarily caught her breath. "They kept me in this room, and I was all alone and they wouldn't let me out. They were going to kill me!"

She used the sleeve of her sweatshirt to wipe at her running nose and then suddenly jerked back from him. "What day is it?"

"Tuesday. Tuesday the twenty-fifth."

She pushed him away, jumped out of the chair, and slammed her back against the far wall. "Oh, my God. Oh, my God."

"Jennifer, calm down. What's wrong?"

"It isn't over. She won't stop. It's not time yet."

Beamon stood and led her to the couch. "Good Friday?"

She nodded. "My grandfather, he . . . he wanted me to be in charge of the church. But she lied to them. She wants to kill me so it . . . it's hers."

"Who's 'she'? Sara?"

Jennifer nodded again.

"It was a religious thing, though, wasn't it?" Beamon said. "Albert—your grandfather—died too soon and she was able to use that to justify killing you. She said that you were the new Messenger and had to ascend in his place, right?"

She didn't seem to be paying attention to what he was saying. Her head was moving from side to side as though the church's forces were going to materialize from the walls at any minute. Hell, maybe they were.

"Jennifer, is what I just said right?"

"Yeah."

He reached out and gripped her shoulders. "Okay, then. Cheer up. All we have to do is keep you safe till midnight Friday; then you'll be useless to them, right? That's only a couple of days—no problem."

He tried to keep his tone light and to make sure none of his doubts shone through.

"Promise?" Jennifer said.

"Promise. You want something to eat? I've got Cocoa Puffs."

"That stuff's just a bunch of sugar," she said, her eyes moving from the door to the window and back again.

He opened the refrigerator. "Well, I've got hot dogs. But no buns."

"I guess I'll have the cereal."

"I love this stuff," Beamon said as he grabbed the box out of a cabinet. "Cuckoo for it." She actually almost smiled at that.

"Do you know anything about computers, Jen?" She nodded.

"Why don't you see what you can do with the one over there while I whip this up."

"What do you want me to do?" she said, sitting down in front of the screen and tapping the mouse.

"Check for voice messages and e-mail."

"Why don't I just make the cereal? You know where everything is in here."

"Actually, I barely even know how to turn the thing on. It's not mine. I was kind of hoping you could figure out how to work it."

"Whose computer is it?" she said, looking a bit nervous again.

"A friend's."

"Where is he?"

"He had to go home. His father's been sick for

years and he took a turn for the worse a couple of days ago," Beamon lied.

She looked up at him for a moment and then turned back to the screen. A few moments later, recorded phone conversations were playing over the speakers.

"Hey! That's me!" Jennifer said when the recording of her call to the Colorado Cyclist came on. Her smile faltered when she heard herself scream and the sound of the brief struggle before the phone went dead.

Beamon laid the bowl of cereal down next to the computer and pulled up a box to sit on. The messages—recordings of the church's phone tap, actually—were still playing, but he wasn't really expecting anything interesting. They seemed to be pretty careful about using the phone.

"What about the e-mail?"

Jennifer clicked on a mailbox icon and the sound of dialing momentarily drowned out the conversation playing over the speakers.

"Seven messages," she said, clicking on the first.

It came up a jumble of letters and characters.

"It's encrypted, Mr. Beamon."

"Call me Mark."

She looked over at him, a dribble of chocolaty milk running down her chin. "You don't look like a Mark. You look like a Mr. Beamon."

He shrugged. "Suit yourself. WrathofGod."

"What?"

"The encryption key. WrathofGod. One word, the 'W' and the 'G' are capitalized."

A moment later the e-mails began rolling off the printer.

The first six were pretty mundane—financial directives, mostly. The last was a rather innocuous-looking note including Ernestine Waverly's address. He wondered if she'd seen it. If she'd known they were coming. His cell phone had rung just before he arrived at the airport. Had it been her calling for help? And if he'd picked up, what would he have done?

"Are you all right, Mr. Beamon?"

"Sorry, I'm fine. Here's the deal, Jennifer. We need to get you to the FBI. I think you'll be better off with a hundred people watching you than just one." He smiled. "Even one as gifted and handsome as myself."

"But you're going to go too, right? I mean, a hundred people didn't find me—you did."

She really was a clever kid. If they were all like her, he'd have actually considered having children. "I'll be right there. I'm going to call a friend to help us and this afternoon you'll have the whole FBI to keep an eye on you till Saturday. You won't have a thing to worry about."

She looked around her at the dingy apartment, gripping the table in front of her so tightly her knuckles turned white. "Maybe we should just stay here. Maybe that would be better."

"You've already been here too long, Jennifer," Beamon said, dialing his cell phone. "There are a lot of people looking for you and eventually they're going to find this place—"

"Hello?"

"Chet! Is that you?"

Michaels's voice lowered into the same whisper D. had employed to talk to him. "Jesus, Mark. Where the hell are you? We got guys from Phoenix crawling all over the office trying to figure out how to find you."

"I'll bet. Listen up, Chet. Do you remember the time you and I went to talk to the guy about that embezzlement case you were working on?"

"Yeah, sure."

"You remember where we ate?"

"Uh-huh. Mark, what the hell's—"

"Meet me there at three. Leave like you always do for lunch. Drive around a little, get a bite, and make goddamn sure no one is following you."

"But you—"

Beamon looked at his watch. "Why are you still talking? I've got eleven-fifty-six."

He heard Michaels sigh over the phone. "I'm walking out the door."

"Oh, and Chet?"

"Yeah?"

"There are three people who have helped me with the Jennifer Davis case. You're the only one still breathing. You still want to come?"

There was a long pause over the phone. "You're going to tell me what's going on when I get there, right?"

"Yup."

"I'll see you in a few hours."

Beamon turned off the phone and looked into Jennifer's worried face. "If you want to get cleaned up or anything, you'd better get going. We've gotta get out of here."

She stood and started for the bathroom.

"Hold on a sec," Beamon said, picking up the shotgun and holding it up so that she could see it. He pointed to the slide under the barrel. "It's really unlikely, but if anything should happen to me and you would have to actually fire this thing, remember that you need to pull this back or it won't shoot."

A look of horror spread across her face. "You mean all that time I was pointing it at you, it wouldn't have even worked?"

"Strictly speaking? No. But it *was* a hell of an effort."

60

IN THE TWO AND A HALF HOURS IT TOOK TO drive from Flagstaff to Phoenix, the outside temperature had risen nearly thirty degrees. The sun that Jennifer hadn't seen in over a month was beating relentlessly on them through the car's windshield, finally prompting her to pull Beamon's parka off her bare legs and toss it into the back seat.

"Can we turn down the heat a little now, Jen?" he asked, wiping a bead of sweat from his upper lip.

"Okay."

She leaned her head against the window and fixed her gaze on the desert landscape as it sped by, but didn't really seem to see it. After perking up a bit at the apartment when she'd first discovered she was free, Jennifer seemed to have withdrawn into herself.

She probably wanted to talk, Beamon knew. About her parents, her treatment at Sara's hands, her future. But he just didn't know how to get things going. He sighed quietly and thought about Carrie. She'd know what to do. How to help.

"You'll like Chet, Jen. He's a lot younger and hipper than me. Just don't mention his resemblance to Howdy Doody."

She remained so still and silent that he wondered if she'd even heard him. Call that a swing and a miss.

Perhaps the direct approach might prove more effective. "Is there something out there that's more interesting than me, or are you just contemplating life?"

He glanced away from the road for a moment and saw that she had turned from the window and was staring right at him. Her face had fallen into an expression of pain and sadness that someone her age shouldn't have been able to produce.

"I was thinking about Eric and Patty."

"Who?" Beamon said, and then remembered. "You mean your parents."

She turned back toward the window. "I mean my keepers."

Beamon wasn't sure how to respond to that. He did have an unasked question that had been killing him since she'd regained consciousness, though. "What really happened that night?"

"He killed her," she said simply.

"Who?"

"Eric."

"Your father," Beamon corrected again.

"He wasn't my father. My father's been dead for years. He was just some guy the church hired to watch me until it was time to kill me."

Beamon wanted to just let the subject drop—he felt like he was forcing her to dredge up memories best left buried. Deep down, though, he knew it was probably better for her to let them out. "So your—I mean Eric—killed Patricia. And then he killed himself, didn't he?"

She nodded.

"Damn," Beamon muttered. There had always been a trace of doubt in his mind about that. He'd have to give that cute little lesbian coroner a firm pat on the back, if he lived to see her again.

"She just stood there, and he killed her," Jennifer continued. "They didn't care what happened to me. Neither of them."

Beamon looked over at her again, amazed at how well she was holding up. He tried to put himself in her place, to imagine what it would be like to be fifteen years old and see something like that. "I don't think that's true, Jennifer."

"You weren't there. They gave him a gun. He could have stopped them, but he didn't." She turned back to the window. "He didn't."

"You're angry right now. And you've got a right to be. But given some time, I think you'll understand that there was more going on there than maybe you see right now."

A bitter smile compounded the pain etched across her young features. "Patty used to use that on me. 'You'll understand when you're older.'"

"I'm sorry to say, I've found that to be a myth. The years come and go and your perspective changes, but I'm not sure you really ever understand more."

Beamon slowed the car and eased onto an off-ramp. "Your—sorry, Eric and Patricia—believed very strongly in God. They didn't show you that part of their lives, but it was incredibly important to them. They believed that you were, well, almost divine. When they did what they did, in a way, they did it for you. They wanted you to leave them behind. To become more than they could ever be. I know it's weird, but really it's what all parents want for their children."

"For some psycho bitch to kill them so she can keep her job?"

Beamon slowed the car a bit more and tugged on her arm so that she would meet his eyes. "I've spent the last month or so doing nothing but working on this case, Jennifer—I know more about it than anyone in the world, and I'll tell you right now that your parents had no idea what Sara was planning. No idea."

"Maybe they should have stuck around and tried to find out."

The restaurant where Michaels was waiting, thankfully, was just ahead. His first foray into adolescent counseling seemed to have been an unsurprising bust. Probably better to change the subject before he did irreversible damage. "That's it. The reinforcements should be just ahead."

Jennifer started to look nervous. Panicked, almost. "Let's forget this, Mr. Beamon." She twisted around and looked through the rear window. "Please, let's just turn around and keep driving."

Beamon suddenly realized what was probably going through her head. Her parents had pawned her off on the church, and now he was going to pawn her off on the Bureau. "Jennifer, we're less than three miles from one of the largest FBI offices in the country. I'm not just throwing you to the wolves here. They can protect you better than I can. And when you're safe, I'm going to stick a knife so deep into Sara Renslier and her church that they'll never be able to hurt you again. I'm doing the best I can."

She grabbed his arm. "I want to stay with you. You can't even run a computer. I could help."

Beamon eased into the parking lot and spotted Michaels standing in the open door of his car. He pulled into the empty space next to the young agent and looked carefully around him. The lot was nearly full of cars but almost devoid of people. The restaurant's lunch rush was probably pretty much over and dinner hadn't yet begun. Most of the cars probably belonged to the patrons of the shops that were lined up neatly across the street.

Michaels's eyes jerked to the left as Beamon stepped from the car.

Shit.

Beamon fell back into the driver's seat, reached behind him and pulled his gun from the exposed holster in the small of his back, but it was too late. Two men with compact machine pistols held low had already stepped from opposite sides of an old panel van.

He looked behind him. Jennifer had slid from the seat and crammed herself in the small floor space in front of it. She was clutching at the armrest on the door, trying to hold it shut as a similarly armed man tried to open it. Beamon grabbed Jennifer under the arm and dragged her over the seats and out the driver's-side door with him.

"I swear they didn't follow me, Mark. They were already here when I got here."

"Shut up," the man Beamon's gun was aimed at said.

"You shut up, fuckhead," Michaels said angrily.

Beamon winced. That wasn't productive. He felt Jennifer's arms wrap around him. "Take it easy, Jen. We're okay."

That wasn't entirely true, of course. The man who had been trying to get at Jennifer though the passenger-side door had circled around and now there were three men, spaced at about five-foot intervals, facing him. Michaels was between them, looking fantastically pissed off.

Beamon looked around him. There was one other person in the parking lot about fifty yards away, but she was oblivious to what was happening, more interested in getting her key into her trunk without having to put her packages down. If they had to, these guys could shoot him and Michaels, throw the girl in the van, and be two blocks away before anyone knew what had happened.

"You're to come with us," one of the men said.

Beamon adjusted his aim toward the man's chest. He looked a couple of years older than the other two, but he probably still hadn't seen his thirty-fifth birthday.

"Yeah? Screw you!" Michaels said.

"Jesus, Chet," Beamon said quietly. "Could you maybe try and be a little more constructive?"

Michaels frowned and bobbed his head as if he'd just been scolded for not taking out the trash.

Beamon looked around him again. The woman with the packages was driving away. The lot was now empty except for them and a bunch of owner-less cars. The man who had spoken a moment before had his firearm aimed at Michaels. The other two guns were on him.

They wouldn't kill her—Beamon was sure of that. Without the religious mumbo jumbo Sara had attached to Jennifer's death, she would just be murdering her messiah's only living relative. A poor career move, particularly with her main enforcer's recent decision to stop a couple of Beamon's bullets with his chest.

Interestingly, he himself was safe from immediate execution, too. Sara wanted the Vericomm tapes and undoubtedly planned on making his life unpleasant enough to get him to tell her where they were.

Now, Michaels had problems. His life expectancy had just gone from fifty years to less than an hour.

"Let's go," the man said. Ignoring the fact that Beamon had a gun trained on him, he reached out and grabbed Jennifer's arm, pulling her to him.

"No!" she whimpered, tightening her grip around Beamon's waist until it actually made it hard for him to breathe.

Beamon grabbed her hand and peeled her off him, letting the man drag her away with a satisfied smirk. "Not quite the man I'd heard you were, Beamon. I expected some theatrics, at least."

"You sonofabitch," Jennifer said, glaring at him. "You promised."

Beamon didn't see that he had many options. Desperate times demanded desperate measures. In one smooth motion, he cocked back the hammer on his revolver and adjusted his aim to center Jennifer in his sights.

The eyes of the man holding Jennifer widened, but not as much as hers did.

"I got it figured this way," Beamon said calmly. "You've been told not to hurt the girl and to bring me back in one or two pieces—but alive." He looked over at Michaels. "Him, well, you'll probably just kill him the minute we get in your van."

"Great," Michaels said in a mildly irritated tone. He sounded like he'd come out of the restaurant to find that someone had scratched his car.

Beamon ignored the interruption and continued. "I know what you've got planned for her. She'll be dead on Friday morning and in the days until then, you'll have her drugged in some room, alone and scared." He shook his head. "If I let you guys take her, I doubt I'll live to find her again. Maybe it's better that we just end it here. Quick."

He turned his head away from the increasingly confused-looking man and locked eyes with Jennifer. "What do you think, Jen? Out here in the sunshine, or on some altar with Sara hovering over you?"

She looked to be completely frozen. The two men who had their guns trained on Beamon looked at each other, then back at him.

"Here," Jennifer said weakly. Her voice seemed to jolt the man holding her and he took a step backward, but he didn't release her arm.

Beamon was dumbfounded by her answer and struggled to keep his face impassive. He'd asked the question just to add a little more drama to his bluff. He was prepared to go down shooting, yes, but sure as hell not shooting at her.

"You—there's no way," the man said. "You're bluffing." The slight stammer told Beamon that he'd won.

"What would make you say that, son? If we go with you we're all dead—and you make the last few hours of my life real unpleasant. And what if I were to survive? I'm out of a job, broke, and branded a child molester. I'd call my prospects limited, wouldn't you?"

The man looked behind him, but his compatriots weren't offering any help. "Look into my eyes," Beamon said. "What do you see?"

The man fidgeted for a few moments and then released his hold on Jennifer's arm.

She seemed uncertain of what to do, so Beamon grabbed her and pulled her to him. She was probably having a hard time accepting the guy pointing a loaded gun at her as her savior.

"Chet," Beamon said, dragging Jennifer around the car and stuffing her into the passenger door. "Get in your car and get out of here. Jennifer, slide over. You drive."

She quickly negotiated the armrest and had started the car before her butt hit the driver's seat.

Beamon kept the gun pointed toward her and his eyes on the three men standing in the parking lot. He leaned in close to Jennifer and said, "Let's get out of here before they figure out I'm full of crap." She looked over at him, her lower lip quivering slightly, and threw the car into reverse.

One of the men was already talking into a cell phone as Jennifer cautiously negotiated the exit to the parking lot and turned out onto the street.

"Let's pick it up a little, Jen," Beamon said, watching the men disappear into the distance a little too slowly. "Get back out onto the highway and head south."

Satisfied that they weren't being followed, Beamon pulled his address book out of his pocket and found the number for Delta Airlines.

61

"BUT YOU'RE NOT GOING TO LEAVE ME, right?"

Beamon rubbed his eyes with his knuckles as the cab pulled away from them and back into the dark of pre-dawn Washington, D.C.

"Right?" Jennifer repeated, wrapping her arms around herself against the cold and uncertainty.

Beamon put a hand on her back and started toward the dimly lit entrance of the German embassy. She was still in the shorts he'd found her in, though they'd managed to find her a jacket with "Phoenix" stenciled across it in the airport.

"I think we've established that, Jennifer—try to relax. You and I are going to sit in this embassy 'til I can gather together some people I trust. We'll be safe here. You know how the Germans feel about the church."

Beamon banged on the front door as Jennifer pressed up against him for warmth. She was starting to shiver, but Beamon didn't know if it was from the cold or just the stress of the last forty-eight hours. The last month, actually. It was amazing she was still walking and talking.

A dark shape appeared on the other side of the glass, moving quickly toward them. A moment later, Hans Volker pushed the door open.

"Come in. Quickly."

The German looked a little more haggard than he had the last time they'd met. His meticulously pressed double-breasted jacket and expensive-looking tie were nowhere in sight, and he wasn't wearing any shoes. But then, it was four in the morning.

Beamon stepped through the door with Jennifer still attached to his hip. She eyed Volker suspiciously.

"Jennifer. This is Hans. It's his job to watch the church for the German government."

"So this is Jennifer Davis," Volker said. He reached out and took Jennifer's hand. "Goodness. Your skin feels like ice. We'll go up to my office. You can wash up there and you'll also be happy to know that I have two big sofas. I've availed myself of them a number of times and can vouch for their softness."

"Is anyone in yet this morning?" Beamon asked as they began to climb a staircase to the second floor.

"Not yet. I've called our security people. They should arrive any moment. There's an office and bathroom that we aren't using in the basement. You can stay there until you're able to marshal your forces. While you're here we'll have round-the-clock security in the building."

"I really appreciate this, Hans. I'm going to put some stuff together that you're going to love."

"I have every confidence," Volker said, pushing through a set of double doors and pointing down a short hall that terminated in his office. "After you."

"Hey, Hans," Beamon said as he followed Jennifer down the hall. "Could you possibly find Jennifer some long pants—actually, a couple of changes of clothes would be even better."

"Of course."

Jennifer went through the door to the office, but only made it about two feet before she began backing out of it.

"What're you doing, Jen?" Beamon said when she bumped into him.

There was something unmistakable about the feeling of a gun barrel being pressed into one's back, Beamon reflected as he felt a cold cylinder bump his spine. Somehow it was easily discernible from any other object—be it pipe, wooden dowel, whatever.

"Please keep moving forward, Mark," Volker said, giving him a gentle nudge with the gun he must have had lying on his secretary's desk out front.

Jennifer pushed back against him. "No," she whimpered.

He didn't know for sure what was waiting for them in Volker's office, but a theory was forming in his mind. One that he should have come up with weeks ago.

Beamon wrapped his arms around Jennifer and whispered in her ear, "I'm sorry, this is my fault," then used his superior weight to force her forward.

To their left, two men stood in the corners of the office. To their right, Sara Renslier was sitting behind Volker's large desk, flanked by another man Beamon didn't recognize.

"Good morning, Mr. Beamon," she said, standing up from behind the desk. "Hello, Jennifer."

Jennifer stepped back as if the words had struck her a physical blow. She continued to press against Beamon for comfort, though he didn't have any idea why. She probably would have been better off on her own. He'd made more bad decisions in the last week than he had in the last ten years. The church had his life so fucked up, he didn't know what the hell he was doing anymore. "Stupid," he said quietly to himself.

"Excuse me?" Sara said, holding her hand up to her ear. The bandage on her thumb had been joined by one on her wrist. Undoubtedly from her struggling against the cuffs he had used to secure her to her airplane. Beyond that, there was no trace of the woman who had cowered in front of him that night. The armed men surrounding him had revitalized her air of superiority and her condescending tone.

Beamon took a deep breath to try to clear the anger overtaking him. Not at Sara, but at himself. "I said I'm stupid. Your fight with the German government. It's just a publicity stunt."

"A bit late, but of course you're right," Sara said as one of the men behind Beamon stepped forward to take his gun. "We discovered early on that Germany wasn't very fertile ground for our recruiting efforts. It just was costing us money, really— churches, recruiting stations, advertising, et cetera. We did bring in a few influential people." She nodded toward Volker. "But on the whole, there seemed to be something in the German psyche that just wasn't compatible with the Church on the scale we were looking for."

"So you changed your tack," Beamon said. "You used the contacts you'd made to focus your efforts on something you knew would be compatible with the German psyche. The fear of the rise of any insular group to power."

Sara smiled. "It wasn't difficult and cost almost nothing."

Beamon slid his arm around Jennifer's shoulders. "You knew that there'd be a violent reaction in the U.S. The fear of religious persecution has been bred into Americans for over two hundred years."

Jennifer shrank away as Sara approached, trying to get behind Beamon.

"I think it's been my greatest success. We've seen a twenty-two percent increase in inquiries from the American public and a fourteen percent increase in new membership. The outcry against Germany and its persecution of the Church has been over-whelming. The media coverage has been far beyond what we projected."

Beamon was only half-listening to what Sara was saying, instead concentrating on analyzing his situation. It was his considered opinion that he— and more importantly, Jennifer—were screwed. He was outnumbered, didn't have so much as a paper clip to fight with, and had been hopelessly outma-neuvered. It was that last one that really hurt.

"Come over here, Jennifer," Sara said. "We won't hurt you. You're more important to us than you could possibly know."

"Don't let them take me, Mr. Beamon!"

Beamon looked at the faces of the men around him and wondered if they knew that Sara had sold their messiah out. "Now that's not entirely true, is it, Sara? Jennifer's Albert Kneiss's granddaughter and a threat to your power. That's all you really care about anymore, isn't it? Your power? This doesn't have anything to do with God or the future of the church anymore. The truth is, it just has to do with you holding onto the little kingdom you've built for yourself."

Sara looked away from Jennifer and directly at

him for a moment. "You just have no understanding of the meaning of faith, do you, Mr. Beamon?"

The pain in the back of his head flared for a moment and he heard Jennifer scream. Then nothing.

62

THE CARTOONS WERE RIGHT—HE REALLY could see stars. They weren't quite as well defined as the ones on TV, though; more like fuzzy balls of light darting erratically in the darkness.

Beamon moved his fingers and heard a quiet rustling over the hum of the car's engine. The entire left side of his body was numb and he couldn't feel his hands, but it sounded like they still worked. Not that it probably mattered much, given his current situation.

The nauseating stop-and-start rocking, the confined space, and the vibration and smell of gas fumes left little doubt that he was in the trunk of a car. On the bright side, though, it seemed to be a spacious Detroit trunk and not one of those cramped little import jobs. The Japanese had just never gotten a handle on how to make a trunk that a kidnap victim could get comfortable in.

His feet were tied with what felt like rope, which was, in turn, looped through the chain between the handcuffs binding his wrists. Hog-tied, they'd have said where he'd grown up.

And then there was Jennifer. The little girl who had held herself together through so much, but now was going to die because he was a fucking moron. Beamon laid his head down on something hard, ignoring the warmth spreading across the back of his head as the gun butt wound reopened.

He'd lost.

By now, Jennifer was probably in the Church's private jet on her way to the Retreat—an inaccessible piece of land in the vast nothing of eastern Oregon. Even if he were walking into the J. Edgar Hoover Building instead of lying around in a trunk with his thumb up his ass, there would be nothing he could do. By the time he convinced the powers that be not to throw him in jail and, even less likely, convinced them of the church's involvement, Jennifer would be long gone.

And the Vericomm audio? As good as gone, too.

He was confident that the church would "question" him with the same efficiency and thoroughness that they did everything else. Not that they would have to. At this point, he might as well do himself a favor and make it quick. Tell them about Goldman's apartment—if they hadn't found it already themselves—and about where he'd stowed the Vericomm disks.

It was probably better this way, he told himself, rocking over to try to jump-start the blood flow to his side. He hadn't been looking forward to his new career as the night clerk at some roadside 7-Eleven—a job he'd only be able to keep until the church got around to informing the store's management about his new history of pedophilia.

He thought about Ernie, transposing his face with hers and imagining himself as a morbidly obese computer programmer trapped in his home by fear and embarrassment. Or maybe holed up in a trailer in the middle of nowhere, hunting what he needed to eat during the day and huddling next to an old wood stove at night, like Jennifer's uncle.

Beamon adjusted his position again and tried to ignore the inevitable headache that was starting to form as his mind cleared. He closed his eyes, but it didn't make any difference in the blackness of the trunk.

The stars that had been swirling in front of him were starting to fade and finally burn out as he tried to let his grogginess take him back into unconsciousness. Better to just admit defeat right now and let them put him out of his misery.

"Goddammit," he slurred through the gag in his mouth when the car lurched to a stop and sent him skidding face first into the spare tire.

The brief stab of pain in his nose pulled him from his self-induced daze. What the hell was wrong with him? This was no way to die. He shook his head violently, amplifying the throbbing that had taken hold there. He might not be able to save her, but at the very least he owed Jennifer his best effort at throwing a big wrench into gears of Sara's church.

Beamon took a deep breath that did little but feed his various aches and pains, and moved his hands toward his pocket. He had to navigate more by sound and resistance than sensation—his fingers felt dead.

The lighter sparked to life and maintained its flame on his third try at spinning the small wheel. Now if he could just keep from setting himself on fire, he might be able to say someday that being a smoker had saved his life.

The red parka that had served him so well for the last month and a half was lying in front of him. Other than that, there were a few books and the spare tire and tools that were fixtures in most trunks.

Beamon tried to pull off the gag secured around his head using the rubber of the tire, but it had been tied too tightly and shoved too deep into his mouth. He twisted to his right until his knees hit the top of the trunk and slid his arms painfully under him. When he heard his fingers rustle against the nylon of the parka, he started the long process of pulling the coat under him. He didn't know how long it took but he finally succeeded, getting the jacket to where he could access the pockets.

Surprisingly, his cell phone was still in the inside pocket. His captors either hadn't counted on his hard head, or hadn't expected the traffic jam they seemed to be mired in.

He passed over the phone, knowing it wouldn't be much use with the gag. Finally he found what he was looking for: his pen. He unscrewed it and pulled it apart, taking the thin metal tube that held the ink and ballpoint from the cheap plastic cover.

It took another five minutes, but he managed to pinch the tube flat and work it into the simple latching mechanism of the handcuffs. How to get out of your own cuffs was one of the first things they taught you at Quantico. He didn't remember all the nuances, but after a few false starts he felt the satisfying pain of the blood rushing back into his hands. Another push freed his wrists completely.

Beamon pulled the gag from his mouth and took a gulp of the cold, exhaust-tasting air. He tried to bring his feet up close enough to untie them, but it was impossible in the cramped confines of the trunk. Whatever he was going to do, it was going to have to be without them.

He pulled his parka in front of him again and felt around until he found his cell phone. He wasn't sure who he was going to call or exactly how he was going to describe the predicament he'd found himself in, but at least he could tell someone what the hell was going on.

He flipped it open with his still-numb fingers, not noticing that the battery pack was gone until the numbers on the keypad didn't light up. They obviously planned to bury him with it. Made sense—it'd be kind of embarrassing if his phone turned up for auction at some church bake sale. Beamon zipped the useless phone back into his parka and flipped the lighter back on for a moment.

Options?

The easy answer was to start kicking and screaming and hope someone noticed and called the cops. The drawback there was that it was freezing cold outside, so none of the cars within theoretical earshot would have their windows down. No, most likely his captors would be the only people who heard him and they'd pull off the next ramp and use the opportunity to test out their tire iron on the back of his head.

Option two would be to escape on his own. That was his favorite, but it begged the question of how.

Beamon moved the lighter to the back of the trunk and examined the inside of the lock. Nothing he'd be able to figure out. The handcuffs had been his best—and only—lock trick.

He ran the lighter along the edges of the trunk as best he could, finally stopping at a black plastic tube housing a group of brightly colored wires. That might be something. He grabbed the tube and pulled hard, breaking the wires free with a small, but satisfying, shower of sparks.

The sound of a faltering engine and the feeling

of the car coasting to a stop didn't materialize. Instead, the car jerked a bit to the right as it changed lanes and accelerated, the engine purring smoothly.

"Goddammit," Beamon swore quietly. The wires probably ran the fucking air conditioning.

He held the lighter in front of him and examined the contents of the trunk more closely. There were six books, all relating to the church in some way and all decorated with similarly inspirational pictures of Albert Kneiss. The spare tire looked brand new, as did the jack. And that was it, except for a dirty rag and an old McDonald's wrapper. No sense in complaining—if that was what he had to work with, that was what he had.

Beamon picked up the books and piled them neatly behind him. They stacked to be about eight inches high. No way of knowing if that was going to be good enough.

The lighter began to dim ominously as he unscrewed the wing nut holding the jack in place. Once it was free, he put the jack on top of the books and inserted the lug wrench that doubled as its handle—a tricky and completely blind procedure.

Now if Ernie's God would just cut him one little break here, the jack would reach the underside of the trunk and force it open.

Working the lever, which was behind him, was a slow and painful procedure, but the quiet clicking told him that he was making progress.

He'd been working it for about fifteen minutes when he had to stop and rest. The contorted position of his arms had constricted the blood flow, and it felt like there were knives in his shoulders and about a thousand needles in his arms.

He flicked the lighter again. The flame shuddered and glowed a dim blue, but it was still enough to see. Only about a half-inch to go before the jack made contact.

He shook out his arms as best he could and started in on the jack again as the car started a slow deceleration. He'd gotten off about ten more clicks when the lever stopped. He pushed harder, twisting his body to put a little weight behind it. "Oh, come on. Don't do this to me," he said quietly.

That was it. The jack was fully extended.

"One stupid goddamn break, that's all I as—"

Beamon's words caught in his throat when he was thrown forward into the spare tire again and the jack slammed into the back of his head. His ears were ringing loudly as he tried to scoot back into the middle of the trunk, but he wasn't sure if it was from the impact of the jack or the deafening crash that had preceded it.

"What the fuck!" came a muffled voice flowing into the trunk on a blast of cold air.

Beamon shook his head as a car door outside slammed. "You ever hear of taillights, you assholes? It's fucking pitch dark out here!"

Beamon managed a weak smile when he realized that the wires he'd pulled out must have belonged to the car's brake lights. He rolled onto his back and saw the slow-moving glow of headlights, clearly visible through the gaps between the severely bent trunk and the body of the car.

"Get back here, you sonsofbitches!" he heard as the car started to move again.

Beamon kicked hard with his still tied feet, trying to get the stubborn latch on the trunk to completely break free. Nothing. He took a deep breath, pressed his hands against the inside of the trunk, and kicked again.

The trunk flew open just as the car cut hard onto the shoulder and began to accelerate. He could see the man who had hit them running back to his truck to give chase.

Beamon grabbed his parka and struggled out of the trunk, hitting the pavement hard and beginning to roll backward across the asphalt. The truck screeched to a halt as Beamon staggered to his feet.

"What the fuck!" the man said, jumping from the cab.

Beamon tried to focus on the front of the old pickup. One of the headlights was shattered, and the bug guard engraved with "Pearson Drywall" was hanging precariously from the hood.

"What the hell were you doing in there? Look at my truck!" the man shouted, grabbing him by the shirt. That, combined with the fact that Beamon's feet were still roped together, knocked him onto his back.

He sat up and reached back to brush his hand against the base of his skull. It came back covered in blood.

"Hey, you all right?"

Beamon looked up into the man's craggy face and at the traffic that was quickly bogging down around them. "Can I borrow your knife?"

The man pulled it from a leather case attached to his belt and flipped it open. Beamon took it and cut the rope binding his legs.

"You don't want to mess with those guys," Beamon said, trying to get up but falling back to the ground. He felt like one big bruise.

The man held his hand out and Beamon gratefully accepted the help. "Tell you what. Mr. Pearson, is it?"

He shook his head and looked at Beamon suspiciously. "Name's Caleb. I just work for Pearson Drywall."

Beamon looked again at the truck. It was still running, though the vibration of the engine looked like it was going to knock what was left of the front grille off at any moment.

"Tell you what, Caleb," Beamon said, picking up the parka at his feet and confirming that the inside pocket still contained the envelope with what was left of his money. "You take me to the airport and I'll pay for the damages to your truck in cash."

63

BEAMON HAD EXPECTED TO FIND THE PLACE a pile of ashes, but nothing had changed.

Goldman's overalls were still in the box he'd stuffed them in, the computers were still humming away, and the half-full bottle of bourbon was still where he'd left it.

Beamon limped across the silent apartment and sat down in front of a computer, leaning his shotgun against a chair. He jabbed at the space bar and lit a cigarette, watching the screen slowly come to life.

He felt like someone had put him in a clothes dryer with a couple of bowling balls. The gash in the back of his head had continued to seep blood for hours, forcing him to keep a handkerchief pressed against it for most of the plane ride back to Flagstaff. That, combined with the black eyes and swollen nose, had attracted enough attention that he could be relatively certain that the church was aware that he was back in town.

He took a slug of bourbon directly from the bottle next to him and winced as the alcohol went to work on the cuts inside his mouth. How he'd gotten those, he wasn't sure, but there didn't seem to be a single square inch of his body that the church hadn't left its mark on.

He double-clicked on the mailbox icon on the screen and pulled up the church's hijacked e-mail. The feed was still working.

It took Beamon a good five minutes to figure out how to decrypt the e-mail but in the end he was rewarded with six completely useless communications from the late Albert Kneiss.

And that was the ball game. At midnight tomorrow, Jennifer Davis's life would come to an end—a well-deserved punishment for trusting in him to save her.

She'd be twenty-four days from her sixteenth birthday.

Beamon leaned back and took a slightly more cautious sip from the bottle, hoping that it would start to go to work on his headache.

Even if he knew precisely where the Retreat was, what could he do? Fly to Portland, rent a car, then a snowmobile, and ride across God knew how many miles of frozen tundra like James-fucking-Bond? Or maybe a dog-sled team would be more in keeping with his technophobe image.

He reached into his pocket and pulled his cell phone out as it began to ring, but couldn't decide if he really wanted to answer it. It was probably just Sara. Wanting to gloat a bit and to make a substantially reduced offer on the Vericomm disks.

What the hell, he decided, flipping the phone open. He'd spent damn near the last of his money on the new battery, he might as well get some use out of it.

"Hello."

"Mark! Oh my God, Mark. I've been so worried. I've been trying to get in touch with you for days!"

Beamon stopped the bottle about six inches from his mouth. "Carrie?"

"Mark, are you okay? You sound strange."

"That's probably because I don't know why we're talking. I thought we said everything we had to say last week."

There was silence over the line for a moment. "I'm calling to say I'm sorry."

Beamon set the bottle on the table but said nothing.

"What's going on, Mark?"

"What do you mean?"

"I talked to a friend of mine—a psychiatrist who specializes in child abuse. She'd never heard of the Child Safety Administration. In fact, no one has."

"No big surprise there, Carrie," Beamon said, finding it impossible to hide his anger. "Their god-damned business card didn't even have a phone number on it. A little unusual, don't you think?"

"Yes. I . . . Emory means everything to me, Mark. You know that."

He did know. It wasn't her fault.

"I talked with Emory and I had my friend talk to her. There was nothing. I knew there wouldn't be, but I had to be sure. I trust you, Mark, but . . ."

"Look, I understand, Carrie. I would have done the same thing."

She sighed over the phone and Beamon fought to erase the image of her that was starting to paint itself into his mind.

"I hoped you would, Mark. Can we start over?"

Beamon watched the computer screen in front of him as it turned from a block of text to a simulation of flying through space. "No. We can't. Stay away from me, Carrie. You don't want to be part of what's left of my life."

"What's left of your li—"

He turned off the phone and laid it gently down on the table. The computer picked up the vibration and the screen turned back to the last e-mail from the church, as if it were mocking him.

There wasn't much left for him now but revenge. He'd play the tapes for whoever would listen and try to tell his story, but the church had left him with no credibility, no money, and no allies. He had a feeling that there wouldn't be anyone listening.

Beamon looked at the text of the e-mail on the computer, trying to find some hidden meaning in the financial report printed there, but there was none. His eyes wandered across the colorful buttons at the top of the screen, finally fixing on the light gray lettering in the button on the far right.

SEND.

Beamon wrapped his hand around the bottle of bourbon on the table but didn't pick it up. He leaned forward, bringing himself closer to the screen.

SEND.

64

HER BREATHING WAS ALMOST INAUDIBLE. THE white sheets, into which her pale skin blended so seamlessly, barely moved as her chest rose, faltered, and fell in a stilted rhythm.

Sara ran the back of her hand down Jennifer Davis's unconscious body. She'd never wake again. When the others arrived, they'd see her lying there peacefully, preparing to become humanity's teacher for the next ten thousand years.

Then another dose of the sedative just before midnight, combining with what she already had coursing through her veins, and the life would fade out of her. Sara's control of the church would be nearly unshakable then, and she would use that power to continue her work. To increase the church's wealth and influence, and with it her own.

Sara looked away from the girl and considered the problem of Mark Beamon, the only thing standing in the way of the future that she envisioned for herself and the church.

He was broken. She'd seen the pain and guilt in his eyes when she had taken Jennifer and reduced to nothing his desperate struggle and his sacrifice of everything meaningful in his life.

She recognized his subsequent escape as a fluke, but was becoming concerned that despite her resources, he was still missing. If he hadn't been located by tomorrow morning, she would call him and make a meager offer for the Vericomm tapes. With nothing else left, he'd jump at whatever bone she saw fit to throw.

And then, when he was at his weakest, she'd have him brought to her and end it once and for all.

The men who had let him escape—both in Phoenix and in Washington—had been severely censured, but had kept their positions. She needed the Guardians to complete the consolidation of her power and to keep the rest of the Elders docile. A replacement for Sines would have to be chosen. And soon.

Sara walked to the frost-covered window and looked out at the empty expanse that surrounded the Retreat. She didn't turn when she heard the door open. "I said I didn't want to be disturbed."

There was no answer.

She turned to face a man wearing a thick black jacket standing just inside the doorway. His name was Thomas. Thomas Nolan. He was only thirty-two, but intelligent and strong beyond his years. His parents had been members of the church since almost the beginning. She'd recognized him for his fanatical devotion to Albert when he was still very young and had personally attended the ceremony marking his entrance to the Guardians.

Now the devotion he had shown Albert would be hers. When this was over, he would be the one to step into Sines's position.

"What is it, Thomas?" she said as the other two Guardians staying at the Retreat walked in behind him and took positions at the edges of the room.

"Get out of here," Sara said, letting the anger

creep into her voice. "I told you that no one but Thomas and myself are to enter this room without my permission."

"No. Stay," Nolan said.

The two men held their ground, their expressions undecipherable.

"What did you say?" Sara said, stepping closer to Nolan and looking directly into his eyes. The reverence that she had always seen there had disappeared. Instead of averting his gaze, he glared back at her. "Tell them to leave, Thomas."

"No."

"What's wrong with you?" She took a step back, confused.

She looked around her at the men standing silently along the wall, concentrating on maintaining her outward calm. None of the Guardians had ever disobeyed her before. She was suddenly very aware of the young girl lying on the bed behind her and the precarious position that Jennifer put her in. Had something happened that she wasn't aware of? No, that was impossible.

"I thought that you would be the one to take Gregory's place, Thomas. Perhaps I was wrong. Perhaps you don't have the devotion to Albert that he thinks you do."

She jerked back when his hand shot out, but not fast enough. He caught her by the back of the neck and pulled her toward him.

"What . . . what are you doing?" she yelled, struggling to break free. "Let me go!"

The two other men followed along slowly as he dragged her through the door and out into the hall.

"Stop him. He's gone insane!" she shouted at them.

They didn't seem to hear, so she turned back to Nolan. "Albert will—"

At the mention of Kneiss's name, Nolan threw his weight back and pulled her head into the wall.

She slid to the floor dazed, blood from a gash in her forehead flowing into her eyes. She wiped at it with her sleeve, still trying to understand what was happening. Thomas Nolan was the most devoted of all the Guardians.

She didn't stand, but held her hand out, trying to calm down and to give herself time to think. Something had happened. What?

The cold rage was clearly visible on Nolan's face as he moved toward her.

"Wait," she said, holding her hands out in front of her.

He hesitated.

"Just wait. There is some misunderstanding here and there's no need for Albert to ever hear about it. It's okay. It's okay. Just tell me why you're doing this. We'll straighten it out."

Nolan didn't answer, but instead grabbed her by the hair again and dragged her through the grand entry hall of the old building and out into the snow. Sara felt the sharpness of the cold in her lungs as she tried to regain her footing on the icy ground beneath her.

"Stop!" she screamed, digging her nails into the arm pulling her along.

The cold was beginning to penetrate her skin as Nolan released her and she dropped to her knees in the snow. She looked up through the blood that was beginning to freeze to her face and focused on the two silent men standing a few feet behind Nolan. "Whichever one of you stops this will take

Gregory's place and will have whatever he wants. Do you understand? Tomorrow I will be the final authority of the church. *I* will."

One of them stepped toward her. She pulled away from Nolan and crawled to the man. She held a hand out to him, but he stopped a few feet away and threw a single piece of computer paper onto the snow in front of her.

To: Nolan@Guardians5278.com
From: ak@compound6758.com

Sara has betrayed me.

I have allowed her attacks on my granddaughter and Mark Beamon, as well as the death of my most devoted follower, Ernestine Waverly. I did this clinging to the hope that she would look into herself and find the strength of her faith. That she would come back to me.

As the day of my ascension approaches, I must accept that all she has found is a consuming jealousy and greed, and that mankind has not come as far as I had hoped. It seems that every time has its Judas.

If allowed to, Sara will destroy the
church and with it, humanity's
hopes and dreams. It is her time to
stand before God and be judged, as it
is mine.

God Bless.

AK

Sara struggled to keep her breathing normal as
the shadow of a pistol crossed in front of her on the
snow.

"This is wrong," she said, turning toward Nolan
and the barrel of the gun. "It's not from Albert. I'm
telling you it's not from Albert. Mark Beamon has
broken the codes we use. He sent this."

Nolan shook his head sadly, but kept the gun
steady. "Those codes have never been broken. We
checked the encryption signature you gave us. It is
from Albert."

"No! Don't you see? That's how Beamon found
her at the airport. He wasn't watching the plane
like we thought. He read the e-mail!"

"No," Nolan, said, reaching out and pulling the
slide back on the pistol. "Albert told him. He was
giving you a chance to repent."

This couldn't be happening. She would not
allow her life to be ended by Mark Beamon, a
drunken nobody whose pathetic life she'd had the
power to destroy with a few words.

"None of this would be here if it weren't for

me, and none of it will survive without me! I *am*
Albert Kneiss!"

Nolan pressed the gun against her temple, grabbing her by the collar as she tried to back away. "That's for God to decide."

65

BEAMON PULLED HIS FEET UP ON THE BUMPER
of the car and struggled to light another cigarette in
the wind. The hood was quickly losing its warmth as
the engine cooled, but it was still better than the alternative. The interior of the car had been closing in on
him.

The fate of the two e-mails he'd sent was a complete mystery to him. What the hell did he know
about computers? It was entirely possible that the
little zeros and ones that the e-mails were constructed from had just been dispersed to the digital
void of the Internet. If that was the case, Jennifer
was dead and he was waiting for no one.

More likely, the e-mails had been received and
immediately reported to Sara, who wouldn't have
had much trouble figuring out who wrote them. In
that case, he was waiting for a church hit squad.

He'd FedExed the Vericomm audio disks to an
attorney who had kicked his ass in court about five
years ago. Meanest, most ruthless sonofabitch he'd
ever met—a man who clearly could be trusted to
carry out his instructions. Upon hearing reports of
Beamon's death, he was to distribute copies of the
disks—and the handwritten explanation of how
Beamon had come to possess them—to twenty-five

484 — KYLE MILLS

major newspapers. And with that final act, Beamon's hat was officially out of rabbits.

He took a deep drag on the cigarette and moved to a warmer part of the hood, thinking about the contents of the e-mails he'd sent. The ironic thing was, what he'd written in them was true. Or at least as close to the truth as he could get. After spending the last month studying Albert Kneiss through reading just about everything ever written by or about him, it had been surprisingly easy to get into the old man's head and create a message in an electronic hand that would be indistinguishable from his. A message that Albert might have composed himself if he'd been able to.

Except for the last part, perhaps—the purposefully ambiguous sentence that Beamon knew the Guardians would interpret as a death sentence for Sara.

And that was the drawback to his plan. In the unlikely event that it worked, he was a murderer. But what choice had he been left with? A breathing Sara Renslier couldn't be trusted to stay away from the girl. And she sure as hell wasn't going to let him stroke out playing bridge in an old folks' home. Or was that just a rationalization that freed him to take his revenge?

Beamon spotted the gray panel van slowly approaching from the other side of the parking lot and slid his hand around the butt of the shotgun lying under a towel on the hood next to him. Those assholes who had shoved him in that trunk in D.C. still had his pistol. If he was still alive five minutes from now, he'd have to see if he could get that back. It had been a good friend.

"Mr. Beamon!"

The van hadn't yet come to a complete stop when Jennifer burst from the passenger door and ran to him. She almost knocked him off the slick hood when she grabbed hold of him.

"I knew you wouldn't let them kill me."

"A promise is a promise," he said, stroking her hair with one hand but keeping the other under the towel.

"She's gone," Jennifer said, beginning to sob. "She was in the snow! There was—" her voice caught for a moment. "There was so much blood. It was just like Mom."

Beamon was only about half-listening, concentrating on the van as a young man he hadn't seen before stepped from it and walked around to face him. He patted her on the rear and peeled her arms from around him. "Go sit in the car, okay? I'll be there in a second."

She pulled away from him, and a moment later Beamon heard the door slam shut behind him.

"Mr. Beamon. I wanted to tell you—" the man in front of him started.

Beamon cut him off, speaking authoritatively. "It's okay. We understand. You were only doing what you thought Albert wanted. He holds Sara solely responsible."

"I only wanted to do what was right," he said looking at his feet. "I contacted the others and told them what happened."

Beamon nodded sagely. "Albert wanted me to tell you he was sorry to put you through what he did—to ask of you what he did. But that he knew you were strong enough to handle it." Beamon slid from the hood. "He loved Sara so much. I think he believed that she would come back to him until the very end."

The man turned and began walking slowly back to the van. Beamon thought he said, "He always saw the good in people," but couldn't be sure. The wind had picked up and carried the man's words away.

\--\-

Beamon adjusted himself in the sofa and looked down at Jennifer, who was lying on the floor in front of the television. "I find it kind of disturbing the way you stare at things but don't really see them, Jennifer."

"Sorry . . . I was thinking."

"Too much reflection can be bad for you. Why don't you come sit up here and have some ice cream?"

She slowly peeled herself off the linoleum and fell onto the couch next to him.

"Oh, by the way, the place looks great."

She'd spent the last four hours scrubbing and straightening the worn-out little apartment they were holed up in, glancing at the clock on the desk every five minutes or so.

He'd tried to convince her that she was no longer in danger, but the fact that his record was a little spotty on that subject, and the loaded shotgun resting on the sofa next to him, made his argument less than convincing.

They both watched as the numbers on the clock flipped over to twelve o'clock. Jennifer sat completely still, ignoring the dented spoon Beamon was holding out to her. It looked as if she was waiting for something. The sound of the church's enforcers rushing the apartment? A lightning bolt from heaven?

"Midnight, Jen. They don't want you as their new messiah. I hear they're looking for someone with a college degree and some practical experience."

Dumb humor didn't seem to be working, so he tried the ice cream again. Women weren't supposed to be able to resist the stuff. "It's Ben and Jerry's.

Cherry Garcia." He stuck the extra spoon in the carton and wiggled it seductively. "Won't last much longer."

She looked like she was going to crumble into another crying fit, and Beamon felt his stomach tense. He just wasn't built for this kind of thing. He hoped to hell that he could get his job back so he could return to the good old days of finding 'em and instantly turning 'em over to the Bureau's shrink.

Fortunately, the spell passed with only a hint of a tear visible in the corner of her right eye. Beamon shook the carton again.

This time she took the spoon. "Thanks. For everything."

66

"WON'T THE FBI BE LOOKING FOR YOU here, Mr. Beamon?" Jennifer asked, lifting herself off the car seat and yanking at one of her pantlegs. The jeans he'd purchased for her were apparently less than a perfect fit.

Beamon looked up at the front door of his condo. "Doubt it. FBI'd probably assume I wouldn't be stupid enough to come back here while they were looking for me."

"So you're a lot stupider than they think."

He pointed to her wide grin as he stepped from the car. "That looks good on you, smartass."

Beamon pulled off his sunglasses and squinted against the bright mid-morning sun. "Can you see my gun?" he said, turning his back to Jennifer and adjusting his sweater.

"No. But this is a problem." She reached over and buttoned his collar. "There. You look good."

He gave a short nod and started up the walkway.

"You all right?" Jennifer asked, following alongside him.

"Why?"

"I don't know, you look a little nervous. You really like her, don't you?"

Beamon rolled his eyes.

"You should tell her you're sorry."

"I think we may be beyond that, Jen."

"Nah. Women go in for apologies in a big way. Trust me on this."

Beamon took a deep breath and knocked on Carrie Johnstone's door. It opened a moment later.

"Mark!" Carrie threw her arms around him and kissed him hard on the mouth.

"Probably don't need to bother with that apology," he heard Jennifer mumble as he tried to keep from stumbling.

Carrie pulled back and turned toward her. "Oh my God. You're Jennifer Davis, aren't you?"

"Uh-huh. It's nice to meet you, Ms. Johnstone. You're all Mr. Beamon talks about."

"I don't think that's really true," Beamon stammered as Carrie put her arm around Jennifer and guided her in the door.

"Are you all right, honey? Maybe you'd like to talk?"

"Mr. Beamon!" Emory squealed as she ran around her mother and attached herself to his leg. He peeled her off and picked her up. "How are you, honey? The Easter bunny didn't bring you healthy candy, did he?"

She bobbed her head as he produced a chocolate moose from the pocket of his jacket and kicked the door closed behind him. "Don't tell your mother."

"Mark, I want to hear everything. Are you hungry?"

Beamon looked skeptically at the casserole cooling on the stove. It looked normal, but he knew that it was a trick. "Uh, sure, Carrie, thanks."

"Jennifer, hand me that spatula over there,

please," Carrie said, pointing to a copper bucket full of cooking utensils.

She scooped a large piece onto a plate and handed it to Beamon. "This is a great recipe. I just make a few substitutions and it turns out perfect."

Beamon smiled weakly and shoveled a forkful into his mouth. "Can't tell a bit," he said through a glob of something that tasted a little like an empty styrofoam cup.

"Mark's such a liar," Carrie said to Jennifer. "He hates my cooking, but doesn't have the guts to tell me. I admire that kind of cowardice in a man."

Jennifer accepted an even larger piece and retreated with Emory to the small table in the kitchen.

Carrie laid her plate on the counter and began speaking in a voice low enough that the girls couldn't hear. "Where did you find her, Mark? I haven't seen anything on the news about it. Are you back with the FBI?"

"You're the only person who knows. And no, I'm not back with the FBI. I may never be."

"You found her on your own?"

Beamon thought of Ernie and Jack Goldman. "I had some help."

She looked over at Jennifer, who was helping Emory cut up the food on her plate. "Is she okay, Mark? Did she actually see her parents murdered? Was she abused?"

Beamon took another bite of the casserole and chewed slowly. "Her parents weren't murdered— her father shot her mother and then himself right in front of her, and yes, she was physically and mentally abused. Not sexually, though." He leaned a little closer to her. "I have no idea what to say to her, Carrie. I've tried, but you've got to help me here."

Carrie waved at Jennifer. "Finished? Why don't you help me with the dishes while Mark takes Emory for a walk and explains why it would be wrong for her to eat that chocolate moose he gave her?"

"You told?" Beamon said as Emory flew off the chair and disappeared down the hall to bundle up. Beamon stepped aside as Jennifer carried the dishes into the kitchen. "There's one more thing I'm going to need your help with, Carrie. Maybe we can talk about it when I get back."

67

THE SUNLIGHT WAS BARELY STARTING TO appear over the mountains as Beamon pulled a Post-it note out of his pocket and slipped his glasses onto his nose. He read the address written on it and checked it against the one stenciled on the neatly kept house in front of him. This was it.

He knocked on the door and waited impatiently as muffled footsteps became audible on the other side. The man who answered was dressed in a meticulously pressed white shirt and gray wool slacks. An unimaginatively tasteful maroon tie was hanging untied around his neck.

It took a few moments—probably because Beamon was backlit by the rising sun—but recognition began to slowly register on the man's face. He tried to back away, but Beamon reached out and grabbed him by the collar, just as a woman wearing a long green robe appeared in the hallway. "Who is it, honey?"

"Excuse me, ma'am," Beamon said, dragging the man through the door. "I just want a quick word with your husband."

"Gary," she called in a worried voice, "is everything all right? Should I call someone?"

"Just finish getting the kids ready for school. It's okay."

Beamon smiled and waved at her, then pulled the door shut.

"You just aren't real bright, are you, Beamon," the man said, trying to jerk away. There was a quiet ripping sound, but Beamon easily kept hold of his shirt. "You still have no idea what you're dealing with, do you?"

Beamon didn't say anything, but dragged him across the driveway and shoved his face into the passenger window of the car idling there, resisting the urge to break the glass with the man's nose.

"You haven't been informed as to the new world order, I take it," Beamon said, looking through the windshield at Carrie. She nodded nervously.

He pulled the man away from the car and released him. Instead of backing away, he stepped forward, bringing his face to within inches of Beamon's. "What're you going to do, Beamon? Arrest me? Oh, no, wait. You can't do that anymore, can you?"

Beamon smiled engagingly and stomped hard on the man's foot. He howled in pain and surprise and limped back a few paces. Beamon turned back to the car and shrugged. Carrie looked horrified.

There had been no prints on the Child Safety Administration's business card other than his and Carrie's, but the eighth stationery store Beamon called had had a record of printing the offending card. "Guess you shouldn't have had the printer mail those cards directly to your home, huh, dumbshit."

The man looked like he was going to charge, but Beamon stopped him by sliding a hand suggestively beneath his parka. The gesture seemed to have the desired effect.

"I have to admit to being a little impressed," Beamon said. "For fifty dollars in business cards and a few hours' work, you could irretrievably fuck up hundreds of people's lives. How many times have you used this little trick?"

The man straightened up and looked Beamon directly in the eye. "As many as we wanted to."

68

"MARGIE! HOW YOU DOIN', HON?" BEAMON said jovially.

Jake Layman's secretary bolted upright at her desk and then jumped to her feet. "Oh my God. Mark! What are you doing here? I mean, they've been looking everywhere for you!"

Beamon put his hand on Jennifer's back. "Margie, I'd like you to meet the girl everyone's been talking about—Jennifer Davis."

The woman's eyes widened as Jennifer fidgeted uncomfortably and tried to get behind Beamon. "Don't stare," he said. "I think she's a little uncomfortable that I bought her clothes in the Junior Miss section of Kmart."

"And . . . and who's this?" Margie stammered, looking at the man standing next to Beamon.

"This is my friend from the Child Safety Administration. He has a story he wants to tell—"

Beamon suddenly noticed that the dull roar of the FBI's Phoenix office had gone dead, replaced by the quiet hush of intermittent whispers. When he turned around, all motion had stopped. It looked like he was viewing the office on a VCR with a stuck Pause button.

"Uh, I hear that the director's here talking about me," he said, turning back to her. "Where?"

"I'll tell them you're here."

"Don't bother," he said. "Just point."

"They're in Conference Room Two."

He stepped back and motioned to Jennifer and the increasingly nervous-looking man who had accused him of child molestation. They started down the hall ahead of him.

"Gentlemen," Beamon said as he walked through the conference room door without knocking. "And Chet."

"Beamon!" Layman said, standing abruptly and almost upsetting the coffee mug on the table. Chet Michaels pumped a fist in the air and silently mouthed, "Yes!" The director just stared.

"Don't look so surprised, Jake. I told you I'd come in when I tied up a few loose ends." He looked out the open door. "Don't be shy."

When Jennifer self-consciously shuffled in, Layman fell back into his chair.

"The first of my loose ends. Jennifer, I'd like you to meet Jake Layman and William Calahan. You probably remember Chet Michaels."

She smiled politely.

His other guest hovered outside the door, forcing Beamon to reach out and haul him into the room. "Sit," he ordered. The man complied silently.

"That's my other loose end, but I'll explain later." Beamon patted the chair next to him. Jennifer sat down and placed the computer disks she'd been carrying on the table in front of her. Beamon nodded toward them, and she slid them across the table.

"What are these?" Layman said quietly.

"Audio from an interesting little setup the Church of the Evolution had going. I figure it's enough to keep your whole office busy for about five years."

"The Kneissians?" Calahan said, speaking for the first time. "What the hell's going on here? And where did she come from?"

"Director Calahan, I—" Layman started.

"Shut up, Jake. I didn't ask you. Beamon's talking now."

AFTERWORD

In writing this novel I had the arduous but fascinating task of creating my own religion. To accomplish this, I borrowed snippets from many faiths and added a healthy dose of my own imagination and the spirit of George Orwell.

Because all faiths have certain common threads, it might be possible to see parallels to any number of present-day belief systems. Let me assure you that if these parallels do indeed exist, they were completely unintentional.

Kyle Mills lives in Jackson Hole, Wyoming, where he spends his time skiing, rock climbing, and writing books. He is the author of *Rising Phoenix*, *Storming Heaven*, *Free Fall*, *Burn Factor*, and *Fade*.